POISON

POISON

—

Susan Fromberg Schaeffer

W. W. NORTON & COMPANY   NEW YORK LONDON

Copyright © 2006 by Susan Fromberg Schaeffer

For information about permission to reproduce selections from this book, write to Permissions, W. W. Norton & Company, Inc., 500 Fifth Avenue, New York, NY 10110

Manufacturing by Courier Westford
Book design by Anna Oler

Library of Congress Cataloguing-in-Publication Data

Schaeffer, Susan Fromberg,
Poison / Susan Fromberg Schaeffer—1st ed.
p. cm.
ISBN 0-393-06101-9
1. Authors—Fiction. 2. Domestic fiction. I. Title.
PS3569.C35P65 2006
813'.54—dc22
2005029597

ISBN 978-0-393-32979-7 pbk.

W. W. Norton & Company, Inc., 500 Fifth Avenue, New York, N.Y. 10110
www.wwnorton.com

W. W. Norton & Company, Ltd., Castle House, 75/76 Wells Street, London WIT 3QT

1 2 3 4 5 6 7 8 9 0

FOR NEIL

And for the memory of Juanita Harris+Rosenberg,

Magicianess,

Turnkey of the turret

For all things have but little stay,
Not least the most we love.

–English folk song

ONE

—

"THE STORY'S OUT in the papers. You can't escape it. The children will hear it in school," Sigrid told her brother. "Now what are we going to do?"

"Take them out of school," he said. "I'll tell them. I should have told them long ago."

So the children were taken out of school, and there they all sat, at the tail end of the weekend, in the parlor, a wood fire crackling in the fireplace, the two children shivering because it was a cold night, and it had been a long drive to get back to Willow Grove. "I have a story to tell you," Peter said.

Oh, good, the children thought. We like stories.

The names of the children were Sophie and Andrew.

Their stepmother was not there. Peter had banished her (her name was Meena) to the turret.

"Once upon a time—" Peter began, stopping, asking them, "Does everyone have his cup of chocolate? Hold on tight to the handle. Don't grab on to the cup. It's too hot, you'll drop it. So," Peter began again, "once upon a time there was a famous giant who was under a curse. You've heard of famous giants who were under curses?"

The children nodded solemnly.

"And this giant really wasn't as gigantic as most giants, but he was well known throughout the country because he was put under a spell—well, a curse, really—and the result was, everyone came to believe he was the most handsome man in the land."

"And was he?" Sophie asked.

"He was not ugly," Peter said. "But because of the curse, or the spell, it depends on what you want to call it, women had a bad habit of falling in love with him. Even before they saw him when they came to his door, they thought they were in love with him. Well, what was the giant to do?" Peter asked.

"Give them a cookie and send them back," Sophie said.

"Yes, that's exactly what he did, but what if they refused to leave? Should he have called the police?"

"If they were strangers, he should call the police," Sophie said.

"But if they came back again?"

"I don't know, Daddy," Sophie said.

"They did come back, and some of those women, they were under a spell, you understand, did very bad things."

"What bad things?" Sophie asked. "Sit *up*, Andrew!" Sophie said. "Daddy, Andrew's not listening."

"He's younger than you are. He falls asleep more easily. And he's not so interested in stories."

"Don't like them," Andrew said.

"What bad things?" Sophie asked again. "Did they trample on the flowers?"

"Worse," said Peter. "Much worse."

"Much worse than that?" Sophie said, her eyes widening.

"Sometimes," Peter said, "they decided to come to the giant's house to stop living. That was the nature of the curse, you see."

"To stop living? How does someone stop living?" Sophie asked curiously. She thought people started up somehow, someone wound them up the way she wound up a top, and they went on spinning forever. Such had been her experience.

"Well, there are things they can do," Peter said. "People can eat bad mushrooms, and afterwards, they stop living. Or they can go for a drive in the car and their eyes grow heavy, and they run off the road and stop living that way. They can decide to swim a river, but then the water is cold, and their legs stiffen up, and they can't swim, and so they drown and stop living. There are many ways people stop living. Some people live so long life forgets all about them, and so they stop living. But most people stop because they made a mistake. They went for a ride on a stormy night and drove off the road into a tree, or they were hungry, and ate the mushrooms I told you about, and so they stop living. You know what's happened when you hear the siren and see the flashing lights and you know the ambulance is there. Probably someone stopped living and the doctor came in the ambulance and tried to make them start living again, but even doctors can't always make someone start living again once they've stopped."

"And the women who came to the giant's house to stop living? Did the ambulance make them start again?"

"No. They wouldn't start again. They stopped living and no one could start them up again. And everyone said, 'It was the giant's fault.'"

"Oh," said Sophie. "Was it?" she asked.

"Well, it's hard to know that, you see. The giant didn't think it was his fault. He thought these things happened to him because he was under a curse." Peter took a deep breath. "His own wife, his very own wife, stopped living."

"What did she do? To stop living?"

"Well, Sophie," Peter said, "you know how useful it is to have a stove? It cooks your dinner and makes your scones and bakes your birthday cakes and can warm up things. But there is something in that stove that can make people stop living."

"What?" asked Sophie.

"Something called gas. If someone lights the gas with a match, that's where the blue lights on top of the stove come from, that's the gas, burning, but if someone forgets to light it, then the gas goes wherever it wants, and the gas changes from a good thing and becomes a bad thing."

"Because someone forgot to light the gas with a match and turn the gas into blue fires?"

"Exactly," Peter said. "That's what happened to the giant's very own wife. She breathed in the gas and the gas made her go to sleep, and the thing about the gas is, it makes you sleep, and you can't wake up, so you stop living."

"What was her name?"

"What?" asked Peter.

"The name of the giant's very own wife."

"Her name," Peter said, "was Evelyn."

"That was my mother's name," Sophie said proudly.

"Yes. It was," Peter said. His voice trembled. Sigrid got up and went to the window, her back to them, and stared out.

"But my mother stopped living because she had pneumonia and couldn't keep on living. She couldn't breathe in any air. You said that, Daddy."

"I was wrong," Peter said.

"Wrong?" Sophie echoed.

"I got it wrong. She forgot to light the match and the gas got into the house and so she stopped living."

"Just like the giant's very own wife?"

"Just like her. And people blamed *me* for it, just as they blamed the giant who was under a curse."

"Are *you* under a curse?" Sophie asked.

"I believe I am," he said. "Because my very own first wife stopped living, just as the giant's wife stopped living. The same thing happened to the giant's second wife. And my second wife stopped living in the very same way."

"You mean Elfie," Sophie said.

"I mean Elfie," Peter said. "And by that time, the curse was much stronger."

"Who put the curse on the giant?" Sophie asked.

"No one knows," Peter said.

"Everyone says you're very famous and very handsome," Sophie said. "Is that what happens when you're under a curse?"

"Sometimes," Peter said.

"Everyone says you're poison to women. What do they mean, Daddy?"

"I suppose they mean that I don't have a good effect on women."

"But you have a good effect on *me*," Sophie said.

"That's what matters," Peter said, smiling. "That's the only thing that matters."

"But Evelyn, the giant's wife. And Elfie, the giant's second wife," Sophie considered, "he didn't have a good effect on them."

"And neither did I on my very own first wife, or my very own second wife," Peter said. "You see, in some ways, I'm very much like the giant. There was even a little girl who stopped living in the giant's house. She was the second wife's child. Her name was Petra."

"I had a sister named Petra," Sophie said. "But not very long. You sent her away."

"Oh, for bloody sake," Sigrid muttered mutinously.

"I didn't really send her away," Peter said. "She stopped living. When people stop living, we have to put them somewhere. They can't go on staying with the others anymore."

"Why not?"

"I don't know, but they can't."

"You don't know?" Sophie asked.

"No one does. That's the way it is. It can't be changed."

Sophie nodded.

"And did the bad giant have a third, very own wife?"

"He wasn't a *bad* giant," Peter said. "He was under a curse. The bad thing was the curse. Yes, he had a third wife."

"And was her name Meena?"

"Her name was Meena."

"And did Meena stop living?"

"No, Meena is still alive."

"Will she stop living?"

"I don't think so. Meena is very clever about matches. She always lights the stove with a match. I doubt she's in any danger."

Sophie stared down at her hands in her lap. She had twined her fingers together, hard, so that the knuckles showed white. She remembered the day before they left for the beginning of term. Meena shouted, "If you keep carrying on like this, Peter, you will have to buy an *electric* range." Sophie had not known what she meant. She had been frightened by Meena's voice.

"What is an electric range?" Sophie asked.

"What?" said Peter.

"Meena once said it. 'You will have to buy an *electric* range.'"

"Did she?" Peter said. "Well, that's an idea. That might break the curse. Or the spell, whichever you call it."

"Does she have to remember everything?" Sigrid whispered.

"I can hear you when you whisper," Sophie said. "The teacher says I have ears like a fox."

"Foxes are disgusting animals," Sigrid said.

"Sigrid!" Peter said.

"So the story is about you, Daddy," Sophie said.

"I'm afraid so. It must be, because whenever the newspapers tells the story, they always illustrate it with a picture of me."

"Of you, Daddy?"

"Well, love, not just of me. They put in a picture of me when I've got my arm around your real mother's shoulders."

"Evelyn," Sophie said.

"Yes, Evelyn."

"You're just standing there?" Sophie said. "That doesn't sound like a very good picture."

"I think people like it because we looked so happy together."

"Bushels and bushels of my friends have pictures like that, and no one puts them in the papers."

"That's true."

"Can I see that picture?"

"Do you want to see it?"

"Yes," said Sophie.

"Here," Sigrid said, taking out the clipping and ripping the picture from the text beneath it. She handed the picture to Peter. That picture, Sigrid thought. That picture is going to last forever. There he is, looking like the sun god himself, with those sleepy eyes, looking as if he's drugged by Evelyn's nearness, and there she is, smiling as if her life depended on it. Sophie's right to conclude that anyone coming on this picture would only think, There's a very handsome man and a very happy woman, two happy people, and that would be the end of it. But no, Evelyn had to stop living. Women everywhere commit suicide and no one ever hears of them again. And all those women must have thought, as they got ready to end their lives, Now everyone will take notice of me. Now everyone will know who was to blame. And no one *cares*! No one gets a posthumous life. No brown bird becomes a peacock once she's dead. If Peter hadn't seen to it that her last book was published! If he'd let the earth stop her mouth once she'd died. But no. He knew better. He owed Evelyn that much, that's what he said. And now look! Someday I'll go to Tesco's and that photo will be on the covers of magazines.

Now Sophie had inspected the photograph and handed it back to her father. "I've seen that one before," she said.

"Yes, everyone has," her father said.

"And my mother, Evelyn, stopped living because someone put you under a curse, and Elfie and Petra stopped living because someone put you under a curse, but Meena is too strong for the curse, and you are under the curse because you are handsome and famous, but you are also strong. Will you stop living?" she asked. She was frightened, that was clear enough.

"Not until I am an old, old man," Peter said, "and have to walk with two sticks. Although no one knows why I'm under a curse. *I* don't know."

"My mother stopped living, and my second mother stopped, and baby Petra stopped, but now no one's going to stop living anymore."

"That's right," Peter said.

"Can I go to sleep now?" Sophie asked.

"I'll carry you up," Peter said.

"Isn't she a little old for that?" Meena asked from the head of the steps.

"She'll *never* be too old for that," Peter boomed out. "Never, ever, will you, Sophie?"

"Never, ever, ever," Sophie said.

"She's awfully heavy. Mind your back," Meena said.

"Out of the way," boomed Peter. "Sophie coming through!"

Later, Peter and Sigrid sat in the parlor. Peter got up and began throwing more logs and branches into the fire. "Well?" he asked his sister.

"I think it went as well as we could have hoped," Sigrid said.

"Time will tell," Peter said.

"I think you dodged a bullet there," Sigrid said, thinking it over.

"Only for a little while. A little while."

"But you *must* take care, Peter. If people are talking like this. If the children have to be taken out of school when writers start taking up their pens to say you've killed your wives."

"Most people don't know anything about Elfie, thank God for that," Peter said. "Or Petra. No one much cares about poor Petra. Just a child and such a young child."

"But Evelyn's presence keeps growing. I had a letter from Adrienne in the States. She said that there's no point in even trying to speak sensibly of Evelyn. She is already a myth."

"Well," said Peter. "I don't see what I can do about that. Evelyn wanted fame and she got rather more than even she would have expected. Although she didn't live to enjoy it. The dead don't read reviews. That's the good part of being dead, I suppose."

"The point is," Sigrid said wearily, "all eyes are on you. Everyone is waiting to see if you make another mistake. You've already made one too many. And now the children are starting to hear about it. You can't tell them fairy tales forever."

"I can try."

"I think," Sigrid said, "you had better spend your time and energy on something else. Taking care of the women you do take in, for instance."

"Meena is all right," Peter said. "I picked her to be all right."

"She's the most dangerous so far. She won't put up with you. She'll be the one to make you suffer, you and the children, and me, and every single member of our family. Can't you see it yet?"

"She's not vengeful."

"Really, Peter, when it comes to women, I think you *are* under a curse. Who's throwing herself at you now?"

"Well, Rose, for one," he said, and burst into laughter.

"If you're laughing now, you'll be crying later, wasn't that what our mum always said?"

"There's always something to cry over, Sigrid," Peter said.

"But those children! You don't want them weeping their way through life, do you?"

He looked at Sigrid with exasperation and shook his head. "Of course not," he said. "That won't happen. We have to let time pass. We can't make it pass any faster than it does."

"It rather speeds up around you, Peter," his sister said. "Don't you agree?"

"Leave it out, Sigrid," Peter said. "Leave it alone."

Upstairs, in their beds, the two children slept on. Meena, who was sitting in the shadows at the top of the stairs, listened carefully to everything. As if her life depended on what she heard.

TWO

—

PROBABLY SHE WAS thinking, How did I get from there to here? At the beginning, a pretty girl among four other pretty sisters and her wonderful cousin, Julian, her only cousin, who was taken in and then adopted by her family when his own family died of the plague in India, a house she felt safe in, not caring if she ever grew up or anything came of her, because, really, she was so content as she was. She'd had that kind of family, her mother, her father, blameless, guileless, perfect. An Indian family, but very light-skinned, very well behaved, who soon took on English names, all except Meena, who insisted on keeping her own, and after a time, it seemed to Meena that no one thought of her, of any of them, as Indian, although Meena had heard Peter telling his sister, "But I *like* the

Indianness of her. It makes her more exotic." And later, she'd heard him telling Sigrid, "It's because she's an Indian. Can't you see it? They were aristocrats in India and here they are in this British mud puddle and they're farmers. So it's not astonishing that Meena has pretensions or whatever you want to call them. Foreigners want to be more British than the real thing. That's an old story." And Sigrid complaining that she, Meena, put on such airs, but Peter said again, "Isn't that to be expected? It doesn't mean anything. I don't mind." But he had minded. Later. And now Meena was probably thinking, I beat them at their own game. Long ago, I stopped being the Indian girl, one of the sisters with the beautiful black Indian hair. But who, really, had any idea of what she was thinking, now or ever? Just then, she was thinking, Now I am a widow. She was also thinking, There are so many important people here. This is the first time I have been called upon to preside over such an assemblage: alone. My husband was always there, attention drawn to him as if he were the sun who had broken through thick clouds.

Meanwhile, she walked and walked around the garden. She became more and more angry as she walked. So many women here to pay tribute to her husband, who is about to be buried. Bury him! Bury him! I hate him, she thought as she walked. Always walking. She could not stop walking and she could not come back to the mourners who crowded her house, those who wanted to express sympathy for her. But, she thought, They don't care about me. They never cared about me. Oh, she knew what they had always wanted. They wanted to draw closer to her husband, they still did, even now that he was dead, and so they treated his wife well. *Dear Meena, look how well you manage things! It's a good thing your husband has a wife who knows how to order things, to keep everything in order.* She wondered, Why must I bother with them? Why did he need them? He would say, "It's part of my job, and if it's part of mine, it must be part of yours. I'm sorry for it," he said. "But you knew, you knew from the start, I told you so many times from the beginning, it wouldn't be easy," he'd made that plain, to be a woman married to a famous man, a man who still refused to explain the many disasters that had occurred in his life before he met her. "You are taking all that on," he said, "if you marry me. Can you bear it? And my two children. Two *motherless* children. That's how everyone looks at them. You'll be the stepmother. Everyone's eyes will be on you. When I look at the two of them, I think, Are they motherless because of me? Is everything my fault? I never stop asking myself all that, you know that. So think twice. So many shadows. Once," he said, "I wanted to talk about what happened when Evelyn died, but no one wanted to listen."

Then *she,* the third wife, decided he was not to talk. What business was it of anyone else's? If he said nothing, and she said nothing, people would forget them. Overlook them. Or so she had thought. And now there was that woman standing out in the rain with her large black umbrella, Julia. She was the one who caused the trouble, she was the one who said to Peter, "If you have a pit in your garden and you leave it open, people will look into it, shake their heads, and think, Why doesn't someone fill it in? And that will be the end of it. But if you take that pit and cover it over with leaves and branches, everyone will want to know what you're trying to hide, if you do not speak, if you do not say what happened. How can the truth be more terrible than people's imaginations?" Was that Julia over there? Was that really Julia? Julia, the supplanter, the one to whom Peter talked, Meena astonished by Julia, who had no interest in creeping into bed with him, who drew Sophie, her stepdaughter, Peter's daughter, to her so easily, as if *they,* those two, were well and truly family, Julia, to whom Sophie went when she was trying to decide whether to attempt entering university, when Sophie was completely mad, her mother, Evelyn, all over again, and all because she, Meena, had said, "I would prefer to have you use another name, not Grovesnor. That name belongs to your father—as a *public* person. What have you done to deserve it? Can you not make a name for yourself? Must you have his? Ours?" And then Sophie began crying, saying again and again, "Am I not entitled to my own name? Is there no such thing as a birthright?" And Peter saying nothing to his daughter. Let the women fight it out, he must have thought. In the end, both of them enraged at him, Meena thinking, I am his wife, Sophie saying, I am his daughter, it's his name and my name on my certificate of live birth. And then Julia, stating her own view: Why not call yourself Sophie Graves Grovesnor, then laughing and saying, "Well, that sounds perfectly dreadful, I'd go for one or the other of those last names, and to hell with Meena." To hell with Meena. Yes, Julia would have said that, and far more than that. Was that really Julia, standing there beneath that enormous black umbrella in the rain? But how could it be Julia? An American. Americans never thought of buying sturdy umbrellas, and that one was strong, enormous, really, its metal spines shaping the rim like upside-down bats. And talented. Peter always saying, "I never know what she'll do next," Sigrid asking, "Is that a compliment, or another of your ways of dismissing another scribbler, just as you used to tell people, quoting Yeats, 'I couldn't have written that myself,'" meaning that the writing given over for his inspection was unimaginably awful. Peter telling Julia, "If you can't think of anything good to say about someone's work, ask, 'What do *you* like about it?' and the person will talk on for hours." He talked to Julia openly in that way, as if he thought of her as one of the family.

—

WHY WERE PERFECT strangers, she thought as she walked, bothering themselves imagining his past life? Or their life together? Asking themselves, Is he happy with her? What kind of a marriage is it? Is this one, the third wife, going to put her head in an oven, as the other two did? Oh, no, she had thought, so many times during their time together, she would not put her head in an oven. *His* head, rather; she thought, perhaps, she was capable of that, under the right circumstances. She told him once, when he returned from London, "I am going to outlive you. But if you make me sufficiently unhappy, I do know how to stop my own heart. I shall not die unavenged." And after that, he said he would not go to London without her, he would not stay any longer in his sister's house, that sister who was happy for him when he took women into his bed under her roof. "Poor Peter," she could hear her saying, "he needs a holiday." And when she said that his two children were to be sent off to boarding school, he could not argue, because she had said she knew how to stop her own heart. She kept a large bottle of potassium pills in her cabinet, kept them on display, sometimes moving them to the sink: the pills frightened him; he knew that swallowing those pills would have stopped her heart. And then he would have three women dead, and everyone would say, He is a man who kills women, and even his children, *his* children, not her children, she had not been able to bear one of her own, would have to ask themselves, Can it be true? Is our father a man who kills women? Who killed our mother? Did he drive her to death? Is that why we are *step*children, is that why we think of ourselves as secondhand? Two motherless children with a stepmother, whose core is ice, a woman who is made of ice. How easy it was to make him feel guilty! Time and again, she saw how a slantwise look, a seemingly harmless remark, would plunge him first into darkness and then into blackness, as if she had forced him into the coffin of his first wife, or his second. She knew he dreamed of them in their coffins; she knew he had terrible dreams in which he slept with one or the other of them in their narrow beds, and the woman in the coffin cried and he tried to comfort her, or she accused him of having brought her to this, to this damp place of darkness where time had stopped when her heart had stopped, and now neither of the dead wives could estimate how much time had passed because for them, the sun neither rose nor set, and in his dreams, the two dead wives did not change or age; they looked precisely as they had looked when their lives had stopped, and they were rosy and beautiful, the gas did that, flushed them, whereas she, she walked, knew she had aged and grown old, and the more time that passed, the less her aging flesh, the reality of her, what people saw when they looked at her (although everyone always said, "Meena, you never change!") could compare with either of the two dead wives. And her stepdaughter, who resembled the first wife so perfectly, she was the cause of so much trouble, not because she did anything troublesome, but because she duplicated her, the first wife, and how often she had seen Peter look at his daughter and a faraway look would come over him, and she knew what had happened, the stepdaughter had reminded him of something the first wife used to do, and Peter was remembering, he was going back again, and if she interrupted him, he would answer abruptly, and then she knew she did not belong, could not be admitted, into that world he visited day and night, during the day, memories, happy memories, of that dead woman would come back, and he would be with her, united with her more completely than any of the women he met so often in London, that woman so long dead. So it was no wonder that she hated the stepdaughter, no wonder that she had become the evil stepmother. Although she had to hide that. Above all, she had to hide that.

So many things to hide and keep hidden, no wonder everything exhausted her, although she had to hide that, too, to keep people saying, "Oh, Meena, you're wonderful. How good you are to cook and clean for us! And how happy you've made him! He deserves happiness, don't you think, after what he's endured?" What he's endured! Was it impossible to see what she endured, day after day? Yes, inconceivable to them, because she did not count, she was not taken into account, she was only Peter's wife; they paid only as much attention to her as they had to, no more. They noticed her just enough to be polite, and they were all polite, and it was not difficult to imagine what they had to say about her when they left. *She's pretty enough, but really, how boring! How does he stand it? Wasn't she a secretary, some kind of assistant, didn't she meet him because she was typing his manuscripts?* And someone would say, *He shouldn't be permitted to choose his own wives. Look how badly he's done.* Once, she heard someone say that. Which of the women had it been? Perhaps it was his sister, after he'd rung her up, and she, Meena, had the bad fortune to pick up the phone and hear just those lines and no more. *You shouldn't be permitted to choose your own wives.* As if she had already failed some kind of test, and what had she done? What? But whatever it was could not be undone.

She walked and walked, unaware of the spectacle she presented, a gaunt woman dressed in black, the rain streaming down, pasting her clothes to her rail-thin body, her hair wet and dripping, and as she walked, wringing her hands, unknowingly wringing her hands. While the stepchildren, Andrew and Sophie, asked each other, "Shouldn't one of us go speak to her? Shouldn't she come back and see to her guests? Shouldn't she put on some dry things? Why is she stalking about in the rain like that?"

"She's mad, love," said their aunt, Meena's sister-in-law.

A bolt of lightning, followed by a crash of thunder, and she thought, as she walked and wrung her hands, But surely we were happy once. Surely he loved me, at least in the beginning.

Surely he would not have married me otherwise? Or would he have?

———

HOW SHE HATED the telephone. One afternoon, when she was still Meena Church, not married to anyone, not yet, she had picked up the phone intending to ring her mother and heard him saying, "Which one should I marry? I have to marry someone to care for the children," and then the unmistakable sound of his sister's voice, saying, "Well, Peter, if you feel that way, neither of them." *Neither of them.* So even then there was another one. Still, the point was clear: he hadn't wanted her enough. But when he asked her to marry him, she thought, Whoever that other woman is, *she* is not the one he wants. He's asking me to marry him. He must love me. Now, as she walked, she thought, He did not want either of us. He wanted someone to take care of his children. How long before she had come to understand that? Not long, because shortly after their marriage, she packed the children off to school. And how they had cried. Especially Sophie. And how exultant it had made her to see it, the child's eyes red, her cheeks shiny, her nose dripping, and how consolingly she had said, "Here, take my handkerchief," so that anyone watching would have thought, Of course that woman is the child's real mother, of course that woman loves her daughter. And years later, Peter saying, "Wasn't there someone in Greek mythology who ate her own children? A woman, wasn't it?" Of course he knew the name of that woman who ate her children, and Meena thought, I've been discovered. He must not find me out, I must undo what he knows, unweave it, like Penelope. By then, living so long with Peter, she had learned a great deal about literature. Although books, what were they for, really, and how could they compare to raising crops and animals? People, she once said, could live forever without ever seeing a book or even knowing what a book was, but they could not live without food, and he had looked at her as if he had just seen a new and utterly reprehensible being, one that resembled a human being, but was not. Still, she had been right. All those books! Hadn't her father told all of them, "Once," he said, "we buried ourselves in books and we knew nothing of any consequence, but now we are farmers and we need never apologize for dirt under our fingernails. The Asad I am now is not the silly Indian man I was before I came here." Asad, her father, who had said what a privilege it would be to rejoin the earth. "The earth knows all the mysteries." Hadn't her father said that again and again? And now her husband was safe in his own earth, like a bulb that would never rise up again, useless utterly, and all these people who had come to mourn him, hungry and needing food. Not books! Of course she had been right. Let them eat books, she thought, as she continued to walk and wring her hands. And now who was that approaching her? The pastor who had known her since birth, who had baptized her, who had presided over her sister's funeral. Why should her sister have died while her husband, now dead, had still lived? But you must not say such things, she thought. More and more things you must not say. And they must not see it in your actions or see it in your eyes. "You must come back to the others," he said, as he put his arms around her and began drawing her back toward the blackening crowd, "and you must not catch cold." And so she came with him; he was so old and he knew her before her husband had come to this part of England, and she knew she was the one he cared for. So she went. Back.

—

AND OF COURSE the first person she saw coming toward her was Sophie, her stepdaughter, the replica of her husband's first wife. Perhaps, Meena thought, it would have been different if she had a child of her own, but that was not so much a question, or even a thought, only part of the static that had long been the background of her days. And nights. She, Meena, the only one of his three wives who could not produce children. Pregnancy, yes, she had achieved that, but then there were the pains in the stomach, she refused to acknowledge them, until she was carried into the car and taken to the hospital and told that the baby had stopped living, was dead, and the child, the thing that would have been hers and hers alone, had to be taken out. And then the bleeding and the infection, the days of delirium afterward, the antibiotics dripping into her blood, the intravenous on her arm, as they all waited, waited to see if she would survive. He was kinder to her after that, of course he was, and for a while she thought they were grieving together. He stayed home, no more trips to London, and then she said, "That is the worst thing, that I shall never have another child," because in her body, her bones, the headaches that now clouded her eyes, the long muscles of her thighs often threatening to let her go, let her fall to the ground, she knew. And her own body, changed somehow, so that in her mirror she saw reflected a leafless tree of perpetual winter. How could she not grieve, how could she not be ashamed? She had to speak of it; if not, the words revolved like sharp shards of grass. Oh, no one knew what she had suffered then. So she told him, she said, "That is the worst thing," and he said, "But you already have two children," and a dark gong was sounded, and the sun that had always seemed to shine down upon her fell from the sky, and as she fell into deep, deep black water, she said, "Yes. But I wanted one who was only mine," and she learned, or came to learn, how unreasonable he thought her, how selfish, and he came to understand that she would never accept his two children, the ones left behind by his first wife, but he must have thought, One day she will feel differently. After all, they are children, the two I already have, and you come to love children by taking care of them. At least that had been his own experience, although when he thought back to his first wife, it seemed to him that she had loved them, each child, even before her body expelled each of them and sent them into the world. And his first mother-in-law, Charlotte, saying of her, of Meena, "I hope she dies, he doesn't deserve children," and then trying to take the children from him, to keep them for herself, especially Sophie, who was her daughter reborn in another body, saying, "I'll take one and you will keep the other," that was her idea of a compromise, but he fought her, that terrible woman, mother of his first wife, a pelican who devoured her young, maniacal, a witch, who was quite sure she could mold the infant, Sophie, into what she had lost, Evelyn, her own daughter, dead now, thanks to him, the mother-in-law, the devourer, who long ago had shattered his first wife like a precious plate, so that no matter how it was mended, it would never be strong again. And when he said, "Either you take both of them or none," the mother-in-law said. "Keep them both, then," a response he could not understand, but for a moment, he had thought, I may yet be free, I may yet travel where I will whenever I will, I will yet lead the life I envisioned for myself; once he had believed he and Evelyn would lead such a life together, when Evelyn had so astoundingly said, "I don't want children, I want to write and paint and travel," and then one day, she suddenly changed her mind.

Still, he thought they had had an understanding: no children. But then she began hatching the first of his two children, and for some time, he was angry and could barely look at her, his genius-wife, but other women came and said, "How much trouble can one child be?" Even as they spoke, he knew they were lying, knew what they really meant was misery likes company, although there were a few, a very few, who were made happy by having children, who did not want to run away from their own husbands and families or sit in a closed room dreaming of foreign lands or dreaming of *him,* how amazed he had been when he discovered women were hypnotized by him, fell in love with him, worst of all the married women who suddenly came to feel their own husbands could not compare with him, who plotted to keep him where he was, in that perfect little town in that perfect little house, with its many acres of daffodils in the spring, and in the early fall, its trees heavy with apples, all of them conspiring to keep him in this small place, this snow globe he and his first wife had chosen for themselves, and now, apparently, he would have to live in it forever, and everything would be fine if he didn't venture too close to the boundaries of the globe. Everything was sharp and clear and frequently beautiful, but if he came too close to the dome's glass wall, if he pressed his nose against the pane, he saw an entire world beyond it, distorted, of course, by the curve of the glass wall, but always changing, roads that went who knows where beckoning him; he wanted to see where the roads ended and the water began, he wanted to cross the water, cross all of the seas, but of course he would come back; why couldn't his wife understand he would come back? And then one of the women in the village who came in to care for the children set fire to the house while his wife wrote in the topmost room, but Evelyn had ears like a fox, she came tearing down and put out the fire, and after that, Evelyn knew, she knew, that she could never be safe enough, could never depend on his constancy, although he was constant then, but she sensed it, his first wife intuited it, his constancy wearing thin, moths black as crows eating at it, black crows tearing at her skin, and they would continue doing so as long as she lived. She grew ever more jealous, suspicious, but she had her pride; she was the one who left him, went to London and left him there with the new woman with whom he had fallen in love, even though she knew he would tire of her quickly, more quickly than she could have dreamed, so that the second wife, too, would use the gas range to stop her own heart, and their child's, and then there was only one full-grown statue, a waxen beauty, and one small one, too small for anyone to say how beautiful the child might have been had she lived, and after those new deaths, the constant rustle of gossip and blame, a few blessed times when the swish and hiss in back of everything appeared to die out, only to rise up with a roar as if a wave had crashed on the beach.

And what had he done? Other husbands had wives who killed themselves, committed *suicide,* that unutterable word, what had he done that was so much worse than other men he knew? And to have it happen twice! Twice! He had tried to explain himself countless times, but it was futile. There were women who appeared to understand, but what they wanted was him; they would say anything, agree to anything. Evelyn, and then Elfie and then Meena, it was incredible, it was a gift, his genius for women, a power over which he had no power, the spell he cast, and if he spoke of all this to other men and it seemed they understood, they would not understand long; they would go home and their wives would poison them against him. They would say, "He must have done something! That kind of thing cannot happen twice in one life," and some of the wives would tell their husbands, "If you had acted as he had, you, too, might have come home to find me cold and white, did you ever think of that?"

His sisters, Sigrid and Sophie, said he was the kindest man in England, but privately Sigrid admitted to herself that he was passive, that he could not resist a woman who was desperate to possess him, that he was a man who never should have married. There was the siren-beauty of a new love, the pristine world that they unlocked to live in together, and then came the recriminations, her fury, his anger, and then he had enough.

It was Sigrid who understood that he was a rescuer, that he could not resist a woman who needed rescuing, someone he could foster up, like a man who restored paintings, someone who wanted the woman he loved to achieve all her dreams and ambitions, and for a while, it seemed to work, but he was too needy, that was what no one understood, although she, Sigrid, understood it, and inevitably, the day came when he grew tired of rescuing someone, anyone, and wanted to be rescued himself. Then he became distant, was less and less available, and the woman who had needed rescuing still needed it, still required the same attention, the same

cure he had led her to believe he could give her, and the black mark was
once more on his forehead, and again there was the shadow, and in it, the
woman so white and still in her bed, the child so white, like quarried marble, both of them staring at him, both of them saying, It will happen again,
and again, and still again, speaking in voices only he could hear. And
Evelyn, his first wife, smiling, her smile evil, saying, I had not thought
death had undone so many.

Yes, Sigrid knew, he was marked. And he had marked *her*, his sister; he
had summoned her from where she lived in Los Angeles. She understood
that he himself was thinking of suicide, he told her he could not care for
the children, wouldn't she come back, if only for a time? And Sigrid, no
more capable of refusing him than the others, came back, a woman who
did not want children, who did not want to stay in the countryside, who
loved the career she had and the man with whom she lived, she left all and
everything to come to his rescue. And how beautiful she had been then!
Tiny, so thin, her skin pale and flawless, her black hair curling about her
face, as if a doll had come alive, how many people used to say that of her?
In those days what man could have resisted her? Very few could. She had
foreseen, she had expected, had every reason to anticipate a remarkable
future for herself, and indeed, in Los Angeles, she had just begun to live it.
"You don't resemble your brother at all," people used to say, but those who
knew her said, "Sigrid is her brother all over again, but harder, much
harder. I'd rather take on Peter than Sigrid." Well, she would take a little
time out, a little time to take care of Peter, and then she would take up
where she had left off. She had not been back long when he found another
woman in need of his particular sort of salvation, and she could see
clearly, as if it had already happened, how it would end. "It will all end in
tears," she told him, "or worse," and he laughed and said, "How many
times can the same thing happen?" "Many, many times," she told him.
"Why assume there is a limit to such horror? When you write a story, do
you believe you will never write another one? Something that happens
once can happen twice, and something that happens twice can happen

three times. Why assume there will ever be an end? Why assume that horror is finite?"

The rain drummed down and the clouds were thick and dark, and
Sigrid thought, I should have gone back to Los Angeles. I gave up my life
for his life, and it did no good. I was under a spell, his spell, was that it?

Hopeless now to ask herself would life have been different if he had not
called her back, if he had not asked her to mother those two children, if
he had not dreamed up the idea of having her act as his business manager,
when really, as she knew even at the time, her job was to protect him, to
intercept those who approached with vials of poison, to intercept the mail
when articles vilifying him were sent to him by "good" friends, to keep
him as safe as anyone could be, to use the strength she had that he did not
have, to survey the world around her with suspicion, to determine what
was harmful and what was not, to use her ability to sum up what was real
in the world, to say, "This world is hell, and I will stand at the gates like
Cerebus, and anyone who wants to pass will have to make me step aside,
and I never will." And she never did, never gave up, tried to anticipate
everything and prevent trouble of any kind, reproved the children, warned
Peter, and in the end, he dismissed her. He said, "So much disapproval!"
as if she had somehow damaged the children, as if she had not been a good
enough mother, as if she had fought too hard and with the wrong tools.

Meena was coming back, crossing the field separating the house from
the churchyard, one of the pretty Church girls, as Sigrid's mother had once
described them, saying to Peter, "What about one of those nice Church
girls?" Those nice Church girls. Everyone called them that. Their parents
had settled on that surname not long after settling in England, Asad
Chandrasekhara saying, "Our names are too difficult for the British. I do
not want to spend hours of my life spelling out my name," and Meena's
mother, Bharti, said, "Yes, all right, then, but what shall we call ourselves?"
and just then the bells in the church steeple began to ring. It was a Sunday.
And Asad said, "There it is! Church! We shall call ourselves Church!" Soon
after, he hired a lawyer, and so their name was officially changed. All the

daughters took good, plain English names, everyone except Meena. "I think I shall stay as I am," she said. And, as bad luck would have it, it was Meena, one of those nice Church girls, who ended up typing Peter's poems after Evelyn died, Meena, now Peter's widow, typing up poems about Peter's first wife, Peter's dead wife, and then taking Evelyn's place in her bed. Elfie. She had forgotten Elfie. Everyone seemed to. Strange fragments repeatedly flew through Sigrid's thoughts. *And what shall we do next, my lord?* But her thoughts veered again, and she, Sigrid, thought back to her mother, who, when she was dying, Peter sitting on the left, she on the right, their mother propped up by pillows so beautifully plumped by Meena, saying to Meena, "Do leave me alone with my children, won't you, dear?" when someone else might have said, "Get out!" her mother beginning to speak as soon as Meena left the room, turning to look first at Sigrid, then at Peter, and saying, "At the end of the day, it all comes to tears," an expression Sigrid frequently used, squeezing Sigrid's hand and Peter's hand softly, leaving them to wonder, What did she mean, their simple mother?

They had never suspected her of harboring a complicated thought as long as she lived. Such an innocent, her mother. Did she mean, as they thought at the time, that everyone who came to the end of his life had nothing to say, only tears, or did she mean that after a death, those who were left behind had nothing but tears, or did she intend to say, "Everyone has to end like this; every life must come to an end"? Was she just repeating the obvious, intending to console them with that truism, because she lived by truisms and clichés, or so she, Sigrid, had believed? Was that all she meant to say: Everyone who lives must die? Or did she mean something altogether different? Had her mother reviewed her life, summed it up, found nothing she could use as a torch to take her into the darkness waiting so close by, expressed it in that tired saying: In the end, it will all come to tears?

She had been a happy woman, her mother, so aptly named Grace. She never changed, not in all the years they knew her, she was free of ambitions and dreams, content with what she had, her husband and two children, her own brothers, surviving all of her contemporaries, Sigrid wondering now as the rain drummed down, had such tranquillity made for a long life? Of course, her own life had not been serene, nor had Peter's. It was too early to be burying him. But she, Sigrid, was still alive, cold and wet in this driving rain, would perhaps, after this, have a cold for a day or two, but really, she was healthy as an ox, strong as an ox. No, life would not let her go so easily. She would remain as a witness to every terrible thing. Was this self-pity? Sigrid asked herself, only to answer that if self-pity stamped her thoughts, nevertheless what she thought was true. She was not destined to be let out of this life early. She would stay in this world and watch, unable to affect anything, as helpless as ghosts were said to be, despairing of what they saw but unable to change anything, helpless to convey what they knew to those who still lived. It is true, Sigrid thought. I am one of the dead. I have been dead for a long time. For how long, I wonder? From the time of Peter's marriage to Meena? No, before that, when Evelyn determined upon suicide, when she left two small children behind, when Peter wrote to her, to Sigrid, making it clear that he himself was suicidal, asking, "Could you bear to come back and look after the children?" knowing full well she would do anything he asked of her, would give up her life in California, her position that frequently sent her to Germany and France, that life that promised to give her everything under the sun, she would give up the man—her first love!—to come back to care for her brother's children, so that, for the rest of her life, she would say, when others complained, disenchanted by their husbands or wives, "Isn't that what the French say? First love is the only love," and if that was a cliché, experience had taught her to believe it.

But when he first asked her, "Come back, could you bear to come back?" she did not yet know, could not tot up or assess all the irrevocabilities if she agreed to come, but she would have plenty of time to add them up as the years passed; she had not foreseen the many kinds of loss, the loss of will, of unbridled hope, a dreamer, she had not foreseen the inability to dream for herself, but only through Peter, as if, in coming back, she had made the firm resolution that her own life was not to count. She would live her life through her brother. After all, would it not be the same thing? What could he have achieved if she had not come back? How, then, could she not think of his resounding triumphs as her own, made possible by her sacrifice, a relinquishment in the name of love so large that, even now, she would never be able to count the cost? And how long had she been back before he married Meena, and the children no longer needed her, so Peter had said, "It would be good, wouldn't it be good, if you managed my affairs? If you took charge?" And Sigrid had protested, saying what did she know about handling literary affairs? But he had insisted, saying there was nothing she could not do if she made up her mind to it, and at the back, like a fog drifting nearer but still far away, there was always the susurrus, the sound of that gossip: Peter had killed his first wife, what a miracle it was that Evelyn had not killed the children, the gas that killed her could have killed everyone in the house, and then that dark look would come over Peter and she knew he was thinking, How much easier it would be for me if I did as Evelyn had done, and then he married Elfie, and she did do what Evelyn had done, the gas, the gas, taking their child with her, and after that she could never put that horror away as if it were a sock buried in the back of a drawer; it could not be forgotten, the beautiful waxen woman, the beautiful child, something out of a fairy tale, waiting for the prince to arrive and wake them, but the trouble was, reality had its own rules. It was the prince who had sent them to sleep, they were not under a spell that could be broken; yes, at the end of the day, it all came to tears. And then Meena. He said, "I have to marry someone. There are these two," and he named them, and Sigrid asked him, "Do you love them?" and he said, "But which of them would be the better mother?" So she knew he did not love either of the women he had spoken of, and she said, "Well, Peter, if you feel that way, neither of them," but her counsel was already less valuable, she was like currency that had been devalued after a crisis, although of course there would be other crises.

He had married Meena, poor Meena, now stalking about in the rain, twisting her hands. In the beginning, people would ask Sigrid, "Do you think Meena might do what the other two did?" meaning, Will all Peter's wives be driven to suicide? and for a time, her rage would well up and she would become uncontrollable, would say the most terrible things, but when enough time passed, she came to say, "No, I think if anyone is to be killed, it will be Peter. Meena would not dream of taking her own life. She might well take my brother's. That would be another matter altogether." And the terrible jokes: If Peter had only gotten a coal stove after Evelyn, then Elfie would still be alive. As if Bluebeard's wives could simply imagine one key to one door to one room that would turn the lock and let them out of this world into another—if there was another world, which she, Sigrid, very much doubted.

Her own mother, Sigrid's mother, what would she have made of all this? And was it true that her mother never rebelled? Had her mother been as simple and good as she and Peter had always assumed? Had there ever been any evidence, the slightest shred, of an impulse in her mother for another life, one more colorful, more dramatic? She and Peter had found no evidence, but now, with the rain falling, lacquering the black trees, she remembered her mother's eyebrows—or her lack of them, shaved one morning so that she would resemble the movie star she so admired—was it Vivien Leigh? Someone like Vivien Leigh. And the eyebrows never grew back. For the rest of her life, she painted them in with an eyebrow pencil once, twice, sometimes three times a day, painted them in with high, thin arches so that she always wore a look of surprise, as if she expected something to happen, something surprising, spent years and years looking as if she expected something astonishing to happen at any moment, but nothing did.

What must have astounded her was how the same thing happened day after day, wake the children, feed the children, feed her husband, wash the clothes, pour scalding water over the doorstep and scour it, insist that the children do their homework, go to school when the teacher summoned her, because Sigrid never behaved, was always reading the wrong thing, a book she had brought from home, hidden inside the regulation schoolbook, and one meeting Sigrid never forgot, her mother saying to the teacher, "You mustn't worry about Sigrid, Sigrid will get married and have children, no need to worry about her," as if her mother had looked into the shiniest of her saucepans and seen Sigrid's life stretching out beyond her, and what did she see? The same life she had lived, and after that day, Sigrid saw that her mother would never begin to understand her, would always look at Sigrid and see her own image in her, the daughter meant to be the replica of the mother, leading the same life she had lived, a life that she, Sigrid, had already rejected. Those eyebrows, drawn in for the last time as she lay in her coffin, the evidence of that single flight of fancy buried with her. Had Sigrid's bitterness begun even then? What had her mother done one day that led Sigrid to knock her mother to the floor, because she had done that, small as she was, was surprisingly, stunningly strong, and she had not felt shame, only fear of punishment. In those days, her father was still a strong man and of course Sigrid was sure that her mother would tell her father what she had done, but she had done nothing of the kind, she had said, as she struggled to her feet, "I must have done something to deserve it, dear, don't you think?" And then Sigrid had felt guilt, as if she were encircled by a whirlwind, as if such guilt would tear her apart, as if it had made her unable to breathe.

Had she underestimated her mother, or at least undervalued what her mother had done for them, for her and for Peter? The steadfastness of her mother's life, which they had taken as a genius for boredom, the stability which they had taken as boredom, what had she required of them? A life spent worshipping in that Church of the Ordinary, those long, unvarying white walls, those white, unending tunnels leading from one year to the next. They knew when they returned from their rambles that their mother would be there, as always, inevitably uncomplaining, as if she had never heard of self-pity or unrest or depression or unhappiness or

misery, a woman who seemed to have one color on her palette, a kind of
whiteness tinged with pink, who had her chores to do and did them and
did not look beyond them, and so was pronounced boring, "the most
boring woman on earth," Peter said, and she, Sigrid, echoed it; that boredom had been the pillar on which their lives were built. That banality had
allowed them everything, had caused their imaginations to take fire, had
led them to dream up worlds of their own, so different from their
mother's, so much more colorful, so *exciting*! The very word *exciting*
caused them excitement, a foreign element in which they had never
swum. They were free to move unencumbered, while their mother, with
her toes twisted by arthritis, and later, her fingers equally twisted, and her
stick, always with her when she grew older and had difficulty walking,
never complained, never used her difficulties to gain advantage, and
always said, if they asked, "It could always be worse, and that's the end of
it, don't you two have something to do? I have work to do, it's a beautiful day outside, make the most of it," and resumed her dustings and
scrubbings and polishings. And never complained about her husband,
their father, who, she said, had been such a cheerful lad. "Yes," said her
mother, "I married a cheerful lad, but the Great War undid him," she
would say no more than that, would never criticize him, although God
knows, there was plenty to criticize. When they came to know their
father, he had a dreadful cough and an even more dreadful visage, the face
of a storm cloud, a silent man, blackened somehow; what had the pastor
said once? That their father's soul was blackened as if by soot in a chimney, but the fire and the smoke was not of his own making; they had to
understand that, he had withstood horrors, he had come back and carried on, so many others had not come back, so many others who came
back had given up, one falling into a well and drowning, then the same
thing happening a year later to someone else, yet another man falling on
his pitchfork after first embedding its handle in the ground. "There are
many things he cannot speak of," the pastor told them. "You mustn't ask
him. You mustn't ask him for more than he can give."

He resumed running his shop, daily taking inventory, carefully dusting the tins and the boxes so that everything appeared new and fresh and tempting, stared into space as if deep in contemplation, and he was, attempting to guess the number of pounds needed of sultanas before Christmas when the villagers made their plum puddings, how many pounds of jelly beans needed at Easter, how many pounds of lard for the scones, how many scones to ask for from the village woman who did the baking, the same thing, daily and daily, until he had it down, as if he were a fortune-teller, always pinning the tail on the donkey, as he said with the grim laugh that passed for smiling. Saying, as his wife said, "It could always be worse," and Peter asking, "In what way?" and he would say, "If I had bought too few pounds of sultanas, and the wives went off to the next town thinking I didn't know my business," Sigrid and Peter thought, as boring as their mother, and thus father and mother well matched. But the pastor said something, their mother must have said something, about sandstorms and *mustard gas*. "What is mustard gas?" they asked their mother, who didn't seem to know anything about sandstorms and mustard *gas*, but she knew Mr. Colter had breathed it in and her husband had breathed in sand during a windstorm. They laughed about the gas, as if mustard gas were something to spread on meat. And his father's friend, Mr. Colter, who grew sheep as his father had grown sheep in his youth, until one day he got up and it had snowed heavily all night, a blizzard, people still talked of it, and went out to tend the sheep and found most of them unable to move in the deep snow, already half frozen. Dead. After that, after Mr. Colter had called upon Peter's father for help, some kind of veil over the world had torn away from his father, and his friend Mr. Colter, but there was nothing to be done, all he could do was help dig out the sheep, the frozen sheep, and, Peter said, all the veils in the world had been ripped from him, the only light was the icy, cold, unfeeling light of fluorescence, a world without shadows, without veils, unforgiving and comfortless. And so Mr. Colter had given up farming, given up the sheep, built his store, where nothing could die, only rot or mold, but not die, because everything he sold was already dead.

—

AND ONE DAY, when his father was in an expansive mood, at least answering yes or no when he was asked a question, Peter said, "After the sheep, what became of Mr. Colter?" and his father said, "Trembling." Because after that, Mr. Colter had never been right again. He trembled everywhere, tremors everywhere; they made his head shake from left to right, and his hands trembled so that he could barely hold on to anything, and his voice trembled as he spoke, but Mrs. Colter stayed by him, saying, "I'm in this for the long run," and he died before her. They all went to his funeral, and when it was over, his father said, "Another soul gone west," because he meant Mr. Colter had been in the war also, and the sheep, that was one battle too many. "You never know how it will take them," his father told his mother long ago. "Sometimes they come home steady as a rock, and someone breaks a dish or a window shatters, and after that, the man doesn't move again, not even to blink, I've known three men *from this village* who went to stone, didn't blink, and the last one gave way ten years after it all ended and we all came home." How angry his father sounded, as if it were all his mother's fault, and probably it was, because she could not begin to understand. And his father went on, more words from him than either of his children had ever heard all at once, not since his father had been demobbed, saying, "That time we first came home on leave, and all the women at the docks were throwing roses, roses! Full of thorns they were, and my mate Colter was hit in the eye with a rose and might have lost his sight in one eye, but they put a patch on him and sent him back, if you could walk, they sent you back. So how is that, then, they give you a greeting like that, everyone cheering and throwing rose petals, and the stupid ones threw the flower and the stem, thorn and all, and nearly blinded he was, well, I think he was afraid of everything after that, wasn't he? I think he understood what life was after that, didn't he just? I thought, well, he started out a butcher's son, he'd do better in the war, wouldn't he? But no, his father said, 'You only think you've forgotten what

you don't want to keep dragging on with.' I forgot how he used to cry
when his father slaughtered a sheep or a cow, or when the boy trapped a
fox, how we used to laugh at him, didn't we? His saying to his father, 'But
we can always get another chicken!' and his father hitting him in the back,
almost sending him down to the ground, but he was stopped by the glass
case for the sausages, telling him to go out and get rid of that fox, get rid
of it! and he crying, and I tearing up with him, and we killed that fox, and
then we *buried* it. I had to swear we wouldn't tell a soul. We never did, not
until now; he shouldn't have gone over, he couldn't stomach it, no one
would have guessed at it, but did anyone ask about things like that, they
asked, 'Could we walk and talk, you can walk and talk, you're in,' and then
he came home, and my mate Colter, he thought, well, now it's all over,
didn't he? And then there was that blizzard and the sheep froze standing
up and that's when the trembling began, and Mrs. This and Mr. That, they
used to whisper to me, why did I have to keep him in the shop? So blackening it was to see him there, trembling, it wasn't good for my business,
was it? And I slammed down the hammer I was fixing the shelves with,
and they didn't say any more, what could they say, I had the only well-
stocked store in the village. So he sat there trembling until he died, didn't
he?" my father said, and my mother said, "He did, didn't he? He never
thought to go somewhere else, did he? How did he manage? Did you give
him something now and then, to tide him over? I don't remember," and
his father said, "He didn't want for much, he had that little pension, it was
enough for him, wasn't it; he spent the day in our store and at night, he
went home to his wife. She made him pay for that trembling, oh, she made
him pay. It doesn't take much to keep a man alive, does it? Takes even less
to break him, though, and that's the truth, too bad, too bad it was," his
father said, and his mother said, "I expect it's right, what you say," and his
father shouted at her, "What do you know about it?" and later, her mother
told Sigrid, he broke down and cried. Could Sigrid believe her father had
ever cried, openly, with someone watching; could she believe it? And when
Sigrid told Peter the story, years later, years after their father had died,

Peter said, "How could she understand? That's why he shouted, she couldn't understand, and all he wanted was for someone to understand, just once, just once is enough, it's enough for a lifetime," and Sigrid, thinking, He's talking about Evelyn, kneeling next to the stove as if at an altar, and the nurse who finally came saying, "It's a good job we got at her when we did, or she'd be frozen in that pose, wouldn't she?" and that wasn't enough, she had to say, "We'd have had to break her to straighten her out, yes, we got her just in time," and Peter shouting, shouting something. It's what people say to you that turns you quiet, that stops all speaking. Sigrid thought, I learned that in those days, learned it once and for all, so that now people say I don't speak much of myself, not unless I've had a drink or two and then God knows what I say; afterwards, people won't talk to me for months, sometimes never again, well, what can I do about that? Peter was still shouting, even under all that earth, so Sigrid thought, shouting and shouting and shouting until the end of time, why could no one else hear it but her?

—

ALTHOUGH THERE WAS the matter of the chocolate rabbit, every Easter, an enormous chocolate rabbit, almost three feet tall, a display, really, but it became a tradition. Every year, someone tried to buy it. Children and parents saved their pence for that chocolate rabbit, and it would disappear a week after Easter. Their father would never say who had bought it, but it would not take long before everyone in the village knew who had bought that rabbit, had spent so much for it, then the others would say, "Disgusting, to eat so much sweets"; and all the time wishing they themselves had been able to buy the rabbit. And then one year—what had happened?—had their mother expected another child? Their mother cried and cried, but Sigrid and Peter could get nothing out of their father or their mother, and late in the evening on Easter Sunday, he let himself into his shop. He did not turn on the lamps, he picked up the chocolate rabbit and brought it home, and they began by eating its ears, and their mother stopped crying and smiled and smiled, and finally laughed, and their father said he was saving the nose for Mother, and he handed it to her, and she took it as if it were a chalice and stared at it in wonderment and finally popped it into her mouth and got chocolate all over her face, and their father took a dish towel and wet it and wiped her face clean and then both of them stared into each other's eyes, and Sigrid and Peter felt their eyes well up, and for years they thought of that day as the most thrilling day they ever had.

Sigrid wondered if Peter thought back to that day, before he died, and she understood clearly as never before why Evelyn had so charmed him, exciting Evelyn, unpredictable Evelyn, an unpredictable storm of moods, of weeping and laughing, a ravenousness for life such as he had never seen before, an appetite for food so great there were days he believed he could never feed her enough, the same appetite for sex, that ravenousness that matched his own, he had never expected that. But the other days came as well, as if a fuse had blown, and she could not move or make a sound, only lie on her bed and weep, and there were times she did not even have the energy for that, and during those times, he learned despair, and just when he thought, It will never end, this greyness, this endless mourning, she would be up and laughing, radiant as if she herself were responsible for the sun's brilliance, rushing up to her study, and he would hear the sound of typing, typing, and more typing, writing more in a few hours than he could in many months, coming down bursting with energy, saying, "It's time to plant the daffodil bulbs, what about tulips, don't you think planting bulbs in the autumn is a sign of faith? How many can we get? Let's go!" And they would buy the bulbs, and when the crocuses came up, and the daffodils, and then the tulips and all the flowering trees, Evelyn did not come out of her room to see them. She was lying on her bed, weeping and weeping, or staring at the wall, always at the same spot, without moving, gone grey and lifeless, and he would say, "They're all out! Come look! Evvy, come look!" But she would not move. Until two nerves moved together, crossed a synapse, rebuilt a bridge over a high place, a ravine, and she was once more on the other side, running down the steps, out of the house, across the meadow, to look at the daffodils and the tulips, looking them over and nodding, as if to say, I was right to have faith. And she loved her children and she loved her husband and she loved her house until it happened again and she went grey and the world must have gone grey with her, and there was nothing to be done. "Scold her, shout at her," Sigrid had said, but Peter answered, saying, "She cannot be helped in that way." And it was true. No one could help her.

Did it always start with a letter Evelyn got from her mother? Charlotte, that rail-thin mother, who could only eat what her daughter gave her, so that Evelyn tore pieces out of her flesh to give her? A woman like a crow or a raven, her beak yellow and sharp. Because when Evelyn stopped, stopped moving, lost her color, grew like one of the dead, grey and sallow, Peter always seemed to see flocks of crows descending on her and ripping mouthfuls from her flesh. And it seemed to Peter that these crows were loosed by her mother's letters, as if each character instantly became a crow, rapaciously feeding on his wife's body. And didn't he think, didn't he think Evelyn would somehow turn into *his* mother? Time would pass, and Evelyn would become as all mothers became, sensible and predictable and sheltering. Because, before Evelyn, that was all he had known. But he soon learned that nothing of the sort was going to happen. Perhaps if she had lived to be fifty, or sixty, or seventy, she would have become such a woman; he still liked to think so. He could not carry on saying that to Sigrid, who stood still, remembering as the rain drummed down, because she would again say, "Peter, wake up! Open your eyes! She will *never* be normal! She is *not* normal!" And he would say, "She is wearing me out." Oh, she understood that! Yet it was incomprehensible that even as Evelyn exhausted him, even as he complained of how she sucked the marrow out of him, he had already chosen a replacement, at least a temporary substitute, an understudy for Evelyn's grey, draining days, a woman even more fragile than Evelyn: that Elfie, beautiful Elfie, already so damaged, already so worm-eaten by guilt. Would he have chosen differently if he had foreseen Evelyn's suicide? If he had known what was to happen, how could he not know that Elfie would not survive Evelyn's suicide, that she would blame herself for it, in turn blaming him, Elfie finally turning against the world, saying, "Horrible, horrible world!" He held her as she kept repeating it over and over: "Horrible, horrible world!" But at the time, of course, he did not know; he had never believed Evelyn would end her own life. Just then beginning his great opus, completely absorbed, oblivious of Elfie, so that Elfie cried and cried, unstoppable, and Elfie's father said, "She has a man she loves and who loves her, she has a beautiful child, why can't she be happy?" Peter himself was busy with his great work, leaving Elfie's parents to manage her, but they could not, and then someone brought the news of Elfie's death and her child's death, and the news that his two children, Evelyn's two children, had seen Elfie dead, the stepmother destined not to last long, and the child, who lasted not even a year, summoning Sigrid back as if she could work miracles and make a broken mirror whole. But for the two children, Sophie and Andrew, the world reflected the cracks in that mirror, and always would. We were under a curse, Sigrid thought. Evelyn put us under a curse.

And now Sigrid seemed to awaken out of that dream of her past, and watched Meena approaching, and thought, She is mad. She has gone mad. She could almost hear Meena's thoughts: How many of the women here at this funeral have taken him into their bed? When he was alive, Meena could keep Peter here, in this house, a showplace, really, a house, he once said, that did not feel like a home, but in those days she had control. Now Meena saw it had only been the illusion of control. He had a talent for escaping her, he won awards simply so that he could receive them, in London, not far away enough, only distant enough for a train ride or a car trip, only a couple of hours and he could be in London, visiting these people who were here now, in the rain, honoring him one last time.

Why had he married her?

Why indeed? thought Sigrid. Had the conventions of the lower class sunk more deeply into her brother than she'd thought, caused Peter to marry, not only once, but three times? Could he not conceive of living together without first marrying? And how, after the first wife, after Evelyn's death and then Elfie's death, could he marry again? He is dead and gone, Sigrid thought, and there is no point in questioning the dead, especially if you already know the answers. But now Meena was upon her, had grabbed Sigrid's arm, was holding it so tightly that Sigrid almost cried out. "He cannot be buried," Meena was saying, speaking rapidly and loudly, for once not caring if anyone else could hear her. "He can never be buried. Don't you understand? Never! It can't be done! These people, all of them who came here, they want him alive! They will remember him, everything he ever said or did. There isn't enough earth to heap on him, to keep him down, he'll never stay quiet underneath this crust of earth, don't you understand? You understand, don't you? He can't be buried!"

Sigrid said, "It is a dark time."

"Not for him! It was never a dark time for him!"

"Meena," Sigrid said, "I don't have the strength. Wait until this is over. Just a little while. Not a long time to wait, is it?"

"You've always hated me," Meena said, letting go of Sigrid's wrist.

"Meena!" Sigrid said wearily.

"He didn't leave a proper will," Meena said. "Do you know he didn't leave a proper will?"

"Meena," Sigrid said again. Did all of Peter's wives go mad?

"He can't be buried," Meena said again, trying once more to seize Sigrid's wrist. But this time Meena spoke matter-of-factly. "It can't be done. It's because he's famous. Don't you think so? Isn't it true? I never wanted to marry anyone famous. And Evelyn was famous, too. She's still famous. You can't bury Evelyn. I know. I've tried."

"You must go into the house and change your clothes," Sigrid told her. "You have guests to attend to."

"Guests?" Meena said, as if she had never before heard of such a thing.

"Guests," said Sigrid.

"And I must attend to them?"

"Yes," said Sigrid. "And you are very good at it."

"I am, don't you think?" said Meena.

"Go into the house and change," Sigrid repeated.

"Change. In the house," Meena said. "Two of his wives died in that house. Why did we stay there?"

"I was against his staying on, you know that," Sigrid said. "We'll discuss all that later. Go into the house and change."

"Yes, change," said Meena, as if she had come to a decision. "I must change. I shall change."

Mad as a hatter, Sigrid thought, as she watched Meena make her way back to the house. The rain poured down as if it never intended to stop.

Sophie came up to her. "It will be over soon," she said.

"Are you on your fourth husband now?" Sigrid asked irrelevantly.

"You know I am," Sophie said, looking intently at Sigrid, her aunt, the woman who had stood in as her mother once her own mother died, and once again after her stepmother, Elfie, died.

"It's only been two years," Sigrid said.

"I love this one," Sophie said.

"Bertold?" Sigrid asked.

"Of course, Bertold. Are you all right?" Sophie asked her.

"We must all support Meena," Sigrid said.

"Yes," said Sophie. "Andrew thinks that, too."

"Where is he?" Sigrid asked.

"Oh, bending down to look at some kind of worm. He never changes. Remember, every time it rained, he was out inspecting worms? Daddy always said he'd grow up to be a scientist and I'd be the artist, but he's the artistic one, so busy with *forms,* those strange sculptures, and I've ended up the mathematician. Daddy had it wrong."

Yes, Peter always said Andrew would be a scientist and Sophie an artist. Of course, his predictions couldn't *always* be accurate. But Peter also said that Andrew was like a pane of glass cracked straight down the middle. "You can't put too much pressure on him," Peter told Sigrid. "You can put a lot on Sophie and she'll take it, it won't be good for her, but she'll take it, but not Andrew. You'll watch out for him?"

"Everyone watches out for him," Sigrid said.

And Sophie had said the same things about her brother a few days ago, echoing Peter's words as if he were speaking through her. Sigrid could not tell anyone about Peter's estimate of his own son. So many secrets, she had been burdened by so many of them. Who else would he tell his secrets to but her? And of course she had not told them to anyone. But to whom could Sigrid tell those same secrets? Secrets had such weight! But she had kept her secrets, allowed them to weigh her down. She shivered violently, remembering. Sophie thought Sigrid was chilled and said, "We had better get in." There was something excited in Sophie's manner. All this would hold up until the last guest left, the excitement, the polished surface, the good face Sophie was putting on things, and then she would begin speaking angrily, about why this one had come, why that one hadn't, she would sound just like Meena, and Meena would be watching Sophie, waiting for a chance to say something cutting, something implying that Sophie was as mad as her mother had been, as mad as Evelyn, and so Sophie had to be carefully watched. If Sophie ate two pieces of cake, Meena would say, "You'd better watch that, Sophie, you've had so much trouble with the way you starve yourself, we don't want to go through that again," and Sophie would say she hadn't been troubled in that way for years, and Meena would nod and say, wisely, "All the same, all the same," and there would be no one to say, as Peter might have, "Let her alone, she's fine."

"You know what I most dread?" Sigrid told Sophie as they walked. "Everyone leaving and then only Meena alone in the house. But that won't be the worst of it. She won't have realized it, that it's final, but in a few days she will, and I dread those phone calls, when she rings up and rants on and on as if it's not Peter's death she's talking about. I think she's mad, love."

"Oh, I don't think so," said Sophie. "Although she probably hates *me*, but then you don't have to be mad to hate *me*, do you?"

"I can't begin to guess what goes on in that deep well that passes for her mind," Sigrid said, "but we must support Meena. We must all support her."

"Yes, we will," Sophie said. "Daddy would have wanted it."

"Although she will be hard to support," said Sigrid, "but it must be done."

"She'll manage," Sophie said.

Was that bitterness in Sophie's tone? Did Sophie know more than Sigrid thought she did? Peter was not always discreet, not with members of his own family. "We must support her, whether or not we believe she deserves our support," Sigrid said sharply.

"Of course, support Meena," Andrew said, catching up to them. "Look at this. I thought it was a worm, but it's a snake. Speckled."

"You stay the same," Sigrid said to her nephew.

"Always jack-in-the-box, popping up with a snake in his mouth," Sophie said, so that the three of them managed to enter the house laughing, to the great disapproval of the guests who had come so far and gotten so wet, and to the immense disgust of Meena, who always insisted that the three of them vied in surpassing themselves to disgrace her, just as Peter had spent their marriage disgracing her with his affairs, once she came to know of them, and the worst of it was that she had gone for so long without knowing what everyone else knew. How Peter must have despised her for not knowing what was happening when everyone else did, the other two, Evelyn and Elfie, knowing immediately, taking their own grim kind of action, well, she would think of all that now when they came in, Sigrid and Sophie and Andrew. And then they were inside the room full of people, "If you are laughing now, you'll be crying in a moment," Meena said knowingly to Sigrid and the two children, her voice loud enough to be heard by everyone in the room, making what she had put up with all these years perfectly clear, what she still had to put up with.

And what a charmer she is, Sigrid thought, watching Meena, as she moved from place to place, from person to person, accepting sympathy again and again, sometimes saying, "These are dark days, I don't know what else to say, but the sun comes up every day and one day I shall feel its warmth and have a light to steer by, I tell myself it's the same blue sky up there, isn't it?" her face pale and haggard, as if it were a trial to speak, but she made that effort, because after all, the person to whom she spoke had taken the trouble to honor her husband, her dead husband, and it had been such a hard march before he died. "He went the way of my sister," Meena was saying now, and Sigrid knew that when this was over, when everyone began to leave and close their car doors against the cold and the rain, a husband who had come would turn to his wife and ask, "How does Meena bear it? I know he wasn't faithful to her, but they were married for so long, thirty years, was it more? How wonderful it must have been to be married to such a man, even though he had his faults, well, we all have faults," and the wife replying, "Yes, we all have faults, don't we all have them, but not necessarily the compensations," and then the husband answering, "Could you have put up with him? Wondering where he was every time he got out of your sight?" And the wife, it was always the wife, thinking, I couldn't say, really, I couldn't, he's asked an unanswerable question, really, because she had not been favored with such a man. If she had been, would she have done everything she could to keep him, crawled on her belly? Wasn't that what Elfie had said? "I crawled on my belly, I begged, I wasn't a woman anymore, just a thing that begged and pleaded, and then I couldn't keep it up, you don't know what humiliation is until you meet Peter," Elfie, speaking as she wept, weeping day after day, as if weeping and breathing went together, ending by saying, "It's useless to even speak of it, if anyone should have known, I should. Evelyn went through it all before me and because of me, and still, I couldn't begin to estimate what I was in for.

"Who can? 'The burnt child fears the fire,' but who knows what the fire makes you feel? Until you put your hand into the fire as I did. But Evelyn had known, he told me what Evelyn had said to him, 'I shall build you a cauldron of fire and you will know what it is to live in it,' but that was Evelyn, I am not Evelyn, I don't have her strength, and where did her strength get her? If I were weaker. . . ." And here Elfie broke down altogether, ending by saying, "I couldn't be weaker, I couldn't be weaker," and Elfie's parents saying, "We'll give her a sedative, put her to bed, she mustn't talk so long," that was Elfie's father, and Elfie's mother, saying, "It doesn't help to talk, when she talks she sees things with more clarity, everything is sharper, believe me, she doesn't need things clearer or sharper, she uses her own words to cut herself, it goes on, deep inside, I don't know how to stop it, and my daughter, my Elfie, the same one who used to laugh and say, 'We manage these things better in France. In France, the priest is a party to the infidelity, the party of the third part, he blesses the unfaithful and tells them human beings are weak. Now, go and sin no more, and the next week, they're back, listening to the same words. Yes, if it weren't for the priest, infidelity could not go on so smoothly,' Elfie used to say that when she first took up with Peter, she didn't spare a thought for Evelyn. I think she laughed at Evelyn, thought it was a game, thought Evelyn would pay all of the price, and now! Look! Look!" Elfie's father interrupting to say, "Will it help if you fall to pieces altogether? To have lived through everything we saw and now to break when our own daughter needs help?"

"Could you have put up with him?" asked the husband in the car, the rain drumming noisily on the car roof, and the wife answering carelessly, "Yes, I suppose, I suppose I could have," her husband slightly turning to her, incredulous, then turning back to the view through the windscreen, saying, "I hope this downpour cleans the car. Why every huge bird has to let its bowels loose on top of this car is more than I can imagine," thinking, but briefly, My wife would have been one of those women—if she could have—had she been? No, impossible, not because she was too ugly, but too sturdy. Peter never went in for durable women. Women with common sense were anathema to him, and his wife, what did she have but common sense? Although capable of a transitory flight of fancy, saying, "Yes, I suppose, I suppose I could have put up with him," the same thing

as saying, "Yes, I could fly through the air and land on the ridgepole," how
ludicrous she was, his wife.

"Well, the last one gone," Meena announced, slamming the front door
harder than necessary, realizing she had, saying, "How everything sticks in
this damp," Sophie and Andrew already beginning to clear off the cups
and saucers, Meena saying, "Clear off the kitchen table. That table is full
of woodworm, but I want it to last as long as I do," Sigrid mutinously
thinking, Peter built that table for Evelyn so that she could write on it. For
years, it had lived in the study up at the top of the house, but when Meena
moved in, she said, in that steely voice they were coming to know so well,
"We'll have that for the kitchen," and Peter and one of his friends had
obligingly hauled it down, along with the two benches that sat on either
side of it, Meena taking up her place on the bench, looking at the table,
her face hooded but satisfied, clearly thinking, Now it belongs to me, so
much for Evelyn and her silly writing; what had come of it? And now
Evelyn was dead and what did she need with tables, with anything, with
her own children, the two she had left behind?

And that friend of Peter's, telling him about a poet whose wife died, and
he was so distraught he buried all of his poems in the coffin with her, but
of course, the man who had done that was a writer, he should have known
better, so Meena thought, even when she first heard the story, "and then,"
Peter's friend said, "time passed and he had her dug up so he could get at
the poems, well, that's a writer, for you, it's a calling, not a profession."
What nonsense, Meena thought. If I died, would I ask someone to bury
my table with me? Although, Meena thought, I could ask them to build a
coffin out of that table, but not planks already drilled through with woodworm, although why not? Wouldn't a coffin be riddled soon enough? A
horrible story, a hateful story, digging up the dead wife to get at the poems.
Oh, they were all the same, these writers, waiting to hear who had died
and why so that they could "commemorate" the event, as if life and death
existed for them to inspire silly words and put them on thin pieces of
paper. They were useful, those thin sheets of paper. She often found them

rolled up and hidden about the house, behind a loose floorboard, fastened inside a chimney whose fireplace had long since ceased working, and she took the papers and rolled them up tightly, lit them with a match, and used them to set the kindling roaring in their wood fires so that the kitchen and parlor were warm. Hundreds of such sheets of paper, covered in letters of thick black ink, some words circled even more thickly. Evelyn never wrote on both sides of the page, unthrifty, those writers, all of them, especially Evelyn, who wrote the same thing out again and again on her typewriter, why did she need so many of the same thing? An entire sheet of paper because she had changed a single word, and how much better she would have been, that Evelyn, if she had put in some good, honest work, although people did say that the daffodils covering the lawns of their house and the lawns of the churchyard had been planted by her own hands, as if there were something remarkable about her hands, as if it were remarkable that she, Evelyn, had done such pedestrian things. *Planting faith*, had Evelyn said that, or had Elfie? Ridiculous, the fuss. You planted bulbs. They came up. They spread. What had faith to do with it? If the bulbs did *not* come up, then you might have to worry about what you had done wrong, then you might consider the words *faith* and *faithlessness*, *hope* and *hopelessness*, no sense of proportion among writers, especially not among women writers. And in the end, who had custody of that table? She, Meena, had it, woodworm and all. Hers. And she would die with it in her possession.

"Well, that's over," Sigrid said, Sophie and Andrew returning to the parlor and sitting down, Andrew always preferring the huge tan leather chair with its wide arms, at the end of each arm an enormous, curved horn, "I always loved that chair," Andrew said. "Who gave it to Daddy?"

"Oh, I don't know," Meena said irritably. "But if you upend the chair, there's a bit of tape with the name of the person written on it. That's how I kept track of what should be moved to the place of honor when the person visited, if that person ever visited."

"If you let them visit," Sophie said.

"I couldn't have everyone who sent your father a gift trampling through the house," Meena said. "You know how he insisted on his quiet, especially when he was working, and he used to say, 'I'm always working. No matter what it looks like I'm doing, I'm working, what I'm doing will turn into part of my writing'; you remember that."

"People trampling through the house," Andrew repeated.

"Andrew," Meena said, "that is indeed a very bad habit. If you cannot think of something to say, do not repeat what someone else has said. Say something worth hearing or keep quiet. I have lived by that rule and it has not let me down."

"The child is quite silent enough," Sigrid said, thinking, If Peter were here, he would say, "Macs on, wellies on, let's go see how poor Pater's doing," Pater the boar, kept by Meena as a pet, and Meena would have said, "Pater is just fine, why must he be bothered?" and Peter would have said, "Let's go! We'll find something to look at. I imagine the river's gone quite high," and Meena would say, "The riverbank will be slippery, don't go too close to the edge, do you hear me, Sophie and Andrew? There's quite a current with all this rain."

"They're not falling in," Peter would have said. "Not floating all the way down to London."

"I wouldn't have thought it out of the question," Meena would have said. "If you have decided, do go."

But now Peter was gone, and these little comments of Meena's, these moods, thought Sigrid, would have their own, poisonous effects.

"It was good of everyone to come so far, and on a day like this," Sigrid said. "It was good to see Peter honored. So I felt."

There was a long silence, and the wood fire crackled and spit. Some brilliant orange sparks flew up like fireworks.

"I used to love watching the fire," Sophie said.

"Didn't you?" Sigrid asked Meena. "Didn't you love to watch the fire?"

"Watch the fire? As if I had time for watching fires!" Meena said.

"Your own cousin told me, oh, it was years ago, that when you were all young, and the others were all busy at something or other, you would sit for hours and stare into the fire. He wondered what you thought about. Dreaming or scheming, I wonder?" Sigrid said.

Meena stayed silent.

"And I remember," Sigrid said, "that first night you came to dinner at this house, when I cooked a dinner. What was it? Fish? And you wouldn't eat it because I made some kind of French sauce, and Peter picked up your plate and took it to the sink and washed off the fish, and then you ate it, although with each bite you screwed your mouth up a little."

"No such thing happened," Meena said.

"But before that," Sigrid went on, "before that, when we were having soup, and everyone was talking about infidelity and that woman, Bridget, who had an abortion and it turned out so badly, but afterwards she said that she could sleep with anyone and there was no more reason to worry over pregnancies, and without any warning, you fainted and fell into your soup. You remember *that*," Sigrid said.

"I fainted and fell into my soup?" Meena repeated, staring stonily at Sigrid.

"Yes. It was a cream soup. I can still see you."

"Hallucinations," Meena said. "Or you dreamed it. My mother claimed your entire family was mad."

"Did she?" Sigrid asked, a dangerous tone, a sound Sophie and Andrew had learned to know very well.

The fire crackled and hissed. The mantel clock ticked and tocked.

"It's time we were going to bed," Sigrid said at last.

"What I simply cannot stand," Meena said, as if she were resuming a subject they had already begun discussing, "is the hypocrisy of them, all of them. How many of them do you think cared about Peter?"

"Well, I think all of them," Sigrid said testily.

"And that's why they came and inflicted themselves on us?" Meena asked. "Not at all, Sigrid. Everyone knew the place would be full of impor-tant people. Peter once said those people went to funerals the way other people went to parties. They were here to remind the others that they were still alive, they wanted to remind themselves that Peter thought they were important once, although he never cared if most of them had lived or died. They were here to advance their sacred goal, their *careers*. To remind everyone here that they were important, that was the main thing. And to see if there were any crumbs they could take back. I always said that in this country, especially in London, for those sort of people, gossip is the currency they care for. When they go back, they'll have something to trade, they'll use whatever they learned here so they could buy more gossip. *And he did what? And she looked like what? And the widow and the sister, how did they get on? And is Sophie still the dead likeness of her mother?* I hope none of you had the stupidity to repeat anything they could take back to town. I *hope* you haven't," Meena said.

Now she will go on, Sigrid thought. Now she won't stop.

"And that dreadful woman and her dreadful husband," Meena said.

"Rose and Robert, you mean?" Sophie asked.

"How can they be so ugly?" Meena asked. "How can they bear to be seen in public? With her horse-face and her ghastly permanented hair and that bad dye job and her hair combed in front of the mirror so that she thinks, Oh, it looks fine, but she never combs the back of her head, you can see down to her scalp, and the husband, where do you begin? If you say, 'Hello,' he starts in grilling you. If you answer and say, 'I'm doing well,' he must know what you mean by 'well.' The rudest man I have ever known. Has he not heard of dentists? All those gaps where teeth would be. How he spits when he speaks! And they insist, both of them do, on speaking with each and every person there. No one can be spared! I suppose he was quieter today. Someone must have hit him with a stick just before he came and said, 'Remember, the person you are visiting is still upset that her husband has died. She may not have the patience for tendentious arguments.'"

Tendentious arguments? thought Sigrid. Who has been teaching Meena such words? Perhaps there's some truth to the rumor. Perhaps she got her own back and had her own affairs, one with someone who used the word *tendentious*.

"And all of them carefully examining Sophie here, to see if she was or was not Evelyn, risen up from the grave. And you, too, Andrew, everyone scrutinizing you to see if you were the image of your father. How I hate them!"

"Why hate them?" Andrew asked Meena. "They don't mean enough to you for you to bother."

"And asking one another, 'Why does Andrew spend his time in hot countries far from his mother, and why does Sophie head straight for Jamaica with whichever husband she's on now?' I heard them talking. I have ears like a fox."

"Shall you be able to manage?" Andrew asked her. "On your own?"

"I have always known how to manage on my own," Meena answered.

"I mean, are you set for money to live on?"

"He means," said Sigrid, "do you have enough bread? Or will the butcher and the baker be at the back door?"

"Of course I have enough," Meena said. "Peter would not leave me with nothing."

No, thought Sigrid. During the last two years, whenever Sigrid saw Peter, he would say, "I have to make more money, I have to make enough to get away from her." And so he had, he who had always said—and how it had infuriated her—"It's only money," so that Sigrid had to say, "But when the roof leaks, someone has to pay to stop it, and in February, if you decide to go to Morocco, someone has to pay for *that*, so how can you say, 'It's only money'?" And Peter, saying, "Money always shows up when you need it," and Sigrid answering, "But it's been showing up less and less, hasn't it?" and Peter saying, "Money will show up," and Sigrid saying, "Oh, dream on. Was that the bell? I hope it's someone at the door with lots of bread he wants to give away."

"Daddy said he left a will," Andrew said out of the blue.

"And on the night of his funeral, you want to ask how many pence you will get?" Meena asked. "Is that why *you* came? All the way from Iceland?"

"You know both of them came because they heard their father was dying," Sigrid said. "Although they didn't hear it from you."

"I saw no reason to upset them, or to upset Peter with their wailing and weeping," Meena said. "I should have thought that was a time to leave him in peace and conserve his strength so that he could hang on as long as he could."

"No, Meena," Sigrid said. "You wanted him to yourself. You didn't want him blabbing about his doings during the last few years. You kept him prisoner. If it had been up to you, they would have come home to find their father dead. As soon as Sophie came in, he began to cry, and don't you try to tell me he was crying because he was unhappy to see her."

"Of course he was happy to see her," said Meena. "I simply thought he could wait a little longer to see her, and for her to see him. It was a question of his *life*, wasn't it? I was in the best position to make such decisions, wasn't I?"

"It depends on what you were hoping to achieve by making those decisions," Sigrid said.

And so life leaks out, Andrew thought, while these squabblings continue.

"Daddy told me he left a will," Andrew repeated.

"Do you think I wouldn't insist on that?" Meena asked.

"And is anyone to know what it is?" Sigrid asked.

"I shall fetch the papers I have," Meena said, springing up from her chair. "Everyone shall have one, since you have all been so concerned," and she ran up the stairs while Sigrid, Sophie, and Andrew looked at one another. Sophie was crying and Andrew's eyes were red-rimmed.

"Where is Bertold?" Sigrid asked, and Sophie said, "He drove someone to the train. He should be back any instant now."

"Thank God for that," said Sigrid. Meena would restrain her comments in his presence.

"Oh, yes, he hates Meena," Sophie said. "He calls her the greatest hypocrite in England. When he's not speaking of her as the most evil woman in the world."

"She has had a lot to put up with," Andrew said.

"Don't try to excuse her!" Sigrid said.

"Must you hiss like that?" Andrew asked her.

"Must you be so thick?" Sigrid asked him angrily. "Do you think the two of them were living happily ever after those last two years, almost three? Do you think they were even living together?"

"Sigrid, he doesn't know," Sophie said, coming to her brother's defense.

"And shouldn't he have tried to find out, when he heard about his own father's illness?" Sigrid asked.

The kitchen latch rose and then fell. "Bertold's back!" Sophie said, her relief evident.

"Yes, Bertold's back," Sigrid said. "And Andrew still doesn't know *anything*. Who is going to tell him?"

"Tell me what?" Andrew asked. "Why am I always the last to know?"

"Because you are the one everyone thinks needs protecting," Sophie said.

"Doesn't know what?" Bertold asked. "Tell me what you want to know, Andrew."

"No," said Andrew. "It's Meena's place, so it seems to me."

"Thicker than two planks, and he always has been," Sigrid said. "If you think you're going to learn the truth from Meena, you're very much mistaken."

"Whatever became of Daddy's leather jacket?" Andrew asked. "The one he's always wearing in the photographs? I'd like that."

"Meena will give that up. Probably," said Sigrid. "I can't see her cousin wanting to wear that."

"If she hasn't already thrown it out," Sophie said. "Remember the little painting of Elfie's, on the wall up on the third floor? The day after Daddy died, she threw it out."

"She thought of this as her home," Andrew said, "not some bloody museum of our father's life and the lives of his first two wives. She should have thrown out a lot of things," Andrew said, "if it had given her some peace."

The rest of them stared, stared without answering, Andrew so rarely said what he thought; really, when he did so, it was stunning.

"You don't know what you're talking about," Sigrid said at last, and Andrew answered, saying, "Oh, but I do, about this I do know, I may not know everything, I may not know much since I'm so protected, but I do know about this." And then there was complete silence while everyone waited for Meena to reappear and the fire continued its senseless conversation, crackling and spitting its way to extinction.

And yet, thought Sophie, there are beautiful days, aren't there beautiful days? Who knows if there won't be one of them already waiting when the light breaks in the morning? She would have said that aloud, but scorn would have been heaped upon her, or worse, Sigrid would have looked at her pityingly and Andrew would have looked away, as he would have done had he been driving in a car and they were about to pass an accident on the side of the road.

Andrew, silent again, remembered Sophie saying, "What *do* you think about? You're supposed to be the educated one. I think that bloody boar of Meena's thinks more than you do. What *do* you think about, Andy? What, for example, are you thinking about now?"

"Leave off," he had told his sister.

"No," she said. "I want to know," and he said that he thought Sophie talked too much; "You know, if you stop talking," he said, "you'll continue to exist," and Sophie said angrily, "Oh, so that's what you think about, is it? That's what someone thinks who went to university."

She met Bertold when he came over from Germany and he stayed on with Sophie and never went back, and he began to teach her advanced theoretical mathematics, he had quite a reputation in mathematical theory himself, and of course he was twenty years older than Sophie, old enough to be her father, so it wasn't surprising he liked to teach her, but who would have thought how it turned out? The pupil surpassing her teacher, when no one thought she had a brain in her head, how bizarre it was, but the surprise of it was that she had an amazing talent for it. "A real idiot savant, is my daughter," Peter said at the time.

Once, at one of Sophie's parties, Sophie introduced one of her friends to Andrew, saying, "She's just come down from university," said it so proudly that, without thinking, Andrew said, "Everyone's gone to university." He hadn't really meant it as a slap at his sister, but she went white, her lips turned a thin line, and she said, "It's difficult to believe, really, really difficult, to believe that our parents produced anyone so intent on aspiring to the consciousness of a stone. No, not even a stone, a pebble!" and he took a look at his sister and said, "I'm going out."

He found himself in one of those empty suburban streets, in London, in the middle of nowhere. Sophie insisted on living "Behind God's back," as Daddy used to say, but Sophie said, "If you drive, it doesn't matter, you can get anywhere in half an hour." He had pointed out to Sophie, who had to do things the difficult way, at least that was how he saw it, that not everyone had a car, not everyone wanted to take the tube to the end of the line and then take three buses, when the buses never ran regularly or predictably back here, beyond World's End. No, not everyone wanted to stand outside waiting for the right bus on a cold, rainy night, the wind playing havoc with that person's hair, but that was Sophie, she wanted drama, she loved slamming doors, she liked being angry, and then it was too much, and it was back into her safe place, just what she had done as a child, no one ever had to say to her, "Go to your room!" or, "Sit in that closet!" because she had her own safe place, and it was a closet, of all things, a sloping, dark thing beneath the steps going up to the first floor, and she would get in there, way in the back, as if no one could see her, as if no one suspected where she was. And after some time passed, someone was sure to say, Daddy or Meena or Sigrid, would say, "Where is Sophie?" and if Daddy was there, not upstairs writing, he'd say, "I'll look," and at times, when he looked in the closet, he did not see Sophie, she was pressed so hard into the back corner, thrusting herself against the darkness, and he'd say, "Give me a torch, will you?" and even then, when he shone the light in, he didn't see her, and Sigrid, if she were there, would say, "Bloody hell!" and Meena would say, "Peter! Don't go out to look for her, not in this weather. This is what comes of putting up with her whims, she'll come back when she's hungry," and then Sigrid would start in, shouting at Meena, "She's not a dog who'll come back for food! She's your *stepdaughter*!" and Daddy would say, "Not again!" and when finally Sophie was ready to come out, she'd have heard them arguing, she'd be afraid, and try to lie, saying, "I was just sleeping, I didn't hear you calling me," and if Sigrid were there and could reach her, she'd wallop her on her bottom, and then Meena would put in her own two pence and say, "*If* I'm to be the child's mother, don't you think I should be the one to do the disciplining? Don't you think so, Peter?" God, Andrew thought, there was never an end to it, and now Sophie had this house in back of the beyond, and it was the cupboard under the stairs all over again, and in it she was sheltered and safe, at least she felt so most of the time, and when she sensed danger, she locked the door and stayed in there, in her own world, in some town or street of her own, unlisted on any map.

It was quiet now in Meena's house, no one in the kitchen saying anything. That was how Andrew liked it, if they were cooking up revolutions, at least let them do so in peace and quiet; if the others were dreaming up poisons to put in the soup, at least they were doing so quietly, and he began to think his own thoughts, noticing that Bertold had put his arm around Sophie as if to keep her unharmed, Andrew remembering what Sophie had said, "*I'll* find the right girl for you, Andy." Well, that was a threat, hadn't it been, and then he began dreaming up one of his "problems."

As a boy, he used to wonder if his mother, his real mother, Evelyn, had died not on earth but on a distant star, how long would the light from that star take to reach this earth, and when it did reach the earth, how could you retrieve the images of what had happened on that other star, images of what had happened so long ago? How long would it take before she would be seen alive, as he had been told so many times she once had been, yet he had no memory of her? "You were too young," his father said the one time he asked, and then he never asked his father again, and he knew better than to ask Meena, who in any case had not known Evelyn, or to ask Sigrid, whom he did ask once. He asked her, "What was my mother like?"and Sigrid said, "Oh, why do you want to open that bloody door now that it's finally closed? You don't *want* to know, love!" But he had, and he did.

So it was theoretically possible for him to see her, even if she were only light, even if she were no more than a reflection in a mirror, the real woman long gone, her molecules long since taken up by new things, trees, rats, a snake, a worm, a scale of a fish. But was that all he wanted? To see his mother, how she had spoken and moved, to catch sight of her, or the sound of her voice, or the smell of her? He remembered *something* when people mentioned her, a yeasty smell, like unbaked dough. If he could smell that again, what would he remember? What would he learn about what he himself once had been like? Surely he had not always been silent and angry. He had to admit he was angry, always angry, as if he were some kind of fire that appeared to have been put out but now burned deep underground, like those coal mines in Pennsylvania, the ground so hot it hurt you when you walked on it. His anger. He knew it existed, but he could not have said what the consequences of such anger were, could not guess whether his mother's anger had been like his, whether, in fact, he had somehow imbibed hers, caught it from her as if it were something contagious, then grown it, as a specimen grows in a petri dish, in which case he was not quite human, was still aspiring to humanity, was not quite there, as if he only seemed to have his own spirit, but really, that spirit was not his; it was borrowed from his mother's. Sophie had accused him of that more than once. "You are not really human, are you, Andrew? So busy with carving those *forms*. They're nothing human." As if Sophie herself didn't burn with anger, as if she knew why she was so angry, although, he was sure, she understood that aspect of her life, the inner things that went on beneath the surface, more than he did. He understood so little.

But the objects he sculpted, those *forms,* what were they but the shape of sorrows, the shape of sufferings? What else was he to carve? And what had his father said after he looked at many of them displayed for the first time in a gallery? "Taken together," his father had said, considering, "they're a portrait. Of something." And then his father looked at him, puzzled, almost frightened, as if he knew who the person was, the one who had somehow posed for these twisted forms, these objects that his father understood, as no one else had, came together to make a portrait.

—

THERE WAS MORE to it. His mother had deliberately put an end to her own life, and to their lives, the lives they had every reason to believe would continue as they always had. She had taken away that certainty, that conservatory in which small children grew, she had smashed it, and he could not bear to look at plants that were left to freeze in the winter, beautiful and green in the summer, spangled yellow in the sun, and in the winter, frozen, black, resembling black banana peels. Yes, there was another problem he would like to solve. If he reckoned up the number of sorrows Evelyn had suffered, sorrows that would endure as long as she lived, if he counted up the wonders, the great moments of happiness that would not fade until her breath stopped, if he multiplied that sum by the particular intensity with which she experienced her own life, moment by moment, would the total be greater or less than others who put an end to their own lives? In other words, would the number be sufficient to justify what she had done? Decided upon? *If* she had decided, because if it was true that his mother had really been mad, as Sigrid insisted she had been, then when she put her head in that oven, she was trying, not to kill herself, but to kill the madness that lived in her. But he did not believe she had been mad. Something worse had been wrong, he thought, something in her not strong enough to withstand the stabbings others inflicted on her. But they inflicted them on everyone, didn't they? Something hopeless, something that made her incapable of receiving balm and comfort, as if she had been born with a substance, a chemical, in her membranes that would not allow solace, or hope, or plain stubbornness. If he could quantify what she had suffered, if only he could say, Yes, I understand, it was inevitable, I can forgive you. If the number were big enough, the number that represented her suffering. But he had always wondered: if she had been sure she would achieve such celebrity in her own lifetime, would that have changed the number? Would it, when he subtracted the vast number represented by fame, the enormous number that stood for the approval of the world, the world taking her in at last, at last no longer the cuckoo in the nest of the world—yes, he knew his mother, Evelyn, had felt that, just as he had, and his father had, and Sophie had—but for his mother to feel that was intolerable—when he had subtracted that number, would it have been small enough to let her live? She would have done anything to feel, even for a day, like an ordinary person. It wasn't enough for her to be a genius of an artist; she had to be a genius of the ordinary. He knew his mother had thought that. She would have wanted life every which way. He knew that to be true because of the small things his father had let drop, the expression on his face when some particular thing was said about her. Still. If she had known she would achieve such fame. And if that number, the one that represented her fame, had been subtracted from the sum of her sorrows, then would the sum have been small enough, have let her live?

"She used to count things," Sigrid said. "How many steps from the house to the church, how many scourings to clean the table when something caked on the wood before she got to it, the pages she wrote, 'I wrote two pages today,' a fortune in her book. And later, 'I wrote six hundred and fifty words today.' She counted the number of hairs in her brush, every single morning, the number of times a wagon wheel revolved when they were taking feed out to the cow, and another time, though this was a singular occurrence: 'It was as if someone very cold had blown in through the window. It seemed like wind, but I knew it was someone who had just died and was on her way somewhere, on her way to London. I was completely sure of that, but whoever she was, she wanted to stop in here, as if to warm up, she wanted to see me one more time, and I tried to work it out, how long she would have had to be out in the cold to grow so chilled, then I could have guessed how long she had been traveling, then I would have known how far away she was when she died, I could have begun to guess who she was, but no one died in the night, do you know anyone who died in the night?'" Sigrid listening to Evelyn, appalled, Peter riveted, he believed in spirits, he believed they had their own way of journeying from here to there, puzzled, saying, "But no one died," and then the phone went, and it was Peter's mother on the phone, saying, "He went in the night. I was asleep next to him for hours. He was so cold when I opened my eyes and saw the way he was staring, he wasn't blinking, that gave it away, and then, of course, when I touched him, I knew."

"But why," Sigrid asked irritably, "would my father have come to you? You never had much time for him and he wasn't the one you loved," Sigrid intending to say, I was the one he loved best, and Peter, thinking it over, saying, "He may have meant to tell you something, something important that you could keep with you for the rest of your life." And Evelyn's rejoinder. "What on earth could that man have to tell me? I mean, of what possible value would something he had to say be to me?" and Sigrid, who considered it, sure her father had, indeed, materialized in Evelyn's room, saying, "I think he went to the wrong room. I think he went through the wrong window, you're the one who always leaves your shutters open, even in the cold, or he thought Peter would be in that room, or me, or . . ." "Or," said Peter, "he was one of the newly dead and not yet practiced in traveling. He got near where he wanted to go, but not exactly where he wanted to be. No, I don't think he intended to visit Evelyn."

"And why shouldn't he want to visit me?" Evelyn asked crankily. After all, someone had visited *her*, and now everyone was trying to take the credit for his visit. "Didn't you say, Peter, didn't you say he thought I was an exotic beast?"

"He didn't use those words," Peter said, "but that was what he meant."

"I think his exact words were, 'I've never seen a bird with such strange feathers,'" Sigrid said, and Evelyn turned on Sigrid in a frenzy, saying, "You take every opportunity to tell me what a bad wife and mother I am!" And Sigrid, genuinely puzzled, saying, "How do you manage to make that out of what I just said?" Evelyn answering, "What you mean to say is that I'm such a strange bird that I can't build an adequate nest, I can't keep my children in the nest, they'll fall out and smash themselves on the ground, I don't know how to hatch my own children, isn't that what you mean? Well, it is, isn't it?" Sigrid taking fire and answering, "I said no such thing, but I can't help but agree with your interpretation, although, Evelyn, for once, for *once*, it would be very much appreciated if you listened to what I said and didn't translate my words into some peculiar language of your own."

"That's enough," Peter said. He looked at Evelyn as he spoke. Evelyn took those words to mean that Peter believed she was at fault. He never stood up for her against members of his family, and she turned and ran up the steps and slammed the door so hard that the house walls shook, did, literally, shake.

—

ANOTHER PROBLEM: MEENA would come down and she would speak of Daddy's will. Andrew did not want to hear it, but he would have to, all the same. Then how long would it take before her words, made up of sound waves, would cease to exist altogether? Easier, really, to think in terms of light. What were the variables? If the words she uttered were waves, and if the waves ran into something thick, how quickly would they die out? If they did not run into something solid, but kept on traveling, how far would the waves go before they flattened themselves into a line and went silent? Would they get as far as Grisleigh? Or London? Or across the Atlantic? Very unlikely. And who would care to gather up those waves made by Meena's words, who would want to hear them? Because it was true that no matter what he liked to think, his real mother and his real father had written words everyone wanted to hear again and again, and in consequence, everyone wanted to see the two of them, bodily, again and again, to stop the film of their lives, freeze them just before they died, give them time to think, give each of them another alternative. Was that it? Yes, something like that, I'm sure it's something like that, he thought. Whereas Meena had never mattered in that way. Andrew had overheard a couple at the funeral, and the husband said, "I miss Peter. It's a great pity," and the wife answered, "Meena seems well. At least *that's* over," and the husband, hearing what his wife had not said, answered, "At least we won't have to bother about *her* again, that tedious, smiling person," and the wife answering, as her voice seemed to drop, but only because they had drawn farther away from the doorway, "Do you call that grimace of hers a smile?"

And all the times he had overheard people saying, "How wonderful to see Andrew, it's Peter all over again," and all the times he had heard people say, "She's strange, that Sophie, but she's the spit and image of her mother. You can't help but be grateful for that," and the inevitable rejoinder: "I wonder what Meena thinks about *that*!" It was true, Meena had always hated Sophie. He should make more allowances for Sophie, but if you did, if you considered why you were making concessions, then you had to feel pity, you had to *feel*. You might begin to weep, you might take up existence in the cupboard beneath the stairs, and then how did you ever stop feeling? Better to stay as he was. He shivered slightly; the fire was going out. The flames seemed right to shiver and be cold on a night like this, but there she was, Meena, a roll of papers in her mouth like a dog with a bone, her arms full of wood, and he started to rise to help her, but she shook her head, No, I'll do it, and she put more wood onto the fire, first the twigs and tiny branches, until they began to roar, and then the bigger pieces. She was not going to let that fire die down, she would not have it said that she had almost frozen the rest of Peter's family on the night of his burial, and the fire leaped and danced as if to defy all of them, distorted their faces with the flames' odd shadows, but Meena had her fire, and she took the roll of papers from her mouth, the imprints of her teeth were still on them, and she said, "I shall read them out, shall I?" and there was to be no way around it.

—

"ARE THERE OTHER copies?" Sigrid asked. "Surely these cannot be the only ones," and Meena, answered, "Of course there are other copies. These are not the originals. I'll read them out, then, shall I, while the fire is still warm?"

"Yes, go ahead," Sigrid said wearily.

Meena liked this. She liked being in charge; she liked marshaling small details, making things clear, floor plans, seating plans, all such things, what a boring, boring woman, thought Sigrid, she hasn't sprung a surprise in, what? In thirty years? How did Peter put up with her for thirty years?

"Let me explain what I have done, and what Peter asked that I do. He did not draw up the kind of will we should have liked, itemizing precisely who was to be given what. This was done to save on estate taxes. He was persuaded, after consultation with an attorney, that it would be best to leave everything to me."

"To you! Everything to you!" Sigrid exclaimed. "When I was the *executor* of Evelyn's estate for so many years! When I was in charge of all his affairs!"

"But he did this," Meena continued, as if no one had interrupted, "on this condition. I was to obey this List of Wish. I will read that out, shall I? 'I leave everything to you, Meena Church Grovesnor, on the condition that, immediately upon my death, you will gift my estate as follows: one quarter to you, Meena Church Grovesnor, so that you will have an income for the rest of your life, one quarter to my sister, Sigrid, one quarter to my daughter, Sophie, and one quarter to my son, Andrew. This is to be done as speedily as possible. Any further income from the estate of my first wife, Evelyn Graves, is to be divided between her two children, Sophie and Andrew, continuing the practice I began upon their reaching their eighteenth birthday. Signed this day, January 17, 1999, by Peter John Grovesnor.'

"Shall I reread anything?" Meena asked, looking up, looking searchingly at each face.

"No, not if you will abide by his words," Sigrid said. "They seem quite clear."

"Very clear," said Sophie.

"Yes, clear," said Andrew.

"The will itself, then, leaves everything to me, but I am to divide his assets into four parts, keep one for myself, and give one quarter to each of you. Do we all agree? Do we all construe his words as I understand them?"

"Oh, yes," Sigrid said impatiently. "And you will immediately set about doing what he asked?"

"In the morning, the lawyer shall be called, and of course the tax people will have a look, but it won't take very long, I shouldn't think, should you?"

The three of them sat, stunned and silent. There it was, the great wooden door slamming into place for the last time, the finality of it. Even Demeter was allowed back, once a year, Sigrid thought irrelevantly. "Not everyone has gentians in his house in December," Andrew said, startling them all, and Sigrid's eyes filled, and she said, "*Blue* gentians, Andrew, it was *blue* gentians, Bavarian gentians, 'Light me a torch, light me a torch,'" she quoted, tears spilling over, while Meena thought, Whatever are they talking about now? Well, they are all mad. Bavarian gentians, torches, does it mean anything, do they mean to say they would like to burn the will or the List of Wish? "Sad Michaelmas," said Sophie, while Sigrid stared openmouthed at her niece, wiping her eyes, then saying, "Sophie, I thought you *never* read, just those silly romances," Sophie smiling and saying, "Yes, well," Andrew thinking, That must have been the shortest sentence Sophie has ever uttered, and Meena saying, "So now it is over. What I would like, Sigrid, Andrew, Sophie, is this. You have Bertold's big estate wagon, so if you will gather up what items you wish to keep, providing they have no substantial value for Peter's estate, I should like you to take those things with you when you leave tomorrow. It would be best for me to have things done in that way. Once that is done, I will dispose of articles about the house and I will rest. Nursing Peter through this final illness was a terrible business, I do not need to tell you, and I am sure you will all want to rest and regain your strength, free from disturbances, and I, too, ache for silence and lack of disturbance in order to restore myself. Have I put it properly? Have you understood?"

Oh, yes, thought Sigrid. You can't wait to see the back of us.

"We understand," Andrew said softly.

"My estimable Andrew," Meena said. "I know I shall rely on you."

As well she should, Sigrid thought, Andrew, that great ninny. One word, and he is taken in.

"Then we must all go to bed," Meena said. "Sophie, you, too. You have never been strong."

"Yes, we all know I have never been strong," Sophie said.

"You are a Graves in every way," Meena said.

"Except that I lack my mother's talent," Sophie said.

"*I* am your mother," Meena said. Sophie kept silent.

"Yes, we must all go to bed," Sigrid said. "You must go up first, Meena, dear. You have certainly had the worst time of it. Go on, Meena. Get some sleep. Where will you sleep?"

"In our bedroom," said Meena. "Where I have always slept."

"Would you like one of us to stay in there with you?" Sigrid asked.

"Perhaps Andrew," Meena said, considering, "but there is only one bed."

"Out of the question, then," said Sigrid.

"Yes, I suppose so," Meena said, sighing, getting up, walking toward the stairs. "Sleep well. You must all sleep well."

They watched her go.

"It has been years since she slept alone," Andrew said.

"Oh, please," said Sophie. "You don't know anything."

"It is time for *all* of us to go up to bed," Sigrid said. "And be sure to remember what you want to take with you in the morning. She won't give you another chance."

As if in disbelief, Bertold shook his head, but then he nodded, acknowledging the truth of Sigrid's pronouncement.

"Well, then, goodnight," Sigrid said, starting up the stairway.

"Goodnight," said the other three, who remained where they were.

The three who remained stayed silent, staring into the fire.

"She is generous with the fire right now, but only tonight," Sophie said softly.

"Do you remember," Andrew said, "how when we were all young, Meena used to walk about the house naked?"

"And ask you to get into bed with her when it was cold, or when Peter was gone giving his readings?" Sophie said. "She never asked me into her bed."

"And a good thing she didn't," said Bertold, Sophie's husband. "I thought she was asking *you* tonight," he said to Andrew.

"She was," Andrew said.

"Why didn't you go?" Sophie asked her brother.

Andrew stood up with his back to them, facing the fire. "Sometimes, Sophie, you are such a dunce. I'm going to bed. In my old room." Then he was gone.

———

THE FIRE STILL crackled.

"I wish Julia had come," Sophie said.

"You know Julia," Bertold answered. "In the States, she holes up in New Hampshire and no one can reach her, or she goes on a reading tour and no one can reach her, and she doesn't get television reception in the middle of those mountains, and she always says, 'A war could break out and if we were in Keene, we'd never know about it,' and I don't imagine, do you, that Meena sent her an invitation? Probably she would have come, but he went much faster than we thought, and she wouldn't have bought a first-class ticket, she would have had to wait until a flight opened up; you know what she always says, she always said the same thing to your father, 'A middle-class mother of two has to worry about money.'"

"Daddy once told me Julia's afraid of everything in this world," Sophie said.

"Nonsense," Sigrid said.

"But she won't give in to her fears, at least not most of the time," Sophie said. "He said that."

"Well," Sigrid said, sitting back in her chair, "Peter was usually right about other people. Not, of course, about the last woman he married."

"He said Julia kept things to herself. He said it was very hard to know her."

"That may well be," Sigrid said. "Most people keep things to themselves. Of course, Julia's not middle class, no matter what she may say."

"I wish *I* could ignore things that frightened me," Sophie said.

"Lovey," Sigrid said, "you and Julia are very alike in that way. Both of you smile and smile when you're miserable."

A silence fell.

"You want Julia here," Bertold said. "Why?"

"Oh," said Sophie.

"Another of your many mothers?"

"You, darling, are everything to me," Sophie said, "but sometimes a person wants her mother."

"And Julia can fill the bill?"

"Yes. If she'll come out of her burrow and come stay in mine."

"She is reclusive," Bertold said. "I don't understand it."

"So was my father," Sophie said. "Everyone else who talked to me always spoke of Daddy as 'Peter,' meaning the great and famous one, but Julia always said, 'Your father' this or 'your father' that, and if she meant Evelyn, she'd say, 'Your mother.' "

Bertold nodded. The two of them stared into the fire.

"Julia *is* a mother," Bertold said. "She mothers everyone. I like that in Julia."

"She's not as strong as she once was," Sophie said.

"She's not strong at all," Bertold said gently. "She takes ten prescription tablets a day, and those are strong. Something to do with her heart, isn't it? And her bones?"

"Her heart and her bones," Sophie said. "And other things as well. Once I asked her, and she counted up the operations she'd had. I told her not to leave anything out, so she started at the top of her head and she hadn't gotten very far before she was listing two surgeries, one for each eye. That's why she wears those dreadful glasses. That's why her eyes look so huge. It's because the lenses are so strong."

"But she is strong all the same," Bertold said.

"I suppose," Sophie said. "I don't want to worry about Julia. I mean, I want to think Julia will last forever."

"I think Julia finds living hard. I don't mean to say she's suicidal, but I'm certain she often thinks, I wouldn't mind if all this stopped. Especially when she was so tired and began to fall whenever she took a step."

"She once said, 'I have to keep on living until the children are grown up,' and I said, 'They are, aren't they?' and she said, 'They never grow up.' Whenever she starts another novel, she always says, 'I'm happy to be doing this one. I wonder what this one will be like, if I live to finish it.' "

"Superstition, warding off evil spirits," Sophie said.

"Maybe more than that," Bertold said. "She'll show up. Or she'll call. She's been coming over in the summer for donkey's years."

"I like it when she reminds me that I once said, 'I want to be rich enough to afford black cabs.' She always took black cabs. I thought she was like royalty," Sophie said.

"And now you use them all the time," Bertold said.

Sophie nodded and kissed Bertold on the cheek. "Stubbly," she said. "Very stubbly. I miss her."

"Call her," Bertold said.

"Now, that's an idea," Sophie said. "As soon as we get back to London. Don't let me forget."

"Meena said Julia wrote her the most extraordinary letter," Bertold said. "She said she'd give it to you."

"In the morning," Sophie said, "when we're gathering up the crumbs she'll let us have, I'll get it. No one has ever wanted me to have anything. Not granny in America. When I went to see her there, she was packing up my mother's letters and photographs to send to the archive in Massachusetts, and I asked her for one photograph to remember my mother by. She wouldn't give me anything. That's when I stole the three I have. And I thought, I still remember thinking it, Who else has to steal a picture of her mother so she can see what her mother looked like? I mean, *I* was my mother's daughter. Who were those people who went to look at pictures in libraries compared to me?"

"Charlotte always had her own take on things," Sigrid said. "She thought, if Evelyn was a genius, and if enough people agreed that she was—and you'd know people thought she was if hundreds and thousands of people bothered going to libraries to read Evelyn's papers and look at her pictures—then Evelyn was entitled to commit suicide and no one could blame *her*; no one could say Charlotte was responsible. People would simply assume that if her daughter was a genius, of course she would commit suicide. That's what geniuses do. Geniuses always commit suicide. It's in the nature of geniuses to kill themselves. Everyone knows that. Charlotte especially believed that. That idea absolved her of all blame."

"Do you think that was it?" Sophie asked. She considered. "I'm sure that was it," she said. "You are a genius, my darling."

"Must I drink poison, then?" Bertold asked.

"Don't say that, not even in jest," Sophie said. She was agitated.

"I'm not going anywhere," Bertold said.

"I'll kill you myself if you even hint at it," Sophie said.

"Bed," said Bertold.

"Yes," Sophie said.

They went up and the house had itself to itself.

THREE

THE HOUSE IS dreaming. No, that is not right. The house is thinking, as inanimate objects do, if there are such things as inanimate objects.
The house waits until everyone is asleep, and then it is free to think its own
thoughts, whereas when the people are awake and thinking or speaking,
the house takes care to take everything in and remember it. The house
knows its own name: Willow Grove. The house remembers everything
that has ever been done to it, remembers back to the time it was first con-
structed, so that the house, in its infancy, consisted of unassembled
planks, bundles of thatch, staring square walls, and iron nails pounded
painfully into its integuments. It remembers when it had no such things

as bathrooms; it remembers every bird in every nest built into the thatched roof. It forgets nothing.

Willow Grove is like many very old houses. At one time or another, the house decided it was going to stand, and it would not allow itself to be destroyed. From that time forward, it was immune to bolts of lightning that might have set it afire, termites that might have eaten through the foundation beams, floods that might have mildewed it beyond repair. The house knew, of course, that it could be destroyed by one of its inhabitants, a lunatic woman carrying a torch, then holding its flames to the curtains, watching the fire climb those curtains toward the ceiling; the house has always known how vulnerable it is to the people who live in its body. And so it has determined to be a good house, a house that people are happy to live in, and it has learned to cast its spell. When the current owner of the house, the queen of the house, began her campaign of altering the house, which had been a cottage, into a kind of squat palace, the house cooperated, showed up all its nooks and crannies, made certain that someone saw the little piles of wood dust left by the carpenter ants. The house was happy to be praised for its beauty.

—

PETER GROVESNOR KNEW that this house would be his when he heard its name: Willow Grove, the same name as his family name. The house knows that. It was inevitable. But when the house began to turn into something of a coffin, one body found dead and cold in the kitchen, another body some years later, and a much smaller body, a child, again in the kitchen, the house began to think, Is he the right person to have this house, must I let him inhabit me? When winds came and swirled about the house, the house found ways of making the sound louder and more threatening. It knew how, it had years, no, centuries, to learn how to loosen a shutter and make it snap, snap, snap against the wall of the house, the walls that constituted the limits of its body. It knew how to starve the grounds around the house of water so that everything the people planted there would wither and die. Surely, the house thought, these people will leave the house and new people will come, people who will be content, and last as long as humans ever last, will come and stay here, because, said the house to itself, and to the trees, when they would listen, I need company, I need permanence, I need to know the people who live in my body so well they will come to understand me and my language, and we will all be happy together. If they stay, if they are immortal, or at least as immortal as humans ever are, I will have time to tell a few of my stories, a little of what I know; I will tell them of the life of the pines and the oaks before they were cut down and made into planks and beams, I will tell them of the joy they felt when another ring was added to their trunks, nature's way of saying, You have endured, you have been good, you have sheltered all the birds who chose to live in you, you have observed those birds, you have noticed that no more than five of those small brown birds will stay next to one another, that if a sixth comes, or a seventh, the first five will fly up and flee; you will have wondered why it is so, why the birds will not allow more than five to congregate at a time; you will have warned people of storms, when leaves turn their white, light sides up, meaning lightning, meaning thunder; you will have dug down with your taproots even through the hottest summer, shading the earth beneath you and everyone who came to shelter in the shadows; you will have observed the rootless people who cause themselves so much pain and who cannot peer an inch into the future, although they think they can see to the end of their lives, when really, the vanishing point of their horizon is perhaps an inch away compared to the miles so distant from your vanishing point, the green trees in summer; the runic trees in winter; you will have tried to tell them, What you are doing is not good, please stop. Or you will have tried to make them know, What you do now is a good thing, please continue, don't stop; you will have told them all these things in the way your leaves rustled; you cannot blame yourself because they have been deaf to your own whispery language; you have no throats, no ability to shout as the thunder shouts, although you have tried to persuade the thunder to boom out the necessary words so that even the creatures who live in the house would listen; you have been good trees, and so you are to have another ring. And you will not lose your ring and want someone else's ring, as the creatures of the house do, you strange, twisted creatures, so beautiful in your green summer clothing, capable only of loving, even the squirrels who eat into your flesh building small caves for their wintery acorns, even the woodpeckers who tap, tap, tap with their surgical beaks, painful, but as you believe, doing a good service by eating the insects that would otherwise so terribly burrow. There is nothing you do not deserve, and when time makes it impossible for you to stand any longer, you do not complain when you are cut down and made into planks, the planks who made me and will make others like me, all of you remembering the words of the songs sung by the rivers close enough to make themselves heard by you, those beautiful rivers, sparkling, sometimes clear right down to the bottom, at times muddy, running green after a storm, a kind of green color you see nowhere else, the remarkable skein of air that grew cooler and more fragrant as it blew through you, that made your boughs lift and drop, that wondrous air that was sometimes cool and clear, beautiful as the skin of a green apple, apple wine, is that the best way to say it? A moist air leaving a thin film of water on the leaves and branches and trunks, a lovely wind that liked to play gently over the elephant-skinned trees of your trunks, wrinkling, aging, touching you so softly, so happily: the wind made clear how beautiful the trees found you, and the clouds going over.

You cannot pay enough attention to clouds, telling their own stories of what they have seen and heard as they traveled the earth, illustrating the many, the endless things they saw as they went, sometimes trying to speak to the earth below, imprinting with those dark silhouettes on the ground, the clouds' reflections, changing as they went, trying to mold themselves into shapes that would convey something of what they had seen or learned or hoped to learn, because like everything that lived, that existed, they saw far more than they could understand, but wanted to, wanted to understand everything, forever saying, Is there no one who can tell me what these things mean? Is there no one who will tell me, if I wait patiently enough, how all these things fit together, into one thing, one single thing? The clouds, the trees, the grasses, all of them asking the same thing, the house asking the same thing, but louder, made up as it is of trees and the memories of clouds and winds and singing water held in their cells, in the wood made into planks which the house is granted instead of bones.

The house has heard everything, and forgets nothing, and had its opinions, and still has them, the house rarely changes its conclusions because when it makes them they are based on so much. The house remembers Evelyn as if she were still in the house, and in fact she *is* still in the house; the house has great fondness for Evelyn and her moods, her happiness, and her glooms that paralyzed her, she understands Evelyn who is so much like a tree or any other creature who lives out in the weather, she endures hot days and cold days, bright days and dark, the house finds Evelyn neither mad nor alien: the house knows her at once as familiar, less evolved by time, more like a tree or a deer than those humans who now pride themselves on insisting they have changed through the years, grown apart from the world the house knows and sees through the window. The house can speak to Evelyn who feels pity for any crack in its plaster, understands Evelyn when she has gone out through the door of the house and found an animal peering out of the woods at the end of the lawns; the house observes the way Evelyn lies stomach down on the ground and speaks to that animal. Evelyn is very good at speaking to foxes; Evelyn and the foxes understand one another, the foxes advance toward her as if they recognize another one of their own; Evelyn will lie there on the ground, one arm outstretched toward the fox until it begins to move toward her, and then she is happy, then she will tell the fox of all her problems, of her husband who refuses to stay with her in his den, who is restless, who always thinks the place he is living in is the wrong place, whereas she believes she must remain, just as the fox does; she asks the fox, Do you have children of your own? and the fox answers her. She asks the fox, Do you have enough to eat? Sometimes, the fox says, I do, and sometimes she says, I do not, and Evelyn asks the fox what she would like. She tells the fox all she has with her is a roll and half an apple, but the fox is welcome to that; she takes out the roll and breaks off a small piece and pushes it until it is somewhere between Evelyn and the fox; then she waits, her eyes wide open, she rarely blinks, in that way she is like an animal who comes out of the woods, and finally, the fox moves quickly, takes the bread, and retreats, and Evelyn laughs softly, and the fox flattens her ears against her head, and Evelyn says, "Come back, please come back."

She has the right kind of voice; few people have it. It is not a voice you can learn; you must be born with it, how well the house knows that, how often the house had seen people trying to coax a fox or a badger or a squirrel toward them, and the animals fled deep into the woods and avoided that voice, that dangerous sound; irrevocable, that animal's decision as it thinks matters over in its den, whereas when the fox listens to Evelyn, she understands her. She moves closer to her; she waits, trustingly, almost trustingly, while Evelyn breaks off another piece of bread and then pushes it toward the fox, not as far as she pushed it the first time, and the fox comes closer to get the bread, has it in her jaws, but stops and contemplates Evelyn, puzzled, saying, "Who are you and why are you bringing me bread?" And Evelyn answers, saying, "Why not?" a response the fox finds entirely satisfactory, and as days pass and then weeks, the fox begins to wait for Evelyn, bounds forward when she sees her coming, and Peter, her husband, watches all this, and thinks, Incredible, and does not know that he will never again see a woman who can do this, but he will find that out. Then he will have something to think about.

And on certain days, Evelyn can do nothing but lie on her bed, cannot move, and then outside she hears what sounds like a baby crying, she knows that is her fox; her fox wants her to come out, with or without food, and she drags her leaden self from the bed, up to the window. Yes, there is the fox, outside, crying. She forces herself out of the room, down the stairs, out of the house, raining or not, it makes no difference. And the fox begins leaping and running back and forth toward the wood and then to Evelyn, until the two of them are within sight of the wood, and then the fox lies down and waits for her, and she lies down, the two of them on the ground, almost curled together, Evelyn telling her what has happened, saying, "When I opened my eyes this morning, I couldn't speak, couldn't move, what do you think it means? Does it happen to you?" The fox gazing at her with her open, glaring eyes of love, pure love. It is a fox, an animal, but all the same it is love, only a fool would doubt it, and Evelyn listens to the fox, and it seems to the house that Evelyn understands what the animal has to say, and then Evelyn lies without moving, as if she has gone to sleep, but she is not sleeping. Instead even her bones have lost their tension; she is beginning to feel motion starting up within her. Finally she has found someone who can understand her. Who can doubt it after seeing the change in Evelyn now that she has had a conversation with the fox?

Because Evelyn knows, or she has come to know, that there are parts of her mind that are not human; she knows that there are parts of everyone's minds that are not human. Others will not accept that, will not believe it, and so they are denied that kind of language, that kind of experience she has with her fox, her fox and so many others like the fox, that part of her mind that can speak and listen to what others insist on calling an *animal,* whereas Evelyn knows that if she cannot speak to other people of what she knows in those nonhuman parts of her mind, she will never be completely content. There is a kind of joy, a mad joy, really, she feels when she speaks to an animal. A person completely besotted by love feels that sort of joy, but it is less reliable, less continuous, more subject to change, than the kind of joy she feels speaking to the fox, or a cat, or a bedraggled, abandoned dog, and what is it, really? Isn't it a kind of speaking soul to soul, because Evelyn has no doubt that animals have souls. She is far surer of that than the common proposition which argues, not very convincingly, she thinks, that all humans have souls. She wonders if human souls, so recently developed, are not still faulty, moth-riddled, whereas the soul of a fox, for example, is expertly woven and durable, completely reliable, an animal's soul, the only thing she has yet found that is so unfailingly constant and good. Yes, the house loves Evelyn, takes Evelyn in as one of her own, understands her deep in its cells.

But the next one, Elfie, was another matter, not the same as Evelyn at all, a voice too deep for a woman's, a voice that could not even hope to soothe her own child, capable of singing and singing well, but when speaking, not melodious, not comforting. And finding everything on this earth alien to her, and menacing, the trees in winter lashing in the wind, the trees threatening to set the house on fire when the lightning struck, the house appearing ready to fall of its own accord when it heard the sound of the thunder, Elfie certain that the rain would cause the river to rise up and flood, clearly seeing her own pale body floating on the current, her head face down as if inspecting the stones of the riverbed, a woman not capable of comforting anyone, or of taking comfort. No, that was impossible; she was too afraid. Incapable of trust. Whereas Evelyn was not exceedingly trusting, but she knew what she could trust, the fox, for example, the house she lived in which she knew, instinctively knew, loved her back. But this one, this Elfie, repeating again and again how the house hated her, insisting that this house still belonged to Evelyn, although Evelyn was resting beneath the dirt in the little plot just before the fringe of the wood, asserting that this house meant her harm; Evelyn's spirit still lived in this house and intended her no good, and Peter saying (the savior, the visionary, the clairvoyant, the writer of genius), "Bloody hell! It's a structure of wood and stone. It doesn't have *intentions*! It doesn't lust after revenge. What's wrong with you? You liked it enough before we married. I asked you before we married. Wouldn't you rather sell up and go somewhere else? No memories. It's the world's advice; leave those memories behind. That kind of advice doesn't come cheaply; don't say *No*, don't refuse, give it some thought, think it over, Evelyn's not here; believe me, she's not here. If you think she's here, we have to go. You can see that, can't you?"

And the foolish woman, unwilling to admit her terror, unwilling to accept the notion that Evelyn's soul, the echoes of Evelyn's will, could triumph over her, saying, "No, we'll stay on, we'll make it our house, at all the windows will be Indian silks, embroidered; they'll blow in like poppy-colored winds. It will be a beautiful house, it will be our house." And Peter saying, how could he have made such a bad job of it, "Don't forget, the roof needs rethatching. Evelyn never cared about that. She'd rather spend what money we had on daffodil bulbs and bread for the foxes. We could go to another house, one that doesn't need repainting or reroofing. We could start over. You'd like that, wouldn't you?" Elfie answering, "Bread for foxes, what are you talking about? Did she breed foxes?" and Peter replying, "It's a long story, it's not worth the trouble of telling it, believe me, it isn't," Elfie immediately rising into hysteria, demanding that Peter tell her about the bread and the foxes. She had to know, she had to be told, Peter enraged, saying, "You see? Would this have come up if we weren't in this house, if we were in another house? It's an old story, what does it mean to you?" But insisting until she heard the story, and then weeping because she, Elfie, knew her own terror of any animal, especially one like a fox, saying, "They can possess people, they're demonic, I'm sure I read that," she told Peter, who was disgusted by her and showed it, Elfie breaking down, saying, "I'll never live up to Evelyn, why did I ever think I could?" Peter roaring, "This is all because you're so set on staying in this house to exorcise her. Let me tell you, Evelyn cannot be exorcized. There are memories in this house. You can't exorcize a memory; you can go somewhere that doesn't call them up, that's the best you can do," Elfie continuing to weep, saying again and again, "You don't understand, you don't understand," just as Evelyn had repeated the same refrain, here it was, back again.

The house wanted her to go, wanted Elfie gone, wanted Peter gone, the house had proven it could not shelter them. It had tried. The house would keep Evelyn there, in the cells that made up her beams and her floors; the house wanted to keep Evelyn with her, not to be distracted by this frightened Elfie, weeping and weeping. The house understood better than Peter could; Elfie believed that if she stayed on in the house she, too, would somehow become a genius. I'm sorry, thought the house, I regret saying it, but life does not work that way. Elfie cannot learn the voice that Evelyn was born with, the voice she used to charm animals and allow them to speak to her, and yes, the house had powers, but not the kind of powers that Elfie wanted or needed. Above all, a house had a genius for memory, for taking all experience into itself, for waiting, through centuries, if necessary, until it solved the problems posed by the people who lived in it. The house had that kind of genius, a genius Elfie already found inimical, and the house tried to tell that to Peter, but Peter had given up, succumbed to Elfie's whims, agreed when Elfie said, "But if we stay here, we'll save so much; we already have the house, we know what's wrong with it, we're not in for surprises, and besides, the house you live in keeps you safe from other people's houses," Peter laughing at that, finding that funny and witty and true, his own will weakened by Elfie's ability to create laughter, something he thought Elfie had lost forever, so that in a moment of relief, of blindness, he grabbed Elfie and held her and said, "Of course we'll keep the house if that's how you feel about it," not knowing, as the house knew in that instant, that he had sealed his fate and Elfie's fate and the destiny of any child born of their flesh. The house weeping in the silent way in which houses weep, trying to make someone hear what it was saying: "No! No! No! Go! Please go! I cannot be responsible!" while the wind blew in through all the open doors, soothing the house, saying, repeatedly, "This is not your doing, they make their own decisions," but the house rejected all consolation, knowing full well that the house was at least partly to blame for what would happen, the house deciding it was not partly, but greatly to blame.

And so they were all upstairs, Meena and Sigrid, Sophie and Bertold and Andrew, dreaming, silent and dreaming, Evelyn dead and gone, Elfie gone in the same way, and now Peter gone. Sigrid was like an old oak. She might live on for a long time. Meena was made strong by greed and jealousy. The house knew there was no getting rid of her, and those delightful creatures who had arrived no bigger than hedgehogs, Andrew and Sophie: they would no longer be allowed into the house. In a few hours, when the light came up, Meena would see them off and then lock the door. It was possible, more than possible, that the house would never see them again. The house took up the wind roiling about the house and made it roar, made it shout down the chimneys into all of the bedrooms, but the sleepers remained asleep and did not stir, and the house would not be comforted, not for some time. Even worse, the house knew with absolute certitude that far worse was to come. I am not a lucky house, it thought. I would protect them all, even that Meena, but I cannot.

Yet it was Meena who had brought the house to such a high standard, Meena who learned quickly, who bought magazine after magazine, who determined that the house was to be more beautiful than any she had yet seen, Meena who had almost succeeded in transforming the house, and in so doing, had driven Peter out, had driven off Sophie and Andrew, had stood there in the kitchen one sunny day, only a few small clouds scudding down the sky, thinking, This is the house as I want it, and what's more, *there are no children in it,* so happy at that thought she had embraced her chest with her hands, her bony hands, because she had grown thin perfecting the house. No one could imagine the nights she had lain awake plotting, adding, and subtracting, until she was sure she would have the money to bring that vision of the house into existence.

Painting and plastering and more painting, Meena thought, awake in bed, lying diagonally, so that she occupied both her side of the bed and Peter's, or what would have been Peter's, but not putting her head on his side, on his pillow, no, not that; painting and more painting, and then moving the furniture back to the just-painted room, and no matter how one tried, one or two or more spots of paint, light green, cream-colored, Indian-red streaks of paint, always such blemishes, always such spots of paint, advertising the fact that the chest or the bed or the chair or the desk was old, declaring again that the owner had not been able to afford the expense of replacing it, and so the imperfect object was back in its room

again. Having learned the hard way that it was best to leave the chair or
the desk as it was, not to scrape off the paint spot either with fingernail
or knife, because the paint would come up with the finish, and then there
was no matching the original color, no covering the pale color suddenly
exposed, the wood as it had been before the owner made it her own. So
many pieces of furniture spotted over with lime green, that favorite of
Evelyn's, the color of early leaves before they fell off and grew darker,
before larger, heavier greenish-black leaves began to unfold, meaning
heat, meaning summer. So many spots of Indian red, carmine, really.
That was the right word for that color, Elfie's beloved color, the house
must have looked like a furnace in those days, so many objects glowing
as if they were live coals. Meena had the bad luck to find the photograph
albums Evelyn had made, and then Elfie after her, and then Meena sat in
front of them, staring at the pictures. Affixed in the old way, to small tri-
angles that had the feel of felt, each picture held there by one embossed
tiny black triangle at each corner, holding the photographs to the black,
brittle pages.

She, Meena, had decided to keep those photograph albums in Willow
Grove, saw them when her own mother stacked them neatly and was
about to throw them out, Meena saying Peter had stacks and stacks of
photographs and nothing to put them in. Let me take them to him, let me
ingratiate myself, because that was what she had meant. Was it believable
that she herself had brought those dreadful things, those photographs,
back into that perfect house, and now no one would entertain the idea of
destroying the albums, so old, "They're so old they hurt," a Jamaican poet
who came to visit at Willow Grove had said, during those years when
Meena still allowed visitors to Willow Grove. No one would allow them to
be touched. Somehow, they had become sacred.

And what color would she repaint the walls now, Meena asked herself,
what should be the spots of color that *she* leaves behind her on the furniture, deciding that she will paint everything white because, after all, white
means purity, and she has lived as a good woman, especially when com-

pared to the women in her husband's family. Yes, she shall paint everything white, to make it clear that she, Meena, had been a saint, still is a
saint, a saint of the ordinary. As she thinks this, it seems to her that the
house shudders, trembles, has somehow heard what she thought as clearly
as if she had spoken aloud. Meena shivers, feels cold, pulls the duvet up
over herself, asking herself what earthly reason this bloody house would
have to resent *her*. But of course it was Elfie's house, and Evelyn's before
hers, while she, Meena, had come last. She thinks again, It is always the
first one who the others love the best. If only I had been the first child. But
her sister, Sangeeta, renamed Susan, was the first. How her parents loved
her! Not that Meena had been unloved. Her parents had loved her pas-
sionately. They had loved each child with passion, but they could never
again love anyone but Sangeeta with such helpless adoration. Sangeeta,
who had come first, who had died less than a year before Peter, reminding Meena of old superstitions, how frightening they were, one superstition particularly, which held that when a favorite child died, it took so
much force from the world, so much of everything, someone else in the
family had to be taken from the world. It had to do with equivalences,
something like that. A person so beloved left a great hole in the fabric of
existence; that hole could not be accounted for simply by one person's
death. Life could make no sense of it, someone else had to die, more than
one person had to die, to make it seem right and plausible that such a gap
had been left in the fabric of things.

Meena shivered again, thinking, Someone else is meant to die,
inevitably someone else will, no doubt one of the people right now sleeping peacefully in her house, so many people who adored Peter, the hole he
left behind, yes, even Meena could see it for what it was. Such a fissure
could not be allowed to remain. It had to be accounted for and so at least
one more had to die. Sophie! Perhaps Sophie. She had never been strong.
But would Sophie be enough? She, Meena, was the strong one, the one
with the great will, she had declared that over and over, was she the only
person who could patch up the hole left once Peter had gone?

This frightens her, really, thoroughly freezes her with terror, so that she curls herself into a shrimp beneath her warm duvet, but nothing warms her; she grows colder and colder, pulls the duvet up over her head; that always works, that always makes her warm, but not this time. This time she shivers as if she had fallen through the iced-over river, and when she looks up, she sees the thick skin of ice, a wall, horizontal above her, preventing her from coming back, from reaching the air. She told herself, Peter must feel as I do now. He must feel just this, deep down there, under the cold earth and the pebbles and all the cold things that make their way through the earth deep below. When I think of it, I have to take a spade and turn up the earth. No, Meena thinks, that is not my job anymore; *I* will hire someone, *I* am a wealthy woman now.

And she was, and the thought calmed her, no longer the scrimping daughter of an immigrant farmer, no longer one of the beautiful *Indian* daughters, no more need to make do as a famous poet's wife, but a wealthy woman, a woman moneyed in her own right, yet not a woman to worry about a camel passing through a needle's eye. She had always known she was better, was somehow chosen to be better and to be recognized as such, and now she was. The fortune, the inheritance she recently had from Peter, that was what had done it.

She has stopped trembling and instead has pulled down the duvet and smiled at the square of blue sky in the window, thinking, once it stops raining, it is hard to believe that it will ever rain again, and with that, she gets up, silently, as is her habit, automatically avoiding the creaking floorboard, going to the door and listening. No, no one is about. She is the only person awake, contemplating that beautiful square of blue, the color of contentment. She is the only one who will feel gratified by that sky. She smiles at the thought. The vanity mirror reflected her face, the face of a happy woman. Indian red or carmine, whatever it was, why should she fret about any of that? She need not bother herself about such things any longer. She waits for the others to awaken, hoping that Sophie, the weak one, will wake first, and would come to see her alone, to be sure she,

Meena, was all right, would walk into Meena's room as if Sophie really believed what everyone had told her for years, that Meena was her mother, as if Sophie, not Meena, believed that *she* herself was the lion tamer, and we all knew what happened to people who felt that, who did that. Meena sat down on her bed and waited for Sophie, willed Sophie to come to her, and she would come. It was inevitable.

FOUR

—

SIGRID HAD NOT slept, not one wink, and would say so when Meena asked, "Have you slept well?" that relentless morning greeting she and Peter had settled on, which in Meena's mouth always sounded like a threat and a reproach, so that, for years, Sigrid had always said, "Oh, I always sleep well in this house," an answer bound to infuriate Meena, reminding her, as it did, that Sigrid had known the house before Meena had ever set foot in it, Sigrid's answer somehow managing to imply that Sigrid understood the house better than Meena ever had or would. Once, in the garden, in the comfortable cushioned swinging chair, Sigrid had asked Meena, "Do you think it conceivable that houses really burn themselves down when they loathe their owners?" Meena looked at Sigrid as if

she had gone mad. "Because yesterday morning, the vicar's wife said that
the Woodhurst house had burned right to the ground, and this witch—
well, a woman who doesn't comb her hair—said that the house had
burned down to spite its owners. What do you think, Meena?"

"I think," said Peter, looking up from his paper, "they burned it down
for the insurance."

"Dead right," said Meena, dismissing the matter, but not before she
scanned Sigrid's face for *traces*, she always found them, those traces, and
she believed that what the traces had to say was always and inevitably and
without exception true. "And the two dead sheep, I suppose they killed
themselves," Meena said, picking up the magazine section, turning to dec-
orating tips. Peter's face appeared briefly over the newspaper, his eyes
laughing into Sigrid's, and then he retreated. He hated to admit it, but
Meena was growing more astute at dealing with Sigrid, not that Meena
would ever be a match for her. Probably, he thought, Meena would kill
Sigrid if it were to her advantage, and he wondered briefly if Meena was
capable of murder, and decided, yes, she was. The kind of murder you
would most dread, not murder inspired by rage or passion, but the cold
wind of intellect. "Watch out for her," Peter had once told Sigrid. "She's
not as harmless as she looks," and Sigrid looked at her brother and said,
"Lovey, how did you ever manage to harbor the delusion that that woman
was harmless? I can see Lord What's His Name now, visiting Meena right
after he is through comforting Myra Hindley."

"Isn't she up for something? Parole or something?" Peter asked, skating
away from thin ice, as was typical of him.

"Meena and Myra Hindley, what a beautiful thought," Sigrid said, and
then insisted Peter take a good look at her garden gnome.

"Why on earth did you ever buy such a monstrosity?" Peter asked her.

"Love me, love my gnome," Sigrid said, while Peter looked at his sister
slantwise, suspecting that somehow Sigrid equated that ghastly statue with
Meena. "If you covered the thing with birdseed, and you should—it has a
lot of nooks and crannies—" Peter said, "then it would have some use."

But Sigrid has lost all interest in the gnome and the garden itself, and was off to something else, like copyright. "Whatever happens," Sigrid said, "don't *ever* let her get her hands on it. She doesn't say so, but she disapproves of everything you've written—well, except for those poems you wrote about farming, and *you don't like those.*"

"I'm not the fool you take me for," Peter said.

And what had he done? *I leave everything to you, Meena Graves Grovesnor, on the understanding that, upon my death, you will immediately set about dividing my estate into four equal sections,* and of course that included the copyright, and whoever ruled the copyright ruled the estate. If she, Sigrid, had never said anything, never given advice, never done anything, never interfered, never made Peter's fortunes her own, could events have come to a worse outcome? So much for the efforts of human beings, so much for intelligence and loyalty and will and energy and smashing your own horizons gorgeous in the distance, accepting instead that unlovely horizon you saw ahead of you. You tried to tack splendid curtains over that miserable view, gold tassels to hold the curtains back, tried to make what you had settled for somehow more dramatic, more pleasing, more like what you gave up your own hopes for before you caved in. And, of course, Peter appreciated it. He said he did. He insisted he would not have been alive had it not been for her sacrifice, her *sacrifices,* and she found such words mollifying and reconciling until she learned that such fulsome praise, such devout gratitude, so freely expressed, was soon to be followed by yet another request, another opportunity for Sigrid to sacrifice herself once more on Peter's altar. And the worst of it, the very worst, was his knowledge, and her knowledge, that she would most decidedly do whatever he had asked of her. Then there was no point at all in Peter's asking, "Would you be willing to do this, to do that?" Asking was, in the end, another way of rubbing it in, reminding her that, yes, this was what she had settled for. So asking itself was a travesty, not politeness, although that was how he thought of it, treating Sigrid as she deserved to be treated, with the most exquisite courtesy. Probably the executioner was extremely courteous, laughably so, when he escorted his prisoner up the steps to be hung in front of a crowd of munching spectators, shouting their approval through their full mouths. And what would she, Sigrid, say when Peter invariably made his newest request? "Of *course,* Peter," because how could anyone who loved him refuse him after the horror, the anguish, that had come to him?

Meena heard the steps coming toward her room, heard Sophie hesitate in front of the closed door, then heard her soft rapping. "Come in, Sophie," Meena said. "Sit *down,* Sophie. We're all so exhausted," Sophie sitting on the chair draped with the lion skin that always sat, would forever sit, on Peter's side of the bed.

"Sigrid's been on the phone to Julia," Meena told Sophie, Sophie wondering how Meena came to know that, then recalling Peter's saying, one day, "Be careful over the phone. Sometimes Meena listens in," and Sophie, stupid Sophie, saying, "Surely not!"

"It must have been very early in the morning in the U.S. when Sigrid called Julia. Julia's a good friend to Sigrid," Meena said, a streak, a tone, in her voice, implying that such a thing was beyond conceiving. "I imagine she'll be coming over, then?" Meena said, and Sophie, answering without thinking, answering quickly, saying, "I hope so!"

"I don't know what you all see in Julia," Meena said. "Aside from Peter's completely inexplicable desire to confide things to her best kept in the family," and Sophie, tired, worn thin, beginning to suspect that she might someday be free of Meena, responded by saying, "He had to speak to someone, didn't he? As far as I know, Julia never gave up one of her secrets," and then Sophie sat back against the chair, the slippery fur of the lion skin. All these animals, dead now, but their skins still harboring the blood-red desire to sink their teeth into a victim, one foolish enough to lean against them.

"Look at what's happened to Princess Diana, not that I had much time for her," Meena said. "All those *trusted, sympathetic, devoted* hangers-on smiling and holding out their hands, waiting to see if someone would put enough money in their palm, and if they did, every one running off to the publishers to write a book."

"I doubt if Julia will be writing a book about us," Sophie said.

"*I* heard her tell Peter, 'You can't trust a novelist. Everything he hears or sees belongs to him and is used by him, by right.'"

"I was there," Sophie said. "She was defending Rose. Sigrid said that Rose should never have written that novel about Robert. She killed Robert off in that book and Sigrid said that was why Robert would never forgive her. Years ago."

"But Julia *said* that you can't trust a novelist," Meena said. "She said it without thinking. She hadn't censored anything, so she said precisely what she did indeed think."

Sophie looked away.

"Don't look away when I'm speaking to you!" Meena said sharply.

"I hear perfectly well, even if my eyes are closed," Sophie said.

"You will look at me when I speak to you," Meena said. Sophie looked straight at her. "And you will *not* glare at me!" Meena said.

"Perhaps I should go out," Sophie said, her voice steely, so that Meena knew she had gone too far.

"It's too much," Meena said, waving her hand, as if to encompass everything, the entire world, the world she knew. The side of the bed, now empty, her pillow that always ended up half under Peter's so that she had to pull it loose, invariably experiencing that tugging of the pillow as an act of aggression, but she did so love turning the pillow upside down and feeling her cheek against the fabric's cool side. And Peter's annoying habit of taking one of the two duvets she put on their bed every winter, so that she had one and he had the other, as if, in sleep, he did not want to share anything with her, so that she, who was cold beneath one coverlet, was forever freeing up part of his duvet and trying to cover herself with it, and then lifting her own duvet and laying it down on top of his. All those things were over, those small annoyances, and the larger, more serious disagreements between them, also over, unsettled now for whatever time fate would give her. But she had expected to battle and win, although in the last year, it came to her with a shock, a shock that had changed everything when she realized she might not win, not this last time, not this endgame. How could she not win the final battle when she had won all the others that came before? His heavy tread on the steps as he came down from his office, less and less frequently heard because he did not always, not any longer, live in the house. He'd found another nest, one he liked better. No one must find out about that, no one not in the family, certainly not Julia, if Peter had not already told her.

The simple, unacceptable fact was that Meena was once again single; that state was not irreparable, although for a time it would be. Convention demanded a certain amount of time pass, at least one year, during which time their marriage ceremony would summon itself up insistently, she wearing a white dress, Peter wearing a white suit, out there in the meadow among the lambs bleating here and there, and the dandelions picked by Sophie, already wilting, even as the vicar spoke the vows that tied them. Sigrid laughing and laughing at something her then-husband had said, or laughing for no reason whatever, wearing a black, billowy dress, laughing before the ceremony (if you could call it a ceremony), saying, "You can't expect me to buy a dress every time Peter gets married!" And then she, Meena, the bride, in tears, Meena's sister wiping up her tears with a cold cloth, taking some strange cosmetic you could only buy from India out of her sack of a handbag, carefully patting it around Meena's eyes, saying again and again, "You look *fine*, absolutely fine!" And could it have been true that Meena heard Peter say under his breath, "Let's get on with it!"

———

BUT SURELY HE'D said nothing of the kind, not then, although later, when they went through the albums and their pictures of that wedding, his third, her first, even though she knew this marriage was to be her first and last, might he not have said that? Because in those days,

Meena never tired of dragging out those wedding albums, such pride in showing them, such love, such triumph, Meena, waving her hand now to indicate how tired she was of the house, and the sticks and stones of the earth itself, and the filmy clouds that tore as they passed through the spiky topmost branches of the trees, how tired she was of the photographs that now no longer reflected anything of reality. It would have been more fitting to have a funeral album. In her parents' house, they had had a funeral wreath made for their grandmother whose black long hair had been so strong, and from her hair, they had woven a garland of roses, and inside the roses, her grandmother's picture, and the small black album her mother kept to herself, only showing it to her daughters or her son on special occasions (and what could those have been? What signal honor had led their mother to open that little album, that casket?), and in it, the death portraits of her grandmother, her mother's mother, three different portraits, one full-face, one profile from each side. In those days, it was entirely common to have such pictures made up. Her mother always said, "Doesn't she look young there? That's how she used to look. Yes, it happens this way in all death portraits. When the body dies, the muscles of the face relax and the face smooths itself out to become what it once was, and you see them again as you first knew them, unless, of course, they died in a terrible agony and then that tortured face was frozen onto them. What a terrible thing it is, to go to one's grave wearing such a frightening mask. I used to think when I saw someone look like that—my aunt did—I thought she died looking as she did because the Devil had already grabbed her by the hair before she died, and when she saw him, that's how her face was changed so terribly. And there's no doubt, she's in Hell now. So I believed. But time went by and I knew better: it was the illness she had. It had nothing to do with the Devil's snatching her to take her down under, nothing at all. She went peacefully, my mother did. That's why she looks as she does, so beautiful, don't you think she was beautiful?" And who among them would have gainsaid her? Still, Meena thought now, her grandmother had never been beautiful, not even when she was aflame with youth—radiant, perhaps, serene, perhaps, but not beautiful. Nor her mother. But serene, patient, long-suffering. Or had her mother been any of those? There are some women who will only turn the silvery side of the moon to their children. Like the moon, they keep their dark side to themselves: if they can. Really, how much did a child ever know about her parent? But Meena thought, she and her mother had known one another well, had grown into one another as friends, had spoken plainly and without artifice to one another. Or had that, too, been an illusion? "You live in illusions!" Peter had shouted at her on the last day before he left to stay with that other woman. "Can't you see it? Can't you see it yet!" But by then his illness had eaten into him. Surely he had not meant it, how could he have, when he had spent the years of their marriage bemoaning the rock-hard nature of her realism, her ironclad common sense. He could not have meant both, so contradictory. When he said both such assertions were true, he was lying. Opposites cannot be true at the same time, Meena thought. It isn't possible. It's a law of nature, isn't it: opposites cannot exist in the same person at the same time. What was that, a law of physics? Two objects cannot occupy the same space at the same time. But Peter had argued against that. If she could remember what he had said! Didn't it have something to do with the nature of being, the difference between, say, a brain and a thought? How tired she became of such discussions, yet it was for such colloquies that he had valued Robert, who would argue any proposition, spitting through the gaps in the spaces between the teeth he never bothered replacing, spitting as he talked, effectively canceling out anything he might say that would be of any use to her, to Meena.

"So tired," Meena said to Sophie.

"Yes," said Sophie.

"We all are," Meena said, as if her suffering and everyone else's anguish were equivalent, whereas, as Sophie knew, Meena believed nothing of the kind. Meena kept her own ledgers and her balance was always greater than anyone else's.

"Yet we must go on," said Meena.

"Of course," Sophie said.

"Although there are times . . ." Meena trailed off.

"There are times?" Sophie echoed.

"Times when you wonder, *why* must you go on?"

Sophie let that stitch drop.

"Have you never felt it?" Meena asked.

"Never," said Sophie. She knew better than to give Meena an opening, something she would use against her later. "Never," Sophie said again.

"I envy you, then," Meena said.

She's lying again, Sophie thought. Why does she bother?

"I suppose we all must divide up our things now," Meena said. "I know Peter wanted you to have the manuscripts of his children's books. He said you loved his pictures."

"Yes," said Sophie.

"So you shall have them?" Meena asked.

"Gladly," said Sophie.

"And Andrew, does he want manuscripts?"

"You must ask him. He may want some of Daddy's letters."

"I intended to give them up with the rest of the archive," Meena said.

So it is happening again, Sophie said. "No," Sophie said. "You must preserve some of them for Andrew. If he doesn't want them now, he will soon. You can give them to me and I will keep them safe."

"And I will not?" Meena said, a sudden flash, like lightning, that anger that was always there, something that lit her from inside, not rosy, but the color of a sharpened sword struck by white light.

"So you will have less that will tire you," Sophie said.

"If you knew how tired I already was by his things!" Meena exclaimed.

"Then give some of them up," Sophie said. "Where is it written that you must keep everything simply because it is yours?"

"And is it better that such things become *yours*?" Meena asked her stepdaughter.

Sophie did not answer. She was thinking, No one knows Meena, not at all. Peter had said it. "Meena lives in an essential unknowability. She could choose to be otherwise, but she will not allow anyone to know her, not me, not anyone, not even, I think, herself."

Unexpectedly, Meena said, "Let us just sit still here, only the two of us, saying nothing. It will be good for the two of us to sit still without speaking, don't you think so?"

Sophie nodded. Of course, she thought, there was something at the bottom of it, some advantage Meena hoped to gain, if only to put her, Sophie, in her place, but sitting still together, without words, yes, the thought appealed to her, soothed her.

A little time went by. The carillon in the church tower struck seven. Seven. At seven in the morning, Sophie thought, I am still up, still working, I've worked through the night, I'm still talking to Bertold. And Meena is also up, already getting up or having just gotten up, beginning to clean a house that is already immaculate.

What, really, do I know about Meena? Sophie asked herself. She is not the deepest person on earth. Why should she be so unknowable? It was Meena who had criticized Julia in front of Peter and the others one Christmas, saying that every word Julia uttered was careful. Even if she were to decide to be indiscreet, she would carefully have decided to be indelicate. "Even Julia's face is careful," Meena had said.

—

SOPHIE HAD GIVEN this thought. Was Julia unknowable? Not, Sophie thought, to her. But Julia opened herself to Sophie; she always had. People said her father had been unknowable. Everyone felt they knew him, but in fact he told them little of himself, precious little of how his thoughts and passions drifted and stuck. What did it mean to be unknowable? Sophie thought, It comes from a kind of despair, from the certain knowledge that someone who is unknowable *knows* he will not be understood.

Yes, she thought, that's it. If Sophie or Peter or Sigrid decided to reveal their own thoughts, the most precious and secret of them, the thoughts that stamped them and made them what they were, they knew they would be misunderstood. And if they were bound to be misunderstood, why hazard what was most dear? Because what happened, as Sophie well knew, was that people listened, and thought, Oh, that is what he means, what a terrible thing to say, when in fact they had completely misunderstood what they had been told. They had been told the truth, but they could not take it in, what they had been allowed to glimpse was a grotesque version, a parody. They had made caricatures out of what had been revealed. If that were to happen, why give anyone ammunition? Why not keep what was true and priceless hidden, safe from the funhouse mirrors of other people's minds? It was time that had taught Peter and Evelyn and Sigrid, and now even Sophie, to be unknowable. Why put down their best carpets to let anyone trample on them with muddy feet? More than likely that Meena had had the same experience again and again, but surely whatever Meena chose to say would be understood straightaway. Or would it? If she had been willing to speak of losing the one child of her one pregnancy, aborted so dangerously by her body, wouldn't others have said, "Oh, that's why she's so bitter, that's why she keeps so to herself. She's a barren woman." Evelyn wrote so many poems about barren women. If Meena had spoken of what it was to live in a house filled with ghosts so much more famous than she was or would ever be, so much more interesting than she could hope to be, wouldn't others, hearing of it, say, if they could, "I pity you. You are to be pitied," when in actuality *she* pitied Evelyn and Elfie, the poor women who had fallen into ghosthood while they yet lived. Women do not give up and die unless they lose something essential to them, unless they are mad. And if people who had known Evelyn or Elfie tried to explain why those two had chosen to open doors no one else wanted to see, much less walk through, if Evelyn or Elfie had tried to tell Meena why they had gone through to the other side, what would Meena have thought then? That such people were fools, romantic idiots corrupted by poems and novels, and how were such people to understand her? She knew that others laughed at her because she kept an old boar as a pet, walked up to it without fear, petted it, spoke to it; perhaps she knew that Sigrid often said, "She would reduce Peter to that boar if she could—a woman with a boar for a pet, it says volumes about poor Meena." Meena had seen visitors to the house, uninvited by *her*, pause and stop at the framed pictures mounting the stair wall to the second floor, pictures of cats she had loved, dead cats, dead dogs, dead parents and sisters, and at the top of the stairs, a huge glass dome with three birds perched realistically on a tree branch, three birds with brown feathers, their heads and necks brilliantly yellow.

"A museum of dead things," Sigrid had said one night, and Meena heard her, and so Meena knew how her sister-in-law spoke of her to others. As if anything that concerned her were the least concern of strangers! As if it were wrong to mourn and go on mourning, although she was not a woman held in thrall by sorrow, simply a woman who did not want to forget what she had once loved, especially those who had loved her to the end, who had not wavered, never looked at her with ambivalence, a word she associated almost exclusively with her now-dead husband. A man who said, "I love you," when what he meant to say was, "I hope I love you; I hope this watery love is enough, for me and for you." The more she revealed herself, Meena had concluded, the more she became obscured. She could, she supposed, reveal more and more of herself, and paradoxically cause herself to be less and less known, but she could not bear the travesty of their understanding. Nor could any of them have opened themselves fully—Sophie, Sigrid, Peter, the source of so much trouble, and the most destructive of all, Evelyn. Whereas Elfie had poured out everything she thought and felt, and so, as was the way of the world, she had grown the most unknowable of all. Because, thought Sophie, what Elfie had had to say seemed so transparent, so ordinary, people paid little attention, and then later when they tried to remember her, when they tried to recall what she had said, after she lay down, her head on the pillow she had first placed in the oven's grill, they could recall almost nothing. There were no shreds, no bits of sentences, with which Sophie could build a scarecrow of Elfie.

If she could, Sophie would build such a figure; she could contemplate it and theorize about her: Elfie. Elfie, who Sophie now thought about as the heroine in a story told to her when she was very young, and in that story, there was a child who continually gave away a piece of her mind, until one day she wanted to give away another piece of her mind and discovered she had no pieces left. It was those who most desperately wanted to be understood who failed to be comprehended, who ended up stamped as unknowable. Julia had been unknowable as a child. Julia had told Sophie that. "It was so much safer that way," Julia had said. But Julia had found others like her, and then she no longer needed to be unknowable. So perhaps it was true to say that Meena had found no one she resembled, except, of course, the members of her own family, her dear ones, the ones who did indeed understand her because they differed so little from her. Although Meena *had* differed, even from them, staring into the fire for hours, thinking about who knew what, while others read or went about their chores, Meena spending hours and hours of staring into the fire without speaking a word.

"Were you always happy as a child?" Sophie said, breaking the silence.

"Certainly," Meena said. "It goes without saying that it helped to know my own parents, to know exactly where I belonged. I wasn't one of those children who dreamed my parents were not my parents, but were really kings or queens. I thought of my mother as a queen and my father as a king. I'm sorry to say you had no such certainty as you grew, one mother after another, until, luckily, you had me, one who stayed. But it rather cracked you, I think, all that rattling about. Children are fragile when they're so small, and you were very small when the trouble all began, not even three, and perhaps Andrew was luckier. He didn't know what he'd lost. But you did, I'm sure of it. Sigrid used to talk of how frantic you grew when you were brought back to Willow Grove after Evelyn died, how afraid you were to go up the steps even if she lit every lamp in the house. She said she had to drag you upstairs. Sigrid thought your behavior very mysterious, but what could have been plainer? You suspected you had lost something enormous, and you knew you would be sure of it when you went upstairs and *she* was not there. What a mess she made out of things! Well, not everyone is made to be a mother."

Meaning, Sophie thought, that if Evelyn had not had children, perhaps she could have gone on, survived. But she had had two children, although perhaps what Meena implied was true. Andrew and Sophie had been the death of Evelyn; Evelyn was responsible for leaving them to the dubious mercy of their stepmother. Meena the wife, the stepmother, the widow. Poor Meena, the evil stepmother. But she had a genius for some things. Whatever she said twisted Sophie's spirit, broke something that had healed once and then twice, until she, Sophie, became quite used to living with a box of broken glass set somewhere deep inside. Yes, that was Meena's genius, her ability to torment without appearing to turn a hair. Unknowable, perhaps in the end, because mad. Sigrid said that repeatedly. "Meena is *mad,* lovey. Don't ask for explanations. Don't blame yourself. Madness has its own rules and ambitions. Your own mother was mad." And how, believing that, could Sigrid comfort Sophie? Or Andrew, who kept himself in a remote world where the name Evelyn Graves meant absolutely nothing, a safe world where Evelyn Graves had never been born or died, had never been resurrected as the genius, the famous poet, so that Andrew was never faced by people who knew what kind of woman his mother had been, never felt as if he had to explain his own place in the scheme of things, or explain Evelyn's fate, as if he could remember the least thing about her, not even a memory or a sound or a scent, although there were times when someone lit a candle, and the smell of the burning wick and the hot wax together reminded him of something—primitive. Fugitive.

They said that his mother used to light candles. When Evelyn first lived with Daddy in Willow Grove, they had no electricity, and so they used candles, and would have used them in any case because Evelyn so loved them, their lit translucent bodies about which she had written so much. The scent of the burning candle, its blackening wick, probably those sights and sounds did not belong to him, were not memories from his early months, but came from a later time when Evelyn was already as waxen as one of those candles, when the light that made her flesh so beautiful had gone out. Perhaps Elfie had lit the candles for the brief time she lived, or his aunt, Sigrid, had lit them. He knew that to be true, but he could not rid himself of his secret belief that it was Evelyn who had lit the candles, and the scent of those burning candles was almost all he could remember of her. So precious to him, that possible memory, how could he speak of it? He knew, he had always known, that he never would or could speak of any of this.

And now Meena decided that she had had enough of people, especially those people, now awake and sitting at her kitchen table. After this, she thought, she would never have to cook for them again, never have to allow them past the threshold of Willow Grove. What did they mean to her, what had they ever meant to her? She had married into this family when she married Peter, and somehow she had thought it would be all right, that she would come to love them and they to love her, but she had not counted on her own nature, on her own violent jealousy, first manifested in her desire to keep Peter completely to herself, and when that failed, she discovered her capacity for hatred—and revenge. And all that before she was made aware of Peter's infidelities, his never-ending betrayals, yet none of them as scalding as many of the humiliations she had suffered at his hands. Oh, yes, someone had to suffer for what he had done to her, and in time, she came to see that Peter was not the one to punish. She had to be careful there. He had been through so much already, and now that he was famous and everyone knew who he was and who *she* was, she was not about to lose any of the spoils of war. There was nothing she was willing to give up. Even at the end, when death sat first on his left shoulder and then on his right shoulder, he continued to believe she was an honest and honorable woman, an Indian, that was true, but time had turned her into a good English country girl, someone he could count on. To have maintained this illusion in light of what he had already come to know! To make, at the very end, an enormously stupid mistake. But then many would argue that he had always made stupendously stupid errors, and they would also say he was never the one to pay for them. He had escaped the consequences of his own actions again, Meena thought, but she knew which people would pay for his last mistake, and all of them were sitting around her kitchen table. She knew what she was doing, she had made her calculations.

She knew how Sigrid hated her, but Meena also knew that Sigrid was loyal, believed in sticking together, would always have done anything for Peter, and would continue to comfort Sigrid now with pleasures large and small because she believed it was what her brother, Peter, would have wanted. Giving up Sigrid—that would be giving up the loyal dog, the strong dog, the faithful one who would die protecting her owner. Sigrid was like the dog in a famous Japanese story, Peter had told her that. Once there was a dog who met his owner at the train every day. The owner died. But until the dog died, it would report daily to the train station, waiting for his owner. Such fidelity had made the dog famous, proverbial. There were statues built of that dog. So if she gave up Sigrid, Meena knew she would be giving up someone who was greatly to be valued. But Meena hated her, wanted no part of her. She would, she thought, simply have to do without Sigrid, the faithful companion, and in so doing—she had no illusions about it—she would instead gain a faithful enemy, one that would never stop undermining her. If it proved necessary, Sigrid would live forever, simply to torment her. She smiled slightly into her cereal, how unlikely it was that anyone would think of building a statue of Sigrid for her loyalty, her faithfulness. Sigrid's faithfulness was the sort that made enemies. She did not count the cost when she protected those close to her, she had given up the only man she had ever loved, leaving him behind in Los Angeles, finally marrying Douglas, that man who now never left the house, Sigrid's house, nothing but a shadow in his room. "And will Douglas be coming to the funeral, then?" Meena had asked, and Sigrid said, "Certainly not. You know he goes nowhere."

"I would not have expected you to take such a *pale* man," Meena said, and Sigrid answered, "He was a beautiful boy. Once."

"Poor Sigrid," Meena told her.

"It suits me down to the ground to have a husband who bothers me not at all," Sigrid said. "It is quite useful to have a husband stashed away somewhere in the house. He keeps off unwelcome suitors. And, of course, I can do *exactly* as I please, as can he. He protects me, you see, Meena. He does me no harm. Every woman should have such a husband," she said, and looked meaningfully at her sister-in-law.

"I am surprised you can still remember his name," Meena said maliciously.

"Meena, dear, everyone remembers *your* husband's name. Has it been a great consolation?"

And she did not answer Sigrid. Checkmate and checkmate again. If she were to answer Sigrid, she would hear something far worse than what she had yet heard. Best to go quiet when Sigrid was present. Deviousness, slyness, Machiavellian planning, all that was alien to Sigrid. Tiny as she was, fragile as she looked, at heart she was an amazon queen; she would be the one who armed herself and strode forward to meet the lion that had been terrorizing the town, whereas she, Meena, was underhanded, covered her traces, was the sort of child who kicked someone under the table and then, when the other one hit her back over the table in full sight, would tearfully ask her parents, "Why did he do that? What did I do?" and was consequently consoled while the other sister or cousin was punished. No slaps delivered above the kitchen table in full view of her mother, not for Meena. Perhaps it was true that she was not intelligent, as Peter and Sigrid had always said, but she was cunning, crafty, full of deceit, and her parents never saw it, never glimpsed it, nor had her sisters nor her cousin. And she had had years and years now to perfect her illusion of guilelessness, her air of injured innocence. "She is a saint, that Meena," so many people had said so, and now she was determined that they continue to say so. She would not let anyone besmirch her image as Peter's perfect wife, and now, Peter's perfect widow. She would be what she had always intended to be—the keeper of the flame. Oh, Sigrid used that phrase with contempt, but Meena had loved that phrase for years, unspeakable years. And that, at last, was what she would be now: the keeper of the flame.

The day he died, Peter smiled suddenly and said, his voice restored, if only for a moment, to its full strength, that voice loved by everyone in the world, as if he indeed had been a kind of siren, an *homme fatal,* he said in that famous voice of his, *Fear no more the heat of the storm, or the some- thing something's furious rages.* How she would like to know the source of that sentence, and the word or words that she could not now remember. But she remembered what she had said after he smiled and spoke those words in his usual, strong voice. She had said, "To tell you the truth, Peter, I think you are quite right to fear everything," whereupon his eyes closed and his hand trembled on the sheet, and the alarm on the monitor went, and the green line that was his heart opening and closing went flat, and he was dead, and what consolation it had been for her to know that those were the last words he heard, *I think you are quite right to fear everything.* What a wonderful secret, to know the last words he had heard, while she told others, tearfully and to such good effect, "He seemed to awaken and grow strong again, and he said, *Fear no more the heat of the sun,*" and she would break down and weep, huge, choking sobs, inducing the same sobs in many of the people to whom she told that story. A small revenge, but very, very sweet.

"Well, then," Meena said aloud in her brusque, efficient voice, "I shall certainly not continue to need such an enormous table in the kitchen." No one knew what to say. What, after all, was the appropriate response to that? *I'll take it?* Anyone who said that would appear unutterably greedy and grasping. And in any case, they knew that Meena used that table as a desk, answering Peter's correspondence and her own, ever more considerable, because lately she had become a patron of several charities, spreading out papers on the table, deciding what letters to keep and what to discard. "I wouldn't do anything, not right now," Sigrid said. "Impulsive actions are always regretted later."

"Yes, I'm sure that's so," Meena said with a great sigh. "I'm sure it must be," while Sigrid thought how lovely it would be to lay Meena out, lifeless, on that very table never to move again or speak again. How many poisonous meals have we all eaten here? Sigrid asked herself.

"But the rest of you must take what you please," Meena said. "Especially your own things. Andrew, I have *all* of your university textbooks in our house. Surely you must want them. Take them or dispose of them, one or the other. And all that clutter from your sculptures in the barn. Once you have cleared it out, I can give the barn a good cleaning."

"But," said Andrew, "I cannot carry everything off today. Those things will not fit in my car."

"Nor in mine," Sophie put in.

"Then they will have to stay where they are," Meena said.

"Well, after all," Sigrid said, "it isn't as if you have a pressing need for a barn, is it?"

"I like things to be tidy," Meena said.

"I'm sure Andrew will be back for his things and the barn will once more resemble a hospital in its cleanliness," Sigrid said.

"There is no need to be sarcastic, is there?" asked Meena.

"Well," said Sigrid, "nothing of mine is still here. Everything of mine is long gone. But the children will have childhood things left about, especially in the attic. Peter took great pains to keep all that in good order. He knew they would want them."

"My Paddington bear!" Sophie said suddenly.

"Oh, Sophie, I don't know *when* I threw that out!" Meena said. "It was dirty, simply filthy. Anyone could see germs swarming above it. Out it went, and good riddance!"

"You threw out my bear?" Sophie asked, incredulous.

"Please," Meena said. "Don't work yourself up. I'm not up to one of your fits. I know you inherited them from your mother and it is inevitable that you have them, but I am simply not up to it right now."

"My fits!" Sophie exclaimed. "Inherited from my mother?"

"Please," Sigrid said to Sophie. "Don't take the worm on that hook."

"And what does that mean?" Meena asked.

"And what *is* left of mine?" Sophie asked, her voice gone the color of storm clouds, threatening lightning, threatening thunder.

"Some small dresses, a few pairs of shoes, very small baby shoes, and a roll of your paintings that you once set such store by."

"The dark red one with the large bird?" Sophie asked.

"Peter insisted we keep it," Meena said, "although he said it was a poor painting and didn't augur well for your later work."

"No one cares what Peter may or may not have said," Sigrid said. Both of her hands were fists resting on the table.

"That is what is left," Meena said. "And there may be other scraps. This is not a warehouse. This is a house. We had to dispose of a great many things in order to make room."

"To make room for what?" Sigrid asked. "There are enough outbuild-ings here to house the Acts of Parliament. What needed so desperately to be thrown out?"

"I suppose," Meena said, adopting her patient voice, "I should have kept all the leaves that fell in the autumn instead of raking them up and burn-ing them."

Sigrid looked at Sophie and Andrew. They looked from one to the other, avoiding Meena's eyes. *Don't say anything,* said Sigrid's expression.

"Well, let's hop to it," Meena said. "Search the attic and your old rooms."

When it came to it, it did not take long. Andrew carried off his old col-lection of butterflies, all caught and pinned himself, a stack of books, and some flat unpainted wooden boxes he had hidden beneath a floorboard, and inside each was what he had then considered an extraordinary specimen of an oddly marbled stone, and a stack of his own papers, primarily sketches for his future sculptures.

"I should look through those," Meena said in her most businesslike way. "Peter liked to put letters into books the way other people put in pressed flowers. I'm collecting all his letters."

"If they are in those books," Sigrid said, "Peter intended his son to have them."

"Oh, no, it was just his habit," Meena said, moving toward Andrew and his small stack of books.

"Don't touch those books, Meena," Sigrid said. At that, Meena seemed to shrink.

"Take them, Andrew, if you want them so badly," Meena said. Sigrid intervened before Andrew, out of guilt, could give them up, and said, "I'll see to these."

"And what have you got?" Meena asked Sophie.

"Just as you said. Some children's dresses and a roll of my first paintings and some notebooks full of equations."

"Really, I should go through all of those," Meena said, contemplatively and exhaustedly.

"Leave them," Sigrid said decisively. Meena promptly retreated. Thank God, Sigrid thought, there is still someone on this earth that woman is afraid of. But she also could hear what Meena would say later to anyone who would listen: "They carved up everything the day after the funeral. I wanted to keep back one or two of Peter's letters, not valuable ones, only inestimable to me, but they wouldn't hear of it. I couldn't fight back, not really, not when I felt they were also suffering. But still! They took everything that could be carried off! Although I must say that they did leave some rubbish in the barn. Well, death is a terrible thing, what it brings out in people, not in everyone, certainly, but in surprising people, those from whom you don't expect it." And she would sigh, and there would be a slight shaking of her head. And people who listened would think, again, "Poor Meena! That woman is a saint!"

"You will look after the will and the lawyer, or shall I do it?" Sigrid asked. "It might be a relief to have all that taken off your back."

"Oh, no, I promised Peter," Meena said. "I promised to obey his wishes. He did, you see, leave it all up to me. It is my last duty to him, surely you can see that."

"Then you will see to the lawyer?" Sigrid persisted.

"Certainly I will," said Meena, her voice gone cold, the voice the three of them all knew so well.

Somehow, they found themselves outside the house, having said their goodbyes to poor, poor Meena, ready to open the car doors and slide into their seats for the trip back to London, when Sigrid suddenly said to Sophie and Andrew and Bertold, "The last time Peter stayed with me in London, he said, 'I should be very happy never to see that woman again.'"

Sophie nodded. Andrew looked stunned.

"Daddy would not say that," he said.

"I've told you before," Sophie said. "You don't know what you're talking about."

"And now," Sigrid said, "she's thinking of raising peacocks. She insists that the noise they make won't trouble her."

"Peacocks?" Sophie asked.

"Peacocks?" asked Bertold. "The woman is mad."

"Peacocks?" asked Andrew. "If she wants peacocks, why shouldn't she have them?"

"I wish she had a violent desire to raise boa constrictors," Sigrid said.

"Peacocks," Bertold said again.

"Please!" Sophie exclaimed, as if, should she hear the word *peacocks* once more, she would start screaming and raking her face with her long nails.

"Peacocks," Sigrid said again, this time playfully.

"Siggy!" Sophie exclaimed. "Don't do it!"

"Peacocks!" said Andrew.

"Peacocks!" said Bertold.

Sigrid pursed her lips as if to say the word again, but at the last instant burst into laughter.

"We are all mad today," Bertold said, and then the laughter grew contagious, and they laughed until their faces reddened, until they cried. And, of course, Meena, the curtain twitched back to see more clearly, watched in a kind of horror. Why were they laughing? When she was so sure she had destroyed any happiness they might have remembered from this last, final visit to Willow Grove, the house that they had once believed was their home.

FIVE

——

WHO DID SHE know in London who would be awake at seven-thirty in the morning? Julia asked herself, looking around the cabin of the plane, almost empty, a plane which should have left at two A.M., but was, as usual, experiencing "delays." No one she knew kept normal hours, not in the United States or in Great Britain, although doubtless there were some of her friends who were awake at seven-thirty A.M., but they would only be awake if they had not yet gone to sleep the night before. Her friend Eliza would be awake, but the man she lived with refused to answer the telephone when it rang in their little house outside of Oxford. Well, that was not quite true, Julia thought, shifting restlessly in her seat. He did not have to choose whether or not to answer the phone when it rang. He had unplugged the ringer, so that anyone trying to call Eliza believed that the phone in her house was ringing and ringing, when in fact no one in Eliza's house heard any sound whatever. Just once had she called that number and found herself on the phone to her friend Eliza, and only because Eliza had happened to pick up the phone just as it would have rung, had it been capable of ringing.

If the plane does not take off within the hour, Julia thought, I will call her. Thank God for cell phones, although she herself never used hers unless she was finished with her work at the university, and then she would call her husband and ask him to pick her up. "I fail to see why," Sigrid once said, "having walked away from all that teaching, all those students and all those papers, you willingly entered into one of those tame lions' dens again," and Julia, patient Julia, as Sigrid so often referred to her, had explained again that she accomplished so much more when she taught. Teaching brought her the familiar pressure of time, an accustomed structure that was like a trellis and kept her climbing. Teaching caused her many panics about having insufficient time, and thus made time far more precious and sent her to her desk far more often than when she was not teaching and could easily say, "I'll start again tomorrow."

"Perhaps I was wrong to have refused teaching," Peter said, the last time he had stayed with them when he came to the States. "You have been so very prolific."

"Well, writing novels," Julia had said. "They keep you company. For years and years."

"I tried, more than once, but it was hopeless," Peter said. "I should like to have written more."

"*You* were the one who told me, 'Posterity doesn't want much of you, one or two good things, *one* good thing, and that's enough.'"

"I said that?" Peter said.

"We were in Northumberland, in that pub called the William."

"Your memory is a terrifying thing," Peter said. "Especially terrifying in a woman, especially to a husband married to a woman with an unerasable memory. Who can argue with a wife like that? She can call up everything, every dust mote that has ever settled as evidence in her behalf. A *typhoon* of information. You know you've already lost the argument when she speaks her first word, because what she's really doing is calling up her witnesses and she has hundreds, and she remembers what each and every one of them had to say. Evelyn was like that, too."

"If people had known her better," Julia said, "if they had known how difficult she was, for herself and for everyone else, well, then, I think people would think of both of you differently."

"Don't kid yourself," Peter said.

"The truth has to count," Julia said. "For something."

"And if someone asked you, presumably on your deathbed so that you knew you could never repeat what you had to say about me, how *would* you describe me? If the truth is to count, that is."

"I would have to admit, wouldn't I, that you had not been faithful to Evelyn, and that itself would not be so dreadful, but you knew what your infidelity would mean to her. So, culpable in that way, I would have to say that. Although she must be held responsible for some of your doings. She married you with her eyes open. You had a reputation before you were out of college, deadly to women, all that sort of thing."

"Would it have warned you off?"

"Absolutely," Julia said. "If I had met you after I had already come across Matthew. But, of course, before Matt, when I was mixed up with Tom, well, at that time I would have been susceptible to you. But no one in her right mind would go through that sort of thing twice. It nearly killed me the first time."

"All the same, you didn't die."

"I forgot. You haven't read all my novels. I didn't bother with stoves and gas. I hoarded up pills and took them all at once and I knew, I *knew* that Tom would not alter his morning rituals, and there was an excellent chance that when I fell asleep on the floor outside of the bathroom, the grain in those oak planks was the last thing I would ever see. But even if I had died," Julia said, "what harm could I have done to him? He already suffered from guilt. His nature wouldn't have tolerated any more. Afterward, when I was in the hospital, some junior psychiatrists came, and one of them told me, 'We asked him what he would have felt if you had died,' and he said, 'Not as sorry as she would have wanted me to be.' Speaking the truth, for once," Julia said. "And of course I was not famous. He might have felt differently if I had been as famous as Evelyn."

"Evelyn wasn't famous, not when she died. Don't you ever wonder? How famous she would have become if she hadn't actually put her head in that oven?"

"Do you wonder?" Julia asked him.

"Always. She would have been famous if she'd lived. I'm sure of it. She was so determined to be famous that she wouldn't have taken no for an answer. It would have taken her a few years, but because she killed herself, she became more than famous, far more. She became mythic. Of course, she was also dead. And so was I, really, caught in that mythic amber with her. Me and my Francesca di Rimini." He laughed harshly.

The two of them, Julia and Peter, sitting on Julia's daughter's bed, a maple canopy bed, its pink canopy above them, the pink bedspread resting beneath them. "If someone could see this," Julia said. "Last night, I saw you from the hall and your feet stuck way out past the footboard and there you were, the caged lion sound asleep beneath this little pink canopy."

"It was too bad to put Anna out of her bed," said Peter.

"She has to learn to share, like everyone else," Julia said.

"The hard voice of the mother is heard in the land," Peter said.

"I'm not being hard."

"I suppose not. I spoil my two," he said. "Who wouldn't, under the circumstances?"

"Does Meena spoil them?"

"She leans in the other direction. She thinks it's her duty to right the balance."

"What is it someone said. '*Benevolent neglect,* that's what children want.'"

"And did you have that?"

"No."

"Well, the whole world knows that Evelyn didn't have it, not with her kind of mother. Evelyn didn't have a chance once her father died. Charlotte always lived through someone. Who else could have done as well as Evelyn?"

"It's too bad, all that," Julia said. "Families. I always say, the same person who created plagues created families. It's the same sense of humor."

Peter smiled and got up. "I'm off to visit Mandy," he said, as if that were an entirely ordinary event.

"Didn't she say she'd come here to the States to be free of you?" Julia asked.

"She is. She's married to someone else and she has three children."

"But still she wants to see you."

"What are you driving at, Julia?"

Julia laughed. "I was remembering that chase through London when Sally or whoever it was decided she was going to give you a galley of her new book, and she kept missing you. She almost dropped down with exhaustion before she found you. It was so hot! Everyone said it was the hottest day in August since they started keeping records."

"She gave it to me when I was with her and I lost it and she wanted to replace it," Peter said.

"Don't even try to sound reasonable, not to me," Julia said, and an immense grin broke over his face.

"She was hilarious, Sally, wasn't she?" he asked. "I rather liked all that in those days."

"She's very famous now. You can see her whenever you want to on *Masterpiece Theatre.*"

"So, shall I be back in time for dinner, or don't you two eat?"

"If you're back by seven, the three of us will eat. Otherwise, the two of us will be eating at the Floridian."

"I'll be back on time," Peter said.

"It's your worry," Julia said.

"Well, you have learned a lot, haven't you, little Julia?"

"How long did it take me to learn that?" Julia asked. "Twenty years? More?"

"But what is it you learned?" Peter said, growing serious. "What did you learn that taught you to say things like that? And mean them?"

"I was cutting up little sandwiches for the English tea at the college, and there was a woman there, very beautiful, you would have liked her; she thought of herself as the Wife of Bath. Until I came, she was the undisputed beauty. When I arrived, she treated me dreadfully. The nastier she was, the nicer I tried to be. And then I sliced a sandwich in half and it came to me. Most people are born knowing the things I needed to learn. Well, I suddenly understood that there were people who would only treat you well if you treated them badly. And so I changed my behavior immediately. I had that woman terrified of me within weeks. After that, whenever I published another poem or gave another reading, she tried to tell everyone who would listen. She exhausted herself trying to please me, and I knew better than to be pleased, although now and then I did allow her a tiny, tiny smile. That's how I learned."

"So you learned how to treat men by practicing on a woman?"

"I learned how to treat *people* by practicing on her. But it's true that a woman usually finds ways to keep a man in line."

"Good God," Peter said.

"I'm sure you have your own ways," Julia said. "Probably you tell the lady of the day, 'Meena will be angry if I don't get back,' and then you have more room to maneuver. I'm sure that's what you do. Meena's just one small but very effective weapon in your armamentarium."

"You can be cold, Julia," he said, contemplating her.

"And what should I be? Madame Earth Mother?" She laughed. "No more. It's too late for that."

"Too bad," Peter said.

"What would you have done with another conquest?" Julia asked, more sharply than she had intended.

Still in the plane, Julia looked at her watch. Eight-thirty in London, and still, none of them would be up. The Great Rebellion, this going to London on her own. She knew herself to be too dependent and so one day she decided she would go to London alone, in the middle of the semester, as if she had a right to do just that. Matt objected. They were at the Floridian, and when, for the third time, he said, "You won't be able to manage the luggage on your own," she put down her knife and fork and said, "As soon as you're finished, we're going to Macy's to find some luggage I can handle." He said he would miss her, and she hoped it would be true, because he was always so sunk in work that she frequently felt as if she lived on her own, more lonely than she would have been had she, in fact, lived alone.

For several years she had thought more about Sigrid than Peter. In the end, she wondered, who was the more interesting of the two? A man who was the male equivalent of a femme fatale, a man with an immeasurable weakness for women, especially those to whom he was not married, a poet who wrote very good poems, or Sigrid, who adored only Peter, who gave up everything for him, who went on fighting and fighting as if, decade after decade, the struggle continued to matter.

I don't really understand her, Julia thought. She is worth understanding.

The year she had first come to London, she had met Sally, the woman who sent a galley all over the city to replace the one Peter had lost. She and Sally had liked one another. It was only a few weeks before Julia's birthday, and Julia said, "It is nice to be almost fifty," and Sally said, "You wouldn't be so happy about that if it weren't for all the women who made it possible for you to think so," and Julia nodded, taking in that comment, knowing how little it applied to her, she who was so reclusive, who had fought her important battles on her own. "You'll go out of town to college over my dead body," her father had said, to which Julia had answered, "If I have to step over your body to get there, that's what I'll do," and the drums began to beat in the family, until they were silenced by her grandfather, who told her father, "If you don't send her, I will." That, Julia thought, looking back, was the first miracle.

"I like Sigrid," Julia told Sally after a sufficient pause, "but I don't know why she gives her life over to Peter."

"I'll tell you a story," Sally said. "I don't remember who I first had it from. Once there was a very old man who could barely move, he was so crippled by arthritis. He hands were twisted, even his toes. And he had a dog, a lovely dog, about seven years old, but very, very lively, what we call *spry*. And then one day, a friend came to call on the old man and the old man leaped up from his chair and ran up and down the steps from the kitchen to the parlor, and the visitor was agape, and said, 'What happened to you? What kind of cure did it?' And the old man said, 'I gave the arthritis to the dog.' And there was the dog, under the piano, barely able to move. 'I gave it to the dog.' Sigrid is the dog," Sally said. Sally had said all she had to say on the subject, and Julia said nothing, did not comment at all, because even then, even when Julia and Sigrid were first getting to know one another, she knew that Sally was right. Sigrid was the dog.

Finally, Julia asked Sally, "And will it work with Meena? Will Meena be the dog?" and Sally said, "It won't work with everyone. You understand why. You don't have to ask me. Think about it."

No, Meena would not be the dog, would never be the dog, because she could not love deeply enough. Perhaps once Meena had loved that strongly, for a week or two weeks, but then when she saw what she was up against in Peter, she uprooted those feelings one by one. She could picture Meena doing it, yanking those feelings out of her soul.

"So you understand," Sally said, who had been watching Julia's face with a kind of avidity. "It's an unlovely thing, isn't it?"

Unlovely. She had never heard that word uttered before. Unlovely. It was too small a word for what Sally had told her, Julia thought. It was monstrous.

She could still make a call. There was a telephone in the back of the seat in front of her. It was nine-thirty in the morning in London. She called Sophie, who went through her usual effusions, said that Julia should come to her directly from the airport, laughed when Julia apologized for calling so early, and said, "How could you wake me? I'm still *up*," and then her voice went desperate and she said, "Julia, I am so happy you are coming, I can't tell you how happy, how are you, Julia, are you well?"

"I still make mistakes when I speak," Julia said. "I'll tell you about it when I get there."

"And did you ever finish that novel about your family?" Sophie asked, and Julia said, "Last week," and Sophie said, "Oh, Julia, then you really *are* all right," and Julia laughed and said, "Sophie! Go to bed! I think the plane may have intentions of leaving the ground."

"I can't wait to see you!" Sophie said. "I can't, I really can't, do you believe me?"

"I do," said Julia, "and no more than I want to see you."

She replaced the phone in its cradle in the seat in front of her, saw the stewardess's grateful smile, waited for the plane to lift so that she could put up all the armrests in her row and cover herself in three blankets meant for three people, for there were very few people in the plane, and then she would sleep. She should have told Sophie, "Tell Sigrid I'll be there by nightfall," but she didn't have to tell Sophie that. Sophie would ring Sigrid and rouse her up from whatever sleep she was granted these days.

SIX

——

"THIRTEEN STAINED-GLASS skylights?" Julia asked.

"I started with one, of course with one, and then when I saw the colors, and the way everything changed all day with the light, I thought, a second one would be just right, and then I saw another, and I decided that one would be *spectacular* in a bathroom, well, the kind of bathroom I was building, more a cross between a parlor and a bathroom, full of plants, you've seen it, Turkish carpets everywhere, and each window was more beautiful than the next, and finally I ran out of ceilings. The thirteenth is in a large closet. I put lights in the ceiling in back of it. It's the most splendid closet in Great Britain, I'd swear to that."

"That," Julia said, "is how I ended up with Oriental carpets one on top of the other. I told everyone it was called 'layering' and I said this is what the Arabs did when they decorated their tents. For a while, I thought about using them on ceilings and two of them did wind up on the walls."

"Sigrid thinks I'm mad, of course," Sophie said.

"Of course," Julia agreed.

"You think I've gone too far?" Sophie asked.

"How can you go too far with things that shine out like that?" Julia asked her.

Julia and Sophie were not unknowable to one another.

"There's one thing I really want to know," Sophie said.

"What?"

"How are you? Really?"

"You mean all those fainting fits after the stroke," Julia said. "I'm fine, as far as I know, and as far as I know, nothing caused them. Two hundred tests later, and the conclusion was that *nothing* caused my fainting. But I was too tired to get from the bed to the chair. And then the last thing that happened, it's still going on, I tend to *stick,* you know, say 'yellow' instead of 'blue,' or 'morning' instead of 'evening,' but no one seems to notice. 'Smudgy' instead of 'Sunday.' They think I'm distracted."

"You must have been terrified," Sophie said.

"Not when it was happening. You know how it is. And then it began to seem hilarious, I started laughing, I couldn't stop, and I suppose it was contagious, and everyone was trying not to laugh, but they did. It was my fault, I suppose it always is. I was the one the teacher sent into the hall, saying, 'You can come back in when you can control yourself,' and I'd come back in, and start laughing all over again. I was sent down to the principal a couple of weeks before graduation, and the poor man looked at me and said, 'Julia, why don't you just go home?'"

"But to mean one thing and say another!" Sophie said.

"I knew it would pass," Julia said. "I had no intention of saying sense-less things for the rest of my life and the words I needed weren't *com-*

pletely stuck. Sometimes I didn't make too many mistakes. But I couldn't read properly. Sentences didn't make sense. Then I got a copy of *People,* and I decided to practice reading out loud, but I didn't want to bother the woman in the next bed reading out loud stories about Tom Cruise, so instead I read the specifications they print next to the ads for prescription drugs. I was afraid to stop reading aloud, so I must have been frightened, but I was reading in a low voice, and I'm sure the other woman in the room must have thought I was mumbling some kind of religious tract, but I wonder what she made of what she did hear, '*adverse reactions, esophageal reflux, tachycardia,*' that sort of thing. I particularly liked the allergic reactions and the contraindications. I thought no one could possibly be healthy enough to swallow that drug. I think it was for acid reflux disease, something like that. It was later, about two weeks after they let me go home, when it really dawned on me that I had been in real trouble. And Matt was still commuting after I got out, so I was left alone for half the week, and I got that lifeline thing. You wear it around your neck and press a button if something goes wrong, or if you fall down, and people come and get you. I was willing enough to get that. Needless to say, I didn't fall down when I had that damn thing around my neck, but I had to get up my courage to get into the shower; everyone kept saying, 'That's how people die, in the bathtub.' That's the kind of thing people tell you after you've had a disaster. The lifeline medallion is back in the country house in the bathroom, dangling from the knob of the closet door. And then there were all those tests in New York. Who knows? They didn't really know. So now I take my poison pills, they're anticoagulants, and walk around with thin blood and try not to bump into anything so I don't turn black and blue, and I've gotten very good at not bumping into things. Now you know everything," Julia said.

Sophie nodded.

"But you, you're very pale and you look exhausted," Julia said. "Is it your father's death? Or what is it, really?"

"Daddy's death was awful, and I had to beat down the door in the hospital to see him before he died, and there was my stepmother barring the doorway, but the real trouble now is an ongoing thing, and my joints swell up, well, like yours. You know what that's like."

"When I was young and sixteen," Julia said, "and hobbling about with what people said was juvenile arthritis, I'd go to the doctor and all the octogenarians would glare at me for taking up their time. I always said old age was not going to be a surprise to me and I was right, although it's got an even bigger bag of tricks than youth, much bigger."

"I thought Daddy would go on forever."

"So did I."

"I'm so glad you are here," Sophie said again.

"I sleep too much," Julia said. "I'm always sleeping. I'll be very boring to have around."

"I sleep all the time these days," Sophie said. "I tell you what. The nicest place to sleep is the bathroom. It has the most comfortable fainting couch. And a beautiful dying swan carved in its back. Daddy loved it. He loved that room. I wanted to bring him back here and look after him, but—"

"But Meena wouldn't have it," Julia finished for her.

"Whatever I could have done, he still would have died," Sophie acknowledged.

"It's worth remembering that."

"Yes," Sophie said. "Are you tired?"

"I had no idea anemia made you so tired," Julia said. "I thought only thin, fragile-looking people became anemic."

"But it's improving?"

"Oh, yes," Julia said. "Last summer when I was over here, Sigrid worried whenever I got out of bed. Really. One day I got up to pull the blinds, the sun was so bright, and I fell between the vanity and the wall and it was a job extracting myself. I don't know how I ever finished that book."

"The book of your illness," Sophie said thoughtfully.

"I hope it doesn't show."

"Daddy used to say that when a book weakened you in that way, you knew you were doing your best work."

"I wonder. Usually I'm completely healthy until I finish the last page, and then I collapse. Really collapse. Visits to the doctor, prescriptions filled at the pharmacy. Writing usually gives me a sort of immunity. Your father once gave me a book about all the psychosomatic illnesses writers suffered with, and they tended to fall into two or three categories, I remember that, and I've been trying to find that book again ever since, but I can't remember a thing about the title or the author."

"Daddy believed real writing came from a kind of possession, a spirit that took you over, and it was usually an evil spirit. It gave you what you needed to write, but it took far more."

"He said that?" Julia asked.

"Meena said I was a hypochondriac. She thought you were, too, and she told Daddy he was just as bad when he began to complain about his stomach."

"People as healthy as Meena can't believe other people really have illnesses," Julia said, and there they sat, twenty years between them, discussing illnesses like two old pensioners in the waiting room of a physician's office. "And Sigrid never understood, either," Julia said, "although now that your father's gone, well, she's started to see the cracks in the mirror."

"Poor Siggy," Sophie said.

"Poor everyone," said Julia.

SEVEN

—

MEENA FOUND HERSELF alone in Willow Grove, alone in the house. If I were to tell someone I was alone in the house, thought Meena, how sorry for me everyone would feel, but I am not unhappy, I have the house to myself, it is *my* house and I can do what I please with it, I can walk into the front parlor and revel in it without anticipating Peter's tread on the steps, the board squeaking just before he walked in, his expression sour, the comment he would make, "Once this was a simple, plain house, a house for plain people, as it was intended to be, and now look at it. Look at it." In his last months, Peter said the same thing, again and again, but out of habit, she thought, without energy. "You know, I still have to repay my cousin for that landscaping of yours," he said every so often, until

Meena snapped at him, "Don't you think I've done enough to deserve a decent garden?" and with his intravenous still in his hand, with the bottle and the stand attached, he got in his estate wagon and drove off to stay with that woman, and she, Meena, had been terrified. What if he had died there, in that other woman's bed? What if everyone heard that he had left her for someone else?

But he returned quickly, only two days after his departure. Meena gave him that much time before she called him. She had known just what to say. "If you do not return before nightfall, you shall not find me here." Almost Evelyn's words. Long ago, he had told Meena that story, Evelyn saying, "When you read this note, I shall be dead," and he tore down to London, pounded on the door of Evelyn's flat, and when she opened it, her hair was neatly washed and she had lightened it until it was almost platinum and was dressed in something stylish he'd never seen before, and she smiled and smiled, and said, "Peter! Do come in!" And how furious he had been, but still, he could not afford to ignore those tricks of Evelyn's, not when she had tried so many times, running off the road on her way back to Willow Grove. Everyone thought she was only a bad driver, and then there was her mother, Charlotte, calling him, saying, "Please take care, she's done so many things," words that needed no further explanation.

But now Willow Grove was hers. She had transformed it. She had chosen the stones for the kitchen floor; she had chosen the paint for the rooms, the draperies, one set for the summer, one set for the rest of the year, the carpets on the floor; she had hinted for them when that Indian author kept coming, presuming that he and she had something in common simply because both of them were from India, and he insisted on cooking up inedible meals in her kitchen, so spicy she could barely swallow them; after all, she hadn't been brought up on Indian food, while he and Peter ate enormously and roared with laughter. "Well, Peter," she had said, "if you will eat food like that, your stomach will hurt," and he had said, "There's some custard in the summer kitchen,

Meena, why don't you go eat that?" meaning, Why don't you get out and leave us alone?

And of course she listened at the doorway when Peter said, "Summer kitchens! Do we need summer kitchens in England? It's February all year round in this country. But she read about summer kitchens somewhere in one of her damn magazines, something about Jamaica, I think it was, and we had to have one, so in July or August, we're out there shivering, you know what British weather's like, especially up here in Northumberland, and cooking up some bland meal she says is good for me, and the summer kitchen comes in handy twice a year, but what a lot it cost! For two days, or two weeks, if it's a very hot season." And Meena, listening, thinking, How dare he talk about me like that? What right does he have to speak of me without my permission? Of course I know about summer kitchens! My mother kept one in India and then kept one in Great Britain. How dare Peter speak to that man about what I think about summer kitchens! Although, in truth, Peter rarely did speak of her, not out of loyalty, oh, no, but out of boredom, out of disgust. It occurred to her now that he might have spoken of her far more often than she had suspected, all those trips to London, to people he'd known for decades, how he emphasized that— *I've known them for decades.* As if that made them worthwhile, as if that meant anything.

The turret is mine now, Meena thought with satisfaction, climbing the steps to it, stopping to admire each shape of light as it fell onto the Indian carpets, the good, unusual Indian carpets. There was the rectangle of gold sunlight, here was the long strip of white light, here was the broad band of greenish light, leaves flickering in it, so beautiful, while Peter, if he had still been here, would have arched his eyebrows, would have said, "Haven't you seen sunlight fall on a floor before? Does it have to fall onto something valuable before you appreciate it?" There he had underestimated her, Meena thought. Such fleeting images meant a great deal to her. But she spoiled everything the day she had taken three of his friends on a tour of the house, stopping at one carpet and saying, "They weave what they see, you know. Those are the tanks and those are the black planes that fly low, but see how they have drawn the planes in with jaws as if they were alive, as if they were birds," repeating what Sigrid had said about those rugs. "Puffing yourself up like a toad, making yourself feel important," Peter said, turning abruptly, going down the hall to his small, plain study and slamming the door.

Had his illness caused such outbursts? Was his fury deepened by his knowledge that he would not be seeing those rugs, those halls, those rooms for very long, whereas she, Meena, would last and last, saying what she pleased as she showed the house to whomever she pleased. Surely he should not have felt so much contempt for her!

Now she has stripped down the turret room, made it hers, taken everything from the room, painted the walls white, a small room, but beautiful, curved, six windows, the panes so scrupulously clean it was hard to believe the windows held panes of glass. If it weren't for the occasional reflection, it would seem as if the glass had not yet been placed in the frames, so beautiful to look through on a day like this one, a scrubbed day, so fresh and clean you could believe the first days of this world looked entirely like this one, and he used to feel such delight when she said such things, surprised, as if he had not expected such things from her, but when he changed, there was nothing she could say that would not be ridiculed. He said, "Oh, yes, a newly cleaned world, and the throngs of downtown London are the window washers of this world. The streets and lanes here are crowded because of all the cleaners," and then to find out that *Evelyn* had mocked him when he went into raptures about the freshness of the world after the rain. It had been Evelyn who had laughed at him then, saying those things about throngs and throngs of window washers clogging the lanes and the streets. Peter had thrown Evelyn's own words back at her, at Meena, the third and least considerable wife. Yes, at such times, Meena thought the two of them had joined together to torment her. But who would have believed he would treat her in that way?

She had broken down once beneath it, and she had said something to Julia, of all things, to Julia. After another argument with Peter, she agreed to let Julia visit Willow Grove. "Can't you see Julia is married the way you believe people ought to be married?" he went on in that voice, awful, cold. "What excuse will you dream up to bar her?"

And why *am* I barring her? Meena had asked herself. I don't dislike her. I won't go so far as to say I like her, but I don't *object* to her. "All right," she told Peter. "Invite Julia."

"Invite Julia?" Peter repeated, incredulously, disbelieving.

"It is you who thinks I hate everyone," Meena said. "You have invented that myth about me. It has nothing to do with me."

And so Julia arrived, and Peter went out alone, walking in the rain, and the two of them were sitting in the turret while Peter was out when Meena suddenly said, "He is cruel to me." Julia looked steadily at her. It seemed as if she were about to say something, but then she made a decision. She kept her silence. "There is something you wanted to ask me," Meena said. "I could see it in your face."

"Well, Meena," Julia said.

She had never heard anyone speak with such sadness, or was it sympathy? Was it possible it was sympathy? "Tell me what you wanted to ask," Meena said again.

"Does he mean so much to you?" Julia asked, slowly, as if groping for words. "Would you say, even to yourself, I will not put up with this? I will not stay with him? Could you ever say that?"

"No," Meena said.

Julia said, "I understand. Meena, I do understand."

"You don't believe he is cruel. How can you believe it?" Meena asked.

"But I do. I do believe it," Julia said.

"Must everyone grow to hate everyone else?" Meena cried out suddenly, uncharacteristically, beginning to sob, knowing how amazing all this must have sounded to Julia, as if an alligator had suddenly begun reciting Shakespeare.

"Sometimes," Julia said. "Sometimes they do. And sometimes they stop."

"But he will not stop. Once he has begun, he will not turn back," and to her horror, Meena continued to sob. "Now you will tell me I must stop crying, it is not good for me to cry," Meena said, but Julia said nothing, simply sat still and waited. "And now you will tell Peter exactly what I have said," Meena went on.

"Certainly I will not," Julia said. "What do you take me for?"

"You will tell him," Meena said hopelessly.

"Must I tell you again?" Julia asked. "I will not speak one word of this."

"Why?"

"*Why*?" Julia asked. "Because of what you just told me. Because now I am responsible for keeping your trust."

"People Peter knows don't behave in that way," Meena said.

Julia said, "Perhaps you underestimate them."

"No. I don't."

"Look, Meena," Julia said. "I understand what you've told me. There are two paths, aren't there? You find a way to live with him, and if you do, you save yourself, or you leave him, and if you do that, you save yourself. He is important, yes, and he is very important to many of us, but he ought not to become so significant and important that you or anyone else is cut off from the light because of him. You *know* that, Meena. You weren't brought up to believe that a person of talent or reputation or beauty was somehow more equal than anyone else. You weren't taught to think that someone has the right to sacrifice someone else. You were taught such things were wrong when you were a small child. Don't lose sight of what you know. Don't do it, Meena."

Meena had ceased sobbing. She sat upright, her hands placed in her lap. "I have chosen my path," she said.

"Have you?"

"I have."

"People change paths all the time," Julia said. "People call that 'living.' "

"That is not my way, Julia," Meena said.

"Then you must do the best you can," Julia said, "knowing it will not be easy."

"You admit that?"

"Of course," Julia said. "It goes without saying."

"I didn't think to hear it, not from you."

"How well he knows his way to the Slough of Despond," Julia said, "and how well he teaches *you* how to reach it. He cannot help being what he is, but you are not doomed to change and become like him in that way."

"I'm afraid I am," Meena said.

"Well," said Julia.

"Yes," said Meena. "Well."

And Julia had never spoken of that extraordinary conversation, not to Peter and not to anyone else. Meena would have known if Julia had. Julia had kept her trust. And now she was sleeping in Sophie's house, in one of Sophie's bedrooms, and soon all of them would be telling Julia of her misdeeds, her *sins*.

"I fail to see why you made an exception for Julia," Peter said in those weeks before his death. "And yet you don't send for her now."

"I make no exceptions," Meena said, turning her face away. But it was not true. She had once made an exception for Julia, now sleeping in one of Sophie's beds, Sophie, now lost to her. It is best not to make exceptions now, Meena thought. It is best, now that I have set my course, to make no exceptions. I must remember that I cannot afford to make exceptions.

—

SIGRID RANG SOPHIE early the day after Julia arrived. "I need help," Sigrid said.

"Oh?" said Sophie.

"There has been this line running through my mind since the funeral, and I simply cannot place it or find it. It begins, 'Fear no more the heat of the sun.' Do you know it?"

"No," said Sophie.

"Naturally not," Sigrid said. "Go wake Julia."

"She's sitting here," Sophie said, handing the telephone to Julia.

"I can't place this line," Sigrid said. "It goes, 'Fear no more the heat of the sun, nor the something something's rages.' I thought it might be Kipling."

"No, not Kipling, Shakespeare," Julia said.

"Shakespeare?" Sigrid said. "Impossible. I know every line of Shakespeare."

"Is this what you're looking for?" Julia asked, and began to recite:

> *Fear no more the heat o' the sun,*
> *Nor the furious winter's rages;*
> *Thou thy worldly task hast done,*
> *Home art gone, and ta'en thy wages;*
> *Golden lads and girls all must,*
> *As chimney sweepers, come to dust.*

"I'm skipping two stanzas, but this is the last:

> *No exorcism harm thee.*
> *Nor no witchcraft charm thee!*
> *Ghost unlaid forbear thee!*
> *Quiet consummation have;*
> *And renowned be thy grave!*

"Is that it?" Julia asked.

"My God," Sigrid said, her voice shaking. "Every so often, Julia, you remind me of why I like you."

"Ah," Julia said. "While you're alive, I know I will never be the worst person in the room."

"Leave off saying that!" Sigrid exclaimed.

"It's true," said Julia.

"*Golden lads and girls all must, as chimney sweepers, come to dust,*" Sigrid said.

"Yes," said Julia. "It's perfect."

"Perfect," agreed Sigrid.

So many voices breaking, so many eyes filling with tears. Why did people live? Why did people die? But some did not live, could not. The living would not allow it.

Julia and Sophie sat in the beautiful room on the outskirts of London. In her small sitting room in another part of London, Sigrid cried silently, got up, picked up the winged wooden carving of a woman Julia once had given her, and sat down again, repeating the words, *Fear no more the heat o' the sun.* Meena sat in her turret, looking out over the meadow as it undulated toward the churchyard. Andrew slept in a friend's spare room, not dreaming, as usual, not dreaming. Phone lines connected them all.

I am so happy to know the lines.

Where is Daddy?

I feel sorry for Meena.

No one thinks of me now.

Do souls travel at the speed of light or the speed of sound?

A parenthesis, silence, exhaustion, a kind of peace: grieving.

—

HE HAD BEEN ravenous when it came to sex. And in the beginning, so was she, she was so young, he was the one who had awakened her. And then he had come to know that Evelyn had been a person of ravenous appetites, emptying refrigerators when she was invited to houseguest, ravenous for information, asking Penelope, renowned playwright and a man who was a great friend of Peter's, Penelope, a remarkable horsewoman, her relatives all known for *something,* some for their pedigree, some for their writing, politicians, oh, the kind of family Evelyn herself hoped to create, Penelope an enchantress: take her to a party and half the men were in love with her within an hour, and almost all of them within two, and so Evelyn asked Penelope, "How do you enchant a man so much older than you are? Are there secrets? Are there tricks? Tell me, tell me!" Almost endearing, Penelope thought, in her ravening curiosity. "Would you dye your hair another color altogether? Would you do anything to look young? Would you try plastic surgery? What would you do? Why didn't you want children? I didn't want children, but then suddenly I did, and now I want dozens, dozens!"

Penelope laughing and saying, "Be a little suspicious of your enthusiasms. They're not the same as intuitions, they're not instincts, certainly not instincts," Evelyn contradicting her, "Oh, yes, they are instincts. Instincts are like weeds, don't you think; they break up concrete to get up into the light, instincts, passions, they're weeds in our natures, they can't be stopped, why try to stop them? Don't you see it? Didn't you see it when you married that boy? He was a boy then. Wasn't that unstoppable? Did it do you any good to ask, Is it a good idea? Shouldn't I wait? No, no, I can't live like that. What's the point? All you do is waste life, waste time. You're going to give in to all that anyway, and if you make a mistake, it's over with faster, and you're still young, don't you think?" And Penelope, laughing and laughing, until she said, "Evelyn, let's heat up the lasagna," and Evelyn's face fell; she had to admit that she'd eaten all of it before lunch, eaten enough to feed eight people at luncheon, saying, "I was *so* hungry," and Penelope, laughing and laughing, saying, "Never mind, we'll all go 'round to the pub for lunch, they make a good roast on Sundays," Peter asking Evelyn, "How could you eat *all* of it?" Evelyn answering, "But I was hungry!" Peter saying, "How can anyone be so hungry?" but smiling;

Evelyn was so huge, so unrepentant in her hungers. And that night, she would be just as hungry again. How could he have ever thought to replace her? Why hadn't he known what he had? But then she died so young. Penelope often said, "Peter, we were all so young, well, *she* was young, definitely she was, even she would have cooled off *a little*; it's inevitable, don't you think so?" and Peter, puzzling it out, saying, "But Meena was no younger when I met her, and she's cooled off, not that she was ever on the boil like Evelyn," Penelope replying, "Oh, well, some flowers bloom fast and fade even faster, but I don't think Evelyn was such a flower. No, more like an ivy, climbing over everything, choking everything," and Peter asking, "Is that what you think? That she would have choked everything?" And Penelope asked, "Didn't she? Peter, didn't she?" All those empty plates and pots and pans and Evelyn never gained a pound. Once Penelope came into the kitchen suddenly and there Evelyn was, licking the chocolate icing from the emptied bowl, her face smeared with chocolate, her eyes ecstatic, no remorse, no guilt at all when she saw Penelope. And of course she had skimmed off some of the frosting on the cake so that in places the icing was thinner, and what could Penelope do but sigh and smile? You had to respect such appetites.

And then Evelyn fell in love with Penelope, not a matter of the body, not that at all, but when Evelyn fell in love with people, she could see no fault in them. There was nothing too small for her to discover about them; she was fascinated by them, and when she turned the hot beam of her attention on whomever was now the object of her utterly uncritical love, that person felt as if a hot sun were warming her, as if something of great importance, precious beyond estimation, had been bestowed upon her. So Penelope went through all that, underwent all of that. She cooked without resentment for Evelyn, who consumed everything, she began teaching Evelyn how to ride because she, Penelope, was a great horsewoman, saying repeatedly, "You must not be afraid of a horse simply because it is the size of a building. You are not afraid of buildings. No?

Then why fear a horse?" Evelyn laughing and climbing into the saddle, falling right off, but in weeks, galloping abreast with Penelope, and one afternoon, Evelyn's mount decided to jump a fallen log, and Evelyn did not fall, she shouted with joy, she laughed, her hair streamed out beneath her hat, she laughed and laughed. And so it went, until one morning Evelyn got up and went to the window where she had heard voices, and there was Penelope and Peter, the two of them deep in conversation, their heads leaning together, and Evelyn thought, *That* is why she has been so kind to me, she has been after Peter all along, and in that moment she turned on Penelope, *saw her for what she was* (an expression Peter had learned to dread, and with good reason), came clumping down the steps still in her flannel nightgown, the one Peter's mother had sewn for Sigrid, but Evelyn said it suited her so much better, would they mind if she took it? Her mother-in-law looking at Peter, then at her own husband, finally saying, "Of course you must have it," already worried because she would have to explain to Sigrid, her daughter, how she had come to give that nightgown up to Evelyn. "We have to go back," Evelyn announced to the two of them, both of them startled, then appalled. "I must go back," Evelyn insisted. "The appointment at the BBC, you remember, Peter?" and Peter saying, "What BBC appointment?" and Evelyn hissing, "How can you be so dense?" Penelope asking, "Have we done something? What have we done?"

"You've done nothing," Evelyn said, "but we must go home."

"At least wait until we've eaten your pheasant," Penelope said.

"That murdered thing!" Evelyn exclaimed. "How can you expect me to eat it?"

"Is that the trouble?" Penelope asked. "I'll make something else. You don't have to eat it. You should have said."

"Ten minutes, Peter," Evelyn said, and stomped back up to her room, the room that had been hers until she heard the voices, looked out the window. And Peter turned slowly to Penelope, said slowly, "Women devour everything. Women make me their world and then they want to devour me, and if I don't want to be devoured, they're worse than snakes; they twist themselves until they begin to eat their tails with their fangs, until they have devoured their own world and there is nothing left of anything. Evelyn has begun her devouring."

"No," said Penelope. "No."

"And once it begins," Peter said, "nothing can stop it."

EIGHT

—

IT WAS INEXPRESSIBLE, how happy she was to be in charge of
this turret, to know no one else had the right to enter without her permission. Of the turret, Peter had said, "You have it," smiling that beautiful,
blurry smile, his eyes half closed as if he were still half asleep. "You have
it. It's the best room in the house." And it was, it was still the best room in
the house. Thatch for the roof above all the other rooms, but slate on the
roof of the turret. Oh, how she had wanted that turret! Not another turret in this town or in any one near it! As children, they walked this far simply to see the turret, her older sister dreaming up stories about the ladies
who lived in that turret, always ladies with very long blond hair, because,
as Sangeeta said, they had to let down their hair so that a prince could

climb up into the turret to claim them, although at times the women of the turret used their long hair to bind flying dragons who attempted to come in through the turret windows. So many stories. Sangeeta was supposed to have lasted forever, wasn't she?

But Meena had said no to the turret, very firmly, without hesitation, because she knew very well that the turret had been Evelyn's before hers, and Elfie's before hers, and the only being who could be allowed in that turret was Peter. Two women dead by their own hands. Each of them still had business to settle with Peter, but they would not put up with Meena. Meena, like others who had grown up in the country, believed in the great strength of spirits who took their own lives. And so Meena said, "No, no. Anyone can see it is your turret. It suits you," but he said, "And it would suit *you*," back in the days when he still wanted to make her happy. She turned the turret down again and again. Finally, Peter said, "You must not say no to so much or the day will come when no one will think of offering you anything." And once more, she had said no to the turret, and indeed the day had come when he would not have dreamed of offering the turret to her, when he sat there in his chair, his back to her, enraged and immobile, until she turned and went down the steps. Those rough-hewn steep steps up to the turret, they were harder to manage now than they once were. Even the smallest and sprightliest and healthiest woman begins to feel it in the knees. Meena felt it so, felt that her knees did not spring from one step up to the next, as if catapulting her up the flight of steps. Well, that strength was gone, but that wasn't so much to lose, was it?

But now, looking through the windows of the turret, Meena thought, I have come into possession of this at just the right time. The huge oaks were level with the tops of the turret windows and the birds were here with her, flying into the topmost branches, the birds so different from what they seemed on the ground, so much plumper, staring into the room so curiously, as if to say, This would be a good nest for *me*. And what kind of birds were these, these grey-feathered birds, their chests surmounted by shiny brown feathers of every conceivable shade, and on their heads, brilliant red feathers. Not cardinals, surely, of course not robins, but what were they? She had never seen such birds before. Yes, you could sit up here, in the wide armchair she had hauled up herself, the arms far too wide for the turret room, its cushions stuffed with down. Someone had treated the covering badly. The fabric of the seat was slashed, but she had found a kilim in the back of Andrew's closet and covered the chair with it, and she would have been willing to swear the chair had been waiting for her all this time, waiting and waiting, she and the chair waiting together, the chair acknowledging that she, Meena, owned this piece of furniture as it had never been owned by anyone else in its life, the kilim, beautiful, absolutely beautiful, transforming it. *You see, you see what I can do?* she said aloud to the ghost of Peter, who would not be happy to see her at peace in this chair covered by her son's kilim. Meena could remember when Peter bought it in Turkey, in the market, and how she had been called out of her hotel room to do the bargaining. Everyone who knew them relied on her to do their bargaining, and yes, she had been good at it, she had been, she went at it with such enthusiasm, and, as everyone acknowledged, such skill.

"Stop that cleaning!" Sigrid had said, because that was what Meena had begun doing when they were first settled in the little Turkish hotel. Meena looked around her, said, "Right, we're not unpacking until I clean," and she had begun to clean everything: Sigrid was sure, Peter was sure, that room had never before been so clean. They were certain that a room in that part of Turkey was not meant to be so clean; perhaps the dirt and the dust had some sort of useful purpose. Meena snorted at that and continued her scouring. "I want to see the sun go down, I want to see the market and hear that wailing the women make," Sigrid said. "You stay here and clean, Meena, if you must." And there were turreted rooms in Turkey, and stacks of carpets, their hues more beautiful than any sunrise or sunset, and all of them were out there in the sun, the sun that was going down, turning the gold sand red, and where was Meena? Inside. Cleaning.

Oh, yes, Meena thought now, he thought less of me after that, for staying inside and cleaning while outside there were such splendors, but who else was to clean? Would Sigrid do it? Did Peter care? But *she,* Meena, had cared. They ought to have been grateful to her. And then, just as the light was dropping, Sigrid came back and said, "Meena, I've found a carpet, I've never seen such a carpet," and without thinking, Meena said, "I'd better come out and bargain with you, shall I? So that you don't waste all the money Peter is going to make by coming over here." And Sigrid ended up with the carpet at half the price, a beautiful kilim, its background the color of aqua seawater, and the flowers, so beautiful, so strangely real, here and there a woven bird that resembled no bird that had ever lived. How strange it seemed to Meena that people who could weave such flowers could not begin to weave a bird that resembled a real bird, an actual bird; how smitten she had been by the carpet, so much so that Sigrid said, "You can buy it off me. If you want," and Meena said, "No, no, that is your carpet." And then, years later, when Sigrid moved from a large house to a small one, she gave up the carpet, not offering it to Meena. No, she gave it to Andrew, and he in turn had given it to Sophie, and Sophie had kept it until she moved to London, and then returned it to Andrew, and so it came to rest in a corner cupboard of Andrew's old room in Meena's house, until one day she found it, found it and covered this wonderful, wonderful chair with it. In the end, Meena thought, you got everything you wanted if you could last it out.

Did she still believe that, after all she had gone through with Peter? Yes, she thought, I do believe it. Perhaps I have wanted the wrong thing and that was the trouble, but what I want now is an opulent life. How she loved the sound of that word *opulent*; she could say it aloud whenever she pleased. She could sprinkle it like salt through her conversations, and there would be no contemptuous glances when she used such words. Wasn't she entitled to use them, wasn't everyone entitled to use words like *opulent* once they knew them? Freedom. A new stage in her life. Now she could have everything she wanted. She would take care to want the right things. And it suddenly came to her. I want *everything*. And I shall have it. I shall go about acquiring everything beginning today. Was life any more complex than that Turkish market she remembered so well? She had complained, after Sigrid bought the carpet, about how heavy it was, saying that half the weight was dust and dirt. "Well, you would say that, Meena," her sister-in-law had said, but she, Meena, was supreme in the market, and why should this market in this remote corner of England be more difficult than that market had been? All of life was a market, really, and, thought Meena, *I am the one who knows how to bargain.*

She smiled, and thought of Sophie and Andrew and Sigrid, and it seemed to her that they were shrinking under her gaze, all three growing gaunt as if starved, and she nodded her head three times, as if to say, It will be done. It has *already* begun.

NINE

———

WHAT, JULIA WAS asking herself, is there left to say about Peter? Not because other people asked her about him—acquaintances—who knew they had been friends for almost thirty years, but the others, his children, his sister, they were the ones who were difficult, and here was Julia, just opening her eyes in Sophie's third-floor bedroom, just moving to the two windows that came together in a V shape, probably the consequence of the man who planned the house deciding that no, he didn't want the house going just here, but wanted it there instead; in any event, it was peculiar, the shape of this room, the shape of the outside wall, and no one could account for it. "But it is just *this* I like about it," Sophie always said, as if someone had criticized a beloved child or a pet. "If this house were any other way, if it were more *normal*, the house would be spoiled, the enchantment would be broken. You can see that, can't you?" And Julia could honestly answer, "Yes, I can see that." That was an easy question to answer honestly, but if Sophie were to ask, as she often did, "Daddy was the kindest man in this world, wasn't he?" how was Julia to answer?

The Peter Julia had known had not been the kindest man in the world. He was always promising things—"I will take you hunting"—but never taking you, instead saying, "On Saturday, I shall be there at eleven; nothing will stop me," and then ringing up at ten-thirty to say he wouldn't be able to come, something about the traffic or the train or a relative who had suddenly dropped by without warning, from Alaska, from Patagonia, from God knows where. "Sigrid, he is impossible," Julia said once, years ago, and Sigrid said, "You can't blame him, love, it's all Meena. He would have been setting out to see you, he might have been in the car, and Meena would have come up to the car window and tapped on it until Peter rolled it down, and she would have said, 'If you go, I can't be responsible,' so he had to go back. That's why he didn't come."

In the beginning, she believed such excuses, but sooner or later she discovered, everyone discovered, he had chosen to do something else. On that day, at that time, you had not been important. It was impossible to know whether or not to hold him responsible, and was it really likely that Peter, who could be so stubborn, had suddenly allowed himself to become a man without will, someone out of *The Day of the Triffids,* his own will canceled out by another's, and by what? A word from Meena? Yes, you came to understand that Meena was part of his technique, part of his strategy for satisfying his appetites of the moment, Meena allowed him to do what he pleased, allowed him to dispense with duty, and loyalty and the unhappiness of the moment, if you could use such mild words for the misery he habitually caused. Meena was his excuse to abandon all promises, to do precisely as he pleased. Because you came to realize that you could never know if Peter had deliberately disappointed you and hurt you, or if Meena, not Peter, was responsible. A slippery man, really, capable of hurting people, telling himself, Oh, yes, he'll survive, or she'll survive, when he above all ought to have known that you could not nonchalantly rely on someone else's survival. He did not estimate what his whims would cost others.

Julia herself had suffered enough from that sort of thing, until she tired of it, came to feel that if he came, he came, and if he didn't, there were many other interesting things in the world, so that when she found him sitting in the audience when she was giving a reading at a small college (and what on earth had he been doing there?) Julia was certain that he would not have come had she asked him. A sadistic streak, surely we could acknowledge that. We did not have to demote such derelictions to passivity, as Sigrid did, and as Sophie did. Poor Sophie banned from Willow Grove when Meena laid down the law, relegated to a holiday visit every other year and Sigrid allowed to visit the next, Meena having put her foot down because, she said, aunt and daughter disagreed on everything, and so Meena refused to have her holidays spoiled. Yes, Julia thought, it was undoubtedly Meena who had decreed that Sophie would come one Christmas and Sigrid the next. But if Peter had insisted, if he had said, "They are both important to me and I shall have both of them there," would they have been banned as Meena insisted? Was it deference to Meena, or did he enjoy people, especially women, fighting over him? So many smokescreens, so easy for him to create, so easy for him to hide behind.

Yes, thought Julia, looking out the windows, there was a time Sophie was critical of her father, but now he had died, and all his faults suddenly had been erased, had never existed. Julia had seen such things happen often enough, she herself had said to her cousin, "Just because my father died, he didn't become a saint," but why should Sophie forgive him for having let Meena deny her her birthright every other year, and frequently, year in and year out, because Peter was working: he had an attack of something or other; he needed quiet; Meena was displeased with his daughter. Any excuse would suffice.

Downstairs, she could hear Sophie moving about, frying pans clatter-ing. It was time to go down, and Sophie would say again, "He was the kindest man in the world, wasn't he?" and wouldn't it be cruel to say, "He was many, many things, and he did so much good, I doubt if I would have begun writing again if he hadn't been able to inspire people close to him, something about his aura: after knowing him, it was not hard to under-stand the man who went to a shrine and claimed his life had been changed by touching a sacred stone; something about him, an aura, palpable, real, apparently not subject to his volition, a matter of molecules and beliefs and radiance, definitely radiance." You came under his aura, and you were bathed in it, that radiance. As she had been. And for some time afterward she allowed him anything, but then she grew older, less willing to be dis-appointed, although she did not go so far as others who claimed Peter humiliated them, deliberately humiliated them, as an editor who had worked with him once said, "It's humiliation after humiliation, large and small; if you deal with the Grovesnors, you'll come to know that," and was it Sally who had said, "Yes, that's right, that's spot on, humiliations large and small, and more often large rather than small." But Julia had not fallen in love with him, under his spell, yes, like everyone else, but then Julia once said, speaking of someone else, "He does not humiliate me. He humiliates himself. Only I can humiliate myself," and that, she believed, was true. Knowing the truth about yourself, knowing what you were willing to accept, what you willingly brought on yourself, that was harder than blaming Peter, harder than knowing what Peter did or did not intend.

And what would she say to Sophie, Sophie who was so easily hurt, Peter's body soon gone to bones, pebbles still settling, falling through his rib cage, deep down in the dark and damp where he now lived? Better not to say anything. But now to have to begin protecting Sophie! When such protectiveness, such sheltering, had stunted Peter himself, had enabled him to go through his life blind to the wreckage he himself caused. Would it not be best for Sophie to take her own measure of the life she had lived with her father, to say aloud, "Just there and there he disappointed me, just

there and there he made me weak; he cracked the cup, the cup that will
never again be made whole"? Because if she understood, if she blamed the
right person, would she not be able to fight? Better? More efficiently, with
more hope? Yet she was so easily bruised, and who was to blame for that?
And was she, Julia, now to join that conspiracy to protect Sophie as Peter
had once been protected? Were the furies never to stop pursuing that family, once a small family, a couple, only two, Peter and Evelyn? Julia would
go downstairs, she would say, "Of course your father was kind," but she
would stop short of repeating the rest of the mantra, *the kindest man in
the world*, and Sophie would notice that omission and she would resent it.
Had Julia not accepted the truth they all lived by? That he was the kindest
man in England? How could Julia not agree and say, "Yes, he was the kindest man in England"?

She shook her head and went down.

But what Sophie asked her, after they had settled into the comfortable
armchairs in the enormous kitchen, was this: "What kind of person was
Daddy? No one will tell me the truth."

And Julia was stunned. Saying, finally, "I can only tell you the kind of
person I knew him to be. Everyone saw him differently. There are people
who still swear he was a saint, had gifts, changed people's lives by one sentence, could do no wrong, that sort of thing, an angel, in other words,
Sophie, but then I don't believe in angels."

Sophie leaned forward. "Tell me what kind of man you knew him to be."

What should she say? Funny? Intelligent? A man who inspired others to
go beyond their own limitations, or, more precisely, to risk going beyond
what she believed to be her own limitations? Cruel? Could she speak of
his cruelty to his daughter? His casual cruelty, not directed at Julia herself,
but she had seen it directed at others, at that editor who had spoken of
humiliations large and small, so that, one night, after he had given a reading, he gave her the wrong directions, took all the rest of them off to
another restaurant on another street, and would have left that editor
wherever she was waiting, but his friend Jeremy, a good and decent man,

would not permit it and insisted on going out in the rain to find her and bring her back. And then, once she was safely seated with everyone else, Peter turned his back, literally turned his back to her, and spoke only to Julia, whom he had just met. Should she tell Sophie that? Wouldn't Sophie say, "But I am also cruel in that way, especially to men," and if Sophie said that, then of course it would be safe to tell her about her father's little cruelties, only the little ones; perhaps they could be hazarded, but not the larger ones.

Instead, she found herself telling Sophie a story.

"He came to see us that summer we lived in Cornwall, right next to D. H. Lawrence's cottage, and he was happy, he was full of mischief, he said if we went down to Seal Island, we would see the seals. They were always there, and I asked him, 'What kind of a trip is it?' And he said, 'Not bad at all, a little bit of a climb down,' but by then I already knew him, and I said, 'It is precipitous and vertiginous, isn't it?' and he said, 'Well, a little steep, but nothing to worry about,' and I said, 'I am staying right here, and all of you can tell me what it was like when you come back.' So he took them off to Seal Island and I stayed behind, and just before the bend in the road, when they were about to disappear, he turned back and shouted to me, 'Oh, ye of little faith!' and for some reason, I changed my mind and decided to catch up and go, because after all, my children were being taken down a sheer cliff. I already knew it would be like that. And it was. It was worse. Not even a path down the cliff, but a kind of shelf, all of us clinging to the cliff wall, afraid to look down, and your father booming out, 'We're almost there! You can look! Be brave!' But we weren't brave, we were terrified. I held on to my *daughter's* hand, for God's sake, the disgrace of it. I was so terrified, and finally we were down on that narrow, rocky beach, and naturally, not a seal in sight.

"So we sat there, on the hard stones, until we could breathe normally again, and then we had to go up, and your father kept on exhorting us, 'It's not nearly as difficult going up as going down, much easier on the knees.

You'll see,' all of us staring at him with hatred, real hatred, hating him as we made the climb back up, and when we got back to the house, falling down on the floor and staying there, because, as my husband said, 'You can't fall off the floor,' and your father, laughing at all of us, at everything we said, and everything we said was about how terrified we'd been, and I knew, I knew before we left, he was leading us into bone-breaking fright and we would never forget it. Well, I never have; I remember every instant of it and I don't like remembering it, even now, and I don't know why he was so insistent. Did he want us to feel that kind of terror? Did he think it was important to survive an experience like that, that we would be the better for it? He liked risk, Sophie, I knew that, but I knew that *before* we made that trip down to Seal Island, and I was furious, absolutely furious, because he had caught our two children up in it, and Anna was only six! She's grown up fearless, you know that; I sometimes think that began with Seal Island; our family isn't known for its fearlessness, at least not in the last two generations, and my son, well, he still believes he saw a seal when he got to the beach, and he still believes he'll see whatever he wants to see. How much is due to that horrible, horrible trip to Seal Island? Did he ever take you, Sophie?"

"No," said Sophie, "he never did. But Meena never saw why he needed to go to Cornwall when he was so happy in Grisleigh upon Shallows; I mean, would Meena find anything of any value beyond the boundaries of Grisleigh?"

"I hated Bishop's Nympton," Julia said. "He found us a farmhouse to rent there, and there was that incredible smell that seeps into everything in a cow farm, and the bathroom, well, I'm afraid of insects, I always have been, and I think he must have *imported* the world's most gigantic beetles and put them in the bathrooms of that house. Oh, I hated it there."

"Meena never would have permitted a beetle to enter Willow Grove," Sophie said. "Never. Willow Grove was paradise and she decided who and what was allowed in it."

"Yes," Julia said.

Silence in the kitchen, and then Sophie said slowly, "So you think Daddy was cruel? At times?"

"Oh, yes, but is that saying something?" Julia asked.

"But more cruel than others?" Sophie asked, persisting.

"Yes," Julia said. "More cruel than others. But he was more of *everything* than everyone else."

"And you believe that?" Sophie asked.

"Yes," said Julia. "I do."

"He must have done *something*," Sophie said. "All those tragedies on his doorstep."

And Julia, astonished, staring at Sophie.

"But at Seal Island, you were all so young, and he changed when he grew older, didn't he?" Sophie said, and Julia thought, So it is coming down to what I expected after all.

"Of course he was changed by experience," Julia said, thinking, Some people soften with age, but others, those who resent aging, they grow harder, they grow more and more bitter, more cruel, although they learn to hide their cruelties, as Peter had done, as she had seen him do.

"Yes," said Sophie, "I believe that. I believe he changed. And when you were all young, was he happy? Did he seem really happy, through and through happy? Because he never was, not when I knew him."

So Julia would have to tell her another story.

TEN

———

WAS HE EVER through-and-through happy? Julia asked herself. She looked past Sophie to the window. Rain had begun to fall, yet the day remained brilliant. She watched as the rain began to depress the leaves like piano keys. It is so beautiful here when it rains, Julia thought, so much light behind the sky, the rain itself silver. What could she tell Sophie that Sophie did not already know? When all of us were young, she wants to know what we were like when we were young. We were like everyone else, Julia thought. We had been mad with youth, drunk on youth, never thinking we were young. It was youth that made us what we were. The young always think of themselves as already wise, or wise enough, never think that it is youth that makes them do what they choose to do. We were merely eruptions of youth itself. It would have been such a help if we had understood that at the time, but then we would not have been young. I told Peter, "We are already what we will be. Being young, what is it? We're painted on with brilliant colors. We'll change as years go by, but we won't *really* change. We'll fade." And he said, "Yes, I think that's the truth of it, I think that's right, I'm a little faded now. Others can't see it, but I see it. There are some who wish I'd already done a lot more fading." But now Julia thought, No, it took him most of his life to fade, and even then there was not much fading; what he did was wear himself out, he stopped being the despair of the women he met, no longer had the energy for it, or perhaps it was something else, perhaps he was tired of the same storms again and again, and one day he looked up and thought, No more storms, no more waves crashing on the shore, I'll write about those storms, I don't want to live through any more of them. The storms were incapable of further novelty, nor those familiar dramas, almost boring; he was not curious about them any longer; why should he be? He knew them too well. What he was curious about now was peace, quiet, small surprises. And so the next woman he met would find a different man, a man tamed by time, a man no longer young, someone who knew what would happen if he behaved as he had in the past. Had Peter been any different in this from any of us? When he was young?

What Sophie wanted were the little films, pictures of Peter young and alive; after all, the specifics were what mattered; at one time, he had done this and this and this, those distinct moments, those were what the mourner wanted to conjure up after a death. Well, there was that night in the club, she would tell Sophie about that, that nightclub where the decorations were black and silver headless mannequins set against a background of black felt walls, the place garish and ghoulish, but all the same, the place to be. Mannequin heads were mounted on the black walls, and two bulbs were screwed into the top of each mannequin head like horns. Those bulbs lit the club, and on the table, blood-red tablecloths. And none of us commented on our surroundings; no one wanted to appear shocked or puzzled; after all, we were young and thought we were used to every-thing, and in the very center of the grotto, because this club was meant to look like a grotto, were silver-painted carousel horses behind the bar. And Jane, who no one had yet heard of, but was about to become very well known, had already finished her book about sex and all its strangenesses, and had already spoken to an accountant about what she should do when her novel was published. Someone had *insisted* she do that, probably her then-husband, the man who was to become the first of six.

What an utterly weird thing to do, Julia had thought, how on earth did Jane have the nerve to go to accountants *before* the book was published? Wasn't Jane afraid of jinxing it by showing so much confidence, so much optimism about her own fate? Julia sitting at the table with her husband of three months, thinking, I don't like Jane. Probably she never would have liked her, not after seeing her on TV sitting atop a claw-footed tub filled with red and silver Hershey's candy kisses and Valentine candy boxes to promote her new book of poems, *Edible World,* Julia wondering, How on earth does she have the nerve to do it? But at the same time thinking, Jane's right to do all this, she's doing the right things, not hiding under the table, peeping out from beneath the tablecloth of her cave, feeling quite safe in it, because who else other than Julia wanted to hide like that? No, it was not so much the sight of Jane and the tub, and the display of the red and pink Valentine boxes covered with lace and red satin that had set Julia so against her, it was the party Julia had given, the party to which Jane had not been invited, but Jane had come anyway, seeming to attend every party that took place in the city, no matter how small the gathering. If Jane did not show up at a party, Julia always said, someone should immediately call the police and then begin dragging the East River. So there was Jane, at Julia's house, and *uninvited,* but still coming up to Julia and complaining because she had wanted to meet Peter. She had discovered that Julia knew him and that he was somewhere in the city, Jane's city.

Certainly Julia had never felt the place to be *her* city; she loathed it, but was careful not to say so. And Jane asked Julia why she hadn't invited

Estelle Lark; didn't Estelle Lark teach English in Julia's department? And then, having complained sufficiently about the inadequacy of the guest list, Jane went up to two young women, students of Julia's, and asked them, "Who are you?" and when they said they were students, aspiring poets, as Julia and Jane had once been, Jane launched into a harangue, saying, "If you're going to be a poet, don't teach, God, don't do that, no, marry someone rich, a man who can support you until you make it, and then get rid of him. Haven't you seen any of the feminists after a party at the Guggenheim when they're getting their fur coats from the cloakroom? They *all*, darlings, they *all* have rich husbands, usually furriers; they're all swimming in money. *They* know what men are for. You can learn a lot from them. I did. I don't let much go by me," the two girls staring at Jane, horrified, one of them both horrified and frightened; the other was spunkier, getting up the nerve to ask Jane, "Is that what you did?" because, after all, the two students thought such advice ludicrous. Later, they called that conversation *surreal*, and Jane said, "I speak from experience. I married a doctor, and does he rake it in, and he's not even a good doctor, but that's not the point. The point is the money," at which juncture Julia seized Jane and said, "You have to say hello to Isabella. She's over there in the corner and she's wondering why you haven't come to speak to her," and of course Isabella was not in the corner, had never been there, but what other way was there to get Jane away from those two shell-shocked girls?

Why, really, had she hated Jane so? What had Peter said of her? "Oh, she's old before her time. But the main thing is, Julia, she's on the make. You still think there are pure things. Like writing. Jane was *born* knowing better. I've known women like that before. They'll do anything, so why be shocked? She's older, that's all," and Julia exclaimed, "She's two years *younger* than I am!" and Peter laughing, saying, "She's an older soul, a wrinkled older soul, well, you'll see it in time."

But then there they all were, in the grotto, most of them having flown over the barrier of the *First Book Not Yet Written, But Intending to Publish It Soon,* into the very much smaller clan of *One Book Published, And*

Intending to Be Famous, Julia there because Peter had dragged her along after Jane's reading, and he said, "You *have* to go," to which Julia had crankily asked, "Why?" and Peter asked her, "Don't you know?"

"I'll go if you will," Julia said, so there they were, wondering what would happen next, sure that something would, Julia already under Peter's spell, admitting that she did want to try writing a novel, didn't want to stop at writing poetry as she had been doing, and Peter saying, "Try it. Do it," so certain that she could do it, and in fact she would begin her first novel the day after he flew back to England, and after that, she would never hesitate again, never stop, *could* never stop, not even when she wanted to. In the nightclub, Jane's voice rose over the amazing din saying, "*Always,* I mean *always,* buy black panties. They don't show the dirt. You can pull them out from beneath a couch and put them on, and no one thinks they're dirty, filthy, really; remember, black panties, black panties." And then she was on to something else, but the place had become as quiet as a tomb; everyone was stunned into silence, but hoping to hear more, and without thinking, Julia leaned toward Peter and said, "I hate her," and Peter laughed so loudly everyone turned and stared at him, and Peter said, "She's the kind of woman other people *would* hate," and Julia asked him, "Do you like her?"

"I would, for some things," Peter said, to which Julia answered, "Oh, well, for some things, yes; I don't have any trouble seeing *that.*"

"But I wouldn't touch her myself," Peter said, turning serious. "There's something not right there. Can you imagine the trouble *that* one would cause?" But he looked speculatively at Jane, as if, in spite of what he had said, he was not quite willing to rule her out altogether. And then Jane cried out, "Look! They've turned on the carousel horses!" Her first husband, the doctor, tried to quiet her down, telling her, "Jane, you're drunk, you're drunk. Those horses aren't moving."

"Aren't moving?" Jane said, staring at him, and she burst into laughter, and the rest of the table started laughing, for no reason at all, trying to stop laughing but starting again whenever they caught someone else's eye.

Well, that was youth, that was being young, and later Peter said to Julia, "You don't see it yet? Everyone wants his niche, his special place, that's what all the exaggeration is about, everyone's trying it all on, personalities, eccentricities, everyone's trying to find out how good they are, pretty, prettier, prettiest? Smart, smarter, smartest? Almost famous, a little famous, very famous? So until they find it out, what that niche is to be, and believe me, most of them aren't going to find anything like what they *want* to find, they're caricatures, all of them caricatures of themselves, surely you can see it. I'm the same, I'm no different, but I've gone further down the path, that's why I can laugh at them; that's why I don't bother hating any of them; they have to go through all this, and you, Julia, you're still trying to be the good girl, the middle-class wife; well, you're not going to succeed, you weren't meant to be the good girl, but you won't turn into Jane, either. The interesting thing is, what we are *now* is what we have *always* been; that's what we can't see, not now." And what neither of them had seen, not then, in the middle of grottos and black panties and first contracts and first reviews, was how reclusive both of them were, and how quickly—in retrospect, it seemed quick—both of them would move into their own, closed worlds.

The horses aren't moving. Well, that was youth, that was being young, Julia thought, as she sorted it all out, and then told the story of that night to Sophie.

"So," Julia said, "there was your father, in the middle of that, having a grand time. A good time was had by all, and a little more than a year later, Jane and I published our first novels, and Peter came out with the collection of poems that put him on the road to the Nobel, and we were all so young and heedless, really, causing accidents right and left, and accidents happening to us, and we didn't care. Who thought about scandal, except to think it was another great thing, another experience, something to look forward to? Heedless, careless, happy people, all of us filled with ambition as if we were carnival balloons, yes, that about sums it up." Julia paused and looked away from the window. "There was so much we didn't know," she said softly. "Not then. And on that night, Peter was there. He wasn't the instigator as he usually was, and it gave him a break. He could watch the others and what they were up to. It was good for him, and he enjoyed every minute of it, and of course, he had me to teach. He loved teaching anyone who knew less than he did, and I was a genuine ninny, really, I was. So that, Sophie, was that."

"Did he sleep with Jane?" Sophie asked.

"I thought he would," Julia said, "but it turned out he really didn't like her. We all went to another party for your father the next night and Jane wasn't invited. She sent a note around to Peter, saying, 'I'm so sorry I couldn't come, but I'm so worn out with these interviews,' as if someone had *asked* her to come in the first place. He tossed it into the fireplace."

"And did you?" Sophie asked. "Sleep with him?"

"Me? No," Julia said. "*Everyone* wanted to, he was, well, it's hard to say what he was, but he had something; I don't know anyone who didn't feel it. But I was just married, and anyway, I remember back in those days, someone used to say that in spite of whatever I said and did, I was really the faithful dog. I was really always trotting back over to the man of the moment, invisible slippers in my teeth." Julia laughed. "Everyone was so funny about everyone else back then, and so accurate. Sigrid still is. That's one reason I like her as much as I do."

"Not everyone likes Sigrid," Sophie said.

"Not everyone likes me, either," Julia said.

"Sometimes I think Sigrid is afraid of *you*," Sophie said.

"Oh, that's nonsense," Julia said. "Sigrid's not afraid of anyone." Only of Peter, she thought, only Peter, and now there's no one she's afraid of.

"So he slept with everyone he wanted to?" Sophie asked.

"AIDS had yet to appear," Julia said. "We were none of us well behaved."

"Except for you and your invisible slippers," Sophie said.

"I only kept them in my teeth when I was in love with one particular person. If there was someone I was with for more than a week or two, I was in love with him; you know that stage, when you're so smitten with the idea of being in love, you behave as if you're already in it, so a man comes along, an innocent man, and he doesn't know he's entered into a relationship that's already been going on, at least as far as the woman's concerned."

"Once Sigrid said something like that, but she was talking about the time when Peter met Evelyn."

"I'm sure she was exactly right," Julia said. "That's how we all were then. Weren't you? You're not that much older than we were then," and Sophie said, "Oh, yes, I am. I'm almost forty and God, do I look it! But it is so nice to think of Daddy happy and young like that."

"All you have to do," Julia said, "is remember what you were like when you were in your twenties and then you won't even have to ask me." But unless someone were to describe something Peter had done, Sophie could not see it. Julia understood that, how impossible it always seemed to peer back into her own parents' lives.

"I missed all that," Sophie said. "I wish I could have seen it," she said.

"You were barely *born*!" Julia exclaimed. "Of course you missed it!"

"If I had a family, two parents, not necessarily both living together in the same house at the same time, separated, whatever, they would have told me stories about themselves, and I would have believed them the way I believe you. Everything would have been so much more vivid and valuable because they told the stories themselves."

"Oh, yes," Julia said. "I know. I heard stories like that from my mother and father, almost always from my mother, although my father was there for the telling, and I don't know how many times a year I think of those stories. Too many times, I think."

"There can't be too many times," Sophie said, standing up suddenly, going to the window. "Here's that huge pigeon again," Sophie said. "She's always here, looking in, as if she thinks she owns the place. Sometimes I look up and think there's someone staring in at us, but it's only that pigeon."

"She? A female pigeon?"

"It's a she. Look how drab she is. You know, Meena's thinking of rais-ing peacocks."

"I know," Julia said.

"Daddy might have enjoyed peacocks," Sophie said, thinking it over, "but naturally enough, Meena wouldn't have dreamt of having them if she thought Daddy would have liked them."

And so it begins, begins again, Julia thought.

ELEVEN

———

WHO IS THERE who has the courage to peer into that claustrophobic submarine that people call a long marriage? So Penelope thought as she stared out of the strict white hospital room at the Royal Marsden. Healthy as an ox all those years, astride her horse, a centauress, having chosen England over America, having gone to doctor's for checkups year in and year out, finding nothing, until the doctors themselves barely bothered to look, so that she stopped going, saw no point in continuing, but what was wrong was hidden deep inside, they would never have discovered it. She discovered it herself, because of the blood and the pain, and the cancer had let her live a good long time now, six years, or was it seven? But she was getting tired of it, the poisoning, the radiation, and if she did live on, what could she be but a bystander? It was all well and good for Sigrid to say, "There's a lot of *stuff* left in you, Penny. Keep on. You'll have a grand time," but Penny didn't believe it, she liked passions blowing up suddenly, then falling to earth like a bankrupt leaping from his skyscraper as people did back in the thirties; she liked all that fuss, all that drama, that was what she lived for. And here she was, over seventy, considerably over seventy, but of course seventy wasn't what it once was, and at the last visit to the plastic surgeon, always the same doctor in California, he said to her, "It's a good thing you started so early; there's hardly anything we need to do, do we? All we need is a little rain to stiffen up the tulips after a dry spell." \

And in fact, men still fell in love with her, men much younger than she was. Well, that was the story of her life, wasn't it? But how could she take a man up on his invitation, when she knew what she knew, knew about that magical little sack deep inside, meant to produce new life but now producing something very different? How scathing Evelyn had been when Penelope decided to remain childless, as if it were a failure on her part, as if choice meant nothing. She would have been a horrible mother. She knew it, so she made her decision. It was something to wonder about, still, after all these years. Would her first husband, M. R. Stone, have stayed with her if she had become pregnant and produced a child, because he thought, everyone thought it in those days, if you loved your husband or your wife, of course you would want a child with them? Had he thought she hadn't loved him enough? Probably Evelyn had thought she hadn't. And in the end what had Evelyn achieved by having children? Two children, both of them abandoned, left to stepmothers. Had Evelyn, who read everything, neglected to read the fairy tales? Or was she too young to understand the truth in those fantastical stories? Because Evelyn had been so young, younger than anyone else her own age had ever been. Everyone was young then, wasn't that our trouble? Penelope asked herself that.

Long marriages, Penelope thought again. She herself had not had one, but she had known many such unions, thirty-eight years, forty-three years, fifty, fifty! After M.R., there had been a long, a very long, liaison. It went on for years. She had been young when it began, and when it ended, she was old. She didn't regret it. She'd chosen a man designed to be an antidote to M.R., someone solid, dependable, in love with *her*, one of those endlessly valuable men who are like ducks who imprint on a woman if she crosses his path at the right time, as she, Penelope, had done, thinking, when she met Michael, *safe harbor*. And so it had been, and so everyone had told her, "How lucky you are, Penny. What are you complaining about, Penny? If he's a little on the boring side, is that something to weep and wail about? Would you rather shiver in a dark room, your arms wrapped around your chest, wondering what flat he was in now, what woman he was entwined with now?" And hadn't Sigrid made the same choice when she married Douglas, although he had faded as a carpet fades in brilliant sun? There were times when Penny thought of Douglas as already dead, embalmed and set on an office chair, and Sigrid was happier with him now than she had been with him in the beginning. *My husband.* Was there a woman on earth who didn't want to speak those words? "My husband" this or "my husband" that?

It was the length of it, the length of the years, the nature of two humans together, so many daily suppressions of one's personality. Even if yours wasn't much of a personality, nevertheless, it needed suppressing, more times than one could count, even in a day, all those negotiations, shall we go out, and if so, what shall we do? Gloom and doom, Michael always predicting gloom and doom, and what a waste of time it was, predicting the inevitable; they were all doomed, they would all be enveloped in gloom soon enough. Why should she curb her extravagance? Why should she hoard up her pennies? Against what?

Did she, Penelope, have children to whom she could will these imaginary pennies? Did she have *anything* but her beautiful jewelry, once so laughed at, now so treasured, those beautiful things Eliza the jeweler had made, Sigrid shaking her head when Penny bought them, saying, "You're mad." And it had been a kind of madness, a kind of frenzy, because if fire-birds let their feathers made of red-gold fall to the ground, wouldn't any-one who knew what they were grab them up? She knew a firebird feather when she saw it; she could say that much for herself. "You could live quite well on those, if you sold them," Sigrid said, turning over one of the huge bracelets, admiring the workmanship, the sparkling beauty of it, and Penelope answered, "And what would happen? I would see them again and buy them again, this time for fortunes," and Sigrid said, once more, "You're mad."

Not mad, but dying. In this perfectly correct, perfectly heartless white room. So newly painted, always newly painted, whenever she was admit-ted here. The Royal Marsden, where everyone goes to die, but each one saying, "Not just now. Wait until I've had my tea." Everyone saying, "Just a bit more time," but for what? What did they intend to do? What did she?

Long marriages. How her mind wanders, as well it might. Is there any-thing she wants to dwell on?

Years spent together, and the two who spend them together coming more and more to resemble two potatoes, because in fact they *are* pota-toes, and why should they aspire to anything else? Not seeing that time shared is not doubled when two people share time, but halved or worse, and surely they must think to ask, Whose life am I living? What kind of life am I living? Are surprises, good ones (bad ones are inevitable), still possible? What long-married husband or wife does not have an eye out for a surprise, something that might upset the balance? The balance is every-thing; they know that, those long-married couples.

She thought of Rose and Robert, married over thirty years. He died just this year, didn't he? Who could have stayed married to such a man? When every word out of everyone's mouth had to be scrutinized, analyzed, inspected, dissected, tested for any trace of careless thinking, even if all you had said was, "Nice morning, isn't it, Robert?" Until the cross-examination became so intolerable that people had been known to scream, literally scream, "I'm sorry I said anything! What I said didn't mean anything! It wasn't supposed to mean anything! It was just noise! So can you let it be! Just shut up! Shut up or I'll knock you down!" As the head of Robert's department had in fact done, in the quadrangle, in front of the students and the fellows and the benevolent man who had come to decide if he wanted to fund Robert's extremely expensive pursuit into the nature of the human genome, which request, believe it or not, Robert had been granted, the patron saying, "The man is a man of genius, but if he goes mad and ends up in restraints or in Holloway, all funds will be withdrawn." And how much better it would have been for Rose if Robert had died far earlier, if he hadn't decided to take revenge for having married her, blaming her for failing to meet his own ambitions.

Afraid, after a while, to say, "What a beautiful morning!" only to find herself mired in dissections of beauty, whether or not *this* particular morning was any more beautiful than any other morning, until Rose ran into her study and twisted the door lock, a very strong lock, meant for entrances to houses. Yes, she should have left him. Penny asked Sigrid, "But how can she bear it? Why doesn't she leave him?"

Sigrid said, "Oh, Penny, she'll never leave him. She's afraid to be alone. She's not like you or me. She's afraid of the world. She can't extend her territory unless she is clinging to someone's arm. For her the world is a great, blank, staring face, a mirror-face, it glares at her, and she won't want to look into that, will she? Well, she never has so far, and why should she start now? Reasons for leaving," Sigrid said to Penny, "they multiply like moths, but she won't leave. I know she won't."

"No," said Penny. "Why should she change? No one wants to change. You can tell in advance who will change. All you need is to ask, What reason does she have for changing? No, certainly Rose has no reason to change. She might, if she thought she could survive on her own for a small period, if she could walk through that tunnel of loneliness you first go into. She's like Alice hovering at the rabbit hole, afraid to go down, but Alice *did* go down. There were not many Alices in the world, and I would not have gone down, either, not voluntarily."

POISON   169

But those arguments that went on forever and ever! When Robert started in, I thought, He is an evil man. The evil comes out of that arguing. I don't know what I went round there for, but it was very cold, one of those summers more like February than August. And there were no other people there, I was the only one, I should have left when I saw that. I never saw him without wanting to strike him. Of course, there was nothing to eat. Making a meal was beneath Rose. She's still the same. So we went to that café across the street.

"All those windows in that café, Sigrid, you've been there," Penny said. "They're like mirrors. I saw Robert in that window, and I thought, Who *is* that? Who is that man sitting there in the corner, the one with his shirt open and his belly hairs showing? Before we sat down, before we had a chance to order something, they were arguing about Peter and that woman he carried on a long affair with. Both of them knew Sally, and Rose said that Peter had told Sally that he wanted to marry her. He was certain. He'd decided once and for all that he wanted to leave his wife and children, and would Sally please find a house for them to live in?

"And Robert started in. Well, Sigrid, you know what he's like. Sally ought to have known better. 'When a married man says he's going to leave wife and children, Sally ought to have known better.'

"Robert wanted to know how Rose *knew* that Peter had said he would leave Meena and marry this woman. Could it not be true that Sally only *thought* Peter had said that? And Rose said, 'I saw the letter!' And he asked her, 'Did the letter say, "I'm going to leave wife and children and marry you?"' and Rose said, 'Of course not! Peter wouldn't have been so stupid as to put that in writing, but it was clearly *implied*.'

"Robert said, '*Implied!* Well, there you are!'"

"He never said he was going to leave Meena and marry Sally," Sigrid said. "He would never have said that. You can say a lot against Robert, but he was shrewd. Why were they talking about Peter in the middle of a café?"

"Did Rose have any choice?" Penelope asked. "You know Robert. So that stupid conversation was meant to go on and on. He cross-examined Rose, he refused to believe Peter had really led Sally on until she began looking for a house. Rose said, 'What woman in her right mind would ring up estate agents and spend days looking at houses if she didn't have good reason to believe the man was going to marry her?' and Robert, needless to say, had an answer. 'You don't understand anything about men and women, you literary women. It happens all the time, a man says this, a man says that, a woman *thinks* he's said something altogether different. By morning, the woman has the man down on his knees, a chocolate box in one hand, a ring box in the other, when all he said was, 'If only I'd met you before I met her! If only I didn't have children!'

"And what did Rose have to say? 'But I *know* her! She's not the type to imagine things!' It was never going to end. 'Type?' Robert said. 'And what type would that be? And what kind of knowledge of Sally do you have? I'd like to understand that kind of knowledge. Describe that kind of knowledge to me, Rose. Explain to me how Sally, a *literary* woman, would not, under these circumstances, *imagine* anything? Isn't imagination supposed to be her stock in trade? But you *know*, whatever that means, that this time, *this* time, Sally didn't imagine things. Would you clear all that up for me, Rose?' "

"Oh, God," Sigrid said.

"Yes, oh, God. *Is* there a more ghastly man on earth? Anyway, this cross-examination was too much for me. I said, '*I* know her! She's hard-headed. Sally doesn't hear things unless people say them,' and he said, 'You literary women! You don't understand anything! If I had a pound for every woman in London who thought a man had said, "Go look for a house," when all he said was, "If only I'd met you before I met her!" God, I'd be rich!'

"But was he finished? No. Was Rose smart enough to let it go? No. Rose said, 'You see? I said in the beginning, it would all come down to *caveat emptor*! It's all the woman's fault! She should have known better than to trust him! So it's all her fault!'

"Rose was right, she was absolutely right. It was all coming down to *caveat emptor*, the woman's fault, because naturally Robert would have liked to believe everything was always the woman's fault.

"But by then Robert had persuaded himself that Peter had merely said, 'If only I'd met you before I met her!'

" '*Caveat emptor*,' Rose said.

"And then *Robert* said, 'Thank you, Rose, all my wonderful thoughts, all my complicated distinctions, reduced to a couple of foreign words, *caveat emptor*, that is really brilliant, how do you do that? If only I could do that, reduce all my investigations to two foreign words, *caveat emptor*, you really are marvelous, Rose!'

"He kept on at her like that, and I kept hearing *caveat emptor* every few seconds, I tried to go into the kind of fogs we used to have here—nowadays you watch those old movies with everyone moving about in those man-eating fogs and you wonder, *What* was that about?—and Robert said it again, *Caveat emptor*. Well, Sigrid, you know *I've* never been well behaved. I picked up my umbrella, the good, stout black one, a big one that wouldn't be blown inside out, and I brought its handle down on his head. Once, twice, three times, it might have been three times, I don't think four. By four, he would have recovered and tried to stop me. Sigrid, he wasn't frightened at all, that was the most surprising thing! He smiled at me! He said, 'That isn't how you literary women win arguments. Assault by attrition, that's the phrase I'd use for it. You're more primitive, Penelope. I admire that. Just hit the man on the head! Don't worry about whether the man is right or wrong. Hit him on the head. Isn't that what women do when they're outmaneuvered? You're the only honest woman I've met! No disguises! Just hit the man on the head! Perhaps you're not a literary lady after all!'

"And what did Rose have to say then? She said, 'Yes, I must get dinner, I have three people to feed tonight.'

"Sigrid, for the love of God! *Caveat emptor!* What holds them together? They hate one another! I gather Rose considers me quite mad now. I *know* I should keep out of it when a couple starts to argue, I *know* I should keep my head down. The way he treats Rose! She ought to leave him! Does he own her? Did Robert buy Rose from her father? You've been married long enough. You always say, 'It's a matter of convenience,' but even so! You understand marriages. *I* don't. I only *know* how married people cling together, at least until one of them takes an axe to the other. But she could have left him voluntarily, couldn't she have?"

"Not voluntarily," Sigrid said.

"And Peter, he would have left all of them sooner or later. He wanted to leave Meena for Sally, but Meena wouldn't hear of it. He *was* motivated," Penny said, "to stay as he was. Not to go through those horrors again. I think he knew his limits perfectly well."

"Why must you criticize him? Why must you make him small?" Sigrid asked angrily. "Why must you remember horrid arguments in filthy cafés? Why if two idiots are angry at each other do they have to bring Peter into it? Is he some kind of touchstone? It's a bad marriage. Someone begins to talk about bad marriages and the next instant, they're talking about Peter. Is so-and-so's husband as bad a husband as Peter was? Is the wife as victimized by her husband as Evelyn was? All that horror, and people opening it up all over London, in grotty cafés, why didn't you stop them, Penny?"

"Stop them? When did you try to stop Robert?"

"Many times," Sigrid said.

"And did you succeed?"

"Never," said Sigrid, beginning to smile.

"Peter or no Peter," Penny said, "you would have liked to be a fly on the wall during that argument."

"It isn't the least bit amusing," Sigrid said, but she was smiling. "*Caveat emptor*," Sigrid said. "I can just hear them, and I can just see them," and then she began to laugh.

"Marriages," Penelope said. "The great riddle. You never can recover from that first love, can you, Sigrid? There must be some people who manage it. Remember how M.R. used to call me Peppy and sometimes Pepita?

No one knows how much I'd like to hear him call me that again. Although," Penelope said, veering in a slightly different direction, "Peter once told me he'd done well in taking Elfie after Evelyn, but in five or six months, he'd changed his mind, begun working on a new book and had no time for Elfie, and it was the gas again. Sorry to mention it, Sigrid, but it did happen. That was Elfie's way of writing *The End* at the bottom of the last sheet of paper. A woman with a genius for punctuation."

And where was Mark, Penelope's first husband, whom she thought about once or twice a week?

"Why worry so much about Peter?" Penelope said. "He could always take care of himself, and Meena can take everyone on. You don't do him a favor, trying to make everyone think he's flawless. Even a giant has faults," Penelope said. "He is your particular blindness. What reason do you have not to see his faults? He will not shrink, become less than he was, because he had his imperfections. To acknowledge them, tell me, what is the difficulty in that? To say, Yes, he was human. Isn't that what he complained of so bitterly? That he was viewed as a monster, when really, he was blamed because no one could see he was human? He was too proud; he should have let other people see him as he was, then they would have said, There but for the grace of God, and all that rot. But instead . . . And you hold on to it."

"To what?"

"To some vision of him, some *version,* that never existed, not even in the beginning. But you will never give it up."

"Because I know the truth!" Sigrid said. "The truth of him!"

"Long habit, that's all it is," Penny said. "Long habit. A simple peasant worshipping her stone saint. How do you differ from Rose? Long habit. An idiot peasant worshipping her weathered gargoyle."

"Peter was not like that!" Sigrid said.

"Well," said Penelope.

Penelope was the one Peter had come to when Evelyn died; she was the one into whom he had poured all his worries. She had kept an eye on him, she had seen how easily he could have gone the same way as Evelyn. Time went by. M.R. was in America. They shared her flat. One night, they stared into the electric fire, snow was falling, and he said, "They blame her for giving in, and the ones who don't blame me accuse the weather! They say it was the coldest winter in England in a century. Pipes froze everywhere. So they did! They froze everywhere! And did they find housewives dead and cold, their heads in the oven? Hundreds and hundreds of dead house-wives, mothers, dead all over London? Because the weather had gone cold! Did women put an end to their lives because the toilets didn't flush? If only I had left her earlier. I would have done. I came back from a meeting in London. We were still living in the country, and there she was, shred-ding my manuscripts. She had reduced them to *fluff. Fluff!* (Or, as his accent had it, *floof.*) No apologies. No regrets on Evelyn's part. She never had them. She was always right. No one else suffered as she did. So I struck her. And the pity of it was, that night she miscarried. Then we were stuck with one another. I often wonder, was that why she put herself in that stove? Did she say to herself, I should have left him then, but I'm making up for it. I'm leaving him now. Because I would have left her then, if she hadn't miscarried, if I hadn't given in and gotten her pregnant again as soon as the doctor gave the word, I had to give her back what I thought I had taken from her."

They deserved one another, Peter and Evelyn, Penelope thought. All married people deserve what they get if they survive together. And now Meena. It was too much to think about Meena. Penelope looked through her window once more, saw the windows in the wing across the cement path from her, saw someone entering a room and crossing to the bed, a new one coming in, faceless, from where she, Penelope, stood, a greater darkness inside a twilight darkness, and went back to her own bed.

First love, Penelope thought, lying down, her pillow softer than she remembered it. If any of them had any idea! It marked you as permanently as a steer branded by the hot iron. Nothing would ever have the same impact again. People, Penelope thought, should take care with their first

loves, choose them wisely. She laughed out loud. That was the very definition of first love: you had no choice. It came upon you like a natural disaster. There should be insurance paid for such a disaster, Penelope
thought, but naturally there was not, all insurance policies specified that
their company was not responsible for acts of God, and what was first love
but an act of God? Usually a very, very bad act, usually causing consequences worse than hurricanes or floods or cyclones. But how beautiful
they were, first loves, when they were occurring, when they were in the
first stages. What kind of disease was it that began with such beauty, such
emotion, such brilliance, before the next stages set in, the rot, the boredom, the infuriating habits, the sad knowledge, and who wanted to have
it, that ability to complete one another's sentences? Yet there were people
who claimed they were kept in thrall by first love for the length and
breadth of their lives, and it held them until they died. Did she believe it?
Penelope asked herself. I wish I did, she thought. I wish I did. But no, she
did not. It was possible to mistake peace and quiet for ecstasy. People did
it all the time, especially people who had been badly wounded. For a while,
after M.R. died, and she found someone new, Penelope told herself, It isn't
first love. It's close. But it *was* second love, and how it held! Now she was
more honest and she admitted, at least to herself, yes, she had found peace
and quiet, and yes, after the second year, somewhere in the third, ecstasy
transformed into peace and quiet; how could she not have seen it at the
time? And she might never have seen it if Paul, her second husband,
hadn't died, leaving her alone and so enraged that she had good reason
to begin reexamining their lives together. Yes, that had been her reason to
change: her uncontrollable anger because Paul had died. Without consult-
ing her, he had put an end to peace and quiet. The two of them were no
longer like those attached houses in Kensington that made up long cres-
cents, those attached, expensive houses, plastered, all cream-colored,
butter-colored, that went on and on forever.

In the end, certainly, he had done her a favor by dying. Already resentments between them were beginning to harden, those brick walls that

grew up between one soul and another. Soon they would begin to blame each other for their failures, for the ambitions they had not achieved. They would not do so openly, not declare open warfare, but instead begin a kind of *Gaslight* behavior, induce as much guilt in each other as possible, and the positions they took toward one another, those would also harden so that when the tragic event happened, to him, to her, there would not be pity enough, not enough sympathy between them, only irritation covered over by wifeliness or husbandliness. The world rehearsed you soon enough in those gestures, those actions, soon enough, and even if one tried to help the other, there could be no helping, and that, Penelope thought, that inability to help was perhaps the most bitter defeat of all, because the bitterness each felt had grown so strong simply because they had a *history* together, had been through so much together, had never forgiven the other for his failures or her failures, that shared history had nurtured them until it now choked what would have been new growth. The unending fury, the successes each resented in the other, the failures, equally resented, if only because the other one had been a witness to those defeats, that violent resentment manifested in so many ways, because nothing changed between them, although they had fought so to keep everything unchanged, and there they had succeeded, had created boredom, had killed off any hope of novelty. Peter had been right about that. There is no poison worse than boredom. Most illnesses grow out of that rich loam of boredom, more hatreds between husbands and wives are fostered up by boredom. It is not the slow ravage of time that sets people apart. That, Peter had said, tended to draw them together, at least if both people could bear to see the ravages time was visiting on them.

And if they could bear those ravages brought by time, they felt pity for one another, and then sympathy. They looked into each other and saw themselves as well as the other person. It was a good thing, that, a great thing. Once more they were growing together equally, one not outstripping the other. People should think twice before marrying someone very much older or very much younger. The pity of the young for the old was not enough, was lethal in itself. Peter knew of what he was speaking. He was on solid ground there, although he couldn't explain why it happened that when one succeeded and the other did not, the one who did not was unable to take pleasure in the happiness of the one who had achieved his desires. Peter had succeeded first, but if Evelyn had been the one to prove herself first? Would their lives have turned out differently? What was it about couples that brought out the worst in them and so rarely the best? Yes, Peter had asked that repeatedly. Had he spent his life elegantly whining and complaining about Meena and her attitude toward him? And done the same before that when he spoke of Evelyn, who had so eclipsed him, or poor Elfie, who had been made so insignificant, so inconsequential, not only deep in Peter's shadow, but also by Evelyn's? Peter had not, Penelope thought now, scrutinized long marriages out of that strange streak of scientific curiosity so strong in him, but had inspected them and spoken of them out of self-pity. His was the old, familiar lament, *Why me? Why me?* When he might have asked, should have asked, "Why did I receive such great gifts? Why should I not be expected to suffer now?" Surely he must have known that suffering was the way of the world. It was impossible to listen to anyone for long without hearing that eternal complaint, *Why me? Why me?*

I am glad, Penelope thought, that I told Julia about Evelyn's miscarriage, about everything Peter told me. Julia will know I want her to pass it on. I had to do something, tell someone, if only to compensate myself for the exhaustion the Grovesnors inflicted on me for all those years. No, I should use the right words for my resentment: for all the humiliation they caused me for so long. I wonder if Julia will choose to tell someone what I said. She won't do it right away, not for some time, and I wouldn't have told her when I did if I hadn't known I was dying. I thought it was wrong to leave this world with a secret like that. To still have such notions of right and wrong! At her age! To make any judgments at all! And to think it still matters!

Once, Penelope remembered, there had been no snow that winter, and she had always so loved snow, and did to this day. She took a strand of crystals out of the dining room chandelier and hung it over the window-pane in her room, and it stayed there like a chain of ice cubes or falling sleet. She kept it there for one year, through one spring and summer and fall, and whenever she looked at it, it cooled her. I wish I had it now, she thought. How long it had been since she'd thought of that, how many years had passed, how rarely since she'd thought of Daddy, scolding her about taking the dining room chandelier apart, telling her how old it was, and for how many generations it had survived without accident, and what was she thinking of? She should let her mind go free, let it drift, find such events and times and resurrect them again, as many times as she still could, which would not be many.

So now, Penelope thought, she preferred to die alone, if only because she had seen what it was to be attached to someone else for a long time. Dying alone, that was what she wanted. She considered, fleetingly, exceed-ingly fleetingly, calling Sigrid, warning her, because Sigrid would miss her, she knew that, but to hear it from Sigrid again, another aria about Peter's tragic life! No, this life was *her* life, Penelope's. This was *her* death, not Peter's. Why should she dilute the last important event she would ever experience? She did not want to share her dying with tales of Peter. In the end, all of us have seen too much. If Penelope could remember that, she thought, turning her pillow over so that the cool side soothed her cheek, she might find this dying very enjoyable. Indeed she might.

TWELVE

——

SOPHIE, STILL IN bed, has been speaking to Evelyn, something she has done for years, something that has grown more important with the passage of time.

"I was frightened by a pigeon today," Sophie told Evelyn. She tends to think that Evelyn hovers there in the great bough just beyond her window. "That's not right. Let me start over. I was working on my computer, and I thought I saw a face at my window, so high up. My room's as high up as your study was in the turret. But it wasn't a face, it was a pigeon strutting back and forth on the outside windowsill. I suppose we will have to put screens up in the spring and summer or we will have an aviary. I remember the screens in Granny's house in America. Do you remember them?

They don't have screens here, not usually. Don't forget me," Sophie said, closing her eyes, saying what she always says when she finishes speaking to Evelyn, "Don't forget me," meaning, also, "I won't forget you."

—

NIGHT IS FALLING over London. It falls so late here, Julia thinks. There's still enough light to read by. I could read the packet of letters Peter sent me, letters he copied over after writing them to his brother in Jamaica. No, I don't want to read anything, Julia decided. I should ring up Penny. Why has no one mentioned her? In the wake of Peter's death, they've forgotten about everyone and everything. Peter was like that, an eraser on a chalkboard, everything obliterated in a fog of swirling chalk dust, the words written on the board, written large a few minutes before, now no longer decipherable. But here are the leaves outside, so beautiful, the way they flicker, the way they write on the white walls as if they were composing a story or a confession in another language. Goodnight, Sophie, she thinks. Goodnight, Sigrid, goodnight everyone I know and love, the way she used to end her prayers as a child, so afraid of leaving someone out when she began listing her beloved people, "God bless Mother and Father, my grandmothers and grandfathers, my aunts and uncles," but had she forgotten someone important? and so she would end saying, "God bless everyone I know and love." Now she says, very softly, "Goodnight, everyone I know and love."

—

PENELOPE IS SOUND asleep in her hated but familiar white room in the Royal Marsden. During her treatment, she was given so much intravenous Benadryl that she was knocked out completely, and is still as unconscious as someone who had been given a total anesthetic. She is dreaming of her first horse, who broke his leg when he made a jump. Her mother said, "He will have to be shot," and her father agreed.

"No," Penelope said.

"He *must* be shot," said her father. "He is a horse. You cannot expect him to walk around like an old man with a stick," and Penelope stuck out her chin and asked, "Why not?" "He is to be shot and that is the end of it," her father said, and she answered, "Then I shall shoot myself immediately after you shoot him." Her mother gave in and said, "Let her have her crippled horse." In her dream, Penelope remembers the horse very well, loping lopsidedly after her, eating the apples she brought him, and in the end, siring a champion. There are so many ways of living well, Penelope thinks in her dream.

—

SIGRID, WHO HAS been up until late reading a novel about a benighted Egyptian family who took a political wrong turn, was almost asleep when a cold wind settled on her. Someone has died or is dying, she thinks. But who? Who now? Not Meena. Meena will never die. But someone who cares enough about me to warn me, or to say goodbye. Someone who had died, or is dying, in the middle of the night. Perhaps it's me, Sigrid thinks. Perhaps it's me who's dying.

—

MEENA, TOO, FEELS it, the cold wind, in her turret, the lights shut down for the night, but can see clearly because of the full moon reflected in all six of her windows. "There is no use going over it again," she said to Peter as if he were standing beside her, "No use. I've made up my mind." Perhaps it was Penelope who died? Peter always said a cold wind on a hot night meant someone had died or was dying. What else could it mean? Hadn't she been told that Penelope was somewhere in London? Penelope, hugging her secret, the only one still alive who knew that Peter had struck Evelyn and caused her to miscarry. When Penelope died, no one would know of it. There would be an end to scandals. Although in the end, Penelope had grown very close to Julia. Did everyone cling to Julia, did everyone speak to her of what they never otherwise spoke? And Julia was staying in Sophie's house, in London, in that completely unfashionable part of the city. Why did Sophie buy a house in such an area? What if Julia knew? Meena was suddenly sure that Julia did know. Secrets don't want to die any more than anything else does, Meena thought. What, though, was the use of worrying when she could be looking out her turret windows, admiring the six full moons in the six scrubbed and cleaned windows? The moon will put me to sleep, she thought. It always does.

—

THERE WAS A wind howling around Willow Grove, blowing down the chimneys. There was rain falling heavily in Northumberland, where the rest of Peter's family still lived or were buried. If there was anything left of Peter, if Peter had anything to say on this particular night, he must have chosen to say it through the wind and the weather, but perhaps he had nothing to say, was remaining silent, doing nothing but listening to the wind roaring over the earth above him. Can it be heard so far down? Do the dead have a special way of hearing? But he certainly could not see the full moon, or the six moons in the turret window. Or was that true? Was there a way some part of him might still fly up to the tops of the trees and look in through the turret windows: like a pigeon, like the brown bird Meena had seen earlier in the day? In spite of having fallen asleep, or almost asleep, Meena thought about that, a fugitive thought, blown into her consciousness by the howling wind rattling the crooked apple trees, causing the great boughs of the oaks outside to lift and drop and lift again. She stirred, and in her sleep pushed her duvet up higher so that her ears were covered, and then she was sound asleep, thinking of nothing, but occasionally, unknown to her, unheard by anyone else, whimpering. Only a little.

THIRTEEN

——

"WHERE WILL YOU BE?" Meena asked. Peter was starting up the steps to his study.

"Isn't it clear?" Peter asked.

"The roof needs rethatching," Meena said. She was staring up at him, craning her neck. She had a neck that was easily strained.

"It can wait," Peter said.

"You said that last week."

"I was right last week, and I'm right now," he said, dismissing her, going up the steps, until she heard him on the landing, and then there was the sharp slam of the door.

He won't be down for a while now, Meena thought. He's so very intelligent, so much more so than I am, or so he thinks, but now because I've
made it seem that I want him to look about the roof, he will spite me
and not come down for hours, which is just how I want it. I want the
house to myself. "You have a more passionate relationship with that
house that you do with your husband," Sigrid had told her over the
phone a week before.

It was true, Meena thought. A house was a woman's other body,
another version of herself. A house could be beautified in a way the body
could not. It could be far more perfect than a body of flesh and bone. A
house, Meena was sure, was grateful for the attention you paid it, did not
criticize the woman who kept it up, was, in some ways, she thought, like
a devoted cat, silent, adoring, always there. Age could be erased from it.
It could grow more and more beautiful with each year, defying time. And
at the same time, the house aged as its owner aged, and the two of them
were somehow always the same age, loved one another, spoke to one
another without speaking, without the need for words. So she would have
the house, that lovely person, alone to herself for how long? Three hours?
Five hours? He had a bed in his study. When it was cold enough, he kept
food on the ledge outside the window. There was no reason to come back
down, not unless he wanted to do so, which he appeared to want to do
less and less. She listened for the tap, tap, tap of his old typewriter.
Everyone told him he would write more if he bought a computer, but he
would not hear of it. He had his Mont Blanc pen and he had a ream of
paper and he had his ancient Remington typewriter, bought by Evelyn
during those years in America, carried by boat to London when the two
of them returned to England.

So he is reading or writing someone a letter, Meena thought. He is up
there like a princess trapped in his castle. And of course he has locked the
door upon himself. So, thought Meena, I am safe.

FOURTEEN

———

PETER WAS REREADING his letter from Martin, his brother who had gone to Jamaica, oblivious to Meena, far from the rest of the world. He kept rereading the middle section of the letter:

> I don't know where my life has gone. I meant to marry and be happy and I married well and I have been married happily. I meant to come here and compose and make something of my music, as you did with your poems, but my music never satisfied me the way your writing satisfied you. When I was at my worst, I judged my work as no better than the plumber clanging on radiators when he fixed the pipes, and then I tried to paint, well, you know how I've

always loved painting, everyone in the family painted, but I was never satisfied and so I went back to music, and I thought, if I could only get the pure, high note I always hear when I see something I know I will remember as long as I live, that would be enough, but the pure note was more elusive than a beautiful wild bird that was never meant to be caught. So I stuck to my music at last, and have wasted many years composing airs no one wanted to hear. Well, two talents is one too many. You fall into that abyss, that cliché everyone speaks of, that ravine, that space described as between two stools. But of course that is not why I failed. There *have* been people who excelled in two disciplines—in more than two! And of course nothing much came of it, a small living, enough to support a man with a childless wife. And now, suddenly, it is over, and I am left asking myself, What have I done with my life? It is a terrible thing to have to ask yourself that question, because the mere asking of it means you went wrong somewhere. People who went right, there must be people who went right, don't come to the end of things asking what they did with their lives. There was so much tragedy in your life, so many obstacles, it's hard for me to believe that you kept going. I would have been broken. But perhaps that's the point. I would never have found myself in such extremis. I was not cut out for the roller coaster, the arguments, divorces, all of that sort of thing. I had a horror of horror and I still have it, but horror has changed itself into its opposite (I think so many things do that), and today as I write, horror is stability and the monotony that makes stability possible, the certain knowledge that I grew up, grew tall, took a wife, filled notebook after notebook with music, and changed not one iota from the child I once was. How can I justify having lived such a long life, only to realize that I have not changed since my infancy? I speak more clearly. There is that, I know more words. I know better than to put my hand on a stove. I can write a correct sentence. And this is all I can say for myself. Better to have never existed than to have come to this. I envy the men I knew who died suddenly on the golf course or swimming in the warm sea here because they didn't have the time to ask themselves, "What have I done with my life? Where has it gone?" And even if I had known it would come down to that, what would I have done? I see now that I was not meant for great things, never should have dreamed of them. The great thing was in leaving England and coming to Jamaica. How daring I thought I was in those days! I must have thought, the musical palette of Jamaica, that's the thing, I need that. I must have thought the melodies of that country would rise up and sing themselves to me and I could write them down; but the country was wilder than I am; perhaps that was the trouble. Now Laura and I live in a house made of cinder blocks, painted over by a layer of stucco, like the natives, living in a house painted livid pink and sky blue on the outside. We look like everyone else, we could *be* anyone else the way we live in the house. Of course, we are not natives, so we live in a compound near Ochorias. Men with machine guns living in grey booths are at the corners of our territory and in front of the gates to the compound, because where we live is a compound. I have good friends here, and when we visit them, we feel utterly safe, but when we get back in our car to return to our own pink and blue house (it is such a cliché, that house. It is not even worth photographing), we are frightened the entire time, because of our white faces and the hostility of the natives who live there. If one of them were to kill us, our friends would be horrified to discover we had been killed. And all the friends we made over the years would lament in their churches, and the pastors we know would make sermons of us, but would one of them press the police to find out what had happened to us? No. Because in the end, we were never truly one of them. That kind of acceptance takes years, genera-tions, probably a good number of intermarriages, and I doubt that even that would have made the difference. We could never really have become one of them. The British who come to see us say, "Oh, you have gone native," but what does that mean? We are still white, still British to the people who live here. I can't count how many times we were asked, in the beginning, "What is Ascot, man? Tell me why you like it so much. More fuss about hats than a church full of women on a Sunday." If I said I didn't know anything about Ascot, had never thought about it, they were disappointed. So I made up stories. I can't remember what they were about, something to do with the British showing off to tell everyone they weren't members of the lower classes, and then they would ask me, "Lower classes?" What counts here is not class but whether or not someone is educated or goes to America and sends back money, or makes enough money in America or Great Britain and then comes back here and lives as if it's plum pudding every day. To sum it up, Peter: living here, I've learned a few things other people don't know, but the knowledge I've acquired isn't worth having. That may be the point: I failed because I couldn't see the worth of what I saw or learned. So I have to conclude I am a person of no vision, and now, well aware that every breath may be my last, or my next to last, all I have to say is, What became of all of it? How did it go by so fast? Why didn't I store something against the coming cold? And then I remember what I have just written you, and I admit—again—that I could have done things no differently. Whatever was needed to make a difference was not in me at all. It makes me very bitter to think in this way, so I have learned, most of the time, not to think at all.

Well, there were three children in our family. At least one of us made it. I tell myself you succeeded for all of us, but to be truthful, I find little comfort in that. In the end, the arrival of your letters to me are the most vivid, important moments of my life. You are my baby brother and you will always be my baby brother, yet I am the one who looks to you. I know that you know you can always depend on me and I find considerable happiness in that. Enjoy your life, Peter. It ends so quickly. I will write more cheerfully next time. My love to the children and to Meena, and of course, to Sigrid. I shall write to her later. I don't like to write to her in this vein. It only makes her unhappy.

Peter stared at the sheets of paper, covered in a script almost identical to his. He asked himself, What can I say to him? Yes, it was true he believed himself superior to Martin, although he would never admit it to another soul, but he did believe he was better, special, marked out by life, because otherwise why had the world singled him out, made such a fuss of him? And did he believe that those who failed, or led ordinary lives of quiet content, were in every way his inferior? Yes, he had to admit he did. Evelyn had been the same. There were times he looked up and saw her watching him in a speculative way and thought, She's wondering if *she* is superior to me, if *I'm* worth it. But of course that was Evelyn, she who could not live in a straight line, so that one moment she adored the person she lived with, and the next moment erased that adoration, and she was filled with doubts, telling herself she could not love a man with such narrow shoulders.

She lived her life like that moment in Anna Karenina's life, when Anna returned from St. Petersburg and saw her husband at the train station and thought, How large his ears are, and the illusion of his perfection was shattered for her and the two of them were destined for separation. When Evelyn looked at him in that way, he was sure that she had decided that his ears stuck out too much, or he had committed a grave sin when he hadn't shaved the hairs on the side of his neck, and he knew she was thinking, He's not the man I thought he was. Then she would give herself a shake, a mental shake, the kind a dog gave itself when it came out of the river, and again he would be the golden, the perfect man. But the time would come, he knew it would, when she could not do it again, when his ears would remain too large or his shoulders too narrow, and she would begin to burrow in, he had no words for that burrowing in, only that it undermined what lived between them, and he believed, he still believed, that she would have left him if he hadn't left her first. Because Evelyn wanted immutability. She needed the changelessness of perfection. Above all, she wanted nothing to change, and he could not bring her changelessness. No one could. Although when Evelyn most loved him, when her love for him was strongest, she had convinced him that he was unalterable, perfect, a man of miracles. At such times, her faith in him had been perfect. He should write Martin about all that, how terrible it had been to lose that, and how afterward, in spite of the awards and the fame, his life had been as commonplace as anyone else's, worse, because he knew he had fallen from a great height and could never climb back.

He would have to answer Martin's letter, make it sound as if he, Peter, were still happy, as if his own fate still satisfied him, because Martin needed him to believe that. But he would know, somehow Martin would know, that there were bitter dregs in the gold goblet. He, Peter, would have to disguise them well enough so that Martin could ignore them, pretend they didn't exist. We are all of us the same in the same way, Peter wrote.

It is true that some of us are granted more than others, but there is always that scene in Shakespeare's tragedy when Hamlet hears the grave digger begin to speak about the skull. If only it were possible to go through life without ever seeing that globe of bone, its black eye sockets! How can anyone not envy animals who don't know what common fate awaits them? Or do they know? Sometimes you see an expression on a cat or a cow, it doesn't matter what it is, but it's clear, even through their fur masks, a look of such sadness. It's enough to believe they do know. And who is to say they don't? I prefer to believe that animals don't know what's waiting for them. They don't know. Their natures don't twist as ours do, deform as ours do, so that, compared to us, they are all angelic beings. Well, I've said that before.

I've been back from Africa for a week. Meena didn't go. She said it would be too hot there, and "additionally," that is her favorite word, there were the flower beds to prepare and the canvas-wrapped tree trunks to unwrap and the usual twaddle she finds to explain why she's decided against leaving this little plot of earth she thinks constitutes the entire globe.

Everything is oversized there in Africa, especially the sun when it rests on the rim of the horizon for the half hour before it begins quickly sinking down. Huge! Molten, a glimpse of what the earth's core must be. And the quirky, bent trees silhouetted against it like tortured, black spirits.

The animals are huge. Until you see them out on the veldt, out in the open, you can't realize how every other image you've seen of them diminishes them, the television that boxes them in like toys, the cages that hold them in zoos stealing their menace from them, but give that menace back to them, and they grow and grow until you feel like an ant beside them. It's their aura, their danger, that makes them so big, as big as they are. Finally you see them as they are. The flowers are the same. After you've seen them out there as they are, as they are meant to be, not neatly set in rows like schoolchildren in classrooms, the flowers of England are poor things. You go to sleep in a tent there, or on the ground around a fire, and you know you could wake up and find a tiger tearing you to bits and it seems right that you would die that way. Natural. You don't mind, or at least I don't—didn't.

When I came back here, got off the ship, found the right train, got back to London, took the right train, got off at the right station where Meena would meet me, I couldn't bear to look at the place, so small, so damp and chilly, such a cheap replica of life as it should be, as it once was, as it still is out there. I was stunned all over again, but this time by the incredible paucity of things, the pallor, the deadness of everything. For three days after I got home, I was quite miserable, but I'm used to that. It's part of what one pays for going to a place like Africa and then coming back. And I always believe I have to come back. When you decided to stay on in Jamaica, I thought, I should never be capable of such bravery. I think you underestimate yourself. You have lived in a land big enough for what you can imagine, what you are doing is what I can only try to imagine, while I have lived on here, in this tiny country, adapting to every possible kind of claustrophobia. Every inch here is accounted for and made use of, no places here where weeds tumble and trees reseed themselves. I liked that immensity about America, the hugeness of it, the untidiness of it, the sprawl, the uncounted acres, and then you return to England, every inch manicured and tended and surveyed—again and again. If I knew I were going to die, say next week, I would like to go back to Africa and let some savage thing devour me. That would seem appropriate and right. It's all in the traveling, isn't it, since when we get down to our last breaths, we're all going to the same claustrophobic little space. And there you are, still in a huge place, an untamed place, with jungles! Jungles that frighten you, but jungles! I envy you those jungles and whatever lives in them, savages on two feet or on four, what difference does it make, as long as they can kill you and give you a death worthy of a human being. Probably you don't see things in that way, but then, why should you? Everyone thinks of me as a savage.

To have had a brother like you, an older brother, someone who has been steadfast and who has never wavered in loving me, what greater gift has anyone ever given me? If only because you achieved an ability to love with such strength, such constancy, you have achieved a great deal and I am there to testify to the enormity of it. I regret so much about my life, although, as you say, there were many reasons for such regret. But I could have done without them, I can tell you that. To live an equable life, who can achieve it? Yet you have. You must not dismiss it as if it were nothing. The sun, as I remember, is huge when it sets on the Jamaican horizon. Don't make so little of what you have. As for the rest, as for asking what you have done with your life, you must know that I also ask the same thing. My great consolation is my writing. I hope it will outlast me. I often listen to one of your compositions and think, Those will outlast him, and how wonderful that would be, but how terrible as well: posthumous fame. Fame is for the living, or should be. But there I may be wrong. How many of us have gone under when the wave of fame hit us and we discovered how badly we swam. Once a day, I think how Evelyn would have enjoyed the fame that came to her after her death. But it is best if I do not think of Evelyn, although I do think of her, every day, all the time, especially when I go up to the turret room which I have claimed as my own, which Meena insisted I take as my own, and now *I* insist upon having it and allow no one into it, not even Sophie or Andrew. Andrew is not so young these days and he's sculpting, another one messing in the arts, but he will not eclipse you, I think. Although if he concentrates on busts, really portraits in marble, he may well accomplish something enormous. Life is intolerably strange. I will not live long enough to see what the children accomplish. Andrew has it all against him, the son of two parents, so famous, or infamous, and infamous is the word I would choose. As for Sophie, who knows what will become of her? She goes at life as if she intended to swallow the world, whereas Andy's afraid to live, that one. I don't know what to do about that. He's seen what happens when people are not afraid to live, and he's done more than that; he's suffered the results.

   It's good, Martin, to measure ourselves against one another. It isn't a competition. It allows each of us to see more clearly what

we are. My love to Laura, to all of the songbirds around your
house that your music really is, and to you, who I have always
been able to love without reservation.

Peter looked over what he had written, sighed, and wrote his name,
black, thick letters, as if a crow had walked across the page printing the
words for him. He was always happy when he wrote to Martin. He did not
ask himself, Will someone reading this years later ask if this letter was
written by a good man or a bad man? He was only writing to Martin, his
brother. Peter moved from his desk to the dilapidated armchair, contemplated the pattern of cabbage roses on its now-thin, faded fabric, ready to
rip or shred if too much weight were put on it, and stared out the windows of the turret. Evelyn, he found himself saying, when you were up
here, were you always writing, as you claimed to be, or were you hiding
from me? Or was it simpler? Were you simply waiting for the glue to dry,
the glue you daily applied to the cracks that shattered you long before I
met you, fissures that began to show when you were not even seven years
old? What was it, Evelyn? I will write you a letter, Peter decided, and I will
hide it very, very well.

FIFTEEN

—

MORNING, AND A brilliant sun was splashing all the bedrooms with gold stripes and coins, and all the women who were connected, somehow, by Willow Grove were opening their eyes and counting their coins, except, it should go without saying, for Sigrid. She used kilims to drape her bedroom windows so that no ray of light could penetrate and wake her once she had finally fallen asleep. But Sigrid, too, sensed the gold brilliance of the light outside her windows, and began reviewing her accounts. They all do the same, every day, at least once a day, although they count different things: Sophie, how long she has until her beauty fades (but it is true she no longer cares as much as she once did, not since she married Bertold, which must mean, she thinks, that she has finally

found a man she can love). And Julia, taking inventory of the many aches
and pains of her rheumatic body, knows her ankle has swollen without
needing to look at it, her shoulder sore because she lies on her side and
her knees rest on each other and the bones don't like it, Julia rotating her
wrists to see if today she will have trouble with her hands, asking herself
every morning, Is it worth the trouble of staying alive? knowing she
would never again attempt to end her own life, not when she still has two
(about to be middle-aged) children. But how difficult would it be for her
to forget her blood thinners and let the congenital malformation of her
heart do its work; no one would ever suspect what she had done, but the
trouble is, Julia thought, there is always *something* interesting to do, if
only the familiar walk down the hill to the warm croissant and then the
familiar walk up the hill to her rooms, Julia thinking, We are brown birds,
no more and no less than the hundreds chittering in the hedges. A few
crumbs is enough for them, a few crumbs is enough for most of us; and
then, having finished her rheumatic inventory, she began her familiar
rosary: how many years will she have to live? She is already in her sixties,
but her grandmother, mother, and aunt staggered a long way into that
great desert called the eighties, none of them with their minds quite
intact. Some years should be subtracted from their life spans because
their minds died faster than their bodies, although her great-aunt lived
to be ninety-six and was probably the sharpest one in the family, and
ruled it until the day she died. I am surprised, Julia finds herself thinking, that my great-aunt agreed to die, not when there were still members
of the family she could blight. Was it possible that she, Julia, so sickly, so
fragile, could do what the others had done and live on into great old age?
Her great-aunt's heart had been damaged in the great flu epidemic of
1918, and for years she was given digitalis, and then suddenly her problems with her heart were over.

   I suppose, Julia thought, my great-aunt concluded that such illnesses
were unnecessary and somehow booted them out the door. Could she,
Julia, do that? She thought not. Although there were times, and this morn-

ing was one of them, when she thought, I am alive for a reason. I came too close to being carried off so many times and here I still am. I must be under the delusion that I keep myself alive to continue writing. Peter had thought that about himself; he had thought his writing justified everything about him, and what a delusion that had been. Or had it? Are all writers, all artists, so egomaniacal, so egocentric? Julia watched the sunlight move on the wall and thought, There are a lot of gold coins splashing about in here this morning. It's not one of those mornings when I wake up and think, I could easily get up, and then a few moments later I think, I could easily go back to sleep. And for a moment, she would be suspended between the two states, sleeping or waking, and it was delicious, making that decision, Should I get up? Should I go back to sleep? Finally being able to have such a decision to make, not having to get up and make breakfast for the children and then drive them to school while they fought all the way there in the back of the car, so that one morning, she thought she heard the radio saying that Yoko Ono had shot John Lennon, and that made perfect sense to her, but when she got home and turned on the TV, it was not Yoko Ono who had shot John Lennon, but some deranged person he had never met, and *that* seemed insane.

She had said, again and again, that she could not wait for the children to go to college, but when her son left, she sat in his room in his chair all day long, barely moving, and later, if she had reading to do, she came into his room and did her reading there, and if there were papers to grade, she graded them in his room, so she knew, when her daughter was ready to leave, when her trunks were packed and shipped to the college she had chosen, she would not be leaping about dancing. *Here we are and there we are,* as Eeyore said.

But how many people like Peter could be subtracted? How many, before you yourself stopped wanting to live? Astonishing, that Sigrid kept on going. Of course, no one believed Peter was dead. No one ever believed that the people who mattered most were dead. It was easier to believe that you yourself had somehow died. Your youth, which you called up so often, as if it were its own savings account, began to seem perilously small. Was it Sigrid who had said, "I'm afraid we are all in for a penurious old age?" And so we are, Julia thought, but it is not money we lack. No, our Great Depression will be brought on by the death of others, and then there will be one particular death, you never know what it will be, you may suspect, but you can never be sure, but that one particular death will occur and everything will unravel, and then she, Julia, would be living on a grate, an emotional grate, out in the cold, begging for pennies, for the rest of her life.

If her husband died . . . Would she ever be able to complete that sentence? It was more difficult to imagine his death than her own, impossible to believe that her life went on without him, just as she could not imagine the world going on after she was gone, although she was coming to understand that the older she became, the easier it was to imagine life going on without her. But a world without her husband—no. She complained about her husband often enough, she complained about him to the *cat,* for God's sake, but she could not imagine a world in which he did not exist. In the end, that was love, not at all what she would have expected. The one precious thing about old age, she told Peter, was that very little could knock you off your feet and take you by surprise. That dark person walking toward you had walked toward you before and knew you had survived many encounters with him.

Yes, Peter said, the same person coming up toward you over the hill, first his head, then his shoulders, then the rest of him, again and again. But at least you were not in for the kinds of surprises that had once almost destroyed you before you knew you could survive such things: when you were young. Wasn't that why many people went under so young? They were agreed on that, Peter and Julia, something immense took place, but you had been through it before, you had survived it before, and you could live through it again. Not a wonderful thing when you knew that there would be nothing new under the sun, but instead you were given something else; you were always given something else, although what you were given was not really what you wanted. You were given a sense of predictability, safety, all those things you had never wanted, even dreaded, when you were young.

Sophie is in her own room, counting her own gold coins, but hers are the real thing, the ones that click and clank and can be turned in at a store or the bank. "*I want this house to be perfect,*" she had told Julia. "This time I'm not going to compromise."

"And did you? Ever?" Julia had asked her.

"I made the most of what I had," Sophie said, "but this time, I don't want to do that. I want to have the best. But it's very expensive to achieve that, don't you think?"

"I certainly do think," said Julia, who was, in her own way, at least as extravagant as Sophie. How strange that the two of them should have been brought together, so similar in so many ways, so many years separating them, so many miles, such odds against their ever having met, but destined to grow together, as if they were long-lost relatives, as sometime Peter had thought, saying they had to be because otherwise how to explain the sympathy between these two?

But now Sophie is almost out of money. It seems to her that she spends most of her time talking to her banker, working out how much she needs to pay the mortgage. But she doesn't want even one boarder in this immense three-story house. She only wants people she invites in, not strangers with their own ideas, poking into the cricks and cracks of her house, trying to gather information about her mother and her father. She doesn't want them. On the other hand, there is the specter of foreclosure. For the hundred thousandth time she thinks: I need a patron. And why should she not have a patron? Everyone has always come to her rescue. Everyone loves her and tries to help her. Except Meena, who does not love her now and never has. Still, Meena may be the answer. If she would bestir herself and distribute her husband's estate, Sophie's *father's* estate, she would not have to worry, at least for a while. She could clear off the mortgage on the house which was so close to being perfect. When you approach perfection so closely, how can you dream of giving it up? And to think that Meena is again standing between her and what she most wants. But really, not very much time has gone by since the funeral. Meena will be honorable and do the honorable thing. She cannot have changed so much since Peter's death. Or can she have? Is wrecking her stepdaughter's life at last reason enough for Meena to change?

I need a patron, Sophie thinks again. Do mathematicians acquire patrons? Or should I become Andy's agent? He should paint portraits of famous people, God knows we know enough of them. The famous and the rich: Do they need portraits done by him? Haven't they already had their own portraits painted, aren't those already hanging on their own, perfect walls? Hasn't Andy himself painted portraits of Meena's beloved pets? Not that he minded doing a portrait of a Persian cat, a cliché wrapped in fur. He found it a challenge to make that thick fur seem to puff out with static electricity and grow alive even though it was made of paint and brush-strokes, but portraits are not what he wants to paint. Now he only wants to sculpt. She would like him to paint portrait after portrait of Bertold. The last one he did of Bertold was large enough to cover an entire wall of their sitting room. Sigrid looked at it and said to Bertold, "You must feel quite small when you sit beneath that picture," and Bertold said, "There are days when it is a relief to be small, but really, Sigrid, even though it is a portrait of me, don't you think it is a great painting?" and Sigrid had to agree that she thought it was.

How on earth did Andy, who had steadfastly refused to learn *anything* about art, who refused to look at other paintings or statues in museums, to read books other people had written, come to be able to do what he now did, and did so easily? He is a mystery, that one, Sigrid thought. It is a good thing Sophie never decided to take painting seriously, although she did go through a phase. Sigrid cannot forget Sophie's coming back from a museum—someone must have dragged her there—and asking, "Why is Picasso so famous when I am not?" Well, as Peter said, that was a conversation stopper.

But the two children had had such peculiar lives, Sigrid thinks. Why should any of us have thought they would turn out to be standard-made?

The bright gold light played over Sophie's walls, and Sophie again began to speak silently to Evelyn. Tell me what to do, she asked her mother, whom she can barely remember, a long braid, swaying, a sound, a certain smell, someone coming toward her carrying a kitten. For years, she thought her mother had died of pneumonia. That was what her father and Sigrid told her. "It was a terrible winter," they said, "the worst winter on record that century, and your mother fell ill and could not recover. She struggled to stay alive for you and for your brother, but her strength gave out," Daddy said. "Sometimes, it happens, no matter how strong the person is, or how strong you thought she was." And for years, she believed it, thought of her mother as Camille on her fainting couch, bravely persevering, coughing her way into eternity.

They knew, naturally, that Sophie would learn the truth, would have to. The truth was there waiting, immutable, incapable of being worn down by the elements, immune to rust; one day, it would be there in the road, waiting for her; why cause the smashup now, when she was so young? Later. Later when she was older, more capable of understanding it. Withstanding it, yes, that was the right thing; it was right to put off telling the children the truth, and meanwhile, they would continue to tell them that fairy tale: their mother had died of pneumonia.

"Send them away to school?" Peter had asked Meena. "Why? There's a school here. I can teach them anything I think they're missing out on. See them only on holidays? I *know* that's how the upper classes do it, but we don't come from that sort of people. My father ran a shop. I never knew one person who didn't say he hated being sent away to school."

"All the same," Meena said. And what could Peter say, really? Could he reply that he had married Meena because he needed a mother for his children? She must already have known that, somehow women always know, but it is one thing to come upon the truth herself, to learn it her own way, and another to hear the plain truth from someone else, from him, from

Sigrid, so that splinters of the truth slid beneath her fingernails and stayed there. He gave in to Meena, telling himself, It may be for the best, knowing it was not, and thinking, I am not a brave man. Giving in to her on this score was the decision of a coward.

And then Meena saw no need to drive the children to the school when Sigrid, who was so close to the school, could meet the two children there and get them settled. "What?" said Sigrid. "You're going to put those two children on a train for the first time in their lives? They have to change trains. I don't think, Peter, they're ready for that."

"*They mustn't be pampered,*" said Meena in the background.

"Put me on the phone to Meena," Sigrid said.

"It won't help," Peter said. "She can't be swayed in that way."

It's no use, he had said of Evelyn. *She can't be helped in that way.* How had her brother managed to find and marry one woman after another, all completely inflexible, who could not be influenced by him? He is weak, Sigrid thought, not something she wanted to admit, not even to herself.

"She doesn't need to be swayed," Sigrid said. "*You* can refuse. You can say, 'If they go, I go.'"

"You know why I can't do that," Peter answered.

"I *don't* know," Sigrid said. "If she wants to have an affair with the gas burner, let her have it."

Now the line appeared to go dead. "Are you there?" Sigrid asked him. "Is she standing right there? Listening to you? For bloody sake, tell her to move off!"

"Will you meet them?" Peter asked finally.

"Of course I'll meet them. What kind of beast do you think I am?" And Sigrid slammed the receiver into its cradle.

"I take it that was a no," Meena said, standing next to him in the already more posh kitchen.

"She said she'd do it," Peter said, still staring at the telephone receiver in his hand, as if he'd never before seen one, then finally seeming to return to ordinary consciousness, replacing the receiver, and walking out without saying a word, going up the steps, and closing the door to his turret study. *Click*. The click of the lock bolting the door. And Meena, shivering at the sound. She would think of that moment again and again, his leaving the room, going up to the turret, fastening his door against her, because that was the first time he had ever done such a thing, that sound, that click. She knew then she would hear it again and yet again, until, really, it was all she would hear.

So the two children were put on the platform of the station to wait for the train. "Now, don't go back inside to buy sweets," Meena cautioned Sophie. "And you must keep an eye on Andrew. He is in your charge, because you are the oldest, and you must ask, 'Is this the train to Royston?' And you must ask the conductor, once you sit down and put away your things, 'Please tell me when it is time to get off and wait on the platform for the Royston train.' Can you do that?"

"Oh, yes," said Sophie, her eyes enormous. Sophie tried to look into her father's eyes, but they seemed to skitter away just as her gaze was about to meet his. "Good girl," Meena said, smiling at Sophie, that smile that took so many in, yet it puzzled Sophie, because although other smiles warmed her, Meena's did not. "Say goodbye to Mother," Meena told them, and then Peter's eyes met Meena's, a searing, searching look Meena turned her face from. And Sophie said, "Goodbye, Mother."

There was still no sound of the train warning them of its coming. Oh, well, we're a few minutes early, Meena thought, and the wind is so wild today it would drown out the sound even if the train were bearing down on us. "You must not eat all of your sandwiches and fruit at once," Meena told the children in the strict tone she reserved for them. "You must only eat two sandwiches before you get off for the next train. There are four in each bag and I don't want you meeting Sigrid with the two of you all queasy and green, or having her think you are starving to death because you ate your sandwiches so quickly that by the time you see her you will be ravenous. You will see to it, Sophie?" Meena asked her. Sophie nodded and then said, "I want Daddy to come," her eyes tearing, and Meena said, briskly, "None of that, Sophie. You know better. You are to take charge of Andrew. You are to be *good*. And if you are good, I will send you a box of these when you have gotten to the school. Sigrid will tell me if you have or haven't been good," and Meena presented each child with a chocolate lollipop, admonishing them not to eat it until they were settled on the train and had put away their things. "And don't put your lunches beneath your feet," Meena said. "You won't like the way they are when it comes time to eat them. Don't put them against the heater, either."

"Was that the train?" Sophie asked in a whisper, looking at her father, thinking, I don't want to go, don't make me go, hoping he could hear what she did not say aloud, would change his mind, would say, "It's only a joke, everyone back in the car." The urgent sound of the train whistle split the air. "Everything ready?" Meena asked cheerfully, looking at Sophie and thinking, What a drab and dull-looking girl, and born of two such parents. Where did she come from, that chubby girl with bad skin and greasy hair, cheeks like a chipmunk's, but of course she, Meena, had not been a beauty herself at Sophie's age. The child might grow into *something* that did not offend the eye. Already it was clear enough that Andrew would be a replica of Peter. When Meena looked through the Grovesnor family albums, she saw Andrew again and again, only to realize, each time, that she was looking at Peter as a child. Well, Andrew was all right, then. "You won't forget everything I've told you?" Meena asked Sophie.

"I will be good," Sophie promised. How hard she tried to please, Meena thought contemptuously. How I hate it when a cat I dislike begins to follow me wherever I go, as if it were too stupid to sense how much I dislike it, and the more it follows me about, the more I feel distaste for it, like that skinny yellow cat that shadows me everywhere, hoping I will pick it up and stroke it as I do the others. Sophie is that cat, Meena thought. Of course she wants to please me. Sigrid had made that quite plain, saying, "She is a motherless child, and what she most wants is a mother of her own, you can see that, can't you, Meena?"

Yes, she could see it, but it didn't mean she liked it. "She will be a real beauty, you'll see," Sigrid said with great conviction. "When she grows up, when she gets rid of that baby fat, she's going to be far more beautiful than you ever were." More ridiculous statements made by the Grovesnors, Meena thought. Sigrid says that to frighten me, but I am not frightened. That child has no more chance of growing up to be a fairy princess than any toad I come upon leaping out of my way when I do my weeding in the garden. What spark, what *splinter* of beauty, can Sigrid see in that dumpy, fat little child? How she hated fat people. When all they had to do was stop eating. Of course, she, Meena, did not have to stop eating. She was always busy at something, polishing something, digging up the ground with a pitchfork, going out to visit her boar, whitewashing another room, sweeping another floor, sanding the old varnish off a wood floor. Of course she was thin. "You are too thin," Sigrid always said. "If you came down with something, how would you fight it off?" and Meena would always answer, "Thin people last the longest," a response that always drew a nasty look from Sigrid, followed by her predictable, involuntary sigh.

"Come on, come on," Meena was saying, hurrying the two of them into the train, Peter right behind her. "Take these seats, they're good ones. We have to hurry. The train's about to leave," and Peter, shouting back as they moved away toward the open door, "Look out the windows! You've never been to these places before! When I ring up, tell me what you saw!"

"Oh, get *off*!" Meena said irritably. "Or we really will be left on the train."

And so the children watched their parents out of sight on the platform, and Peter stood there in the wind, his scarf flowing through the air like a banner until long after they could see him.

"Satisfied?" he asked, turning to Meena, and Meena said, "It was the right thing."

"Then you're satisfied," Peter said.

And of course they had been sent into the great, wide world with their little bag of crumbs, sent into a world neither of them could control or predict. "Well, Peter, we all live in that kind of world," Meena said, and Peter mumbled something about *special circumstances*, and then retreated to his study in the turret, and the invariable, because now it *was* invariable, click of the lock.

—

THE GOLD SUNLIGHT plays over the walls of the strict, square room in the Royal Marsden. Penelope is trying to wake up. She hears the women's voices, the nurses coming and going, floating somewhere on the surface as she sinks deeper and deeper toward the ocean floor. The rainbow fishes go by and stop and stare at her through her porthole, and something she's never before seen goes by, swimming with all six feet, and then a shark stops and looks in, and then indifferently swims away. I must go up, up, thinks Penny, I can't live down here. I won't be able to breathe down here much longer. "Any change?" asks one of the voices, and another voice answers, "Not yet."

So, thought Penelope, they think there is still hope. She struggled harder. She conjured up her farmhouse in Tuscany, the wildness of it, the heat in the summer, the thick stone walls keeping in the cool from the night before, beginning to give up that battle by four o'clock, but by then the sun was weakening and the temperature was already dropping. The owls that flew back and forth, speaking in their own tongues, and the green parrots who had nested near her house, building their enormous nests, their *condominiums*, as her first husband had called them. He had not liked the parrots. They made so much noise. They disturbed him at his work. How unreasonable they all were, husbands, lovers, acquaintances. When the woods were full of starlings, and was there anyone who made a more unlovely, harsh sound than a starling, and such a loud noise! Much louder than the cries of the parrots. Penelope called the parrots to her, and they came, a storm of green parrots, blocking the windows, the green color the skies turned before a thunder-and-lightning storm. Parrots. She saw them; they blocked out the scene outside, that dreadful wing of the hospital opposite her own, a honeycomb of small square rooms, the people inside not wanting to die, still fighting to stay alive. I'm glad you came, she said to the parrots. Very glad.

Through them, she can see the hills of Tuscany, the relentlessly bright sun, her whitewashed walls, the roof in need of repair, the upstairs room no one went into any longer because of the leaks when it rained, and the sound of someone coming up the steps to her bedroom.

"Mark!" she exclaims, and there he is, that young Adonis who shares her bed, and she turns her face to him, and the parrots send up their chorus of noise, a B-minor mass of noise, but deafening, and Mark is saying, "Here I am, I told you I'd come back." Penelope breathed deeply in relief, and the nurse near her said, "She's gone. Call the doctor and get ready to strip the bed," and the nurse in the doorway paused and said to the two of them in the room, "I wonder if she died happy."

"She was smiling," said the nurse near her bed. "But probably it was only a reflex. You know how it is. Probably it didn't mean anything."

"Still beautiful, even at her age," said the nurse in the doorframe. "More than I can hope for."

"Oh, Jean," one of the nurses said.

"I am certain she died happy," said the nurse in the hall. "Look at how she smiles."

No one commented on the fact that Penelope died alone in an anonymous room, into which she had brought no mementos, nor did they mention Penelope's refusal to call anyone she knew. Most people who die alone are not happy, thinks the nurse who will have to strip the bed. But I think this woman may have been. You don't know. You never know.

———

THE BRILLIANT GOLD sun had gone behind a cloud and had been replaced by thick clouds the color of mercury. The new buds on the leaves, half-opened, were darker, yellower. In a moment, the rain would come down. Julia loved rain and snow equally. Peter used to say of her, "You love weather."

"Not hot weather," Julia would say. "I hate the heat."

"That's true," Peter would say.

"Heat," Julia would say, "is not weather. It's weight." Sophie, on the other hand, reveled in the heat. Rain was what Sophie disliked, pouring-down rain and thunder. It unsettled her, made her aware of something just at the outer rim of consciousness. When raindrops began to hit the windowpanes, Sophie's thoughts always turned to Evelyn's death, her mother's death, as if Evelyn had died on a day when it rained, and on such a day, on *that* day, Sophie had seen something she was not meant to have seen. But hadn't Sophie been told that it was not raining when Evelyn died? Snow had fallen during the night she died. It had been far too cold to rain. Nevertheless, when she heard rain, Sophie thought of her mother's death, and each time, she would try to summon it up, as if she might discover some detail, some clue. She suspected, each time, that her mother's spirit was against such investigations, as if Evelyn's spirit were still alive, watching, attempting to interfere, to protect Sophie for her own good, because hadn't everyone said Evelyn, while she lived, was an excellent mother?

The large drops of spring rain began to fall and hit the windows. Sophie bent her pillow in half and used it to prop herself up higher, the better to watch the rain. Was that why she tried so hard to imagine her mother's death? Because she believed she would summon up her mother? If asked, Sophie would have said she half believed, half did not believe in spirits. She knew her father had, and that Sigrid still did, and she had been told of their many attempts to summon up the dead through Ouija boards. When Sophie had asked her father, he said, "They listen, but they don't speak." Such attempts ceased with Meena's presence. Meena pronounced the Ouija board unholy and what was more, a colossal waste of time. "You upset yourself and you upset everyone else," she told Peter, looking meaningfully toward Sophie.

As time passed, Meena took the train to London more and more often. She worked for various charitable causes, frequently ending up as committee head. Peter saw her to the train, and when he saw the train pull out with his wife on it, he drove back to Willow Grove, and out came the Ouija board. Sigrid, his lifelong accomplice, was either already present or about to arrive in her blue car, probably late.

Sigrid appeared particularly proficient at summoning up her father using the Ouija board, whereas Peter invariably attempted to raise Evelyn's spirit. What he had wanted to know, soon after her death, and what he still wanted to know, was this: how serious had Evelyn been about wanting to die? Before that final day, she had played so many tricks, made so many lame attempts. At the time, he had insisted to all who would listen that her attempts were not cries for help, that worn-out platitude, but were attempts to frighten Peter into doing what she wanted of him.

It was raining, a pouring-down spring rain, and Sophie, who was frightened of Ouija boards, afraid that they might indeed speak, and might actually lie deliberately, because, in Sophie's experience, everyone lied sooner or later, and again, she conjured up her own mother on that night and day in London when all the pipes froze.

She sees Evelyn standing in the parlor, her long hair loose, unwashed, in Sigrid's long flannel nightgown she had been so proud of, the nightgown she had taken when they went to visit Peter's mother and father in Northumberland, and for a while, Evelyn stands quite still. Then she moves to the window, looks out, and sees a light snow falling. At this, she goes back into the room and perches on an overstuffed armchair, as if someone were already sitting in the chair itself. She sits that way for a long time, her eyes traveling to the little flight of steps leading to the bedroom where her two children sleep soundly, then back to the little kitchen and its well-scoured stove. What is it that will tip the balance? Sophie asks herself. Once more, she sees her mother look at the little steps leading to the bedroom and its two children, of whom she, Sophie, is one. Evelyn's eyes rest on the dead, black Bakelite of the phone. It does not ring, nor does

Evelyn seem to strain toward it in any way. Some time passes. Evelyn is wearing nothing on her feet and finally she begins to rotate her left ankle. Probably it has fallen asleep because she has stayed in the same position for a long time. She gets up and goes to a cupboard, opens a drawer, where she finds a thick roll of broad tan masking tape, an old, but clean, well-bleached towel, and a children's scissors. She is like a surgeon, taking up her tools, but this time, she is going to use them on herself. A fugitive thought makes her smile: doctors should not practice on members of their own family. And then, oddly enough, she goes to the chair, sits down, and spreads her things out on her flannel lap. Perhaps she has decided against the plan for which she needed the tape and the little scissors with the red handles? But she is only reviewing it, thinking it through again. She does not want to make any mistakes. This time when she gets up, she works with deliberation and purpose, the sort of purpose that intends to reach its goal.

She begins to tape up the front door to the flat until there are no open spaces, until it is entirely sealed up. Then she goes to the window, the closest one on the right, and tapes that one shut, then the next window, and the next, and on into the bathroom and the kitchen, until all windows are taped closed. When she finishes, she sits down on the chair again, sits there as if exhausted, but a smile is beginning to play about her lips. She looks toward the little flight of stairs leading up to the children and listens to hear if a child is crying or wants something to drink. They are sound asleep. Evelyn prepares a tray for their breakfast, goes up the steps, opens the door quietly, leaves the tray just inside the room. But before she leaves, she picks up the large roll of tan tape she had placed on the tray. Then she closes the door, quietly, and begins taping up the door to their room. She uses twice as much tape to shut this door as she expended on any other door or window. She goes back down the steps, sits in the chair, and waits, listening for the children. Is anyone crying? Has Sophie come to the door and tried to open it? Silence. She has made those two children the arbiter of her own life. If they cry, everything will be postponed. When she still hears nothing, she takes up the towel and goes toward the kitchen, stopping at its threshold. It is as if she has never seen such a room before. Taps arched like the necks of swans through which good water will pour if you turn a knob, the sink the color of snow, so often scrubbed and bleached, although there is a halo of rust around the drain.

Since the two children came to exist, she has feared germs and diseases, and feared the stove, so often turned on in this time of bitter cold, but now dead and cold itself. Right now she would not mind a little heat, what she is about to do makes her cold, but she cannot light the stove, not if she intends to proceed with her plan. Instead, she goes back into the large sitting room, takes up her red sweater, full of moth holes, but warm, and puts it on over her flannel nightgown. She thinks, That's better. When she returns to the kitchen, she takes up the well-washed, overbleached white towel and spreads it on the bottom rack of the oven. She is well aware of the telephone, knows it is in order, has long ago memorized the phone numbers of everyone she cares for, but she has no desire to use them. She stands next to the oven, looking into the parlor, looking again at the little flight of steps, listening for her children crying. It is four in the morning and completely silent. She sighs, says aloud, "It's done, it's ready, what am I waiting for?"

Then she turns her back on the other rooms, kneels beside the stove, she is an acolyte of things like stoves, and places her head on the lowest rack of the oven. Too hard, too uncomfortable. She does not want the discomfort to undo her resolve. Back again to the parlor, where she finds a large stuffed dog the color of the rich earth in her mother's back yard, picks up the dog, and carries it with her back to the oven. At least the dog will be safe from her. She kneels down again, puts her head on the rack, places her left elbow on the stuffed brown dog; now she is comfortable enough, stands up, switches on the gas, kneels down again, first puts her arm against the dog; it is comforting, having the dog there, puts her head down on the rack, and wonders how long it will take before the gas takes hold, before she grows sleepy, but when the gas begins to do its work, she is unaware of it. She is so tired she is already sleepy, and peaceful. From the minute she knelt down that last time, she was peaceful, peaceful enough to sleep, gas or no gas, and is asleep before the gas begins to bond with her red blood cells, is only dimly aware that she is going to sleep very well tonight, thinks, so vaguely it is barely a thought, I should have revised my last poem on the desk, but all that is far away, is like an iceberg that has drifted away in the fog, and she has stopped listening for the children's cries, she will never hear them again, not after tonight, she sighs deeply, turns her head on the stove rack but feels no discomfort, does not see the sun lightening the window and the room, and she is gone. The last thing she thinks, or believes she thinks, is, Don't let anyone wake me, or, He can't wake me. Either of those thoughts, or both mixed together, the last of her thoughts—they may be strong enough to reach Sophie through the Ouija board, those thoughts will not reach her husband who is summoning her, nor Sigrid, if she is calling her up, but her own son or daughter, perhaps they will be able to do it.

Her spirit drifts about the room for a short time, longer than usual because the windows and doors are sealed up so well she cannot escape easily, but then someone comes and breaks down the door, and she can move so quickly! Then she is gone. She does not stay to listen to the cries, the frantic dash up to the children's room, her husband on the floor, trying to lift her, she stays for none of that. She is gone and wants to be elsewhere, or nowhere. It was a mistake to have come in the first place, to this jigsaw world where no amount of pushing and pressing would let her fit in. Yes, thinks her spirit, she wants to be nowhere.

Fear no more the heat o' the sun, / Nor the winter's furious rages.

I think, Sophie tells herself, that was her last thought, her unraveling, shredding thought, as she sailed out the door and the little flat we lived in.

Come back! she cries to Evelyn's spirit. She can see her mother's face. Evelyn is crying, but she is obdurate. She will not come back.

Safe in her room, warm in her bed, Sophie thought, Today will not be a good day. My stomach pains me and my ankle is sore. How could she admit that Evelyn's refusal to return to her has summoned up a great storm of rage? Sophie has never admitted to her rage and cannot do it now. Nor can she acknowledge the rage she feels for her father. She does sometimes think he was like the priest who helped two women and one child into the sacrificial oven, but always with the best of intentions—to prevent an even worse disaster. Sophie turns angrily away from the window, knowing better than to get straight up and speak to anyone else in the house, not in this mood, when she would say terrible, terrible things even she did not believe.

—

"YOU MUSTN'T TELL anyone," Rose said. "Promise me you won't."

Julia did not answer at once, instead thinking, I get mixed up with too many things. "Why?" Julia asked finally. She had learned that, at her age, and much earlier, people do not often ask the unadorned question "*Why?*" They sneak their way toward asking *why*, find ways of finding out what they want to know without ever using the word *why*. But to Julia, it always seemed so much simpler to ask "Why?" when "Why?" was really your question, and in any case, why must an adult person pretend to understand every strange thing in the world? Julia knew people were unnerved when she baldly asked why, even thought she was impolite, if not downright rude, but she also knew that people she cared for would eventually become accustomed to her, would not react to her asking "Why" as if she had just committed a kind of verbal assault.

"Because," Rose said, "if people think Robert is mad again, they won't invite us to parties."

"Are parties that important?" Julia asked.

Rose said, "I would go to parties day and night if I didn't have to make a living by my writing."

"Incredible," said Julia, who would go to almost any length to avoid anything of the sort.

"Well, you must admit that you are intolerably reclusive," Rose said.

"It's the only way I can get anything done," Julia said. "You can get up early, do your writing, and then go out for lunch and go home and work until it's time to go out for dinner or go to a party. I can't do it. One thing a day is enough for me. Actually, one thing a *week* is enough for me."

"For a while," Rose said with considerable urgency, "no one asked us to parties. Robert would corner people, no matter who they were, and no one could escape him. He said very strange things."

"Why didn't you go alone?"

"Robert *likes* parties."

"Does he still corner people?"

"Does the leopard change its spots?" Rose asked. "But now they think he is quite sane and they remember he almost won the Nobel, and I think they feel complimented by his attention. Even if it is torture."

And it is, Julia thought.

"I like to see all the other people who do reviews, and the new editors, and the feature editors who might give me work. I want them to remember I'm still alive."

"Ah," said Julia. "Networking."

"Well. I have to make a living by my writing," Rose said. "Robert should have had a pension just as you do, but somehow when he retired, it was gone. All of it gone."

"Terrible," Julia said.

"*You* have a pension," Rose said. "I wish I had a pension."

"I have a pension," Julia said, "because I taught for thirty-five years. If you had chosen to teach for thirty-five years, you would also have a pension. You don't envy me having taught for one-third of a century?" She was furious at Rose, but she had, as someone had said, a careful face. People could not read her. How dare Rose envy Julia her pension when she had worked so hard and Rose had spent years doing exactly what she wanted, nothing more, because *she* was privileged, *she* was a real writer. And hadn't Peter shared the same attitude? Hadn't he persuaded Evelyn that she ought to take the risk and rely entirely on her writing, and hadn't they both promptly developed writer's block: although Peter's had not lasted very long, but Evelyn's had lasted so long it had almost killed her. *I shall put an end to my life if I cannot begin to write in the next month,* Evelyn had written in her journal. What a position he had put Evelyn in, giving her nothing to rely on but her writing. Why hadn't he seen that money was not the main concern; Evelyn needed far more than poems to keep her aloft. When Evelyn felt her world beginning to crumble, as it sometimes seemed to do several times a day, would ten poems, or twenty, or thirty have been enough for her? Why hadn't he seen she needed something more than her own writing? "You pull your own insides out when you write, your own insides covered with your own blood," Peter once said to her. Why hadn't he seen that Evelyn was a bleeder, that she could not keep it up, writing and writing? It was more than exhausting herself; it was more like losing blood, and the only person who could give you more blood was you yourself, the one who had done the bleeding. Well, he had had his way. They were young, and the young are always so certain of everything.

"Remember," Rose said, returning to the purpose of her call, "you mustn't let anyone know that Robert's mad again."

"I daresay they do know, but I won't tell them," Julia said. "Anyway, if you keep saying there's nothing in the world wrong with Robert, people will believe you. People tend to believe what they're told."

"That's what I think," Rose said. "I'm going to a party tonight. At Sally's. She'd be so happy to see you. Why don't you come?"

"No," said Julia.

"What will you do instead?"

"Watch *EastEnders,*" Julia said. "Talk to Sophie. Try on each other's jewelry."

"She won't talk to me. She thinks I'm going to write Peter's biography."

"Are you?"

"Well, yes, I need the money, and I've written several biographies. I know they weren't well received in the States, but here they made quite a splash."

"There you are," said Julia.

"There I am?" Rose asked. "That's why Sophie won't talk to me?"

"No, Sophie doesn't talk to people if she doesn't know them well."

"I don't know how you got to know her well," Rose said irritably.

"Accident."

"For a person who never leaves the house, Julia, you have a great many such accidents."

"I do, don't I?" Julia said.

"Could you speak to her for me?"

"No," Julia said.

"But it would make such a difference!"

"That's not the kind of influence I have over her," Julia said.

"Oh, you do," Rose said, her voice sour.

"And what is Robert doing right now?"

"Oh, he's corralled a man who writes about dogs and how they communicate, and he wants to know what kind of communication dogs have, and if there's any such thing as communication, and what does the concept of communication imply, the usual thing," Rose said, starting to smile. Julia laughed and stirred her cappuccino.

And now, thought Julia, watching a sun spot dance on the wall, Robert was dead. Sigrid had told her that last night on the phone and Julia asked how Rose was managing, and Sigrid said, "She goes to parties, but leave it to Robert to get his timing wrong and leave her in the shit. He was getting weaker and weaker after that heart attack, and going up the steps was harder and harder, so he finally persuaded her to sell that flat in Islington and buy a much smaller garden flat so he wouldn't have to manage the stairs, and she hated that flat, it was in Muswell Hill, the worst part of it, and they were not in there two weeks when she came back from a lunch with Sally, and he was sitting up in his chair watching the telly, not moving, so Rose thought she was in for another excoriation, but not that time, he was dead. Completely dead. Their own children told her she was better off without him, but she cried for weeks, really weeks, and I knew right away what she was crying about. She was crying about having lost the Islington flat, and lost it for no reason. He spoiled everything for her, right up until the end. He was a spoiler, Robert, even though I liked him, but still you can't really blame him, all those medications, and the way they misdiagnosed his damn liver. They *made* him mad, the doctors, I mean. If you live here and you get yourself into the hands of doctors, you can learn to hate this country. Peter used to insist that the doctors here were fine, and look what they did to him. Funeral to be held two years earlier than necessary. Doctors here should post a notice like that in their waiting rooms."

"Is she still dyeing her hair?" Julia asked, and Sigrid said, "Oh, yes, she's taken it back to its original color, and it prettifies her; that color, the red shade she used made her look so yellow, I always thought she had a touch of jaundice, but now she looks younger by the week. He was wearing her *down*," Sigrid said. "He was wearing her *out*. It was his revenge on his wife being so noble. I used to say he'd outlive us all," and Julia said, "He was a very sick man."

"Yes, he was," Sigrid said. "But she, she's healthy as a horse."

"So she's out of danger, now that he's gone," Julia said.

"I'll tell you the real danger, Julia. The real danger is that she'll live long enough to outlive her reputation and have to see that reputation for what it's worth. Most writers I've known who went through that would rather have died before they had to see that happen. You can live too long, can't you?"

"Yes," Julia said. "But most people stay alive hoping to see their fortunes take a turn for the better and wanting to see what it's like when it happens."

"Idiots," Sigrid said.

"Yes," Julia said. "Idiots."

"She's a dim bulb," said Sigrid, "but a good girl. She tries hard."

"I hope she tries hard when she writes Peter's biography," Julia said.

"WHAT!" shouted Sigrid.

Oh, I am in for it now, Julia thought.

"I'll put a stop to *that*!" Sigrid shouted down the line. "A pygmy writing about Gulliver! It's more than anyone can bear to think of!"

"I think," said Julia, "the ink's already dry on a contract somewhere."

"I can't bear it!" Sigrid said. "I cannot bear it! There are already five madwomen working on biographies of Peter, and *now* there's a sixth! Six crazy women writing biographies! Six *stupid* crazy women writing biographies!"

"She needs the money," Julia said gently.

"Blood money? She needs blood money?"

Julia kept quiet. She found herself thinking, Once again, it is Peter causing trouble. And then she asked herself, Is it disloyal to see someone clearly? Because I can see him clearly, or saw him clearly, and I always did. If he had seen himself clearly, so much would have been spared.

So many! I had not thought I had undone so many! Peter roaring in the pub, having drunk more than anyone could possibly drink, so much more than one could believe, even if it had been only water, which, of course, it had not.

SIXTEEN

―

PETER IN HIS turret, reciting, for some reason, "Little Miss Muffet." Lately, Martin's letters had been quiet, full of peace, but he knew better than to believe in appearances. He hoped his brother had come to some sort of understanding with himself, was no longer asking himself, What have I done with my life? One of those questions better left unasked once one passes forty years of age, he thought. He would write Martin in the usual way, without having second thoughts and third thoughts and tenth and fifteenth thoughts until he was worn out before he set pen to paper.

Martin, he wrote,

I have been thinking about Evelyn again, and what I told you I was thinking of last time. I know other people revisit their memories, and take out photograph albums, and sit there and look at pictures of those who have died, but I don't look at the albums; I can still see her so clearly. I would like to stop rehearsing and rerehearsing those days, as if there were something in them I could change. Sometimes I think, If I wrote about her, wrote the truth about her and me as I saw it and still see it, I wouldn't keep going back to those same days and those same events. It's worth the experiment, if that's all it is. But Meena continues to be dead against it. I mentioned it again this morning, and she looked out the kitchen window as if she actually expected an answer to appear in that blankness, and I saw what she saw, a huge crow resting on a branch, peering in at us, and she said, No, Peter, I can't allow it. I can't even look at a crow without thinking of her and what happened to her and everything that happened after she left. After she left! Not that Evelyn *died*, but left, like one of those village women who says, I won't let that man beat me anymore, I'll hop the next bus, and I'll find a better village. I'll dye my hair red and no one will find me. How do you deal with a woman like that? To have gone so far down the road with me and still to understand so little. But all the same, I have tried writing bits and pieces, and it seems it does exorcise her: a little. So I think I shall continue. I've heard enough of "I can't allow it," heard it too often and given so many things up so many times until now I find myself thinking, I'm too old to be bullied. The truth is, it's a matter of indifference to me: what she does or doesn't do. I'd be quite happy never to set eyes on that woman again.

My first wives died so young and so fast I had no idea of what it was like to tire of a woman, no, that's not right, I didn't have the time to learn to loathe a woman and still be tied to her, year after year. Have we stayed together all this time because, in the end, it's been a matter of asking myself, "What would the neighbors think?" I never put it to myself that simply, but if that's what I was worried about, what the neighbors thought, and the newspapers, and the critics, and my children, then I'm a coward. I've lived a coward's life. Haven't you yourself suspected me of it? That your younger brother is a coward? Meanwhile accepting all the tributes offered me for my courage, for going on in the face of all that horror, those are Sigrid's words, when there was no courage in it. After all, what choice did I have? Before Evelyn, it would never have occurred to me to do myself in. I was too happy in myself, too full of myself, Evelyn said that frequently enough. Put an end to my own remarkable life? Why? Could I have done something deserving the ultimate finality of that bloody oven?

I reproach myself for good reason. I was unutterably stupid. I swallowed whole Evelyn's gospel. We were one soul who had been split into two, there was nothing we could not share and should not share because not revealing everything to each other would unbalance our lives which were so perfectly balanced, well, everyone wants to believe something like that when you've just escaped from your potato parents, or, in Evelyn's case, from that black witch, Charlotte, who was always incapable of understanding a single thing about her daughter.

So, like a damn fool, I took her to see the slaughterhouse. It meant a lot to me, that slaughterhouse, it was a living metaphor of what life was built on: brutality and blood and the need to survive that justified the way the men hit the cows on the heads, smashing their skull bones into their brains. I would go there on butchering days, the day before the market, and watch, and think, Don't forget. This is what life is like. Evelyn got wind of it, and of course she had to go, and like a fool, I took her. There are fools and there are fools, but there was never one greater than me. She couldn't even stomach the smell of fertilizer, and I brought her to the slaughterhouse. She *insisted* I bring her, but I could have said no. Like our father, I could have said, "I am putting my foot down." Do you remember that? *I'm putting my foot down*, and how we used to laugh when he said it, going outside, far enough so he couldn't hear, and laughing until we cried, asking each other, Where else would you put your foot but down? What a fool! Then how ashamed we were, laughing at him, so we ended up doing extra chores because we felt sorry. I think of that more often than I like to remember. Well, that is the way it is between parents and children. He was always putting his foot down and I was never putting mine down, and who turned out to have gotten it right? Mum used to tell me, she said this before Evelyn died, "You won't make my mistakes. You'll make your own mistakes," and I was foolish enough to ask myself, Why should I make mistakes? *Any* mistakes? So we are paid back for our arrogance, eh, Martin? When I could have said to Evelyn, It's a beautiful day. Why don't we sit in a meadow and make daisy chains? She would have liked that, she would have been content with that, instead of watching adorable little animals smashed on their bloody heads and reduced to someone else's bloody supper.

When we got up in the morning, we could have stayed in bed and talked on after the storm of it, that storm of bodies; she was a passionate creature, probably everyone knows that, or has come to, why did I have to get up and start moving? What was there that couldn't have waited? And into what day was I hurrying her, that big red sun on the horizon, always threatening to burn everything up, that was how she saw it. And if she did get up, and make breakfast, and rush up to her study because she knew I thought it was best for her to get straight to work, then what a failure it was if she couldn't write anything. And her eyes, accusing me as she came down, as if I had set her up to fail. When what I should have said was, If you don't write anything today, you'll write tomorrow, what's the hurry? Sooner or later, you'll write something. Go take a nap. You're exhausted. If I had taken that tack. But Sigrid always says there was no tack to take. If I had said, Forget about writing today, Evelyn would have countered, saying, You don't believe I have it in me anymore; you think I'm finished. Which is exactly what she did say when I said, Let it go for today, let the pressure build up, and tomorrow you'll write something twice as good, maybe ten times as good, because you skipped a day. But she would ask me, What are *you* going to do today? and I'd say, I'm going to feed the animals and turn them out into the pasture, and then I'll go up and write. And that little twist of her mouth, as if what she meant to say was, *You* have something to write about, your talents don't run dry, but I'm only a little poet, isn't that what Sigrid calls me, doesn't she tell people, Oh, he's married a *little* poet, and now you believe it. You've lost faith in me. After that, days spent in her room, in the dark, the blinds shut, and if I tried to come in, it was *our* bedroom, she'd say, Go out. It was better to go out, I soon learned that. So I never got the trick of her.

And after Sophie came, I thought she was happy. She threw herself into all that mothering business. No more dyed hair. She let her hair grow until it reached her waist, plain brown hair, nondescript, that's the right word, and I looked at her and thought, She's happy, she doesn't need that shining gold hair anymore. And when she stopped washing it often enough—she'd been so scrupulous before—I thought, She's busy with the baby. She gets up early to write, she has no time. Depression, hopelessness was written large, all over her, and I didn't see it, didn't even suspect it, until I met Elfie, and then I saw everything I had overlooked in Evelyn, and more. Well, they say love is blind, but as usual, mild people put everything too mildly. Love rips out its own eyes.

The thing of it is, Martin, should I write about her, write it all down, say to Hell with bloody Meena? This isn't a rhetorical question, you see. If I have a genius, it's one for making a mess of other people's lives. You wouldn't think I'd have trouble answering a question like that. I ought to know: the odds are if I want to do something, it's wrong.

That's enough of that. Now on to the two hundred questions I want to ask about you and Laura. Ready or not, here I come. I do wish life could be as simple as it was when we played that game.

—

"JULIA," SOPHIE SAID, her eyes red-rimmed, "why do you think she did it? You must have thought about it. Charlotte says it was like a roll of the dice. Well, she doesn't use those words, she says my mother woke up one day and it was a bad day and she gave in to it, whatever it was, the exhaustion, the disappointment, fear, whatever it was. Does it happen that way?"

"Some people wear themselves out. They think they have more strength than they have, and they wake up one day and they know they can't take another step. Maybe it was something like that."

"She did it to punish Daddy."

"Probably. That, too."

"But," Sophie persisted, "you tried something like that. You were ten years younger than she was when she died."

"Well," said Julia.

"Did you want to die?"

"I wanted someone else to take the decision away from me. The man I lived with, the doctors at the hospital, I couldn't stand it anymore, so I spun the wheel."

"And lived," Sophie said.

"No one would play Russian roulette if everyone died each time," Julia said.

"But there must have been things holding you back."

"Oh, yes. I had two white rats named Daisy and Ophelius, and I worried about what would become of them."

"*Why* do you think she did it?" Sophie asked, going straight back to the first question.

"Who knows? I don't. Your father never knew. He once said she was addicted to her dream of eternal sleep, but I don't know how seriously he meant it. She was serious, we know that. All that taping closed of windows and doors. She meant business. I imagine she couldn't conceive of things changing for the better, as simple as that. If it was more complicated, I can't begin to guess."

"So, some live and some die," Sophie said.

"Exactly."

"I am going to live, no matter what," Sophie said.

"Good," said Julia. Just then, the sun went behind a cloud, but they beamed at one another.

"But Meena is not likely to do such a thing?" Sophie asked.

"Oh, no," said Julia. "Not Meena."

SEVENTEEN

—

THE DAY IS washed, and blue, and brilliant with sun, but Sigrid has shut it out. She sits on her overstuffed chair which she long ago covered with an indigo kilim to hide the cigarette holes in the chair's fabric, but now there are so many cigarette holes in the kilim, they are even more obvious than the holes in the chair were before, if only because the kilim itself is so beautiful and draws attention. And she was smoking, "that filthy habit," as Peter used to call it. "Did you ever wonder where she got the golden color for the woodwork?" Peter asked Julia once. "It's pretty, isn't it? You know what it's from? Nicotine. It's all that nicotine. The woodwork used to be white." Exhaling puff after puff of smoke into the room, like a kind of dragon about to begin breathing fire.

Rose, *Rose,* intends to write Peter's biography. Is there no bolt of lightning that can strike down a bough and crush Rose under it? Is there no drunken driver who can flatten her on Haverstock Hill? Nothing in her refrigerator harboring botulism that can carry her off? Is there no God? Of course there is no God. If there were a God, there would be no such thing as Rose. I hope you are satisfied, Sigrid says aloud to Peter. The least you could have done was outlive Rose. No one expected you to outlive Meena, she's so much younger than you are, but Rose is as old as I am, Peter, for bloody sake!

So much disapproval.

She heard his voice saying that outside in the wind. It must be a terribly windy day, Sigrid thinks, but she has no desire to open the curtains and look for herself. You should be turning in your grave like a pinwheel, Sigrid says, addressing her brother's voice. But perhaps, Sigrid thinks, is it possible he finds it funny? Is he laughing? Is this the laughter of the gods, the laughter of the dead who no longer have to care about consequences? I will show her about consequences, Sigrid thinks. Rose will not get away with this. Then she turns on Peter's spirit, his voice, whatever it is, saying, It is not enough to turn over in your grave. No, you should be pounding on the roof of your coffin with both your feet; we buried you in good, stout shoes, what foresight, you should appreciate it now. Peter, start your pounding. Get started pounding. She stubs out her cigarette and laughs aloud. If all these people, Peter and Meena and Sophie and Andrew, were not related to her, she would find all this hilarious. She would revel in their doings. Instead, all this has driven her to distraction again and again and again. She ought to give it up, fall, figuratively, on her sword, but then she remembers what people say. When it comes to Peter, Sigrid is too harsh, she is far too cruel to anyone she thinks has hurt him. But then Sigrid decides, No, I can never be too harsh or too cruel in that way.

Instead, she looks at the clock and sees it is eight o'clock, which means that both Meena *and* Rose will be up. A little sliver of gold light escapes into her bedroom, and Sigrid asks herself, Why should either of them be enjoying the day? Whose day should she blight first? Well, of course, Meena's.

She dialed the number, "the most changed telephone number in the country," as Peter used to say. When she heard Meena answer, Sigrid bypassed *Hello, how are you? I hope you are keeping your days full,* and instead said, "You can't let Rose do it, I won't stand for it, she'll make such a botch of it, and if she gets hold of what's gone on these last two years at Willow Grove, *you'll* never live it down!"

"Sigrid?" Meena asked.

"Of course, Sigrid," she answered.

"What on earth are you going on about?"

"Rose, you fool! Rose is going to write Peter's biography!"

"I am the executor of the estate," Meena said in that infuriatingly calm voice that led people to make her the chairwoman of charity boards. "I shall tell everyone not to cooperate with her and I shall deny her permission to quote from either Peter or Evelyn's work. I shall tell the same thing to the others who intend to write Peter's biography."

"That won't be *enough!*" Sigrid shouted. "She will finish first! She'll be finished in a month or two! You have to get it out of Peter's publisher, find out who Rose's writing the damn thing *for,* and then bring pressure to bear to stop her!"

"I think that will probably be hopeless, don't you? She'll publish that book in a comic book format if she has to, don't you agree, Sigrid? What I *can* do is refuse permission to quote and let people know that I consider her inadequate to the job."

"It isn't *enough!*" Sigrid shouted. "Don't you understand what harm she can do? Peter's at the height of his reputation. Rose will smash it, she'll smash everything!"

"I doubt very much if Rose is capable of doing anything of the sort," Meena said. "She's recently lost her husband."

"What?" Sigrid shouted. "What does that have to do with anything?"

"If you carry on shouting, I shall have to put down the phone," Meena said.

"Don't bother!" Sigrid shouted. "Gas bag! Idiot!" And she slammed the phone down so hard that she hurt her wrist.

She dialed Rose's number. "Up early, are you?" she said, greeting Rose's sleepy voice.

"I get up early every morning. I have to earn my keep," Rose said.

"You should have less to earn now that Robert's out of the picture. One can live far more cheaply than two."

"What are we discussing?" Rose asked, her voice wary. "You're not worried about how I'm making ends meet. Or are you?"

"No, Rose. I've just heard that you intend to write Peter's biography."

"That's true," Rose said.

"How dare you!" Sigrid shouted.

"Let me pull up a chair and explain it to you. I've written *several* biographies. I knew Peter for years. A publisher came to me and asked me if I'd like to write Peter's life. I know his work, I know all the same people he grew up with, I've written well-received biographies, quite esteemed, really, and I agreed. Who better than me?"

Sigrid was left speechless. "I can hear you snorting over the phone line," Rose said. "Don't forget to breathe."

"I wish *you* would stop breathing!" Sigrid said.

"More shouting," Rose said. "Look, Sigrid, *someone* is going to write a life of Peter Grovesnor. Why not me? Who better than me?"

"There are times," Sigrid said, "when you do take my breath away. Can you have so little understanding of your own ability? Your translation of that Italian poet: even the writer himself complained to Peter about it. If he'd lived longer, he would have had someone else do it again! He intended to include a preface! Not *thanking* people, as other people do, no, he intended to name *you* as the person who had ruined his reputation!"

"He had quite a good reputation when I finished ruining it," Rose said. "Before I translated him, no one ever heard of him."

"He said he wished no one ever had heard of him if they had to hear travesties of his poems!"

"Everyone was quite satisfied," Rose said.

"And to do a biography of Emily Brontë, someone as bloodless as you are!"

"Everyone quite liked the biography," Rose said. "The reviews were excellent."

"Only because you regurgitated perfectly good scholars who had gone before. And your translations from the Urdu! Is there a soul on earth who doesn't laugh at them? No, Rose, your gift is to wait until all the intelligent people have done their work and come to sane, intelligent conclusions, and then you write your little fluffy thing on top of theirs. If you wait until some good people write on Peter's life, then you can write your own little thing. But to do the first biography! It will set literary history back for a century! You can't do it! You mustn't!"

"I'm quite sure Peter would give me his blessing," Rose said. "He often said lovely things about my poems. They're still there, on the jackets of my books."

"Rose," Sigrid said, attempting to speak normally (her voice was going hoarse), "he said those things because I was your friend, and I *begged* him to say something nice. I *begged* him! I said you were a good girl and you tried very hard. *I* wrote out those little compliments you're so proud of! I wrote them and posted them and Peter copied them out in his hand-writing and sent them back to me, and I sent them in to the publisher. Where would you be without those little compliments? Don't you owe him something?"

"I'm quite sure he wrote them himself," Rose said. "It was impossible to bully Peter into anything."

"I didn't *have* to bully him, you bloody fool!" Sigrid shouted. "I had to beg! I had to remind him of what it was like for you living with Robert! I told him to do it for me! Of course he would do it for me!"

"You are not taking Peter's death well," Rose said.

"What does that have to do with anything?" Sigrid shrieked, beside herself.

"Peter would not be happy to hear you roaring at people."

"You don't know anything, not a thing, about Peter! You *can't* know anything about Peter! You're like a turnip talking to the sun, asking it to tell you how it shines. You have to give it up!"

"Don't be silly," Rose said. "I need the money, and what's more to the point, I'll do a good job."

"But you *can't* do a good job, Rose! Don't you understand how small your intellect is? Think. What would Robert have said?"

"He said, Sigrid, that it would be a splendid thing, to do a work of non-fiction. I would be forced to stick to the truth, not get lost in a garden of weeds, which was all fiction was. You know what Robert would have said."

"And he thought it was a fine thing for you to do Peter's life?"

"Yes, Sigrid, he did."

"Well, he was mad as a hatter, wasn't he?"

"Sigrid, I'm going to put down the phone," Rose said.

"Who is publishing it? Who has the nerve to publish this travesty?"

"I have no intention of telling you," Rose said, "especially not when you're in this state. When you feel better, I'd like to interview you and Sophie and Meena, too, if she'll give anyone the time of day these days."

"*No one* is going to speak to you!" Sigrid shouted into the phone. "Can you understand that, you stupid cabbage?"

"I'll ring off now. You're coming down with laryngitis," Rose said. Sigrid stared at the dead, beige telephone receiver. She hit herself on the right side of her head with it. Then she realized that she had hit herself quite hard and all she would have to show for her effort would be a swelling the size of an Easter egg.

EIGHTEEN

—

MEENA WAS IN her turret. Her cousin, virtually the only person allowed to visit Willow Grove, had begun to worry. Not only did she not leave the house, she rarely left the room. In the mornings, she would carry up a string bag with half a loaf of bread and some cheese and a large bottle of water, enough, she believed, to see her through until the next day. Now she sat on the low bench in front of the six windows and looked out. From the turret, there was very little that rose up higher than her place of ascent. The turret room was higher than the roof of the church in the meadow that adjoined Willow Grove, but the church spire was higher than her perch, which was, as Meena thought, as it should be. Up there, she was on eye level with the very tops of the ancient oaks and elms. The birds flew differently up here, she saw, no longer afraid of the people on the ground. It seemed to Meena that the birds here sang louder and more frequently, although, she noticed, today there seemed to be no birds about. But there had been a strong downpour in the early morning, and probably, she thought, the birds were still sheltering beneath the leaves on the boughs they trusted. Then there was a loud flutter, and an immense crow flew into the oak directly in front of her. The crow ruffled its feathers as if to dry itself, then settled into immobility, its eyes fixed, it seemed, on Meena. A crow, she thought. Of course. Peter had so loved crows. What was it he had said? *I admire their rapaciousness.* Was that it? Their beaks can take out a man's eyes in seconds. Was that what he had said? Was that why he admired those immense black birds who so expeditiously ate the grass seeds she put down every spring?

Could it be true that Rose was going to write Peter's biography? Of course she would stop it. In the past, Sigrid had stopped such attempts by refusing permission to quote. But these days, so it seemed, people were less frightened and more brazen. They quoted without permission. The head of Peter's publishing house had warned her. She had a significant amount of money, but she would soon lose it if she sued everyone who she thought had committed an infraction of her rules. "And, of course," he had added, "you know you cannot claim that a dead man had been libeled or slandered."

"Surely not!" Meena said. "Surely everyone is not free to say whatever they please simply because Peter is dead."

"I'm afraid that's rather how the law works," said the publisher, and Meena had said, "We'll see about that."

But Rose! And Rose was a friend of Julia's. And Julia had been a friend of Penelope's. They will conspire against me, Meena thought. How could they not? She picked up the telephone and rang Sigrid's number. Engaged. Then she rang Sophie's. Also engaged. Beyond doubt, the two of them were on the line to each other. Talking about her, deciding what to do about her, determining what they would tell Rose. Julia was a sly one. Why did no one understand that? Julia would tell Rose just enough so that the "biographer" thought she was going home with a full stomach, and it would never occur to Rose that she had kept the best parts to herself. Or perhaps Meena had it altogether wrong. Julia would tell Rose all sorts of dangerous tidbits, dangerous to her, to Meena, and out of her envy for having been Peter's wife, Julia would see to it that she put herself, Meena, in the most dreadful possible light. None of those literary women from London had forgiven her for excluding them from Willow Grove, for making it so difficult to gain access to Peter. Although Peter had seen to it that Julia always knew what his X-directory number was. Meena would change their number once again, and the next day Julia would call, asking Meena how she was, was her sister better than before, was it as cold in England as it was in the United States, apparently willing to talk to Meena for hours, until Meena interrupted, saying, "Shall I give Peter a shout?"

To which Julia would always answer, "Why not?" She was not one to make Meena feel like an inconsiderable, insensible thing. No, she had gone to great lengths to appear interested in her and what she had to say. Perhaps she had cared about her. Probably she cared a little about everyone she had ever met. There were such people. Meena knew herself not to be one of them. She cared for very few people, *her* people, of whom Peter used to say, numbered no more than three. And now with the threat of Rose's allegedly unstoppable biography, was it not likely that Julia and Sigrid would ally themselves, bind themselves together more tightly than before? Take Sophie into their charmed circle with them? Draw Andrew in, take him in, make common cause against her? Who were her natural defenders? She had none.

On the great black bough, still shiny with rain, the crow raised one foot, put it down, and then raised the other, putting it down. Probably his feet are wet, Meena thought. One assumes that wild creatures do not mind the wind and the rain. They mind cold, of course they do, but one takes it for granted that everything else is a matter of indifference to them.

What, really, did she fear? Meena asked herself, staring into the crow's eyes as if he would be able to tell her. Peter was asleep with his secrets. Penelope, God willing, had had the turf pulled up over her before she had time to tell anyone anything. What did Sophie have to say that could damage her? Sigrid, she was the danger. She knew everything, on the phone to Peter almost daily for more than forty years, and if she did not ring him, he rang her, or worse, got on the train and stayed in her little house overnight, and sometimes more than overnight, until she began to suspect he never intended to come back, until she had to ring him and say, "You will be back tomorrow, then, or you shall have to leave me behind." Then he would return, ever more sullen, more sarcastic, more cutting. Sigrid, that secret agent, who would say anything when she grew angry enough. There had to be a way to keep Sigrid quiet, to keep all of them quiet. Well, she had no power over Julia, but perhaps there was a way. Meena considered that new problem as she took out her loaf of French bread, and, on the table that had been Peter's desk, spread out a large sheet of brown paper. Yes, it would be the cheddar, she thought. How many pounds of Cambozola had she eaten during Peter's reign? A good, plain red cheddar, that was what she wanted. She cut off a slab of the cheese, slid it into the open jaw of French bread, and began chewing slowly. She should have seen it before! Right there, under her nose! And it was Peter who had given her the weapons she needed. His final words gleamed like surgical instruments in the autoclave, neat, precise, clean. The will! The will was all she needed to keep all of them in line, especially Sigrid. She would finish eating her bread and cheese, drink a good glass of water, and think how best to approach her, her sister-in-law, who, up until now, had been so sure of defeating her.

—

"PHONE FOR YOU," Sophie said, handing the receiver to Julia.

"For me? No one knows I'm here." Was it her imagination, or did Sophie seem disturbed? "Probably Matt," she said, because Sophie's telephone number was taped to the refrigerator door in New York and only people already in her house would know how to contact her. Sophie shook her head.

"Hello?" Julia said.

"I'm Nigel Banninster," a male voice said. "You bought some tiles off me from eBay, but you paid me for them twice. I thought I'd better ask you what you wanted me to do rather than write you a great big e-mail. So. The tiles."

That voice! Full of suppressed laughter just beneath the surface, and what was most unnerving, that accent, that exact timbre, that same way of finishing a sentence and saying nothing, giving you time to frame your response, if you wanted to offer a response, and if you did not, giving you time to enjoy what he had just said, or simply allowing a moment for the pleasure of knowing yourselves once more joined, once again hearing each other's voices. "What is the weather like there?" the voice asked.

"It was clear and sunny, but now it's pouring down rain," Julia said. "You're voice is so familiar. Are you from Northumberland?"

"Lancashire," Nigel said. "Well, North Country, anyway. I tried to call you in the States, but they give me this number. It's about the dark green tiles, you see. You've paid for them twice. But I think you wanted red. Did you want red?"

She didn't care if the tiles were to be dark green or ruby red. She wanted Nigel to keep on talking. There was Peter's voice again, that beloved voice, which she had either forgotten or was unable to summon up. In the States, she had bought several recordings of Peter reading his own work, started to play one, and then took the CD out of her computer and threw it across the room. The voice was hard and tinny, not Peter's, not Peter's voice as she'd known it. "I thought it sounded *exactly* like Peter," Sigrid had said at the time. "Can't you hear him when you play that record?"

"Not on that disc," Julia said, thinking, His voice has been recorded over and over; it doesn't sound like his voice, not to me, I'll never hear that voice again. But she was hearing it now. Of course! The disc hadn't reproduced the hesitancies, the odd, expectant silences between small utterances, the seductiveness of his voice, and now that Peter was no longer there, she understood that his voice had been a great weapon, a seductive voice affecting men and women alike, so that now she wondered, Did everyone from his part of the country who spoke with his accent and in his timbre have the same ability to cast a spell simply by asking, "Did you want the red?"

"Although I was born in Yorkshire," Nigel said out of the blue. "What time is it there, then?"

"The same time as it is where you are," she said. "I'm in England."

"Oh, I forgot. I thought you were still in the United States, you see. I thought I called you there. Confusing, all those time changes."

If it wasn't Peter on the line, if really this was someone named Nigel, a man who sold tiles, then Peter had somehow taken possession of this man. Otherwise, why were they still speaking of red tiles or green tiles or time differences? Why did she want to keep him on the line, talking? "I can refund the money, or I can send you two sets, but I don't know which color you want, you see."

"Either one is fine," Julia said, when in truth, more dark green tiles were the last things she wanted. She wanted the ruby red. But it seemed so ungenerous to insist on them when he had somehow let Peter come all the way back from wherever he was, simply so that she could hear his voice one more time. She did not want to stop him speaking, but apparently Sophie had call waiting, and an odd beeping began and then continued in the background. "I had better let you go back to whatever you're doing," Julia said. "Still jet-lagged, then?" Nigel asked. "And hungry, I don't doubt. That's the way it is with humans. They've proven it. You take a trip in a car or a train, and your instinct tells you, some part of your ancient brain tells you that you may not find anything to eat there, so you eat up while you're going. That's what it's about, that ravenous eating."

Aloud, she asked him, "What do you do? For a living, I mean."

"I sell tiles," he said, laughing softly. "And now and then try to write the occasional mystery novel, but I never succeed. No talent, you see."

"I see," said Julia.

"So it's the green tiles, then? Two sets?"

"Yes, two sets," she said. "Thanks so much for calling."

"I thought, not a great long e-mail, you see. It was easier to ring you up."

"I can confuse anyone," Julia said. "Calling was better."

"Well, goodbye, then," the voice said, but he was still on the line; she could feel the expectancy.

"Goodbye," she said. What else could she do? She put down the phone.

"You've gone completely white," Sophie said.

"Have I?" Julia asked, and then, as if to forestall further questions, she launched into a story about a student, one of the best she'd ever had, a black woman, who came in one day and *she'd* gone white; she hadn't thought it could happen, not when her skin was so dark, but she was white all the same, as if she'd been powdered, and when Julia asked her what had happened, she said, "Food poisoning. We all went to a Thai restaurant, cheap, you know, no refrigeration. It's on Coney Island Avenue. Don't go."

"Julia," Sophie said.

"What?"

"That man who called up. When I answered, he sounded just like Daddy."

"He was born near where your father grew up."

"And do you think that accounts for it? I've known a lot of people who grew up in Cornwall. Was he a Cornish man?"

"He said Lancashire. North Country."

"I think it was him," Sophie said. "I think it was Daddy."

"We're both still half asleep," Julia said. "Someone with an accent like your father's, yes."

"You wouldn't have gone white like that if you hadn't thought it was Daddy."

Julia took a deep breath. "It did sound like him," she said.

"What did he talk about?"

"Tiles," Julia said.

"Tiles?"

"I bought some while I was still in the U.S., and apparently I paid for the same ones twice."

"How did he get this number? I'm X-directory."

"He called home and my daughter was there and gave it to him."

"And he went to the expense of calling you in the States to say you paid twice for some tiles? Will he call me?" Sophie asked.

"What?"

"I mean, if it was Daddy."

"If it was your father, he would have called you first. I'm sure of it," Julia said.

"But he called you instead."

"Because he wanted to settle the *tiles*."

"He never put me first," Sophie said, her eyes welling up.

"Sophie! For Christ's sake! It was a perfect stranger! A man selling tiles! Are you interested in tiles?"

Sophie turned her back and stared out the window. Rain poured down like little rivers, each rivulet taking its own, torturous path. "You wouldn't lose your temper at me unless you knew I was right," she said.

"It wasn't *him*, Sophie! You'll hear him again. You'll dream about him and then you'll hear him."

"And have you dreamed about him?"

"No," Julia said. "But then I never dream about people I loved." She was remembering the tapes she'd made, almost two decades ago, of her own father answering questions she'd asked him about their family, and how comforted she'd been when she summoned up his voice by depressing a button on the tape machine. But when she played one of the tapes for her mother, she said, "It doesn't sound like him," just what she had said to Sigrid after listening to Peter's recorded voice reciting his work. If you cared enough about someone, you heard his voice, his true voice, only when he spoke directly to you. Otherwise, there were the mufflings, the veils, the echoes, life's static, changing the sound of the words even as he spoke them.

"*I* dream of the dead," Sophie said, a sharp edge to her voice. "You're right. I heard him just for an instant, asking if you were there and if he could speak to you."

"It wasn't *him*," Julia insisted. "Meena always said everyone in your family heard things that weren't there."

"Now you're agreeing with Meena?" Sophie asked. "Then you know it was Daddy."

"It certainly sounded like him," Julia admitted.

"Why couldn't you have said so in the first place?"

"Oh, Sophie," Julia said.

"Everyone always wanting to keep bits and pieces to themselves."

"Oh, *Sophie!*"

"Right. Oh, Sophie. As if it's my fault, as if you don't want to keep the truth to yourself."

"What truth? We're talking about *tiles*, some strange man who sells tiles!" There were times, Julia thought, when she could understand Meena and her rages.

"I wonder if he calls Meena and speaks to *her*."

"He didn't want to speak to her when he was alive. I doubt he'd start now."

"If you could ask her. I mean, maybe he *has* spoken to her," Sophie said.

"No," Julia said. "She already thinks I'm mad. She thinks we're all mad. Why give her an opening?"

"But—" said Sophie.

"No," said Julia.

—

SIGRID WAS DREAMING up tortures for Rose and for Meena, Rose because she was threatening to write her brother's biography and Meena because she had insisted on thrusting herself into his life and then persistently staying on in that life long after Peter had wanted her gone.

She conjured up an enormous storm of thunder and lightning, the winds so violent that huge boughs were torn down and thrown at both women as if a Greek god were hurling arrows at them. But even that was insufficient punishment for Rose and Meena, and Sigrid, staring out the window, imagined the wood behind Willow Grove rising up like an army and beginning to move on the house, and Meena, for some reason not seeing what was happening, continued to go on with her weeding, until an immense shadow fell over her, and one of the great oaks stretched out its arms and embraced Meena until the branches began cracking, and the tree bough pressed Meena harder and harder until the life in her stopped, never to start again. May all of nature rise up against her, she intoned in a deep, quavery voice, her wiggling fingers pointed in the direction of Willow Grove, the same gestures she and Peter employed when they were children and wanted to cast a spell, a long time since Sigrid had even thought of such a thing. Years had passed during which she never thought of casting spells, no longer believed in them, although she thought Peter had, right until the end. *Why is he wiggling his hands like that?* the nurse had asked her. *Is it because of the pain?* And when the nurse went out, both Sigrid and Peter burst into laughter, pain or no pain, morphine drip or no morphine drip, asking her brother, "Who are you casting a spell on now?" Peter replying, "Far but not far enough, the word for something that tries to reach heaven, but cannot go up, who has a small sword that pricks like a needle, who does not mean anyone well. Unravel the clues and the spell will be completed."

That ancient game they used to play, although what reason did they have back then to set spells on other people?

"Guess," Peter said again.

"Meena," Sigrid said.

"The spell is cast and now must bind her, nor can we revoke it," Peter said, deepening his voice, wiggling the fingers of both hands, and the two of them laughing heartily, when Meena walked in. "What is this all about?" she said. "Sigrid, I shall have to bar you. He has been ordered to rest."

"If you try to have her barred," Peter said, "I will have them bar *you*."

"Of course, he doesn't know what he's saying," Meena said imperturbably. "It's the morphine. That's what causes the trouble."

"I'll be resting day and night long enough," Peter said. "If I sleep a few less hours, nothing will change. Whoever rolled the dice is holding them down."

"You see?" Meena said. "Now he's talking nonsense about gambling!"

"Bloody stupid cow," Sigrid said. "Bloody beast."

"And I shall bar Sophie," Meena said, as if she had not heard Sigrid's insults. No, of course not; she would not deign to respond to such nonsense. "Sophie comes into this room and tells him of troubles he doesn't need to hear. She agitates him so that he cries after she leaves. She gives him poems she's written about his death and she wants him to evaluate them. It is not the *time* for it, Sigrid."

"What *time* will be the right *time*?" Peter asked his wife, still his wife despite of all his efforts.

"Well, Peter, since you ask, there may not be a right time," Meena said. "But I intend to spare you unnecessary pain."

"Then go back to Willow Grove and leave me to the mercy of the doctors," Peter said, his voice once more strong.

"You see?" said Meena to Sigrid. "You see how you have upset him?"

"Get *out*, you bloody cow," Peter said, suddenly fighting for breath, his voice gone down. Sigrid quickly occupied the molded plastic chair near the head of his bed. "Go get a cup of coffee, will you?" Sigrid asked Meena. "I shan't be staying long."

"She'll never go," Peter whispered. "She wants to be here when I close my eyes. She wants to tell the papers, 'I stayed with him until the end.' The noble wife, the woman who loved him until the end. That's what she wants people to believe. And of course, I must be here, the great man who loved *her* until the end. What a joke!"

"One sugar or two?" Meena asked.

—

PETER, WIGGLING HIS fingers. Sigrid, interfering as always. The rain threatening as it had since daybreak, but now it came down, thunder and lightning crashing and flickering, as if the world were about to lose power and go dark. And then a sudden flash of lightning, an almost unendurably loud clap, the sound of burning and sizzling, and an immense oak bough tore itself loose and smashed through two of the turret windows, missing Meena by inches. Only inches. The note Peter had written to that woman he wanted to live with once he was rid of her, of Meena: "Don't worry," Peter had written. "She's my wife in name only. Only my keeper." And in that little fishing village on the Cornwall coast, that woman beyond crying, knowing only that Peter could not return to her, would never again sit on the windowsill of the deep window, such thick stones used to build her cottage, staring out at the display outside the glass pane, rigid with grief. Her name was Clare. A grown woman, who, when she was young, asked her mother, "How must I know what is the right thing?" A good, simple girl who grew into a good woman, who understood what people intended to say without having to hear the words. And now she was left alone with no one to understand her as Peter had understood her. Meena was irrelevant to her. They all were. Whether she understood any of them or not, Meena or Sigrid, was a matter of indifference to her because the one person she had understood, and intended to continue understanding forever, had gone first, leaving her alone. She might have complained—if she had been one to complain. If she had thought to lament and grieve, what would she have said? The same thing everyone else had to say under the circumstances: "Why did you die and leave me here alone?"

It comforted her to remain still, to remain at a fixed, predictable distance from Peter. It would be so much easier for him to find her if he got loose as he had told her he would, laughing, saying, "I will come back as a spirit, an unmarried spirit," laughing, both of them, laughing, Peter long

ago having noted her indifference to what was said about his first two
wives, even incurious about what he wrote, completely heedless of things
like "reputation," "ambition," "a place in the canon." What mattered were
the tides and the height of the waves off the rocky coast that began where
the meadows ended, and whether the men who went out with their nets
would come back, and if it was true that there was no longer enough plaice
in these waters. And Peter mattered. He had fallen into her life like a bolt
of lightning, a white-hot jagged line of lightning the color of mercury in
a thermometer, splitting open a seam in the world she knew, allowing just
enough space to let him in. The wind was whipping the new trees. They
bloomed so much later here in Cornwall. They were twisted and deformed
by the endless winds blowing over, the wailing women Peter had called
those trees, and she said, "No, they are the tortured spirits of both men
and women," and he answered, "Men *and* women, Yes, why should I
assume that it is only women who are tortured?" and they smiled at one
another. And what a blessing it had been, at his age, to come across the
correct woman at last, so much time wasted with the others, thinking, If I
had met her first, we would have been completely happy from the beginning, but even then mocking that idea, as if destiny would have allowed
such a fate for him, but still: safe harbor. He had reached safe harbor at
last. And then he thought, I have to make more money, I have to make
much more money. I have to have it to get rid of Meena, and so he had
decided to break his own, self-imposed silence, and write about Evelyn
and how things had gone between them, and it would not be hard, he
thought. He had written down so much of it already, in his journal. And
Meena had begun by saying, "If you do that—" but before she could finish the sentence, Peter had said, "I am going to write this book, and if you
don't like it, you will have to leave me behind." When it came to it, when
he had to decide, to take another risk, he concluded he had take it. After
all, everyone needed his chance at happiness, and would he have another?
Not at his age. He was going to take that chance, and if Meena decided to

befriend the gas range, so be it. He was too old to care. Or too worn out, or perhaps the two amounted to the same thing.

Clare looked out at the new green leaves, chartreuse, really that was their color, and it seemed to her that in this light they were not lovely. Livid. That was the right word. Their color in this light was livid. Nature was displeased.

NINETEEN

———

THE PHONE WENT, and Sigrid picked it up. "Don't try to explain it," she shouted down the line. "Don't call me until you can tell me you've given up the whole mad enterprise!"

But it was not Rose. "Don't you think it best to learn who is at the other end before you begin shouting down the phone like a madwoman?"

Meena.

"I'll put down the phone and ring again, and we'll start over, shall I?" asked Meena. Meena the Perfect. The phone went dead. Sigrid replaced the receiver and waited to the phone to ring once more.

"Well," Sigrid said.

"Much better," Meena answered.

"What steps have you taken?" Sigrid asked. "To stop Rose's biography."

"None at all," said Meena. "I've rung you up to discuss something a bit closer to our hearts. Enough time has gone by. It's time to execute Peter's will. Unless, of course, you don't want me to, in which case I will delay."

"Of course I want you to begin," Sigrid answered. "It's time to take care of this. I don't foresee any complexities. We tot it all up and divide by four."

"That's it exactly," Meena said. "Except for a few problems."

"What problems?" Sigrid demanded. "Peter made everything perfectly plain."

"Nevertheless, there are problems," Meena said. So calm. A dangerous sign, Sigrid thought, always utterly calm before she drops her bombs. What an infuriating woman she is.

"What problems?" Sigrid repeated.

"Well, of course, the List of Wish was very short, and the will even shorter. Everyone who understood Peter will understand why. He had only hours to live, or minutes, he was on that morphine drip, he didn't know what he was saying. I thought the thing to do was keep it short. But of course we spoke of other things he didn't have time to write down."

"What *are* you driving at?" Sigrid asked.

"You know how Peter valued his privacy, how both of us did. We spoke of how best to protect mine, as well as my memory of his life, before he died. Surely that does not come as a surprise, surely it doesn't," Meena said.

"*What* are you talking about?" Sigrid demanded. "He was in his right mind until the instant he died. He wrote the will and the List of Wish hours before he died and a nurse witnessed it. I spoke to the nurse. She said his mind was clear as a bell and his hand trembled, that was the only weak thing about him. What are you trying to concoct now, Meena?"

"Why should I concoct anything?" Meena asked in her infinitely reasonable voice. "He left everything to me so that I could divide the estate into quarters, and we agreed that I would do so immediately, provided the three of you agreed to our conditions."

"Conditions? What conditions? There were *no* conditions. I have a photocopy of the documents in front of me."

"Yes, but there were verbal conditions. Of course there were. He was so weak that I hadn't the heart to make him try to write it all down, and if I had, I doubt if he would have lasted long enough to finish it."

"Verbal conditions? He was barely willing to speak to you."

"Nevertheless," Meena said. "There were."

"And what were these verbal conditions?" Sigrid said, pressing her hand against her heart, reminding herself to breathe in and out.

"As I said, they had to do with continuing our custom. Of protecting our privacy. Of protecting *my* privacy once Peter was no longer there to defend me."

"You kept after him, making him write letters to the papers, threatening to sue whenever his name was mentioned," Sigrid said. "Is that what you have in mind by 'conditions'? Am I now to carry on writing to the papers and threatening to sue if someone mentions something that displeases you? Is that what you intend?"

"No," said Meena. "Something far more simple. If each of you will sign a confidentiality clause, I will release your shares of the estate at once. Peter and I agreed on that."

Sigrid was momentarily silenced. "A confidentiality clause?" she asked finally. "Peter told you we were all to sign a confidentiality clause?"

"He most certainly did. He was thinking of all of you, not only me."

"I don't believe you."

"Then you're calling me a liar," Meena said. "No one has *ever* called me a liar."

"My brother, the one who said, 'I hope everyone is entitled to his own life,' asked you to bind the rest of us with a confidentiality clause? And what did he want us to be confidential *about*, Meena?"

"Anything to do with family matters. He didn't want them public, you see. There's nothing new in that. You yourself fought battles to keep his privacy intact."

"You realize that Peter talked rather openly to his friends in the two years before his death," Sigrid said.

"If he did, and I'm not certain he did, he would only have spoken to friends he completely trusted. There was a tacit understanding that they were not to repeat anything he said about his family life. You know that is true, Sigrid."

"It may have been true once, but I doubt very much that he continued on in that way to the end. I know at least five of his friends with whom he was very open. Friends who knew he was living apart from you, that he was no longer willing to stay at Willow Grove, and that he stayed in a stone cottage in Zennor down in Cornwall and only came back when you made a scene. Those friends were told about the fisherman's daughter, they were told that Peter said he needed money so he could buy you OFF!"

A silence fell.

"I see now why he was so intent on the confidentiality clause," Meena said smoothly. "How guilty he must have felt for breaking our rules and telling perfect strangers about our lives. Especially when he knew he intended to return to me, as he told me himself."

"Meena, I am sure he never said anything of the sort. I have the last notes he wrote to that poor woman in Cornwall. He never intended to return to you. Those notes make all that perfectly plain."

"And you would use them against me? You would create another scandal? Aren't you worn down by them?"

"You forget that the others are involved. Sophie will *never* sign a confidentiality clause, and why should she? She's as stubborn as her father or her mother. And someday she may want to try writing. Even you can understand that she can't agree to such a thing as a confidentiality clause. Peter would never have asked it of her. He told her, and I was right there, 'You're your own person now and your life belongs to you, and you must use what you find in that quarry because in the end, that quarry is all we ever have.' He would *never* have tried to hobble his own child in that way!

You *are* a liar, Meena! Don't think any of us will fall for this nonsense! I won't, and I'll see to it that the others won't."

"Then you will be breaking the terms of our agreement, and I shall have to go to court and explain that the List of Wish is completely without value. I shall know how to do it."

Sigrid had moved beyond shouting and had now gone cold with rage. "Aren't you forgetting a little something? Me, for example? Do you think I will stand by and watch you disinherit those two parentless children? What an interesting story it will make, how you borrowed money from Peter's cousin to remake your *garden,* and then you wouldn't let Evelyn's children in the house. Yes, I think the whole story of Evelyn Graves's estate and what became of it should be reopened once again, this time when I have all the files at my disposal. I lost them for a time, as you well know, but just last week I found them again. That, and a will of Peter's, made out in his own hand, signed by him and countersigned by me. It will all make such interesting reading!"

"And who will listen to you?" Meena asked. "You who have spent your life huffing and puffing against any word uttered against Peter! People will say, you know they will, 'Oh, it's only that Sigrid person, going on about her brother again. It's all she has to talk about, she has nothing more in her life.' You could bring out diagrams Peter drew up—all in his own writing—for nuclear devices meant to level Buckingham Palace, and no one would pay the slightest attention. You are the boy who cried wolf once too often, Sigrid, surely you can see that. People will speak openly of your monstrous passion for your brother, while before they kept silent. They kept quiet out of respect for Peter. Out of sympathy for me. You were the gate, the way in to Peter. People had to respect you, but only while he lived. If they wanted access to Peter, they had to put up with you. But all that is over. Now *I* am the gate to Peter! I am the one people write to, asking permission to quote from his writings or to see his private papers. I think it would be best, Sigrid, if you went along with me. It would be for the best. You are not growing younger, you know."

"Not growing younger, no," Sigrid said, breaking the silence that had fallen. "But wiser. I was born wiser than you are now. And even if everything you say of me is true, I will find a way around it. You must know that, Meena. You have seen me pull a rabbit out of a hat so many times. I can still do it. I know how to work through others as well as anyone on this earth and I know people who are even more clever than I am. I am more than the boy who cried wolf, Meena. I *am* the wolf! Do you really want to tangle with me?"

"I am the widow. I am the one people will pity. Whereas there is an army of people resentful of you because of how you bullied them."

"To protect *you*. And Peter. Don't forget that," Sigrid answered.

"An army of people, all waiting for a chance to come at you."

"All waiting to read the piece Peter wrote about your love for your pet boar," Sigrid said. "An extraordinary piece of work. Someone said that the woman pictured in that piece of Peter's put Medea in the shade. I won't need to say a word, not about that. I have my own hooks and my lures, and you, Meena, are the bait. Don't think I'll hesitate to use them. Don't think I'll forget Peter's charging me to look after the children. Surely you know me well enough to know what will be coming. And my hand won't be seen in any of it. It will be Peter's hand, reaching out from the grave. He's rung people up since you buried him, you know," Sigrid went on, dropping her voice. "He rang up Julia, pretending he was calling about tiles."

"Calling about ties?" Meena said incredulously.

"*Tiles*, not ties," Sigrid said. "I gather they had a quite enjoyable conversation."

"You are mad," Meena said. She had gone cold and her hands trembled.

"*I* wasn't the one who had the conversation. Sophie told me about it. She heard him herself. She was very, very put out because he hadn't asked to speak to her. I very much doubt that he'll want to ring you up, Meena. I think he said something about pounding and banging, and what you ought to do if you hear it. It will be the sound of his shoes hitting the roof of his coffin. When I heard that, my blood ran cold. But you know better than to believe in such nonsense. Still, there are so many credulous people! Imagine what they would make of a story like that showing up in the *News of the World*. I don't suppose you get that paper, do you, Meena? Although, as I remember, it's very popular in Northumberland. But never mind. The *News of the World* is the last thing you need to worry yourself about. When will you be releasing my share of the estate, then, Meena?"

I cannot frighten her, Meena thought. No one can frighten her. She knows the worst that can happen. The worst that can happen is that someone will kill her, and she's said often enough that she's lived too long. Does she really have manuscripts Peter wrote about her, about her marriage to Peter, hidden away somewhere? It's just the sort of thing the two of them would have been up to, Sigrid and Peter. Everyone taking her as so much worse than she was, everyone taking Peter as so much better than he had any right to pretend he was. No, Sigrid is not the one to attack, certainly not directly. The children cannot take on legal fees, not yet, not until they come into their share of the estate, and I can afford to take my case to lawyers and delay the children receiving so much as a pound.

"After I deduct the legal expenses and settle the will, you will be the first to receive your share," Meena said.

"Yes," said Sigrid, drawing out the word. "How glad I am to hear it. But don't forget the other two. Peter's two children. You remember their names, do you?"

"It would be better for you if you did not threaten me or pressure me further," Meena said. There was her true voice, naked as steel and colder than ice.

Oh, yes, Sigrid thought. I will be very quiet until she lets go of the money.

All the same, it had come as a great shock to Sigrid to realize that Meena had never intended to abide by Peter's wishes, never had any intention of distributing the funds of the estate as he wished it, despite his very clear wishes. We'll see about that, she thought. And just when she had thought it was over, she would have to drag herself into armor again. Was there no one on this earth to pity her? Activity keeps you alive, Peter said. Had said. But Peter chose to delegate those activities to her. He would want her to take over now. And so it was beginning again. I think, Sigrid told herself, I shall sleep all day and let the answer phone cope with messages. No wonder she never opened the curtains of her bedroom. If anyone ever needed a cave, I do, Sigrid thought, sighing, sliding beneath the duvet, waiting for one of the cats to settle itself on her hip.

TWENTY

———

CLARE HAD PUT the kettle on. In a minute, she would have a cup of tea and could settle herself in her chair, in Crows' Nest, where she had lived all her life. She now had fifty thousand pounds in the bank, because, as Peter had insisted, he wanted her to be free of money worries, never to find herself reduced to relying on the dole. He had arranged it carefully, gone in, spoken to the local banker, brought letters of credit, written up a kind of will attesting to the fact that the money was irrevocably hers, taken a lawyer in hand to be certain no one could challenge this "gift" and no one could accuse her of theft or forgery, taking it very seriously except for the moments when he burst out laughing, saying this was the first time in his life, his entire life, when he had actually planned ahead, done the prac-

tical thing. "And of course there will be interest," the banker had told Peter
and Clare. "This is an interest-bearing account and you need not move
any of it into a personal checking account unless you see the need to do
so, and even then, it is an *interest-bearing* checking account. Mr. Crane is
distinguished for his financial acumen, and I have gone to him as you
wished, and asked him if he would look after Mrs. Tartikoff's finances. He
will do a good job, and we will advise him of any information along those
lines that he does not already have. Are there any questions?" the banker
asked, leaning forward.

What a shiny bald head he has, thought Peter, who had already grown
bored with all this. They say bald men are more potent than the men with
lions' manes who keep their hair into the grave. He wondered if it was true.

"Don't you think," Clare was asking the banker, Mr. Goodfellow, a
name, she thought, more appropriate for a funeral director, "the amount
is rather large?"

"When the tax man comes to call, they will certainly have questions,
but," Mr. Goodfellow said, "Mr. Grovesnor has seen to that. He has put
away two years' worth of taxes, although we doubt that you will need to
touch that money. We've arranged an annual stipend to keep you far from
the long arm of the tax man."

"That's a great relief," Peter said confidently. "Isn't it, Clare?"

"It is," Clare said, a little faintly.

"You're not accepting this money against your will, are you?" Mr.
Goodfellow asked in a jocular tone.

"Oh, no," Clare said. "I trust Peter in everything."

"Then I believe we're finished for the time being," Mr. Goodfellow said,
"although you're to call at any time you require advice and everyone here
will assist you, and it goes without saying that there will be no charge for
our services. You understand all that, Mrs. Tartikoff?" he asked her. "No
questions at all?"

"None," Clare said.

"And, of course, there is the small sum Mr. Grovesnor set aside for medical emergencies. That you cannot touch. We can release those sums only upon the authority of a medical man. But you look like a healthy woman, Mrs. Tartikoff. I knew your father. Is he still alive?"

"Both of my parents were, until the storm last April when the cliff gave way."

"So had it not been for fate, they would have gone on to their centenaries," he said. "As will you, I'm sure, Mrs. Tartikoff."

"Can we go?" Peter said, standing up abruptly.

"Of course, of course," said the banker.

"It's just that Mrs. Tartikoff is not accustomed to discussing finances and I don't want her overburdened, you see," Peter said.

"I see, of course I see," said the banker. "And Mrs. Tartikoff understands that the funds are available from this moment forward. She does not need to wait until—"

"She doesn't need to wait until she sees the obituary," Peter said.

"Yes. Quite."

It was, Clare thought, a beautiful, wood-paneled room, the dark wood gleaming, a beautiful plastered ceiling, a very high room, and chandeliers suspended above each end of the long table, reflecting themselves in the table surface.

"It's a beautiful room," Clare said, dazed.

"Yes, isn't it?" the banker replied. "The walls have heard a good many things in here, I dare say."

"If walls could talk," Clare said, thinking over that saying. It was a new thought, one she had never before contemplated.

"Well," said Peter, who shook hands with Mr. Goodfellow, who produced a copy of Peter's last book out of the air, saying, "If I may," proffering his beautiful Mont Blanc pen, the same pen as Peter's. Peter hesitated a moment, then sat back down and signed the book.

"It's very good of you," Mr. Goodfellow said, a little more ardently than strictly necessary, Peter thought. He put his arm around Clare and steered her out of the room.

Outside, it was a beautiful summer day, a surprisingly cool wind blow-ing in over the sea toward the cliffs. "What do you want to do now?"

"Are you peckish?" she asked Peter.

"No," he said.

"Then you want to go back to the tin mines," Clare said. "Don't you?"

"Yes."

"A woman came here almost a decade ago, and she was full of stories about the tin mines, and one afternoon she decided to climb one of the hills, and you can imagine what happened. She was never seen again. She was warned. My mother herself warned her. She is in there somewhere, inside one of those vertical shafts."

"So there she stands, upright for all eternity," Peter said.

"At attention, as it were," Clare said.

"And if someone were to find her, could they bring her out?"

"These are different times," Clare said. "They don't send children down into the shafts anymore. I doubt if anyone here would risk his own child to find an American woman who managed to disappear into a mine shaft. And she *had* been warned. Local people usually skip giving warnings. We don't need tourists, is what they think. So if someone disappears into a hole in the ground, they think, That's just as well. All these hills, riddled with shafts from the old mines. You don't see them before you come upon them, that's the trouble. That scrubby undergrowth is very dense. Everyone who lives here knows better than to go walking on those hills. Anyone who decides to go all the same takes a long, stout stick, and they give a good poke at the earth before they take their next step, and even then some of them dis-appear without warning."

"And if a local disappears?" Peter asked. "Do they search then?"

"Oh, they make a show of it. An hour or two around the base of the hill, where they know the location of the shafts, and then back to the pub for the rest of the day. What they think is, a local man, if he goes for a walk on one of those hills and does not come back, well, he wanted to disappear, didn't he? It's not as if he didn't know what he was doing. Quite an acceptable way to do yourself in, all things considered. People say, 'He must have slipped. He must have come across a place on the hill where the shafts were too close together; he wasn't prepared.' No one worries about a local man or woman starving to death in one of those shafts. They're very deep. Whoever fell in would certainly be knocked out, and he'd be so deep down there'd be no animals to go down after him, so, really, it's quite an acceptable cemetery. And it saves a funeral and all the expenses. You know, there are still families here who put their dead out to sea in skiffs on stormy nights and call that a funeral. Otherwise, the costs would break them."

"I think that's rubbish," Peter said. "That's the stuff of old romance novels."

"Well, then, my grandmother went to sea in a romance novel," Clare said.

"I would love to see Meena pushed out to sea," Peter said.

"Everyone pushes out soon enough," Clare said.

"Can you take us up to the top of that hill?" Peter asked her. "Do you know the ground well enough?"

"Oh, yes," Clare said. "You know what they call it here. 'The honeycomb of death.'"

They began their careful climbing.

"It's safe right here," Clare said, indicating a log resting on the ground. "There are no oaks up here. Someone brought this log all the way up."

"Better than contemplating a skull," Peter said, sitting on the log. "'They carve their words in stone,'" he said, quoting.

"What, love?" Clare asked.

"Another line that came into my head and flew out again," Peter said. "As in, 'I am Ozymandias, King of Kings.'"

"Oh, I know that one," Clare said. "When we get back, will you look that up for me?"

He would look it up, read it out, pretend he didn't know it well enough to recite it aloud without a book open in his hand. Why make her feel small over nothing?

"Take me out on the water," he said suddenly. "On a stormy day."

"*Not* on a stormy day," Clare said.

"Oh, so you go against my wishes," he said, and she laughed.

"But the light is going, you see it is, and going down this hill in the gloom, well, even for me, it's a little daunting."

He agreed that they would go back.

"Just one stormy day?" he asked her.

"Forget it," she said.

He laughed out loud. How American she just sounded! "You watch too much television," he said.

"I keep the TV on in my study," she said. "And the experts say that if you watch four hours in front of the telly, every day, day in and day out, you develop very strong muscles of the eyes."

"The things you come out with," Peter said.

"But doesn't it ring true?" Clare asked, and laughing and chattering, they made the rest of their way down.

Now, sitting in her chair in the topmost room, Clare thought, Perhaps it would have been best, taking him out to sea on a stormy day. He had no love of hospitals, none of nurses, their blank white uniforms like staring white pages, like priestesses of writer's block; he had called them that. She had needed *that* explained. She had asked, "And does it make that much difference if you don't write?"

"Not don't write," he said, "*can't* write. Yes, it makes all the difference."

"Why does it?" she asked. "Because of the way the soul is attached to the body," he said. "By a very thin thread, much flimsier than sewing thread, and if you let it out too long, if you don't use it up, if you don't keep it close to you, it snaps, and then what do you do? Without your soul? That," he said, "is writer's block, or the consequences of it, anyway. Do you see?" She nodded, although she did not see, but she saw no reason to have him explain it again, not when he got so tired in those days.

There were still two fingers of tea in the cup. The tea had gone cold, but she sipped it slowly all the same. "I'll warm up the tea, shall I?" she would say to Peter in those days, not really so long ago at all, but he always said, "No, don't get up. Liquid is what we need, not something hot or cold. Sit still! Leave the tea things in the sink! If you could imagine how much I like to see tea things sitting in the sink, not having them rushed out from under your nose and washed before you'd finished!" So she left the clutter, waited until he fell asleep to clean things up, and often fell asleep herself, and the sink was full in the morning, grease caked on the dishes, a brown ring beginning to form inside the teacups. "Beautiful, uncleaned things!" he exclaimed, sometimes saying, "I'll clear off," as if washing dishes were something he had wanted to do for years and years, but an evil witch had prevented him.

So now there was nothing to do but stare out of the window and remember. He would not come again. People would not ring up and speak of him. Instead, she sat still, taking note of how a person's, a life's, image faded. Already she could not summon up his voice, although she could remember its effects, the warmth of that voice, like drinking wine for the first time, everything warm inside, the promise of laughter regardless of what he chose to speak about, the confidingness of that voice, telling you things he had never told anyone before, how privileged you felt to be told these secret things, even if they were of no consequence, but they were of great import because those words had been his, spoken by him, and she took up each word as a crow would take up a glistening thing it took to its nest and cherished, even defended. But the voice was going, there was no doubt about it. She could not summon it up.

And soon the image of his face would go. She could delay that little death, continue to look at his picture, smiling into the sun, his eyes squinting, a shock of hair falling into his eyes, the eyes of a young man, not a man approaching his seventies, that rugged face, the White Cliffs of Dover, she always thought of that when she looked closely at his face, until one day she told him her secret name for his face, and he laughed, and then suddenly grew serious, saying, "I wish I were as impervious as those stones, I wish I had a chance of lasting that long." But then they started up laughing again, at anything, a black ant climbing the white wall and disappearing when there appeared to be no crack into which it could vanish, a spiderweb without its spider: everything could be woven into a story, and usually it was, and how she had loved those stories, no one had ever told her stories. Well, there was Postman Pat, such things, but her parents were not ones to dream up stories. They would peer into the mists when the wind howled and you couldn't see past your own windowpane, and it always seemed to her that they were caught up in stories of their own, stories that had already happened and whose plots they knew well, whose endings they knew well, stories they would just as soon forget, as people who are haunted by ghosts learn to put up with them after vain attempts to reason with them. The mists that swirled around the Cornwall coast in the winter, that endless howling, that was story enough for anyone, or so she had thought.

But his body. She could summon up his body without hesitation, the feel of it, the particular way he slept on his side, the half sentences he uttered in his sleep, never enough for her to work out the rest of what he was saying, the sweetness of those words, rising up from the cauldron of his being, how she would have liked to know what he was saying. She never asked, not ever, when he opened his eyes. And the way his frame had emerged as the flesh grew thin, as the illness ate at him, how young he suddenly looked, as if he had never lived through those years he so often told her he regretted, years he ought to have lived differently. "Well, it's too late, of course it's too late," always ending by saying, "But of course I have *you*." Odd that she could remember the timbre of those words and no others. Probably those words came to her in her sleep. And now she was alone with her regrets, wishing she had met him years and years earlier. She might have stopped some of the trouble he had found himself in again and again, but maybe not. She would have happily suffered through whatever trouble he had brought her. Or so she wanted to believe.

The phone went, and it startled her. Very few people called her. She was a solitary person, Peter had said that many times, and it was true. She was not unhappy if no one called for weeks at a time. She picked up the phone hesitantly. Who could it be? "Hello?" she said tentatively.

"Are you busy?" asked a female voice. "Sleeping?"

"No, I was drinking my tea," Clare said, mystified. Someone wanting to sell something, no doubt.

"I haven't called before," the voice said. "It's taken me this long to get your number from Sigrid."

Could it be Meena? What reason would Meena have to ring her up, now that everything was over and done? Why would she call? Could Meena be foolish enough to expect comfort from her?

"Oh, I'm terribly sorry," said the voice. "I'm Sophie. Peter's daughter."

"Sophie."

"Yes, Sophie, his daughter. Did he ever mention me to you?"

"So many times, I feel as if I know you."

"I feel the same," Sophie said.

"Yes," said Clare. "Of course."

"And you are there alone? In Crows' Nest?"

"Yes. Alone," said Clare.

"You should have some company," Sophie said. "He would have wanted you to have someone with you."

"I think he knew I could manage," Clare said.

"But still!" Sophie said.

"Yes. But still," Clare agreed.

"I should like to come and visit you."

"It's a long journey," Clare said.

"I have a car and I drive far too fast. I can be there quite quickly."

"I see," Clare answered.

"The trees seem to be singing so loudly just now. It's the wind, I suppose. I listen for it, but now that the branches are down, I rarely look at them."

"Yes," Clare said. "It's a loss."

At that, Sophie began to cry.

"Oh, please don't cry," Clare said. "Come and see me. If you must cry, we can cry together instead of crying alone."

There was a long silence. "Hello?" Clare said.

"You are just as Daddy said you were," Sophie said.

"Well," said Clare.

"Something very strange happened a few days ago, and I would tell you, but I'm afraid you would be distressed. You must decide if you want to hear the story."

A story! How long it had been since she had heard a story! She thought all stories had come to an end.

"I would like to know," Clare said.

"A man rang up here and asked to speak to Julia, a friend of the family's. It was Daddy's voice. We were both sure of it. He said that his name was Nigel and that he sold tiles."

"Ties?"

"*Tiles*," Sophie said irritably. "Sigrid thought I had said ties as well. I think Meena thought Sigrid was talking about ties. But he wanted to stay on the line with Julia. He wanted to know what the weather was, and what she was doing, and he was very, very amused when Julia, that was the woman he had called, said that his voice sounded just like my father's."

"I see," Clare said.

"That's the whole story," Sophie said.

"And has this man called anyone else? Speaking of tiles or of any other thing?"

"No," Sophie said. "But I have gone on hoping."

"You want to hear that voice once more?"

"Yes," Sophie said.

"I would give anything, anything!" Clare said.

"Would you?"

"Anything," Clare said again.

"Can I come and see you? Is there a time when you're free?"

"I'm always free," Clare said. "Come whenever you like. The door is always left open here. If I'm not in the house, go down to the pub at Zennor. Someone will have seen me and will tell you where I am. People keep track of one another here by their cars. Everyone knows my car, a rusty Morris estate wagon with wooden strips. Or you can go in and wait for me to come back. I'm never gone for long."

Clare could hear Sophie crying again.

"Why would I not want to see you?" Clare asked. "Peter's daughter. Of course I want to see you. Of course it would be no trouble. You must come. What a blessing it would be."

"Oh, I will come," Sophie said. "I will be there sooner than you want me."

"I will be waiting. Do you eat much?"

"Yes!"

"Are you a vegetarian, like the new generation?" Clare asked.

"No."

"Well, then, when you come, we shall shop at Tesco and I shall lay on a feast. You will definitely come?"

"Oh, yes," said Sophie.

"And will you bring others?"

"No. If you don't object, I would like to come alone."

"I had hoped for that," Clare said.

"You must stay well," Sophie said.

"Of course. And so must you."

The wind had begun howling around Crow's Nest. Both of them could hear it plainly.

"Goodnight, Sophie," Clare said softly.

"Goodnight, Clare," Sophie said.

Clare put the phone down. She thought, She used my name. This made her smile. She picked up her cup and saucer, took them to the sink, turned on the tap, was about to begin washing them when she thought better of it, and left them in the sink unwashed.

TWENTY-ONE

———

SIGRID WAS ENJOYING the absolute blackness of her bedroom. The doorbell had rung early that morning, unforgivable, but it was the package she had been waiting for: room-darkening blinds, and she put them up at once. Not one splinter of light could enter into her bedroom from the glary outside world. She liked this complete blackout. It reminded her of the Second World War and school drills, all of them putting on gas masks while they sat in shelters until the all-clear sounded. A terrible war had been raging, and yet existence had seemed a great deal simpler to her then. Life would be simple once more, Sigrid thought, if she refused to leave this blacked-out room. What had Peter meant to her back then? Her brother, *a* brother, someone to protect, someone who neglected to do his homework because he was outside, roaming and watching birds and whatever animals he could discover. *She* had been the better student then. She had always been the better student. But her superiority was wiped out when he began to write. Talent counted far more than intelligence, she learned that soon enough. Only Julia had tried to persuade her that she, too, had talent and should put it to use. She cited Sigrid's letters, insisting they were masterpieces in their own right. But there was a question of intention, of determination, and Sigrid had never intended to make herself known through her talent; she hadn't had the confidence for it, the bravery, and it was a relief to her when she discovered that her brother had more than enough to set his course for fame. She would go along as his first mate. But if he had not been there, if Peter had not struck out on his own, would she, in time, have clamped down and set herself the same course? There were times when she thought she would have, had she not been preempted, but that was the wrong word—she had not been preempted—she had been relieved of her duty.

"Throughout time," Julia had said more than once, "women have lived through their men, made that decision to live through them," a statement which never failed to throw Sigrid into a rage. *Everyone* knew Sigrid to be an untamable force of nature, everyone but Julia, who insisted that she, Sigrid, was like the good woman behind the great man, and what a pity that was, when she could just as easily have been the great woman who stood alone needing no one behind her to give her strength. If there was anything in Julia's estimation of her, then Sigrid had been undone by laziness. What more did she require than a good book and a quiet room? She was the person everyone called, asking, Have you read this one? Have you read that one? What do you think of it? When Peter stayed in the little bedroom at the top of her house, he took home the books she had just read. Laziness, as Sigrid repeatedly told Julia, did not lead to greatness, nor even to mediocrity. Mediocrity, Sigrid insisted, was probably harder to achieve than greatness, just as, so Sigrid believed, it was harder to write a bad book than a good book. A good book cooperated with you, whereas a bad book was difficult from the beginning, required changes in points of view, endless rewritings of intractable passages, characters that insisted on lying about in corridors like dead bodies instead of moving from room to room. A bad novel was as hard to move as a truck that needed pushing uphill, whereas, as Julia well knew, a good book drove over mountains taking the driver with it. Sigrid was a lazy woman who liked to shop, to frequent good restaurants, to discuss events with intelligent people, to play bridge, to decorate the rooms of her house, and very occasionally, to vacuum. When it became necessary, when not vacuuming became something of a disgrace. Her mother, pouring scalding water over the doorstep: she had inherited none of that. Meena was such a woman, and Peter had hated her for it. "*A kind of madness,*" he insisted, "*a storm of cleanliness, a disease in its own right.*" But he was happy enough if someone dropped by and found the house spotless, although it was also true that if someone had happened by Willow Grove and then had to climb in through the rolls of dust, he wouldn't have minded.

TWENTY-TWO

———

IT IS A POOR idea to settle on a favorite bench at the top of Parliament Hill, Julia thought, if only because there will be so much competition for it. Her favorite was right at the very top of Parliament Hill, the highest spot in London, and from her bench she could see right across London and beyond to hills that were, from that distance, only a wash of ink indicating their existence. From there, on a clear day, when the sun was just beginning to set, the city appeared immaculate, its little mazes set out scrupulously and shining, not a speck of clutter anywhere. How distance cleans things up, Julia thought. Straight ahead were the red-tiled roofs of Highgate, and to her right, the city center itself.

Her bench was in the middle of the kite-flying arena. Every day, year in and year out, people came with their kites and sent them flying. Some of them came from generations of kite-flying families. It was impossible to predict when the most extravagant kites would be brought out and begin flying overhead. One was flying now, a biplane trailing long tails of butterflies like colored smoke, so that the kite looked like a plane that had been hit by a gunner in another fighter plane.

The sight of that plane made her uneasy. I should get up and change my seat, Julia thought, but she stubbornly stayed where she was. It was going to swoop down and hit her, she was sure of that. She continued to watch the roofs of Highgate, but kept an eye out for the kite's progress. A large kite could do serious damage, she knew that, but all the same, she wanted to see if the kite would hit her, as she sensed it would, and she saw the fighter begin its precipitous fall, straight toward her, as if it were obeying her summons. It struck her on the left side of the head just above her ear. Immediately the kite fliers began running toward her, Papa Kite, Baby Kite, Sister Kite, and Brother Kite. "Are you hurt?" asked the father. "There's a little bleeding there. Laura, take out a tissue and give it to the woman, that's a good girl."

The child solemnly unwrapped a sheet of paper and took out a few tissues kept enclosed in it. She handed them to Julia. "Oh, thank you," Julia said, thinking that her head, when it began to hurt, would really do a good job of it. "No, no, I'm fine, *fine,*" she insisted to the father. "People who will sit on these benches must expect a good knock on the head sooner or later."

"They've been trying to ban kite flying up here," the man said. "I'm afraid they'll succeed. There's some kind of neighborhood watch."

"Not one I intend to inform," Julia assured him.

"That's good of you," he said.

"I enjoy watching the kites."

"I see," the man said, beginning to smile. "You should be safe now, though, at least for a time. We're going back. Homework, you see."

"Please don't worry about me," she said, her head beginning to throb. "No damage done here."

The family and its kite departed.

I have this *thing,* Julia admitted to herself, and I hate to let anyone know. It sounds so ridiculous. If you were to tell someone, I saw a particular kite and I knew it was going to strike me, nine times out of ten the person listening would answer by saying, "If you stand under kites long enough, it's bound to happen. It's a matter of statistics. It's almost bound to happen." But how to explain the certainty she'd had that *this* particular kite was going to hit her on the head? She had never before looked at a kite, sure it was going to strike her. There was no way to explain how she had known. Peter would have understood because he believed in all those sorts of odd things, but Julia would not have told him about this incident. He believed in premonitions, extrasensory perception, animals conveying messages to humans who were receptive to what they had to say, but he himself did not experience such events or such foreknowledge. He must have waited all his life to experience such a moment. Probably he was still waiting even when he knew he was about to go under and die, because he had been told so often that before your own death you saw and heard differently, saw strange things at the very moment of your death. Still, she doubted if Peter had seen anything more than a dimming, or perhaps a flaring up of what appeared to be a presence, a phosphorescence, that lightness at the end of the tunnel reported by so many, when all synapses fired at once. That, she thought, was what the dying saw, nothing more. Why should a dying person suddenly develop a special ability, second sight, whatever it was, when according to Julia, everyone was better off without it?

One thundery afternoon in the spring, before Julia had finally been banned from Willow Grove, she and Peter were waiting for Sigrid to arrive. They knew they might be waiting for hours. Sigrid was known for her inability to appear at the agreed-upon time. People who knew her well would only meet her at restaurants, so that if they were tired and hungry they could sit down, and if worse came to worst, they could order and begin their meal alone. "You know," Peter said that day, "in Scandinavian countries, when someone was lost, a person would send a bird, usually a raven, to search for the lost person, and whatever the bird saw, the person would also see it."

"Hmmph," Julia said. She was tired and hungry, annoyed by waiting, once more, for Sigrid.

"Do you think there's anything to it?" Peter asked.

"You do," Julia answered.

"Yes. I do," he said.

"Do you know any ravens?" Julia asked.

"If we did, if we knew how to speak to them, I'm sure a raven could find Sigrid."

"I'm sure the *police* could find her. All they'd have to do was look for a woman who couldn't avoid semi-articulated lorries."

"So you don't believe in the ravens?"

"I don't have an opinion one way or the other."

"At least you're not dismissing it out of hand," Peter said.

The next summer, Julia's dog came back from the veterinary clinic. Smoky was lethargic and disconsolate. "What's wrong with you?" she asked the dog. Then she thought of the Scandinavian ravens. "What happened to you?" she asked the dog. The dog's ears perked up. "All right, let's see," Julia told her. She pressed her head against the dog's muzzle, and immediately her own living room disappeared, and she was seeing something else, something she could make no sense of until she understood that she was seeing everything from an unusual perspective—as if she were no taller than her dog. From that vantage, she saw cages whose roofs were cut off, metal doors and walls that did not reach the top. Farther down the hall was another, smaller cage, and in it was her black and white cat, Alfred. "I thought you were in the same cage together," Julia said. "The vet said he'd put you in together." Smoky whimpered. "It's all right, it's all right," she told the dog. Alfred was still at the veterinarian's. For all the dog knew, the cat was never coming back. Peter's ravens. The dog was speaking to her as Peter believed ravens could speak. Against common sense, she called the vet's office. "This is Julia Ouslander," she said. "You had my dog in for a few days. My cat, Alfred, is still there. Can you tell me if they were kept in the same cage?"

"Oh, no," said the attendant. "We would never allow that. Our insurance wouldn't permit it."

"I see," said Julia. "Please ask the doctor to call me as soon as he can."

They had been separated. "Alfred is coming back in the morning," Julia told the dog. Then she put her head against the dog's muzzle once more, but this time no strange scene rose up in front of her. Smoky jumped down from the couch and walked into the kitchen. *Food*. Then it might be true. Ravens could be sent to look for people in a white, snowy landscape other people could not reach. Ravens, who could fly above everything, fly quickly, seeing everything, could lend their eyes to people. After all, she had just borrowed her dog's eyes.

I ought to tell Peter about this, she had thought, but she decided against it. There was already enough gossip about Peter's belief in the occult, in his practice of the I-Ching, his belief in messages from the Ouija board which people thought Peter had used to manipulate the very impressionable Evelyn. "He drove Evelyn to it, him with his black spells," a woman from the churchyard told everyone who would listen. Every Sunday, the woman came to church, and when the sermon was over and people began filing out, she began to talk about Evelyn, done, if not to death, to madness, by Peter's black masses. All that nonsense would have dispersed like dust if Peter hadn't believed that he had, in fact, driven Evelyn into a deeper kind of madness than the insanity caused by the swirling furies with which she habitually lived. It was futile to tell him, "Stop saying, 'It was my fault, I drove her to it. I didn't know she was so—so—breakable,'" and when enough time went by, and he stopped publicly blaming himself, it was too late. The damage was done. "And the irony of it was," Peter said, "I myself saw nothing, heard nothing, but it was Evelyn who had the gift."

"For bloody sake, don't repeat *that*!" Sigrid said. "'He's trying to wiggle out of what he did'; that's what everyone will say."

"Peter, don't say *anything*," Julia said. "Wait until things die down."

"They've died down," he said grimly.

And then, suddenly, there was Meena, always in the middle of everything and anything, admonishing, banning anything further, announcing, "We're not speaking of *that* again."

Too late, always too late, as Sophie said. The same as in that fairy tale, the one about the man sworn to secrecy, but his secret was so hard to keep, he told the waters of the creek, and wherever the creek's water ran, it told everyone, which is why we now speak of babbling brooks. What fairy tale was that? Sophie asked Sigrid, who said, "Ask your father. He remembers that sort of thing."

What story was it? Julia asked herself now. Was it Midas? Who was it? It's not that secrets won't remain hidden. It's that no one can keep them.

TWENTY-THREE

———

ROSE SHOVED A stack of magazines from the couch onto the floor. What was it that made Peter so fatal to women? Of course, she had felt that power herself, had given herself over to it quite shamelessly that summer when they both taught a workshop in Northumberland. When he spoke to her, she laughed like a young girl, at everything. I imagine, Rose thought, looking back, I made quite a cake of myself. Why hadn't Robert been there? Oh, yes, it was pleurisy, wasn't it? But he said, "Go on, Rose. We need the money." Thrusting her out into the cold, as she thought of it then. "I shall be quite miserable there," she said, but Robert answered, "The *money*, Rose, we need the money." And whose fault was that? Not hers, the faithful wife.

Was there ever a wife more faithful than she'd been? It was *his* fault. He was the philandering husband who'd somehow lost his pension, or was about to lose it, she wasn't sure, not anymore, of the timing. So she went alone.

And every woman was in love with Peter by the third day, if indeed it had taken that long. An old woman who walked with a stick mooned over Peter. The young girls jumped out of their vases like cut flowers suddenly animated. Everyone hung on his words. She had been no better. And now he was cold and quiet and she was writing his biography. Right, she told herself, I will get to the bottom of it. It can't simply have been sex. There were other men who were as beautiful and at least as sexy.

Probably Julia had some idea. She always had ideas. Rose had called her and asked her. What was it, that hold he had over women? And Julia said, "Not just women."

"Then what was it?" Rose asked again, and all Julia said was, "Make me a child again, just for one night."

"You have to explain that," Rose said. "You can't just leave it like that."

"It's a clue," Julia said.

"But *to what*?" Rose asked, her voice rising.

"I wish I knew," Julia said.

"You are envious. You are envious because I am writing Peter's biography and you are not," she said.

"What an extraordinary approach, insulting me so I'll give you more information," Julia said. "Really, Rose, quite extraordinary."

"You're mocking Robert!" Rose exclaimed.

"Am I? I suppose I am. But I do have to go now," Julia said, and she rang off, leaving Rose infuriated, thinking, That enraging woman. What, really, does she know? She's not, after all, the sphinx. But Rose could not give it up. She believed that Julia did know the answer to riddles, at least this particular one. About Peter. "It is *unearthly*," Penelope once said, "the way Julia can see into Peter. When she doesn't really care. I mean, of course she cares, but not in the way women usually do."

Rose had to learn what Julia knew. As Robert used to say, "Rose could wear down a stone." I will not be defeated, Rose told herself. Robert is dead and I see no reason why I should ever be defeated again. She went into the bathroom and carefully combed her hair so that the grey roots did not show. She should have made an appointment at Shapes and had it done weeks ago, but really, once it was properly combed, the roots were almost invisible. Satisfied with herself, Rose sat down at her desk. She had not thought to comb the back of her head, because she could not see it, and would have been shocked to see how her hair parted naturally down the middle, and how clearly the white stripe of undyed hair, like a skunk's, was so plainly displayed. But such weaknesses endeared Rose to people, although Rose herself would not have been happy to know of it.

—

"WHAT DID YOU wish for?" Peter asked.

"I know what it is," Julia told Peter. "It's clear, to me."

"Then tell me," he said.

"And break the spell?" she said, laughing. "You have to guess."

"You won't tell me? Not even me?"

"Not even you," she said.

"Will you tell Sigrid, then?"

"Not Sigrid, either."

"Sophie, then?"

"Someday. Probably. She may need to know someday."

"I see," Peter said.

"Do you?" Julia asked.

"Not really. Unless she thinks I dabbled in the black arts. You wouldn't like her thinking that."

"I wouldn't," said Julia, who refused to say another word.

"Tell!" he said, diving at her, but in those days, Julia was fast on her feet and was out of the room before he could catch hold of her.

—

"I'M GOING TO see Clare," Sophie told Julia. "You think that's wrong, I know, but I want to know her."

"Why would I think that's wrong?" Julia asked.

"Well, a betrayal of Meena," Sophie said.

"You want to talk to Clare because she was the last person to really know Peter. Why shouldn't you go speak to her? He didn't let anyone else come close to him those last few years."

"What I want to know," Sophie said, "is the answer to the question that Rose asked you. Where did Daddy's power come from? I felt it, but he was my father. Of course I felt it. But everyone else! Where did it come from? Sigrid says it was magic. Why don't I have it?"

"You have enough magic," Julia said.

"But not the kind my father did, not his power!"

"I think it was a small enough gift, but enough. It was enough," Julia said, tugging her comb through her curly hair. "He turned you back into a child. Something about the way he stared at you, as if he'd forgotten there was anyone else in the world. Well, everyone mentions that. Though that wasn't the important thing. What was important was how safe he made you feel. And that laughter of his, barely hidden, no matter what you were talking about, so you didn't carry on feeling serious for very long. And that voice, completely soothing, as if you'd known it once before, nothing to do with his accent, or its pitch, not anything like that, but its essence of soothingness, if there's such a phrase for it. A mischievousness, completely incorrigible, and a way of drawing you into it, as if the two of you were children together, but he was still the safe and protecting one; he was both things at once, the parent and the child. Oh, I don't know, but that's what it was like!" Julia said, throwing her comb down. "I'm sorry," she said. "I miss him. But you know," she went on after a pause, "he could be such a nuisance! When he was in a bad mood, I mean. You'd go into a restaurant and all of a sudden there was nothing on the menu he wanted to eat, and that way he had of staring and staring at the menu, until you wanted to pick up your menu and swat him with it. And those fits from out of the blue when he was sure he was dying of something like a fatal hangnail and whatever you said made it worse. I used to tell Sigrid that he would have been absolutely fine if he'd married a real harridan, and if he didn't get home in time for dinner, she would have broken a plate over his head. I believe that, you know.

"Everyone was too nice to him. A good smack on the head with a broom handle, and he'd have known what he could get away with and what he couldn't. But as it was, he didn't know. He didn't know where the boundaries were; all the rest of us know them only too well, but he didn't, so he kept testing, trying to find them out. And that way lay trouble. His life would have been happier, maybe *happy*, if he'd had a wife who met him at the door with a plate full of cold chops and green peas and smashed it down on his head. Robert needed the same kind of wife. Rose married the same kind of man as your father, except, of course, he was missing what Sigrid calls the magic, or what I call the charm, or what anyone would call attractiveness."

"You wanted to hit him over the head with a broom?" Sophie asked.

"Many times," Julia said firmly. "But, you know, he was so tall, and I wasn't nearly as strong as he was, so I *said* things instead. And afterward, he behaved a lot better, I can tell you."

"But he was so kind!"

"Sophie!" Julia snapped irritably. "Grow up!"

"I'm sure Clare never wanted to hit him on the head with anything!" Sophie exclaimed.

"What do you want to bet?" Julia asked. "Pick something. Let's bet!"

The two of them stared angrily at each other, and then suddenly burst out laughing.

"You see?" said Julia. "Tell me how many times you wanted to hit him on the head with something! Don't try to pretend you never wanted to!"

"I didn't. Well, not very often. Only at Christmas, when he said I

couldn't come down because Meena wouldn't have it. There were important people coming, and she refused to be disgraced."

"Your father! First he should have hit Evelyn on the head, then Elfie,
and then he should have done the same to Meena," Julia said. "Then there
might have been some peace."

"I wonder if anyone ever did hit him," Sophie said, considering.

"I daresay Evelyn did. I don't think she ever was afraid of him. She was
the kind of woman who could have wound up behind bars wearing
stripes—if she'd been unlucky. She would have picked up anything she
could lift and thrown it at him. Sophie, Peter said that himself! He said she
threw things at him. What husband are you on now? Third? Fourth? You
never threw anything at one of them?"

"I hit one. Or two," Sophie said. "Not that hard."

"Well, I did, and hard. I lived with someone for a good long time. That
was before I met Matt. And when everything was falling apart, I picked up
a stone Mexican statue. Ordinarily, I couldn't even lift it to dust the table
it sat on, and I threw it straight at his head. I missed by an inch, if that
much. It hit the oak doorframe, and later, when I looked at the wood, the
statue had taken out a big chunk. If I'd hit him, I'd be wearing stripes and
a number right now. After that, he behaved himself—for a while. But if
you have to throw things, you know the man won't start to behave, and it
was over, really, when I threw the statue. If I hadn't known it was over
before, I knew it was over when I did that. I needed a man who'd be faithful. I'm an American, after all. I remember Peter's old friend Mark saying,
'We weren't surprised Peter married an American, but we were surprised
he married such an *American* American.' A puritan, I suppose that's what
he meant. Not all wives are cut out for infidelity, not even in France," Julia
finished.

"Would *you* have been happy with him?" Sophie asked.

"I just told you," Julia said. "I'm also an *American* American. Matt
always knew that the fastest way to get a divorce would be for me to find
out he'd had an affair. *He* was an *American* American. And he came from

the same kind of place as me, and the same sort of family. Middle-class, also like me. I *loved* the man who made me throw things. It was a passionate business, but I never wanted to have children with him. That always means something."

"It's hard to imagine you throwing statues," Sophie said.

"Yes, well," said Julia. "And when he was late for dinner, I'd pick up his plate and put the whole thing in the freezer compartment—for later."

"Life," said Sophie, "is hard."

"Yes," Julia said. "It is."

TWENTY-FOUR

———

MEENA KEPT A sharp eye on the weather. Stormy weather soothed her, and at the first sound of raindrops pelting the windowpane, she would go straight up to the turret and sit in her chair watching the storm while the rain poured down, kept at a safe distance by the windows, leaving her safe and dry. It was too quiet. It's been quiet for too long, Meena thought. They think I don't have the nerve to move against them. They think their silence will wear me out. They think the boredom, the lack of phone calls, their arguments arriving in the mail saying everything belongs to them, they think all those things will wear me down. Nothing will wear me down. This time, she thought, they've miscalculated. I've been to the solicitor's. I'm going to court to swear that the List of Wish meant nothing and that Peter intended to revoke it but he hadn't had the time. I'll swear he wasn't in his right mind when he wrote out the list in the first place. I'll say he told me I must use my own discretion in everything. Everyone will believe me. Everyone always does. I've tried it out on people who knew Peter well and they believed me. Peter wove a spell, but no one ever felt they knew where they stood with him, whereas everyone believed they knew where I stood. And that was true, for a good, long time. But no more. Any nature can be distorted. Peter used to say that of me, "You aren't the woman I once knew. Time has distorted you." As if time had anything to do with it! As if wind and weather had anything to do with it! As if Peter himself wasn't enough to account for any change in me, especially anything grown distorted and ugly. Then if I am distorted and ugly, Meena thought, I shall act according to my new nature. Then we'll see. Thunder and rain and lightning, lightning tearing oak limbs and throwing them. That's the weather I want. That's the weather I shall give them. And I shall stop them. There will be no stories about that woman in Cornwall. I will stop everything I don't want known. He is gone, and there is nothing I cannot do now, and he himself handed me the tools. He handed me the power. Fool! What a fool! I always knew him for a fool! But I never dreamed to hope for this! And now I will take advantage of his foolishness. Because he never expected it of me. He underestimated me time and again, and now he shall pay. And I shall not feel so much as a splinter of guilt. He made me what I am and what I do now is what he made of me. What I do now is what he has made me do.

The lightning split the sky and the thunder rolled and rumbled and shook the foundation of the house and Meena smiled and smiled and smiled.

—

THE SAME RAINSTORM was shaking London. Even through her windows, Sigrid could feel the violence of the weather. Meena is not, she thought suddenly, doing nothing. She is acting against us. It would be use-less to call Willow Grove and try to get anything out of her. Far better, she thought, to go up there herself and speak to the people Meena knew there, people she herself knew well. Sigrid wasn't entirely sure her driver's license was valid, but if something happened, what difference did it make? She grew more and more nearsighted by the day, and it was only a matter of time before she would be barred from driving. Yes, she would drive up to Willow Grove, stay at the pub, and do some investigations of her own.

—

"I THOUGHT," SOPHIE told Julia, "I'd go to see Clare tomorrow. If you wouldn't mind being left alone."

"I have to read a tower of books about half as high as you are, so no, I don't mind. I never mind. Especially in this house with its thirteen stained-glass skylights. I'll end up spending all my time looking at them. When will you leave, do you think?"

"Probably around five in the morning. Maybe four. If I decide to leave early enough, I'll stay up until it's time to go."

"Get a little sleep," Julia suggested. "So you make some sense when you get to the other end."

"I don't think I'd make much sense either way," Sophie said.

"Precipitous arrivals," said Julia, sighing. "They run in the family."

—

THIS STUDY, JULIAN thought, looking about at his whitewashed room decorated only with black and white photographs he had taken on his various trips to India, was very orderly, very efficient, very pleasant to contemplate on a perfect autumn day which for some reason was occur-ring in the middle of the winter, something perhaps a little unsettling about this collision or confusion of seasons, but of course, this was Great

Britain and what else could he expect, although Julian would have been happier if everything, even the weather, was predictable and orderly; his world was orderly and methodical, even the flower beds of his gardens were geometric, neat, white flowers here, red flowers there, no mad mixing of colors, his wife exactly what one could expect of a well-to-do housewife living in Northumberland, his children's aspirations tidy and entirely appropriate, a life not likely to yield surprises, upheavals, catastrophes; of course, such things might happen, a serious illness might disrupt everything; Julian knew such things could happen, everyone knew how capricious human bodies could be, that was simply the nature of a mortal being. Without such events, life was conventional, routine, even boring. Oh, yes, Julian thought, I have an appetite for boredom. It suits me.

Yes, I prefer everything orderly, as Meena's life is not, as it had never been since she married Peter, and during that time when Peter was dying, and Meena was in the hospital, in the middle of the corridor, fortunately late at night when no one but a few nurses could possibly have heard her, she burst out, "It's like being in a car, and you're driving, and something shatters the windscreen, and you can't see anything properly, everything you look at is fractured, and bright lights everywhere covering the world with cobwebs, and an instant later the windscreen is whole, just as it was a few moments before, and you think, Yes, I will make it home, I'm not too far from home now, and the glass shatters again and there's an oncoming car, and you think, I can't make it, there's no point; I might as well take my hands from the wheel, and the world comes together just when you've given up expecting it, and just as you think it's over, it won't happen again, it starts again; it's horrible, you can't imagine how horrible it is, there's simply no imagining it until it happens to you; has anything like that ever happened to you, I hope it never does!" and then she burst into tears, great choking sobs; he gave her his handkerchief, but it was soon soaked; he said, "You must get ahold of yourself; you will do yourself no good," but she was beyond getting hold of herself, and finally he said, "Come out of this place, come sit in the car, at least you'll be calmer," and that was what they did. They sat in the front seat of the car and he said nothing until she was quiet.

"Can't you let it all go?" he said to her at last. "Now that everything's ending, now that there will be no one to upset you; can't you let go of it?" and she stared at him as if he had been transformed into a serpent beneath her eyes. "Yes, yes, I know," he said; "I know what you went through. You were never meant for that kind of life; remember, your mother said, 'A good, sensible man, that's what you want, what good will all the glory in the world do you if there's to be no peace?' but you didn't want peace, you said you wanted excitement, you wanted love, you wanted to be *important*, and you were important, as Peter's wife you *were* important, but where did it get you?

"You take after your father," Julian said, "but I am like your mother, at least in some things; it was your father who said, 'I will make them forget I came from India, I will make them admire me,' but your mother said, 'What do I care what any of them think? What do I care about those lords and ladies? What do I care about the queen? Our family is more distin- guished than the queen's, more ancient than any of the *gentry* of this lit- tle country. Impress them? Why should I care to impress them? What are they to me, can they lay claim to *my* family, the fortune we once had?' She said, 'Of course we lost it, but once it was ours, once people came to us begging for favors, they waited outside of our beautiful gates, so many of them waiting, as if a procession had come to a halt in front of our house, and haven't you seen the pictures, the mountains where we lived, miles away a tiny train steaming its way along, and all of that land, all of it between our house and that railroad, and beyond, beyond! belonged to us! And now you grovel before these little people, and why? Because you came here from India!'"

"I remember," Meena said. "I told my mother, 'But this is where we live, the people here don't know what we once were; to them we are only farm- ers, people who have dirt beneath our fingernails, less than the lowest because we come from India; we're not wanted; we can never be as good as the least of them; that's what they think, no, I want more from them than that, I shall take my place among them, and it shall be a good, high place, I shall *force* them to give me that place,' and my mother said, 'You might as well ask pebbles and bushes to admire you; none of them are worth your admiration, and Peter Grovesnor, the son of a shopkeeper, if you marry him, will you have a good, high place, because he is a writer and is admired? Yes, yes, you love him, you love him *now*, better to marry a man who will worship you; you should be worshipped, the woman should stand on the higher pedestal as I did, my family was greater than my husband's, he knew it, he was always a bit afraid of me; you should marry in the same way, do as I did, but this Peter Grovesnor, he will not worship you, very far from it, I am sorry to say.' "

But Meena's father had been happy, very happy, when she married Peter; after that, people would know his family was better than people here liked to think; once she had married Peter, *his* family would glitter like gold bangles. After all, this was what he had wanted, not only to be accepted, no, that was not enough, but once more to be a man of consequence. When what he really meant, what he really wanted was to *condescend* once more, to disdain others beneath him, as he had done in India, although whenever he looked at his wife or a member of his wife's family, he knew he was the one who was frequently disdained, disregarded, even though when he first married, his family had the great fortune; his wife's had the rank. But to have lost both rank *and* fortune, to have fallen so far, to have been blamed for things he had not done, so that the only thing to do was leave the country of his birth, how had he survived? And Bharti, Meena's mother, told her, "Your father will never forget what he has lost, but what, really, did he lose? Can he lose the bloodline, that ancestry that made others bow down before him, could I lose my ancestry, so much more illustrious than his? Will I run after a dog because it wears a crown on its head? And you, Meena, you are like him. Better to know yourself of higher quality than those people you run after, because in the end, they will never accept you, unless, of course, they like you, but you do not think of their liking or disliking; you think of beating them into obedience and they will not be beaten in that way; they will think of your father as a coolie man and me as a coolie man's wife and you as a coolie man's daughter—unless they like you, and the people of this country, they pick you up like a flower you see by the lane and they throw it back down again, and why do they throw it down? Because they *can*; they take people up only to throw them down, that is the game they play, how often have I seen it, they take someone up and then they are through with him; they are children, useless and cruel, and yet you must run after them!"

And, Julian thought, Meena had spent her life running after such people, Peter's people; they had pretended to take her up; they had never wanted her, and so they had thrown her down—long before Peter's death; why hadn't she seen it?

"Can you not see it?" Julian asked Meena. "Don't you yet see it? Your mother was right," and Meena had turned on him, her lips a white scar, her face purplish, lit by the fluorescent streetlights, saying, "She was not right! I shall never admit that she was right! I shall make them bow down to me!" and he said, "It cannot be done," said it sadly, because long ago he understood that Meena's mother was right, and so he had settled on a proper life, respected ordinary people who valued him for his very uninteresting but useful existence; he hid his intelligence and his ability to coldly calculate, and he knew he would never be like that flower his aunt had so often spoken of, the flower that was picked up only to be thrown down. "And now you will drag me into all of this," Julian said bitterly. "And in the end, both of us will suffer."

"We may suffer, but we shall win," Meena said, said it with such conviction that he was persuaded, utterly persuaded, if only because her will was so strong—so much stronger than his—that he could not believe she could conceivably be wrong.

—

THE RAIN POURED down over the turret room. A particularly brilliant flash of lightning lit the windows. As if the light itself had triggered Meena's thoughts, she suddenly sat up straight, ran back down the steps, hesitated for an instant, remembering all the times she had been cautioned about using the bath or the telephone or the telly in a thunderstorm, and dialed Julian's number, Julian, her cousin, the attorney.

"Will you come over?" she asked him.

"In such weather?"

"At once," Meena said.

"It won't wait until morning?"

"I would have called in the morning if I thought it would wait."

"I'll be right there," Julian said. "If the car starts."

"It had better start," Meena said grimly.

—

ROSE WAS STILL smarting over Julia's recent dismissal of her inquiries about Peter's life. They can't get around me so easily, she thought, sitting bolt upright in bed. The lightning flashed and she saw the wrinkles Robert had left in the bed. When she changed these sheets, the last traces of him would be gone. She had never understood why people changed their sheets so often. When Sigrid still spoke freely to her, she once told her that Meena not only washed her sheets, but ironed them.

"And did she starch them?" Rose had asked.

"Well, Rose, I don't know, but they always felt new to me," Sigrid said.

"When Robert and I were first married," Rose said, "we couldn't see the point of washing sheets. We bought new ones."

"Very dear, that habit," Sigrid said.

"Not when we bought them in the monthly jumble sale. We knew the people selling the sheets would have washed them first, so we often bought

our new sheets in that way. But then when the children came and money
was tight, we stopped all that. And Robert had to stop throwing out his
shirts and buying new ones."

"Throwing out his shirts?"

"He didn't see the point of spending time on laundering shirts any
more than he did on washing sheets. 'A waste of time and spirit.' You know
he always said that."

"So," said Sigrid, "on the days he went in to university looking like he'd
grabbed a shirt straight out of the dryer, the shirts weren't even clean.
They certainly weren't ironed."

"We tried finding someone who wanted to iron. You'd have thought it
was easy enough in those days, there were so many refugees, but no one
wanted to iron. Or to wash windows. But the Polish woman we have now
irons everything. I feel so smart these days."

"You left it a little late," Sigrid said. "Robert was an eminence after all.
You ought to have seen washing and ironing as an expense of the job, don't
you think?"

"He went through a phase of taking everything to the Chinese laundry.
He'd gotten it into his head that the laundry man had been rusticated for
some offense against the Communist party, not in England, of course, but
in China, and he'd been admitted to this country as a man who'd escaped
persecution. So he went there all the time. He looked quite decent while
that went on. Too decent."

If, Rose thought now, there are probably skeletons like that in *my* very
boring closet, what must there be hanging from the hooks in Peter's? But
no one here will speak to me. Sigrid's put out the word, and I hear that
Meena is rigid with grief, seeing no one. Probably it's a good time to get
something out of Meena. I shall draw her out. I'm sure I can. Of course, I
shall drive. There's only one decent pub up there, and if it's full, I'd end up
sleeping in my car, and really, I've gotten too old for that. I have so much
more money now that Robert's died, she thought wonderingly. Yes, I definitely will go up there, she decided, and if the pub is booked up, which I

doubt, I shall find a good bed and breakfast. Or Meena may decide to put me up. It's not impossible, no matter what Sigrid may think.

Everyone, Rose knew, worried about how she was bearing up under Robert's death, when the truth was, she had spent so much time dreading it that his death, when it came, was something of an anticlimax. While he lived, she had cried herself to sleep at night on the couch, trying to imagine what it would be like to live alone, until finally she decided that the problem would not be loneliness, nor an inability to manage, which was what people seemed to expect in her. No, the problem would be that she could no longer refer everything to Robert. She had set her course by his reactions. She knew, for example, that if he greatly praised something she had just written, there was something wrong with it, seriously wrong, not a matter of mere editing or moving paragraphs about, switching the ending and the beginning. No, the writing needed to be thrown out and she needed to start again. When she did that, and rewrote what she had written, and again gave it to Robert, and he said, "As usual, Rose, you have managed to miss the entire point; you have thrown out everything that was good and substituted that feminist claptrap," *then* she knew she had gotten the piece right and it was as she wanted it.

Now, though, she had only her own opinion to rely on. For several months after his death, Rose was afraid to write anything, certain that without Robert's reaction she was lost in a wood, and he had gone to his grave with the only compass she had ever had. But passing time taught her that what she wrote was received as well as it always had been, if not more enthusiastically, and each month gave her a stronger sense of herself, a feeling of wonder, an exhilaration that arose because she could do anything on her own. She had never before enjoyed that sense of ownership in her own work. She had always half attributed her accomplishments to her father, and then to her husband. She had gone off to college, and within weeks of leaving her parents' house, she and Robert were inseparable. I have never been my own person, she thought. I thought I was, but I was wrong.

And she flourished, and others saw that, and spoke of Rose's bravery and flexibility and courage, and said aloud that they hoped they themselves would do as well if a similar catastrophe befell them. She had her unsteady moments, her panics, when the words slid from her pages and formed a conical heap on the floor, but everyone had them. She knew they did. The blank spells, when she could think of nothing, when all she wanted to do was scream and continue screaming, they were occurring less and less frequently, and Rose had no doubt that they would soon disappear altogether.

I am a *widow*, just as Meena is a widow, and so we shall have something in common, Rose thought as she got in her car and slammed the door which did not lock quite properly, allowing the rain in as it had done since the day Robert put the car in the wrong gear and rocketed backward into the car behind them.

Her plan was to ambush Meena. Of course, Sigrid had warned her about such attempts, saying, "The one thing Meena loathes most is surprise visits, and if she sees you approaching, she will not come down."

Then it would be necessary, Rose thought, to take her entirely by surprise. Robert used to say that she had a genius for tactical maneuvers, and what a pity it was to have wasted such a talent. Had he spoken sarcastically? Really, for years she had never known. But she had learned to avoid *him* and to keep clear of his skirmishes, all the little traps he tried to lay for her. She would stay at the pub they liked so much. She was sure they would have a room. It was not yet high season. She would check in and spend the night there, and in the morning she would drive to the church near Willow Grove, where she would leave her car and walk up the lane to Meena's cottage. It was best to arrive at ten o'clock in the morning. How well she remembered Meena's contempt for people who slept late when they could be busy doing something, anything, without requiring electricity in order to do it. The weather was warm. If it was not raining, Meena would be weeding in the garden or planting something or other or spraying her roses to keep off the Japanese beetles. There would be no question of Meena's trying to pretend that she didn't see her standing there. Then she could speak of what it was to be a widow, and could say, with great diffidence, that she intended to write Peter's biography, and offer up this sentence: "English literature owes its own special debt to Meena Grovesnor." She would tell Meena that she had already written those words in a eulogy she had written for Peter, and Meena would be won over. Surely it would happen precisely as she imagined. And so she drove happily, hour after hour, making her way to Northumberland and Willow Grove, with no one in the car to insult her or argue with her or insist she turn left when she knew she ought to keep straight on. And meanwhile, she thought smugly, Meena is sound asleep, anticipating nothing.

TWENTY-FIVE

———

"YOU CANNOT TRUST that woman," Sigrid told Sophie. "I have to see Meena myself."

"You will only end up shouting her down," Sophie said, "and then she will truly be intractable."

"I don't shout. When do I ever shout?" Sigrid asked indignantly.

"*Please,*" said Sophie.

"I will keep my temper and flush her out and find out what her game is."

"You already know. We all know. She's decided to hang on to that money until we have to beg, and I myself will not crawl on my hands and knees for money."

"How like Peter you sound," Sigrid said. "But when it came to Meena, your father knew she was capable of anything."

"Still, regardless of how you look at it, you are going to see her to try getting money off her. She'll be expecting you."

"She's already agreed to pay me my portion."

"Once she's deducted legal expenses and God knows what else," Sophie said. "You're not in the clear, not yet."

"It's not *me* I'm worried about, you stupid goose! It's you and your brother!"

"Don't shout at me, Sigrid."

"Someone has to wake you up! It's not simply a question of whether she *gives* you money or doesn't. It isn't *hers* to give. It's Peter's money, and he wanted you and your brother to have it. He wanted the two of you to supervise what became of his estate. She's already making decisions that ought to have nothing to do with her, selling his library and his manuscripts to universities in the States."

"There will be records," Sophie said. "She'll have to divide up that money with the rest of us."

"Don't be a fool, love," Sigrid said. "I watched her bargain for rugs in Turkey."

"Well, that's it, you see," Sophie said. "I don't want to haggle over Daddy's money."

"You don't have to haggle. How can you be so thick? The money is already yours and she's deliberately keeping it from you. I know what she'll say when I get there. She'll say how extravagant you are, hopeless, really. She'll start talking about the thirteen skylights. Really, Sophie, did you have to let her see them? Didn't you notice she was counting them as she went through the rooms? She'll bring up every penny Peter ever gave you, the money he gave you when you bought your first house in Northumberland, the money he gave you when you first came to London, the school fees when you were sent away to school. She's probably got a ledger totting up what you cost in nappies! Don't you know what she is?

I know she was the only mother you ever had, but she wasn't really a mother to you. Even your brother says she's always hated you. Don't you know it? Can't you admit to it? What in the world was your father thinking of when he entrusted the estate to her? *An honorable woman.* He did think that of her. He would never have expected *this.*"

"All you'll do is wear yourself out and come back and sleep for three weeks. Or four," Sophie said. "And the more we pressure her, the more she'll dig in."

"That's what we need to *know!*" Sigrid said. "If she's going to dig in, we have to do some digging of our own."

"Useless," said Sophie.

"What does Bertold say?"

"Bertold says she's a monster and should hand over the money, but he says she won't, and life is too short to spend it trying to wring so much as a pound out of a woman like that. And other times, he's so angry at Meena for ignoring me that he turns red in the face."

"So he won't mind if the bailiff comes to the door when the two of you can't pay the mortgage?" Sigrid asked her.

"Oh, it won't come to that. Money always appears out of somewhere."

"Peter used to say the same, until he wanted to be rid of Meena, and strangely enough, all the money trees in the garden had died. Otherwise, do you think he would have published that book about Evelyn?"

"He always intended to publish it."

"So he said. After he discovered he had *no money!*"

"I will not go to Meena, and we cannot afford solicitors' bills."

"The *threat* of solicitors may be enough to turn her," Sigrid said.

"If you want to waste your time trying to make that woman see sense, I can't stop you. You won't get anywhere, though."

"It's *your* money!" Sigrid shouted. "It's your *father's* estate and how posterity will see him! You must care about that!"

"Sigrid," Bertold said, suddenly appearing, "so nice to see you. You came to see how the addition to the house is progressing?"

"Money, Sophie, *money*," Sigrid said. "Renovating houses cannot be done without money."

"There won't be any more skylights in the addition," Bertold said.

"You think it's funny *now*, but wait until you start dealing with the bank."

Bertold and Sophie exchanged glances.

"You *have* had dealings with the bank!" Sigrid said triumphantly. "And do you like it? What will you do? Surely you have a plan?"

"We're getting in a lodger," Sophie said.

"A lodger? A *lodger*? A lodger won't even pay for your taxi bill! Be serious, both of you!"

"It always comes out well," Bertold said. "Sophie always manages."

"She managed before because she had Peter to rely on, but now it's Meena she has to deal with. Can't you see? You *have* to do something!"

"Sigrid, darling, with all possible respect to you, we *do not* have to do something about Meena. Don't worry yourself. Enjoy your time. It will all work out, you'll see," Bertold said.

"It will all work out if *I* work it out for you!" Sigrid said. "I've got to go. I'm leaving for Northumberland tomorrow."

"By train?" Sophie asked.

"*Not* by train," Sigrid said, refusing to elaborate further.

—

I SHALL STAY at the Prince Albert, Sigrid thought. None of the family ever stayed there before, so I shall not be expected. Meena might actually venture farther than the town center if she knew I was coming. When she reached Willow Grove, she would not shout. She would not even lose her temper. She would explain to Meena why Peter's last wishes had to be honored, and, of course, if she refused to see reason, she, Sigrid, would threaten. Hadn't Julia repeatedly said that she, Sigrid, ought to write her own autobiography? Perhaps she should begin with that. "I've begun on

my autobiography," Sigrid would say. "So many people have been plead-
ing with me for it, and Sophie in particular. You know how she says the
truth will all die with me." Of course. Why hadn't she come to it earlier?
It was bad enough, in Meena's opinion, that the living spoke without her
permission, but the idea that someone might disapprove of what Meena
had to say, and write that *in a book*: that was entirely unacceptable.

Sigrid got in the car and turned the key in the ignition. The engine
sputtered, then roared into life. I must take care driving, Sigrid thought.
The road is lined with such large cars these days. And what about that
"extraordinary" document Meena had spoken of at the funeral, a document Julia had written? In the end, it had turned out to be no more than
a letter of consolation. "I am so sorry," Julia had written, and other such
predictable things. And then Julia wrote, "I've been remembering that
time when both of you came to New York and I was walking with Peter
and you were walking with Matt. I was unhappy, but I didn't know why,
and I told that to Peter, who said, 'You're bored.' It was true. And then I
said how much happier I would be if we could afford a place in the country. I hated the city, all that concrete, so many memories of my life as a
child. And Peter said, 'It's only money.' It's only money! I said, 'That's a big
thing if you don't have it,' but he said again, 'It's only money,' and within
six months, it turned out that I did have the money and we bought the
house in the country and now we live in it all the time. At the time, I
couldn't understand him, how he could say it was only money? We had
two young children then. Well, you've been through all that. And then one
day I realized that what Peter meant to say was that when you wanted
something enough, you found a way to get it. And shortly thereafter, you
wrote me and said, 'We are creeping toward winter in front of our wood
fire,' and when I heard the news about Peter, I remembered all that, and
how happy we all were then."

For once, Sigrid thought, Julia had been unable to peer through the
mists. When was it that Peter had dragged Meena off to New York? He had
issued Meena an ultimatum of some kind. Julia had not known about that

then. But Sigrid knew that he had decided to separate and then divorce Meena if she did not go. That must have been in the early seventies when Meena was so beautiful and could easily persuade others to believe how happy she was. Astonishing, that she had taken Julia in, but in those days, no one had the slightest idea of disturbances in the marriage. So here it was again, Peter saying, through his will, 'It's only money,' and Meena bristling like a hedgehog at those same, fantastic words. How odd, Sigrid thought, that Julia had written to Meena reminding her that Peter had said, "It's only money." Those words must have been *scalding* to Meena, or if they hadn't been so at the time, certainly they would be now.

Why was she waiting for the car to warm up? It wasn't very cold. But she hated to get in and out of parking spots. Sigrid put the car in gear. The man who owned that red car in front of her wouldn't mind a few more dents in his fender, and she was in a hurry to get on the road. One or two thuds, then a screech. There, thought Sigrid. That wasn't too bad. I'm sure the man was sound asleep in his bed. That light that just went on in the window across the street, whose house was that? Well, it has nothing to do with me, Sigrid thought, another restless soul, up late at night, wanting a drink of water—or something stronger, as she usually did. And then there was the wind coming in and whipping her thick hair this way and that, and *La Bohème* on the tape, and Sigrid remembered once again why she had always so enjoyed driving. Not a good place to stop and get a bite along the way, but Trusthouse Forte wasn't too bad. They had very good flapjacks and other forbidden foods. She sailed off down the road, following the signs to the highway.

TWENTY-SIX

———

"YOU SEE," MEENA was telling Julian, "I want to stop them taking everything. How can it be done?"

"You want to leave them with nothing? Is that it?" Julian asked his cousin.

"Nothing but bleached bones," Meena said. "After all, I was scarcely out of my teens when I married him, and now I'm in my forties. I'm still as trim as I ever was, but my face is ravaged, and so am I. I'm not young any longer, no matter what people say. I can't bear children. That's been true for decades, and even if I had done, I wouldn't be able to do it now, and the kind of men I might want won't want me, unless they're interested in the money, and I certainly don't want to buy a husband. I don't want to give the money up. I'm through with compromising. From now on, I do exactly what I want. I'll buy nothing costing less than two hundred pounds. When I go to parties, I shall forget about resale shops and if I want to have the house worked on, I'll call the best workmen there are and I won't count the cost."

"But the real reason is Peter and what he did to you," Julian said.

"Of course. That goes without saying."

"Just so you keep that well in mind," Julian said. "So there will be no wavering."

"So then what can we do?"

"You will have to go to court, and not lie, but you have to *color* the truth a little. You know, put it in the best possible light. Especially when it comes to the List of Wish. I know such a list has no real legal standing, but many people, including judges, act as if it does. It's got a long history. People abide by it. Families agree on the List of Wish to avoid paying heavy taxes and then the executor, in that case you, gifts the money to the remaining relatives, and everyone keeps much more. It's a very English document, Meena, and many people treasure it. Last wishes sound so much warmer than last words."

"Shall I say he wasn't thinking clearly because of the pain and the morphine and that I wrote only what he dictated to me? Will that do?"

"You've been working it out," Julian said.

"Who else will do it for me?"

"Here *I* am," Julian said, his tone injured.

"But will that be enough?"

"It should be," Julian said. "But it's folly to anticipate a judge, even worse to predict the outcome of a jury. And there's one tiny problem."

"Problem?"

"Well, I've looked over the documents. The will itself and the List of Wish were dated and witnessed on the same day. It's his signature on both. I can even recognize the pen he used. If you argue that he was not in his right mind when he dictated the List of Wish, anyone can argue that he was also out of his senses when he wrote the will. The same day, the same time, no indication of which he wrote first, he could easily have written the List of Wish first, that was the more complicated document, and then, having settled his mind about the list, gone on to write the will. Two interdependent documents, as it were. What might tip the scale in your balance is the quasi-legal status of the List of Wish. People do treasure the list, as I said, but these days people are very careful, and tend to have proper wills or a List of Wishes loaded down with witnessing persons and stamps that automatically record the time of signing. There's none of that to support the List of Wish, only your signature and some little nurse's who no one's ever heard of. All that may well be decisive and work in your favor. So if you go into court to slant the truth a bit, you must bend it very skillfully. You don't want the judge or anyone else to decide that the actual documents need to be examined and reevaluated."

"Oh, but surely the will is weightier. It is, as you say, a legal document."

"Yes, but surely you see it depends on the judge's angle of vision. Perhaps he will think—and I think something like this must actually have happened—that Peter dictated the List of Wish and then thought, This may not have sufficient standing. In that event, he would have wanted an unassailable will that couldn't be set aside if the List of Wish was challenged. He must have looked at you and thought, Oh, she's a good girl, and will abide by his wishes. So to Peter, both documents were the same. He thought it didn't matter if you obeyed the List of Wish or the will. He expected you to divide up the estate just as he wrote in the List of Wish. I suspect he would have written a far more detailed will if he hadn't been in such pain. Or if he hadn't felt he'd run out of time." He paused, looking at Meena. "Isn't that exactly what happened?"

"It was such a confusing, such a terrible time. I don't know if he'd have written a more detailed will if he hadn't been suffering and if he hadn't been certain he was going to die at any moment. I rather think that he thought the documents were fine as they were."

"I can testify to the truth of what you say."

"Won't that appear a bit prejudicial?" Meena asked. "You are my *cousin.*"

"I'm rather more than your cousin. You forget. I'm a barrister. That counts for a great deal in a court of law. Of course, you must be represented by a barrister other than me. Everyone would assume I was prejudiced in your favor."

"It's true," Meena said. "Can you prepare a list of suitable barristers? Then we shall get the matter on the docket."

"Here," Julian said, sliding a sheaf of papers over to her. "It's done. The petition, the statement of evidence. I prepared it before I came."

"How wonderful you have always been, Julian."

"Keep them safe, Meena. Keep them out of harm's way. Don't let them lie about in the house. You don't want Sigrid or the children, or anyone else, for that matter, reading these."

"Yes," said Meena. "I've already thought of that. But they've already read the documents. Still, I've barred them. For my own health, that's the reason I've given."

"Very good," her cousin said. "Very, very good. The frail and grieving widow. You don't get to play that card often."

"No," said Meena, sinking back in her chair, staring at her cousin. "No, you don't."

"Just stay out of their way. That's all you need to do. I'll take care of the rest."

"Yes," Meena said. She sat, unmoving, in the chair. A pity she hadn't had children, Julian thought. Her claim would have seemed, legally speaking, so much more . . . legitimate. She needs to sleep. She looks, Julian thought, taking a careful look at her, like an unstrung marionette. Yes, a pity she hadn't had children.

—

ROSE KNEW THE day would be hot even before she opened her eyes. She had carefully closed all the curtains. She dressed in a wool paisley skirt and a light cotton blouse, the usual kind of outfit for London, when summer turned to winter and back again without any warning. "No one really needs summer clothes here," Julia frequently said. "Ten days in a summer at most." Rose took a purple sweater that she thought went rather well with the coral paisley skirt and set off in hunt of her prey. She followed her plan and parked her car at the bottom of the street that led up to both church and cottage alike. Better to approach at an oblique angle, Rose thought. Animals always do. At least they did in documentaries she had seen on TV. She began climbing the steep street toward Willow Grove. Funny, she hadn't realized how careful you had to be on these paving stones. A person could break her neck. She'd had the same thought that morning at the Prince Martin, a pub she had dearly loved one or two decades ago when she had stayed there, but this morning she noticed the way the first floor twisted and turned without reason, causing you to climb up a small flight of steps, and then climb down another on her way to the main stairway, and she thought, This is exhausting, Why did I never notice it before?

I don't remember this, either, Rose thought. Surely the street was never so steep. She was panting slightly as she climbed, and threw her sweater over her shoulders. It seemed less heavy than carrying it over her arm. There, at last, was the archway to Willow Grove. It looked exceedingly peaceful. There were birds twittering everywhere. Oh, yes, Rose remembered, Meena always fed the birds. There were green metal arches almost hidden in the hedges, and suspended from each arch was a bird feeder which Meena carefully kept full. If Meena was not here, surely she had been here a short time ago. Birds eat so fast, Rose thought. She stood still, catching her breath, and then marched through the metal archway into Willow Grove. There was the same white gravel shining its way to the

kitchen door. Rose had always wondered why those stones stayed so obe-
diently in place instead of straying all over through the grass, but now she
saw that there were wooden slats sunk into the earth, and they rose slightly
above the level of the grass, holding everything in place as it was meant to
be. As usual, everything as neat as a pin, smoothly running, all proclaiming Meena's presence, but there was no sign of her. She went up to the door
and rang the large cowbell Peter had put up there. He had said, "It's for
the children, you see. I want to be sure they've heard me ringing for them.
They make up such excuses when they've found something interesting, and
the one they like best is that we didn't hear them calling. They'll have
to hear that bell when it rings."

"It is an unusual bell," Rose had said.

"Just the way I want it," Peter said, and it seemed to Rose he was a bit
curt. Probably, she imagined, because his new book wasn't going well.

There was no sign of Meena. Rose sat down on the doorstep. That
stone gets very hot, she thought. When she looked up, she saw small
brown birds diving into the thatch of the roof. Then a black, iridescent
crow flew out. There must be a lot of insects in that thatch, Rose thought.
That's what the birds came for. Peter had no fear of insects. Rose did.
Twenty years ago, when she and Robert would drop in without warning,
the house would be neat as a pin, but Rose would stare about when she
thought no one was watching. Spiders! Ants! Things that stung! "You
don't belong in the country, Rose," Peter told her, laughing. "You must
never try it."

And Robert said, "She won't leave the city for long. She feels safe from
wildlife there. Even though I told her that no one is ever more than ten
feet from a rat in that city."

"You shouldn't say that to Rose," Peter said. He is taking my side, Rose
thought at the time. Someone is finally taking my side. But no, she should
have seen it sooner. Peter was keeping them to the subject. And then he
said, "It's seven feet. Seven feet from a rat."

"Really, Peter, I think that's quite sufficient," Meena said, and Peter subsided. Then was Meena taking her side? Probably not at all. Probably she was only playing the part of the good hostess.

"Are *you* afraid of rats?" Robert asked Meena.

"Certainly not," she said. "I have a pet rat, now that you mention it. I found it half-frozen in the snow. I quite like it. Rats are very intelligent, more than cats or dogs."

"*Where* is the rat, Meena?" Peter asked her. "Tell them where you keep it."

Meena said, "Peter, you must not leave everyone with the impression that you can only think of rats when the very idea of rats so disturbs your guests."

"*Guest,*" said Robert. "The rest of us are undisturbed."

"Anyone who mentions rats again shall have no pudding," Meena said. They all laughed, surprised by her wit. But she had not meant to be witty. She had meant what she said.

"And what shall pudding be?" Robert asked her.

"Blackstrap molasses on stale toast," said Meena.

"Oh, that is serious," Robert said.

"Indeed it is," Peter said a little sheepishly.

"He wants his pudding, you see," Meena said, and they all laughed again. Meena finally smiled.

"Where have those children gotten to now?" Peter asked.

"Probably looking for toads," Meena said, and then she looked over at Robert and glared. For once, Robert decided to keep still.

It was nice in those days, Rose thought. She stood up. Probably Meena was now in one of the gardens. That was where she had expected to find her, after all. Evidently, Meena had been to Sissinghurst recently. There was a white garden and a red garden and one that mixed blues and purples. In none of them could she see a woman stooped over to do her weeding. She saw a sunflower in the distance and made her way in that direction.

"Well, well," said Meena, appearing out of nowhere, "uninvited guests. What a surprise."

"Not an unhappy surprise, I hope," Rose said.

Meena was smiling and her smile remained uninflected. "Not at all. Only these days I'm not used to visitors."

"It doesn't do to get too isolated," Rose said. "I went through that when Robert died."

"Yes, yes," Meena said, her voice soothing. "We are both widows now. Come back to the house for an early tea, well, a *very* early tea. It's so hot. Soon we shall all have to take siestas, as people do on the continent. I can easily give you iced tea." When they were settled on opposite benches of the long kitchen table, Meena began worrying a hole in the wood with the nail of her small finger. "Woodworm," she said. "Peter used to say, 'I hope it lasts as long as I do.' Do you remember?"

"Yes, I do," Rose said.

By now Rose was shaking her tall glass of iced tea back and forth. The tinkling of the ice soothed her. "When I was young, I had wind chimes that made a sound like that. I wish I had them again," she said.

Meena tried to suppress a gesture of annoyance, but Rose noticed it.

"We lose so much on the way," Meena said.

She has become quite smooth, quite sophisticated, since I knew her, Rose thought. Sigrid never prepared me for this.

"So we do," Rose said softly.

"Well, Rose, here we are, two widows, and we both know how each of us has suffered. But that need not prevent us from speaking our minds. I understand you want to write a biography of Peter. Is that correct?"

"It is," Rose said. Now she felt on surer ground. She knew how to negotiate; she was, as Robert had never tired of saying, good at wearing people down.

"I suppose Sigrid must have told you that there's to be no biography," Meena said. "He didn't want it. I promised him I would stop all such attempts, just as he had stopped them when he was alive. I intend to carry out his wishes. I'm sorry to be so blunt, Rose."

"Let me be equally frank," Rose said, her back stiffening. "You know I've written four very well-received biographies. You know I knew Peter rather well, almost from the time I entered college. Who better than me to write his life?"

Meena stirred the long glass of iced tea in front of her. "It pains me to say this, Rose, it does, but Peter did not think highly of those biographies. Nor did Sigrid. I'm sure Sigrid told you so. Peter would not have said anything to upset you or insult you, so of course he said nothing, as well he should not have. You know how writers must behave. Peter used to say, 'It is a small country, and to survive at all, we must become master hypocrites.'"

"When he praised me," Rose asked, astonished, "his praises were nothing but hypocrisy?"

"He thought you very industrious," Meena said.

"Industrious!"

"You cannot expect me to rewrite history, Rose. If I begin twisting what I know Peter said, I will soon lose my ability to hear his voice altogether."

"You mean to say he thought my work was worthless?" Rose asked, genuinely flabbergasted.

"He never used those words," Meena said. "I know only that he did not think highly of them. I remember those precise words. 'I can't say I think highly'—or perhaps he said 'much'—'of those biographies.'"

"But you know anyone can write his biography without your permission. If it is not an official biography, as I can see mine will not be."

"We did discuss that, Rose," Meena said. "He said, 'If it must be done, there are two or three people who might do it. One was a very old friend he knew from his days in America. Another was a scholar who has spent years studying his work. I think there may have been a third, but perhaps not. There are five women now beginning work on biographies of Peter, and I shall not help them. He did write down a list of those he did *not* want to write his biography, and Rose, I'm afraid you were at the top of that list."

"I don't believe it," Rose said flatly. "You are only saying that to discourage me. Now that Peter is gone, you can put whatever words you like in his mouth."

"If you feel that, Rose, then you must ask Sigrid. He told her the same thing."

"Then you won't help me?" Rose asked.

"How can I go against my husband's wishes?"

"I've recently lost my husband. Surely you have sympathy for that?"

"Of course I'm sympathetic. But we're talking about apples and oranges. I can't allow my sympathy to stand in the way of Peter's wishes."

"Peter is dead!" Rose blurted out.

"We know that only too well. Rose, you will have to excuse me. My cousin is coming to see me about Peter's will. It's all a matter of procedures and barristers and editors and what books must come out next, but it must be done. I must see to it. I'm sure you understand."

"I've made you angry," Rose said. "I've upset you. I didn't mean to, you know."

"You've done nothing," Meena said, her voice smooth, her smile unchanged. "Nothing at all."

"Nothing!" Rose said. She did not like the sound of her own voice. Of course I am angry, she thought. Of course *she* has insulted me. Probably Peter said none of those things. He always admired me. He told me so. I was right. Sigrid and Meena have put their heads together.

"If I may risk upsetting you once again," Rose said, knowing this was her last chance, "you do not really understand the world of writers and books and publishers. I think you make a mistake in putting me aside."

"I'm sure I've made many mistakes, and will make many more," Meena said, rising. "Let me see you to your car."

"It's at the bottom of the road," Rose said.

"Let me see you to the gate, then," Meena said.

"I wouldn't have expected this from you, Meena," Rose said.

"What I want makes no difference. It's what Peter wanted. I appear to have trouble making that clear," said Meena.

"Oh, you've made it very clear," Rose said.

"Have I? I'm glad," Meena answered. "Take care going down. Everyone who's grown older complains of those flagstones."

"I'm not doddering yet," Rose said.

"Of course you aren't," said Meena, the other widow.

—

AS ROSE WAS slowly making her way down, watching the flagstones, she thought she saw a familiar figure striding up, so familiar that the person advancing toward her took her breath away. That woman coming up the street was wearing a trench coat and a scarf was wrapped around her head, obscuring her neck, face, and hair. But Rose could see through the disguise. It's Peter! she thought. How much shorter he looks! So he's not dead! He pretended to die and now he's going about disguised as a woman! *Now* it all made sense! Meena was keeping Peter's continued existence a secret so that Peter would be left in peace at last. Of *course* she had said those horrible things to warn Rose off. She was determined to protect Peter's privacy, as she always had done.

The two of them were not within ten yards of one another when the climbing person suddenly raised her head and saw Rose walking down. "You!" said the person. "What in God's name are you doing here?"

It was Sigrid. This, Rose thought, was too much to bear. To have gotten her hopes up so, only to have them dashed so horribly!

"Sigrid?" Rose said. "Is that you?"

"Who the bloody hell do you think it is?" Sigrid asked. "What are you *doing* here?"

"I came as Peter's biographer," Rose said. "I owed it to myself to appeal to Meena."

"And when did you have that brainstorm?" Sigrid asked. "I told you that no one would talk to you. Did you think I meant everyone but Meena? Oh, Rose, what have you done? Always puffing yourself up, always thinking you're better than you are!"

"I've had quite enough of that for one day," Rose said.

"Then you weren't met with open arms?" Sigrid asked. "What a fool you are, Rose!"

"She said all sorts of silly things about how Peter thought badly of my work," Rose said, waiting to be corrected. But Sigrid did not contradict her. What a ridiculous, what an imperious, self-important person Rose had become, Sigrid thought.

"I warned you," Sigrid said.

"But you will talk to her all the same?"

"There is almost nothing in this world that Meena and I can agree on, but your work, Rose, is one of them," Sigrid said.

"But you were the one who discovered me, who fostered me up!" Rose exclaimed. Surely, Sigrid could not be saying these things.

"You worked so hard and you had all those girls to raise, so I spoke to Peter. I've told you this before. I never suffered from the delusion that you would do splendid work. Never, Rose."

"Don't say such things!" Rose cried. "You are angry with me and in the morning you will regret having said all this!"

"I regret your having come," Sigrid said. "I have my own concerns, important concerns, matters concerning Peter, and now that you have gone to see Meena, *in spite of my advice,* she is going to think we are making common cause. Do you really think that paranoid twit is going to believe that the two of us just happened to come to Willow Grove on the same day? That it was all a coincidence? You have done a great deal of damage, Rose, and I am done with you."

She wrapped herself in her scarf and swept past Rose, climbing quickly up the hill, not looking back.

"Sigrid!" Rose called out. "Sigrid!" But she knew that Sigrid was not going to turn back and speak to her again, and so she kept calling out Sigrid's name, until she saw herself as if she were a bird high up on a tree, and from that distance, she knew she resembled an abandoned child. Then she began making her way down the street. If you could consider that miserable lane a *street*.

———

SIGRID HAD REACHED the gate to Willow Grove, and went through it without hesitation. She rang the cowbell, but no one answered. Out putting flowers on Peter's grave, no doubt, everyone from the church watching her piety and fidelity. She went through the first of the gardens and spotted Meena digging in the blue and purple garden she had begun several years ago. "Meena!" she called out.

Meena stood up. "*Another* visitor?" Meena asked her.

"I had no idea she was coming."

"Well, I did," Meena said. "I asked the people in the Prince Albert to tell me if anyone from London was staying there. I knew it couldn't be *you*, I knew you'd expect to stay at the house, and I remembered your warning about Rose and the biography. I suppose it could have been someone else, but I was quite sure it was Rose."

"I spent the night in that nice pub near Grisleigh," Sigrid said. "No one called to warn you? From the Prince Albert?"

"I shall put that pub on my list," Meena said. "If you are here to plead Rose's case, although I can't begin to imagine why, it's of no use. None."

"I have more important concerns to discuss," Sigrid said.

"You mean the will?" Meena asked. "I've told you. It's in the hands of the courts and the solicitors."

"I should like to see those papers, Meena," Sigrid said.

"I will not submit to your bullying. I put up with it when Peter was alive, but no longer."

"You understand, Meena, that I know all about Clare. I know that Peter moved out of the house and kept an apartment in the town, saying he worked better in solitude. I know precisely when he moved from that apartment to Crow's Nest in Cornwall. I *know* Clare, Meena. I have letters Peter wrote to her. Do you want all that in the papers?"

"Peter's reputation must be sacred," Meena said. "Which is why I am demanding a confidentiality clause from all of you."

"If you persist in such nonsense, at least where I'm concerned, I shall go right to the papers myself," Sigrid said. "Really, Meena, you know better than to threaten me. It's mad, really, the way you go on. And in any case, we've already agreed about my share. I'm here about the children."

"How like a crow you are," Meena said. "Peter said that of you. Last week, when I went into London, I looked about at the houses in Belgravia and thought, the pigeons rule the heights up there. The crows stay down below, atop the high streetlights, two stories up, but not on the roofs. Isn't it odd? I never took proper notice of it before, the way the pigeons take over the highest places."

"Because they know no one will bother them up there," Sigrid said. "It's not a mystery."

"Then why don't the crows go up there as well?"

"Is there something you're talking about?" Sigrid asked. "I can't catch the drift of it. Are you trying to imitate the way Peter carried on a conversation?"

Meena's smooth surface reddened. "I think I am entitled to mention pigeons," Meena said.

"Anyone may speak of pigeons," said Sigrid.

"I suppose you will want a cup of tea?" Meena said.

"Unless you want me to make it myself. All day, a refrain from a song has been running through my mind. Do you know it? 'But all things have but little stay, not least the most we love.'"

"I do know that," Meena said. "It's from a folk song. Peter used to sing it all the time in his last months."

"That's it. Now I remember. Clare used to sing that song to him when he was in pain."

"I see," Meena said. "Well, of course you would remember that line, just as I do. You know, you have always felt too at home in this house, Sigrid. Once I came, it was no longer necessary to take care of the children. You were not needed."

"You mean I was not *wanted*."

"Follow me," Meena said, as if Sigrid had somehow forgotten how to get back to the house. She followed Meena's steely back as they made their way.

——

"OF COURSE YOU know you are upsetting Sophie dreadfully," Sigrid said. They were sitting at the worm-holed kitchen table. "You know how easily upset she is."

"She takes people in," Meena said unsympathetically. "She has had *years* to perfect her impersonation of the poor stepchild, the poor little orphan. I must say, her mother set her a good example. She has studied up on Evelyn. Sophie does a rather good impersonation of her, I think."

"Don't get your hopes up there," Sigrid said. "Whatever you have to say about Sophie, she is not one to take her own life. She'll stay alive out of spite. And now that she has Bertold, she's quite a lot stronger than she was. You don't see it yet, but you will."

"If *only* she wouldn't use the family name," Meena said in exasperation. "A mathematician. When she can't add two and two!"

Meena was, Sigrid knew, trawling for information.

"Peter thought her work, her mathematical work, was quite good. He couldn't judge it himself, of course, but experts in the field think she's a genius. You are quite behind the times, Meena. She *has* made a reputation for herself as a theoretical mathematician. She made a splash in something called the topology of H spaces and she's gone well beyond that. Something about string theory. Bertold says she's celebrated, really. And she improves at such a rapid rate, just like Evelyn, exactly like Evelyn in that way."

"And her poems?"

"Poems?" said Sigrid. "I didn't know she wrote poems any longer."

"Poems about her evil stepmother, so I understand it," Meena said. "An entire book about her evil stepmother."

"I don't know where you get such outlandish information," Sigrid said.

"I shall read it by next week," Meena said. "*If* it exists."

"How very odd," Sigrid said. She became absorbed in stirring sugar into her tea. "When she still wrote stories, she invariably submitted what she had written to me. But, Meena, this rings a bell. I think she did give Peter a poem to read. Right at the end. Although at the time, I didn't think *she* had written it. But after all, it's to be expected. The artistic daughter of two great writers, you would expect her to try her hand at writing. I'm sure she's quite good."

She stared into Meena's eyes. Meena was the first to look away. "I understand," Sigrid continued, "she *was* writing a story, about a woman whose husband was dying, and the wife decided to help him out of the world, his situation was so pitiful. But Sophie may have given it up. She is so busy with her maths. And she has that huge stipend from some kind of foundation. They send her theorems and proofs to inspect. I don't understand any of that, of course. And she has to prepare a paper to read at a German university. Apparently she has proved some kind of impossibly difficult theorem."

"She can't be very good," Meena said. "I was told that maths prodigies started early. As I've said before, Sophie can barely do her sums."

"*You* were the trouble there," Sigrid said. "She *was* precocious as a child. She was sent from school twice because she kept her own maths books inside the ones the school provided when she should have been reading the books prescribed."

"Putting silly romance novels inside her maths book!" Meena exclaimed! "Of course I had to rebuke her!"

"But she *wasn't* putting silly romance books inside the schoolbooks! She put books on *mathematical theory* inside the standard textbooks. The books they gave her bored her to death. She was reading mathematical theory when she was a child! Although would *you* ever have bothered to find that out? You always expected the worst of her. And that time Jamie came to Willow Grove—you remember him, the famous mathematician?—and Sophie went up to him and the two of them went off into Peter's study, and when he came back, he went up to Peter and said, 'She found a more elegant solution to my problem than I did. You've got to do something with her.' And *you* sent her to her room because she was bothering the adults. If it hadn't been for you, banging on and on about how she couldn't add two and two, Sophie wouldn't have *hidden* her talent. She's never stopped working on math theory. She was working on it *before* she met Bertold. She used to apologize for it. She'd say, 'It's only a hobby. Like doing the crossword.' But I know what Sophie thought! She thought you hated her for having a special ability, when your greatest accomplishment was working out an excellent table plan. And if Sophie didn't understand that at the time, I did!"

"*You* knew she was a mathematical wizard, then?" Meena asked sarcastically.

"If I didn't, it was because you'd done such a good job shaming her whenever she did anything remarkable. It was always you, Meena. You were always the trouble. Don't think Peter didn't come to see it."

"Be that as it may," Meena said, "if Sophie publishes a book impugning me, the law will be brought to bear."

"For what? What has she done? She hasn't seen you in years and years. You banned her from Christmas at Willow Grove and you rarely came along when Peter came into London to see her. What does she know about you? Why should *you* be her subject? She has her own friends. Really, Meena, you see spectral beings in bright sunlight. A friend of Sophie's suffered through her husband's dying. It made a great impression on her, as one would expect. If you go about crying libel, people will begin thinking that you have a reason for trying to stop your own stepdaughter from doing her own work. People may conclude that poor Sophie, disinherited by her stepmother, has been driven to desperate measures. Sophie does not hold up well under financial distress. A mathematician does not make a fortune, after all. She may be trying her hand at something literary in order to supplement her finances."

"And is that to be laid at my door? Am I to spend the rest of my time living like a church mouse so that spoiled child can buy skylights? *Thirteen* skylights!"

"I knew the skylights would stick in your throat."

"They would stick in *your* throat if you were expected to pay the bill!"

"Well," Sigrid said, drinking the rest of her tea, "I imagine she will comfort herself with Clare when she goes to visit her. She's spent her life looking for a proper mother."

"You must not let her know about Clare!" Meena said, whitening. "I forbid it!"

"I'm afraid Peter told her all about that long ago," Sigrid said. "When Sophie was last in hospital, Peter went to see her, and Clare waited downstairs in the car. Sophie guessed. She said, 'Daddy, you have a girlfriend! Is she here with you? Bring her up!' But he said no, Sophie needed her sleep, not excitement. He promised to bring her round to meet her later, but we all know why *that* didn't happen. Instead, he told Sophie all about Clare. He made it quite clear, how happy he was with her, how he believed he had found the right woman at last."

"Peter would never have spoken of such things in that way," Meena said, tapping the fingers of her right hand against the wooden table. "He would not have told her."

"Then how did she know about Clare, and well before I did? That would be very difficult to explain."

"You mean to say that she knew about The Difficulties, but she intends to meet Clare?"

"I believe she may already be visiting her. She left last night, before I did. It must be the stars, because Rose also left the same night as I. We didn't plan it, Meena. It *is* the stars. When so many things happen in the same way, there must be intention behind it, don't you think?"

"No, I do not think," Meena said. "And if Sophie is so concerned about money, she should turn back before she reaches Crow's Nest."

"Have you ever seen the place? Crow's Nest? It's beautiful. I recognized it when I first saw it, I couldn't understand why. And then I realized. All those paintings done by Lawrence Frost, always the same landscape, the same landscape of Crow's Nest. Such a beautiful place, Meena. You quite lose your bearings. Everything is upside down, the sea looks like the sky, the sky looks like the sea, and the two of them reflect each other. Enough to convince you the Buddhists are right and the world is a dream and there is no real up and no real down. It made me dizzy. But I never wanted to leave. Did Peter speak to you of the tin mines? They worried me, all those vertical shafts, graves, really, waiting for their bodies, not a place to go for long walks, as you like to do, Meena."

"I have been to Cornwall, of course," Meena said.

"Then you must have seen Crow's Nest."

"I may have passed it. I was taken so many places."

"Even after Peter began living there? With Clare?"

"After that, I had no desire to visit Zennor. That strange little town. There was a pub next to the church, wasn't there? That woman is welcome to Cornwall. But she is not welcome to my daughter."

"Do you mean Sophie?"

"Certainly I mean Sophie."

"You speak of her now as your daughter," Sigrid said. "Only because you don't want Clare taking anyone else from you. Sophie hasn't been your daughter for years. If she ever was."

"She was. Most definitely she was."

"How time changes our memories. For a time, Sophie believed I was her mother. She was too young to remember Evelyn. All she remembers of Evelyn was tugging at her apron when she cooked in the kitchen. She's sure she remembers that. That memory is very clear. But otherwise she remembers nothing. If a stepmother had been a true mother to her, Sophie would have taken to her as if to her real mother. These days, she tells people she did wish for just that, *even if she was secondhand.*"

Meena stood up abruptly and began striding up and down through the kitchen. How enormous this kitchen has become since Peter first bought Willow Grove, Sigrid thought, as if seeing it for the first time.

"I will not have Sophie going about saying such things. I've had more than enough to put up with through the years! She must be warned! I will not tolerate it!"

"I'll be sure to tell her," Sigrid said. "I'll say, 'Sophie, Meena refuses to tolerate the things you say.' I'm sure that will do the trick, don't you think?"

"I am very tired," Meena said, suddenly sinking down on the bench. "I think you had better go. In future, I shall want a warning before any of you arrives. Otherwise, I shall have you treated as stalkers."

"Stalkers!"

"Yes, stalkers," said Meena. "Don't drive me to it."

"You don't want to see Julia? She's in London. Or do you now consider her in the stalker category?"

"I don't have time for Julia."

"Once you did. Of course, things change, as you said. Well, Cornwall is lovely this time of year," Sigrid said. "Perhaps I should join Sophie there. Such a beautiful place, don't you think? Not so predictable as your part of Northumberland."

"You are free to go anywhere you please," Meena said. "But not here."

TWENTY-SEVEN

—

EACH TIME PENELOPE went into hospital at the Royal Marsden shortly before she died, with the exception of the very last time when she knew she would not leave again, she always brought certain items with her, small totems that conjured up her life as it had been many years before. One of them was the famous black and white photograph of Evelyn Graves and Peter Grovesnor. It was not so much that she treasured the memory of those two, but rather the associations they both had for her. When Evelyn and Peter were young, she herself was still married to a young and famous playwright, Mark Heath, a man considerably younger than she was. She and her husband often lent their flat to the Grovesnors, as Penelope and her husband called them, and simply to see the two of them together in a photograph was to call up the time of her marriage so vividly that it was, for Penelope, still going on. She had loved other men since Mark left her, but never had she loved anyone as completely and, as she had to admit, so ruinously. When she first began her reluctant stays in hospital, she would bring a picture of herself and her first husband, Mark, but that simply made her regret the past she had lost, and looking at it made her suffer for the loss of her youth. It was the picture of the other two, Evelyn and Peter, that brought back her life as she had once lived it, who brought the past back, all of it, so poignant and still so mourned. For that reason, the photograph was essential to her. In hospital, Penelope would study the picture of Evelyn and Peter as if the riddle of life itself were contained in it.

This is the famous photograph. No one famous took the picture. The person who snapped it was not even a gifted amateur. There was too much sky showing above the couple, their arms intertwined. Taking the picture must have been a problem. Peter was so tall, so much taller than everyone else, so that, to photograph both their faces, their beaming faces, the person taking the picture must have had to shoot up at them, and in consequence, it appeared that both of them, but the girl in particular, somehow seem to lean back against the air behind them. Probably Peter's actual face was little changed by the perspective in the photograph. The viewer saw his face straight on, but Evelyn was looking up. Someone viewing the photo would see Evelyn looking up at Peter as if in complete adoration.

They were wearing what appeared to be quite ordinary clothes. Anyone could date the photograph by what the two were wearing: it was the late fifties or the early sixties. Evelyn was wearing a starched and ironed white blouse. The waist of her full skirt, cotton, printed, was bound by a wide cinch belt. His outfit was equally nondescript, and therefore impeccably proper. He was wearing a cotton shirt, also unwrinkled and very clean. Presumably, he was wearing chinos. It was hard to tell.

Her hair was blond and the sunlight caught it. It was long, a halfway-to-the-shoulder length that was popular at the time, and it was waved, gently, the kind of waves that were in style then, considerably fuller and looser than the tight marcelled waves so popular in the twenties, but suggesting that previous time, hinting that not so much time had passed as one would think, that what people wanted thirty, almost forty years before was still what they wanted now. She had learned to subdue her hair, to suggest loveliness, propriety, correctness, although somehow her hair, like her clothing, did not really suit her. Perhaps no one's hair and clothing did, not in those days. In several years, the sixties would advance and all styles would change, even those governing the courtship of couples.

His hair—what was there to say about a man's hair, really?—unless he had grown bald at the top, drove a sports car, and wore a ponytail—but those times had yet to arrive. His hair was under restraint, savagely contained, but a shock of hair fell forward over his right eye. There was something about that rebellious shock of hair that made the entire picture more alive.

Such timeless smiles in that photograph! She was wearing lipstick, which in the picture looks very dark, but was probably bright red, the preferred shade of the decade. Probably she had been wearing the same shade for years. It was a black and white picture, but anyone who continued to look at Evelyn and who knew her hair was blond, almost platinum, and that her lipstick was a vivid red, would see her come alive: a young girl, a young woman of her time, attractive, intent on appearing as attractive as possible, but taking care to remain within limits. Extravagance of any sort did not do in those times, suggesting looseness, *that kind of woman,* even madness.

His face in the photograph did not invite speculation as to his coloring. His hair was dark. That was clear enough. It had always been his face that drew people toward him. A rugged face, a rock-face of a face, suggesting romantic heroes, ultimately earning him the name of another Heathcliff, as well as other, more unsavory labels. But there was nothing in the photograph to suggest disturbance or unhappiness or changes that would be later bought by time. Time and the passage of time: these ideas were banned from the photograph. Anyone looking at the picture would not think, Someday these two will grow old. The picture announced the impossibility of such an idea.

Their smiles would be commented on again and again. Hers was a smile of rapture. Perhaps the dark light of retrospect caused the viewer to see something that shadowed the blissfulness, the triumph in it. But the rejoicing was there, and the viewer had no way of knowing from what that triumph arose. Was she ecstatic because she had found the man she always dreamed of, and now she had him? Had finding him made her believe that it was really possible to begin a life again, to erase the very short one that had gone before? Were all these questions the picture brought to the surface the result of hindsight? Everyone knew what had become of them. Was it possible that there was no trace of triumph in her brilliant, brilliant smile? Only a cynic, or a depressive, might look into her face pictured there and think, That can never last. Shining things like that never last. *Brightness falls from the air; queens have died young and fair.* A singular viewer, eccentric in some way, might have thought such things, especially if he had seen them near the time the photograph was taken.

His face was the one that haunts. Much later, after the young woman was gone, after she was dead and buried, not much older than she was when this picture was taken, his face would be the one that was remembered. It was, as everyone said, especially women, so remarkably attractive. The rough-hewn face contrasted so sharply with his eyes, so often remarked on, those hooded eyes, in this picture, half closed, half dazed, and made drowsy with happiness, as if declaring to anyone who looked at this picture, No one can be happier than this. In the photograph, he was quite sharp, his face in perfect focus, but all the same, his face had something blurry about it, as if all the muscles in his body were relaxed, sated and drunk with happiness. He must have been holding tightly to her, because she was pressed so hard against his chest and shoulders. That must have been the consequence of desire. Or it may have been something simpler. The photographer may have said to them, "Get closer together so I can get everything in."

It was always hard to know what subjects felt at the instant a photograph was taken; everyone who had looked through his own or family photograph albums knew that. Everyone always looked so happy. There was the picture of the young woman soon to be told that the man she loved no longer loved her and wanted to leave her, and hours later, she would be swallowing the sleeping pills she had been hoarding for months. But in the photograph they looked so happy, as if they could never stop being happy. There were the members of a family, the small children grinning ferociously, the parents smiling happily as if there were nothing but tranquillity in the world, and one of the children, seeing the photograph later, would think, Were we ever as happy as we seemed in this picture? And if that grown child remembered his childhood well, he would think, How did we ever manage to look so happy? When that time was not at all happy. And then he would go back to the older photographs, scrutinizing his parents when they were younger, before he was born, and think, But they were happy *then,* surely they were happy then! And if he saw something less tranquil, something the photograph had managed to capture, he might go back further and further, back to the albums whose black pages have the feel of felt, where the photographs have deckled edges, back and back, and the further back he went, the happier the couples seemed. Everyone smiling in photographs, even in pictures taken a few months after coming into this world! Smiling through birthdays, birthday parties, smiling from the saddles of ponies securely tethered at Coney Island, smiling during sweet sixteen parties, kneeling with friends at the beach, standing up in their finery at their own and others' weddings, always happy. Thus the world conspired, lied, tried to tell each new creature that there was nothing in the world but happiness, even when tragedies were destined to occur immediately after the photographer snapped the picture.

How much better, how much more sensible, more honest, more truthful, were the pictures taken in the nineteenth century, those Victorian

times, when the photographer was called in to make a mourning picture
of someone who had just died, that last photograph completing the long
series that began with the infant in his christening gown, all the family
members dressed in their finest, the women all wearing their jet jewelry,
black, shiny, sometimes iridescent, the color of well-fed crows, that jet suggesting, even in the midst of such happiness, that other, darker, black seeds
were being sown. The arc in a family picture album, always the same,
delineated in the series of photographs of each person, so that each person knew how he would progress through life, how, whether happy or
unhappy, the last picture taken of him would be, with God's grace, a formal portrait the photographer took of him when he lay in peace in his
own home, in his own, last narrow bed.

The happy couple in the picture: Evelyn and Peter Grovesnor.
Someone could easily reconstitute such a photographic arc, a photographic album, for either or both of them. There was Peter's, the first picture of the thin, frail, croupy child, destined to grow into a strong man,
not more handsome than many other men from his part of the country,
but far more magical, more capable of charming; then the young boy, his
face smeared with dirt after digging in the earth looking for something
he would not disclose, *Tell me, tell me, and I will help you look for it,* refusing to give up any information; next the older boy at school, looming
over the others, a mortarboard tilted dangerously on his head, happily
holding tight to his diploma, *You'll never get anywhere, you don't look at
those books, you'll be sorry when it comes time to go down in the mines
because what else will you be fit for?* The young man, barely a man, leaving for university, turning back to wave goodbye to someone in the house
who at that moment had a camera, then the mortarboard again, once
more a mortarboard; finally a young man in a suit too small for him, a
slightly shiny suit from Oxfam, but it had been made clear to him that
employees in his office must wear suits, still without a briefcase, only with
a plastic carry bag from Dillons, and then the photographs began to thin
out, until he began to appear with Evelyn, pictures of him reading as he

sat at the bottom of a bed while Evelyn was curled up at the top, pictures of picnics, always with Evelyn, always with the checked tablecloth she brought with them, and finally the famous photograph taken on the day after their wedding, the wedding pictures missing, but existing some- where. Peter always thought they would find them, those photographs of the two of them, he in his shiny suit, Evelyn in her beige lace dress and her off-white pillbox hat, both of them uncomfortable, but happy: who could doubt their happiness?

And there was a last photograph: it would have completed the arc, the photograph taken by his daughter as he lay in his narrow hospital bed in the white room in the Royal Marsden, an intravenous drip attached to him like a leash, the rails of the bed up, not because he was in danger of falling from the bed, but because he was so weak and the needle in his arm pained him as every part of his body did, so that it was easier to find a comfort- able place if he could rest against the rails of the bed, or use the rails of the bed to pull himself to one side or another, or pull himself toward the pil- low, a ravaged man, pale, still striking, irreversibly attractive, even nearing death. This time the pallor is unmistakable, the creases in his cheeks so deep they cast their own thin shadows, and this is the last card in the deck. Did he accept it, what fate was offering him, what fate had made him, the number of days fate had doled out to him?

Probably he did. Most people who suffer badly do. They feel the destruction as it takes place in their bodies. The pain they feel makes them know what is happening to them. Did he think, as so many others did, I have been worn out by all this, worn through? I am willing, more than willing, to have it stop? Because there were some who were not willing, and many would say such people died terrible deaths. Had he not told his daughter that he wanted to die a good death? Then probably he did want to stop. And there was that morphine drip with its button that he kept carefully in his hand. Was he himself the one who delivered the final dosage, the one that would put an end to his heart's beating? Wouldn't someone else have had to do it? Or had he pressed the button when he felt his energy ebb and had known that if he pressed the button now, he would never have to press it again?

But before that, there was his daughter, with an Instamatic, having gone down to the gift shop when she saw how weak he was, when she knew beyond doubt that she would not have such an opportunity again. So that now that last photograph exists, preserved in Sophie's own house, a photograph that belongs only to her, the last moments of her father's life, which no one but she can see.

And, of course, the series of Evelyn's pictures, not as long a series, naturally not as long. She came to a stop so much faster. The smiling child coming forward for her awards, as many—more!—than her birthdays, kneeling at the beach, her skin tanned, her hair bleached, the golden girl, as people called her, then the photos of her, so thin and bruised after her suicide attempt. And after that, the photos of her and the man she chose, Peter, a man she never believed would die, a man who looked as if he had been carved out of stone, no more vulnerable than a statue, so that regardless of how she tried to imagine his death, no matter how hard she might finally come to wish for it, Peter's death, she could not believe he would ever die. Pictures of Evelyn and her children, her hair now long, often twisted into braids and then pinned brutally against her skull, so that she looked like someone's Polish grandmother. Still smiling in her pictures, but now there was no denying the tremulous look, the anxious expression, the difficulty in smiling. Although she did try. Wearing a printed dress of indiscriminate design, a simple necklace she must have worn day in and day out, a thin chain and one pearl suspended between her prominent clavicle bones. Attesting to something, but what? But now, instead of looking into the camera, beginning to look down toward the heads of her children, a graceful pose, but one that refused to expose her face completely, what could be seen of her face proclaiming, *Everything has gone wrong. Will someone please tell me what has gone wrong?* And no one to tell her, not even people who had been through all this before. What could they do but shake their heads, meaning to say, *This is what life is, wait and it will pass,* but no one to tell her where the strength came from to wait, to let time pass. And if she did not believe she could wait for time to pass, then why torture herself further? Why not end her life now, because what it had become was what it would always be, because she had no strength to change. Or so she believed.

Was there, is there, somewhere a photograph of her as she lay quietly in her own final, narrow bed, while her husband cried and cried, and she slept on, undisturbed? Somewhere there may be one. There may have been such a photograph once, but wouldn't her husband have destroyed it? In those days immediately after her death, when he destroyed so many things because he could not bear to look at them? Or did he hide many such things, knowing that the day would come when he would want to look at them again? And then time passed, and he forgot about them, as some women preserve one photograph of their first love and keep it, fading, cracking, but kept safe, somewhere hidden, but easily found, no matter what. That picture traveling from house to house, throughout the storm of childbirth and raising children, throughout their own passions for their own husbands, throughout all the illnesses, preserving that one photograph as if it were a lifeboat, as if once they had known what they wanted, as if once life had been perfect, and if it had been perfect once, then it could be again. But if such a picture of Evelyn existed, Evelyn, once she had breathed in the gas rising from her own oven, as if the gas were the only mother's milk she still believed she might drink, no one knew of it, no one knew if it existed. If Meena had found it, it would not have survived. Is there any person who knows Meena, who knew Meena, who would believe it survived? So Evelyn's arc ends abruptly, at the high point, at high noon, before her life begins its steep decline, before the body inevitably succumbs to the pull of the earth, before the bones begin to hear the songs of the earth, calling and calling, until, finally, those songs become the most beautiful melodies there are. Not a long flight through the air, poor Evelyn. Her children have flown longer and farther. Even her daughter has flown long enough to begin worrying about losing her youth. Well, Evelyn didn't have to worry about *that,* Peter said to Sophie. "She is eternally beautiful, your mother. She would have liked that. She would be nearing seventy if she had lived," Peter said. "Can you imagine it?"

No one could. No one would ever be able to compete with that eternal, tragic, youthful, inspired figure of womanhood and maternity. The unchangeable genius, the woman she became when she turned on the gas. And yet: what a sordid way to die, her head in an oven, what an unforgivable thing, to leave two small children. Suppose, people said, my mother had done that to *me.* And in the end, the miracle was that so few people chose Evelyn's way. They found another way and went on. No wonder so many thought of Evelyn as a saint. Yet their thoughts about Evelyn were hopelessly muddled. After her death, her life had grown to be a cautionary tale; her destiny had warned and saved others, who had thought of Evelyn, and moved back from precipices of their own, who looked at the famous photograph of Peter and Evelyn and thought, I am not meant for sainthood. I do not want to pay such a price. And still: many would also think, Yes, Evelyn Graves was a true saint. She endured such misery, but she created astonishing beauty out of despair; she spoke for *me,* if I could have written, I would have written the same words she wrote.

And eventually the viewer always notices the slight tracery of black branches in the photograph visible somewhere above their heads, not distinct, almost like cobwebs, the two of them in their spring clothes, no sweaters, no coats, but the trees behind them proclaiming, *Winter.* Winter and the death of everything.

TWENTY-EIGHT

———

SIGRID WAS BACK in her own house, thanking God that she had a house and a roof, a leaky roof, but still a roof, and had to depend on no one. Her first husband had been dead for almost twenty years. He was the one she had loved, not Douglas, her second husband, forever holed up in his study, never raising his voice above a whisper, never asking for anything, content only to breathe in and out as if that were more than enough life for him to bear. She often asked herself, Has Douglas had a nervous collapse? He never went out, never wanted to go out, although it is true that he did occasionally venture out for the occasional paper. But she invariably concluded that *she* could not undergo a collapse, not when there was anything left in her. Her first husband had died in France when the two of them were no longer together. He was tall and strong and hand-some, but also addicted to alcohol and their fights were still talked about by people who had known them. "I'm well rid of him," Sigrid used to say when he left for France, but when the news of his death came, she was des-olated. Every year, without fail, an Egyptian friend would send her a letter of consolation: *Remembering you in your time of loss.* Each time the card arrived—she knew it from the handwriting—Sigrid would smile, open the card, put it down on the table, go off and make a cup of tea, come back and stare into the garden thinking of Allen who had died alone in France. After a time, those memories changed from bitterness to a wistful sense of loss, reminding her of the soft chartreuse colors of the trees when they first begin to leaf out in spring. Then, one day, perhaps ten years after Allen's death, another card arrived from Cairo, and when Sigrid opened it, she thought, What is this all about? And she realized that the mourn-ing was over; the little altar she kept had been bricked up, and there was no longer space for him. Gone at last, not so much a memory as a story she had once known well, and still knew well enough to tell to others without disturbing herself, the flesh and the marrow gone out of it, Sigrid thought.

How were memories dulled, as everyone invariably said they would be? Were there stages in that process? In the aftermath of a death, was the lost person summoned up again and again, until the sharp edges grew dull, and then began to erode altogether? Julia had given her, oh, years ago now, a daguerreotype of an old woman sitting upright in her chair, staring straight into the camera lens. "Be careful of it," Julia had said. "Don't expose it to light. Don't keep it open on the mantel." And when she asked Julia why it had to be treated with such care, Julia said, "It's the silver that makes the picture so fragile," she said. "The silver tarnishes. That's why they went to such lengths to make the case. See that little embossed leather case? And inside, the puff of velvet with a design burned into the pillow; that's to pro-tect the glass plate, and when you've finished revisiting the woman in the picture, you close the case and fasten it with those two brass latches."

"Like a little coffin," Sigrid said.

"It is," said Julia. "And the face inside the little coffin begins to decay just like the real one did. The image starts to tarnish and the margins turn bluish black and green and begin moving in. Like algae in a pond. They were very careful because of all that."

Yes, Sigrid thought, it was the image of the person, particularly the face, that faded fastest. Already Peter's face was fading. She could summon it up for an instant, and then it was gone. But she remembered, saw that face sharply, when she saw his image in a photograph, and after that, it was the face in the photograph that she remembered. And which photograph did she usually look at? The famous picture, Evelyn and Peter, their bodies pressed against one another, that picture, that icon of happiness. He *was* meant to be happy, she thought, she'd always thought that, but now she began to wonder. Was it true? If happiness was what the world had intended for him, why had everything turned out so badly? Was his choice of women his Achilles' heel? More like a leg than a heel, she thought. Did he secretly crave unhappiness? Once or twice before, Sigrid had thought as much. But today, after her visit to Meena, it seemed evident. But what did he have to be unhappy about? Had an appetite for unhappiness been born that rainy summer in Cornwall when none of them had anything to do, when customers came in infrequently, deciding against braving the rain, choosing to remain dry and warm in their own houses, making the best of what they had? The children came into the store sporadically, flying in like a flock of birds, laughing and talking, buying sweets, then leaving as quickly as they had arrived.

When Sigrid thought back to that summer of endless rain, she remembered Peter sprawled on the floor at her father's feet, asking him question after question, none of which their father ever seemed to answer, but evidently he had done so, once she left the room, asking question after question about the war, the mustard gas, the sandstorms which had brought their father down, irritating his lungs, infecting them, scarring them, so that he spent the rest of his life short of breath, asking about mustard gas, asking about the first time tanks were used in battle. The first time he had seen British tanks in battle, what an incredible sight they had been, like something out of a book of horrors, knocking everything down, shaking the earth, causing the enemy soldiers to run in terror, telling Peter that he would not be alive, none of them would have survived that battle had it not been for the tanks, ending by saying, "To this day I love tanks. Love them. Avenging angels, they were. Great, lumbering grey things, they were. You wouldn't think anything of it today, times change so fast, you see, no, you wouldn't think anything of them today." And after weeks of bothering their father, Peter turned to the three uncles who had returned from France and Germany, and asked them his endless questions, only this time with far greater success because after his conversations with his father, he had learned what to ask, where to begin. No, thought Sigrid, it was not what his father and the uncles told Peter that fanned his appetite for misery, of course not. His mother had heard all the same stories, heard them in greater detail, heard them orchestrated by great, gulping sobs, and she had not changed, not really. Their mother had always known there was misery in the world. She did not have to learn that by listening to other people's tragedies.

There must have been a time, Sigrid thought, when Peter really believed the world was perfect and golden, when he believed that this perfect happiness was his to keep forever, when he was certain that everything belonged to him by right. And then what was buried deep in the bone began to sprout and take root, that big tree of despair and the fatal shade of its leaves. What was it? Something too small for anyone, not even Peter, to recover or understand? One of the fairy tales that marked him? Something found dead in the lane? Those spring mornings in Cornwall when a sea fret settled in and no one could see beyond his nose, and his endless walks and what he saw there? A lane with a sheep dead on the ground, black birds going for its eyes? Farther down, skeletons of animals who had drowned or frozen, emerging from the mist on the ground at the grass's verge, the bones of small animals that had gone missing in the winter. Was that the skeleton of a cat? Mrs. Bolster had lost her cat right after Christmas. That could be her cat. But Sigrid had gone on the same walks, sometimes on her own, sometimes with Peter, and not until Evelyn died had she discovered an appetite for despair.

Where *was* that photograph of the two of them? Sigrid got up and riffled through the packed, senseless drawer of the dining hutch. There it was, a stack of those photographs, xeroxed, down at the bottom of everything. She picked one up and looked at it, pulled out the scissors, and cut Evelyn from the picture. Oh, I have seen you often enough, too often, she thought, crumpling the sheet of paper and violently throwing it into the trash. But, as Sigrid soon understood, that exorcism had done no good.

—

IN THE LITTLE house she hated from the first time she laid eyes on it, Rose went straight to her study. The trip to Willow Grove had shaken her badly, but as Robert would have said, had he been alive—had he gone with herto protect her, and now who was to protect her?—"Why must you pay attention to everyone's opinion? Will you start asking the postman what he thinks of your books?" She *was* weak in that way, and so had built around herself an almost impenetrable smugness and certainty about her own great ability. "If it is a wall, it is a wall with crenellated turrets," Robert used to say. "You can hold off an army with turrets like that. But be certain, Rose, be *sure* that you do not build it out of wood." "Why?" asked Rose, and Robert had answered, scornfully, as was his way in their last years together, "because, Rose, of flaming arrows. Have you never heard of flaming arrows?" and Rose said, "No, I hadn't given flaming arrows very much thought."

"Don't give too much thought to anyone, Rose," he said. "You know it's a mistake."

How had she survived all that? When they had begun so happily. *Begin as you mean to go on*, that great blueprint for life. And so she had. But he had not followed the same path.

Once, she had believed Julia was her great friend. One afternoon, the two of them were sitting in the café across the street from Rose's flat, and Rose asked Julia, "Do you and Matt have that hate thing between you?"

"Hate thing?" Julia answered.

"It's probably too early for you," Rose said, "and your husband hasn't retired, but when he's home all day and has nothing to do, and you become the only thing he concentrates on, that's when it starts. Every phone call you make, every bill that comes in, anything anyone says who stops by, that's when it starts."

"Hate thing," Julia said again, thinking it over.

"There's no other word for it," Rose said. "There's no one else around, so he hates you for everything that's gone wrong, and you hate him for hating you. And when he *sees* you hate him, he hates you even more. That's why we travel so much. It's better when we're out of the country because he sees new things and his attention veers away from me to other things. And then we come back, and I'm jet-lagged and go to sleep, and when I open my eyes, there he is, saying, 'Not the same old Rose again.' But you are ten, fifteen years younger, so you haven't run into it yet."

"I would imagine he had always been difficult," Julia said.

"Yes. But he had a whole *university* to be angry at, schedules, grants to write, all of that. We were happy enough in the beginning. We were. My idea of perfect happiness was to find a man who wanted to spend every moment of his time with me, and only occasionally would he venture out into the world. Well, you know what they say about wishing for what you want and then getting it. I've had what I wanted for almost ten years, or is it twelve? It seems like centuries."

"Funny," Julia said. "That's exactly what I once wanted. Probably that was what broke up my first relationship, not that we could have lived together even if that hadn't been a problem. He counted every penny and

I was extravagant. If an infant in the crib can already be extravagant, I was. A few years ago, I had to give a reading in the city where he's lived for years, and I stayed with a friend from college who'd known him, and you know how it is with old friends. You start to behave as if you're both the same age you were when you first met. She wanted to show me the house her ex-husband lived in, and then she wanted to see the house of that author she likes so much, so we drove there and sat in the car staring at her house, and then I wanted to go see the house where the ex-love of my life lived, and it was a huge house, probably very beautiful inside, but even from where we were sitting, across the street, a very wide street, it had the look of an unfurnished house. We couldn't see anything on the walls. If there had been things on the walls, someone would have had to buy them. I often wonder, those men who are so passionate about minimalism, is it an excuse not to spend money? I mean, it doesn't cost anything to have *nothing*."

"Well, that was never Robert's problem," Rose said. "He blamed me because the house was such a mess, but he didn't see the point of hiring someone to clean. And when he saw something, he bought it, so we have that stone temple lion in the middle of the parlor. Every so often, I try it out in another place, but it only makes matters worse. And then he wanted an especially good stereo system. So there it all sits, and there do I, Aida in her tomb. My own study is just as bad, but I stop at books. A few posters on the wall, but otherwise only books. When I was younger and stronger and he went boating with the children on the canals, I'd drag things down the steps and out into the trash and when he came back, he never mentioned they were gone. But now if I take down the trash, he wants to know what's in it. 'You might have thrown out an important bill, could I look through that bag, Rose?' I started using the big, black trash-bin liners, the kind meant for leaves when you rake things up in the fall. I thought that would dissuade him, the enormity of looking through that, but instead it gives him something to do. He never finds anything, but he keeps it up hoping to shout at me about something."

"You should move out," Julia said. "For a while."

"Oh, I can't do that," Rose said. "In ten years, you'll see that you can't do it, either."

"Is it just habit, then?" Julia asked her.

"Habit is far more complicated than people think," Rose said. "Far, far more."

—

ROSE WISHED SHE could ring up Julia, ask to meet her at the same coffee shop, talk things over in the same leisurely way, as if time were a bolt of cloth that would never come to an end, but Julia, she now saw, had never liked her, not really. Julia had been bored by her or angry at Robert, but all the same, relentlessly polite. Rose ought to have seen that politeness for what it was. Was there anyone else but Julia who would argue with Robert without losing patience or her temper? But one night, the two of them nagged Julia and Matt into going out for dinner, and Robert kept on and on about some subject so utterly arcane that even a specialist on the subject would have been bored, until Julia blew up and shouted at him, saying, "You're not interested in the truth! You're interested in making everyone around you unhappy! And what is a good man, by your definition? According to the definition you've just framed, you ought to be hanged!"

"Julia," Rose had put in, rather feebly she knew, because, to tell the truth, she was so delighted to hear Julia speak out like that.

"A *good* man has some compassion for others," Julia went on. "A good man does not continue even when someone at a very good restaurant picks up his steak knife and threatens to drive it through his own heart simply because you will not stop." There was no silencing her. When she finally finished, she looked at her husband and said, "Matt. Let's see about the check."

"I didn't realize you intended to pay," Robert said, finally shamefaced.

"And would that have shut you up? If you knew we were paying the bill?" Julia asked him. "Would anything?"

Afterward, just as Rose had expected, Julia was always busy when she called. Finally, Rose called one time too many, and she asked Julia why she was so busy. Couldn't she take even a short break? Wouldn't the time away be good for her work? and Julia went silent, and then said, "Rose, I can't tolerate it anymore. I cannot stand listening to one more diatribe of Robert's."

"But we could meet alone for lunch. At the café," Rose said tremulously.

"Doesn't he follow you about these days, like Mary's little lamb?" Julia asked. How hard her voice had become, as everyone else's voice grew sooner or later, although Julia had lasted far longer than most.

"I can't stop him coming," Rose said.

"It's better if we don't meet. You'll pay for it afterwards, Rose, you know you will. You must have paid quite a price for that last dinner when I lost my temper."

"No. Just the reverse. When we got home, he was full of admiration for you."

"I don't care whether he admires me or doesn't," Julia said.

"So I am to be left behind?" Rose said.

"I wouldn't call it leaving you behind."

"Then what would you call it?"

"Protecting my sanity," Julia said.

"You're as steady as a rock!" Rose exclaimed.

Julia said, "Rose, you don't understand me at all. The bell's ringing. Surely you can hear it through the phone, and I'm late. I'm still not dressed. I can't go out on the street like this."

"You're going to meet Sigrid for dinner, aren't you?"

"Yes, I am."

"And if I accidentally dropped by?"

"Don't do it," Julia said. "Matt would walk out and I'd have to go with him and there'd be a problem paying for the check. Sigrid wouldn't be pleased, either."

"So that's it," Rose said.

"Don't make it worse than it is," Julia said, and rang off.

Well, thought Rose, there was no point in rehearsing those days. They were dead, gone, and she had work to do. Somewhere she had a list she'd made of things to do. At the top of that list, she now remembered, were a number of questions she had meant to ask Sigrid, small things. Had Peter gone to dances? When did he first begin to write? She knew what Peter had said in interviews, but could she tell her when he *really* began to write? Hadn't someone said that he decided on writing because he knew he could get himself admitted to Oxford if he began publishing poems in the school paper? Not much chance of getting answers out of Sigrid now. Sigrid would blame her for everything that went wrong in her family because she, Rose, had had the temerity to make her way to Willow Grove against Sigrid's advice. Life really was impossible, especially if you let other people in. When Robert was very depressed, he used to say that very thing, and she was beginning to wonder if he hadn't been right all along. She opened the long, shallow drawer of her desk. On top of papers was a newsprint photograph of Evelyn and Peter, the same photograph the newspapers always ran. Surely their lives had been happier than people thought. Peter had always seemed so happy, so *imperturbable,* whenever she'd met him. Of course, in those days he was usually sloshed, but as Robert said, Peter was one of the world's great drunks. He simply became happier and happier, more and more excitable, as if he had discovered new colors in the spectrum of human emotions. And Rose thought, If I had been that happy, even for one day, surely it would have sufficed. I could have lived on that one day for the rest of my life. Just one day. It would have been enough. Why hadn't it been enough for him?

TWENTY-NINE

———

IT WAS LATE in the afternoon when Sophie reached Crow's Nest. She stopped halfway up the lane leading to the house on the rim of the hill above her, turned toward the sea, and looked out at the sky. There was the landscape of one year of her childhood, the setting sun reflecting in the sea, the sun seeming to set in the sea, that familiar sensation of the world having been turned upside down, a scene always vividly evoked when she upturned an hourglass. Really, it was so beautiful here. Why had her father ever left? Julia always said, "It doesn't do to spend your life too close to the place where you were born," but then Julia was always quick to admit that her own childhood had been a horror. The farther from your own birthplace the better, Julia always said. Sophie's back hurt. It

was such a long drive. She got out of the car and stretched herself, leaning against the car's warm body. No reason to greet Clare for the first time
as if she were ninety-nine and bent double with arthritis. She had forgotten, she always forgot, how tropical Cornwall was. Each time she came,
she was astonished to find palm trees growing as happily as if they had
been planted in Jamaica. And the trees, tortured and tormented out of
shape by the wind endlessly pouring over the hills and then down. She
loved it here.

When she finally arrived at Crow's Nest, no one was about. The stillness was comforting. A gravel path led up to the front door and she followed it. There was no bell, only a huge wind chime and a placard in her
father's writing, saying, *Ring the chimes*. She pushed the chimes over to the
left. What a beautiful sound, the same sound a spring wind would have if
it had a voice of its own. There was a small sign that said *Clare Tartikoff*,
and below that, another sign, in larger letters that said, *The Light House*.
Had she stopped referring to the house as Crow's Nest? That would be too
bad, Sophie thought. The house had had that name for centuries, certainly
for as long as she could remember. Her father had told her that.

Was that the sound of someone coming toward the door? It was, and
the heavy door swung open.

"I'm Clare," said the woman. Her long grey and black hair was piled up
on top of her head, and she wore a black sweater and black pants.

"There are little bits of wire stuck in your hair," Sophie said, unthink-
ingly pulling one out.

"Oh," Clare said, flushing. The flush began at the base of her neck and
traveled upward until her face was scarlet. "I make chandeliers, you see.
The wires get everywhere."

"I love chandeliers," Sophie said.

"Would you like to see mine?" Clare asked. "They're not lovely, sparkly
things like the ones in the London shops, but one day I found I had too
little money and I made a few of them, and they sold very well. So that's
what I do. Perhaps your father told you?"

"No," said Sophie, smiling. "Probably he thought I had far too many chandeliers."

"Well, come see mine," she said. "Although, really, there's nothing remarkable in them." She led Sophie down the hall, down two steps, and into a long room whose far wall opened on the ocean. For a moment that was all Sophie saw, the great portrait of the sea framed by the immense window. "I made this my workshop because I needed the light," Clare said.

Sophie looked around her. On the left and right side of the room, chandeliers hung from rafters, one after another. "You sell them?" Sophie asked inanely.

"Yes. I never thought I would."

"I didn't mean, well, I didn't mean to say no one would want to buy them," Sophie said, her own face reddening.

"I didn't think you meant that," Clare said. "Would you like me to show you my wares?" In her own workshop, Clare was most at ease. A queen-sized mattress and spring had been placed on the floor to the right of the entrance. "Your father liked to stay in here when I worked," she said. "He liked looking out at the sea."

"He always said he missed the Cornwall coast," Sophie said.

"Yes. He did. I have some lemonade and some cookies and a tin of candied ginger. Your father used to bring that down each time he came. And of course I have tea and digestive biscuits."

"Tea would be lovely, and a few pieces of ginger. My father hoarded candied ginger. My stepmother was annoyed by it. She called him greedy."

"Everyone is greedy about something," Clare said. "I'll be straight back."

Sophie sat down in a red butterfly chair and looked out at the sea. Why had her father moved to Northumberland when he could have lived here? This was a house that spoke of warmth and beauty and comfortable silences in which people discovered what they truly thought. The windows were open, and a small breeze, slowly turning into a wind, was cooling a room that was almost always hot in the summer. The large wall of windows at the far end of the room took the sun's heat and amplified it, so that the wind, when it came, was a ribbon of warmth moving sinuously around everything it touched. The chandeliers slowly swayed back and forth in the currents of air, as if the room, or the house, required hundreds of these pendulums to keep its machinery going. The finished chandeliers, or those that seemed closest to being finished, hung immediately inside the entrance to the room, while the others, under construction, sparkled in the light, and beyond those were the undecorated wrought-iron chandeliers, the skeletons. When the wind picked up a little, some of the crystals already wired in place clicked together like wind chimes.

I have never seen a more perfect room, Sophie thought. I feel as if I've lived in it forever. How my father must have loved this room! With its litter of snipped bits of silver wire, its heaps of crystals set out in clear acrylic bins, its rows of crystal pendants, some fluted, shaped almost like angels, others like crystal daggers, crystal bunches of grapes in all colors, everything in a controlled profusion in the racks beneath the chandeliers, and a children's wagon, painted in yellow, red, and indigo, filled with cones of crystals, all sizes and shapes, waiting beneath an unusually large chandelier. This is where chandeliers come from, Sophie thought dreamily. This is where the world's chandeliers come from.

"Here we are," Clare said, returning.

"Lovely," Sophie said. "But take me on a tour of these chandeliers."

Clare flushed again, but then she laughed softly. "All right. Let's start with the ones on the left. I'm not sure they differ from the ones on the right, but there you are. You see they're full of little photographs," she said. "I used to call them 'The Family Tree,' but we changed them to 'Family Light.'"

"We?" asked Sophie.

"Well, your father liked dreaming up titles for them, you see."

"He would have done," Sophie said. "And the frames for the faces, those little frames, they're exquisite! I've never seen anything like them. You could sell each picture frame separately."

"Yes, well," Clare said, "but I like chandeliers. When I began, I had almost no money, but at the end of the season, I'd go about looking for abandoned fixtures and I decorated them, so that's how I began. When Penzance became such a beehive and the wealthier sort began to move in, the new people threw out the old fixtures. I haunted the trash looking for them. And then I thought, what I need are bits and pieces. People threw out old silverware, broken wine glasses, brooches that didn't fasten, anything that lost a stone or wasn't perfect.

"After the season ended, really ended, when the fogs began coming in, I went from village to village looking at jumble sales. You can find the most beautiful things, a red jade fox once meant to be a hair clip, so I'd take that, or a spray of jeweled flowers. I found one of those once, and later I found they were diamonds, so after that, I was careful, little carvings missing arms or legs or a head. Of course, if I found a figure intact, it was dear. Well, dear compared to the things people gave away free. I took all of those. People were happy to be rid of them. Two large silver turtles, they began as earrings, you see. There they are, closer to the window. Then one day I saw someone with a stall of little frames meant to be filled with photographs, meant for snapshots taken by tourists, and I thought, A family tree! Why not a chandelier filled with people's faces? People's faces radiate so much light, well," she said, reddening again, "so it's always seemed to me. So I got a little camera and took photos of everyone I knew, and made frames for the pictures. In the beginning, I bought the frames and glued things onto them, but then I began to try out copper wire, it was all I could afford, really, and I made little flowers and little wreaths, fantastic shapes. Well, everything I made was *supposed* to look like real life, but in the beginning, I was hard put to make a tree resemble a tree, and then once I had this *suggestion* of a tree, that was all it was, I'd decorate it with whatever I had, usually pieces of shell and small pearls. People threw out so many pearl necklaces, not real, of course. It was the end of the summer. I suppose they had better things they wore in the winter, and bits of crystal beads and rhinestones I pried out of broken brooches and bracelets.

Earrings were wonderful. Everything in them was so small. I hardly ever got two the same. But once someone threw away a rhinestone belt, very old, but everything sparkled like the sun on the water, I lived on that belt for a long time, that was a treasure, and then, you know, you get better at it, and you begin to buy silver-plated wire. You don't think you'll ever manage to buy pure silver, but you do get bits of coral, all the things the shopkeepers can't wait to get rid of for pennies when the season ends, and transparent stones, if they were stones and not plastic. It's always been a surprise. Come sit down and have your tea," Clare said abruptly, as if she'd just realized how many sentences she had strung together. "Oh, no, the tea will be cold! I don't usually go on and on like this. I *am* sorry!"

Sophie was fascinated. "This chandelier," she said, pointing to the one closest to her, "is this typical?" She had asked about a chandelier covered with small photographs in elaborate frames.

"Oh, that one, yes. People used to ask for those soon after a wedding. I don't know how people came to learn about me. But someone would come and say she wanted a picture tree, that's what people called them, of her mother and her father, and her aunts and her uncles, and, of course, the same for her husband's family, and I'd always suggest they leave one or two branches bare so that there would be room for new pictures. I meant pictures of children, of course, but I didn't say that, and besides, a tree always has some dead branches, doesn't it, branches that don't bloom? If we left some branches bare, the tree would look much more interesting, and later, if someone wanted more pictures and more frames, I said I'd do them for her. That was the beginning, a kind of sparkly wedding album, and I found out about the open crystal bowls they use in real chandeliers, and if people were willing to pay for them, I'd order them up, and they could use candles to light up the chandelier, the way people used to do. I would have given them the cups," Clare said, flushing again, "but I didn't have the cash. So I had to charge them.

"And then I began to see that some people really wanted a Tree of Light to remember people by, all the people they once knew who were dead. A woman came in one day and said, 'I don't know where all my friends have gone to. Really, I can't find their addresses anymore, or all the ones I have are wrong. The post keeps sending everything back, you see. It's a small country. You'd think you could keep track of your friends. I can't even find my brother!' and while she was talking in that way, I thought, of course she can't find them; they're all dead. But I couldn't say that to her. It was so sad. So I suggested that she let me make her a Tree of Life if she still had pictures of the people she couldn't find, and that way she would *always* know where to find them, and she marched straight out of here and straight back with the photos. So then I saw that there could be funeral chandeliers, and I thought, Those should be the most beautiful ones of all, and I was earning some money by then. I took the train to London. A jeweler here told me where to look, in Covent Garden, I think it was, and I asked for Austrian crystal. That's what everyone said to come back with, and that's how the funeral chandeliers began. And those are always the most beautiful ones. Sometimes I can't sell them for as much as they cost, so I keep those." She fell silent, and stared out at the water. "Not much left of the light," she said. "See the sun, resting on the horizon, out there where the sky meets the sea and the sea looks like the ground? It will flare up when it starts to go down and all the chandeliers will sparkle as if I'd fired them. That's the part of the day I like best, that last blaze of light."

"Did you make a Tree of Life for my father?"

"Yes," Clare said, her neck turning scarlet. "Of course I did."

"Can I see it?"

"It's in the room at the very top of the Crow's Nest," she said. "A lot of steps to climb to see that one. If you're not tired."

"No," Sophie said.

———

THERE IT WAS, her father's Tree of Light, suspended from the great beam in the middle of the octagonal room, revolving in the breeze, chiming wildly. How could a chandelier make so much noise? But then you saw the brass rods suspended here and there, always two together, so that when the wind stirred the chandelier, they struck one another. They chimed. What a beautiful sound, more beautiful than any harp or organ.

"I tried something new this time," Sophie said. "I'd thought of brass chimes before, but I was too lazy to work it out. So I went to the bell maker. He casts the bells for all the churches in Cornwall, or he repairs the ones that crack, and I told him what I wanted, and he looked at me and said, 'I suppose you're after getting a beautiful sound,' and I said I was. 'A happy sound?' he asked me, and I said, 'Happy, yes, but, well . . .' and he rescued me. He said, 'A mournful, happy sound?' So then I said, 'Yes, that's just what I want.' He told me to go home and come back three days later, and he'd have some chimes to try out. He'd have to cut the rods to different lengths because that would make a difference, and the thickness would make a difference, and the way they chimed together would make a difference, and I didn't want to hear any more. He was making me dizzy, and I thought it couldn't be done. But he'd gone to so much trouble and he was willing to do more, so I came back.

"And when I did, he must have had twenty or thirty pairs of chimes, and each one made a different sound, and one was more beautiful than the next, and then he struck *those* rods, and they were more than beautiful, those were the ones I wanted. It did have to do with the differing lengths of the bars, but I didn't understand about that, only that it made all the difference. So I said, 'Those are the ones I want,' but first he wanted me to listen to all the other sets of rods, and there were some that belonged in weddings, and others that were high and maddening, they sounded like early days, you know, like youth, so I thought, From now on all the chandeliers will have chimes unless people don't want them, but they do, you see, most of them do, although it adds a great deal of expense. We'll go into the room below here a little later, because right now they'll all be chiming at once and it's a little mad down there. A little deafening. 'A joyful noise,' your father used to say that. But look at this one. Don't be afraid of it. There's nothing that will break. I don't want my things to break."

And there it was, that huge chandelier in three tiers, and there was Evelyn, Evelyn large and Evelyn small, Evelyn playing in the sand on the American beach, Evelyn's grandmother at her gardening, her father beaming out at her, Sigrid as a young girl, thin as a stick, her own grandmother and grandfather, she could barely remember them. She would have sworn that she would not have been able to identify their faces, but she knew at once who they were, Andrew as a child, Evelyn holding a child in each arm and beaming up into the sun, squinting because of the light, Evelyn wearing a lace suit and a pillbox hat, her father's picture frame next to hers. He wore a suit, a little shiny, probably a trick of the light, little pages of manuscript reproduced in splendid frames, a poem about a sparrow, she could barely make out the title, but then she could, "In Honor of a Sparrow, Dying Young." Her father must have written that out for Evelyn. She was the sort of woman who would mourn a tiny bird. Her Uncle Martin, so beautiful in the beginning, but in his later years balding, taken to wearing a pince-nez, the image everyone had of an accountant, one extremely displeased by the sum at the bottom of the long row of numbers when everything was totted up. And there, astonishingly, was a snapshot of her father at Meena's wedding, and a photo of Meena holding each child by the hand as they walked down the dusty lane in Northumberland, Meena somehow managing to look as if she were walking alone, the two children, Sophie and her brother, slightly befuddled as if someone had given them instructions they didn't quite understand. Then Meena with her black hair still very long, and later, Meena in her tailored, expensive suits, her hair clipped neatly, her face already hardening, and later pictures of Meena standing in the garden with other human trophies, the Nobel award winners who seemed to congregate at Willow Grove along with her father, one Nobel winner among so many.

And there she was, Sophie, a chubby child, swollen eyes and her fists raised to rub them. There Sophie was marrying, again and again, four different men, and each time Sophie was more sophisticated, and finally, there she was with Bertold, Sophie dressed this time in a gown of her own making, beaded, thousands of beads sewn on one at a time, "staggeringly beautiful," said one of the reporters who had covered the ceremony, because by then she, Sophie, had become worthy of notice in and of herself, a mathematician, well known, often asked to appear on TV when an authority in her field was needed. There was Sophie's dog, that white puff of canine fur, referred to by her brother as "the designer dog," and endless little photographs of the rooms in their house. How had her father gotten those pictures? She remembered Bertold saying, "We have to photograph everything, Sophie, for the insurance, everything, because once something goes, how are we going to prove it was ever there? And we should get someone in to appraise it all. What if we were to have a fire? How would the insurance people know what a heap of ashes were once worth? It has to be done," and he had set about photographing the house, room by room, shelf by shelf, wall by wall. Even the smallest carpets were photographed, and many of Uncle Martin's scores, photographed one by one. Her father must have gotten hold of the photos somehow and then asked Clare to use them and she must have had the pictures shrunken down to fit these miniature frames.

—

EVERYONE SHE HAD ever known, everything she had ever been. Everything her mother had ever been, and her father, and her brother, all suspended in that three-tiered chandelier of sparkling, singing light, all those colors, that fantastic explosion of color, crystal pendants, emerald green, ruby red, imperial purple, indigo blue, clear crystal, aurora borealis sending the spectrum of white light in thin daggers everywhere. There were chains of crystal draping this way and that over the arms of the chandelier, each tiny frame decorated, the frames created by weavings of silver wire, in places crocheted into a kind of flesh, at times resembling parts of

a medieval knight's armor, pieces of cut silver intertwined with the crocheted silver wire. Little flowers made of crystal, so tiny, fashioned into
bouquets and set in tiny vases of twisted silver wire, really, the chandelier
was an impossible thing, not something that could have been created in
this world, existing somehow beyond the confines of earthly beauty, so
that watching it, Sophie felt it might at any moment disappear. It was
more precious than anything she had seen before, shaming the diamond
nestled in the indentation between her clavicle bones, making her ask why
she had ever thought precious stones were the most beautiful, the most
worthwhile stones there were. Ropes of amber crystal, rose, peridot,
chunks of amber here and there, red amber. Hadn't that once been her
father's present to Evelyn, that necklace seen sometimes in the few photographs of her that survived her lifetime? A ribbon, didn't it look familiar?
Intertwined by chains of aurora borealis crystals, so tiny. Were they crystals? No, they were Victorian buttons, so minute it was difficult to imagine anyone using them. Only a surgeon could open and close a garment
fastened by such buttons, tiny flower-shaped buttons, and then tight clus-
ters of seed pearls, bits of opalescent shells encrusted by crystals. How long
it must have taken to adorn each shard, how transformed the shells were.
You would not think it possible, ideas of shells, illusions of shells, shells
that had fallen from another place, from another sky, not the durable blue
canvas above this one. Oh, the chandelier was a miracle. A stronger breeze
blew through the room and the chimes sounded, spelling out the words
the wind always spoke but that were destined to remain indecipherable.
The sights and the sounds were too much for Sophie, who sank down on
the floor and began weeping as if she had seen a marble statue move, crying again, but differently than before, crying almost as if she herself were
singing the song of the chimes, the words of the wind. And how soothing
it was, what a relief it was, perhaps, she thought, it was even salvation.

Clare watched her, saying nothing, saying nothing to comfort her, above
all, not saying, "Don't cry. There's nothing to cry about," only waiting for
Sophie to stop crying and to stand up, which, of course, she finally did.

"It is so beautiful," she said, wiping her eyes. "It is the most generous thing I've ever seen."

"Generous?" Clare asked.

"To put in those pictures of my mother, but to put in those pictures of *Meena*, how could you do it? I couldn't have done it. I wouldn't have wanted to do it."

Clare sighed. Time passed. The chimes' remarkable voices counted out the minutes.

"That chandelier was meant to be the Tree of Light. We called it that. Everything of Peter's—your father's—had to be in it."

"Where are *you*?" Sophie cried suddenly.

"There," she said, pointing to a large carton, a smaller one next to it. "I'm still doing the frames for our pictures. I thought, I was the one who came last, so it seemed right that I leave my own pictures until the others were done." She picked up one frame from the small box. "That one's nearly done," she said. "It only needs some seed pearls at the top and bottom, a kind of crown shape, very pointed. Most of them are finished. Each one still needs one more thing. When they're done, I'll be finished."

And there, Sophie suddenly saw it, was the famous photograph of her parents, Evelyn and Peter pressed against each other, that picture she had photocopied from the newspaper, had retouched and made sharper and fastened to the inside of one of the doors of her Moroccan mirror, the one Sigrid had brought back for her, that wonderful mirror, the photo hidden from view by two closed doors, so you decided whether or not to open the doors and view yourself in the mirror, you could not be ambushed by accidentally walking past that mirror, raw and shining with light, pitilessly reflecting your accidental face, your wild face, not the tamed face she always preferred to show to that staring, blank mirror the color of mercury on a grey day. *There they are*, Sophie thought, safe in this chandelier. There all of us are, even Meena. Look, there's even a picture of Rose! A picture of Julia! All of them. Meena, Sangeeta, another sister who died young, before she could pronounce her own name, all of them, angry, greedy, famous, failed, all of them, together and infinitely beautiful.

"I would very much like to have a picture of this chandelier," Sophie said, attempting not to cry, knowing from long experience that if she continued trying to stop these tears her throat would begin to tighten, and within hours she would have a terrible sore throat, and then she gave it up and began to weep quietly.

"You can have the chandelier," Clare said. "And then you won't need the picture."

"I am a greedy thing. Probably Daddy told you what a greedy thing I am, but I am *not* going to take this chandelier out of Crow's Nest. This chandelier is the heart of the house. It is where it belongs."

"Then I will make you another one," Clare said.

"Would you?" Sophie asked.

"To tell you the truth," Clare said, flushing—she must be terribly shy, Sophie thought, Daddy had always liked shy people, although he was most quickly taken in by the flamboyant ones—"I had already begun one for you. Your father thought you might like it. He said you were very fond of chandeliers."

"I see," Sophie said, beginning to laugh although she was still weeping, and then began choking. "I miss it so very much, that mockery."

"Yes," said Clare. "And I had thought of Sigrid. Would Sigrid accept a chandelier?"

"I *know* she would love it!" Sophie exclaimed. "She's always the one who's left out. People paid so much attention to Peter. Meena did her best to push Sigrid into a dark corner and keep her there. So many people have tolerated her because they knew they could get to my father through her; they pretended to care about her but they never bothered to know her, if they had, well, her life might have been very different, but she kept people off. She knew people weren't interested in her, wanted to get through her to Peter, except for Julia. Julia knew Peter before she met Sigrid, so she had no suspicions on that score. Oh, all that's another story altogether, but yes, Sigrid would be out of her mind with delight! I know she would!"

"She won't see me as the—what is the word? The interloper?"

"I think," Sophie said, her voice hardening, turning cynical, "she wishes you had loped in *years* before you did."

"I hope it's true."

"It *is*!" Sophie insisted. "You wouldn't," Sophie asked suddenly, struck by a dreadful thought, "think of making a chandelier for Meena?"

"No. Surely not," Clare said.

"Because she deserves neither light nor life."

"It's getting dark in here," Clare said. "Usually the light's the last to go in this room. Should I light the candles in the chandelier? I haven't done it yet."

"Please," said Sophie.

"I have a lamplighting thing," Clare said. She produced a wand and slid up a lever on its handle so that a flame appeared at the far end. "Just like a cigarette lighter, only meant for candles, or, I suppose, for fireplaces," Clare said, and began setting the candles alight. "*Now* it will sparkle," Clare said. "It's not too bad, is it?"

The chandelier chimes sounded their agreement and there seemed to be nothing for it but to sit on the floor against the wall and gaze at the chandelier, which had now come alive and created an air of expectancy, as if the dead would now begin to speak, or as if something beyond imagining, completely unforeseeable, were about to occur. "I like chandeliers," Clare said softly.

The chimes may have had an answer to that, but Sophie and Clare sat still, as if struck dumb. A short time passed and there was the sound of thunder. Imperceptibly, the two women moved closer together. Anyone looking in would have thought they belonged together. Somehow.

The chimes sounded again. The two women turned to one another and smiled.

THIRTY

SHE HAD BEEN in the turret since early morning, before the sun rose, one of those nights when darkness fell, but sleep would not come with it, and there had been many such nights, too many, in the previous two—or was it three?—and a half years. Now a pale greyish sky was casting its light into the six windows of the turret, but inside and outside there was still no color, only a barely discernible hint of yellow in the vast daffodil beds, and even then, she was not sure whether or not she imagined it, that color, any color. But now the light would continue brightening.

A crow flew into the tallest of the trees and began his screaming. He was looking for his mate, that must be it. Meena was right, because within seconds a smaller crow flew into the tree and settled itself near the large one. Then the two of them stared into her room. *You're not getting in here,* Meena said aloud. *This is my room.* Then she wondered if she were, perhaps, speaking to herself too often. Many people she knew told her, "Now that I'm all alone, I talk out loud to myself, even though there's no one else to hear." She had heard that repeatedly. In those days, she could think of nothing more golden than silence, no one pressing his or her demands on her, asking her if she would organize a small dinner party, more Nobels! Who would have thought there were so many of them!

She had run the children down to the Activity Centre so they could rehearse the play Sophie had written. As she remembered, Sophie's plays tended to be about shipwrecks and pirates. A dreadful storm would blow up near the Cornish coast, a ship would be dashed against the rocks, and the people of the town would climb down and find everything precious and bear it away. Somehow, a young girl very much like the author would perform a heroic act and that heroine was asked to choose whatever she wanted from the ship's treasure, and the last scene inevitably, or it seemed so when Meena thought back to it, saw the child triumphantly bearing off her goods. Either that or there was someone so fiendish that even Sophie, or the character very like Sophie, could do nothing with the villain, and so the evildoer was thrown from the cliffs and usually dashed against the body of the wrecked ship. That, all the children agreed, was usually the best part. They competed for the distinction of being the villain who was thrown against the rocks, flung themselves about so violently that one named Luke—could he have been named Luke?—pulled down the scenery, exposing all the other children doubled over with laughter in the wings, the pulleys and the unpainted rafters, and instantly he became the hero of the village children, all thanks to Sophie's violent, swashbuckling plots, not the sort one would expect from a young female. *Not,* thought Meena, a very easy child to like.

On the tree bough, the birds shifted their weight from one foot to the other.

A thin mist wreathed and coiled through the gardens below her, and Meena saw the boy on his bicycle, and then the satisfying thud of the paper as it hit the heavy wooden kitchen step and slid down to the door stop. She never consciously decided to go down for the papers. The steps were dark, and downstairs it was even darker, but she could easily move through the house with her eyes closed. She had practiced that particular skill longer than she could remember. Once back in the turret, she watched the leaves brighten. The early, frothy chartreuse blooming was gone, and now the heavy, bottle-green leaves had unfurled and kept her screened from everyone below, almost screened from the crows. Yes, she would like to be screened from the crows, but if she were, she would miss them. They had become a kind of company. Did I go down for the papers? Meena asked herself. Enough time had passed so that her body had gone back to its resting state and the slight pounding of her heart caused by her climb had returned to normal. *Thump, ump, thump, ump.* "You have a slow pulse, Meena," Peter always said when he counted it. Why on earth had he been counting her pulse? In the months she was briefly pregnant, was that it? Past remembering, so many things, and just as well. Her memory was quite good, good enough to cause her sufficient and more than sufficient misery.

—

OF COURSE I brought up the papers, she thought. There would be the *Daily Mail* and their own local paper. The local paper was always the one she opened with the greatest enthusiasm. The doings of the butcher and the baker were, to her, the only true stories. They were about people she knew. The local paper was really a letter from all the villagers to one another. She had lived in the vicinity of Willow Grove forever, far longer than Peter had ever done. She knew everyone for miles and she herself was known by everyone in exchange. As a child, she had known the farmers and the shopkeepers, been afraid of everyone, assumed they disliked her because she came from India, and worried especially about the upper classes and what they thought of her. She had worried that she would never learn to dress as they did, could never hope to be so tidy, to look so *smart*. She concluded that such women were born as they now looked. That look was born in their bones and inherited from their ancestors and so she knew she was hopeless. But time had taught her a thing or two. Money was at the heart of everything, and ambition. You needed ambition to spend the time searching out the right dress or the right suit, safest to buy what you would wear from Harrods, or Dickens and Jones, when she came to learn of them, brand names were safest, not, of course, the names sewed onto the collars of high-fashion designers; then, if you didn't know what you were doing, you could easily become a laughingstock, and everyone *would* laugh at you. But she had learned the tricks of the trade. She was now mistaken for a woman of the upper class, perhaps a lady. An aristocrat, certainly. She adjusted her behavior and her speech slowly as she studied the others who came in droves after Peter won his Nobel, and in the end, she made most of those women insecure when confronted with *her*. She smiled to herself, nodded to the two crows, well aware of what she had achieved. And it was an accomplishment. She had seen so many people try and fail to achieve the same thing. She was not like Julia, not like Elfie before her, who had a flair, not only for the original, but for the dramatic, Elfie, who arrived in a flurry of scarves and capes, vibrant colors everywhere, you would have thought such colors in combination would have been quite unspeakable, but people in their perfect Jaeger suits would turn to Julia or Elfie in envy, and ask, "Where did you find *that*? It would be perfect for a day at Ascot," and Julia would laugh and say, "Well, some of it," Julia said, "comes from C. and A." Everyone knew better than to shop at C. and A., such cheap things, flashy, meant for the very young or those who knew no better. "And some of it comes from Camden Lock." How did Julia even dare admit to such a thing, shopping at Camden Lock, when her mother had warned her against markets like Camden Lock, saying everything you see there runs or falls apart in the wash, and some of it's been worn before, and all the fabric comes from countries where the plague still rages. "And one or two things are quite dear, really," Julia said. And then someone would say, "That is a beautiful brooch," and Julia would say, "A reproduction. Eighteen dollars. Twelve of your pounds," a price which would have meant, of course, that such an object had to be ruled *out*. "But it's beautiful," someone was sure to say sadly, and Julia knew the whole history that went behind that sigh, would smile, make note of who the woman was, and if it was a woman she liked, the very same brooch would arrive in the post a few days later, soon to be worn on that woman's Jaeger suit, although it did not have altogether the effect it achieved when Julia wore it, but still, some of the glamour hung on, or so the woman, pinning on the brooch, thought. Perhaps a purple scarf? that woman would think. A brilliant purple scarf trimmed with gold embroidery, almost like sari material, followed by the harrowing thought that perhaps Julia's scarf *had* been made of sari material. Julia was capable of such a thing.

Really, Meena thought, the empress of such outfits was Sophie, who had sewn her own ball dress when she was invited to Buckingham Palace, a ball dress made of parachute fabric, and had apparently, to Meena's disgust, spent the evening answering the inevitable question, "But where did you *find* it?" And had worn the gown, naturally, with a rhinestone necklace of the type favored, it was said, by drag queens. But Sophie had been quite a success, photographs in all the papers, and after that, it did seem that the world was determined to see more of her.

Well, the paper. It was lying on Meena's desk and when she looked down, a small photograph caught her attention. A chandelier. Not another chandelier, Meena thought. I'm sick of them. They're like cotton candy. A person can have too much of it. She didn't think she could survive with a chandelier of any sort in her own house. But she saw the words *chandelier* and *Cornwall* and *artistic* and raised the paper to take a better look. Another article imported from London's fashion columns. We could all do without another of those, Meena thought, reaching for her spectacles, rimless, slightly rose-tinted.

"Oh! Good God!" she exclaimed aloud to the crows. "It's that woman in Cornwall!" She began reading. *Clare Tartikoff, well-known locally for her "Tree of Light" chandeliers, now making quite a splash at Liberty's. The new darling of the Sloane Rangers. Her work bought by a member of the royal family to hang in Highgrove.* Highgrove! What did Clare *Tartikoff* have to do with the royal family? "This is beyond endurance!" Meena exclaimed. "I will not allow it!" But fate had already allowed it! She looked out at the crows, as if expecting sympathy. Impenetrably, they stared back at her. "But *who* can have caused this?" she demanded of the walls. And, as if she had been the queen in the fairy tale, the one who asked, "Who is the fairest of them all?" and the answer came back. Sophie. Of course it was Sophie. Sophie had been to Cornwall, Sophie with all her aristocratic connections; how little time it had taken Sophie to conquer what she, Meena, had thought unconquerable, Sophie who had said of her dinner parties, "It's a performance. If you understand that, then there's never any difficulty," Sophie, that pudgy, oily-skinned child, grown up to be the fairest of them all, that clumsy, despicable person with an instinct for saying the wrong thing, endlessly disgracing Meena, her long-suffering stepmother, but now, moving through a room, leaving a wake of golden happiness in her path! Sophie! Sophie! And again, Sophie! Meena burst into a storm of utter exasperation and fury.

Look at the picture, she kept telling herself repeatedly. At least there is no photo of Clare Tartikoff in the paper! In the *local* paper. It was a large picture, really, and the more Meena looked at it, the larger is seemed to become. When, in the beginning, it had seemed the size of a postage stamp!

She pulled her spectacles down on her nose and inspected the chandelier. Oh, so *now* she saw why the local people, the *Grisleigh upon Shallows Chronicle,* had picked it up! It was plain to see. There, suspended on the black chandelier branches, were the pictures, quite clear, really, if one looked, and of course, everyone *would* look.

There was Peter, arms around Evelyn, beaming out of the tiny frame. There was Sophie and Bertold, arms twined together, there was Sigrid! Not

Sigrid! And Andrew! And there *she* was! How had that Clare Tartikoff dared to put in a picture of her? Yet there was Meena herself, looking like grim death, stony-faced but smiling, looking, Meena thought, as if she were eighty years old! Was it possible she really looked like that? And all the other women in the pictures, even Julia, even Sally, appearing better-dressed than she was, or, if not better-dressed, at least displaying some *flair*, whereas there she was in her cliché of a Jaeger suit, as if she had stopped in to say hello and found a party in progress, and she, Meena, were the charwoman, the drabbest of them all, a poor brown and grey bird in an assemblage of peacocks and parrots! *This* was too much! Nothing could be worse than this! As if the chandelier were announcing to all and sundry, *Meena Church Grovesnor* is only one of many, and the least estimable of them all. The pictures were the proof.

Meena turned the page in a rage. She would be soothed by the announcements of births and weddings and deaths, to see who had been granted the long obituaries rather than the short notices, the listing of who was visiting whom: these never failed to soothe her. But what was this? Snapshots of a party held by Lady Anne and Sir Evan McClarren! Her closest friends! The ones she had most often invited to dinner, the ones she had not resented coming when they arrived at Willow Grove. Not to have invited her! It was intolerable! What had she done to deserve such treatment? Might Lady Anne have heard of The Difficulties? And if she had, who would have told her? Sophie again, certainly Sophie, hobnobbing at Highgrove in a parachute gown. Of course it was Sophie again. But would she have told the McClarrens of The Separation? Sophie had no discretion, but even she knew where to draw the line. And was it reasonable to assume that Sophie was rushing about London, indeed, rushing about all of England, to inform people of The Separation? To tell everyone about *Clare Tartikoff*—Tartikoff, for God's sake! Oh, no, much more likely for Sophie to have met the McClarrens at some exclusive club, to have droned on and on about her financial difficulties, the new addition to the house, the thirteen stained-glass skylights (how she hated that word, *skylight,* hated anyone who installed them, as ludicrous as someone who had decided to deck her house in éclairs), and then Lady Anne would have said, "Oh, but surely you have a mountain of money your father left you?" And she could see it, her stepdaughter was standing right before her as she said, "Well, it didn't quite work out that way, you see."

And Lady Anne, so fond of Sophie, so sure that she was entitled to say whatever she pleased, to interfere in whatever she pleased, because after all, what was rank if it didn't grant such privileges, would say, "Whyever not? Did something go wrong?" And Sophie, that smooth one, would say, "Not precisely *wrong,* Anne." Sophie always addressed her as Anne, such impertinence, and the worst of it was how Lady Anne liked it, as if they were two young girls together. And Lady Anne would ask her, "Wasn't it Peter's intention to leave his old family house in Cornwall to you?" Sophie smiling ruefully, and Lady Anne saying in tones that might have frightened armies, "I shall look into this, Sophie, indeed I shall." And Sophie would have said, "Oh, no, Anne, no, really, these days it's best not to disturb Meena; she isn't—" And then she would break off, so that Lady Anne would continue, saying, "You mean she's not right? Her head is not right? Or do you mean I should not disturb a nest of snakes? Oh, I saw your eyes flicker at that! I shall look into this, Sophie, be sure of it. Snakes, indeed! I don't know why he married that woman! A man's heirs must be given their due. Surely even Meena, mad as she may be, will see that!"

"Best to leave her alone, Anne," Sophie would say. "You don't want that sort of trouble!"

"Am *I* to be afraid of that upstart?" Lady Anne would exclaim. "Then you don't know me, Sophie. Really, after all these years, I would have thought you would know me better than that!"

That, thought Meena, was how she came to be left out of this party. What was the party for? For Lord and Lady McClarren's fiftieth anniversary! It must have been the party of the season! Of the decade! And she had not been given the chance to decline! Lady Anne would have known how to appear to proffer an invitation, at the same time making it perfectly clear that she, Meena, would rue the day should she accept it. This was more than a snub. It was an insult, delivered full force, as if Lady Anne had taken down one of the crossed ancestral swords mounted on her dining room wall and with all her might smitten Meena with it. So the fact of her widowship had, finally, counted for nothing. How could she counter innuendos, slight changes in Sophie's expression, Sophie's seemingly innocuous words revealing vistas of betrayal heaped upon Meena by her a stepdaughter? Oh, Sophie had backed her into a corner. Hadn't Peter warned her time out of mind? "You underestimate Sophie. In the end, Sophie will have what she wants. Sophie loves victory, any victory, even a pyrrhic one. That means, Meena, Sophie will always have the trump card." And time and time again, she had dismissed Peter's warnings. The crows on the bough would have understood his words faster than she had. "Too proud," she had overheard Peter telling Sigrid. "That pride will be her ruin." Talking about her, as usual, discussing her as if such a thing were permissible, but despite all that: she ought to have listened.

She looked at her watch. Seven-thirty. Surely, Julian would be awake by now. Her parents had trained everyone to get up just before the cock crowed.

"Oh, it's you, is it?" said her cousin at the other end.

"I've come to a decision," Meena said.

"Seen the papers, have you?" Julian asked.

"Can you come straight over?" Meena asked.

"Of course," Julian said. "At your command, as always."

"Don't be cheeky," Meena said.

THIRTY-ONE

———

"YOU COULDN'T HAVE done worse than ask for a confidentiality clause," Julian said. "You know what they're like. What the bunch of them are like. And I'm sure they'll find friends who are also like them."

"It hasn't gotten into the papers," Meena said defiantly. "Nothing about Clare Tartikoff."

"You will stick at that," Julian said. "Even after you've just seen her chandelier in the *Grisleigh upon Shallows Chronicle,* even after you've seen the chandelier with your face hanging from it. A little lower, I might add, than *her* face. Not to mention Clare and Peter together, quite a bit higher up the tree than you are."

"What difference does it make where the pictures are?" Meena snapped. "If people see that picture, they'll want to know who she was."

"And you still mean to tell me that nothing about Clare Tartikoff has gotten into the papers, and the Grovesnors will keep the separation a secret, as well as the affair, a very long affair, let me remind you, and the letters Sigrid seems to have, and Sophie's apparent acquaintance with her, they will keep all that quiet? Don't you think that photograph of Clare's appearing in the paper had something to do with Sophie?"

"Of course it did!" Meena snapped again. "Do you think my mind is altogether gone?"

"Your self-delusion is still very much intact, I'd say," Julian told her.

"Meaning what?"

"Meaning that you still believe you can control them. But they are intent on eluding your control. Otherwise, they would have signed the papers you sent them long ago. There's only one thing for it now."

"And what is that?"

"I think you must punish them. That's all you can do. Punish them first. Or they are sure to punish you and keep on punishing you."

"Not if I gave over their shares of the estate," Meena said, almost in a whisper.

"That," said Julian, "is the last thing you ought to do."

"Then they'd have nothing to persecute me for. What motive would they have?"

"Better to ask what reason they would have *not* to continue persecuting you. Even if you gave them their share, do you think they've forgotten the past? Does Sigrid ever forget anything? And now what you can expect of Sophie is beginning to come clear. Years of trying to make you love her, and in her interviews she speaks of herself as a 'secondhand' child. She's finally turned on you, Meena, and that sort never turns back and forgives. I've heard rumors that she intends to write a book that will skewer you, at least if she has her way. She intends to write her autobiography."

"An autobiography, at her age! And what is that book to be called?"

"*Poison*. If I'm not mistaken. But she'll change the title if she can think of a more venomous name for it."

"She cannot be permitted to publish such a book," Meena said. "I will stop her."

"How?"

"I will go to law."

"She has already submitted a few chapters to a specialist in libel and slander. He told her it was quite all right to go ahead and publish it. So, you see, there is nothing standing in her way."

Meena had gone white.

"Don't dig your nails into your flesh like that," Julian cautioned her. "Your palm is bleeding."

"To have this go on and on!" Meena erupted.

"I warned you about the confidentiality agreement. You might as well have thrown firecrackers into the wood fire. What did you expect? They're a family of artists."

"Sophie an artist!"

"You can be as contemptuous of her as you please, but she is well known in her field. People seem to take to her. You don't, but others do. She is becoming quite a celebrity. Last week, her shoes were photographed when she was at a party. The pictures were in the Style section of the *London Times*. Soon people will want to read about her grocery lists. I've been keeping track. I don't like surprises. And in her own way, Sigrid is an artist, an artist of strategy and vengeance, the same word you used. You cannot hope to win over her."

"Then what *can* I hope for?" Meena cried out.

"I've said it before. You can punish them. They care for money. They may not believe it, but it's true. Peter wanted money at the end. No one thought so before then. That thirst was hidden, because up until then he'd always had more than enough. And Sophie is more extravagant than any-one even believes. As for Sigrid, one Christmas she said that when one got older, what was one to look forward to but trips to exotic places and treats, the more treats the better, many treats every day. That would be the goal. I remember her precise words. For that she needs money, and so does Sophie."

"But I have given over Sigrid's share!"

"But, thanks to me, you are still reining her in. I saw to it that you didn't gift the money to her outright. Everything she gets has to go through you. You are the one who decides what portion of the legal costs are hers to pay for, you are the one who decides what the tax on her share will be, and you withhold that tax, you are the one who stipulated that upon her death her share will not go to the children. So she is not free of the reins we placed on her."

"That's true," Meena said, thinking. "But it is not enough."

"Lady Anne's party," Julian said, reminding her.

"So many years stroking that woman!" Meena exclaimed. "And now she treats me like a scullery maid!"

"No, she has more respect for you than that. She treats you as an enemy."

"But I wanted her favor! I wanted her protection! I kept Sophie from her. But I now see that *Peter* did nothing of the sort."

"Sophie is capable of drawing people in. Anyone, I think. She's been to Highgrove, or so I've been told. With Bertold, that superannuated flower person."

"To Highgrove!"

"So I've heard. I can't swear to it."

"To Highgrove!" Meena exclaimed. "*I* go to Highgrove. *I* am the one who belongs there!"

"Not your decision to make, darling," Julian said. "It's a big place. Both of you can visit there."

"At the same time?" she asked, horrified.

"Not necessarily."

"I think," said Meena, stiffening in her chair, "I must take this to court."

"I believe you must."

"But to sit in front of those people, in front of a judge! And to . . ."

"To lie?" Julian asked. "Of course you must tell the truth—as you see it."

"I don't tell lies," Meena said in a low voice.

"That was true. Once," said her cousin. "But you may see things quite differently than others do. And of course no one's memory is entirely reliable, especially under difficult circumstances."

"I am to march into court and tell the judge some poppycock! And swear to it?"

"How far would you get if you went to court and told the judge the wrong version of the truth?"

"Oh!" Meena exclaimed, throwing herself about in her seat. "You see what they have driven me to?"

Julian said nothing.

"And the important thing is, I must make them believe that Peter changed his mind after he wrote the List of Wish, because when he wrote it, the illness and the morphine meant he was not in his right mind. And I must not let them reflect on the interdependence of the will and the List of Wish?"

"We already agreed on all that."

"Can I do it?"

"Wear a Jaeger suit," Julian said without a trace of irony. "Think of it as your armor. Try and wear something pink. Go into London and find someone to advise you on makeup. You must appear soft and helpless and ravaged by grief. I thought of all of it before I came. I have a number," he said, digging through his pocket for a piece of paper. "The actresses go here before auditions and important events. Sophie went there before accepting one of Peter's posthumous awards."

Meena, her eyes shiny with tears, accepted the piece of paper. "I shall write this down," she said.

"Not that you *need* help," Julian said. "But you want to appear in a certain light. Think of it as a performance."

"The very words Sophie used about social occasions, " Meena said.

"She is extravagant, but she knows the ways of the world," Julian said. "You *have* to know them to keep up such extravagance."

I wonder if she will do it, Julian thought. I wonder if she can manage it.

"Pink?" Meena asked.

"Pink," Julian said.

"I know just the shop in Hampstead," Meena said.

Ah, thought Julian. By all means, let her get her own back if she can. I should have liked to go to Lady Anne's party myself, he thought, but I suppose that part of our lives has ended. Lady Anne rules this part of the country, and she reigns over most of England thanks to the invention of the telephone. We shall be shut out, he thought. He amended his unspoken sentence. We are already shut out. Irretrievably so. Unfortunate, yes, but we did have a good run.

"Pink," Meena said again, in wonderment.

"All sweet women wear pink," he said.

"I suppose," Meena said. Her mind was already on something else, probably the shop in Hampstead. Sigrid would not be caught dead in a Jaeger shop. "You cannot go wrong with Jaeger," Meena once said, and Julia had answered without thinking, "What a terrible thing to say!" and Sigrid had roared with laughter. Those two!

THIRTY-TWO

———

"SHE IS TAKING us to court to set aside the List of Wish," Sigrid said. "I'm certain that article did it, the one about the chandelier."

"I hoped it would," Sophie said.

"You see now that we must institute our own legal proceedings," Sigrid said.

"No," said Sophie.

"Now, *immediately*," Sigrid said. "We could have waited. *She* would have waited. But you don't think before you act. You never have. You went to see Clare. That was fine, but you had to rub it in Meena's face and help place that story in the paper."

"I am *particularly* proud of that," Sophie said. "When my headaches act up and I can't leave the house and I know that it is Meena making me ill, I find great satisfaction, not to say peace, in knowing about that artist in the *Grisleigh upon Shallows Chronicle*."

"You're mad," Sigrid said. "You act on impulse and you don't know what you're doing. You never imagine the consequences, or if you do, you imagine all the wrong ones. You're no chess player, Sophie."

"But I am," Sophie said.

THIRTY-THREE

———

FOR NO REASON that he could explain, Andrew, who had business in London, had decided to stay at Sophie's instead of obeying his usual habit and ringing Sigrid's bell, so that now he was installed in the smallest room on the third floor, the least decorated room in the house, probably, Andrew thought, because Sophie knew this room was originally meant to be a nursery. "Take any room on the third floor," Sophie had said. "Use all of them if you like," but the other rooms were decorated so beautifully he felt as if he were suddenly living in *House and Garden*. He could almost smell the perfumey cloud that invariably arose from such magazines, liberally strewn about the house. He liked the little room; its walls came down at odd angles and he would hit his head if he moved about too quickly, so there he sat, on the narrow bed in that room, sitting on a plain red duvet, although, he supposed, it was made of Thai silk or had a tag from a famous designer, and he looked around the room, only one small table and a chair, both painted white, white curtains at the window, but red carpeting, and the red duvet; he was reminded of a scene from a fairy tale and thought, If it started snowing in here, I would not be surprised, staring unfocused at the white-painted bookcases, and then something caught his eye, a title of a book that demanded he look at it: *Evelyn Graves: Her Life and Work*. He was tired, but he got up, hitting his head as he did, and crossed the room, picked up the book, went back to the bed, and opened the book at random, and there it was, a photograph of his mother and his father, "the famous photograph," as both Sigrid and his father had always referred to it, and there they were, his parents, radiating happiness, and Andrew thought, This is why realistic art is useless; it never represents reality, I need to find a form or a collection of forms, things that show emotions, forms that incarnate those emotions so that they can be seen for what they are. For example, the truth of the two people, his parents, in this picture, although perhaps their happiness *was* realistically represented in that photograph, at least at the moment the photograph was taken.

I have to do something, Andrew thought. I have to decide what I must do about Meena and I must settle my feelings about Sigrid and Sophie and Meena, the woman I thought of as my mother for so very long, but how am I to do that? *Start with the forms.* Isn't that what Daddy would tell me if he were here? Start with the things you're sure of. But really, Andrew was not sure of anything. He had a talent for realistic portraiture; Sophie went on and on about that, but she had no idea of how he hated a realistic portrayal; what was it but a mask? No, he wanted to sculpt what writhed and twisted beneath the surface; someday, he might someday believe that some people's surface did not hide impulses that twisted and writhed; such people would be serene. What an accomplishment it would be to sculpt such serenity! Even to glimpse such a thing as serenity. Unimaginable!

I can try, he thought, putting down the book and taking up the sketchbook he always kept with him, and he began sketching, and then he thought, Why do I feel such hatred for realistic portraits? Why don't I feel the same hatred for people's faces? After all, they are nothing but masks; the faces he hated the most were ones that gave nothing away. Meena's was such a face, and Andrew realized that he had always feared Meena, he had always feared her porcelain face, how like a doll she could look, wasn't it Sophie who feared dolls because she said they looked like people that had no souls? Then she might well have been speaking of Meena; had he always seen Meena in this way or had he this instant come to look at Meena in such a way? Yes, a frozen form, Meena was a frozen form; I must do something about Meena, he thought, his eyes burning, I must oppose her, but I cannot imagine that; something will have to happen, my hand must be forced. Oh, I am such a coward, Andrew thought, and what would happen that could be large enough to rouse him to action? He could not imagine anything of sufficient magnitude. The habits of a lifetime were against him; she was his *mother*; could no one understand that she was his mother? Why did he, why did Sophie, try to think of Evelyn as their mother? Evelyn was gone long before he had been able to hold a cup, before he began to walk, but always, always Evelyn prevented him from reaching conclusions about Meena. Meena, the mother, when the very word *mother* stopped all thought, obscured all rational thought as if the word itself became a dense fog that spread and spread, obliterating everything. He looked at the famous photograph again and thought, They had no right to be so happy, not even for one second; think of the consequences of their happiness! and then it came to him: that is why I can never think badly of Meena; she was less harmful than Evelyn; wasn't it true? But did that absolve Meena—because she had caused less suffering than Evelyn? Yes, he thought, this is what has always stopped me; Meena was the better mother, she was the one who had done less damage. But Meena had done damage all the same and she intended to do more. I must help stop her, Andrew thought, and he lay back on the red duvet and looked up at the ceiling. But how can I? he asked himself. I can't do it, not now. Something has to happen. He stared at the small hairline cracks in the ceiling: more subsidence, but easier to read the meaning of those cracks than try to peer into the future to see what might make him able to oppose Meena: his mother, or at least the mother he had settled on, telling himself, This is my mother; Meena is a good mother to me. Cracks in the ceiling, he said to himself, tell me what to do. Tell me what a mother *is*.

THIRTY-FOUR

—

AS USUAL, SOPHIE believed that Andrew was living in cloud country. He was always the one for whom people felt sorry. He was the one with the dreamy look, the astonishing resemblance to their father, his aura similar to their father's, although, naturally, not as strong. But her brother had no idea, no idea at all of the effect he had on them. His life should have been no easier and no harder than any other member of the Grovesnor family's, but he had taken his father's example one step farther, and instead of living in Northumberland, out of the way of journalists and the obsessed strangers who wanted to know anything at all about his mother and his father, he had moved first to Argentina, then to Greenland, and was now threatening to go farther, perhaps to Iceland. He was a sculptor interested in forms he saw in nature, especially those that survived in extreme cold or extreme heat, so that when Sophie accused him of running away from the family, inevitably his rejoinder was simple enough. It was abundantly clear that his work would not allow him to stay on in England, where it was neither cold nor hot enough. He had seen everything there was to see in this country. He was at once Sigrid's delight and eternal exasperation. "Does he know what happens around him, or do you have to be an exotic stone to compel his attention?" Sophie would ask, and Sigrid would say, "He isn't strong enough to live any other way."

"But," Sigrid would tell Sophie, "Andrew's hiding may be your father's doing. He heard Peter say often enough that he would disappear if he could. I think he meant it quite literally. There were things that happened"—here she invariably became vague—"and I thought he might take Evelyn's way. I don't know how many times he wrote out his will, had me witness it, and keep it safe for him. So I don't understand, I can't make sense of it, why, in the end, he wrote out a useless will that relied on Meena's integrity and goodwill. He must have been off his head."

"There may be a different reason for looking at Peter's desire to disappear and Andrew's wanting to do the same," Julia said one afternoon when Sigrid was talking to her over the phone. "When Peter visited us in New York, he felt safer. He talked more. He told me that he had a besetting sin, a real fault, a desire to make everyone happy, and in the end, he said, all he did was make everyone miserable. His old friend, what was his name, Justin, the one he used to drink with, told me not to believe people if they said Peter was too kind. Too good. It wasn't kind to try to please everyone, especially since he already knew what the consequences would be. Sophie always says, 'Daddy was the kindest man in England,' but how can she believe it? If he'd been that kind, he would have had the strength to be *unkind*. But he never had that strength, I don't think he did. Meena banned this one and that one, and when she saw she could get away with it, she banned almost everyone he knew. She insisted that he hobnob with the 'great people.' And then she put her tiny foot down about going to

Egypt. 'I don't see why I need to go that far to see sand,' she said, and he caved in, and after that, it was India. She might have been born there, but she didn't want to see starving people. She didn't want to be in a country where people worshipped rats. And then it was the United States, and what was wrong with *that* country? Evelyn was born there. The cultists lived there and didn't mean either of them well. Meena said, 'If you want to keep on in the way you like, you shall have to leave me behind,' but what could he do then? He'd already set the pattern. He had to agree to what laws she set down. Was that kindness? Did that make for happiness for his children? Because she was all too willing to bar *them*. I'm sure he had something to say on that subject, but what good did it do? They couldn't come to Willow Grove. So, the kindest man in England, Sigrid. I don't think so. I don't see it. Instead, I see Andrew beginning the whole thing again. He doesn't want to make anyone unhappy, especially not himself. So he keeps out of everything, and there are times when all of you need to defrost him and have him take *some* kind of action."

"It's true," Sigrid said. "He doesn't have the stomach for any of it."

"It's more than that," Julia said. "Sometimes you have to say, 'This far, and no farther.' And now with this business about the will. Sophie's eating herself up alive."

"Oh, Sophie will be all right," Sigrid said impatiently. "Sophie is always all right. She's a Graves, just like her mother."

"And look what became of her mother," Julia said. "On top of that, she's as bad as I am. You can point at any part of her anatomy and there's something wrong with it. It's not hypochondria. Beyond doubt, it isn't. I've gone to the doctors with her. She's not dreaming up strange illnesses fishing for sympathy. All things considered, she downplays what's wrong. She's had troubles you've not heard of, Sigrid. She doesn't tell you. She doesn't want to frighten you. She understands you better than you think. She knows you'd be frightened. You think she talks all the time, but she keeps many things to herself. Who's left of her family? Evelyn died early and now Peter's gone. She has you and she has Andrew, but he opts out.

He says he's tired of all her hysterics. You should *drag* Andrew into this fight, because if you don't, one day he's going to wake up and he'll be very sorry he didn't stand with the rest of you."

"I doubt that," Sigrid said. "He's happy with his cold stones and pieces of driftwood."

"He *isn't!*" Julia insisted. "How can he be? He adored his father. This is about what both of them owe their father. Because they do owe him something. It's *not* only money. There's the work he spent his life on, and how will Meena deal with that? What does she know about books and literary people and editors and reputations and keeping Peter's work in the canon? She can't be the one to take that on. She's over fifty. It's time for those two to take over. Or at least take part in the decision making."

"Yes," said Sigrid. "I've said that from the beginning."

"And what's happening? Isn't Meena blocking all of Peter's unpublished work?"

"She won't let anything he wrote about Elfie go into print, and she certainly won't have anything published if it concerns Clare. There are three books there, unpublished, maybe four, and they won't see the light of day. She's going to do another collected poems. She thinks that's enough."

"Well, there you are," Julia said. "Andrew has to be dragged in."

"And could anyone ever drag Peter?"

"Yes. They certainly could. He was dragable, I know he was."

"Who will drag Andrew, then?" Sigrid asked.

"I think Sophie. Sophie is the only one who has a chance."

"Impossible," Sigrid said. "You're dreaming."

"I can't do it," Julia said. "I barely know him."

"No, it must be Sophie," Sigrid said, considering. "Sophie! To have everything in her hands!"

"But as it is now, you have one child saying, 'I will fight Meena for my father's sake,' that's when she's not saying she won't fight at all, and the other one saying, 'I'll stay out of this for my own sake.' If this goes on,

Meena won't need to put up a fight. If she knows how they feel, she knows she's already won."

"Over my dead body," Sigrid said.

"If you want Sophie to take her brother on, you can't have her thinking that she can't manage it. She *has* to feel she can deal with it."

Sigrid nodded.

"I can help with Sophie," Julia said.

"I know you can, love," Sigrid said. "But don't you get your hopes up too high. Just when you think you've got Sophie where you need her, she slams a door. She thinks she's locked someone out, someone like Meena, but she's wrong, and by the time Sophie knows she's locked herself *in,* it's too late. It will be too late for all of us."

"Sophie will manage," Julia said.

THIRTY-FIVE

———

ANDREW WAS NOWHERE to be found, and he did not want to be discovered. He had driven to Penzance, found the map of scenic walks, and decided to walk from Penzance to Zennor along the steep cliff paths. He had his rucksack, a large loaf of wheat bread, a great wedge of cheddar cheese, a box of Sultanas, and two canteens that dangled by hooks from the rucksack on his back. So he set out.

The day was hot and the sky was the particular shade of blue that announced summer rather than spring. A beautiful day. So much climbing. In short order, he stopped, sat down on a rock, stared out over the sea, then opened the rucksack and pulled loose a chunk of bread and a bit of cheese. Then he began to eat in his own particular, distinctive way. He took a bite of the bread, chewed it a little, and then took a bite of the cheese, and kept this up until everything he had taken out was gone. "You still eat like a child," Sophie never failed to tell him. "I went to a lot of trouble with that sauce. Don't eat the asparagus and then drink the sauce like a soup. The tastes are supposed to blend together." But that, he thought, was the trouble. An asparagus stalk should taste like an asparagus. The sauce should taste like the sauce. And was it so childish to want to taste the pure asparagus, undiluted, undisguised by the sauce? It wasn't as if he carried on in that way throughout the whole meal. At a certain point, one which only he recognized, he thought it quite safe to eat asparagus and sauce together. Sophie would be sure to notice and say, "Well, thank God for that. I went to a lot of trouble making that sauce, Andy, I can tell you. Someone would think you had something to fear from that sauce." From one extreme to the other, his sister, first playing the pouting, flirty child, next the fussy grandmother, carrying on about a sauce and incapable of paying attention to the many wars breaking out in the rest of the world.

It's true I'm afraid of asparagus and sauce, he thought, staring out over the water. He wanted to know what things were, what they really were. He didn't want things disguised or prettied up. His *life* had been asparagus with sauce. For years, Sophie had gone on and on about Meena and how little she cared for her, how she despaired of making Meena love her, but he had never questioned Meena's affection for him. He had always been sure she loved him. She took him into her bed when he was ill or frightened; she confided in him, and so he knew when his parents were not getting along well together, and he knew why. "When you are grown, and women begin to love you, you must think, will you hurt them by loving them? You must be careful and not let anyone think you care more than you do. It is not fair to women to lead them down the garden path," Meena told him.

Garden path? What garden path? The path through the little gardens in Willow Grove?

"You are a handsome boy, Andy, and women will fall for you, and you must take care with them. You will be the living image of your father, and, Andy," she said, dropping her voice to a whisper, "he has not always been careful."

Women falling for him? Falling how? Falling where? Would they hurt themselves?

"I hope no one will fall because of me," he said.

"Oh, they will, they will," Meena said wearily, not understanding how little he had understood, how frightened her words had made him. "But all the same, you must try, my darling."

"I shall do," he promised.

"Oh, my good boy!" she exclaimed, and wrapped him tightly in her arms. "I know you will do the right thing."

Now, thinking back, he asked himself what on earth Meena had been doing, and even if he had understood precisely what she meant, why had she been speaking to him in that way? Surely it was inappropriate.

"She never let *me* in her bed," Sophie once said.

"I don't think that's really the point," Bertold said. "Not the point at all."

"She ought to get a dog," Andrew said. "To keep her company."

"I don't think a dog is what she wants," Sophie said. Again, that steely voice.

"Woof!" said Bertold. "Woof!" Sophie began to laugh. Her brother joined in. It was a contagious laughter, and Bertold was laughing along with them. Sophie laughed until she cried. Just then, Meena came in wearing her white apron. "What's so funny?" she asked. "Tell me!" and of course that made them worse. "I will commence breakfast and you'll eat what you're served since you're all incapable of speaking," she said, stalking out. The hilarity in the room grew into a crescendo. Meena heard it in the kitchen, scrambling eggs, weeping into them as she beat them up with her whisk. They will never let me in, she thought. They never wanted me. And to make it so clear the morning after the funeral. I will never forgive them. Never.

Yes, thought Andrew, looking out over the sea, it was always asparagus and sauce where Meena was concerned. He had never understood her rightly. He remembered now, and understood now, why his father had watched Meena cooing over him, his look contemptuous, beyond hiding. And he had thought his father was contemptuous of *him*. His childhood would have been different, certainly his present life would have been different, if he had known Meena for what she was, if she had not been, like the asparagus, covered in sauce. Yes, things ought to appear as they were, he thought. It was no wonder he had taken to sculpture. Once he thought mathematics was the answer. There would be right answers and wrong, everything in black and white, no shadows when adding two and two. But then he found that maths were far less precise than he thought, and if possible, there was often less and less certainty in mathematics than in literature. So he had given up on maths, and everyone had said it was too bad, he had a gift for it. Everyone expected that he would have some kind of gift or another. He was the offspring of two geniuses, after all, if they *had* been geniuses. He had never been sure about that.

He looked up to see a head begin emerging, slowly, from the cliff beneath. A bald old man, the sun glistening on his bald pate.

"Mind if I sit on that rock?" he asked, indicating another flat rock nearby.

"Not at all," Andrew said.

"You may wonder at my stamina," the old man said. "I was put through my paces during the war and I've been going through the same paces ever since."

"Admirable," Andrew said.

"You seem fit," the old man said.

He thanked the man. Meena had trained him to be polite.

"But I've seen young men who appeared happier. In a dilemma, are you? Not making up your mind about a girl you've gotten in the club?"

"No, nothing like that," Andrew said.

"No? Then out with it," the old man said. "We cliff-walkers have our rules, you know. We can say what we like to someone we've never met when we're out walking from one place to another, and you can do the same to us, and the rule is, we don't let anyone else in on what we say. That's why," he said, leaning forward confidentially, "we walk as much as we do. I can't tell the missus about the war. She won't hear a word about it, never would. But when I feel the urge to confide, I put on my good thick-soled shoes and set out on the cliff path and I always find just the person I want."

"Do you want to talk about the war?" Andrew asked.

"Not today. Today I came out hoping to hear something new. It's not the old lady's fault, but I've heard her stories time in and time out. A little like the queen's Christmas speech, if you take my meaning. But you have something you want to say. I can almost hear it, I can."

"Family trouble," said Andrew. "Nothing very interesting."

"What's more interesting than family trouble?" the old man said. "Every family has it."

Andrew was about to leave, about to repack his rucksack, when he heard himself saying, "It's my father's will. He died and he left a will and no one can agree if he meant what he said. He said one thing in his will and another in his List of Wish."

"That kind of trouble," the old man said, nodding. "When I was growing, no one had anything. This is how a will was in those days: 'To Anne, my good black dress. To Rachel, my jet brooch. To Emily, my warm crocheted shawl.' And that was the end of that. Before the body cooled, the rest of the family bore off the hutch and the flour scoop and all the rest of it. Everyone knew what was what. People took the clothing straightaway. It was a simple thing, a will, in those days. But I suppose your will had quite a lot more in it—your father's did, I mean to say?"

"A great deal more," Andrew said, and he was soon telling the old man the whole story.

"Well, well," the old man said, stopping him several times, each time saying, "This was a good day to go out walking."

"And that's it," Andrew said, astonished at having told someone else everything he knew. "My sister's disappointed in me. She thinks I could do something."

"Oh, she's right there," the man said. "A man can always fight. If he thinks what he believes is right. You know what you think is right? Or you're still, so to speak, deciding?"

"I think I know what's right," Andrew said.

"A man must fight for what he believes is right. We all found that out the hard way, when we put on our uniforms and walked up the planks to the big grey ships. You can stay behind with the wharf rats, but then what will you make of yourself?"

"Not much," said Andrew.

"Then don't disappoint your sister," the old man said. "You don't get too many sisters in a lifetime, not these days. And even back then, you started out with a lot of them, but most of them didn't last it out. Mine are gone, all of them. You've got one that's criticizing you, but she's alive. You can let her down, but you'll regret it, won't you?"

"Yes," said Andrew. "I will."

"And as for stepmothers," the old man said, "I have one last thing to say. They're not of your own blood, then, are they?"

THIRTY-SIX

——

JULIA HAD FOUND a little flat to rent on the top floor of a family house and moved into it. The house was off Parliament Hill and she had to climb up to the fourth floor to reach what had once been the nursery and the nursemaid's quarters. She had gotten on well with Sophie, just as she always had, but Julia's appetite for solitude grew with every passing year. After some time in Sophie's house—she was grateful to Sophie, but ravenous for silence and complete freedom. The flat was tiny. One miniature parlor, one extremely small bedroom, so small that when she got up from the bed she had to do so carefully, or she would find her face knocking against the plaster wall, and a very small bathroom with a large mirror on the back of the door. Everything had been painted white. The curtains were sheer and white and the crocheted bedcover was white. The bedding was white and the wall-to-wall carpeting was grey, almost startling. The little room reminded her of the room at the top of Sophie's house. It was exactly what she wanted.

The white telephone rang and she knew it was Matt before she answered it.

"How are they doing?" he asked. "Who's winning?"

"It's hard to say. Meena's going to court to set aside the List of Wish. And Sigrid's busy. She's up to something. And Rose is upset at all of us because of things Meena said to her, although she isn't very forthcoming about what Meena *did* say, but somehow we're supposed to intuit it, and no one's really speaking to Rose because she went to visit Meena after Sigrid forbade it. So all in all, it's a draw. Where the money is concerned, anyway. Although I don't think Meena can win this one, not if the rest of them stick together. Each one of them can seem like a formidable little mob."

"But you're happy there? You aren't exhausted by them?"

"Their lives are not my life."

"And so they're keeping you busy?"

"They certainly are. Sometimes I try to remember how this all began."

"Because I asked Peter if he'd give a large reading for small money to a working-class college that could barely pay him."

"That's right. That's how it began. Such a long time ago."

"Almost forty years," he said. "He hadn't even married Meena then."

"What's the weather there?" Julia asked him.

"Hot. Very. You're not missing much. Weather alerts on the radio and on the computer news. Stay inside. Drink liquids. Don't fall asleep in the sun. And over there?"

"Freezing," Julia said. "I went out and bought a pair of wool socks and a huge green wool sweater. I sleep in it at night. I thought I saw Meena in the High Street, but it couldn't have been her because she didn't recognize me. I don't think she'd pretend not to know me. If it was Meena, that is."

"Does she know you have red hair? And it's cut short?"

"No. I haven't seen her in five years and everyone's been too busy to tell her about me, and no one would have told her, because no one's speaking to her except Andrew and we barely know each other."

"So how could she have recognized you?"

"She couldn't have."

"Where was she?"

"Coming out of the Jaeger shop at the top of Haverstock Hill, across from the Everyday. She was holding a large carry bag. She'd been shopping. Successfully, by the look of it."

"And you? Have you looked in at Jaeger's?"

"Don't be silly," Julia said.

"So it's still Camden Lock for you?"

"Of course."

"And what did you find now?"

"Strange velvet scarves."

"You have enough scarves."

"Really, I go to see what the young designers are up to now. There's always someone just starting up. Do you miss me?"

"Not desperately. Work's keeping me busy."

"Will you be happy to see me?"

"Of course."

"Of course," she repeated.

"I'm glad you went," he said. "Why should you be bored because I'm busy?"

"No reason. But Matt, I feel so *scrubbed* in this little white place. It makes me happy."

"Then don't fill it up with clutter."

"You couldn't fit so much as a wish in this room," Julia said.

"Take Sigrid to the Chinese for me," Matt said.

"A good idea. I will."

"What's Andrew like?"

"Exactly and exactly and exactly like his father. He looks like him. He is like him, only, I think, more scrupulous. A lot more scrupulous."

"Don't fall in love with him," Matt said.

"You'd have to worry if I were twenty or thirty years younger."

"Would I have to worry?" he asked.

"No."

"And you're keeping away from Rose?"

"Believe me, *that's* no trouble," Julia said.

—

JULIA LAY DOWN on the little white bed in the little white room. The white telephone rang again.

"He's changed his mind!" Sigrid's voice exclaimed. "He's going to try mediation with Meena."

"I don't understand," Julia said.

"Andrew! He's going to see what he can do."

"That's wonderful," Julia said.

"All because he went on a walk to Seal Island. You remember those cliffs? And he met an old man and they talked, and it seems the old man talked him into getting his feet wet, and he's *doing* it, Julia, he's *doing* it."

"Let him have his head and don't expect too much. By the way, I thought I saw Meena coming out of the Jaeger shop."

"She's smartening up for court," Sigrid said. "Julian's coaching her. I'm sure of it."

"She looked pretty grim to me, a little like my idea of Myra Hindley."

"When she's finished, she'll go into court looking like Princess Diana, and next to her, Mother Teresa will look like Scrooge, and in the end, everyone will say, 'You're so *marvelous*, Meena!' She knows her stuff. *Why* did he have to marry that woman?"

"Let's wait and see what Andrew accomplishes," Julia said.

"Could *you* be so vengeful?" Sigrid asked her.

"Well," Julia said. "Of course."

"I think not," Sigrid said. "You'd drop two stone and get out your hunting spear and find another man."

"That may be, but first I'd finish off the man who had the affair," Julia said. "That's why men don't want a divorce. They know how vengeful women are."

"Well, Peter wanted one."

"Then you shouldn't be surprised by Meena," Julia said. When she rang off, she turned on her side and looked out the two windows. The people who had built the house must have been dwarfs. The bottom windowsills came almost to the floor, the windows set at just the right height for a small animal. And those windows were so close to the edge of her narrow bed that anyone suddenly springing up could fall right out of the window and it was a long way down to the cement sidewalk. From the two windows, tall and thin, and from the feel of the air coming through them, it was evident that it was a beautiful day, one of those autumn days that would not come to the States until October or perhaps November.

It was seductive, a day like this, whispering that nothing should resist the soft, shining air outside. But Julia was happy inside the narrow white room, and it seemed to her that she could enjoy the day even better if she stayed where she was, looking out through the windows framing the day. Everyone will be outside but you, Julia thought. She nestled happily, more deeply into her bed. Matt would not approve of this room, she thought. He would have pronounced it a cell. If he had been a writer, he might have thought differently. When Peter moved out of Willow Grove and into a flat in the village, he set up a study in a closet, a closet with a window, an oddity that bespoke many renovations throughout the generations. Julia had also used a closet as a study when she first married, a closet painted Wedgwood blue, just big enough for a card table and a chair, but it had the other necessary requirement: a window. Probably she could have written anywhere no matter how small the space; she could have written suspended from a swing provided the space afforded a window. She had long since concluded that no one could write staring at a wall. A window was an essential object. Peter hadn't found windows terribly important. For him, a study had to be so small that only one person could occupy it.

There was nothing so delicious, Julia thought, as deliberately staying inside on a beautiful day. That was true extravagance, that was optimism, the willingness to believe, or at least behave, as if time were both elastic and plentiful, and so there would be other, beautiful days, that there was no urgent reason for not wasting a day like this. This ability to waste time was one of the precious things granted by passing years. And that was what Evelyn had lost, and Elfie after her, the time to waste a day like this, knowing there would be more such days later.

THIRTY-SEVEN

—

MEENA WAS UP in the middle of the night, primping, adjusting. Her hair was secured by a hairnet that had once belonged to her mother, and when she had picked it up and saved it and took it home like a demented pack rat, she wondered why on earth she was making off with it, because surely she would never need it. No one wore hairnets any longer. These days, there was styling spray that kept hair in place, kept it hard as a rock. How sallow her face looked in the mirror, but perhaps it was the lamplight. There were no photographs of Peter to be seen in the bedroom, and for a moment this worried Meena. What if the judge should discover that she had banished all photos of her husband from their marital room? But she had many such pictures, in ornate silver frames, all over the parlor, and in any case, there was no reason for the judge to enter Willow Grove, and even if he did, it would be easy enough to explain the absence of conjugal photos. She would say, "It's too painful, having them here when now I'm alone, too easy to look from that photograph to my new life and measure how much has been lost." Yes, she quite liked the sound of that. And she would end by saying, "Come see the photographs downstairs! I have some lovely ones there. It's so much easier to look at them in daylight, don't you find?"

Well, the pink suit. Just as Julian had said, Jaeger had the perfect pink suit, a rough-weave linen suit, beautifully tailored, the sort of suit that never goes out of style, so the saleswoman had said. It would not announce itself as something new, something she had acquired to make an impression on the court. Anyone in the court might think Meena had had the suit forever, searched through her closet, and decided, Yes, that will do, and had taken it out, giving little thought to making any particular kind of impression. All in all, she thought, a perfect purchase. And of course she should wear a brooch, the kind of brooch that would have belonged to her mother or her mother-in-law. Had she such a brooch? Yes, the one she had taken out the day before was perfect, a little spray of enameled lilies of the valley, no stones at all, nothing extravagant. Her people had had so little money. Everyone in the court would know that and be reminded of that when they saw only little seed pearls standing in for diamonds, perfect. She lay the brooch on top of the suit. But she would need earrings, small ones, but ones that gave her a finished look, because she had come up in the world, after all, and everyone knew that, too.

The little pearl studs surrounded by diamond chips, those would be perfect. These days no one believed anything was real. Everyone wore copies of the originals, zircons replacing the diamonds locked in the safe or the bank's vault. And her wedding ring. Nothing to worry about there. She'd never taken that off and never would. She would take that ring to her grave so that if Peter's spirit chose to visit her, he would be infuriated all over again. Why should vengeance end with death? What else? Shoes.

She was a tall woman. Flat shoes were in order, tan leather, did she have them? Yes, there they were in the corner of the closet. Not really cold enough to require a coat, but she did have the black cashmere cloak Sigrid had brought back from France. It dwarfed her, that cloak, but that was best, best to appear fragile and buffeted by life. As indeed, Meena thought, she was.

Meena switched off the light and sat in her chair. Outside, the moon was still bright and round. She was accustomed to staring out, observing the doings of animals and birds. The loose shutter which had clattered and had driven her to such distraction until she finally began to dream of it, in her dreams sure that the sound of the *thud, thud, thud* really was the knocking of Peter's heavy shoes against the coffin lid—that shutter had been fastened. It is not like me, Meena thought, to let my imagination run wild. And yet, now, sitting in the chair, looking out, she dreaded that noise starting up again. But how could it, she asked herself, now that the shutter had been fastened, now that all the shutters had been inspected and fastened with new, iron hooks? She stood up and went to the window, looking down on the grounds of Willow Grove, hiding herself behind the draperies, as she had so often done through the years. She had a sixth sense; she knew when intruders were about. She had that sense now. All those intruders through the years, usually women who wanted to catch a glimpse of Peter, the man they believed had murdered Evelyn. But sometimes they were women who had met him during receptions given after his readings in London, and finally, an Argentinian woman, who had followed him all the way from Rio de Janeiro after he read there. "I think that is enough of your globe-trotting, Peter," Meena had said at the time. "Half of London sneaks up here trampling my tulips, and now, it seems, the whole world is to come!" For a short time, he had stayed at home, even surrendered his passport to her, only to agree to read in Capetown. He had appeared in her little study, which was painted blood-red, a place where she went to settle accounts and pay bills, write bread-and-butter notes, and read contracts. She found contracts clear and not at all difficult to understand, and he asked, rather shamefacedly, to have his passport back. *The Bloody Chamber,* that was what he had taken to calling her study. But when he referred to her room in that way, she said nothing. By then they were not on good terms and it was simpler not to speak.

It seemed to her now, looking out, that there was another intruder loose on the grounds. She saw him moving just inside the fringe of trees at the far edge of the field. He would move forward, as if he intended to approach the house, then change his mind and move back into the darkness. He kept this up until Meena shivered in terror. It is not a person, she told herself. It is a tree branch pushed forward by the wind and then falling back again. Yes, she thought, probably that was what I saw. Yet whatever it was seemed to move as Peter had, striding forward purposefully, but only for a few steps, then retreating just as decisively. Meena picked up the mohair throw she always kept on her chair and wrapped it about her. It would be useless trying to sleep if she went back to bed. Julian would be here soon enough and she would send him out to look for any footprints, any telltale signs. People went mad in solitude, Meena thought. Yet she had prayed for solitude for so long, prayed, really, to have the house alone to herself—in other words, prayed for her husband's death. Peter must have known that, Meena thought, drifting into sleep in her chair; he must have done. He picked up her thoughts before she herself knew what they were. Something caused her to jump in her chair, and she opened her eyes to see a white face at her window. She screamed, once, twice, but there was no one to hear her, no one to tell her that she had only seen the moon reflected on the windowpane, but finally she did realize it, settled back in the chair, her heart thumping. She gave up all hope of sleeping, and as she did so, fell deeply asleep. She fell into a dream she would not remember when she awakened, but she heard Peter saying distinctly, as if he were standing by her chair, *When you give up hope completely, that's when you get what you want.* Had he said that to her, or had she heard him say that to Sophie? When he spoke in that way, she had always believed that what he said was true. Meena stirred in her sleep, thinking, or was she answering him? "Why should I give up hope?" she said.

—

"ARE YOU PREPARED for this?" Julian asked Meena as he sat at the kitchen table eating his usual breakfast, scrambled eggs, fried toast, three strips of bacon, and a separate plate of fried tomatoes. "It would be better to plead nervous exhaustion and reschedule than go into court and give inadequate answers. The tide may be turning against you. Lady Anne has not kept her suspicions to herself."

"Lady Anne!" Meena exclaimed.

"Her opinion carries a great deal of weight," Julian said.

"Last night, I thought I saw a man lurking at the edge of the woods."

"Oh, please!" Julian said. "Last week, it was Peter, hammering at the lid of his coffin, and of course it was a loose shutter."

"I know that *now*," Meena said.

"I wouldn't have thought you'd be so susceptible to hysterics," her cousin said.

"Of course I'm not," Meena said. "But I did see a man, and later, I thought I heard his voice, although I can't be sure of that. By then, I may have been dreaming. I wish you would go scout it out, Julian. At the edge of the woods, where I keep the row of birdhouses."

"There was no one there," Julian said. "But if you let me finish my breakfast, I'll borrow Peter's rubber fishing boots and go out and look. Where do you keep them?"

"Under the cupboard beneath the steps, as I always keep them," Meena said absently.

"You should throw out all of that stuff," Julian said.

"I may do," she said. She was watching the plate of tomatoes, slowly vanishing into his mouth. Had he always eaten so slowly? She had cooked too much. Really, he ate too many fried things. Peter had been so careful

of what he ate. He checked his cholesterol level whenever he went to a doctor's office. In the end, he could have lived on cheese and bacon and it
would not have made the slightest difference. It was Meena's axiom that
you never died of what you most feared. "Aren't you finished yet?" she
asked Julian.

"I can see there's no eating in peace here," he said. "Leave the tomatoes
on the plate. I'll eat the rest when I come back." She nodded, stared at the
clock on the wall, the swaying of its pendulum, always the same motion,
never changing, poor clock. She heard the door slam. The door slammed
again and Julian was back, looking disgusted. "Not a sign of so much as a
butterfly touching down," he announced, and picked up a piece of a
tomato and popped it into his mouth. "You must get yourself under better control. You are too young for dementia. It's nerves, that's all it is. You'll
see. When you're through with the court, there will be no more slamming
shutters that sound like dead men's feet and no men walking in and out
of the woods. What would they be doing here? You need a good dog. I'll
find you one. A *big* dog with a deep thunderous voice, an Alsatian, I'd say.
That's all you need, a big dog."

"I *had* one," Meena said, "and look at all the good it did me."

"You mean Peter," Julian said, laughing and then starting to choke on
the next bite of tomato. "You had the wrong sort of dog."

"It isn't amusing, Julian. All sorts of things come out at night."

"Usually they come out when lonely people can't sleep and spend their
time staring out of windows into the dark," Julian said.

—

THE COURT BUILDING had existed forever. Twice the villagers
had defeated proposals to tear it down and replace it with a newer, more
modern building; the general opinion was that a court was bad enough to
enter without it also resembling a hospital, as new buildings tended to do,
and so it had remained untouched.

"Now, this is not a jury trial," Julian reminded her as the two of them climbed the brick steps. "Although if the judge is suspicious, he may suggest a jury trial, so it would be best if you could stop everything here. He will ask you questions and you will give suitable answers. You won't speak of shutters or other nonsense, will you?"

"Of course I shan't," Meena said with asperity. "You're too anxious to think me mad."

"Most people would willingly believe it," Julian said. "They believe Peter drove Evelyn mad, and then Elfie. Why would they not think the same was true of you? I believe," Julian continued, "that you know Peter meant you to divide the estate, and now you suffer from guilt and think Peter is pursuing you."

"Or Evelyn," Meena said, pausing at the top of the steps.

"Evelyn?"

"After all, a good deal of the estate came from her earnings. I was looking through the accounts last night. Her books sell far more than Peter's. It occurred to me that she would want her children to have the lion's share of the estate."

"Evelyn is *dead*," Julian said, staring intently at his cousin.

"Of course she's dead. Everyone knows she's dead. But no one lets her rest in peace."

Julian opened the heavy oak door to the court building.

"Sit down on that bench," he told his cousin. "And what do you mean, they won't let her rest?"

"People don't behave as if she's dead," Meena said.

"And what does that mean?"

"Her gravestone. They won't leave it alone. They keep prying off the letters of the Grovesnor name."

"Yes, we know that," Julian said.

"But last time, last time, someone got into the plot, got over the spiked iron fence, and managed to pry almost everything loose so that it read *Evelyn raves*. When, as you well know, it should read *Evelyn Graves Grovesnor*."

"And now you're worrying about that?" Julian asked. "After almost forty years of the same nonsense? Do you see why I'm afraid a guilty conscience will undo you in there?"

"Evelyn raves," Meena said in a low voice.

"That," Julian said, "is enough of that. You should never have allowed him to move you into that house. You've spent far too long in a haunted house."

"*I* was the one who insisted on living there. From the time we were small, I always admired that house. We saw it every Sunday when we went to church."

"He should have dragged you away from that place," Julian said.

"*I* would never have allowed it. And now I am entitled to it and everything that comes with it."

"So long as you bear that in mind," Julian said.

"It is all I bear in mind," Meena said.

"At least if you prevail in here, you'll have enough dosh for a good long rest cure."

"That's *enough,* Julian," she said.

"Ready, set, go?" he asked her.

"Ready," Meena said. She straightened her pink suit. Even she could not look like a uniformed general in a pink suit. A sweet, harmless woman, a brave widow, still with youth in her, but not too much youth left, a woman who had spent her life taking care of her husband, now a deserving widow, just as she had wanted to appear.

THIRTY-EIGHT

—

"THEN YOU BELIEVE," the judge asked her, "that the List of Wish was not, finally, what Mr. Grovesnor wanted?"

"I do believe that, yes," Meena said.

"And he himself asked that you repudiate it?"

"Yes. He did," Meena said.

"And his motives for declaring that document invalid?"

"He had been on morphine, you see, and as I said, his mind was not clear. But during those two hours when he did not require pain medication, his mind was quite sound, and it was his desire that I be taken care of properly, and I was only to make gifts to the others in the family which I myself wished to make."

"So, a radical change of heart?" the judge asked.

"I argued against the change," Meena said. "I thought the List of Wish was best for all concerned. If everything was divided into quarters, then there could be no possible arguing. I had proposed the List of Wish myself. I did not want it voided."

"I see," said the judge.

Meena looked straight at the judge, nodded her head, and moved her clasped hands slightly up and down.

"And was there anyone who witnessed the drawing up of the will and the List of Wish, or anyone who heard Mr. Grovesnor attest to the fact that he desired to revoke the List of Wish?"

"There was no one to hear the discussion," Meena said. "We had two nurses working around the clock, and I often gave the nurse time off to rest. I knew how exhausting such work is, you see. If I intended to remain in the room, and if I planned to watch over my husband, I would send the nurse out for some coffee or a little nap. During one of those times, my husband awakened and his mind was quite clear and he appeared free of pain, which I took to mean that he had little time left to live. It was then that he spoke of revoking the List of Wish. As I said, I argued against it, but how could I bring the full force of my will to bear when he was so weak? When I refused to agree immediately, my husband became agitated. He had me swear that I would revoke the List of Wish, and he wanted someone to attest to his change of heart. It was his idea to have the List of Wish revoked and to have the nurse witness it. But before the nurse could return and do as he asked, he . . ."

"He . . . ?" said the judge, prompting her.

"He had died," Meena said, beginning to weep. She unclasped her hands and pressed them to her cheeks, then moved them upward to wipe away the tears.

The judge himself looked stricken. "Then you are willing to swear that Mr. Grovesnor wished to revoke the List of Wish?"

"It was what he desired," Meena said.

"And will you now abide by the List of Wish?"

"In principle," Meena said. "It is my belief, as sole executor of his estate, that his children should inherit some part of their father's estate, just as children do in France, but the estate is not as large as we believed it to be. My husband believed there would be a substantial sum, enough to keep all four of us for the rest of our lives once we had paid our taxes. But the preliminary indications are that the size of the estate will be much less than he believed. Above all, he wanted to be sure that I should be well provided for during the remainder of my life. My husband was, in many ways, quite a conventional man. He knew that I had spent my life taking care of him and his children, our children, and he believed that when a husband died and left a widow, that widow ought to inherit his estate. If I hadn't intervened and asked for the List of Wish, there would not have been such a document."

"You yourself suggested he add it to his will?" asked the judge.

"I did," Meena said. "Perhaps I should not have meddled in legal matters, but at the time, I understood the sum of money to be greatly in excess of my own needs, and so I had him draw up the document."

"And that was drawn up on the same day as his will?"

"Yes. It was."

"And did you also, at that time, ask him to write up his will?"

"I did. I know what havoc can be wrought when one dies intestate. My husband's first wife died without leaving a will and the complications continue to this day."

"So I understand," said the judge.

Behind her, Meena heard a woman snort loudly.

"So you see, I wanted a legally proper will, and a written statement of his wishes. Unfortunately, his wishes changed immediately before his death, and there was no time to revoke the List of Wish before it could be rewritten and witnessed."

"And you will then swear before God to what you have just testified?"

"I will," said Meena.

"The clerk will prepare the documents and you will sign them. That will revoke the List of Wish. It is not, in any case, a binding document, as you know."

"Yes. I do know," Meena said, again beginning to weep.

"By all means, take a seat," the judge said.

The woman who had snorted before now went toward the door. Meena turned and saw Lady Anne leaving the room. How had she gotten here? And what was she doing here? She would go straight to Sophie and repeat everything she had heard word for word. Eventually, Lady Anne would speak to the judge, with whom she was socially acquainted, but by then, it would be too late to alter his decision. She had won and the List of Wish was now invalid.

—

"YOU DID VERY WELL," Julian said when they came out into the sunshine.

"I should go to the constable and complain of trespassers and stalkers," Meena said. "Evelyn's grave continues to be defaced, which means that there are still people who do not wish Peter well, and in his absence, I believe they have settled on me and decided I am to be his stand-in."

"I should leave it alone," Julian said. "For a while. People might think the stalkers are members of the family whom you have just disinherited."

"It suits me to have people believe that the family is persecuting me," Meena said.

"And so it would, if others had more sympathy for you and less for them," said Julian.

"And you think they don't?"

"I think the spectacle of two orphaned children is a bit much for most people to stomach," Julian said. "Especially since everyone knows how devoted to the children Peter really was."

"How devoted was he, really? He went to Africa because it suited him, and Peter particularly liked watching the big cats. He went years without visiting Sophie, even when she lived quite close by. And when Sophie went out to Jamaica and stayed with Martin, he didn't fly out to see either of them."

"As I remember, you were against his doing anything of the sort," Julian said.

"No one knows that but you," Meena said. "And you are not about to tell anyone. If a will can be changed once, it can be changed twice."

"If you really intend to change your will so that, upon your death, nothing goes to his sister or his children, but goes instead to my family, you must go to a good lawyer in London and keep the details of your will secret. There must be no leaks. The confidentiality you need most must belong to your solicitors."

"An attorney is bound by privilege to say nothing."

"I am a barrister, and I know how loosely lawyers talk," Julian said. "On this point, you must take great pains. If you intend to have your fortune revert to me and not to Peter's children, everyone will know that your aim was revenge. It will not do to let others know that you intend to disinherit the children entirely. It is one thing if people believe that you yourself need the means to live, but quite another to think that you hold on to the estate simply to keep them from it. Everyone knows that Willow Grove was Peter's long before he married you, and that Willow Grove was the children's home. If you will it to me, people will talk. And not nicely, Meena."

"Oh, I understand!" Meena said irritably.

"And you must stop speaking of intruders and stalkers. People *will* think you've gone round the twist."

"Even if I am telling the truth?"

"Even if you *think* you are telling the truth," Julian said. "Have you heard from any of them recently?"

"The children? Sigrid? No, they've gone very quiet."

"I don't like the sound of that," Julian said.

THIRTY-NINE

——

IN CORNWALL, IT was unusually cold and rainy, what Peter would have called a palette of greys.

"It might as well be February," Sophie told Clare as they sat in Crow's Nest, watching the great Tree of Light sway from its chain. Every so often, either Sophie or Clare would stand up and push it as if it were a swing, and the chimes would ring out.

"In February," Clare said, "all the tourists will be gone and I will have gone to work filling all their orders. I'm like a tulip bulb, really. You plant me in the fall, and I stay underneath until the spring, and then I emerge again. Along with these things," she said, reaching up and tapping the chandelier so that its chimes rang again.

"Yes, the winter is for work," Sophie said. "Daddy always said that no matter what he did, he always finished his work in May, just in time for spring."

"Did he, then?" Clare asked.

"If you could have whatever you wanted, " Sophie asked, "what would you ask for?"

"Now?"

"Yes."

Clare considered. "If I could have whatever I want," she repeated. "Well, what I most want is what I can't have. But if I could have one of the things I most want, I would want to see Willow Grove. I've never seen it, you see, not even driven past it. I'd like to go in and see where your father spent most of his life."

"Never? You've never seen it?"

"Never."

"We should be able to do that for you," Sophie said. "The obstacle, of course, is the dragon at the gate. Meena rarely leaves the place, or so I understand."

"I know it's not possible," Clare said. "We were only playing wishes."

"I think it might be done," Sophie said. "The trick is to get Meena out of there."

"Your father never accomplished it," Clare said.

"He was defeated by her, you see. Or worn out. It comes to the same thing. But there might well be a way. Meena is a nobility worshipper. If someone important were to invite her round, she might well go. She might well do," Sophie said. "Yes, I think that's the answer."

"What is?"

"Her beloved Lady Anne. The woman's cut Meena off and now no one in her social set will have her anywhere. She's caught up in a grim Jane Austen novel."

"Your father said you never read," Clare said.

"He had to pay my school bills, so he must have known I read *something*,"

Sophie said. "We'll be going to visit Lady Anne on the weekend," Sophie said. "I'll see to it."

"I'm not counting on it, you see," Clare said. "I thought of Willow Grove as an enchanted place and an evil witch had cast a spell keeping me away."

"We will just see about evil witches," Sophie said.

———

"AND," SAID LADY ANNE, "she swore, absolutely swore, that she herself had persuaded Peter to draw up the List of Wish, and that he himself was the one who wanted it revoked," Lady Anne said. "You should have seen her there! Butter wouldn't melt! In a pink suit! Only missing Paddington Bear to clutch in her arms! Swearing on oath that the revenue of the estate was so much less than she or Peter had anticipated! When I *know* that is not the case!"

"Anne, how do you know?" Sophie asked.

"Bankers," Anne said. "We all bore ourselves silly at the same eternal dinner party. It's gone on for over fifty years. If anything new comes up, I want to hear it, and so I do."

"And of course poor Clare wasn't given a cent," Sophie said.

"That may not be true," Lady Anne said.

"Anne, you're blushing! What do you know?" Sophie asked.

"He might have given her a small sum. *She* had nothing."

"And does Meena know?"

"Certainly not!"

"That's to the good," Sophie said. "She's down there in Cornwall, and she can't make much out of those chandeliers."

"She doesn't charge enough for them, that's one thing," Lady Anne said. "I've commissioned one and the price was ridiculous! I said I wanted to pay twice the price and so have a chandelier worth twice as much, but all she said was that she'd make the chandelier bigger. So I told her to make it bigger."

"She's not a businesswoman," Sophie said.

"No," said Lady Anne. "She was most definitely not after Peter for his money."

"I've tried to help her," Sophie said, "but she has only one wish, and I can't help her with that. She wants to see the inside of Willow Grove, but of course you can't pry Meena out of there with a lobster fork."

Lady Anne tilted her cup of tea back and forth. "I can never drink anything hot," she said. "I'm always the last one finished because I wait for the tea to grow cold. Well, Sophie, I have an idea, and I suspect you've already thought of it."

"Yes?" said Sophie.

"She would come if I invited her. For a weekend of titled guests. And if she were suddenly possessed by a great desire to return to Willow Grove, I would ring you at once and warn you."

"I don't have her telephone number," Sophie said. "She's changed it again. She thinks people intrude on the grounds. The vicar told me that."

"Crazy as a loon, and getting crazier," Lady Anne said. "I shall ring up Julian, and he will hand over the number. He can't afford to lose clients, not those in our set."

"You could get her out of the house? For a few days? Do you think it would work?" Sophie asked.

"My dear, you know Meena," Lady Anne said. "She will go flapping after anyone with a title."

"When could it be done?"

"Why, next week," Lady Anne said. "She'll jump like a flea fast enough, I daresay. I'll invite two or three couples, all titled, of course, and she'll be there. Sophie, you are a great tonic! People like me never get to do anything mischievous! At least not at my age. I feel as if I'm twenty again! Silly, but young! That is worth many thousands of pounds, and you, Sophie, are priceless!"

"Then, Anne, would you try?" Sophie asked.

"Hand me that leather address book," she said. She found Julian's number and dialed it. "Yes, yes, Julian, it's Lady Anne. McClarren, who else? I don't have your cousin's phone number. She's gone X-directory again. Give it to me, please." She picked up a pen and scribbled the number down. "I had hoped to find her free next weekend. I've never seen such weather. We're all bored silly. I'm quite sure Meena would be a breath of fresh air. *Would* she? I do hope so. I know what she has to put up with. We will cheer her up, I guarantee it. Yes, she is to be there by noon on Friday and stay until noon on Monday. See to it that she gets there, will you, or I shall be very, very insulted. Then it's settled? Good. I'll ring off now, Julian. I must call the butcher; you know how many details need attending when you have guests."

"Well, that's taken care of," Lady Anne said with satisfaction. "And Julian is pleased as a peacock. He was in court, watching her lie herself silly. I daresay he thinks his coaching saved the day for her, and so the whole world of Northumberland believes his cousin to be a perfect saint. So now is the time to plot your break-in. I only ask one thing, Sophie. I should like to meet Clare. She was most pleasant and gracious to speak to when I rang her up."

"Oh, there will be no trouble about that," Sophie said fervently. "No trouble at all. Anne, thank you so much!"

"Come for a week, the two of you," Lady Anne said. "There are so many empty rooms here. One can be fitted up for her if she wants to work. The people who come to me take their cue from what I do. Everyone will want a chandelier! Or I shall gift each of them with one! Yes, a week would be wonderful!"

"But Bertold would miss me," Sophie said.

"My dear Sophie, I assumed you would bring Bertold with you. You know we can accommodate all of you."

"Anne, have you ever counted the number of rooms you have here?" Sophie asked, laughing.

"My dear, what is the point? I know they're all here. They don't come and go, you know. I'm sure one of the servants knows. Shall I ask?"

"No, Anne, I like thinking of your house as an endless catacomb. I like thinking that there may be tribes of trolls living in the cellars, all quite sure they won't be disturbed."

"You are a strange child," Lady Anne said, smiling. "You do keep me amused. Peter said you might."

"Always happy to oblige," said Sophie, laughing again.

"Youth and laughter," said Lady Anne. "There is nothing like it."

FORTY

—

WILLOW GROVE WAS still and silent in the heat that had descended the day before Clare and Sophie arrived. The leaves of the great oaks and elms were motionless in the air. Even the birds seemed exhausted by the heat and only occasionally cheeped on the branches. A black and white cat came toward the cottage, and, seeing two people it didn't recognize, went back into the wood again.

"Well, there you are," Sophie said.

"What a beautiful roof," Clare said. "The way it's molded. How hard that must be to do."

"You want to get inside," Sophie said. "Let's see if she still keeps a key in back of that Portuguese tile. No, she doesn't. We have to get in another way. She's put locks on the ground-floor windows. But not," Sophie said, craning to look, "on the second. We can get in through a window on the second story. I can, I meant to say. I was forever climbing into the house at night when I was younger."

"Is there a ladder?" Clare asked nervously.

"If there's a ladder, she's locked it up. No, I can get in the usual way. Come around to the back."

"She keeps her most beautiful roses back here out of sight," Clare said. "I suppose she wanted them to herself, to herself and to your father."

"I don't think he cared much for her roses," Sophie said. "All that fuss over yellow-leaf and Japanese beetles and all that spraying of poison, he never liked it. 'If it will kill an insect, what will it do to you?' he used to say. Well, Clare, the only thing to do is to climb this apple tree."

"Climb an apple tree?" Clare said doubtfully. "Apple trees are not strong when they age."

"I know this apple tree very well," Sophie said. "You see how the branches hit the windows on the ground floor? My father wouldn't allow her to cut it. He said he knew the apple tree was the spirit of the house and great harm would come to all of us if the tree was cut back. He was sure of it, you see, and whenever he believed strongly in something, everyone soon believed he was right. So there are several boughs that will take me straight to the window."

"I don't know, Sophie," Clare said.

"I do," Sophie said. "That's why I wore jeans and sneakers," and in a moment she was climbing the tree as skillfully as any tree rat. "I'm almost there," she called down to Clare. "The windows aren't locked."

Clare heard Sophie pounding at the window frame. "It's stuck," Sophie called.

"Please come down!" Clare pleaded.

"No, it's open now. I'll go in and then I'll come down and let you through." Sophie disappeared from sight, then stuck her head out of the window. "Come around to the kitchen door," she called. "I'll meet you there."

The kitchen door opened. Sophie grinned at Clare. "Welcome to Willow Grove," she said.

—

IT WAS CONSIDERABLY cooler inside the house, and dim. It was also completely still. "I don't think I've ever found it so silent," Sophie said. "There was always some kind of sound, if only Daddy banging away at his old Remington. It's like a tomb in here. She's closed all the shutters. You don't normally feel like you're underwater in here," she said uneasily. "I'm opening the shutters in here," Sophie said, and when she did so, sunlight flooded into the room. "There, that's more like it." She sat down on one of the benches on either side of the kitchen table and motioned for Clare to do the same. "The famous wormwood table," Sophie said. "Daddy used to tell us he wanted the table to last as long as he did, and if anything happened to him, he wanted one of us to take it. He built it for my mother, you see. The lumber for it came from an old house that was pulled down after a fire. There's a scorch mark somewhere, but I think it's under the table. At least, that's what I remember. Maybe there was no scorch mark. Daddy may have dreamed it up so we'd spend our time looking for it while he was cooking something. He used to cook one meal a day when Sigrid was here, usually luncheon, because he got up early to write. There wasn't an armchair in here then, I'm sure about that." She got up to inspect it. "Jumble sale," she said, sitting back down. "Fraying on the arms, and that awful print of sunflowers. Meena would have thrown it out or had it reupholstered. I imagine he got it when he knew how ill he was. Nice to have an armchair in the kitchen. I should have thought of that."

"It's a huge kitchen," Clare said.

"They broke down a wall," Sophie said. "The far part of the kitchen used to be a nursery."

"Oh," Clare said.

"And the plaster walls were full of cracks, and so was the ceiling. Daddy said you could read the cracks. The cracks were like letters and the house used the cracks to tell its stories. I loved those explanations, but Meena didn't care for them. She'd say, 'Time to get the plasterers in, Peter!' Good Lord," Sophie said, looking around her, "the place brings back memories. I remember coming back here after my mother died, I didn't know she had, but I remember coming back with Sigrid, and I remember being told to go up the steps and turn on the light, but I wouldn't go. I was afraid of spiders. Sigrid hit me and I went up and turned the switch on the landing. That's the only memory I have of those times. I was too young to remember much. I knew something was wrong, something was missing, but I didn't know it was my mother. I don't know where Daddy was when Sigrid told me to go upstairs. Probably he was unloading the car, something of the sort. Andrew doesn't remember anything. I don't think he'd started to crawl yet. He was very slow, Andrew, about everything. Everyone worried when he hadn't started to speak by the time he was three, but the doctor said there was nothing wrong with him and he'd speak when he found something worth saying." She fell silent, staring about the ceiling. "Well, in those days, it didn't look like this, I can tell you. I remember the floor was packed dirt, hard as cement. And we had an icebox, the real thing, and a little man who delivered the ice twice every week, more in the summer. He gave us shaved ice, and Daddy poured sugar water over it. He let us pick whatever color we wanted. He had a shelf full of little bottles of food coloring. Andrew always wanted his ice to be blue. Now there's that double stove and that double refrigerator. They belong in restaurants, really. I don't know why Meena ever needed them. She complained all the time, but she never did very much cooking, not that I remember. She soon had the Prince Edward trained up. She'd call up and tell them how many people were coming, and whether it was to be lamb or beef or fish, and she'd given them all the recipes, but if there was to be someone exotic, another Nobel coming, then there had to be something special. She favored apricots and meringue in a raspberry sauce. She'd drop the ingredients over herself. Sometimes she'd make something like that herself, but it wasn't long before she'd stopped bothering. She said it was too much trouble, and who were those people to her? They used to fight over that, Daddy and Meena. Now the kitchen's got recessed lighting and a ceiling fan and spotlights trained on the tabletop. She used to pore over American fashion magazines. Well, anyway, I'll take you on the tour. Next, the parlor. Daddy used to like that room, but he said it got too sleek and started looking like a trap."

"A trap?"

"You know, a room full of curiosities, so people would sit still and ask questions about where things in it had come from. Very, very posh, so there was nothing someone like Lady Anne could turn her nose up about." The two women hesitated in the doorway and then Sophie went in and opened one of the shutters. "African chairs with arms made from tusks, some black African masks on the wall, those cost a fortune. I don't know who gave them to Daddy, but he liked them, especially the figure in the corner, the one that looks like a skeleton. He always did like that. Meena tried to make him get rid of it. The dead man sculptures are down in the cellar. They used to be in the garden, but Meena couldn't stand them. His friend Clyde is famous for those. I suppose now she'll sell them off, if she hasn't already. I didn't notice the nude woman outside when we came in, so probably that's gone."

"In the cellar?" Clare asked.

"Daddy loved them and said Clyde never did better work, and Clyde thought so, too. "

"Animal skins everywhere," Clare said.

"Everywhere," Sophie said. "Each of them with a story. And that polished floor. Meena was always down on the floor there, polishing. She didn't trust anyone else to do it. And I was down there with her. She said I had to learn proper cleaning, and there were arguments about that, because Daddy said I should be reading a book he'd given me, and I always ended up with wood slivers under my nails, and one of them got infected, but Meena said it was nothing, and by that time the finger was red and swollen and Daddy took me to the surgery, I had blood poisoning, and after that, I didn't have to do the scrubbing anymore. 'Haven't you ever heard of gloves?' he asked Meena. So she was angry at me. Everything was always down to me. Let's go up."

"Take care not to disturb anything," Clare said.

Sophie's hair was down. Clare followed behind her. She had seen pictures of Evelyn before, and Sophie looked just like her, at least seen from behind, with her straight hair down, falling almost to her waist.

"The Bloody Chamber," Sophie said, throwing open a door near the top of the steps. "It's funny about that room. My mother painted it deep red. After she died, Sigrid had it painted white. But when Elfie came, it became her room, and she painted it deep red all over again. She put up a little painting in the corner of the room, right there, right above the baseboard, so that my half-sister could see it, two cows and a dog, and one cat up a tree. It should be here, under the drapery," Sophie said, and pulled the curtain aside. "She's taken it away," Sophie said. "Daddy liked the idea of keeping something to remember everyone by. Upstairs, there's a sheet of paper with a poem written on it and Daddy had it treated so the ink wouldn't run, and then it was glued to his study wall, and he lacquered it. He loved that poem. You'll see it when we get upstairs, if the poem's not already gone, but it may be there; it must be worth quite a lot. Meena wouldn't throw out something that was worth money. Funny, he didn't find anything of Meena's he wanted to memorialize, but maybe he only did that after someone had died, and there was never any chance of Meena dying before him. Sigrid never liked these *death things,* that's what she called them; she said the Bloody Chamber was the right title for that room. He was turning all of Willow Grove into Bluebeard's Castle, all those things to remember his dead wives by. She used to be scathing about all that, Sigrid, although she did say the little painting of Elfie's was 'rather sweet.' "

"Why do you think he kept them? If they upset Meena?" Clare asked.

"Maybe *because* they upset Meena," Sophie answered.

"I think your father hated to let things, well, not *go,* but go under. I think if he kept something of theirs alive in this world, their spirit would know how to find their way back if they needed to return."

"Did he ever say that?" Sophie asked sharply.

"No, but he would fall into a fury when he heard about the letters on Evelyn's stone being pried loose. He was going to take down the stone and bring it here, into the garden, and if Meena wouldn't put up with it, he'd keep it in his study. That last attack on the stone, *Evelyn raves*— he wasn't going to put up with it any longer."

"I never knew he felt that," Sophie said.

"He said many times that he would have liked Evelyn to come back one more time and tell him why she had done what she'd done, and why she couldn't have put up with him, you know, given him time, because he'd have settled down with time, and then they'd have been happy."

"I don't think he would have calmed down enough to suit my mother," Sophie said. "I mean, look at what did happen. He found *you* three years before he died, and by then he was well on his way to seventy."

"He wouldn't have calmed down. I used to worry, you see. Each time he came back, I expected he'd say, 'Clare, I have something to say to you,' and he'd tell me the name of the new other woman. He said it would never happen. I don't know. Some men wear themselves out and then they're perfect husbands. Maybe he'd gotten to that point. I don't know. Maybe he didn't have the energy for that tomcatting, as Sigrid called it. Or it might be that he was really happy. I don't know. It would have been a great thing to find out. As things fell out, I had no regrets on that score, the tomcatting, I mean. But I would have been happy to be able to stay together longer. I used to wish for that."

Sophie nodded and went back into the hall. She opened the doors to the bedroom that had once been her parents', then the small guest room where the walls sloped down at crazy angles. "That used to be my room," Sophie said. "I never liked predictable places, square rooms. If I had this house now, I'd put a huge chandelier in this tiny room, and you'd barely be able to get in it and get to the bed. You'd think you were *living* in the chandelier, like a bird in a nest of light. And Meena, if she still had anything to say about it, would snap at me and say, 'Sophie! You can barely fit a naked bulb in that room!' She is completely conventional, that woman. Sigrid always said that we didn't get on because both of us were Aries and dragons, but Julia is an Aries and a dragon, and we get along very, very well. Do you believe in it? Astrology?"

"Peter did," Clare said absently.

"Up to the turret, then," Sophie said. The stairs up were tall and narrow and the climb was steep, a flight of steps you could kill yourself on. "'Be careful,' Daddy used to say to anyone he took up to see it.

"She hasn't shut *that* door," Sophie called back to Clare. The stairwell going up was not well lit and Clare had been coming up slowly and carefully, exactly as Sophie's father would have told her to do.

"Oh, it's been changed, she's taken it over!" Sophie cried out. "It's all white walls and not one book in sight! The *desk's* gone! There's nothing in it, just that old armchair. That used to belong to my mother. She found it somewhere in London. Someone had put it out on the sidewalk, and she made my father get a taxi and take it back to their flat. She used to nurse us in that chair, that's what Daddy said. I wonder if Meena knows how that chair got here. The poem is gone! The one I told you about! It was right here!" she said, pointing to the wall to the left of the chair. Clare came up and looked at the wall.

"She took a razor and cut it loose," Clare said. "See those thin scorings? Four lines forming a rectangle? Only a razor would do that. She didn't throw it out. She put it somewhere."

"You mean she sold it!" Sophie said, bursting into tears. "She sold it!"

"Perhaps not."

"She might have burned it, her own private cremation," Sophie said. "She would have liked that. She was always threatening to burn up something or other. 'There are too many manuscripts in here, all they're doing is gathering dust, let's burn them when we burn the autumn leaves.' 'We

don't have to pay to take that away. We'll burn it on the lawn after it rains.'
I can smell the smoke! That's her perfume, Meena's fragrance! The smell
of something burning!"

"You mustn't upset yourself on her account," Clare said. "Think how
happy she'd be to know she'd upset you. Was it a mistake to come back
here?"

"No!" Sophie said violently. "I haven't been allowed in here since the
funeral. She's made it plain that none of us would ever enter this house
again. But it's *my* house, too! It's my second skin!"

"Of course it is," Clare said.

Sophie threw herself into the chair. "Look," she said. "There are two
ravens on the branch out there. They're staring in at us, probably wondering where Meena is and why they can't gouge out her eyes."

"We should go back," Clare said gently.

"Not before we play Daddy's music," she said. "It would be here somewhere, under a floorboard near the window." She got up and crouched
down, pushing on the floorboards until one creaked. "Ah. This is loose,"
she said. "Here it comes." Beneath the floorboard was a lone audiotape. "I
brought a little tape recorder," Sophie said. "Do you mind if I play it?"

"Of course not."

"I hope it still works." She lifted the tape from its plastic case, put it in
the tape recorder and depressed the play button. Immediately a strange,
high voice began to sing, "Come Ye Sons of Art."

"Daddy loved this, but Meena thought the singer was freakish, a man
who wanted to sound like a woman. She had no use for countertenors. Do
you know what they are?"

"No."

"Oh," said Sophie, who launched into an explanation of how such
singers had been created and then prized. "Although this one," she said,
"was not castrated first."

One side of the tape played, then ended, and Sophie got up, turned the
tape over, and they began listening to the second side. "It gets hot up here,"

she said, and jumped up again, opening the window. She opened it easily, knowing how to press the window when it stuck, as if she had been opening the window day in and day out. The music began winding around the room and then trailing out of the house like smoke, dissipating in the woods.

"I hope Daddy can hear it from here," Sophie said. Clare nodded, and they retraced their steps, Sophie closing each door she had opened, until they were back in the kitchen. They stood still, looking around the room. "It must have been hell for her, living here," Clare said suddenly.

"You mean Meena?" Sophie asked.

"She was so young when she came," Clare said. "When you're young, you don't want to come into a play already beginning its third act. If she'd come first, or if she'd been older . . ."

"Don't waste your time pitying her," Sophie said sharply. "That's all sentimentalism. If you'd known her, you wouldn't think that. She wanted this house, she got it, and she'll hold on to it with those lobster claws of hers."

Just then, the phone went.

"Come *on*," Sophie said. "Either that's Lady Anne warning us she's coming back, or it's Sigrid, ringing up to ask how things are going. If Julian tries to call Meena and the phone's engaged, he'll know someone is here. We better go," she said, opening the kitchen door, and the two of them stepped outside into the late afternoon sun, and the heat hit them as they ran down the graveled path toward the car. The music was still drifting toward them when Sophie turned the ignition and the motor started up.

—

"SHOULD WE HAVE left the music on?" Clare asked nervously.

"Oh, yes, I think so," Sophie said. "Home again, home again, licketysplit," she said, as they drove precipitously down the steep street and into the town. "Home again, home again, jiggedy-jog, the cat's in the cradle, the pig's in the frog."

Clare turned toward her with shining eyes. "Your father always used to say that when we left to go back to Crow's Nest. It changed every time."

"Odd," Sophie said. "I thought *I'd* invented that. I've been saying that forever."

"It could have been your mother. She might have thought of it."

"That's true," Sophie said. She drove quickly and well. "I wish," she said, "we could still hear the music. I wonder how Meena's doing. Not well, I hope."

———

AND, IN FACT, Meena was not doing well. The last notes of the music playing in the study were just dying out when Meena thought, Nothing here is what it seems. Everyone is as polite as ever, more polite, much too polite. It seemed to her that people's smiles were slightly glazed when they smiled back at her, that those smiles slid into an odd, mocking expression just as she began to turn her head away. But, she told herself, all that is imagination. All that comes from having lived such a solitary life for far too long. She saw Lady Alexandra lean toward Lady Anne, whisper something, and Lady Anne said something in exchange, and then both women began laughing together, a peal of laughter. Was it Meena's imagination, or had they looked her way before the laughter began? I should never have come, she thought. Surely Lady Anne is up to something. To have snubbed me so over her party, and then to throw a dinner party in my honor, really, it makes no sense. She had a sudden, sharp sense of danger. But I must not give in to this, she thought.

Some time ago, she had been standing in Peter's study. A piece of paper lay in the middle of the desk. He'd put his pen down without closing the cap, in such a hurry to answer the phone before she did. Now he had his own phone number and she did not know it. She'd tried to find out, asking the pub owner, "Would you write our phone numbers down? We've changed it again," she said, and she laughed, hoping he would not see what she was doing, that she herself didn't know both telephone numbers, but he obligingly wrote the telephone number she already knew. "And the other one?" she said, handing the little sheet of paper back to him. "The other one?" he said, puzzled. So the second number was meant to be secret, known only to him, to him and that woman who called. Instinctively, she knew the second phone number was not meant for her.

She picked up the paper and read it:

> The red sun rose up like an eye,
> Bloody, all capillaries burst apart
> From the difficulty of the last night's birthing,
> The canal of darkness narrower than ever before.
> He could not see properly.
> He saw birds, all black.
> He saw black buildings and black fields and dark grey stones
> All in a row, all askew.
> He knew this was the day,
> This was when it would happen,
> Had to happen.

He is going to leave me, she thought when she had read it. He intends to leave me. What a bad poem it is! she thought. Just last week, he had said, "While I stay with you, I will never write another good poem." How could she argue about that? But this! This meant that he was going to leave her regardless of the consequences. Oh, by now she understood his language, the secret language of his poetry. She herself had turned the world black for him, blacker than burnt wood, she had bloodied the sun. He was willing to give up its light and his sight in order to escape her. "This was when it would happen / Had to happen." So he had decided, he had changed his mind, there was nothing more she could do. He could be so cowardly, so passive, but now he had resolved to act. He had *resolved* to leave her. Oh, it will not be so easy to get rid of me, she thought. She picked up the sheet of paper, took up the little paper book of matches, struck a match, and held the fire to the paper. It took fire, and the orange flames leaped up. She was holding the paper by one end, but when the flames came too close to her, she dropped the paper on the old, thick wooden desk. The rest of the paper burned itself up, turned to flakes of ash, and scorched the surface of the desk. *Now* live in the canal of darkness, narrower than ever before, she thought. Now find out what it's like to live in that canal. She looked at the paper, reduced to ash, and then quickly left the room. He would find the ashes, not the paper and its first draft, when he returned, and he would not dare to say a word about it. Not yet. Not while he was still in this house. She knew that Evelyn once had waited for him to come back from London, and when he was late in arriving, she took up a stack of his manuscripts and set them on fire. All his wives do the same thing, she thought. She felt no guilt. Why should she? He was lucky none of his wives had set fire to *him*.

"*You* seem to be having interesting thoughts," Lady Anne said, coming up to her. "Tell me, tell me."

"Only the usual widow's thoughts, I'm sorry to say," Meena said.

"But they're *your* widow's thoughts. I think they must be very interesting," Lady Anne said. It was unmistakable, the smugness in her voice, the subtle menace, the undertone of contempt. Then why did she invite me here? she thought. Why bring me here only to enjoy my unhappiness? "Come and circulate," Lady Anne told her, as if there were nothing askew in the world.

—

"I THINK TODAY was a good day," Sophie said to Clare as they drove back to Zennor and Crow's Nest.

"A wonderful day," Clare said. "Thank you so much for it."

"Damn!" Sophie exclaimed. "I left the tape recorder there. I meant to put it back before we left. It's sitting there on the floor right beside her chair."

"Shall we go back?" Clare asked.

"No, it's too dangerous," Sophie said. "Let her find it. She always left frightening things for all of us to find. Now it's her turn."

"But I wish we hadn't forgotten it," Clare said.

"I didn't really forget it," Sophie said. "You know what was most odd about the turret?" Daddy always had a draft of a poem on his desk when you came up there. There wasn't one this time. There wasn't even a desk." She called Sigrid on her cell phone and explained how she had happened to leave the tape recorder.

"Are you driving while you talk to me?" Sigrid asked.

"Yes, yes," Sophie said impatiently. "Should I do something?"

"You already have done," Sigrid said. "And good for you," she said. "Did Clare enjoy it? Seeing Willow Grove?"

"Yes. She did."

"Then drive carefully and don't make any more calls until you stop the car," Sigrid said sternly.

"Yes, Sigrid," Sophie said.

FORTY-ONE

——

THE PARTY, MEENA thought, had not ended well. In the past, Lady Anne had always arranged for someone to bring her back to Willow Grove. This time, however, she seemed to have forgotten. On Monday, after breakfast when everyone gathered around the immense table in the gaming room, Lady Anne had called out, "Someone must be driving toward Willow Grove," but everyone who was going toward Meena's house answered that this time they had taken their two-seaters, or what a pity it was that they were going straight on to their children's homes, and it sounded, to Meena's ears, like a chorus of rehearsed voices singing a song of rejection. "I am sorry for it, Meena," Lady Anne said, "but we shall have to put you on the train. There's a taxi that will take you from the train, is there not?" And Meena had said, "I'll just call Julian and he'll collect me," her voice cheerful and unperturbed. But of course she had been humiliated as if stung, no, whipped, by a cat-o'-nine tails. She had, of course, not called her cousin. She was too raw with shame when the train pulled into the station, and so she had taken a taxi home. She could afford it, she thought, and it came to her, as she paid the fare, that Lady Anne had taken the change in her finances into account.

But there was balm in the sight of Willow Grove, standing still in the coolness of a fresh morning, that house and the intense brightness of an early morning that promised the stifling heat to come in the afternoon. One bird warbled sadly. Probably the bird feeders were empty. In the past, quite some time ago, that had been Peter's job, filling the bird feeders. He found the birds' frantic activity amusing, their swift swoops out of nowhere from the branches on the trees fringing the meadow, their instant competition for the seed that inevitably fell to the ground when he poured in the birdseed. Now, of course, she was the one to fill the feeders, and she could now do it with less trouble, having told the gardener to hang the feeders lower so that she could easily reach them. Even so, it was an exhausting job. The birds ate so many seeds, and so fast. Her husband used to say that he intended to deduct the cost of the birdseed as a charitable expense. The feathered deserving poor.

She hesitated before opening the door and going in. For the first time since she had become the mistress of Willow Grove, she felt as if she were being punished by having to return to it. Lady Anne threw me out of her own house, Meena thought, and she did it shamefully. She would not have put any other guest on a train unless that person had insisted on being taken to the station. Really, it was a mystery. Why, Meena asked herself, invite me at all, only to throw me out? That may have been the point, to throw me out in full view of the rest of the assemblage. I am ruined in society here, Meena thought.

She changed her mind, and instead of going in, walked to the arbor halfway between the house and the woods. She herself had stained the arbor once Peter had built it, and he had insisted on a chair big enough for the two of them to sit in. There had been a beautiful wisteria vine that Meena kept well, and they often sat in the arbor seat, defying the wasps that tended to swarm through the greenery clinging to the arbor walls. They had never been bitten, and Peter had dubbed the place the Bower of Bliss. He loved giving titles to people and to things. He created imaginary titles for imaginary shops. Julia, who loved marcasite and often wore a suede trench coat, was to have a shop called the Marcasite de Suede. He had dubbed Eliza, the jeweler, whose work he admired whenever he saw Julia wearing it, Sparkle Plenty, although he had not been very satisfied with that effort, and occasionally tried out a new title whenever he saw Julia wearing something Eliza had made. Sophie was the Twelve Dancing Princesses, because she bought everything by the dozen and had enough energy for a dozen people, and Sigrid—what had he called Sigrid? She Who Disapproves. He had called Sigrid that, but that title had been supplanted by another. Whatever had it been? No doubt, Meena thought, grimacing slightly, he had dreamed up a very unappealing one for her, although he hadn't told her what it was. But Sophie must have known, and probably Clare. No one was about to tell her. Long ago, there had been attractive titles he invented for her, ones known to the children, others secretly held between Peter and herself. But looking back, it now seemed as if things had gone bad rather quickly.

Still, Willow Grove itself beckoned, as it always did. Once inside, the cottage would seem to ask for a promise to stay, not to leave even for a day. The cottage had become, somehow, like a child. It no longer liked to be left alone, although there were times when Meena believed the cottage, like everyone else, was scheming to be rid of her, hoping for a new mistress to come as had happened so many times before. Meanwhile, there was no question. The cottage wanted company, reassurance.

She walked back and opened the kitchen door and went in. It always surprised her, the stillness and strangeness of the air inside after she had left the cottage alone for even a few hours. She stood in the kitchen, star-

ing about the room, thinking, This house I love is to be my jail. If Julian
had been here, if I had said this aloud, he would have answered that the
house would remain a jail only as long as I insisted on living in it as if I
were serving out a sentence. It was a large cottage, full of guest rooms;
there were people to be invited, and many doors leading out, many places
she could go that she had not yet seen. Unlike Meena, Julian liked traips-
ing about. Best to stay in one place. Then you knew where you were.

But now it seemed to her as if the house had been disturbed somehow
in her absence. When she left, had the benches along both sides of the
kitchen table been askew like that? Out of the question. She invariably
straightened them so that they were precisely parallel to the long table
itself. How Peter had hated that rage for order, as he called it, pointing out
that the benches would be moved again in a few minutes when he sat
down or when the children came, or when the woman who lived above
the church came down to clean. Now, however, no one but Meena moved
the benches. She would not have left to visit Lady Anne unless the benches
had been straight. In fact, she remembered straightening them. A black fly
had died and fallen to the wooden table. She had picked it up, thrown it
in the trash, rinsed her hands, and straightened the benches. This was,
Meena thought, upsetting.

She went up to the benches and put them in order. Then she sat down
and looked about her. Surely there was an odd strong scent in the kitchen,
not the odor of food that had gone off or a rodent dead in the walls. This
was a pleasant smell, floral, light but penetrating. Perfume. Certainly it
was perfume. A woman had been in here. But Peter is gone, Meena told
herself. There is no further reason to worry about women creeping into
the cottage in my absence. She had forgiven, or appeared to do so, Peter's
tomcatting (was that Sigrid's word or had she herself first begun to use
it?). She knew full well that Sigrid approved of his doings, had said to her,
"If you will stop at that, there will be no hope for the two of you. He can't
be changed." She had had no choice, but when he began bringing women
into the house, into their bed, even the appearance of forgiveness was out

of the question. He had especially enjoyed bringing other women to the cottage. He knew what a violation he committed, made all the better for the woman of the week, who quite enjoyed the thrill of coming in, asking questions about Meena. What she was like? Who in the world hung that gold birdcage from the bedroom window? Who kept things so clean? Unbearable. But there was no mistaking the scent of perfume. Peter was gone, but there was the penetrating scent of perfume. It was uncanny. Perhaps the woman was still here!

Meena took the sharp, long-bladed knife from its drawer—she never kept out such a knife, never left it visible on a shelf or a table; it was too suggestive a weapon, too tempting for anyone inclined toward assault— and she went up the steps. The scent was stronger on the landing, but all the doors to the rooms were closed. Meena went into the bedroom. It was just as she had left it. Nothing there had been disturbed. Thank God for that. She opened the door to the Bloody Chamber. Untouched. Her list of things to do lay precisely in the center of her French provincial desk, just as before. But what was this? Was there a rose petal on the floor? She picked it up and turned it over, inspecting it. Browning, but it had once been yellow. Oh, yes, she had cut some roses and put them on her desk several weeks previously. A petal must have fallen and it had escaped her sharp eye. Her eyes, she thought, were no longer what they once were. Two years before, even one year before, she would have seen that petal and dis- posed of it. Peter quite liked fallen rose petals. In the beginning, when the flowers began to go, he would throw out the flowers, but leave the petals that had fallen or those that fell when he carried out the ones that were no longer fresh. He knew she objected. When the petals began stiffening, he would gather them up one at a time and put them in the trash bin. "We have," he used to say, "the largest trash baskets in the whole of England." Meena had not approved of them, either, and took to spraying the inside with roach and ant poison, not when Peter was around to witness it, no, never then.

Meena had better look in the turret.

There, the door to her room was open as she always left it. She never left the room without promising herself to return within minutes. She went in and sat down in her chair and stared out the windows. The scent of perfume was sharper than ever. Was she being haunted? Peter and Sigrid believed such things were possible. Were the two crows outside on their usual tree or had they gone elsewhere? Harder to see them now that the dense foliage of leaves had turned the trees into feathery screens. Yes, there they were, on their familiar branch. They must have a nest some-where about, Meena thought uneasily, then wondered at her sense of unease. I am less and less tranquil, she thought. *Sister Anne, Sister Anne,* she recited to herself, wondering where the line came from, no doubt from an old story her father had read to her as a child. *Sister Anne, Sister Anne.* She had been reading a book just before she left. Where was it? She reached down to see if it had fallen to the floor. She felt something cold and hard. Her heart pounded. She stood up, faced the chair, and stared down at the floor. A tape recorder! A portable tape recorder! Had that woman, that Rose, gotten in here looking for atmospheric details? But *how* would she have gotten in? All the doors were locked and the windows were fastened on the first floor. It made her smile, imagining Rose trying to climb a ladder to let herself in through a second-story window. But, she thought, even if Rose had not done so, there were others capable of climb-ing to the second floor and letting themselves in. But who would do such a thing? When the vicar might have been up in the steeple, seen an intruder, and begun ringing the bells, or simply gone over to the cottage to inspect the place? He would have had a good view of the cottage and he kept an eye out; he'd told her so. *Sister Anne, Sister Anne.* Was she now to be annoyed by that phrase for days? And who was Sister Anne? There was Lady Anne, but the refrain did not refer to her.

Now that she had seen it, she had to pick it up, that little silver tape recorder. She didn't recognize it. Perhaps the owner had left a name and address on the machine somewhere? Return in case of loss? A ten pound reward if found? Nothing. No trace. Was there a tape inside? She was frightened. Had someone left her a message? What kind of message? Who would break into her house to leave her a message? She pressed the eject button. Yes, there was a tape inside. She closed the tape door, rewound the tape, and pressed the play button. Immediately, Peter's music began to fill the room, the music he always played when he wrote, always the same thing. In the beginning, she had bought him other tapes thinking he would like a change, but he had explained that this music belonged to the writing, and as soon as he heard it sound out, his pen began to move across the paper as if of its own accord. Peter has been here, Meena thought with horror, and he brought a woman with him. The music continued to play. Inconceivable that Peter had set it going simply to torment her, and for what? Because she was alive when he was not? Or, she thought uneasily, for other reasons?

They were in an apartment in Massachusetts, honored guests at a small dinner party, at Harvard, a university, very important to go there, Peter had said. And so they went. That was very early in their marriage, before she refused to go to such events. There was laughter, conversation, people shouting to make their point, Meena smiling enigmatically, hiding the fact that she was terrified of strangers and in fact had nothing to say. Suddenly there was a lull in the conversation and a strange whirring, a *click, click, click,* from beneath the couch they sat on. "And what's that?" Peter shouted, jumping out of his seat, flinging himself down on the floor, and reaching beneath the couch. "Come out of there, you!" he boomed in that voice already famous for its power, already known by its accent. And what had he extracted? A tape recorder! "So what is that doing there, then?" Peter asked the scarlet hostess, who stammered, "Well, I was going to ask you about writing a biography."

"Mine?" asked Peter. "I've barely begun to live!"

"Well, not yours, actually," the hostess and would-be biographer said—what had been that woman's name? An odd name these days—Henrietta? Abigail? Agatha? Lucinda? Something of the sort. "Evelyn Graves. I thought I'd try a biography of Evelyn Graves. But of course I'd need your permission."

"You would! You would!" Peter had boomed out, slightly horrified, vastly amused. "But you thought you'd begin collecting information first? On the off chance?"

"Something like that," said Henrietta Abigail Agatha Lucinda.

"A *short* biography?" Peter shouted out. He was, Meena saw, utterly drunk. Hopeless to caution him; he would only grow worse. "Because, after all, it was a very short life!"

"It was," said Henrietta Abigail Agatha Lucinda. "But I *am* asking your permission."

"Have you written anything I can read?" he asked her. She said she had. Why was he talking seriously to a woman who would hide a tape recorder beneath a couch during a party? What kind of person could she possibly be?

"Yes," the woman said, a girl, really; we were all so young, Meena thought.

"Well, let me have it," Peter boomed over the party noise. "Only don't give it to me now. I have to carry everything back by plane. Mail it to me. Give me a piece of paper and I'll write down my address."

"Peter!" Meena had hissed beneath her breath.

"It's all right, Meena," Peter assured her in stentorian tones.

Eventually, he gave her permission, and she'd begun on her biography, but nothing came of it. Why not? Oh, yes, she began and she'd had a nervous breakdown and ended up in the same mental facility where Evelyn had been the summer before she came to England where she had the bad luck to meet Peter. Afterward, Peter always warned anyone who wanted to write about Evelyn, "Don't do it, love. They all end up in the madhouse, you see." He had said that to Julia when Sigrid began pressing her to write *Le Biography*, as Peter's sister referred to it. "We *need* a good one," Sigrid kept on saying. "People are writing unauthorized lives and Peter always comes out very badly. We need a good one, not one by a suicidal, would-be poetess who thinks she's another Evelyn."

"Don't do it, love," Peter said to Julia, who had said, "Good! I don't want to write biographies. And Evelyn's life was so short. It seems to me

anyone can understand what happened without first reading a book."
How *that* comment had endeared Julia to Meena! You had to say this for
Julia. She wrote her own books and didn't lean on the lattice of other people's reputations. Peter was her friend and that was the end of it. "Real
friends are hard to come by in my position," Peter had said, and Meena
had not disagreed.

The music stopped. The tape stopped. "I shall have to call Julian and
ask what he makes of this," Meena said aloud. She would ask, discreetly. If
anyone had come to the cottage, someone would surely have noticed.
Here, people knew where everyone was by your car. When people saw your
car, they waved, knowing you were in it. She would find out who had come
to the cottage. Then she saw the slight unevenness in the floor, and the
loosened floorboard. Could it possibly have been Rose, the would-be
biographer? Of course, she couldn't have climbed in through a second-
story window, but had she hired a child? *Why* had Peter always referred to
Meena's study as the Bloody Chamber? Why had he ever mentioned it at
all? Did he have to tell everyone who came in how much time it had taken
her to paint it? The white woodwork against the blood-red. Had Rose gotten it into her head that there were horrors to be seen inside, in rooms she
had not seen? Whoever had intruded on the cottage had known Peter.
Such a person would have meant no good. If only Lady Anne were well
disposed toward her still! She could ring her up, ask for advice, set Lady
Anne to questioning her network of spies. But if she were to call, she
would make herself the object of ridicule, whereas now she was only the
object of distaste. Lady Anne must not be called. But she would like to ring
up someone who was *not* Julian. Out of sheer frustration, Meena burst
into tears. The tape player had stopped, but Meena still heard the music.
How well she knew it! How she had always hated it. Was she destined to
spend the rest of her life trembling in her chair? Wondering if everyone
was now discussing the crumbs of their lives together? If everyone was
beginning to speak of her study, indeed the cottage itself, as the Bloody
Chamber? Did everyone want to look in hoping to find bodies hanging on

hooks? There were still those who continued to hate Peter, still those who insisted he had driven Evelyn to suicide. Then they would not want his widow to be happy, would they? Would a woman have broken in because of her hatred of Peter, or was it one of the lunatics who helped perpetuate the cult of Evelyn Graves? She could not endlessly turn over the same ground, or she would soon find herself breaking into her own house, not knowing who she was. No, it had to stop, or she would go quite mad.

FORTY-TWO

———

WHY ARE THERE so many hot days lately? There were never hot days like this long ago. And why are there so many wasps? Rose asked herself as she struggled with the opening pages of Peter's biography. She was reduced to working in the kitchen because if she worked in her study and turned on the light after dark, the wasps came in, and she had already been bitten twice. Rose was extremely careful when she moved about the drab little house, her eyes usually riveted on the floor, especially near windows, especially the floor beneath the kitchen window, because when a wasp died, it tended to fall there, and she had discovered that it was just as painful to step on a dead wasp's stinger as it was to be assaulted by the living insect, and so she walked through the rooms like a two-hundred-year-old woman who had not taken her calcium pills or drunk enough milk, so that now she was doomed to perpetually stoop over, her head to the ground, as if her bones themselves insisted that she contemplate the earth which awaited her, not the sky, not the heaven from which she was certain to be barred. When she met her young writer friends—you had to remain friends with the young writers; they were the ones who had to remember you when you were gone, who had to judge how much you were worth, because, even if she had hypnotized most of her contemporaries, critics her own age had a most annoying habit of dying without setting a successor in place—she always asked, "May I sit in that chair, dear? I have trouble with my back," and then she would explain the misery to which the wasps had brought her. To which *time* had brought her, no husband to repair the VCR when it shorted out, no one to scold her morning, noon, and night; at least then there had been noise, at least there had been another presence.

There were the completely inscrutable forms sent by the tax man (Robert had always taken care of that), but surely it was not a good thing to receive so many letters about tax, saying *First Notice, Second Notice,* and at last, *Final Notice.* Nevertheless, even though final notices kept arriving, no one seemed to *do* anything about them, and in a vague way, Rose believed that she would not live long enough for the tax men to pull themselves together and go after her. In her Job-like list of horrors, the wasps were by far the worst. As it was, she kept a large can of wasp spray on the kitchen table. A friend from America had brought it. It was not so easy to come by wasp poison in England, at least one that worked. Her dread of the wasps had become very nearly paralyzing. Once again, she was thinking of selling the house. The market had gone very high. She would get a far better price for the little house than she had paid for it, but the flat she had given up in Islington so that Robert would have a garden and not have to struggle with the steps was now completely beyond her range, although she still hoped that when she finished the biography, everyone would buy a copy and at last she would be financially sound. As things stood, she had to keep herself on a tight leash. Robert had left her with nothing but their mutual debts.

She had no pension of her own, not as Julia did, and how unfair that seemed. Julia had actually *enjoyed* going to a job, teaching, that blight of the spirit, as Peter always called it, and Rose had been quite happy to agree, having been, one had to admit, an indisputably terrible teacher, the students bored, their eyes on the huge round clock high above all their heads, while Rose tried out all her ingratiating ways. They worked so very well at parties where everyone stood about with a glass of wine in his hand, but in the classroom *nothing* worked; nothing ever did. Even if she maintained her chipper, if not chittery, air throughout the class, even if she offered the students up bits of gossip to which they were certainly not entitled, at the end of the hour there would be, not simply a sense of relief when the long hand of the clock reached number twelve on the clock face, but a very audible sigh of relief. Why, she had asked Robert, did all of her charms not work their spell on students, when she was so spectacularly successful at cocktail parties?

Robert had insisted that students were *in*humans. "They exist in two modes, really," Robert said, "the horrible, grubby larvae you see sitting lined up in seats in front of you, and the butterflies they become the moment they touch the air outside the classroom door. Extraordinary, really."

Robert himself was reputed to be one of the most hopeless of all teachers, a brilliant man, everyone agreed on that, even the students, but incapable of pursuing a thought that could be written into a notebook, veering off onto tangents, entire worlds, where no one could follow. Students were said to prefer the Pakistani man who taught the same subjects, although what he had to say was partly incomprehensible thanks to his difficulty with the English language, not to mention his enraging habit of writing out, on the chalkboard, half of an equation and neglecting to write out the rest. In spite of that, or because of that, there were always groups of students buzzing about after class, probably, Robert said with contempt, asking the man to tell them the second half of the equations he had not thought to write down.

"If I were prettier, or younger," Rose used to say, only to have Robert remind her that when she had indeed been younger, students resented her because they were older than she was, a disrupting effect caused by a reversal of what was expected in the generations, and then he would point out how many other teachers there were who were astonishingly ugly but beloved, and in whose classes places were sought after fervently. Like wasps, all of them, Rose thought. She could not face entering the teaching arena again. At first her students would be respectful and quelled by her "reputation," but kept in order for no longer than three class sessions, and then they would evince the hostile silence she so well remembered from previous terms. And so she had given up the privilege of teaching them, giving up a tenuous financial stability in exchange for those dewy mornings before anyone else was stirring, working at the kitchen table to avoid disturbing Robert, because in those days they could afford no study, but in the morning she was aware, she sometimes thought, of the sound the trees made when the leaves began to grow from their bare branches. She had seen too many writers disgruntled, embittered, and then destroyed by teaching, whereas she had escaped all that.

"It's not *you* who were not meant to teach," Robert said. "It's the fact that *they* were not meant to learn." She had quite agreed with him. She had taken comfort in his view of the teaching profession, far too much comfort, she now thought. Now, if she came upon an ex-student, a member of that inimical tribe, she could not repress a sense of triumph shot through with bitterness; *they* had not appreciated her, but she had flourished and they had not. They were bankers, advertising people, finance managers, estate agents, but they were not writers and they never would be. Although, Rose had to admit, these ex-students often seemed disgustingly happy. But then probably she herself seemed so to them.

The phone went. It was eight-thirty in the morning. No one Rose knew called at that hour. Most of her writer friends would not have dreamed of calling before eleven. But perhaps there was an emergency, someone in need of comforting, or it was one of her children, stranded on the road when the car overheated. It ran in her family, she thought, cars overheating, cars pulling over to the side of the road, steam escaping from under the bonnet, pouring out of the suddenly opened windows.

"Rose," said a deep and definitely stroppy voice, "what color is your hair these days?"

Sigrid.

"Color?" Rose said, "The same color it's always been."

"You haven't gone and dyed it red?"

"Certainly not," Rose said. "Why are you asking me such a thing?"

"And you haven't been round to Willow Grove? Again?" Sigrid asked, her voice menacing.

"I have other things to do, Sigrid. I have to write a biography of your brother. Although, I must say, it is pretty hard going."

"Hard going?" Sigrid asked in astonishment.

"Well, you have to admit," Rose said, "that his childhood was frightfully boring. All that dancing out onto the moors looking for birds to shoot. No family tragedies, nothing like that. It doesn't make for fascinating reading."

"I'm sorry we neglected to commit the occasional homicide," Sigrid said. "We would have done if we'd known we'd need you to write Peter's biography."

"Oh, please," Rose said.

"Are *most* people's childhoods fantastically interesting? Aside from women in Brontë novels?"

"Well, mine wasn't," Rose said. "But then I've never wanted to write my own biography. Autobiography, I mean."

"All you've ever done is write your own life," Sigrid said. "You must have killed Robert in at least three novels."

"Robert was never the model for any of my characters," Rose said. "Why are you asking me about Willow Grove? I told you. I have no reason to go back there and find myself insulted again."

"*Someone* has been there," Sigrid said. "Did you put someone up to going?"

"What *are* you talking about?" Rose asked.

"Well, there is a rumor," Sigrid said vaguely.

"A rumor?"

"Meena believes someone was in the house. You've had nothing to do with it? She's very agitated."

"I'm sorry to hear that, Sigrid, but what does that have to do with me?"

"Perfectly true," said Sigrid. "Nothing. Please remember that." And she rang off without warning.

The whole family has gone berserk, Rose thought. What's left of it. But then Meena was never really part of that family. I must write that down. I mustn't forget that, Rose thought, looking for her notebook. Where had it gone? She had put it on the table as she did every morning, and next to it a ballpoint pen. There was the pen. Now what? she asked herself, and, standing up, lost her balance when her foot landed on the notebook, which had somehow made its way to the floor, as everything in her house inevitably did. "Meena was never really a member of that family," she wrote in the retrieved notebook. "Perhaps her Indian ancestry told against her." *That* looks interesting, she thought. On the other hand, Peter *did* gravitate to foreigners of any sort. Evelyn was born in the United States. Elfie was born in Germany. I must rethink what I've just written about Meena and her Indian ancestry. But before I go on with that, I must ring up Phil and ask him what sort of birds were shot by hunters in Northumberland. Surely not crows or robins. They would be too small to shoot, in any case. Vultures? Were there vultures in England? Hawks? What did she know about hunting? Why *should* she know about hunting? Her subject was the usual distortions of the heart, the wayward passions. There would be plenty of that later in Peter's life, but first she had to get that far. He could not spring into being as a man in his late twenties, although why not? Why not write *The Portrait of a Marriage*? She rather liked that title. But she had signed a contract, after all, yes, she could not forget that contract. They had been very specific. The Americans were like that. Her book was to be a biography of Peter's entire life. It was to begin at the beginning and end when he ended. It was to portray his life from his first breath to his last. What a pity. There was no way around it.

At eleven, she rang up Phil and asked him, "Phil? When you went shooting, what kind of birds did you shoot?" and he answered, "Well, really, Rose, anything that moved. You're speaking of young people, children, I take it? Because by the time I grew older, people had given up shooting ducks, you see. Too many people were killed by mistake."

"How could anyone mistake a human for a duck?" Rose asked.

"It didn't happen that way," Phil said. Really, now that Robert was gone, talking to Rose was almost as hard work.

"What did *you* hunt?" Rose asked.

"Lizards. You know, chameleons. And frogs. The shiny ones."

"Using a gun?" Rose asked.

"Of course not," Phil said irritably. "Rose, someone's ringing the bell."

How rude everyone's become, Rose thought. And he didn't even think to ask me how my book was going.

FORTY-THREE

———

WHAT ARE THE truths of a life, and how is anyone to know them? Isn't it in the nature of things to have the slate erased daily as nightfall erases the sun-filled world? Sigrid had been thinking of that, and so was Julia, who had come across an old toy somewhere at the market, the Magic Slate. Was that what it was called? A cross between a sheet of paper and a chalkboard, you wrote on it with a stylus of wood, whatever you wanted, words, pictures, and when the shiny upper sheet was lifted, everything written on it disappeared. The Magic Slate, was that it? All children loved it. She had had one herself. Peter had one later. Everyone had one once. And the Magic Slate was a lesson in life. You wrote what interested you or what you thought was important, and you knew that what you wrote there could not last, although it always seemed—hadn't it done?—that whatever you wrote on that slate, whatever you drew there, was better, more significant, more skillful than anything you had written on paper. Sometimes you took the slate to your parents to show them what you had created, but on the way something always happened. You lifted the sheet of plastic by mistake or the wind came up, and the sheet came loose from the backing, and what you had written was gone. Through our toys we learned the most important things. Today, Sigrid thought, all her days appeared to have been written on sheets from the Magic Slate. Night would fall, sleep would come; new things would be written on another kind of Magic Slate; those were called dreams. Then the light would come back, the dream paper of the Magic Slate would be lifted, and everything would vanish. The light, now it was back, would present you with a clean slate, and you would write on it, and when the light faded, the words would vanish, and the whole thing would begin again.

And not only individual lives were like that. Families were like that. A long night would come for one member of the family. The others would try to remember her, to tell those who came later what she had been like, to remember as many details, as many events, as many consequences of her doings as possible, and no one listened, or if they did listen, could not seem to remember long, and in spite of all efforts, the Magic Slate's page was lifted. That person was gone, until finally an entire branch of the family was gone. A little bad luck was all that was needed; a daughter who grew up and could not bear children; a son who grew to maturity and did not want children, and when those two were gone, so was that branch of the family. Was there anything more pathetic than a family tree? So many people researching, creating that tree, and finally there were the branches that ended nowhere, leaving nothing but empty space, and not even one person to wonder what had become of them.

If it was true that a family, an entire family, could vanish without leaving so much as a memory, then what chance was there to preserve a single life? No one to say, This was how her dying was; this is why he lived,

this is what she thought; this is what he made of the world. How was anyone to find even a splinter of truth about the dead? It couldn't be done.
Was that why people seemed to have an instinctive worship for writers, a
reverence that has existed from the beginning of time? Because writers
defeated the Magic Slate, managed to keep some of the fragments they
wrote alive, managed to make themselves heard through the clamor and
babble of the years. Became mythic, were searched for, as if they had gone
underground like everyone else, but only for a season, like Ceres, and
could appear again and again when someone opened the books they had
written, grew brighter with passing time, finally blazed with the light of
centuries, their words a measure, a yardstick, a comfort, saying that even
then there were these sorrows, even then there were these joys, these
defeats, these victories. Everything does not disappear, only the individual
event, the singular person, that singular person created time and again,
year by year, decade by decade, century after century, until finally he is
eternal, the person alive in his or her own time, resurrecting the ones so
like those who had lived before, vanished before, but now back again.
Stock characters, really, cast in the same roles, the only roles ever available,
each playing out the same role in the same plot, the only play anyone had
ever invented. Picked out, one or two, by good luck or bad luck, by no particular volition of their own made sacred, something far beyond what the
words *famous* or *fame* could ever convey, dragging other minor characters
back into the light, the people who spoke one line, *What ho, Octavius?* preserved in the magic wake of the one whom time had turned to myth. "My
Lord, a message!" That messenger preserved forever until the Magic Slate
lifted the page for the entire species. *Sir, she is dead,* saying no more than
this, but her name preserved for history. Earthquakes could not destroy
that name. *Sir, she is dead.* Part of a story that would not die, and she herself unaccountably preserved, as if an entire splendid gown had rotted
way, the jewels adorning it buried or lost or stolen, but one sequin, one
fragile bit of glitter preserving itself, picked out, put in a glass case in a
museum, endlessly visited, finally given a name: Bathsheba's sequin. You

knew where it was. You wanted to see it, and if you did not, you were taken to see it with or without your own will, would be taken to see it when the school trips were scheduled. Tumbled out of the coach having brought your boxed lunch, paid your pound, marched off to see Bathsheba's sequin, and in the end, after most of your years had passed, expired, really, that was a better word, you still remembered it, how it had looked, what its name had been: Bathsheba's sequin. Unaccountably, you had created a story around it, knew who had worn it and why, knew why the gown had been lost or saved.

Because a particle far smaller than a fingernail had been preserved, and you had been to see it, and space was all around it, and that space had to be filled in by a story, by a sequence of events: this happened and that happened, and finally all that was represented by Bathsheba's sequin. And could it comfort Bathsheba to know that stories had sprung up around that sequin not remotely resembling Bathsheba and the once-real life she had lived? Would the woman who once held that name recognize anything about the truths of her own life, if she knew, somehow knew, what was said of her? Was she tortured by the half-truths, the untruths, the travesty her legend had become, because, Sigrid thought, all such legends were inevitably travesties, travesties that were, at the same time, true because no one could invent anything that was *completely* untrue, because if they had, something so clearly false would long ago have vanished: an oddity, a curiosity, a person with three heads, in the end, so strange as to be ultimately uninteresting. The true things were distorted, falsely reported, but believed, because of the one sequin of truth left in them, the truth that everyone invariably recognized.

And Evelyn and Peter, what of them? The myth of their ecstatic first love, as if they had opened their eyes each morning seeking only the eyes of the beloved other, no one to say that both of them were badly flawed, no one to say that Evelyn could not continue to love, not continuously, not in a stable way, after she discovered a flaw in her beloved, or needed to invent one to explain her sudden swerve from love to hate. There was no one to explain how small that flaw was, but all the same, it was a flaw in the perfect surface she required, a flaw which, once seen, could not be unseen. She returned to it again and again, dwelled on it, until what had been barely visible began to spread, threatened to cover everything. When she looked at it, and saw it, that flaw was all she saw, and what sense did it make then to speak of love, the love she so reveled in, so delighted in describing to others?

Then the weather would change, or the stars would move in the heavens, and Evelyn could not see the little scar, the little flaw, and then he would again be the perfect man, the only man who could make her happy, and again she made a god of him as only she could. And he was happy then, because who else would ever deify him as she did? That was evident in what she said to him, in how she touched him, and he returned that passion, not something he could bear to lose, because he believed, in those days, no one else would ever look at him as she did, no one else would ever value him again as highly. It was in the nature of young things to grow toward the light, no matter how hot, not to think about the scorching, the withering that could follow, not to take care.

What flaw did he have? Were his flaws what drove her away? Perhaps there was no flaw, perhaps her estimation of him, her swerves in perception, changed because her own moods changed, and she could not understand what caused her moods to alter so abruptly. Was her unsteadiness too great to permit her to see it? Did she blame him because she was unwilling to blame something in herself, something she sensed was too terrible ever to be remedied?

And the nature of their night ravenings, Evelyn had hinted at it, but of course no one had been in the bed with them. Nevertheless you could guess at it, the sex, both of them so insatiable about food, either one of them capable of clearing a refrigerator as if a tide of fire ants had swept through leaving only the scoured, chalk bones inside, so that it was reasonable to assume that they had fallen upon each other in the same way. Wouldn't it have been enough for Evelyn simply to acknowledge the power of her hunger? But she would have had to accept that hunger and she could not, so she would have had to believe that such passion arose from him, could only come from him. She had to say Peter himself had inspired it, and only Peter. She would have made a religion of that passion, or was it love, as she made a religion of everything that mattered to her, her writing, her cooking, her motherhood, the raising of her children. So many gods to appease! Exhausting herself, draining herself beyond hope, until even the marrow of her bones cried out against the assaults she made upon herself.

Whereas Peter adored her, had the strength to respond to her passions. But really, he was not the initiator. There was always something passive in him, an enormous hunger which Evelyn filled and was happy to fill. She loved to eat and she loved to feed people, and he, like a new nestling in the nest, opened his beak as largely as he could. Peter and Evelyn, possessing enormous passions, but ungovernable, really, not quite capable of being controlled. Why had Sigrid never seen it before? Two ravenous infants in the guise of a grown man and a grown woman. Yes, that was it, two ravenous infants who were each other's toys, and who inevitably tore those toys to pieces, because isn't that what infants do? And yet people measured their own lives by Peter's and Evelyn's, sure they knew what they were measuring themselves against, because, after all, had those two not been geniuses? Two geniuses, together in the same house?

And how did Peter and Evelyn differ from anyone else, except in the fact of their genius, in the strange nature of their toys? And ignored was their all-too-traditional, familiar, really mundane behavior when they grew angry and smashed up the toy the other loved most. And would it have been such a disaster if each one of them had not been the toy of the other? Peter's many affairs, about which everyone now knew: Had he been trying to prevent that foreordained smashup? Had he looked for other toys so that his passions were not always trained on Evelyn? Because from the beginning, he could see the massive energy of that woman, the blazing intensity of her, but nothing like his own stamina, she did not have that, she could not hold it before her like a shield, like a—like a what? Like a snail shell, of course, Sigrid thought. An unpleasant image that would come to mind when she thought of Evelyn, but all the same, like a snail who, once out of her shell, could not get back in. And how like a snail she had proved to be, Sigrid thought bitterly, leaving her trail of slime, coming out into the sun after the enormous storm she herself had caused, her own children, future generations, Evelyn's mother, Charlotte, everything devastated in her wake, the devastation continuing still. And now it was working through Meena, her own nature now still distorted by Evelyn's power, Meena continuing to destroy what was left, the only thing worth leaving, the two children, Sophie and Andrew. *Avaunt thee, witch, the rump-fed runion cried.* The things that flew into her mind when she thought of Evelyn, Sigrid thought. Oh, as hopeless now to cast spells, to try to cast Evelyn out, as it had been then!

And Julia, who never tired of repeating, "Sigrid, you're the only one who really understood them; you owe it to them to write about them. You don't have to use your own name. At least write it down for the children!" But did the children need to know what their parents had been like? And how could she be sure she was right in her conclusions? And why did Julia not write what she knew, because surely she understood them as well as she, Sigrid, did, although Julia had not known Evelyn, only met her once, but all the same, Julia had the sense to be distrustful of her, to think Evelyn dangerous, and Julia assumed that like sought out like, and had concluded that Peter, too, was dangerous, possibly untrustworthy, not a man on whom you wanted to stake your life. Well, then, perhaps not Julia.

Julia had married well and knew she had. But she had already learned what it was to lash yourself to a man of unreliable emotions. "Not many men really like women," she had said once, eyes averted, speaking, clearly, from experience. Perhaps Peter hadn't. Sigrid rather suspected that Julia would say that of Peter, believed that, in spite of all appearances, he had not liked women. *That* was a puzzle. Here was this man, this genius, this Peter, this great lover of women, and what did he do? He chose women he was likely to destroy, not intentionally, but when he acted according to his own nature, destruction was the unavoidable result.

She had seen Julia unravel Gordian knots. "Look at the results," Julia used to say. "The results are the motive. If you want to know what you really want to do, look at what you are doing." For example, Rose? Was she suffering, struggling to support Robert? Then she wanted to suffer. She needed to expiate the guilt she had stored up during all the years she had let him support her. And in order to continue suffering, she had portrayed him in her novels as a monster of inflexibility, knowing she would cause him to strike back at her. You had to give it to Julia, Sigrid thought. She had a point. She had a logical mind, but she was all too likely to abandon logic or rationality, so that Sigrid often thought of Julia as a benighted gypsy from the medieval age, like Evelyn in that way, every house with its totem spirit, bouquets of flowers made up of sparkling brooches, set in an old pharmacy bottle placed in a sunlit window so that, even on the darkest, grimmest February days, those bouquets sent rays of light stabbing through the dull room. Yes, there were many reasons she continued to like Julia. *We are two faithful hounds,* Julia had once said, and it was true.

The phone went. Julia. Should they go to the Chinese? And then Sigrid said, "By the way, Martin has sent me one of Peter's letters. He's sold all of his to a university in the American West, a Dakota, I think, North or South, does it make any difference? I wonder why he saved that one out for me. He doesn't have much money, but still, selling off his brother's letters! He might have asked me first. I would have tried to buy them myself. He wrote so freely to Martin and anyone can read those letters if they have an academic letterhead. Rose will be beetling back over there to read them. I hate to think of it."

Julia was silent for a moment and then said, "Maybe, just maybe, the truth will be better than silence. In the end, I mean."

"Better? For whom?" Sigrid asked.

FORTY-FOUR

———

Brother Martin,

Not the usual run of things this time. I've married the American girl I wrote you about. She wanted to be married, and it seemed to me I was old enough. I think it will be all right. You remember I used to promise that I would never marry? I underestimated the determination of a woman who wants a ring on her finger and a shackle on a man's ankle. I think it will be all right. It will have to be. She is a collection of paradoxes, very strong, but also very fragile. I've told her plainly that I don't want children, don't want domesticity and want to spend my life traveling and writing. She tells me that's exactly what she wants. Let's hope she's telling the truth. I haven't been around long, but long enough to know that a woman will say whatever she wants you to hear. I've been honest about my character, such as it is, but even if I hadn't, I've seen her talking to other women I've spent time with, and so she must know about my reputation, my "appetite" for the ladies, and all the rest. She isn't, technically, going into this blindfolded. I think she's heard about every sin I ever committed, and then some, but she was determined. I admire her, to have such determination and such courage, and to want me as much as she does. I doubt that I'll find anyone else like her again. Last night, she said, "It's too bad we have to have bodies." I've thought the same thing many times, especially when Mum was dying. Talking to Evelyn—that's her name—is as close as I'll get to talking without any barriers. She says that in time we'll be able to speak to one another without words. We are that close.

This morning, we got up early—she gets up even earlier than I do—and found ourselves in the middle of a thunder and lightning storm, the likes of which I've never experienced. Two apple trees went down behind the house and now there's only one left, the one that taps on the bedroom window when the wind is up. The storm electrified her. There was nothing she could think of that we couldn't do. She began planning our successes while the lightning flashed all about us and she put her head and shoulders right out of the window so that she was thoroughly drenched and looked like a wet cat, but the harder the rain came down, and the louder the thunder sounded until it sounded as if it were exploding right outside the window, and the more the lightning flashed, the more excited she became. It was dangerous, leaning out in that lightning storm, and I told her so, but she only laughed and leaned further out until I had to drag her in. She couldn't stop talking about what we were going to do for the rest of our lives, and then we went to bed, and when we got up for the second time, there was

something, I don't know how to say it: changed. An odd, almost
scornful expression on her face. There was nothing for it but to go
into the village and come back with a bottle of wine and something to eat that was sticky with sugar, and she watched me go,
still with that strange expression. She is very changeable, and I
would be hard put to say what causes her to change as she does.

When I returned, driving through the fat rivers of rain pouring
down the windscreen, she said the weather upset her and she
was, literally, under a cloud. There was nothing I could do to cheer
her up. She no longer wanted the wine or the sticky buns and
instead she kept asking me if the roads would flood and would we
be isolated here, quarantined by the weather. I'm writing from the
turret of Willow Grove. She loves everything about the place,
especially its remote location; she keeps saying she can't get far
enough from society, and she won't hear of the difficulties we face
here, the lack of plumbing, the lack of running water, the need to
drill a well, all of that. She said we would be pioneers and create
our own world.

Even so, now there are endless complaints about hauling water
up and down from the first story to the third, and she is already
shuddering at the thought of going out into bad weather to drag
back pails of water. Sigrid thinks she is pregnant, and if not, will
soon be. She says that accounts for her—what shall I call it?—her
flickering. I think sometimes her soul is like a firefly. It winks on and
off. Or she contains two souls, soul A and soul B, and when soul
A is in the ascendant, I want to worship her. Soul B is another matter altogether. She is a demon intent on punishing those who are
not good enough, and I do not measure up to the standards of
Soul B. I find all that *flickering*—I cannot find another word for it—
worrying and ask myself what I have gotten myself into. But I *am*
in it and there is no getting out of it, and to tell the truth, I have no
desire to be taken from her or to leave her. I cannot even imagine

such an eventuality, at least when soul A is present, although this week there were several incidents when I could begin to believe that such an outcome might not be entirely undesirable. I wonder if you understand any of this. I'm not sure if I understand it myself. Between asking myself, "What have I gotten myself into?" and "How did I find such great good luck?" I am mightily confused. Sigrid says time will sort everything out and if we make mistakes we can correct them, but I wonder if she believes what she says.

Right now the rain is falling only gently, the lightning has stopped assaulting our patch of earth and has decided to spare the last of the apple trees, clearly the spirit of Willow Grove, and there is only the occasional, fading rumble of thunder. Of course, the quaint thatched roof is leaking madly, and I shall be in for it when Evelyn comes down and finds we don't have enough pots and saucers to put beneath the leaks in the roof. The puddles on the floor will make her cry and she will cry because she says the water on the wood will cause the floor to warp, and all this will continue until she decides it is time to go back to her writing, or begins writing something new, and then she will forget about the leaking roof and the warping floor, and when she comes down, she will expect me to have sorted everything out, as if I knew what to do with a leaking roof. A leaking roof would be no problem if we had the funds to fix it properly, but we barely have enough to live on, and we agreed that we would work on the house as money from our writing began to come in, but of course now Evelyn is impatient.

Her mother writes her from America exhorting her to find a good, tight, modern house, as if there were many such things in the country where we now are, as if we had not used up what we had in buying Willow Grove, and then she sends a check to fix some windows, or install a bathroom, and of course I don't like it. It feels like charity, and I've said so, but Evelyn insists that her mother's greatest joy is looking after her, and we should not be proud. Am I proud not to want that money, knowing full well that Evelyn's mother wishes I were deep beneath the soil, that I had never been born, that I had never taken her daughter across the sea and set her down so far from her? There seem to be a great many complaints in this letter, but the truth of it is still this: I am happy with her and believe I would be miserable without her, although there are days when my patience wears thin. I am more patient than I expected to be, but I am no saint, which will come as no surprise to you.

I hope you will consider coming back from Jamaica and will stay with us at Willow Grove. You will no doubt like Evelyn very much, and as long as we have no rainstorm, she will probably be all sunshine and daisies. She has gone at the garden with a vengeance and cadges bulbs from whoever is not on the watch. I tell her that one day she will be bunged up for breaking into people's gardens and leaving with a wheelbarrow full of daffodil bulbs. She is quite mad about daffodils, but her vegetable lust now seems to be veering toward tulips. When the crocuses were out, she coveted crocus bulbs. She wants whatever she sees, anything she deems beautiful. All that is, I think, an extension of her very strong appetites, for which I am grateful, although, as is the case with the leaking roof, I cannot always gratify them. I imagine we will be in for some storms of our own, but I never wanted or imagined a sedate, exemplary marriage. I saw too much of that when I was young. Either you are seduced by your parents' lives or you turn from them, and I did the second. Well, there are only two responses to one's childhood, and although it might have been better to have aimed no higher than what I had already seen, that was not what I wanted, and I still cannot imagine wanting it. We are all punished by our choices, so Evelyn says, although she refuses to elaborate further on that one, but she has had her own experiences, and they have led her to that conclusion. In time, I imagine I will discover why she says such things.

But do consider coming here, and by all means send many postcards of Jamaica. The pictures I have seen of it so far are just the sort of thing to fire Evelyn's imagination, and if she determines to go, then both of us shall get there and we will have great times together. Please be frank about what I have told you; tell me what you make of it, as Sigrid does, although listening to her is a bit like having your ear washed out by a cat's tongue. In a moment, I will hear Evelyn on the steps and I will hear the door of the turret room opening, and the pots and pans await, so it is time to strengthen myself for the coming battle. Tock, tock, tock go the raindrops falling into the kitchen, and Evelyn will hear them as she is coming up the stairs. All my love to Karen.

Did you have to board up all the windows against the hurricane, and was it as bad as you were led to believe it would be? Odd to be setting out on my new life in such a leaky boat. It is difficult to leave off writing, but write soon. I depend on your letters. Evelyn would not be pleased to know I felt that.

FORTY-FIVE

———

THEY HAD ALL received identical letters, each arriving within minutes of the other, although they could not have known that at the time. The signature was not Meena's. But there was a cover note that came with the letter in her handwriting, saying only, "The person who has trespassed upon Willow Grove is known by me to have been there." There was no further elaboration. The envelopes had been addressed by Meena, but there was no postmark, which meant they had been sent by messenger.

"Not that round-apple writing again," Sigrid said aloud, reading the note. She read the note again, snorted, and tossed it, crumpled, in the bin.

"What is she talking about?" Andrew said aloud, immediately deciding to return to Cornwall and once more make the walk from Zennor to

Penzance. "Should I call her to ask what the trouble is?" But then he remembered that she had not given him her new directory number. She's changed, he thought. Even when she would give it to no one else, she always gave it to me.

"Does she think I'm going to commit crimes in England?" Julia said aloud, going toward the telephone and then ringing Sigrid, whose line was already engaged. Probably talking to Sophie, she thought, and dialed Sophie's line, only to be answered by the expected busy signal.

"How did she get my address?" Clare asked herself, wandering through her chandeliers, occasionally tapping one of them as she went by so that the chimes rang out as consolingly as church bells, which, in her part of Cornwall, were said to scare off evil spirits.

"Not that again!" Rose exclaimed. "Does she really think I have nothing to do but climb about the walls of Willow Grove? I've been there often enough! Why would I need to break in to soak up the atmosphere? I shall have *my* solicitor send a note to hers. I have an alibi for whatever day it is she's talking about. I've been round to see people every day for the last two months! Intolerable!" While the ghost of Robert whispered, "Intolerable, Rose? Do you really wish to choose that word? When you are flourishing and are clearly finding nothing *intolerable*?" Nevertheless, Rose thought defiantly, *intolerable* is the word I shall use. Surely she cannot feel free to assault people's peace! Peter might have gotten by with such behavior, but that stone-faced widow, no, she must think twice and thrice again.

"She knows it was me," Sophie was saying to Sigrid. "Or she thinks it was me, which is quite bad enough. I suppose right this moment she intends to see to it that Andy and I are disinherited, but we already *are*, you see. It's too late. And look at that handwriting! All the rest of us form letters like crow's feet, but she has that pretentious *beautiful* writing. I always wondered why my mother never developed it, you know, that kind of handwriting that signified an artistic temperament, all beautiful curls and curves and the *e*'s always made to look like the *e*'s in printed books. She was so careful about everything, but she had a scrawl as bad as mine or Daddy's. And here is this *pretentious* woman with her beautiful immaculate handwriting!"

"Don't respond," Sigrid said. "She'll take any communication as an acknowledgment of guilt. I wonder if she's pinned the same note to your father's gravestone."

"Oh, don't!" Sophie exclaimed.

"If she has, I hope *he'll* respond," Sigrid said. "Have you heard from Andrew?"

"No. He's hiding somewhere. He'll find the note when he comes back with his twisted roots and oddly shaped stones and maybe one rigid, very dead snake."

"The two of you will soon be the only family you have left," Sigrid said. "You must get on better."

"I try," Sophie said, her voice gone sullen.

"Try harder," Sigrid said.

"And who will scold Andrew?" Sophie burst out. "Is he never to blame for anything?"

"I'll speak to him," Sigrid said. Did this squabbling never end? She, Peter, and Martin had not squabbled until they were in their sixties. "I wonder," she said aloud, "if she sent a note to Lady Anne."

"Oh, don't be ridiculous," Sophie said. "First of all, she was staying with Lady Anne when this so-called break-in took place, and can you imagine Lady Anne climbing the tree with her sticks like a spider? Or being winched up by footmen while she sat in a velvet hammock? Meena would *never* do anything to alienate Lady Anne. She must know how things stand there, but if I know Meena, and I *do* know Meena, she still hopes for reconciliation. She still cares for the Great and the Good she knows in London. She won't want Lady Anne whispering a little word in their ears."

Terrible, to be so obsessed, Julia thought, the note suspended over the trash, but then she changed her mind, folded it in three, and carefully put it back in her address book, where it stuck out like a bookmark.

FORTY-SIX

———

"WELL," SAID MEENA to Julian, "they will all be sorry now."

"It was a mistake to send it," he said.

"They will know I will not be trifled with," Meena said. "I was not defanged by Peter's death."

"I very much doubt that they ever entertained such a notion," said Julian.

"Now they will know better," Meena said smugly.

"No, now they will publish that note. One way or another, they will, and since you did not see fit to sign it, I don't see how you can very well sue. *They* can sue. They can make a case against you for sending them libelous letters, I daresay they can, although I don't suppose they will."

"Sue *me*?" Meena asked incredulously. "*I* am the victim!"

"Ah," said Julian. "There we have the beauty of the law. What was your solicitor thinking of when he let you send those notes round? And in your own handwriting. Why didn't he consult with me? The man must be mad. Stop that crying! The chicken is already flying through the air caught by the hawk's talons. A little late to regret it now."

"Do you think they will sue me? Sigrid? Sophie?"

"I doubt if they think you're worth their time," he said.

"Oh!" Meena exclaimed in a rage, stamping her foot, and then yelping with pain.

"You'd best leave off that stamping as well," Julian said. "You're not as young as you were. You'll fracture a bone."

"Oh!" Meena exclaimed, banging her fist against the wormwood-ridden table.

"You'll soon be in a body cast," Julian said unsympathetically.

"But who else can I rely on but you?" Meena wailed.

"Well may you ask," her cousin said.

"There are bones in the hand, you know," her cousin said.

"If you could show some sympathy!" Meena complained.

"If you could show some common sense and restraint," rejoined her cousin.

———

INSTEAD OF THE expected prompt flutter of letters, all professing innocence, all in one way or another placating her, Meena's notes met with silence. "I think you have to understand that in the past," Julian said, "their rush to apologize and make things right was not motivated by love of you or fear of your power, any more than the expensive gifts they gave at Christmas were given out of love or a genuine desire to please. They wanted to keep the peace because of Peter. They never cared about you."

"Andrew did! Sophie did!" Meena insisted.

"They are not children anymore," Julian said. "If, indeed, Sophie ever was."

"But if they no longer cared for me," Meena argued, "they would already have moved against me. Moved dramatically so. I *know* affection for me has kept them from attacking. The children would not attack me! They still care for me! Of course, I knew it was another matter altogether where Sigrid was concerned, but the two of them, I knew I could use their feeling for me to my advantage."

"If you lose Andrew's goodwill, you will lose everything," Julian said.

"Shall I call him? Invite him round to dinner?"

"Let him alone," Julian said. "You don't know what the others are telling him."

"He listens to no one. He keeps his own counsel."

"And you think you will sway him?" Julian asked. "Doesn't this rather challenge your influence?" He threw down the magazine section of the Sunday paper. "Look at page twenty-one," he said.

"What now?" said Meena, taking up the paper. "Dear God!" she exclaimed. "I want an explanation of this!"

"I daresay. And I also doubt that anyone will have the least interest in anything you have to say. People are still free. They can write about what pleases them, and what a fool you would seem if you objected to this. What would you object to? The existence of this woman?"

Meena was staring at the double-page spread. There was a picture of Crow's Nest set in a circle—so that was what the house looked like!—and to the upper left of the first sheet there was a picture of Clare. In the middle were colored photographs of her chandeliers. The photographic centerpiece was the chandelier that had first appeared in the *Grisleigh upon Shallows Chronicle*. "But, but," Meena spluttered, "you can tell who those people are! Anyone can recognize Peter! And Sophie! She spends all her time posing for photographs when interviewers get to her! You can *see* that Clare is the woman in the picture with Peter. How long will it take before people put two and two together?"

"Not very long, I should think," said Julian.

"This is unendurable!" Meena exclaimed.

"It may well be, but there is nothing you can do," Julian said.

"To flout me like this! Who does she think she's dealing with?"

"I doubt if you're dealing with that woman, or vice versa," said her cousin.

"Who, then?"

"One of those children who are so devoted to you."

"You mean Sophie? Of course you mean Sophie!"

"I would think she was the most likely choice," Julian said mildly. "What did she say to you the last time all of you got together? 'There is more than one way to skin a cat.'"

"No," said Meena, "she said, 'Hair by hair, you can strip a tiger bare.'"

"Peter's maxim," Julian said.

"So," Meena said slowly, "one of them has turned on me. Although, no doubt, Sophie has fits of remorse, but not enough to stop her, not any longer. We must secure Andrew's allegiance."

"Pursuing lost causes is not particularly rewarding," Julian said.

"*Andrew* is *not* a lost cause," Meena said.

"Then see what you can do," Julian said.

—

THE PHONE RANG late at night, just as Sophie was nearing a proof for a difficult mathematical theorem. She had been working in dim light and her eyes burned and watered.

"Hel-lo," she said, answering the phone in her best society voice.

"Just tell me what that was all about," Andrew demanded at the other end of the telephone.

"Do I get a hint?" Sophie asked rather merrily. Once this tired, she had a tendency to say whatever came into her head.

"Why are there pictures of Daddy and a strange woman in the Sunday magazine?" Andrew demanded.

"What strange woman? What magazine?" Sophie asked.

There was a silence. "Do you mean to tell me you haven't seen it?" he asked.

"That's what I mean to tell you. I haven't the slightest notion of what you're talking about."

"Then let me explain. There's a spread about a woman in Cornwall, a Clare Tartikoff. You've never heard of such a person?"

"What are you talking about now?" Sophie asked.

"Apparently this Clare Tartikoff person knows you," Andrew said. "There's a picture of the two of you together?"

"What?" said Sophie, putting down her pencil.

"In a frame dangling from a chandelier."

"Oh, *that* chandelier!" Sophie said. "I think Daddy commissioned it. I think it's called the Tree of Light. It's already been in the papers. Didn't we show it to you?"

"No. You didn't," Andrew said.

"Why is the picture in the papers now?" Sophie asked.

"Apparently they're quite the new thing," Andrew said. "They're selling like mad."

"I saw one and I thought it was rather wonderful," Sophie said.

"Who is that woman in the picture with Daddy?" Andrew shouted.

"Her name, as you just told me, is Clare Tartikoff, and I believe she makes a living doing chandeliers."

"All right," Andrew said. "I know you think I'm a shadowy thing. I *am* a shadowy thing. I know all of you think I'm weak and need to be protected, and I may be weak, and I may need protection, but don't you think I should be told what's going on? If someone were to ask me? Must I always appear to be a fool? With my head in the clouds?"

"I thought you quite liked being seen in that way," Sophie said.

"*Who is that woman?!*" Andrew demanded again.

"We would have told you before this, but you have a habit of vanishing. Has anyone heard from you lately? Did anyone know how to reach you? Where are you now? Probably on a cliff in Cornwall dialing from your mobile."

"That is exactly right," Andrew said.

"Then how were we to reach you?"

"*Who was that woman?*" Andrew demanded again.

"She is the woman Daddy wanted to marry. *If* he could rid himself of Meena, *if* he could get enough money to pay Meena off so he could be free of her. They lived together for two years. Daddy moved out of Willow Grove three years ago, but he went back for appearances' sake, not very often, I must say. He kept a small apartment in the village. He called it his office, but he didn't stay in it unless he had just been to Willow Grove and left in a fury. He was living with Clare Tartikoff in Crow's Nest in Cornwall. That's the woman in the picture with Daddy. That's the woman who makes the chandeliers."

"You've known about all this for three years?" Andrew asked.

"Actually, only two. When Daddy's cancer came back, he told all of us. He didn't want us banging on about how he ought to stay at Willow Grove and let Meena take care of him. So he told us the truth."

"Us?" Andrew said.

"Well, Sigrid and me, and, of course, Bertold."

"But not me?"

"He didn't see why you needed to know. He thought it would only upset you."

"How like him," Andrew said, his voice gone to stone, "to let me think all was going well between the two of them. Meena and Daddy, I mean. He didn't want to be bothered by my opinions. He knew I'd take Meena's side."

"Would you have done?"

"Certainly," Andrew said. "Hasn't this family had rather enough of his famous passions and *our* consequences?"

"Well, if he knew you would react as you have, no wonder he didn't tell you," Sophie said. "And do you still take Meena's side?"

Another long silence ensued. "No longer," he said. "I don't care about the money. I'd like to walk away from it and forget I ever knew about it. But Sigrid's right. Daddy's work must be protected, and Meena doesn't want that or care about that. If Daddy hadn't given people copies of everything he wrote, she'd already have burned it all. I am sure of that. And whether we care or not, Daddy did ask that she divide the estate into quarters. I would have sworn that Meena didn't have a selfish bone in her body."

"Her *skeleton* is selfish," Sophie said.

Another long silence. Sophie was accustomed to Andrew's silences; Daddy had always done the same thing, fallen silent over the telephone when he had nothing to say, although he had been told that his silences frightened people. The person waiting for Daddy to speak thought that Daddy's silence signified that he had taken offense at something, but now it seemed to Sophie that the nature of Andrew's silences had changed. "What?" she asked, prompting him, her voice softer.

"Is there no haystack big enough, nowhere distant enough away, for me to hide under?"

"Is there one big enough for me?" Sophie asked.

"But when people see you for the first time, they don't say, 'You're the living image of your father.'"

"No," Sophie said. "They say, 'You're a dead ringer for your mother.'"

"But you don't try to hide. You don't go off to Africa. You don't sit on the cliffs thinking about India and how big a country it is and how no one could find you there."

"I think about Jamaica," Sophie said. "I've exiled myself to Jamaica for years at a time."

"But you came back."

"As did you. There were reasons for coming back. I missed Daddy. I thought I missed Meena. There was Sigrid. There was my work. I've always thought I was put on this earth to do my own work."

"Or you were put on this earth to finish your mother's work, or both of their works."

"No," said Sophie slowly. "If I thought that, I wasn't aware of it. Surely not."

"But I've never wanted to make a name for myself. I've never wanted 'to make it.' How I hate that expression. I never wanted my name in the papers. I never wanted anyone to know who I was. I thought the *postman* was too well known by everyone in his own neighborhood. A brick among other bricks, that was more than enough to satisfy me. I don't suppose you understand that."

"No."

"That lust for fame, for ambition, for all of that stuff, none of that was beaten out of you when you began to learn about Daddy? And Evelyn? I never thought of her as my mother. I thought of Meena as my mother. I thought she did love me, just the way she loved the orphaned kittens she fed and took in and watched over until they died and then she put their pictures up on the wall going up the stairway. I thought she loved me at least as much as she loved them." His voice turned angry. "Who else was I to love? Daddy was always up in his study writing, or off giving readings. Who else was there but Meena? We called her Mummy, for bloody sake! She insisted on it! And the things she said about Sigrid. Was all that to keep us away from Sigrid, so we would cling on to Meena? Only to turn on us when Daddy died? If she couldn't make Daddy suffer enough for having been married before he met her, was she waiting to take it out on us? God, she's done a good job!"

"I think . . ." said Sophie, "I think you should come back to London and stay with us. I think it would be best, Andrew, really, I do think so."

Silence. "Stay with you?" he said finally.

"With us. Yes."

"Will we fight? Argue all of the time?"

"I hope not. But I have heard that brothers and sisters tend to do that, you know."

"Have you?" Andrew asked. How like Daddy he was, Sophie thought. When he smiled, the smile was audible in his voice.

"Yes. I have. Do come up."

"How much notice do you need?"

"Ringing the doorbell should be sufficient," Sophie said.

"I'll come," Andrew said, and her phone went dead.

Sophie sat in front of her notebook and cried. On his cliff in the dark, the breakers crashing on the cliffs down below, Andrew wept silently. Then he heard the roar of the waves and it no longer seemed necessary to be so quiet and he cried and coughed and made as much noise as he cared to. "Daddy is dead," he said aloud, and, for the first time, he believed it. Well, then, the dead did not need avenging, as Sigrid so often appeared to think, but, he thought, they did need protecting. Meena would have to be confronted, and who better than he to do it? Regardless of what she thought, Sophie did not have the strength for it. I've let people underestimate me too long, he thought. I can't wait until a cancer diagnosis comes down before I do what I think is right. *There's strength in suffering, but I've never been good at it,* his father once said. The wind wailed over the cliffs and he wailed along with it.

FORTY-SEVEN

———

THE RAIN WAS pouring down and houses were growing damp and sour. "Every day for the last fifteen days," Bertold said, and Sophie looked up from her notebook and said, "That's England." Bertold went back to his work and Sophie returned to her equations. "Just think what it must be like in Cornwall, or in Wales, all those creatures drowned in the lanes," Sophie said a moment later, without lifting her eyes from her page.

"Still," Bertold said, "there's something to be said for this weather. It's a good excuse for staying inside alone."

"A very good excuse," Sophie said. "Should I give up on this proof for a while?"

"Let the problem solve itself later," Bertold said.

"I can't do that," Sophie said. Bertold smiled at his sheet of paper and kept going. "Was that the bell?" Sophie asked.

"I think it might have been," Bertold said. The two of them continued with their work. Then the house bell chimed once, twice, and then three times.

"*That* was the bell," Sophie said, jumping up. "That must be Andrew."

"How long is he staying?" Bertold asked.

"As long as he likes," Sophie said.

"Good," said Bertold without turning around.

Sophie flung open the door and found a drenched Andrew standing on the other side.

"Come in, come in," she said. "You must be freezing. Are you hungry? You must be. What can I feed you?"

"A cup of tea is fine. Or some hot water with lemon."

"Is that what you learned in Cornwall?" Sophie asked, helping her brother off with his rucksack and oilskin.

"Someone has gotten the world wrong and put the sea where the sky was supposed to be. I've never seen such rain," he said. He followed his sister into the kitchen. "You know," he said, "when we're together, do you ever think about it? Do the gods look down on us and think we're Evelyn and Peter all over again?"

"I suppose they might do," Sophie said. "A grizzly thought, Andy. I wouldn't expect it of you."

"I may not talk much, but my mind works all the same," he said.

"Come back into the parlor," she said. "Halfway through the summer and we have a wood fire raging. Bertold," she said as they came in, "I'm going to throw you out. I want to have a talk with my brother. He's half frozen."

"Well, we swore there'd be no working in these rooms," Bertold said. "Call me if you want something," he said, putting down his pen, and he promptly disappeared into the black square leading to the back steps.

"Turn on the light or you'll break your neck!" Sophie called after him.

"I know where I'm going," Bertold called back.

The two were left alone. "So," Andrew said to his sister, "it looks as if you like this one."

"I do. You should find one of your own," Sophie said.

"You mean a wife? I don't mean to marry. Well, not unless I want children, and I don't, not yet. I'll wait until I get someone pregnant."

"What an idea," Sophie said.

"Do you ever think about it? Why our mother wanted us?"

"I've spent quite some time thinking about it," Sophie said. "You know I never wanted children. I must have told you so. I didn't want them until I met Bertold, and then it was too late."

"You could adopt," Andrew said, but Sophie waved her hand in dismissal. "So you have to keep the bloodline going?" he asked. "Is that so important?"

"I suppose it is. To me. Considering that we're dying out so fast, we Grovesnors. But you should have children. You'd be a good father."

"Why? Because I look so much like Daddy? That's a recommendation for not having them."

They looked at each other, and both shook their heads. "It's been years since we had a real conversation," Sophie finally said.

"Not since we were small children," he said. "After that, there was always so much in the way."

"You mean Meena," Sophie said.

"I never believed she caused difficulty," Andrew said. "I never saw how she preferred me to you. Now when I think about it, I feel guilty, I can tell you."

Sophie nodded.

"You knew, didn't you?" he asked.

"I hated you for a long time," she said.

"But you never let on."

"I'm not sure I knew why I was so angry at you," Sophie said.

He got up suddenly and stood by the fire, then turned back to look at his sister.

"Sometimes," Sophie said, "you look exactly like Daddy. Not just your face and build, but the way you move."

"I wish I didn't. You probably know that. You must have been a reminder for Daddy. Of our mother. You'd get up from the table and he'd stare as if he'd seen something uncanny."

"Uncanny. Me."

"You could see it in the pictures. When you got older, I mean. If her pictures hadn't been black and white and yours in color, you couldn't have said who was who. Meena once said you must have eaten our mother and that was why you resembled her so much. She used to say terrible things, but at the time I thought they were true. She wanted me afraid of you. *She* was afraid of you, the way you reminded Daddy of Evelyn every time he looked at you."

"But what did she think she was doing?"

"Saving herself, I imagine," Andrew said. "It's funny, how it's all coming clear."

"Sigrid always said she was mad," Sophie said. "You remember Lady Anne? She was in town yesterday and I had tea with her. She's heard rumors."

"Rumors?"

"Apparently Meena thinks that Daddy comes alive at night and jumps out of the woods at her. But he never comes all the way to the house. As soon as she sees him, he goes back into the woods."

"I hope that's not true," Andrew said. "We've had enough madness in the family."

"Do you blame our father?" she asked suddenly.

"Sometimes," he said.

"I can't do that. Even though I know he must have done *something*."

"I think it's safe to assume that much," Andrew said. "But we all do *something*. What our mother did was worse."

"To us, you mean?"

"To everyone," he said.

"Sometimes," Sophie said slowly, "people have no choice."

"Do you believe that? Do you believe you have no choice when it comes to living or dying?"

"It's not what I believe about myself. It's what she believed about herself. Or had to believe about herself. Not everyone is strong. Or brave. Or sees the point."

"Yes, sometimes it's hard to see the point," he said. "That's when I think about moving to India and worshipping rats. They're very intelligent and they're kind to their families. You had one as a pet, if I remember correctly."

"I did," Sophie said.

"And Meena made you keep it in the barn, even in the winter."

"And I used to climb out the window and go down the apple tree and stay there with him. Ophelius, his name was. I named him Ophelia, but he turned out not to be a female rat."

"Yes. I remember that. Daddy said, 'That's why you need to learn languages.'"

" 'Because otherwise you wouldn't know how to change his name properly,' he said. I remember all that." They both laughed.

"Sophie," Andrew said, startling her, he so rarely used her name, "we have to decide about the will and the List of Wish. Not just because Sigrid keeps on about it, but because what Meena's doing is not right. It wasn't what Daddy wanted. Even if he hadn't cared about us, he would have cared about his writing. 'That writing kept me alive,' I don't know how many times he said that. Where would we have been without him? So we owe him something for that writing. If that's what kept him going, I mean. You understand?"

"Of course," Sophie said. "I couldn't agree more."

"I don't think you should be the one to face her," Andrew said. "You've been up against her long enough. It's my turn."

"You know what Sigrid thinks. She thinks you'll see Meena and remember she's your mother, the one who raised you, and you'll give in to whatever she wants."

"It won't happen," Andrew said. "Whether or not I remember she was my mother."

"Was?" Sophie asked.

"Was," Andrew said.

"You sound so sad when you say that," she said.

"Losing another mother, well, it isn't easy. But I can do what's necessary. I'm the only one who can. She doesn't suspect me. She can't believe other people change, certainly not me. I've been completely blind for so long she's come to rely on my walking around with my eyes shut forever."

"So you would be doing it for Daddy?"

"For Daddy, yes. Principally for him. But for you, too. You were the one she was always after. By the time she was through with you, I was pretty safe. Except from her stories."

"You would ask for mediation?" Sophie asked. "You'd go into that cage with her?"

"What choice do I have?"

"We didn't tell you about Clare," Sophie said, "because we didn't think you could bear it. But I never told you about what Meena did when she knew Daddy was dying. Lady Anne got hold of the nurse at the hospital, the same nurse she'd had when she had her cancer, and she rang me up in Jamaica and told me. She said, 'If you want to see your father alive, you better get there fast.' We took all the money we had; I borrowed money from Uncle Martin, Bertold emptied his bank account to get back to England to see him, and Meena didn't want us to see Daddy. She said he needed his rest, and really, his condition wasn't so bad. But I got in there. I had to *push* her out of the way. And Daddy was so happy to see me he cried. Well, I'm crying now, aren't I? I called you and told you he was dying, but I knew she'd be on the line to you saying there was nothing wrong with him. That's why Sigrid wired you the tickets. We wouldn't have done it, we would have let it go, but we saw he couldn't last long, and I thought you should see Daddy one more time. Once more, because it would be the last time. And Meena was so furious! She was white with rage. Her mouth was a like a white scar. And Sigrid was ten minutes away, and she didn't have the least idea. Meena was hoping to have him alone at the end. So he couldn't see Clare, so he couldn't talk about anything, say anything she didn't want him saying. She almost had it all her way. 'You mustn't tell Andrew. He's not up to such things.' That's what she said, word by word. I didn't think you'd get there on time, I can tell you. He waited for you. The doctor kept saying, 'I don't know what's keeping him going,' but it was you, he was waiting for you. So in the end," Sophie said, her voice breaking, "it was the two of us he wanted."

Andrew had put his hands to his face, and shook his head. "What was she thinking?" he asked. "What on earth was she thinking?"

"To be fair," Sophie said, "there'd been so many *This is it*s. After enough false alarms, she probably thought, well, she *could* have thought, but I doubt it, she could have thought that he wasn't dying just then and he'd come to himself, the way he had so many times before. It's possible."

"Anything's possible," Andrew said bitterly.

"I'd read things to him and he was so weak that he couldn't speak, all he could do was press my hand, and a few hours later, all he could do was look at me, and even that was hard. And his mouth was always open even though he was propped up with pillows, and that rasping! And he was so thin! One of the nurses put her arms around me and said, 'You must be brave now, Sophie. When you see that face, the open mouth, the flesh sinking in, the sound of his breathing, that bluish tinge, what is that? Don't you know, really? It's the death mask. It is. Don't let it take you by surprise. Don't set yourself up for the full shock.' She was right, you know. It was better to be prepared. But you, you had to walk right into the middle of it, into that horror, that battlefield, with no one to warn you. Because there wasn't *time*. If the plane had been on time, maybe I could have done something. I wanted to do something. Bertold was ready to talk to you before you went in, but there wasn't *time*. I hate her for that! She took away what little time there was. Blood-eater! A beast with blood on her mouth! When I think about Meena, that's what I see." Sophie waved her hand, stopped speaking, and began to cry.

"Don't cry," Andrew said. "Not so hard. You'll choke."

"I won't," Sophie said.

"When you were little, you used to choke when you cried like that."

"Did I? I don't remember."

"You did. I remember," he said.

"I didn't think you remembered anything," Sophie said. "I thought you refused to remember."

"I tried," he said.

"But you won't try anymore?" she asked.

"I'm not going to excavate everything I can about the past, but I'm willing to remember. And to put two and two together."

"So then there are really two of us," Sophie said, beginning to cry again. "Would you sit here by me?"

He hesitated. Then he stood up and sat next to her on the couch. "A comfortable place," he said. "The most comfortable chair in England," he said, smiling. "You remember that?"

"Daddy always said that about the swinging chair in the garden," Sophie said.

"Yes, that chair," Andrew said.

—

THIS RAIN, MEENA thought. This rain. There will be mudslides. Trees will fall over. Rivers will overflow. People will drown in their cars. Something is wrong, has gone wrong, I feel it. What can have happened?

Julian is asleep upstairs. No one has died. There's no one left to die. But something is wrong. A balance has been disturbed. It must be the rain. What else could it be? I must eat. I must eat more. I am too thin. I must marry again. I am an heiress. I must remember that. But what can be wrong? Why does the rain insist that something is wrong?

FORTY-EIGHT

———

Dear Martin,

I've been to Northumberland again. I took Evelyn, the new one
I wrote you about. I always thought I'd end up in Devon, always
wanted to, as you know, but Evelyn dislikes it. She says what I've
always said, it's too tame, every inch of it accounted for, every bit
of it manicured and prettified, too tame for her. "How can there be
any surprises in a place like this?" she asks. "Where everything
looks like it's been scrubbed clean every night by giant housewives
with giant brooms. Surely your imagination would shrink, everything would shrink, passions, everything, in such a tame place." So

there is no point at all in taking her to Devon. She's bored by the
very sound of the name. But what place would be properly
untame? We went down to Cornwall and Morvah because she
wanted to see where I'd been born and she was full of questions.
Why were there huge mirrors stuck at the edge of driveways?
There must be car accidents all the time, the lanes were so narrow, and you couldn't see around corners in the road—that was
when she understood the need for the giant mirrors—I thought her
quite fascinated by the place and the tin mines and their shafts
going down, and I thought, this was a place to return to, but the
next time we went back, well, I don't need to tell you about
Cornwall, the season was changing, the whole place was
shrouded in that mist you can feel on your skin, and the wind was
howling, so I took her to see Lawrence's cottage, I knew that
would interest her, it's right above the cliffs, and the wind was up
that day and howling like a wolf, and we spent most of our time
sitting on a stone wall while she wondered how Lawrence had
stood living in such a ghost-ridden place, no wonder that he and
Frieda had ended up chasing each other around the cottage. Frieda
wielding a knife. Evelyn hadn't understood it before, but after a
couple of hours there, she did. So we waited until the mists
cleared off a bit and went further down the meadows so she could
see the waves crashing down below, but then we got tired, and
climbed up on another wall. When we climbed the wall, there was
nothing in the world there but us, but I imagine you already know
what happened. Is there a place on the coast where cows are not
raised? So we were suddenly surrounded by cows, all of them
interested in Evelyn's sneakers. I said, "Get down. They'll move off,"
but she didn't have the nerve for it. She said she would sit there on
that wall until they all went somewhere else. Still, the nature of cows
hasn't changed since we played in those meadows, and more and
more cows came to see two people sitting on the wall, and in the

end, we were entirely surrounded. I waited to see how long she would stay there before she got up the nerve to go down, but when I saw that wasn't going to happen, I got down and drove them off. Then Evelyn got down from the wall and we went back through the meadows, while she turned back the whole time taking care that the cows were not following us. So Cornwall is not a place for her, either.

But she feels differently about Northumberland, just the right mixture of tame and wild. "If I could find an abandoned church and live in it, this would be perfect," she said when we were sitting in the garden of an abandoned house. "As long as you could see the sea. I grew up near the sea. It was right at the end of the street. All you had to do was walk to the end of the block." There are no "blocks" in Northumberland, not when you move out of the big towns, not very good hospitals, either, as you remember, but that made no difference to her. She wanted an isolated place, and there was a train to London. She could get a lot of reading and writing done on the journey down. Of course there was a train. She nodded, in that way I am already coming to know, decisively, very decisively. Anyone who wanted to live with her was going to live in Northumberland. I looked around and thought, You could do worse, but my heart wasn't set on it. She asked about abandoned churches and scandalized the estate agent we got a list of properties from. Then we went about on our own and stopped at vacant houses. We came to one with a sign that said "Willow Grove," and a sea fret had come up, but the apples were still red and burned through the mist, and Evelyn, that's her name, Evelyn said, "Those are my apples!"

You asked me why I wasn't married yet. What is it about you newly married men? And women? No sooner do the shackles click over your ankles than you want to hear that clanking sounding everywhere. You remember the times we used to go hunting, and on the way back we'd stop and talk about what we'd do in the

future, and we always said, "I'm never going to marry. If this is marriage, I don't want any part of it," meaning, of course, our parents.
Just a few weeks ago, I would have repeated the same thing and
meant it, but now I don't know. A wife can be quite a relief, I think
now. I tend to dither. Men tend to dithering. But women are decisive. They say, "This is where I want to live," and the whole matter
is settled. What a weight would come off to marry a woman like
that! Finally, I can see an advantage in it, in marriage. .

And, I think, the end of boredom. Women can make an opera
of everything. Two days in the house because of the rain and the
house is suddenly a crypt. So many things to worry about! All of
a sudden the world is stuffed like a Christmas stocking. I quite like
all of that. Cornucopias of kittens and puppies and rugs and
Victorian draperies and washstands that need sanding and
restaining and moldy grouting between the tiles that must be
scrubbed clean or dug out altogether and then redone. And these
nesting attacks. Ever since Evelyn saw the house in Northumberland, she casts a covetous eye on stone walls that have fallen
in and says, "If I had that house, I'd carry those stones back and
make a place to sit out back," and as for plants and flowering trees,
she's barely safe around them. "I'm sure we could root them up,"
she says, "if we had to. Well, we would, if we had a place to live."
Women, they're like spring birds who suddenly learn to speak. "I'll
just have this twig and this piece of straw and this bit of rag. What
a nest it will make." I should find it quite terrifying, really, but
instead there's something precious in it, for once the spark of life
making itself visible in this carrying off of stones and tulip bulbs. It
quite stops you from asking the big, unanswerable questions I was
asking earlier: Why do we live? Why do we go on? Because when
you see a woman at work, you understand that they don't stop to
ask such questions, they simply go on ahead. So they must
already know the answers, and by considering women, you can

find them out. Is it only men who are baffled and who continue to ask such questions throughout their lives? Why did I live? A man must still go on asking that even as the funeral director comes in the door asking for orders. Or, as was true in Cornwall in particular, he continues to ask himself that same question even as he hears the workman hammering his coffin outside his bedroom window. But I'm not marrying anyone, so that's enough said. Still, the word *marriage* is not the terror and black spell I once swore it was.

I wonder about some of my assumptions. If I am to write, is it so wise to covet a gypsy's life? If life is too full, too exciting, how do you ever take time to work? Evelyn thinks the best method is this: you rush about, in and out of cities and countries, devour as many people and scenes as you can stuff into yourself, and then retreat into your own cave and write in isolation, perhaps even seeking out boredom, so that when you come to write, nothing will distract you. But no matter where I've gone, distractions spring out of the ground. Like weeds, really. There are no perfect, green lawns that refuse to admit weeds. The fewer such weeds the better, Evelyn says, if only because distractions will rise up out of the ground and why must one encourage them, or put oneself in a position to meet too many of them? She craves isolation. If she could have it, she would write, and write and write. I see the attraction of the life she envisions, first frenetic activity, and then retiring to a monastery or a nunnery, but is it such a good thing to court isolation? How much did we accomplish when we had nothing but time in the long, long Cornwall summers? Everything I accomplished was finished and done during term in the middle of writing papers on Roman aqueducts and exams set to be studied for, and a store to be managed when Dad took ill, in between Mother's saying, "Be a love, and run to Boots with this doctor's note, and on the way back, one loaf of whole-grain bread and a pound sack of sugar. It's all in the store, just bring it back, it won't take but a second," and despite all that, I covered page after page. What makes us tick, really? As for Evelyn, don't start listening for church bells. She keeps me amused, that's all it is. And she's an American, and she says she wants to go back there to teach when she finishes up here, and America's not for me, land of shiny refrigerators as tall as skyscrapers and ovens big enough for a family to live in. So all in all, I have to say I think I'm quite safe.

Your bachelor brother,
Peter

FORTY-NINE

———

"SO," ANDREW SAID, looking around the table, his eyes resting briefly on Meena's and then moving on to the other faces, "if everyone is here, we might as well begin."

"Julian is not yet here," Meena said.

"Then we'll wait for him, shall we?" Andrew said.

"Yes, we must wait for him," Meena said. Andrew shifted impatiently in his chair. What was he wearing? Had she ever seen Andrew wearing a suit before? Yes, of course, at the funeral. That suit had not fitted at all, the jacket arms and trouser legs were too short. But this suit, this was expensive. If she guessed rightly it was an Armani, but how would he have managed the expense?

"You must go to the mediation dressed like a lord," Sigrid had told him.

"I should go looking like a pauper so everyone would feel sorry and give me enough money to get home."

"Everyone thinks they'll be given more if they come in looking like a vagrant," Sigrid said. "Julia thought the same thing. I'm telling you what I told her. Go looking like a pauper, and they'll give you what they think is proper for a pauper. Go looking like a lord and they'll be ashamed to offer you less than what a lord deserves. You must have an Armani suit. I'll put it on my card. Call the cab. There's a little store in Hampstead."

"A little store," Andrew said. "Fortunes have gone into your little stores."

"And still, I am not yet living on a grate," his aunt said.

"The best you have," Sigrid said grandly when they entered the shop and pushed Andrew forward. "He must look *rich*."

"An actor, madam?" asked the salesman.

"Yes, he shall be. In that suit," Sigrid said. "Navy blue?" she asked Andrew. "Black is out of the question. *You're* not going to a funeral. This is to be *her* funeral."

"I'm sorry, madam?" the salesman said.

"He wants navy blue," Sigrid said. "And the tailoring must be done in the morning, and I shall be back to inspect it, and everything must be *exactly* right, is that clearly understood?"

"Very clear, madam," the man said.

The fitting began. "Stand *still*, Andrew!" Sigrid said, bristling with annoyance. "Don't stoop over! How can he measure if you keep stooping over? Stand up *straight*, Andrew!"

"And how is that, madam?" the man asked, when he had finished chalking the trousers and putting straight pins in place.

"You look simply grand," Sigrid said to her nephew. "That will do," she said to the man. "And now, Andrew, you must treat me to a cake and some tea. No, *I* shall pay for it. This is my day to do things for you."

"I'm not hungry," Andrew protested.

"What does that matter? This is a *ceremonial* tea. Order something and don't eat it, but order *something*."

"What will you have?" Andrew asked her as they were seated at a table in the Hampstead Café.

"The almond cakes are very good, quite like Spain. I recommend it."

"Two almond cakes and tea for two," Andrew said.

"With or without milk?" the waitress asked.

"Just set down everything, love," Sigrid said. "That's how it's done. Don't *flush*, Andrew," she said as the waitress moved off. "She has to learn how to behave or the shop will throw her out."

"You're never very kind to waitresses or shopkeepers," Andrew said.

"Or taxi drivers," Sigrid said agreeably. "You will feel far more confident in that suit. You'll see it yourself."

"I expect I shall," Andrew said. "If anything were to remind me that the meeting is about cash and power, it would be that suit. Actually, it would be *any* suit. I never have reason to wear a suit. Well, I did, for Daddy's funeral."

"After this, I predict you will have many occasions to wear that suit," Sigrid said.

———

PERHAPS THEY POOLED all their resources, Meena thought. I wouldn't like to think my money had paid for that suit. She looked around the room: three of her attorneys and one representing the children.

"Ah, Julian," Meena said as her cousin slid into his seat next to her. "Now we may begin. Andrew, I understand that you wish to speak first?"

"I'll keep this short," Andrew said. "The will is clear, as is the List of Wish. We want to adhere to both documents. We also request an accounting of your finances. We understand that you claim you will not have enough to live on if we are each given the share our father specified. There has been far too much loose talk about how great or small a sum is involved here. We want an accounting of the estate's assets, and an accounting of what assets you have already received. Additionally, we will not agree to a confidentiality clause. If you are to insist upon that, I should get up and leave now and the mediation must end. There will be *no* confidentiality clause. My sister's life is still developing, and she is entitled to whatever material she wishes to make of her own life. I am entitled to the same privilege, as is Sigrid. We shall not agree to hold our own lives hostage simply to inherit the money our father intended to bequeath to us. Meena?"

"You think of me as a captor holding you hostage?" Meena asked, her eyes filling.

"I believe I said that if you continued to insist on a confidentiality cause, we would indeed view you as a captor holding us hostage, and we will break off negotiations," Andrew answered.

Meena and Julian turned to one another. He read horror in Meena's eyes.

"But this is a *mediation*," Julian said. "Surely you are willing to give way on *something*."

"Not on a confidentiality clause," Andrew said. "That is not negotiable."

"Everything is negotiable," Julian said.

"Then you may continue negotiating without me," Andrew said.

"About what are you prepared to negotiate?" Julian asked.

"Percentages," Andrew said. "After a document of financial disclosure, we might consider dropping the percentage of the estate due us in accordance with the List of Wish."

"What amount would you agree to?" Julian asked.

"Perhaps twenty-four percent."

"Twenty-four percent!" Meena exclaimed.

"And twenty-four percent of any interest accrued since my father's death," Andrew answered.

"Interest!" Meena burst out.

"Be *quiet,* Meena!" said Julian, rounding on his sister. "It would be best for my cousin if we could come to an agreement today. This is very hard on your mother—"

"Stepmother," Andrew interrupted.

"This is very hard on Meena," Julian continued, "and the sooner we bring this to an end, the better."

"Then you have instruments of financial disclosure available for us to see? I can fax them directly to Sophie and to Sigrid."

"You are joking, surely," Julian said. "These documents will take time to assemble."

"*If* they are to be assembled at all," Meena said.

"We cannot negotiate—or undergo mediation—in a vacuum," Andrew said. "Nor will we."

"How can you speak to me in this way?" Meena cried.

Andrew looked down at his hands, and then looked up at her. "I should rather not discuss this at all. My father's documents were abundantly clear. Why is further discussion necessary?"

"Have you forgotten who raised you?" Meena cried.

"I have forgotten nothing," Andrew said. "All that is beyond the scope of this proceeding."

Julian leaned close to Meena and whispered into her ear. "We are in trouble here," he told his cousin. "He has turned. Agree to something. Anything. Say you will have an accounting presented to them."

"We will order an accounting made," Meena said. "Financial matters shall be disclosed. Are you satisfied now?"

"Not at all. Nothing can be accomplished until such documents are forthcoming. How can I know if you are simply delaying and appearing to cooperate? If you will rescind the demand for a confidentiality clause, and do it today, have it sworn and entered into evidence, then I will be somewhat satisfied."

"You shall not order *me* about!" Meena said, standing up, upsetting the cup of tea in front of her. "I shall not stand for this!"

"Will you or won't you rescind the confidentiality clause?" Andrew asked. "By six o'clock this evening."

"Entirely out of the question," Meena said coldly, sitting down.

"Then," said Andrew, standing up, "I think we are finished." And he began gathering up his papers, tapping them into a neat pile, and, opening his briefcase (He has a briefcase! Meena saw, stunned), proceeded to place them inside and close the lid. The lock of the case clicked shut. "I will inform Sophie and Sigrid," Andrew said. "As you know, Sophie is very busy with her new work and Sigrid is soon to return to Italy. We will let you know when the three of us will be free to assemble again."

"You will lose everything by this, you fool!" Meena burst out.

"None of us is starving," Andrew said, staring hard at her. "All of us are too old to be bought." He nodded curtly at the faces around the table, and went to the door and disappeared.

"Come back here, Andrew!" Meena shouted.

"Meena, for God's sake, be quiet!" Julian said, his voice rising.

"He left. He simply left," Meena said aloud to the room. "He as good as said I could go to Hell! He's walking out on all that money!"

"Meena, if you say one more word, you can find yourself another advisor," her cousin said.

"But what will they live on?" Meena asked, her voice gone small and bewildered.

"They don't appear worried, do they?" Julian asked sardonically. "They are their parents' children, after all. One Graves and one Grovesnor. You've taken on all of them."

"*But I will win,*" Meena said, her voice low and poisonous.

One of the solicitors cleared his throat. "If they take you to court, a judge could well uphold the List of Wish," he said. "It has been known to happen. The List of Wish is a venerable institution."

"But you told me it had no legal validity!" Meena exclaimed.

"Not technically, no," said the solicitor. "But judges have been known to honor it. So there is precedent. Of very long lineage, I might add."

"Keep silent, Meena!" Julian hissed into her ear.

"They shall never take me to court!" Meena exclaimed.

"It could well be," said the solicitor, "that they are relying on the Court of Public Opinion. If they win in that arena, what could be more powerful?"

"Happy now?" Julian hissed. "Satisfied now?"

FIFTY

OH, SHE'S FINE. Really quite fine. During the day, she's quite fine. A little shaky at night, but that's to be expected. But otherwise very fine, very well. Getting accustomed to the man who lives in the woods and steps in and out especially when there's a moon. Yes, of course, I know there's always a moon, I meant to say a moon clearly visible, shedding moonlight, making things clearer even at night, that kind of moon. What does he look like? I don't know, I've never seen him, tall, thin, apparently, always keeps his head down, tall and thin, that's all I know. Could it be a woman? I suppose it could be. But with that kind of menace, it doesn't seem to be a woman. They say she talks to crows? I'm sure not. She's fine. Really fine. There are crows everywhere this year, I've never seen so many crows. No one gets close enough to hear what she's saying. That's all nonsense. The things people dream up! Although they do say she's afraid of the papers, leaves them just in front of her door for days on end and then drags them in all at once. Says she never knows what she'll find. Just like the rest of us. Never know what I'll find. Can't worry about everything, you know.

—

SHE WAS SITTING in the turret room, staring out, trying to explain what happened after a death, what death did, how you never knew how it would take you, how you never knew what someone meant to you until that person was well and truly gone. There are people who are so much part of you they can't leave without the whole wall tumbling. Who was Humpty Dumpty? Oh, it turns out you were, but you never knew, not until you fell or until the wall fell. Sometimes she's the wall, sometimes he is, but you don't know, can't know, until it happens. *Then* you have some-thing to cry about. Before she died, Sangeeta said, "Meena, you have to stay alive so you can remember my childhood." What a thing to ask! To stay alive for someone else! But she didn't believe her sister would die, not really. Her sister must have meant to say, "You're the only one left who remembers my childhood; who will I come to when I want to speak of it— if not you?" I'm sure that's what she meant.

Death and cold, they go together, she thinks. I've never been so cold, even on these terrible hot days. I know they're terrible because the ther-mometer says how hot it is. But I'm so cold, my feet are so cold, and my hands. Even when I go out near noontime, I put on my heavy woolen socks. At night, I wear my socks, and over those, Peter's hunting socks, and I'm still cold. Like the last inches of water suddenly swirling down the drain, the warmth does the same; it swirls away into a dark hole and I can't coax it back. And old. I see it when I turn the light on, I see myself reflected, even in my window, old and cold. Wearing a woolen bathrobe over my slacks and heavy sweater and still I'm cold. It's the emptiness at

the core. That's what Peter said, he used to say that, I remember, he did say
that. You can't warm the emptiness at the core. Have I always been cold?
It could be true. Too busy to notice, I suppose. Cold, snowy days in winter, the roads too icy for driving, so we stayed inside wearing our winter
coats, and even then I wasn't as cold as I am now. The strangest things
bring on the cold. A stiff wind that sets the swinging lawn chairs going
back and forth like pendulums. You start to remember everyone who once
sat in those chairs. It's too cold to go out and sit there, not now, not even
when the radio warns against the sun, how it's burning people, killing
them, a terrible thing yesterday—or was it the day before?—a man went
to the shops and left his dog in a closed car and came back to find the dog
cooked, its skin sliding about like boiled chicken skin. There are times
when cold and heat feel the same; what times *are* those? I've felt that so
often. When you touch ice in terribly cold weather, it feels hot, doesn't it?
When you burn your hand on the stove, afterward it feels cold, doesn't it,
is that right? The living protect and warm you; even your enemies do that.
No wonder deaths go in threes. I've always thought three is too small a
number. Deaths go in bunches. The ones left behind keep walking in the
snow, they keep going, looking for the ones they know, and it comes to
them, there is no one left, no one they know, that's when they stop in their
tracks. Families cling together, they warm themselves over one another,
they keep themselves warm, as if they were fires, all warming the others.
So many reconciliations after deaths. I've seen it so many times. And so
many people throwing everything up and going their own way, saying,
"He's dead. Now we don't have to pretend anymore. Now we can do as we
please." And all the threads of the web give way. A spider swinging from
the one thin thread left. It isn't right to pity oneself. After all, I have the
crows! And that's all I have!

Better to be angry. Anger keeps you warm. But I'm too tired even for
anger, so I shiver and tremble alone in this house. People would come if I
let them, as they once came to Sigrid after her first husband died. They
would say, "You must be lonely. Let us help." But they mean, "Give us per-

mission to read Peter's letters. Where are Peter's new poems? And his new stories? Did he sort them out? Did he have a table of contents for a new book? Could I look at a page? Just to see what it looks like?" How many times can you listen to the same song? Creep out a little from your hiding place only to find someone rifling through Peter's old desk, looking for unpublished work, or worse, Evelyn's diaries. They exist somewhere. Why not in this house? Am I the one that has them? Turning me into Sigrid now that Sigrid's finished with all that. I would remarry. If I could. But I am the faithful servant, the one who polished his shoes every morning. Brick by brick, I built that legend up, a brick room with high walls like the walls of a well, and I forgot to build a door, so now I must stay here.

If those children do not belong to me, I will not give them anything! I would rather stand here in the howling wind! They think I will weaken, but I will not. I will stand up through an ice age rather than give them an ember, rather than give them a twig for their fire. Let them know what it is to be cold. But they don't seem cold. Julian was right. They seem quite safe and warm. Andrew was flushed during the mediation, because of the heat, but I was cold. I would have gotten my coat and put it on, but he would have seen it as weakness, as well he should have done. And that woman with her Trees of Light. Do they warm her, I wonder? On warm days in Cornwall, does that room they showed in the pictures become intolerable? Does she have to go out into the wind coming from the cliffs to escape the heat? I suppose she is warm. I suppose she sweats and wipes the perspiration from her brow. I suppose her hair curls up in the damp heat. But my body stays dry, cold and dry. Even last year, my hair curled tightly, but now it doesn't. It lies on my skull straight and dry. Animals are warm, much warmer than we are. I must think about a pair of dogs. I must train them to lie quietly in my bed. Bed warmers, Peter called our dogs, all of them dead and gone. And cold. Of course cold. Yes, more cats in the bed after they've had their jabs and the treatment against fleas. You can keep fleas from you these days. They can do so much these days. But not for

Peter. They did nothing for him then and what can they do now? I get quite close to people running fevers, I should like to run one myself, a high one, to push away the cold, but even that does no good. Last week's high fever made me shake and freeze.

Once you start to lose, you cannot stop losing. Evelyn said that to Peter not long before she left him. Why did she? She ought to have known he would have come back to her. In the end, what difference did it make? He liked all women. He married her. Why would he not have come back to her? But she said many true things. I never liked to admit to it. *Once you start to lose, you cannot stop losing.* A principle of life, a rule, and she stated it so clearly, so simply, whereas I go in circles until I tangle my feet in my own string. Now I prove her axiom. Now I would like to speak to her, to ask her things. I would ask her, What must I do? She is the only one I would trust, but she is dead and cold. How long did she shake with cold after she left him? A few months, no longer. She put an end to it, put an end to weather. That would be the worst, to die and never feel weather again, never see it change from one minute to another. In the end, the weather means more to me than any human being. It is true to say I have always most valued the nonhuman world. I have loved it the most. I was born knowing I could rely on the weather, on the fact that there would always be weather. The weather cannot leave you. But I do wish it would warm me. Perhaps it will. Perhaps it will warm me quite soon.

Is that man waiting in the shadow of the woods? I think he is. I think I know who he is. I think he has something to say. I don't want to hear it.

—

"WHEN HE DIED," Clare said, "I never thought I would acquire a family. I never dreamed it."

"A family of your own," Sophie said softly.

"A family of my own," Clare said wonderingly.

—

"HAS ANDY GONE to sleep?" Sophie asked Bertold.

"He looked exhausted. I think so."

"I'll just look," Sophie said, and went up to the little third-floor room. Andrew was asleep on the narrow bed, his long legs sticking over the end of the bed. Sophie shivered. It was a cold night, cold in that room. There were duvets in the cupboard. She took one down and unfolded it, then softly covered him with it. "You have no tread at all," Peter used to say of her. "You come and go without a sound. Meena finds it unnerving." Sophie smiled in the dark and looked at her brother. He didn't move for a few minutes, and then, as if sensing the warmth of the duvet, he turned on his side and pulled the cover with him. Sophie smiled again and left the room.

—

"MUST YOU BUY a house in Greece?" Sophie asked. "It's so far away. Or is this just another brainstorm?"

"You know how I feel about the sun," Sigrid said. "I always think, I will die in February if I stay through the winter in London. It hasn't happened yet, but now that I *can* go, I think I must."

"Old turtle, sunning on a rock," Andrew said.

"And so I am," Sigrid said.

"I hope I live as long as you have," Andrew said.

"I'm not dead yet," Sigrid said tartly. "You can come stay with me. The planes still fly."

"And if there's a war?" Sophie asked. "They say there will be, and then how will you get back?"

"You've done well enough without me before," Sigrid said.

"Go to Italy," Andrew said. "No one's attacking Italy."

"Morocco," Sigrid said, considering.

"Very warm there," Andrew said.

—

"BUT SURELY MEENA will let me quote from Peter's letters to Martin," Rose insisted to Sigrid.

"She will not," Sigrid said.

"She doesn't *own* those letters," Rose said indignantly.

"Rose, that's hardly the point. As you very well know, the person who wrote the letters owns the copyright. Now *she's* the one who owns the copyright. She owns every word Peter wrote that wasn't already copyrighted when he died. She'll sue you and she'll win."

"Scholars would rise up against her!" Rose said.

"And you will lead them? You will be Stalin, overcoming everything?"

"Must you try to make me ridiculous?" Rose asked.

"Why do you make it so easy for me?" Sigrid inquired. "You can go to that American university and read the letters, and get a sense of them. You can even take *notes*, Rose. You say it won't be the same as the actual words, his cadences and intonations. But you are not doing an edition of Peter's letters to Martin. Try to remember that, Rose."

"I hope you do go to Greece!" Rose exclaimed. "I hope you go to the ends of the earth."

"I'm not going that far," Sigrid assured her. "There's no hope of that."

FIFTY-ONE

——

"I CANNOT THINK of Peter," Julia said, "without feeling a chill."

"Julia, it's what death does," Sigrid said. "I've never been so cold before. I used to think, back when I was young and given to imagining things, that you went cold after a death—in sympathy. Trying to feel what the dead person feels. Things spoil more slowly when it's cold. I was very ghoulish when I was young, you know. I used to show Peter how different things rotted, first the white spots on cheese, then the spots going blue, the soft spots on tomatoes. He had to see them. Then the soft spots collapsing in, and all the colors the bright red flesh turned, 'painted by death,' I think I said, maggots swarming over a bird dead in the lane, I took him to see that. He didn't like it. He was such a cheerful child. He didn't like any of that stuff. It upset him, really. What was I thinking of? And *why* was I thinking of all that? I never had an appetite for the *memento mori*. I rarely give thought to such things. And what happened? They became Peter's great subject. Death and all its dominions. Useless to predict anything," Sigrid said. "He always thought I'd be the one to write."

"And so you should have," Julia said.

"Don't start in on *that* again," Sigrid said, genuinely exasperated.

"I have so many of his letters. If I were generous, I'd let Rose read them."

"Meena would still own the copyright."

"That's true," Julia said.

"Don't give them to her, don't let her read them," Sigrid said. "Peter trusted you. He wrote you about all those lawsuits and the problems with the children. Rose won't understand any of that. She won't understand your attitude, either. She doesn't know that you and Matt stopped his publishing Evelyn's letters until all of them were properly edited. You remember all of that? 'Poor Sophie has no winter coat, and I don't have money to buy it for her, and Peter gives me nothing.' 'He was to have come down to London with our potatoes, but he's eaten them all himself.' 'I can't go out these days because of the snow. I have no boots and my one pair of shoes leaks and I can't afford to repair the soles. He manages to give Elfie all the money she needs, but he has no use for his own children, and I am nothing but the mother of those children, the ones he never wanted, and does not want still.' You can imagine what a dinner Rose will make of those letters. I don't know why you still have copies of the letters Peter suppressed when Evelyn's letters came out. She'll turn that silly book of hers into another biography of Evelyn."

Julia nodded.

"For God's sake, don't let her make you feel sorry for her," Sigrid said.

"I think that's out of the question," Julia said. "What *do* you think will happen to Peter's estate?"

"The children are resolved not to give in."

"People are already talking," Julia said.

"Keep that fire warm," Sigrid said. "You know how to do it."

FIFTY-TWO

———

Dear Bloody Martin,

What the bloody hell have you been bloody well doing? Just thought I'd remind you of how we used to stoop beneath Mum's kitchen window when the window was up and try to shock her by cursing away. We thought she was deaf because she didn't straightaway start scolding, so we shouted louder and louder, but she never said a word. Why didn't we twig to it? We shouted ourselves hoarse and she never heard a word. But Daddy heard it; he was the one who came at us with the paddle. I got up this morning, thinking about the two of us shouting obscenities under the kitchen window. It made me laugh, and then finally it came to me, after all these years. She wanted us shouting so Dad would hear for himself and go after us. She had no heart for smacking us. We were so sure she was thick as two planks, who would have thought she'd be clever enough to work it so that Dad was the one to punish us?

Things are fine here, everyone is fine here. I should have begun by saying that straightaway. I guess Aunt Betty's death gave Mum a shock, but the funeral went off without a hitch, and no one started fighting across the hole dug in the ground, so Mum thought it was a very good funeral, if you have to have funerals, as she said. She came back reminiscing about other funerals that hadn't been so nice, that one where one of her brothers jumped across the grave hole and attacked her other brother, and both of them fell in before the coffin got lowered, and the whole family ended up in hysterics. Now, she says she has absolutely no idea at all of what that was about. Which led her to say this extraordinary thing. I'm sending it along to see what you make of it. "I thought of getting a divorce, once, I did, but after all of you were gone to school, Daddy was my whole life." Mum? Divorce? She must have been to see a film and thought she was the heroine. She's getting a bit fuzzy, Mum is. But tell me what you think of that.

To your question. Am I as certain as I seem? No. Didn't know I gave off that impression. I'm not even certain that I want to write more poems, although now everyone expects it of me. At the start, I saw the poems would get me into Oxford. I found them so easy to write, and I didn't have much else to recommend me, certainly not my distinction in the exams. I quite liked writing those early poems, really, never thought of other people reading them, I mean people reading them who I didn't know, who might have their own opinions of what was wrong with them and had their own ideas about how they ought to be redone, and would say, This word must be taken out and another one substituted. I got used to all that fast enough, if anyone knew how to turn a deaf ear, I surely did, and when I began, I was wild with joy when something got into print, but then I saw how many people were going to have something to say, and they would say it, whether or not I valued their opinion, or thought they had one single brain cell. I told Jake publishing wasn't what I thought it ought to be. I should like to approve anyone who intended to read something of mine, and he said, "My dear Peter, you seem to have missed the meaning of the word *publish*. What do you think publication means?" Then Marianne Moore was dragged here across the pond and had this to say: "It's not enough to have talent. You have to have talent for having talent." I don't know if that was original with her. An American girl here thinks an actress originally came up with that one. Anyway, this Marianne Moore was in quite a fury about the famous phrase "imaginary gardens with real toads in them," insisting that she was quoting someone else, Shakespeare, I think, She had not written those words, yet all her life had been praised for them. To be so famous, and so bitter about that one line! Well, of course she was saying her own work would never live up to that one line she'd never even written in the first place. And all of us dangling on her every word, and I've got to come clean—if she didn't write that line, I didn't and don't think as much of her as I did. Ought she not keep quiet? If I found myself famous, would I have a talent for talent? I think not. Not many people came to greet her before she read. I was dragooned by the Resident because our house was sponsoring the reading. There were three of us there. So this is what it means to be famous, I thought. Everyone knows your name but no one wants to meet you and likely no one reads what you've written. Or cares. Or reads it and shrugs, unim-

pressed, definitely unimpressed, saying, My opinion's as good as
anyone's.

It would be different if I had something to say, you know, if I had
a subject. These young girls starting out have a subject. Themselves. I don't see that's enough. If I were to be my subject, and I
were to start writing stories, pretty empty and vacuous they would
be, I think. But the women, anything they think of or feel, that's
more than enough subject for them. I can't see making people my
subject. I'm not interested enough in them, not to write about, you
see. Why memorialize someone's grief over a death when everyone's been through the same thing? So it seems to me. We're
mayflies, all of us. What interests me are the great forces that
throw us this way and that, the big tides that drag us under or
throw us up to the surface again, coughing, our eyes bulging. But
forces, well, they're hard to write about. Even I see they have to
be embodied, but in what? In animals, I think, not because they're
so interesting in themselves, but because a human with his beady
eyes and small brain can see the big forces at work in the way animals behave. If animals can be the magnifiers, the embodiers,
then I might have something to write about. A subject! A subject!
But without a subject, I have nothing, am nothing. Better, then, to
exalt gossip and worrying and complaint, to eavesdrop on the
neighbors and go down the road for a pack of Benson and Hedges
and tell the little world in there what I happened to hear that day.
Are animals enough? As a subject, I mean? In the way I've spoken of them? Do you know what you aim for when you try to com-
pose? Or are you still fighting with technique and what
instruments go with what, and how the notes must go together?
I've found quite a good book for you, about Michelangelo's use of
pigments, and I think you can apply what he says about painting
to music. I'll send it to you. If you find a recipe book for poetry (and

for fiction, because I begin to think I may well try that), do send it my way.

As for women, there are a lot of them. The tide throws them up on my beach. People say I've got a reputation, all of it bad. I can't, it seems, settle down. I seem to hold out so much, they don't say what that might be, but they mean marriage. What else could they mean? And then I snatch the hope away, so I'm a heartbreaker. Best to steer clear of me. The word *marriage* is a dirty word. Wouldn't shout it beneath our mother's kitchen window. Wouldn't so much as say, Our parents were married for fifty years. You so much as think the word, and they're home writing out invitations and asking their parents how much they can afford for the celebration. They walk around in invisible wedding gowns waiting for the invisible groom to make himself known. Is there a woman who doesn't fit that bill?

Maybe the American girl here. She hasn't heard that English girls are supposed to be like female birds and make themselves as drab as possible. No, she has shiny platinum hair and wears lipstick! Lipstick! Bright red lipstick! And perfume that smells like lilies of the valley, Mum's perfume, but on her it has a different effect, especially here, since no one wears perfume and all you smell is talcum powder over unwashed skin. But this one must spend all her time in the bath. She always looks—and smells—washed. Jake says that's an American for you. They have to be in a body cast to stop bathing. She laughs a lot but she doesn't say much. When she does, she doesn't insist, but all the same, I can't help but think she knows what she's talking about. It makes a nice change. I thought of asking her to the pub, to ask her what kind of refrigerator they have in the States, does she use a typewriter or a yellow pad, all the dumb things people who don't write always ask you, but I saw her gabbling with a group of other female students, most of whom already know me, so this very clean girl with her lily of the valley smell has no doubt heard of me and been warned off. Everyone's still jawing about the night Jake and I got so drunk we found ourselves standing in front of Penny's hall, and I, bellowing for her to come down. Caused quite a stir, it seems, as the girls thought I might suddenly crash down the door and rush up there and take them all. Can't make people my subject, you see. Too complicated. Whereas if a bull happened along and crashed down the gate and got himself into the meadow with the cows, we'd know what that was all about, might even find that interesting and not at all frightening, no thought of blaming the bull, nor thinking him very frightening in the end. Well, they would think him frighten- ing, but not freakish, not mad. People are frightened of every- thing other people might do, as if they were taught to think that humans existed to behave like meringues, so they dismiss any- one who isn't a meringue, saying "He's mad," but it's quite all right to speak of the freakish whims of animals as if they were expected to have them, as well they should be. So here I am, back to that subject again. Subject! Perhaps it is a subject. If it turns out that way, I'll go on with the writing.

You realize, Martin, if you were here, I'd have nothing to say but would go about *silent* and *mysterious*, the words women here like to use for me. But you're over there in that hot country where no leaves fall, and so I write altogether too much. Or is it that, were we together, I'd have said all these things, but a little at a time, a splinter here and there, and if I'd written it all down when the sun set, it would turn out to be pages and pages, as this letter is. Got to get out into the air and howl at some woman's digs and keep my reputation up.

All great things to you, Martin, you will be the one to make our name. Or maybe Sigrid. She has it in her. I'm a pygmy next to the two of you. Blame this mood on the rain. I shall be buried in the rain, how's that for a poetic statement any woman might make? Or admire? I shall tell that to the next woman that interests me.

Peter

FIFTY-THREE

—

THE RAIN WAS pouring down. Lightning was crashing, and thunder sounded out with little intermission, the rain so thick on the pane that the window appeared to be covered with ice. As Sigrid and Sophie well knew, Julia was inclined to stay inside and watch such weather. It put her into a kind of trance, and she often took the phone off the hook so she would not be disturbed. She believed, as Peter had, that it was dangerous to use a telephone in a lightning storm, and both of them had sworn that many people had been electrocuted when they insisted on using the phone while lightning split up the sky. But that evening Julia had left the telephone on the hook, and so it rang. She hesitated. The lightning flashed, and she hesitated again, but then she picked up the receiver.

"You have to stop her! You have to make her stop! This is ruining every-thing!" a voice sobbed into the telephone. Julia moved the receiver away from her ear.

"Sophie?" she said tentatively.

It was Sophie, who launched into a rambling speech about how Sigrid had once more insisted that Sophie stand up to Meena, and every time Sigrid called, Bertold would agree, and when Sigrid rang off, Bertold would insist that Sophie apply pressure to Meena. "Meena's an evil woman," Bertold would say. "Your father wanted you to have your inher-itance, and I want to see that you have it!"

But, Sophie said, she couldn't bear dealing with Meena and could sur-vive only by forgetting her. Merely thinking about her opened deep wounds. The money, Sophie said, wasn't important. She could always earn her own way. She had fled to Jamaica to escape Sigrid's unending pro-nouncements and now Sigrid was ruining Sophie's marriage.

Not again, Julia thought. Bertold can't have found another woman. It can't be starting over again. "Sophie," she said, "you have to stop crying enough so that I can understand you. Who is ruining your marriage?"

"Sigrid!" Sophie cried. "Sigrid! Sigrid! Sigrid!"

"But Sigrid likes Bertold. She entirely approves of him."

"She'll end up by taking him away!"

"You don't mean to say that Sigrid is interested in Bertold? Romantically, I mean?"

"I told you. She wants me to take on Meena. But I can't, she knows I can't, and she won't stop asking!"

"It's been that way from the start," Julia said.

"You don't know," Sophie said. "You don't know what it's like."

"Can you start at the beginning?"

"Well, Meena. You know what she's done. Daddy's will, you know all about that, don't you?"

"Yes," Julia said.

"It started there. With Bertold."

"Bertold? What started with Bertold?"

"He *hates* Meena! He and Daddy used to talk about her, about how horrible she was. Now Bertold's worse than ever."

"I don't understand," Julia said flatly. "I'm afraid you have to spell this one out."

"It's all I can do not to make myself sick over Meena, I go into such rages! And then all my troubles act up and I'm in bed for days. I can't even wake up. Then . . . then I drag myself out and do some work, very slowly, but work all the same. I'd be all right if no one set Bertold off. He used to be indifferent to her. But he's changed. All someone has to do is mention her name—"

"I see," Julia said. "Tell me what the trouble is with Bertold. This is the first I've heard of it."

"I thought you knew."

"How would I, Sophie? You always seem so happy together."

"Because he's glad to see you. Because you don't talk about Meena unless I bring her up. The last time you had dinner at the house, remember how angry he was about Meena? And you said, 'I think that woman is a monster,' and he went on and on about her and how she torments me and how she hates me and how sinful it is to ignore Daddy's last wishes, and how illegal it is to ignore them, and he went on and on. Don't you remember?"

"You think he overdid it?" Julia asked. "I agreed with him. I remember that."

"But when you talk about her, you don't go at it the same way. You listen to what I say and when I stop, when I say I can't talk about her anymore, you don't keep on."

"Well, no," Julia said. "You know how I feel about Meena, and I know how you feel about her, and if I go home and dream up schemes to punish her, it makes me feel better, but I don't think it's a good idea to call you and tell you what I've been thinking about. But Sophie, if you were *my* daughter, I don't think I'd keep so quiet."

"What kind of schemes?" Sophie asked.

"Oh, you know, nonsense, Sophie. Ideas about throwing her into that well at Willow Grove and closing the lid, if there is a lid. Poisoning the Christmas pudding, going to the butcher and asking for a chicken full of salmonella, idiot things like that. But they cheer me up. I like to think of her *writhing*. I have such a nasty streak, I'm too old to pretend I don't have it."

"None of those ideas would work," Sophie said, disappointed.

"No, they wouldn't," Julia said firmly. "Is that what Bertold does? Think up schemes to do Meena in?"

"Worse," Sophie said.

"Worse?"

"He goes on and on about how awful she is, how hard it is on me to be de-mothered *twice*. I can barely stand to think of it myself, but when I hear him going on like that, as if he's shouting at me . . ."

"I see," Julia said.

"You do?" Sophie asked.

"I do see," she said. Sophie spent enormous energy containing her fury at Meena, indeed, against the whole world, but everything Meena did reminded her of her own mother who had left her, and now Meena was going off and leaving her, but in an unexpected way, and when Bertold started in raving, it was as if an echo came back at her and struck her, and it was coming from Bertold, the one person from whom she needed safety and comfort. It was very clear and very terrible.

"If you understand, why can't Sigrid?"

"Sigrid believes in justice. She wants your father's last wishes followed, and she wants what's best for you. *And* you're her flesh and blood. She wants to protect *you*."

"By winding Bertold up? With all her talk about Meena? And her taking us out to the Chinese and going on about how I say I'll do things, but I don't, and how I'll let Meena make off with Daddy's estate because I won't be bothered?"

"I'll talk to Sigrid."

"It won't do any good. You know it won't. You know what Sigrid's like. But Julia, if *he* keeps on at me in that way, I can't bear it! I'll have to—"

"Have to what?"

"I'll have to live somewhere else," Sophie said.

"That can't happen. That can't be allowed," Julia said.

"But I don't see how to stop it!"

"Give me an example. Tell me one thing that made you say that."

"What?"

"That made you say you'd have to live somewhere else."

"Well, Clare, you met Clare? Yes, you did, of course you did. She sent me a snow globe. You know how I love snow globes. This is my favorite one, some bare black and brown trees and snow on the ground, deep in the country. There's a switch on the bottom and when you turn it on, there's the sound of wind and one loon calling to another. I've used up three sets of batteries listening to it. It's the best thing I have. It puts me to sleep. Well, you know what it's like to fall in love with things. I keep it in my study. On Monday night, I had it on, and Bertold came in and heard the sound. It really does sound like the wind, and the loon sounds like an owl calling out. I would have thought it was an owl if the label on the bottom hadn't said it was a loon, and he looked at the globe and picked it up and said, 'That's the sound of Meena's voice, cold and calling out, trying to tempt someone into those woods so he can die there in his thin clothes without any food,' and he went on and on, and when he began to run down, I picked up the globe and threw it across the room and it smashed and there was glass and water everywhere, but the sound of the wind and that bird kept on and on, and I'd broken it, that thing I loved so much. I'd broken it myself, so I screamed at him, I told him to get out, but he tried to make me feel better, I don't know what he was saying, I couldn't hear him, I was screaming, 'Get out! Get out!' And he finally did get out and I slammed the door and locked it and I stayed in there all night and he was back on the other side of the door every few minutes all night long, whimpering like a dog about how sorry he was, but I couldn't forgive him. I still can't. Because he made me break that globe and I loved it so much. That was the kind of thing Meena did. I can't go through it again. I can't.

"Andrew thinks Bertold's after my money. Bertold's not. He thinks he's protecting me. He thinks if he shows me how angry at Meena he is, I'll know how much he loves me."

"Does Andrew know what Bertold thinks?"

"No. But Andy's likely to tell Bertold, and then what?"

"Hearing that might be the shock Bertold needs," Julia said.

"I don't think so," Sophie said. "I don't think anything will help."

"You know, I think more and more of Andrew as time goes on. He told Meena off. He did the right thing, don't you think?"

"He's the only person still in his right mind."

"He walked away. Does he regret it?"

"He says he did the right thing and he doesn't care what Sigrid or anyone else has to say."

"Bertold probably thinks Andrew let you down. But you didn't want him to fight. You don't want to keep on fighting. Do you think Andrew let you down?"

"He didn't let me down," Sophie said.

"Who else is in the house with you?" Julia asked.

"No one. Well, Andrew is out, but he's coming back in a couple of hours."

"And where's Bertold?"

"I don't know where Bertold is, and I don't care! Probably he's at Sigrid's."

"Let him stay there," Julia said. "He'll see what it's like to be whacked about by stories about Meena. Probably he doesn't know what effect he has on you."

"He does! I've told him."

"Sometimes, Sophie, people are bitter about this thing or that thing and half the time they don't know what they're bitter about, or even know they're bitter, and something happens, and that bitterness fastens itself onto one particular thing. It can be useful, you know, only one particular thing you fasten your hatred on so you can go on loving everything else, but sometimes it happens that you fasten on one thing that isn't good to latch on to: because that particular thing hurts other people."

"You think that's happened to Bertold?"

"Yes," Julia said. "I can't be sure, of course I can't, but I think that's what happened. I believe that."

"So all we have to do is move him on to a different thing?" Sophie asked.

"That's *all* we have to do?" Julia asked

"If that's what has to be done, I'll find a way to do it," Sophie said.

"If you can't, no one can," Julia said. "Besides, you have a very happy marriage. Except for the trouble about Meena."

"That's true," Sophie said. "It *is* true."

"And right now, all this trouble is being caused by people's very best impulses. Sigrid is protecting you because she loves you, and so is Bertold. It's a pity. Everyone means well."

"I'm so tired," Sophie said. "If you don't mind, I'll ring off and go to sleep."

"First take your pills," Julia said. "It's important to *me* that you take your medicine."

"I promise," Sophie said.

"Good," said Julia.

"I'm hanging up now," Sophie said.

"Okay," Julia said. The dial tone returned. You spend a lot of time, Julia thought, mistakenly lamenting your lost youth, but in the end, no matter what your age, youth finds a way to drive you around the bend. Somewhere when time first began, someone discovered youth and how much unhappiness it could cause and decided to make everyone else who came into the world suffer in the same way, fixed it so that even when your own youth, that disease, that fever, was over, a much younger person would come down with it and you'd have to go through it all over again. Damn that Meena! Damn that Bertold! Damn that Sigrid! Damn that snow globe!

FIFTY-FOUR

———

Dear Martin,

Since early last evening, it's been a punishing, angry, scouring wind. We've had winds enough like this in Cornwall, but I can't remember the like of this. I spent a little time trying to describe the voice of this wind—it really does whistle—but it's too large, it defeats me. When the first light made its way here, the birds were calling one to another. Their cries made me think they had been blown off course and were trying to find one another. Then there's that inevitable, wise-looking crow I wrote you about. So far, he's ridden out the storm on his usual bough on the cherry tree at the fringe of the woods where he stares at anyone who goes up into the turret. Yon raven has a greedy look. He watches the turret room as if he's still measuring its worth for his own nest—can make you feel quite guilty at times. Evelyn doesn't like him. She takes his proprietary look seriously and keeps the windows closed when she's up there. She's sure that if we don't take care, he'll get into the turret and from there he'll take over the house.

The wind isn't dying down. Instead the boughs of the great oaks are bending down as if salaaming their own God, then snapping back up again, but the next gust brings them further down and leaves keep them down longer before they come up again. So it's up and down and side to side and the leaves are full out—reminds me of seaweed and its dances under the wild waves in Cornwall. Makes me feel quite at home, really.

I thought the apple tree might go off in one of those gusts, go pinwheeling down the meadow like some kind of crazy gymnast, but it's stood up; it's still there. I've wasted an hour or two going to look at it and see if it's still standing since this windstorm began. Of course, all this took place in pretty dim light. We still have no electricity, unless we use the generator, and we save that for emergencies, so there's a lot of candles lit in times like this, but the house is so full of cracks. I'll be walking up the stairs, and another gust puts out the candle I'm carrying. Matches everywhere. Charlotte's sent Evelyn a cardboard carton full of long matches, the kind meant to light stove and wood fires, so they're finally getting a good workout. A telegram's sure to arrive today or tomorrow, Charlotte saying that Evelyn should immediately pack up and come home and get out of this bloody weather, as if she's never heard of tidal waves or tornadoes in America. They only menace Evelyn if she's in England stuck here with me. Charlotte's presence, of course, would protect her daughter.

Last night. There was no sleeping, so I thought up a contest.

She won the first round. I couldn't think of anything to say about the wind and its pronouncements. So then it was on to what the storm might portend. I won that one, I think, rhyming about the end of the world and such like, that was an inevitable victory, that's one of my themes, not too many other people who could manage as well with it, nor would want to. Then it was the people in the house and the effects of the storm, and of course she won that one. She always would win with that as a topic. Something about the wind having scoured the moon down, turning it to sand, one moment of angel dust and then total darkness, no bells ringing out of belfries, all the big bells filled by that sand that once was the moon. I wish I'd kept that one around so I could copy it out for you, but she made off with that one straightaway, put it in a safe place so the wind couldn't get at it if it uprooted the entire house. Then came the last theme, the animals in the wood, and of course I won that one. She set that topic; she should have known I'd win. But when she read out the words on that sheet of paper, she went into one of her rages, crumpled up the page and threw it at me, hit me on the head with it. It couldn't hurt me, of course, but I had the distinct feeling that she wished the sheet and its poem had been a rock that would have knocked me silly. I suppose I'm competitive enough, no point in lying about that, but why does everything playful turn into a fight to the death? She's like that, you see. I read a poem by someone who's just starting out, who may not even begin, he's so young, and I think, They just keep coming, don't they? There's always another wave right behind us. Probably one of them will swamp us, put us in the shade forever.

But why should that madden either of us? When we've been turned to stone and bone, who's going to read what we've written? I try to persuade her that these young ones are the readers of tomorrow, and in the event, they may never show anything more than that one spark of talent she's so depressed about. It doesn't help. Nothing helps. There's a kind of mad exclusivity in her. If she won't be the best, why should she write at all? Well, we all know that state. But I rather thought you went beyond that when you got older. And yet she has an unholy adoration of those who went before, the Shakespeares and Yeatses and Keatses. They comfort her, their works do, as if they wrote everything for her. Last winter I asked her if Yeats would be sick to his heart if he read some of her best poems thinking he'd now be eclipsed. She looked at me as if I'd gone mad and wanted to know what on earth I was talking about.

Of course these idols of hers are dead and buried. It's the living she can't tolerate. So you already know where this is heading. How can she tolerate the recognition that's been coming to me? She types up my things, she sends them out, she scours the magazines and the papers for announcements of new prizes, and another manuscript of mine goes out, taken, by her, to the Grisleigh upon Shallows post office. She's like a mad Penelope, typing and retyping the same thing again and again. She will see my poems in print, but when she does see them printed, it's days and days in bed with that black cloud stuck to the top of her head like a balloon. So I come to dread my own success. Left on my own, I'd wait until I had a good, thick stack and then I'd send out a few at a time. There's not so much invested in each one, you see. And perspective counts for something. A little time works like a good pair of spectacles. I see things much more quickly when time has passed. This word weighs too much. That syllable is too heavy. What we need here is an "and." But no, it must all be rushed into the great maw of editors and everyone else in the world. I don't want anyone playing Ezra Pound to my T. S. Eliot. I don't mean to say that I want to spend the rest of my life revising what I wrote when I was young and strong. But I'd just as soon let it stay there, brewing. For a while. But Evelyn won't have it. She tells me it's laziness. We must earn money now that we've decided writing is to be our living. I talked her into that, of course, and now if what wasn't a mistake for me is a mistake for her, I'm already paying for it. It's not my nature to think that I have to write to justify my life. I never did bother about justifying myself. I was enough for myself. Maybe the trouble is my conceit. I don't see it, but most people do agree that they need to justify their lives. I prefer animals and flowers. Especially predators, any kind of predators. Wolves kill shamelessly, as well they should. Nature obeys its own laws. If I were walking in the lane and came upon a self-justifying wolf, I'd beat it to death myself. The hawk doesn't open its talons to justify its claim to life. It doesn't open its talons to make a dumb show, meaning to say I can take this chicken because I can justify my life. It takes what it can carry off and it eats happily, without conscience. The violets in the hedgerow don't send up an aria of self-justification. They drink up the rain and they exist, and we don't, at least so far we don't, think they need to justify their petals. As you can see, she's filled me with her guilt. That makes her happy, but I won't stay there wringing my hands and tearing my hair. I'll be out with my reel and fishhook for days and to hell with poems. After three hours, walking or fishing or sleeping for no reason, if it takes that long, she'd be at me saying I was wasting time as if I were spending her money. I can't see how to live that way. Don't say I must ask myself if I can live with her, because I must. I don't want to leave her, to rid myself of her, as you thought after you read my last letter. She is four years younger than I, and at our age, what a huge amount of time is that difference! Sigrid says life will knock the edges off her. The trouble is, I'm not sure I want them knocked off. There are enough smooth creatures about. I think of other people as an army of darning eggs. I don't want one for myself.

But you asked why I'm producing so much work. Evelyn. Of

course, Evelyn. She believes that to be a professional writer, she must spend six to eight hours a day writing whether or not she has anything to write about. So she goes up to her study and closes the door and soon discovers she has nothing to write. But she can't come out of the study during these six or eight hours, because if she's a writer, she *must* be writing, and so she writes in her journal. Pages and pages. They're the hidden treasures, you see, veins of ore that must be turned into gold. Once, only once, I sneaked a peek at them. I'm sorry I did. I was like a surgeon opening a body and finding the dissolution and decay had begun and maggots were already swarming. The most *incredible* self-loathing, writing as if she were already dead and looking back at herself as if she herself were obliged to watch all the processes of decay and putrefaction, pages of the stuff, as if they'd been written by a posthumous person, and she is, sometimes that's what she seems, a posthumous person. Horrible. A lot upsets me, but that's the worst. So now when she gets into a mood, I know what's going on in there, because I peeked into those journals, the worst thing I could have done because I can't exorcise the images. They're going to stay with me, and they've done me damage. You can't unsee what you've already seen. I like to think you *can* unsee what you were never meant to see, I wish I could believe it, but of course, I don't. I remember Dad. He never stopped seeing what showed up in front of his eyes during the war.

Then I try to think how I can make some money, not a lot, but enough to keep me going if I come to a dry spell. I thought of growing avocados. People are suddenly mad for avocados. But some of the farmers say it can't be done in this climate. Possibly part of the time in Cornwall, in the summer, but I don't want to go back there, not yet. I just got out of there. What do you think? About avocados, I mean. Or importing Mexican tiles? Sigrid says this is the wrong country for exotic things. She goes on about beige being an adventurous color here, and if I had the money, by all means buy Mexican tiles and store them up because time marches on, even here, and sooner or later, England will wake up out of its white-painted sleep and everyone will start shouting, "Mexican tiles! Mexican tiles!"

Evelyn doesn't think much of my schemes. When she thinks of money she thinks of school and chalk dust. I tell her that teaching school has killed more hearts than any war, but she thinks differently, so I fancy that one day she's going to wake up and say, "Pack up all your stuff, we're going to a good old American college and we'll have a good old American refrigerator that's taller than I am." We did all right putting things in the river when we were in Cornwall, at least in the winter, and a lot of time in the summer, too, where the current ran cold, and we could do the same thing here, but she won't hear of it. She wants to know if I can't think of something less foolproof for preventing botulism because according to her, the whole British population here ought to long ago have died off from food poisoning The whole thing about two countries, the two cultures that you worried me so about, that's no problem. It keeps me amused and not a lot does these days. Although that Puritan work ethic, I rather dislike that, but I never put up with the British work ethic, even though we all know there's no such thing, especially for two boys who grew up in Cornwall with our mother.

I meant to write about the last few books I'd read, to tell you I sometimes do get away from Shakespeare and do stick my big toe into the moderns, but I've spent all this time covering pages about a silly contest we played in last night's windstorm—which is still going on, by the way. Right now, the sound of the storm's changed; I'd mistake it for planes going over. It reminds me of the war and the way we used to climb up on the cliffs to watch out for

German raids. I'm glad that's over, and the ration books, all of that. Did we ever realize how lucky we were to be children of a shop-keeper? Everyone else half-starved or fat and starchy, while we looked better with every week? I suppose we're set to live forever. Remember all that butter we ate? And the bread Mum baked? And the meat we had, when everyone else was eating canned sardines and trying to think of a relative who'd gone to America and could send them packages? And those terrible grey green peas that came out of a can and tasted of nothing but the can? Evelyn says everyone in America ate those, too, but not because there was nothing else, but because two servings of vegetables had to be eaten a day, and by the second serving, it was too much trouble to clean or peel them and easiest to open a can.

Well, the wind is screaming and Evelyn will be up, huddled beneath the duvet that she claims is too thin, and it is, really, but now it's our own kind of war because we've chosen a life that doesn't give us a heavy pocketful of coins, and if I mention it, if I say we should buy another duvet, spring for it, why should she spend another winter shivering under that thin thing, she'll say, "Only if I write more and get more things accepted. I must write more stories. I must crack that market," and it's more than I can bear, that kind of talk. But if now she's cold in her room, she won't forgive me for not coming in to comfort her, as if I could order the wind to die down—I wish it would keep up; it gives me ideas; it shoots energy into the marrow of my bones—as if there were something I could do to make it warmer. And I could make it warmer if I'd climb into that bed with her. My body's always warm, but hers is always cold, her hands are so cold it's like taking the hand of a dead person between your two warm ones, but it's the right sort of day for going about in a wind like this, the kind of wind you get once in a century or half-century, so I'm going out. But if

I stop and go up to the bedroom, I will end up in the bed, and then I'll be the resentful one, and she'll say, "You're in a black mood, aren't you?" and say it accusingly enough so it stings to hear it.

Not cold there in Jamaica, are you?

My next letter will be more cheerful and about something.

Love,
Peter

FIFTY-FIVE

—

JULIA AWAKENED EARLY, delighted to find that the lightning and thunder were still making nuisances of themselves. In the new light, everything was silvery, almost phosphorescent. Very mysterious, a light like that. She turned on her side so that she faced the windows and prepared to enjoy the morning. Inevitably, she found herself thinking about Sophie. She would call any minute. But perhaps she had some time for staring out of the windowpanes. Sophie couldn't have gotten much sleep last night.

Sophie was in the back seat of their car, driving back from Massachusetts to New York, back to Julia's and Matt's house. She had visited a friend of her father's, and then been to visit her grandmother,

Charlotte, and, during that visitation, her grandmother had refused to let Sophie take away any photographs of her mother, so that finally Sophie had stolen four or five of them. She had been barely twenty then, already once divorced, completely unsure of what she wanted to do, and so Peter had suggested that Sophie be sent to Julia. "See what you can do with her," he said. "I surely can't."

"What's the trouble?" Julia asked him. "Give me a hint." She waited for the pause that immediately followed.

"She and Meena are at each other's throats," he finally said.

"I'd say that's enough of a hint," Julia said.

Two days later, she and Matt found themselves waiting at Kennedy Airport, waiting for Sophie's plane to land. "Pay attention," Julia said nervously. "We only met her a couple of times."

"She'll remember you," Matt said. "She called you the Duchess of Windsor."

"She didn't mean anything by it."

"She said it was because of your hair." Julia nodded. In those days, she had black hair she wore long, parted in the middle, and twisted into a French knot. From the front, she did resemble the Duchess of Windsor, and in those days, Peter, who was careful to remain thin and to dress well, largely at Meena's insistence, had been sitting next to Julia when Sophie snapped a picture of them with her Polaroid. "The Duke and Duchess of Windsor," Sophie announced happily when she saw the picture developing.

"And what an unholy couple they were," Julia said.

"They didn't hurt anyone," Matt said.

"No? What about the whole nation?" Julia asked. How lucky, she thought then, to have found Matt, and she was about to say something to that effect when the passengers began to disembark. "Stand up, stand up!" Julia said, still afraid they would miss her and leave her stranded at the airport.

"There she is," Matt said. He towered over Julia and caught sight of Sophie first. Then Julia saw her. The young girl with the blond hair neatly pulled back into a ponytail was nowhere to be seen. Instead, her hair was very long and red and tumbled around her shoulders, halfway down her waist. "You won't have trouble spotting her if you have to meet her in the city," Matt said.

They took her home and the long conversation that was to last two weeks began. Sophie had not yet settled on maths. What name should she use if she began to paint or write? Because surely she would do one of those things. Should she call herself Sophie Graves, or should she call herself Sophie Grovesnor, or should she use neither of those names and invent a surname of her own?

"Isn't there a painter named Freud?" Matt asked. "Wasn't Sigmund Freud his father? What should the son be calling himself? With all respect to your parents, Freud's name is even better known."

"I don't know what to do," Sophie said.

Julia understood that the difficulty was not in the name. The burden lay in taking up a profession in which she would be measured against either or both of her parents, and would they mind her competing against them? "Your father won't worry about competition, even if you end up doing better work," Julia said, "and your mother isn't there to worry about anything. You may *think* she's hovering about somewhere feeling jealous of you, but she isn't, and I doubt if she'd be unhappy to see you try."

"She would, I think," Sophie said.

"*If* she were alive," Julia said.

"Sometimes I think she is," Sophie said, her voice going soft and haunted.

"She's not. Unfortunately," Julia said. By now Julia had a sharp understanding of Meena, and Evelyn was someone she had comprehended from the beginning. If Evelyn were alive now, Julia thought, she'd make short work of Meena. Not even two bites and that would be the end of her.

"So you think I should try?" Sophie asked.

"*Must* try," Julia corrected her. "And we'll have a séance and speak to Evelyn. I'm sure she won't mind."

"A séance?" Sophie asked, her eyes lighting up.

"You know how your father likes such things," Julia said.

Then they had two days off when Sophie went to see her grandmother, and when they picked her up, and she was back in the car, she described what the visit had been like, and suddenly Sophie stopped speaking in the middle of a sentence, stopped abruptly in the middle. Julia and Matt looked at one another. They turned around and saw Sophie, felled, sound asleep on the back seat, her red hair tumbling over her face, down toward the car floor. She looked, Julia thought, like an Irish setter who had been subjected to unspeakable experiments. "The grandmother," Julia said. Matt nodded and kept his eyes on the road.

But when Sophie went back, she met Bertold, and he enjoyed teaching her mathematics and she admitted to her love of the subject and she did so well that she was soon a growing eminence in her field, an eminence with no degree.

"She'll have an honorary degree in no time," Matt predicted.

"I don't understand it," Peter had said. "I can't credit it. She must be an idiot savant. Who would have thought it? We looked to Andrew for mathematical genius."

"Well, you were looking the wrong way," Julia said.

And Sophie had taken her mother's name, so that now she was known as Sophie Graves. "Not a cheerful name," as Matt had often observed.

—

OUTSIDE, THE GREY light had gone brighter and moved up the sky so that just above the rooftops there was a stripe of brilliant, shining silver. I haven't called Eliza, Julia thought remorsefully. Really, I have to get myself out of this room and go around to the galleries and buy up enough of her jewelry to satisfy me until I next get back here, but just as she was considering getting up and getting dressed, the phone rang.

"Sophie?" she said tentatively.

"No, it's Sigrid. Can you go around to Sophie's house right away? She doesn't want to talk to me and I can't go through it again."

"Go through what?" Julia asked.

"Bertold was here, and he called her to ask how she was, and she's hysterical now. I don't know what he said, but she's trying to find something in the house and she can't, and it's Evelyn all over again. I can't go through it again."

"I'll go over," Julia said. "I'll call her first."

"Yes, call, or she'll think it's me or Bertold. She's shrieking, so I don't know if she'd even hear the bell go."

"I'll call her," Julia said again. She called Sophie's number. The phone rang and continued ringing. Just as she was about to give up, someone answered and a shrill voice screeched into the telephone, "I don't want you over here! Where are they? Tell me where they are! That's all I need to know!"

"Sophie?" Julia said.

"Julia?" Sophie said.

"Weren't you supposed to call me this morning when you got up?" Julia asked.

"I can't find them!" Sophie said. "Can't anyone understand? I can't find them!"

"I'm coming over there. I'm getting a cab. Just be sure to let me in. Sophie? Did you understand me?"

"Yes!"

What can she be looking for? Julia asked as she hurried into her uniform of the season, a pair of black velvet slacks and a black sweater. She supposed she'd find out soon enough. She poked under the bed until she found her handbag, thrust her feet into her moccasins, and started down the stairs. "Taxi!" she called the instant she was out in the street. And one magically appeared.

When she got to the house, the front door was open. She went in and closed the door behind her. She heard the door latch. Inside, she heard

sobs. Sophie was not going to be hard to find. The commotion was coming from upstairs. She went up slowly, favoring her sore right knee. The
sound was louder, but not loud enough. All the way up to the third floor,
she thought. Halfway there, she heard the sound of banging, someone
shouting, "Bloody fucking hell! Where did he put it? He put it somewhere!
He wouldn't throw it out! Where did he *put* it?" She went through the
enormous bathroom into the study that lay beyond it. A thin young
woman bent double was pulling things out of a chest of drawers and
throwing them behind her. They sailed into the air and joined the bank of
things already on the floor.

"Sophie?" Julia said.

The woman stood up. It was Sophie, her blond hair tangled, her face
red and swollen, almost unrecognizable, distorted by rage.

"What are you looking for?" Julia asked.

"My marriage photos!" Sophie shrieked as if that were self-evident. "We
had photographers take pictures. *And they're not there!*"

"They're somewhere," Julia said. "Where's Bertold?"

"At Sigrid's. She thinks I need a keeper!"

"Oh, I don't think so. You know how your aunt overstates things. What
she means is that you should calm down. What started all this?" Julia
asked. "Move over. I'll help you look for the pictures."

"Is *that* how they say *calm down* these days?" Sophie shrieked. "Look for
the pictures?"

"Look, Sophie," Julia said, "I haven't done anything to you. I haven't
said you need a keeper. I don't have the vaguest idea what you're talking
about. I don't know what the pictures look like. I don't know if we're looking for an album or a paper sack of snapshots. Give me a break."

Sophie sat back and swiveled to face Julia. "Sigrid didn't tell you what
this is about?" she asked.

"She told me you were in a state, that's all."

"And you came all the way out here because she said I was in a state?"

"Do I need more of a reason?" Julia asked.

Sophie burst into racking sobs.

"Well, it has something to do with Bertold, I can see that," Julia said, "or you wouldn't be looking for your wedding pictures. If you find them, what do you want with them? Do you want to cut him out of the pictures? Cut out his face? Scratch them out with a pen? What?"

"Are *you* mad?" Sophie shrieked when she got her breath.

"Not yet," Julia said. "But I'm losing patience."

"I want to see those pictures," Sophie said, her voice dropping, becoming metallic, "to see if he looked like the liar he is now."

"Well, that certainly clears everything up," Julia said.

"I asked him when he was coming back, and he said not until I'd laid down the law. To Meena! He wants me to lay down laws to that woman!"

"I suppose he should know better than that," Julia said.

"And Sigrid put him up to it! How can you be her friend?"

"Sophie," Julia said. "I don't know if you and I would be friends if we were also related."

"Help me find the pictures!" Sophie shrieked again, going back to digging through the bureau drawers.

"What's going on here?" asked a male voice behind them. Andrew. Thank God! Julia thought.

"Um. Your sister's a little upset," Julia said. "Sigrid told her she thought she needed a keeper."

"What?"

"That's what Sigrid said, although I think that's a bit hard."

"I've not been gone for even twenty-four hours," Andrew said, staring at Sophie, "and the whole family goes berserk."

"Well, it's nice to see you're in your right mind," Julia said.

"Sophie," Andrew said, moving until he stood over her, "tell me what happened. Right *now*."

"You'll only side with the rest of them!" Sophie screamed.

Andrew looked at Julia. "You tell me," he said.

"I'm not really sure. I can't say for sure. But I think Sophie and Bertold had one of their arguments, about Meena, I mean, and Bertold went to stay at Sigrid's."

"Out of the frying pan," said Andrew.

"That's it!" Sophie shrieked. "That's it exactly."

"What were they arguing about?" Andrew asked, again addressing Julia.

"He thought Sophie ought to lay down the law. About Meena."

"Sigrid's the one who told him to say that!" Sophie screamed out.

Andrew sat down on a cedar chest near the far wall and riffled his hair with his hand. A shock of dark hair fell over his right eye.

"Sophie. Your turn," he said.

"Try and make some sense," Julia put in. Sophie looked murderously at her, but then thought better of shouting at her.

"You know how furious I get at Meena?" Sophie asked.

"Lower your voice," Andrew said.

"Why? Because the neighbors will hear me?"

"To hell with the neighbors," he said. "You're giving me a headache."

"You know how furious I get at Meena," she said again.

"Yes. Everyone does," Andrew said.

"You may not know that *Bertold* gets even *more* furious and then he stabs it all into me!" Sophie shouted, her voice rising.

"Bertold gets more furious about Meena than you do?"

"Yes."

"And then he shouts at you because you don't punish Meena?" he asked.

"Finally!" Sophie shouted triumphantly. "Finally he's gotten it right!"

"Sophie!" Julia said.

"Don't waste your breath," Andrew put in. "It won't do any good, not when she gets in a state like this."

"She doesn't *have* to stay in a state like this," Julia told him.

Meanwhile, Sophie had dived back into the last of the bureau drawers. "I found it! I found it!" she stood up, triumphantly waving something.

"And what is it?" Andrew asked.

"My wedding album!"

"That explains everything," he said.

"You think Bertold's after my inheritance! Sigrid told me."

"Maybe he is," Andrew said. "All you two have is debts."

"*He doesn't want Meena's money!*" Sophie screamed.

"Well, he wouldn't mind having it," Julia put in mildly.

"But that's not why he goes on about Meena!" Sophie shouted.

"If you carry on screaming, I'm walking straight out," Andrew said. He sat on the chest and waited to see what would happen. "I thought he might be after your money. I had no clue that Daddy's inheritance was causing this kind of trouble."

"Nor did anyone," Sophie said. "I don't go around telling everyone when Bertold and I have trouble. Meena's going to be the end of my marriage."

"Don't be silly," Andrew said, to Julia's great relief. Now she would not have to say that herself. "What we can do, and what we should do, is walk away," he said. "Now, that seems like an even better solution. If you're really strapped for money, I can lend you some. Not much, mind you," he told his sister. "I know how you go through money."

"And if she handed over the money she's supposed to give us?" Sophie said.

"If you continue saying things like that, Bertold will persist in pressuring you about Meena," he said. "Is that idea beyond you? Right now?"

"Of course not," Sophie said, collapsing onto the small mountain of clothes on the floor and opening her wedding album.

"What do you want with that?" he asked her.

But Sophie had already opened the album and was absorbed in it. Andrew got up and stood over his sister, staring down at the album. "That's you and Bertold," he told her, slightly puzzled.

"You can't see it in his eyes," she said. "The lying. He promised. He said I'd have whatever I wanted."

"Meaning what?" Andrew asked her.

"When we got married, he said I'd have whatever I wanted," she said, crying softly. "He'd see to it that he made me happy. And now look!"

Matters were slowly becoming clearer to Julia. "Everyone says that before he gets married," Julia said. "Matt told me the same thing."

"He *did* make you happy."

"He helped to make me happy," Julia said. "But someone can't make you happy when you're not."

"He's *deliberately* making me unhappy!" Sophie cried.

"No, he's not," Andrew said. "He thinks he's doing the right thing. He thinks you won't be happy unless you fight Meena. And win."

"I can't!" Sophie cried.

"I know," Andrew said. "I know you can't."

"You believe that?" Sophie asked her brother.

"Of course. That's why I'm stepping in. I had to when I saw you couldn't do it. You'd been trying to deal with her long enough. Fair is fair."

"You believe me?" Sophie asked again.

"I told you," Andrew said.

"Your father used to say, 'All I ever tried to do was make people happy, and the result was I made everyone unhappy. I tried to please everyone, and in the end I pleased no one,'" Julia said.

"He said that?" Andrew asked Julia.

"Many times," Julia said. "He was never really a fighter. Isn't that why you're all in trouble now?"

"He said that," Andrew said softly.

"Yes, yes," Julia said. "Many, many times. But he couldn't change what he was."

"And everyone thought he was such a monster," Andrew said wonderingly.

"Maybe it is monstrous, trying to please everyone," Julia said.

"He was never monstrous," Andrew said. "I would have said weak."

"And you would have been right," Julia said.

"He was *not* weak and he was *not* monstrous," Sophie said, rounding on Julia.

"Then it's probably also true that Bertold is not a liar who wants to destroy you," Julia said.

"She has a point there," Andrew said to Sophie. "You're upset and confused. I'll make you a drink. Can you drink these days?"

"Watered-down sherry," Sophie said.

Andrew went off to get it. "Why did you say those things about Daddy?" Sophie asked Julia.

"He said them himself. I'm only repeating what he said to me."

"I'm so confused! I'm so unhappy!" she cried out.

"Sophie," Julia said, "I'm getting tired of telling you to calm down. It's time for you to calm yourself down." Sophie fell silent and stared at Julia, and then stared at the floor. Ah, thought Julia. Silence.

"Right-o," Andrew said, reappearing. "That will be the day, Sophie. When you learn to calm yourself down."

"At least I have the nerve to upset myself!" Sophie exclaimed. "I don't go through life pretending to be a stone!"

"He's not the one you're mad at," Julia said. "He's trying to help."

"He lives in a cloud!" Sophie exclaimed.

"I can certainly see why he wants to help you," Julia said. She looked up in time to see Andrew smiling at her. My God, Julia thought. He is the image of Peter. Then she looked hard at Sophie. She was the image of Evelyn, her mother.

"So," Julia said, shaking her head slightly as if to clear her thoughts, "what do we think of this plan?" she asked Andrew. "You accuse Bertold of harassing Sophie to get his hands on Meena's money."

"It sounds like a riddle, the way you put it," Andrew said.

"Nevertheless," Julia said. "What do you think?"

"I don't know. Sometimes I do think so," Andrew said. "I may bring it up again when I next see him. I should have talked to him before this. Maybe he doesn't know what people think. If he doesn't like us thinking he's after Sophie's money, that might stop him in his tracks and then Sophie can get away from his horns."

"So now I'm the matador about to be run down by the bull, and the bull's my husband?" Sophie asked.

"Exactly," Julia said. "Isn't that how you've been feeling?"

"Yes," said Sophie.

"She can pack more sulkiness into a single syllable," Andrew said. "Our father used to say that."

"He was right about a lot of things. He used to say, 'Very dollar-tropic, is Sophie.'"

"She is," Andrew agreed. "Very dolor-tropic as well."

"Don't speak of me as if I'm not here!" Sophie exclaimed. "But it may be that Bertold *has* changed. He does go on about money. It would be terrible if he had changed. I want him the way he was."

"Let me tell you a story," Julia said. "This is a story about my friend Eliza. Penny knew her as well. It's a story about marriage and it's a story about character. Do you want to hear it?"

"Oh, yes," Sophie said. "Daddy was always telling us stories. Now no one does."

"Remember my friend Eliza, the Swedish woman, the jeweler? She told me this story. After seventeen years of living with Ian, a divorced man at least ten years older than she was, she wanted to marry him, but he refused to take the chance. So, in many respects, the man she lived with was the opposite of your father. In any case, from the beginning Eliza knew there would be no children, and in the beginning, that hadn't seemed an obstacle. Eliza had her work. She had a reputation to establish, and she had Ian. What more could she ask for? He had been working, but he retired early, did everything for her, the cooking and the cleaning, always told her how excellent her work was, carefully judged each object she produced. It was early days, and she paid little attention to what she considered minor eccentricities—his refusal to harbor a cat because cats killed birds, his complaints when she sat on the edge of their bed, because the mattress would begin to sag near the edge. He would never answer the telephone and said that most calls were trivial and interrupted one for no reason, and so he would unplug the telephone so that the ringing would not trouble him.

"One day she rang me from her workshop and said that the strangest thing had happened the day before. She had stayed home to work, and while she was up in her room soldering things, Ian was outside underneath his Range Rover. Eliza said that the Range Rover was so old that Ian spent more time communing with it than he did with her. He had long ago built his own platform on wheels so that he could slide back and forth beneath it.

"While he was under the car, he saw a pair of woman's legs in very high-heeled shoes, very flash. Evidently, he assumed that the woman had her own reasons for stopping just there, and he didn't come out from beneath the car to see if she wanted directions or anything.

"*Then* the woman said, 'You haven't moved since the day I left you.' It turned out to be Flora, Ian's first wife. He rolled himself out, but he didn't get off that platform. He stayed where he was and looked up at the woman. And she said, 'I thought I'd see how you were managing,' and he said, 'As you see.' Then he got up so he could get a good look at her face.

"He said she looked just the same, but now she had brassy blond hair and her hair was curly, not long and dirty blond, the way it used to be. And she had an attaché case, so that made him wonder why she needed that. But of course he didn't ask. And when she didn't seem to have anything to say, he said, 'Well, I'll get on with my work then, shall I?' and she said, 'I can't believe it. When I left you, you were beneath that car, and you're still beneath it,' and he said, 'I do come out now and then. Especially in cold weather.' Then she asked him, 'Are you married?' and he said, 'No,' and he had already slid back beneath the car, you see, but when she saw that, she was angry and walked away, and he saw her legs going down the street in those flash high heels. And a handbag so colorful it made her look as if she were carrying a tame parrot, or a dead one.

"He went back in, and when Eliza came down later, he told her what had happened. She said she'd have liked to have seen his first wife, but he said no, that wouldn't have been a good thing. Eliza would only have asked him which one was prettier and was the first wife thinner than Eliza was. She would have asked him if he was sorry she had ever left him. Eliza would have asked all those things and more. But he couldn't be bothered, and there was nothing more to be said. Eliza asked me what I thought of it."

"What *did* you think of it?" Sophie asked. "And what does it have to do with me and Bertold?"

"Well," Julia said, "now when I think about it, I'm sorry for the first wife, the woman with the high-heeled shoes, and how it had turned out—to go back to the house where she had once lived with him, to find him older and very much heavier, his hair snow-white, and worst of all, unchanged. As if nothing had happened. She must have felt as if she'd never left, because there he was, still beneath the Range Rover, tinkering at something or other, as if she had never really gone away, as if life had gone on exactly as it was before, as if her leaving had not left so much as a seam, her ex-husband no more communicative than the day she left, only telling her he wasn't married. He wasn't interested in whether or not she was. He wasn't interested in *her*, not in the least. Wearing the same kind of clothes, even that, all the same. All the ex-wife saw were the same two legs dressed in jeans, protruding from the same Range Rover. So you see," Julia concluded, "people don't change easily. If they change at all."

"Sophie," Andrew said. "She's just like Daddy. She goes by way of China to make a point about what's happening here."

"Oh, yes, it's a story with a moral," Julia agreed.

"You think he's changed? Bertold?" Sophie asked Julia.

"Did the man under the Range Rover change?" Julia asked.

"No," Sophie said.

"Well, there's your answer," Andrew said to Sophie. "That story should cheer you up."

"It does, but it's a bit terrifying all the same," Sophie said.

"That's another problem altogether," Andrew said. "The next time you think you want to change Bertold, think about that story."

Julia laughed and then so did Sophie.

"I think," Julia said, "you ought to go downstairs with your brother and I'll clean up here."

"Oh, no, you don't," Andrew said. "I've heard all about your knees and other ailments. Well," he said, smiling at Julia, "Sigrid has to talk about *something* in the middle of the night while the two of us play canasta, so why shouldn't we talk about you?"

"Canasta," Julia said. "My grandmother played canasta. I can't even play gin. Well, I can play gin, but I don't know how to count the points."

"You sit on the chest, and Sophie and I will clean up, and then you can lie on the bed while we go downstairs and talk things over. Agreed?"

"Wonderful," Julia said feelingly.

"You drink this watered sherry. I brought two glasses," Andrew said, handing her a glass. Julia drank the sherry down, and then sat down on the chest. It was covered with pillows, and it suddenly seemed as if it were meant to be slept on. She lay down on her side, watching the two of them. They worked quickly and efficiently. Order would be restored at once. "Your father once thought about growing avocados," Julia said. "To make money."

"Avocados in England?"

"He said you could grow them in Cornwall," Julia said sleepily.

"Julia, please get some sleep. I've kept you up all night and then I woke you this morning."

"You didn't. Sigrid did." She felt tipsy.

"Go to sleep," Sophie said.

She's smiling at me! Julia thought. They were both smiling at her.

"Here," Sophie said, coming up to her with something golden in her hand. "It's a little bell. Ring it if you want something."

"That's very nice of you, Sophie," Julia said. She turned toward the wall and was promptly sound asleep.

"So that's Julia," Andrew said to his sister.

"That's Julia," Sophie said.

"He used to listen to her," Andrew said with wonder.

"You see why," Sophie said.

FIFTY-SIX

———

THE BIRDS DISLIKE this wind, no one likes this wind. There are great boughs fallen on the lawns. There will be gashes in the trees. I'll be out there with a tar pot and a brush keeping the sap in so the tree can't bleed to death. Everyone looks at a tree and thinks, it lasts forever, people make houses out of its wood; it's strong, wooden houses go on forever, and then something stirs the air, wind, that thin veily stuff that yields so fast you forget it exists, stirs it so hard it whips the great branches of trees, makes you run into your house, tears things out of your hand, sends your hat spinning down the lane and into mud puddles, and the rain drips down your neck and inside, against your back and waist, and gives you the kind of chill you were always told would give you your death, but what if you want to catch your death? Could you catch your death if you stayed out in a wind like that? No, it only happens if you don't want it to happen. I could go out there now and wait for the lightning to hit me and wait to catch my death, and what would happen? I'd come in scoured and clean, no one to sympathize with me, and no one would, not with what I'd look like.

And the papers. Would the rain wash the papers clean? Sophie wants to write a book. At least Sigrid thinks so. Someone might publish it. *Stop the book! Stop the book!* I told Julian, but all he said was, "Keep quiet and no one will think it's you. If you don't say anything, no one will make the connection, surely not." And they wouldn't. He was right. But he forgot about interviews. Everyone loves to see pictures of Sophie. She will make perfectly clear what she thinks of me. She will speak of the terms of her father's will. She will speak of my hatred of her, how she always knew she was second-hand, but still, she hoped; how I wanted to keep Peter all to myself even though I didn't have him in the end. If she writes that, someone will look into it—but no one has looked into it—still, someone might. They might find out about Clare. Why would anyone read Sophie's autobiography? She is not important. But if for some reason people were to read it, they would find it all there, all Sophie's resentments, all Sophie's hints about how I stole chunks of her flesh, the stepmother who ate her children. They would see me as Medea. What an indictment that would be!

I can't dismiss the two children out of hand. No, they're stronger than I thought. But we can't all exist in the same world. It's really between the two of us, Sophie or me. She's younger, she's prettier, but she's not as strong. She has that one great weakness. She wants me to love her, even still she does, even Andrew still does. They cry off saying they won't struggle over a dead man's money, but who can resist it? Money is money. Everyone wants it. They're not made of finer stuff than the rest of us, they'll want their share, they'll come after it. It's like baiting a trap for a wolf, that money. You always know the wolf will come, but there *are* wolves who bite through their legs to get free of traps. They might be capable of it, Sophie might, and Andrew!

I never thought he could stand up to me, but now he does, even though I make myself the wind that howls around Willow Grove, the gale that tears down boughs hundreds of years old. He dares defy me; how could it happen? It must be Peter, speaking through them, his will loose at last, the weakness in him dead when he died, but the strength was turned loose, and when his skin broke open deep in the ground, the strength worked its way up, beetled its way up, slowly, through roots and rocks, reached the surface and began to howl, became this wind, every night howling around Willow Grove. Other people say they can't hear it, but it's inside; it's in the turret window; it follows me downstairs, it howls from dusk until dawn, it turns back into Peter, his face averted, hidden, walking out of the woods, the fringe of the woods. There's no wind when he's about, coming out and going in, but when he goes in for the night, goes in for good, then the wind starts up again. The dead bell, you can hear it in the wind, all the people who ever died, you can hear it, all of them blaming me, as if I have existed since the world began, as if the world implicates me in all those deaths, not only human deaths, but animal deaths, plant deaths, droughts, the death of everything: the wind says I'm to blame.

You think like this when you don't sleep, isn't it so? It isn't anything to worry about, isn't it so? The two crows on the bough, in the morning: they'll agree with me, isn't it so? Look, the light is coming up. I'll ask them, "Crows, it's because I don't sleep, isn't it so?" And when I ask them, the two crows turn their beaks toward one another, and the big crow turns back toward me and says, "*It is not so,*" and the smaller crow says, "*Stop the wind, it's your fault, you're tearing down the nests,*" and the big crow says again, "*It is not so.*" But the armchair will soon speak; it is striped, powerful things are striped, as are spotted things, not dirty spotted things, but naturally spotted—those are powerful as well. When the armchair speaks it will say, "*It is so,*" and I shall fall into that chair and sleep a deep, restorative sleep and the man will stop coming out of the woods and the wind will stop howling, or howl as winds are meant to howl, saying nothing, implying nothing. How can wind make accusations? It cannot, it cannot do it. It's so, isn't it so?

—

"MEENA, YOU HAVE to do something," Julian said into the phone.

But Meena was in the middle of preparations for the evening's dinner, to be shared with the widow of another Nobel winner. "I'm making salmon," she said irrelevantly, or so he thought. "I have a freezer of it left. I can't stomach it myself, you see, but everyone thinks so much of it, especially when I tell them Peter himself caught it."

"You have to do something!" Julian said with considerably greater irritation than before.

"I *am* doing something," Meena said. "I'm just going to run down to the village and buy a loaf of bread for luncheon sandwiches, and then I'll ring you back."

"Meena—" Julian said, and the line went dead. "Are you there, Meena?" No answer. She'll find out soon enough, he thought spitefully. She can't say I didn't try to warn her.

—

THE LITTLE MARKET appeared deserted when Meena opened the door. Good, she thought. I'll be back before Bettina opens her eyes; she'll hear the coffee brewing in the pot and she'll find my note. She looked at the woman next to the till, smiling. She had known that woman all her life. But Mrs. Ladderstall did not return her smile. Instead she stooped down, picked up a large stack of magazines, put them out on the counter, and began sorting them. The pile of magazines closest to Meena was *Elle*.

"I wouldn't think so many around here would have need of fashion advice," Meena said cheerfully.

Mrs. Ladderstall, a stout woman who wore her hair in the old style, braided and then molded to a crown on top of her head, looked at Meena, and said, "Is that so?"

"Have times changed so greatly?" Meena asked, refusing to take note of the ice in the woman's voice.

"Fashion's for them who can afford it," Mrs. Ladderstall said, finally turning to look at her. "The High Street's not for me. It's Oxfam I need."

Oxfam? Meena thought. Now what? "I'll just have a loaf of your good whole wheat bread," she said.

"If that's *all* you want," Mrs. Ladderstall said, "it's where it always was, back round near the Mr. Kipling's." There was no mistaking the strange note in her voice. Was it sarcasm? No, Meena thought, as she stooped down to pick up a bread. It's contempt. Contempt for me. How extraordinary. "Then that's all you want, then?" Mrs. Ladderstall said as she went back to the front counter. And it seemed to Meena that she pushed a pile of *Elle*s closer to her as if she were inviting her to take the whole stack.

"A very interesting issue, is it?" Meena asked.

"Some might say so," Mrs. Ladderstall said.

"I'll just take one, then," Meena said.

"Only one?"

"Only one," Meena said firmly, although by now she could feel an attack of what she called "The Trembles" coming on. "I don't need one, let alone two." She pushed a five-pound note across the counter and waited for the change. In exchange, a plastic sack was also pushed toward her. Well, well, Meena thought. How things have changed. Before, she always bagged what I bought. So, Meena thought, I have fallen in her eyes. How strange, she thought again. "I see you still have chocolate rabbits," Meena said. "Usually they sell right out."

"Used to be that parents bought them for the little children," Mrs. Ladderstall said. "But you wouldn't know about that."

"No, mine have been gone for some time, flown the nest, as the Americans say," she answered quite gaily, for which she was greeted by a snort. "Well, I'll just be going," Meena said, her voice shaking slightly. "Another busy day. Almost like a day when Peter was still here." Surely the mention of Peter would bring the woman to herself.

"Grmmmph," said Mrs. Ladderstall, quite literally sniffing at her.

Meena fled the shop and went back to her beige Range Rover still safe in the car park. When she had gotten in and slammed the door, she pulled out the magazine and looked at it. Goldie Hawn on the cover. Nothing strange about that. Then she looked down at the printed line near the bottom: *SOPHIE GRAVES TALKS ABOUT LIFE AFTER HER FATHER.* Oh, my God, Meena thought. She searched for the table of contents, cursing at fashion magazines that thought it so chic to hide what lurked in their pages. So close to the front, not buried in the back! Why would a glossy magazine like this one, reeking of perfume, put an article about Sophie up front? Something about the queen, something about Prince William, Goldie Hawn, then the latest fashions for fall, and Sophie! Coming even before an article about what to do when your man loses interest! I shall drive home and read this, Meena thought, but she thought of Bettina, waiting for her, right this moment, no doubt, probably eating a croissant and slathering on homemade cherry jelly. No, no, I shall read it now, she decided, and opened the magazine to page twenty-two. There was a huge picture, a portrait, really, of Sophie. She took up an entire page. She was standing in her red parlor with its white trim, and in back of her was the grand chandelier she remembered so well, and in her arms, she held her little toy poodle. She wore a gold gown of some sort, beautiful but not formal, but all the same, Meena had to concede, quite commanding. Stunning, really. The side was fastened by brown velvet bows, a sure sign that Sophie had made the gown herself. She should have gone to a proper shop. How like her to be photographed in *Elle* wearing a creation of her own making, when if she'd wanted to help out one of her many friends slaving away in their boutiques, she could have used one of their dresses. *An entire page!* Meena thought. Standing there as if she were the Queen of England! And what was that silver rope full of seed pearls twining around her long neck like a snake? Oh, of course! A creation of Eliza the jeweler! So Julia was somewhere nearby. Was Julia up to something? Was she helping Sophie? I'm ignoring Julia at my peril, Meena thought. But Julia never gives up her secrets. Peter used to swear by that.

Then her eyes caught on a paragraph in the middle of the first column. "It doesn't fall to everyone to lose a mother *twice*, but such things happen. You adjust and go on. What makes it hard is knowing that your mother— well, you thought of her that way, even if she was your stepmother—has turned on you and wants to strip away everything your father left for you. My father's death was a dreadful blow, but this is even worse, as if my *second* mother—because, after all, that's how I did think of her—doesn't think I'm worthy of having a snapshot to remember him by."

I shall have her killed! Meena thought. I shall ring up some of the local toughs and have them fire her house! They've always been loyal to me! We all grew up together! But her eyes were stinging, and she now understood Mrs. Ladderstall's treatment of her. Of course. Sophie and Andrew grew up here together as well. They played with all the other local children, and now one of them, Sophie, was announcing that she, Meena, was stealing from her. How could that rag print such a thing! Surely they had heard of libel? She would get straight on to her solicitor. Meanwhile, her eyes again settled on the page. "Of course, my brother is not to be given anything my father specified. My *mother* refuses to allow him back into the house to repossess his old books." What was this, a court deposition? What was the magazine thinking of? What was in that box on the next page?

It was the List of Wish! Of course, some things had been cut out, but not much, not as far as she could see, and predictably there had been some paraphrasing, but there it was, virtually word for word. She's not going to get away with this! Meena hissed aloud, and burst into enraged tears. Someone going by—Mr. Ladderstall—stopped, turned, took in the scene, and looked at her with curiosity. I've got to get out of here, Meena thought. I've got to read this carefully. But not in front of Bettina! I'll drive to Julian's. No, I can't do that. I can't leave Bettina there as if she were an old relative. I have to go back. I have to finish reading that bloody article. She started the car, made an abrupt right turn, and found herself at the entrance to a curved track that ran up to an immense summerhouse, pulled in, and cut the motor. More about a book Sophie planned to write, *Poison*; oh, why had she not seen the meaning of it sooner! People thought of her, of Meena, as the keeper of the flame, a *venerable* person, someone of importance had said that, *who* had said that? She would have to rally her supporters. *More* about Sophie's many illnesses, made worse, evidently, by her stepmother's refusal to admit they were real, although an ambulance had been needed to take Sophie and her imaginary ailments to the hospital each time she felt ill. More about *Evelyn*? What could Sophie possibly know about Evelyn? All she remembered was seeing her from the back while she was washing dishes or doing something of the sort. Now Sophie is saying, "Of course, after my mother's death came a long line of women all wanting to take her place, and my father's single weakness was marrying the worst of the lot." Well! That disposes of both of us, Meena thought, Elfie as well as me, and something about a prize Sophie had just won, proceeds to be donated to Children's Relief. Donated! When she hasn't a bean!

For a wild moment, Meena considered the idea that this might be the *only* copy with such an interview, no other such copies existed, but then she remembered Mrs. Ladderstall pushing the substantial pile of identical magazines toward her. If I drive very quickly to Julian's, I can discuss this with him and not rudely leave Bettina waiting. These Europeans, she thought. They behave like aristocrats. She was about to turn the key in the ignition when there was a sharp rap at the window next to her. She jumped in her seat and her elbow somehow hit the horn, which blared out into the stillness.

"What are you needing here?" asked a rough voice. "This isn't a public thoroughfare, you know." Meena turned toward him. Mr. Brown, caretaker of this estate and so many others. Long ago, she had wondered at it, how immaculate the owners of second houses kept their grounds even when they did not intend to return, perhaps not for years. Of course, she had approved of the tidiness, if not the expense. What did people need with two nests? Best to have one house, fit it out splendidly, and if it became necessary to spend time in another place, for a short time, of course for a short time only, then a rental was the sensible thing, everything taken care of for you, no taxes to pay, no repairs to arrange and pay for, and you left without a backward glance whenever you pleased. She had expressed this opinion often enough, and undoubtedly Mr. Brown came to hear of it. She more than suspected he held the same opinion, but he would keep it quiet; his income depended on the spendthriftiness of these country house owners. Why hadn't Peter thought of becoming caretaker of the wealthy instead of dreaming about raising avocados, she'd never seen an avocado in her life until she met him, and doubted if most people here had, either, except for the visiting local gentry. Peter would have been the perfect caretaker and he would have enjoyed every moment of it, all the conversations, how he loved listening to other people talk, especially if they didn't include his own wife.

"Oh, Mrs. Grovesnor, it's you," Mr. Brown said. "I guessed as much from the Range Rover. You've gone out of the way." Could it be true? Did she hear disapproval in his voice? Did he read *Elle*? No, of course not, but every other house he looked after had people in it who did.

"I thought my tire had gone flat," Meena said. Mr. Brown walked around the car and said, "Tires are just fine, Mrs. Grovesnor. You can go on. Any news of the children?"

"So you will insult me!" Meena cried out, backing up suddenly, making a U-turn, and roaring back out of the track, leaving an astonished Mr. Brown in her wake. "How dare they feel contempt for *me*!" Meena shouted as she drove fast down the roads, finally pulling into Julian's track. He was outside, holding a trowel, puttering with something. "Put that down!" Meena said. "Have you seen this?" She threw the copy of *Elle* in his direction. Julian sat the trowel down on the granite stone to the left of his door and opened the magazine. He found the article and began to read it. When he finished, he looked up at Meena, and said, "Well, now you see why they were in no hurry to agree to a confidentiality clause."

"But they're losing everything!" Meena shouted.

"But look at the satisfaction at least one of them is getting," her cousin said.

"I'll put a stop to that!" Meena said.

"You yourself opened the door," Julian said.

"What are you talking about?" Meena shrieked, beside herself.

"You are now in the Court of Public Opinion," Julian said.

"I'm a widow!" she shouted at him.

"No one has yet weighed the value of a widow against the value of an orphan," Julian said. "Not in the Court of Public Opinion. Or weighed a child against a grown woman, a *stepmother,* who has ignored her dead husband's wishes."

"But I swore I did nothing of the sort!" Meena said, distraught.

"I am no expert in the Court of Public Opinion and its precedents," Julian said. "Wasn't it your principal solicitor who warned you? But I rather think Sophie may be. An expert in that court, I mean," he said.

"I've got to get back to Willow Grove and Bettina," Meena said frantically.

"Leave that magazine here," Julian said. "Unless you want to hand it over to her."

"Oh, God!" Meena exclaimed. She ran back to the Range Rover, jumped in, and reversed the car so fast that a spray of gravel rose up. Then she was back on the road to Willow Grove.

—

"HELLO, THERE!" SHE called out cheerily as she went in through the kitchen door, carrying her paper sack and its loaf of wheat bread.

"I thought you'd quite deserted me," Bettina said, coming out of the parlor holding a half-eaten croissant. "Did you make this yourself?" she said, indicating what was left of the crescent.

"No, no," Meena said, a bit distractedly, "I don't appear to have the patience I once did."

"It's misery, my dear," Bettina said. "Since Vladimir died, I've come to believe that food comes from waitresses and hostesses of summer homes. Come, let's sit and talk. You're flushed, you know. Is it hot?"

"No, chilly, really," Meena said. "Odd, for this time of the year."

"I never know what time of year it is these days," Bettina said. "I don't go about as much as I should. It seems enough to hear rumors of the rest of the world, and even those exhaust me."

"I know," Meena said feelingly.

They sat on the benches of the kitchen table. "You see all these little holes?" Meena asked. "Woodworm. Peter always said he wanted the table to last as long as he did. Now I find myself wishing the same thing."

Bettina gave the tabletop a good hard knock with her fist. "It's sound," she said. "It will last you out, and perhaps the children as well."

The children.

"How are *your* children?" Meena asked, who was then treated to a long dissertation on their recent successes, triumphs, really, and Bettina's worries over Tatiana, who was, she believed, frail and far too susceptible to illnesses of every sort.

"Children," Meena said, sighing dramatically.

"My dear, they keep me going," Bettina said.

"I'll just shell some peas and do a few things for dinner," Meena said, standing up and moving to the kitchen counter.

"Good," Bettina. "I'll just read that magazine I got on the plane. If it weren't for planes, I wouldn't know what was going on outside my door," she said, and to her horror, Meena saw Bettina lean over in her seat and pull something from her large handbag. It was a copy of *Elle*.

—

"I'M IN THE apple orchard," Meena hissed into the mobile phone.

"Don't want Bettina to hear you?" Julian asked.

"Dead right," his cousin said. "We have to do something. Although why I think to ask for your opinion is beyond me. This is entirely the consequence of your letter-writing campaign."

"You agreed to it. You wanted it. You said something had to be done, just as you're saying now. Too many things were leaking out. You wanted to put your side of the story. 'I want to put my side in people's way,' that's precisely what you said."

"Do you think," Meena asked horrified, "that my e-mail, or rather, the e-mail *you* drafted, led to this article?"

"Well, as I said, Meena, you rather opened the door, didn't you?"

"*You* advised me to open it!"

"*You* said something had to be done!" Julian responded. "The language was as neutral as possible. We went over it together. The solicitors went over it. 'It is not the practice of the Grovesnor estate to comment on matters of a personal nature.' Do you remember wanting to begin in that way? Then you reproduced much of the List of Wish. I thought *that* was a mistake. Then you wanted the will in, but you didn't want the list in, and you took out the list. I thought people would find that suspicious, and I'm sure they have. Then you wanted to know how to send the letter. You had some worry about sending it through the mail. It might be thought more libelous, at the very least more self-justifying. When I suggested e-mail, because you could deny you had ever sent it, you leaped like a salmon at the chance."

"Oh, so now I am to blame!" Meena shouted at him.

"Meena," Julian said, now speaking carefully, "who do you have left? You've been indiscreet. I don't mean about the letter. But was it wise to tell Mrs. Edwards that a man lurked in the woods at night and would step forward a very feet and then step back into the shadows again? Now the whole world knows about it. And was it prudent to tell the vicar that at night you thought you heard Peter's shoes pounding on the roof of his coffin?"

"The vicar? The vicar!" Meena said, aghast. "The vicar is bound by oath to keep his silence!"

"Oh, yes. But what about Mrs. Brown? She comes around to tend to his bees before she sees to yours. She was in the back changing into her clothes and she heard you talking."

Meena was momentarily struck dumb. "How could she have heard?" she at last whispered.

"You know what the acoustics of that church are. Everything magnifies and echoes. Unless I miss my guess, other people must have heard the very same thing. You keep this up and soon every last soul will think you're mad. You know the people around here. Once they get an idea in their head, you can't get it out. Do you really want to alienate me, too?"

"Too?" Meena repeated.

"Because you will," Julian said. "If you continue on in this way."

Meena sank down and covered her face with her hands.

"I think you must give them something," he said.

"In my letter, I said that I was saving the money for them," Meena said, looking up at him.

"*Saving* it for them is not *giving* it to them. Lady Anne would know that. I doubt if Bettina would be happy to hear you were *saving* the money for the children."

"In trust! In trust! Because they're not responsible!" Meena said.

"You're shouting at me again," Julian said. "Let me speak frankly. *No one* is going to believe you're saving the money for Peter's children. I know, for one, that the will has been read by others. These people, those people who were Peter's friends, each of them is fully capable of reading a simple sentence. What he said was, 'Upon my death, you are immediately to—' "

"I know what he said!" Meena interrupted him.

"Then you needn't wonder why people don't believe what you say now," Julian said.

"What am I to do?" Meena said.

"Give them something. On account. However you want to think of it."

"Over my dead body!" Meena exclaimed. "They shall have nothing! They broke the confidentiality clause!"

"They never agreed to it," Julian said.

"They broke the spirit of our family's beliefs," Meena said. "That is just as monstrous."

"I doubt that the law would agree with you."

"To hell with the bloody law!"

"Meena, I tell you again, if you keep on in that way, there will be nothing that I—or anyone else—can do for you."

"And is there now? Is there anyone who can?"

"If what I do counts for nothing . . ."

"Don't threaten me!" Meena said.

"Stating a plain truth is not the same as threatening."

"I have to get back," Meena said, and abruptly switched off the phone.

Let her go straight to hell, Julian thought, replacing the receiver in its cradle. But she is, after all, a widow, he thought. And it will work to my advantage if she refuses to let them have anything. If she keeps on as she is, I'll be the one to live the longest. My children will do the inheriting. Unless, of course, her behavior becomes so extravagant that the court decides to look into that will again. There are holes in that will. I cannot understand why Sigrid and the children have not as yet brought her to court. Peter was a cowardly man; I always thought so, and the rest of them are cut from the same cloth, aren't they? Julian thought. At least, he assuredly hoped they were.

FIFTY-SEVEN

———

JULIA DIALED SOPHIE'S cell phone and waited for Sophie to answer.

"Hello," Sophie said abruptly.

"Did it work?"

"Did what work?" Sophie asked, sounding wary.

"Did Andrew talk to Bertold?"

"Tell me your number and I'll ring you right back," Sophie said.

"Oh, he's somewhere nearby," Julia said.

"Right," said Sophie.

The phone rang again. "I'm out in the garden," Sophie said. "I said I was going out to look at what the builders were up to. God, it's like life with

Meena all over again. Daddy was always calling from somewhere in an apple tree. I think it was an apple tree. Or am I misremembering?"

"It was Death that got into an apple tree and wouldn't come down because he was up too high," Julia said. "And because no one wanted to cut the branch down, everyone else kept on living."

"You've got the story all muddled up," Sophie said. "But not to worry. I don't remember it, either."

"So *that* was why he was always ringing me back," Julia said. "I should have realized."

"He probably assumed you knew how things were. He and Meena once got into an argument about you, and he said, 'She *knows* what goes on here,' and after that," Sophie said, "there came the explosion. You weren't supposed to know about anything that went on in that house."

"Andrew," Julia reminded her.

"Yes, yes," Sophie said. "He told Bertold what we agreed he'd say, and Bertold was so insulted that he left the house and went straight back to Sigrid."

"Oh, no!"

"But," said Sophie, "Sigrid called and said, 'Bertold's been wondering if you shall let him back in the house.' And I told Sigrid to say, 'Let him wonder!' He's back now, and I must say, he's in good form. Hasn't mentioned Meena once, or said *anything* about money except to say, 'Darling, we ought to ring up that man who wants you to give a lecture if you think we've gotten enough done since this time last year,' and I said we hadn't, so we had better get cracking."

"Then things are going better?"

"*Much* better," Sophie said, "although he's still on a short leash here, and he feels Andy is keeping an eye on him and he knows it. Andrew's still staying at the house."

"*He* can't be very comfortable," Julia said.

"I think he's quite enjoying it," Sophie said. "It's not often he gets to play the villain, not deliberately. Meanwhile, I'm the princess in the tower and they're the two dragons keeping watch to see that there's no sign of Meena. I do wonder, though, if Bertold isn't appeased by the check *Elle* sent me. It really was quite sizable. I was at my wit's end, trying to think of what to tell the builders. And there is some really good news. Lady Anne gave me a rundown of what everyone is saying about Meena. I suppose no one will soon be offering Meena the management of a great charity. I imagine she is *displeased,* as in 'I am quite displeased with you, Sophie,' a sentence that always rolled trippingly off her long, forked red tongue."

"But Bertold?" Julia insisted. "You don't think he'll start up again?"

"Andrew's words gave him quite a scare. Not to mention having Andy and me in agreement. I've never had an ally who wasn't Bertold before. A real shock to him, I must say."

"So Andrew's standing firm?"

"Immovable," Sophie said. "*Now* he reminds me of Daddy. It's quite funny, really, everyone at table trying to prove that he's the one who cares least for Daddy's money. When in all probability I care more about it than both of them together, although it's quite pointless to go on about it, so I don't, but it is good to be the perfect one."

"Keep it that way," Julia advised.

FIFTY-EIGHT

———

Dear Martin,

See what you make of this. You can see straightaway that I haven't written this, this is an entirely different hand. And there are little pictures in the margin and sometimes at the bottom of the page, as you'll see. I don't tend to that, either. It's from Evelyn's dairy.

I don't know how to be happy. Some mornings, I wake up and can't bear to open my eyes because I know, if it's sunny or if it's storming, I'll find everything I set my eyes on makes me fit to be tied, furious, really. I may not realize I've gotten to that state yet, but as soon as someone says anything to me—Good morning, Slept well, did you?—I'm in one of my rages. Then I think, I'll fall back asleep, I never have enough sleep, I try to blame that on everything, and I lie on my right side and stare at the wall, and suddenly I realize I'm rigid with hatred. Nothing for it but to make the most ghastly grimaces I can. In another mood, I'd smile thinking of what someone watching would make of me, but not on days like this, when all I can do is lie there hating myself, for being so ugly, for not having washed my hair, for not sleeping enough, for not falling asleep, for being afraid of reading what I wrote the night before, for greeting the day as if it were a sheet of paper on which I know I'm going to have to try and write. Those haunted hills in Cornwall, the shafts going so far down. I live in that landscape, afraid to take a step, I have always lived in such a place, but I never knew it actually existed somewhere, so on days like today, I think, it wouldn't be that hard to take a train or a bus and walk the rest of the way and climb one of those hills and close my eyes as if I were playing Blind Man's Buff until I started to fall. And what a relief it would be, to fall, and that cheers me, thinking about the others searching for me on the hill, shouting my name over and over, while I listen to them down there, and don't answer.

Peter said today I can't be comforted in these moods and I shouted at him and said he didn't try very hard, did he? But the truth is, no matter how he tried, it wouldn't make any difference. Nothing ever does. Nothing did. I wait for him to say something I can argue about, something that justifies my flying into a rage, but he's getting cagier. He gets out of the house and goes off to the cliffs and writes, no paper, no pencils. He just writes things down in his mind, and keeps it there until he gets back, and I asked him, How do you remember? What you wrote when you were up there?

We were in a good mood then, having a good time of it, a little
wine helps me, I think, but not much or it sends me back over the
black cliff, and he said that he memorizes a list of images, or
words from the images, until he has an image chain, and then he
writes it all down when he gets home. And when he gets home,
and it's clear enough he's had a good time, I think, he hasn't cared
about me, he hasn't thought about me, he hasn't wondered
whether or not I'm in complete despair left all alone as I am, and
I have to spoil it for him, pick on something he says, or something
he didn't say, or ask, blandly, did he buy a pack of digestive biscuits, and if he says he didn't, he never thought to get over to the
market, I say (in a tone even I despise), I really did want them, you
know, and he says, I'm sorry, and I say, I really did want them, you
know, and again he says, I'm sorry, and then I ask, Did you mail
those letters? I know he won't have mailed them. He only went as
far as the cliffs. Where would he mail a letter from the cliffs? and
he shakes his head and says, I'll mail them tomorrow, and I say,
in that same despicable tone, Tomorrow will be too late, and if he's
not on the edge of exploding at me, I ask, How did you get that
tear in your sleeve? Didn't I just mend it? And he says, The fabric's so thin, of course it was bound to tear if I stretched my hand
out to get something, and then I lose my temper and want to know
if he thinks I have nothing to do but mend his clothes, don't I have
any work of my own to do, is it my fault that I'm not as strong as
he is, is it my fault I write so slowly, is it my doing that I have to
stay in and write whenever I feel quite well, don't have the time to
go climbing about on cliffs, until he finally gives way and shouts,
Will you stop! It's intolerable! I can't bear it! And then I start to say
what I should have done in the first place, I say, I'm angry, I'm full
of hatred, I don't know where it comes from, but I've driven you
beyond reason, and he shouts, You are anger! You are hatred! and
I shout back, saying, When I try to tell you anything, this is the

result, is it any wonder I hide beneath the blankets, the blankets don't talk to me in this way! and he shouts, Then lie there under the blankets and see if the blankets don't have something to say after a few more days of this! and he storms out of the door, and I get on the phone, sobbing to my mother, who says, "Come home, Evvy, come home, I'll take care of you," and if that doesn't snap me out of it, nothing does, the idea of being back with her and her ministrations, of being back there again, it's an electric shock, worse, so I calm down, really calm down, and the bad luck of it is, he always comes back in just then and sees me talking on the phone, and says in that thin voice, You've found someone to talk to, and storms out the door again, and there's my mother, still on the other end of the line, saying, "Evvy, darling, come back, come back, Evvy, he's not the right man for you, I saw that the moment I laid eyes on him," and I get so enraged, I hang up on her and run straight out the door in my nightgown regardless of the weather, rain storming down, blazing sun, calling, Peter! Peter! knowing perfectly well he can hear me, but he won't answer, he won't come back again now, not for some time. Now he's gone to the pub. He's rounded up some of his friends. They'll be back late, after I've fallen asleep, shouting stupidities at my front door, waking me up. I'll get up and put on a heavy woolen robe and come out and offer to make a pot of coffee for all of them, but they'll all start stammering and saying, No, no, we have to go, we have deadlines to meet in the morning, that sort of thing, and when they're gone, Peter will roar around saying, You got rid of them fast enough, didn't you? Did you have to make it so clear, how much you wanted them gone? And I say, All I did was offer them some coffee! He doesn't even answer, just storms up the stairs and slams the door shut and in the morning, it's not hours away. I get up with all good intentions: Today I'll be cheerful. Today I'll be friendly, and he says, Where did you put my boots? and I say, What? and I hear my tone

of voice, and he shouts at me, I'll find my own bloody shoes, and
in spite of myself, I ask him, Are you taking a bath this morning?
Because if you are, I'll take one in the afternoon, I don't mind the
cold water. And he knows what I mean is, Aren't you ever going
to take a bath? Don't Englishmen ever bathe? How repulsive you
look. And he's got his boots on and I ask, When will you be back?
and he says, You'll see me when you see me, and then I go into
a rage, shouting, Pig! Beast! Selfish slug! And even when he's out
the door and getting into our car, I'm still shouting, and he knows
when he comes back I'll say, You left me here alone all day. What
do you expect me to do here all day when I can't drive anywhere,
when I have to wait here and see if one of the lobotomized popu-
lace deign to stop by. You may find them interesting, but I don't.
Thank God we didn't settle in Demonshire. This is bad enough.
And it can go on like this for weeks, all because every morning
when I open my eyes, I have one instant of, not happiness, simple normalcy, it all turns, and there it is, that smell, rotting cheese,
something acrid, pouring from me, one of two faces, the oily one
so I look like a side of pork ready for scalding, or the dry face,
white, chalky, dead, bits of skin flaking off, not a rash, something
worse. If that goes on, I will go down to the bone. That's all that
will be left of me, some foul-smelling bones. I am only foul-
smelling bones, faceless, I don't have a face. I never had a face.
It took so much work to make people think I had a face, a body,
one like other people's. Rotting, yes, as theirs is, but theirs is rotting slowly, whereas I will be putrefaction by nightfall.

As for the Northlumbering people, that's the word I use for
them, what would they say if I opened the door and let them see?
They mustn't see me. I must stay hidden. But this morning, I
opened my eyes, and even before I let an image rest on my reti-
nas, I knew a switch had been thrown. This was to be a good day.
I can feel it, I touch my face and it is a real face, it's not necessary

to look in the mirror I keep next to my bed. I am a human being, a real human being, and this is a day I can make something of. And he comes in and says, Spending another day in bed, are you? And I begin to cry, I say, But I'm fine! I'm really fine! Let's go somewhere! But he's out the door, getting as far from me as he can, and the motor turns over, and he's gone. I can't shout loud enough to call him back. Even if I could, he wouldn't come back, and tomorrow, what will tomorrow be like? If I could promise, if I could say, for two days I'll be fine, as happy as I am now, or for three days, or four, but I can't promise it, you see. I can't promise anything, all I can hear is that voice, deep beneath my brow, inside my skull, chanting again and again, Ruin everything! Ruin everything! Leave nothing alive! And when he comes back, who knows what he will find? And even if he comes home, late, at night, with the Northlumbering men he cares for so much, even if I greet everyone cheerfully, they won't notice. I seared them so many times before, and what can I promise? More of the same? That's all I can promise, the only vow I have to give.

I wanted you to read that. I can go on and on trying to explain Evelyn, but I think it's not possible. You say I must help her. She can't be helped. That is what I have concluded at last. She will not speak to a doctor, so I have been myself, to an old woman, a psychoanalyst, who works at the Tavistock and who did great work during the last world war. She appears to have devoted her time to lost causes. I took these same pages I've just sent to you and gave them to her. When she finished reading, she said, "Your wife is a very sick woman. She needs treatment." I explained that my wife refused to consider any treatment and that I had been trying to help her. "And have you had any success?" she asked me, and of course I had to admit that I hadn't. The only hope she could offer me was remission and the passing of time. She tells me there are spontaneous remissions that have lasted for as long as twenty years, but these are unusual cases. I asked her what she thought about pregnancy, since there are days when Evelyn is so sure that bearing a child will cure her, although she never uses the word "cure" because that would imply or acknowledge the presence of disease. The doctor said she thought, in a case like this, we ought to be very cautious, because even the steadiest women went into rather dramatic depressions immediately after the birth of a child, and that was certainly a consequence she would not rule out; rather, she thought, she would rule it in.

As I am almost certain that Evelyn is now pregnant—her body has a different smell and they say that happens when someone is pregnant—you can imagine how happy I was to hear that. The psychiatrist said that therapy might help, and it must be tried, as there is no other avenue that might afford relief. But I am against it, as you know—I can't help the way we were brought up, and I still believe that only the raving mad belong in psychoanalytic therapy—and I don't see how we can afford it. Moreover, there's the difficulty of our situation. I did not think to find many trained psychoanalysts in Northumberland, and the old woman analyst confirmed my guess. "There is no one." That was bald enough. Then she went on to say that it was lunacy—worse than useless—to attempt to treat her myself. She said, Your wife will already have come to see you as one of the major figures that caused her illness. She will not trust anything you say and indeed, if you attempt to influence her or interpret her symptoms to her, she will, inevitably, turn upon you and then she will have no ground on which to stand. I told her that I believed all that had already happened.

The doctor—she has a medical degree, she keeps the certificate above her chair and above her desk—urged me to reconsider our situation in Northumberland. If you are set on keeping the house, she said, rent it out, and rent a place in London so you will have resources. There are people here that can help you. But as you well know, Evelyn herself is against returning, insisting, as she does, that the solitude and the good country air will be bracing and inspiring to her as soon as she gets over this latest bout of "spells." And, Martin, to tell the truth, I would just as soon she stayed where she was. If she stays in Northumberland, I can go down to London and find translation work and some advertising work, and go back there and finish what I've caught on my hook in the city, and then return again to London and bring the stuff back in. It's not just that London affords opportunities for work. You know me better than that. I want some time away. I want some time with women who make no demands and who laugh and eat and sleep as if life itself weren't pure torture. And everything else I can find when I'm with a woman who has a simple nature. When Evelyn falls into those waxen or dried states she describes so well, there is no getting into bed with her, much less attempting anything more, so that when she comes out of one of her spells, and turns quite ravenously on me, I must do a kind of double-take as my reaction always makes her laugh.

And, beyond doubt, I have gone too far with one of those women of blessedly simple nature. I was so relaxed I forgot to keep a good rein on my tongue which of course ran away with itself like a horse, and I told her—her name is Sally—that if I ever left Evelyn, I would marry her. Sally said, "Well, if you decide upon leaving her, do ring me up," and she went on to the next thing. But no one, certainly not me, says something of such great import unless there's something in it, and the more I've seen of Sally, the more I think I could live very happily married to such a woman. Evelyn herself is forever saying I should have married a waitress in a fish and chips shop. She's quite precise, Evelyn. She doesn't say I should have married a waitress in a high-class establishment, someone who would never complain and would be able to anticipate what I wanted. No, she thinks the sort of waitress I'd be truly happy with is the kind who does nothing but go from table to table, filling up the water glasses. I'm getting in too deep with this Sally, I know. We're quite a couple in London, another reason I don't want to bring Evelyn to London, not even if she wanted to come, or would agree. She's quite something, this Sally.

You know how I wrote you about Evelyn's saying that when she was ready to leave a dinner or a party she'd kick my foot? I was to jump straight into the air as soon as she kicked me. The trouble is, she doesn't really kick. She slithers her foot over to mine, and so I find it very easy to ignore her kicks. But if she keeps it up, and I don't want to go, I say loudly, "Why are you kicking me?" and then the whole table knows what's up, and there's no question of leaving just then. As soon as we're outside, I hear about it. Then she begins. How can I be so stupid? Why can't I just admit I'm trying to make a fool of her? I never had any intention of leaving the party early, not when I was having a good time; and she goes on, saying it's the last time she'll ever go to a party like that again; next time, she wants a list of all the people who will be there and why they'll be there, and she's serious. And if there's a single woman there, I'm sure to be cross-examined. Who is that woman to me and what is she doing there, and how long have we known each other and in what way did we know each other? Until, of course, I'm utterly sickened by the idea of the party and am ready to throw it all up.

But somehow, we get to the party and Evelyn begins her slithering, and the whole thing begins again. If this were played out on stage, it would be hilarious and I would be roaring with laughter, but instead I end up red in the face with fury, and Evelyn sits across from me with a face like Medusa. Except, I think, that Medusa must have seemed a good deal kinder and more pliable.

Last week, Sally and I were at a restaurant with another couple, and I thought I'd flirt a little with the other woman there—she was quite attractive, really, and seemed ripe for the flirting—and suddenly I was kicked in the shin and I let out a pretty ghastly howl. "What was that for?" I demanded, and Sally smiled and said, "I'll kick you every time you forget who you came in with," and she kicked me again, in the same spot, and when I got back to Northumberland, I was limping and made up some fairy tale about catching my foot in the door of the train when it started pulling out before it was meant to do.

But to get back to Evelyn. Probably you're wondering how I got you those sheets from her journal. It wasn't hard. Sometimes she writes on loose sheets of paper and dates them, and puts them in between the bound sheets of the journal. The sheets I sent you were like that. She won't notice they're gone. She rarely goes back and reads over what she writes in journals. They're part of the six to eight hours a day she believes she must put in working on her writing. Although there are times she does go back to reread accounts of her "spells," mainly to remind herself that they do, in fact, come to an end. But now that I've begun raiding those journals trying to keep an eye on her emotional fever charts, I find entries I simply cannot bear. I don't want to remember them and I don't want her to remember them. I'm a dab hand these days when it comes to excising entries with a good razor, and I keep that razor well hidden, as you can imagine, in a waterproof box, hidden under some stones, the whole thing wrapped in an oilcloth. Because there are times I think she'd be very pleased to get hold of that razor and use it on her beloved husband, and she'd feel the better for it, I'm certain of that.

I think you did well in settling on Karen. At least you don't send me excerpts of her mad journals and you don't worry about hiding homicidal objects. Have you thought any further of coming back and helping me with my scheme to raise avocados? There's

enough land for farming here, and not too dear to get a hold of,
but once I got it, I wouldn't begin to know what I was doing, and
Evelyn is adamant: she'll live in a house with no central heating
and no plumbing, but she will not be a farmer's wife and go chasing after the plow when it's time to sow the seeds for whatever
crop I think will make a profit, and says things like, "You'll be the
first one to try growing cotton in this climate." She's also started
giving names to places she doesn't like, names and places, so
Devon becomes Demonshire, and the people of Northumberland
become Northlumbering—things like that. Well, you saw some of
that in that piece of hers that I sent you. She has a very sharp
tongue, Evelyn does, and she will use it, and I must say, most of
the time it's a relief to hear her mocking away at things about
which I feel the same way but am too timid—yes, timid is the only
word—to say such things aloud.

Martin, please don't write me and tell me I shouldn't read
Evelyn's journals and shouldn't invade her privacy so blatantly.
She has no idea of what I'm up to. I know she reads every scrap
I write and searches out every shred that comes into this house,
but this isn't tit for tat; I feel I must read what she writes to keep
ahead of her, to prevent some catastrophe from befalling her. You
will say I would do better to avoid the many kicking Sallys I spend
time with and I should avoid other women altogether, and I do try,
but somehow I don't succeed. Just as I police Evelyn's journals,
she strives to police my life. She's set spies to observe me in
London, but so far, none of them have happened upon Sally or
any of the others, but those women don't last long. In a day or two,
they're gone, so if one of Evelyn's spies searches one out, whoever it is is gone so fast there's not much point in making a report.
And I suspect that that Evelyn's spies know who they're dealing
with and are unwilling to upset her. Sally's not about to say a word.
She says if I want to come to her, I know where to find her and it's

not her job to extract my wife from my marriage as if she were a rotten tooth. I rather like the expressions she comes up with.

Probably all this sounds like my life's become a demented kind of Restoration comedy, but it's not amusing. I wish it were. I wish I could help Evelyn and had less desire to go far from home. But as they say, If wishes were horses . . . Now that the doctor's fore-seen nothing but trouble for Evelyn, which means, of course, noth-ing but trouble for me, I find myself groping through a pretty thick mist. If you see a way through, write and let me know what you've come up with. Meanwhile, consider avocados. People are paint-ing their bedrooms that color—avocado green, I mean. Avocados are the coming thing. If you decide to come back, I'll straightaway go out and buy some land.

What does Karen think of returning to this country? I know she doesn't much care for trouble with in-laws, but our parents are glass animals compared to what they used to be. Last week, Mike came round—he brought some beer for all of us, so Evelyn appre-ciated that. It wasn't going to cost us anything. she's always sure I'm paying for the whole county—and started in talking about the trouble he was having with his mother who was unwell and living at quite a distance, and I put in a few shillings of my own. "I don't know how to help with my parents now that they're so infirm," I said, and Evelyn smiled a brilliant smile, looked at the two of us, and said, "I always wanted to marry a happy orphan." That stopped us dead, I can tell you.

Anyway, Martin, avocados. Surely they are no more trouble-some things in this world than wives.

Love, as always,
Peter

FIFTY-NINE

―

"MORE INTERVIEWS?" SIGRID asked, aghast. "I think we've had enough of Sophie going on about her ailments. The British Empire must think she's Queen of the Hypochondriacs. It doesn't do to whinge on about one's symptoms. Everyone's got them. And what's worse, if she goes on in this way, who will give her a university position? Considering that she's on one of her many deathbeds."

"There may be a way. I've got an idea," Julia said.

"*That* strikes terror into my marrow," Sigrid said. "Tell me what it is so I can disapprove."

"Nope," said Julia. "I'll try it out and see if it works."

"If you're thinking of running naked through Regent's Park with *Meena Grovesnor stinks* written all over you with lipstick, Julia, I have to tell you you're too old for it."

"I hadn't thought of that," Julia said. "But *Sophie* isn't too old for it."

"Not one word to her," Sigrid said, "or it *will* be Lady Godiva wearing a placard and going through the streets."

"Sigrid, *you* owe it to Sophie. *You* be Lady Godiva. She's overworked. You do it for her."

"Oh, what a thought! *Finally* Meena would get the sympathy vote."

"I'll let you know if I think of something that's useful," Julia said. "I'm going to ring off and then go to a few galleries and see if Eliza's got any more jewelry in the shops."

"You're mad," Sigrid said. "Buy them off her. Don't pay store prices. She'd be happy to sell things to you."

"Not if she hasn't kept up stocking the galleries. She has to keep up with them. I come last."

"A customer is a customer. I don't see the difference," Sigrid said. "Call me later if you get back in time for dinner and we'll go round to the Chinese."

"Right you are," Julia said. She hung up and dialed another number. "Rose!" Julia said. "I'm just free and I swore I'd call you as soon as I was."

"Did you?" Rose asked suspiciously.

"I did. And are you still working on that biography?"

"Of course I'm working on it, Julia. I have a *contract*." She said the word *contract* as if it were sacred.

"Have you gotten up to writing about Meena? I know she was unkind to you—"

"Unkind!" Rose exclaimed.

"I know she was unkind to you when you went to Willow Grove, but I know you, Rose, you won't want to put anyone in a bad light. You're so kindhearted, and you know you may need that person later. I wish I had that foresight."

"You don't *need* any more foresight than you already have," Rose said. "What are you up to now?"

"Up to?" Julia said innocently.

"Why are you asking me about Meena?"

"Oh, I just wondered if you were going to write about Peter's separation from her, or if you were going to suppress all that. It *is* unsavory, I suppose. I suppose some people might think so."

"Whatever are you talking about?" Rose asked, irritated, but she had nibbled at the bait. More than nibbled, Julia saw.

"Oh, you're just being coy. You know all about it. I *hate* it when grown women are coy. Anyway, I know you know all about it."

"I honestly don't know what you're talking about," Rose said.

"You know. That long affair of Peter's. He would never have published that book of poems about Evelyn if he hadn't needed the money. He was going to buy Meena off. Of course, he didn't count on the cancer coming back."

"You seem to be saying that he tired of Meena and wanted to go off with another woman," Rose said.

"He wanted to *marry* her. I never heard of a man so anxious to get married."

"Why are you telling me this nonsense?" Rose asked. "Sigrid put you up to it."

"She *couldn't* put me up to it. I knew all about it. From Peter. He said, 'This time I've got the right one. It's taken me a while, but I've finally done it.'"

"You can't be serious," Rose said.

"But surely you know," Julia insisted. "I mean, as his biographer. How could you not?"

"If it were true, I would know," Rose said smugly.

"Well, then I won't say another word about it," Julia said. "Ignorance is bliss, but probably not in a biographer. I'm sure you know all about her. Clare Tartikoff. The one who makes the chandeliers. The one who's always in the papers. Why do you think she's always in the papers? It's because people know. It's because Sophie wants people to know. She wants everyone to know."

"Clare Tartikoff," Rose repeated. "I just read something about her. One of those articles at the back of the magazine where an artist describes what her day is like. I thought, What's she doing in there? What's she done to deserve it? A chandelier maker. That's not an artist."

"They are very beautiful chandeliers, Rose. Peter loved them. Did you see a picture of the chandelier? They always show one of the big ones, the Tree of Light. It's full of pictures of Clare and Peter. *And* Sophie. *And* Andrew. *And* Evelyn, pictures of Evelyn no one's ever seen. In fact, Rose, I think there's a picture of you and Robert."

"What? I'm in a chandelier!"

"Didn't you put on your glasses when you looked at the photo? People *pore* over those pictures. The pictures on that chandelier constitute a high society of literary types."

"Is there a picture of you in it?" Rose asked.

"Yes. Why not?"

"I don't know why you want to play a trick on me," Rose said sadly. "It's bad enough that Sigrid's gone off me, and you have, too, but really, mocking me! I do think that's a bit much."

"It's true," Julia said. "And you know it is. You won't admit it because you're suspicious of *me*. Don't you still have last week's *Guardian*? It's in the magazine. There's the article on the last page of the magazine and there's the picture of the chandelier right opposite it. Take a look for yourself."

"If I have time," Rose said. "And now I'm getting back to work. I have to work for a living, you know. I don't have a pension. I don't have time for silly tricks." Rose rang off.

Julia sat down on the window seat and smiled into the garden. I give her five minutes at most, she thought. The phone went after two.

"I found it," Rose said. "How that family manages to keep everything secret is one of the puzzles of my life," Rose said. "Why don't we meet at the Chinese across the street from my place?"

"I'm supposed to meet Sigrid at the Chinese on Haverstock Hill," Julia said.

"Then let's meet at Café Flo," Rose said. "I know you don't like it, but it's the one place I know where we can get in without a reservation. Two o'clock?"

"Two o'clock is fine," Julia said.

—

"DO YOU WANT to sit inside or out?" Rose asked Julia.

"Inside. It's too bright out. I'll end up with a headache."

"I want you to tell me everything you know about the affair and the separation," Rose said. "Just to be sure that my version tallies with yours."

"Of course you want to know that," Julia said. She looked happily around the restaurant. Half of London's editors seemed to be eating there. And what terrible acoustics the place had! Everyone inside could hear every word. How perfect to be in Café Flo on Haverstock Hill.

"Well?" said Rose. "Just start at the beginning. I'm starving. Don't make me ask two thousand questions."

"I wouldn't dream of it," Julia said.

It would take, Julia thought, three to four days for all of London to get the news. In England, so Julia had always thought, gossip was far more valuable than any other currency. When she got back, she would ring up Sigrid and tell her there was no need for Sophie to worry about giving incriminating interviews. If Peter was an unquiet spirit, he would soon be a great deal more peaceful.

SIXTY

WHAT A SEASON of windstorms! Julia thought. I could stay in my room and watch this forever. She turned off the small light in the parlor, just enough to navigate by, and went back and sat on her bed. When the next bolt of lightning struck, she could see the immense trees swaying. But what was that in the next garden? She pulled the small chair up closer and waited. Another bolt of lightning, and what looked like a beast lying on the earth, its arms raised to heaven. What in God's name was that? Then the obvious occurred to her: a bough had been shorn off one of the trees. If branches were falling in this weather, and boughs were so close to the window that leaves went back and forth across its panes like windshield wipers, she had no reason to stay so close to the panes, but she decided to remain where she was. She could easily recite a history of family deaths whose occurrence seemed predestined, if one assumed you were likely to die of what terrified you.

—

LIGHTNING, MEENA THOUGHT, opening her eyes, shuddering at the brilliant flash. Now I'll be able to see the dark man when he moves in and out of the wood. She went to the comfortable window and looked out. Why had she never realized how close the trees were to the house? Hadn't the boughs been trimmed back after the last storm? What *was* that at the edge of the wood, smaller than a man's fist? Oh, a tree rat. And what was it doing out in weather like this? They disappear when it rains. And they're silvery, not white. Someone's rabbit. Probably someone has gone on holiday and the vicar has taken in the rabbit, a pet of someone in the congregation. Why would he let a rabbit escape into such a storm? She would have to speak to the vicar in the morning. She was tired, and in spite of the chaos of air and water beyond the windowpanes, her eyes began to close of their own accord. She was jolted into awareness by a terrible, stabbing pain in her left shoulder. Death! A heart attack! But it was not a heart attack. It was a broken tree limb that had jumped through her skin and had entered her body like a dagger. I have to get up and summon help, Meena thought. It took all her stamina and all her courage to pull herself back in the chair, and, in so doing, the sharp branch pulled itself out of her. Good, it isn't bleeding much, Meena thought, feeling for the wound. A puncture. That's bad. The blood won't flow enough to clean it. She got to the telephone and called the hospital. "Oh, Mrs. Grosvenor! Can you drive yourself in?" asked the nurse at the other end. "Yes," she said, but when she tried to stand up, the world seemed to tilt and quaver. "I mean, no," she said. "I'm dizzy."

"We'll send someone to Willow Grove," the voice said. "You're there, aren't you?" she asked. "Can people get in the house?"

"The doors are locked," Meena said.

"Is there someone who can unlock them?"

"Yes," Meena said unsteadily. "I'll call him. But send someone. I'm losing blood inside. I'm sure of it."

"Yes, dear, don't worry," said the voice.

Meena was dizzy, but angry. "What is your name?" she asked angrily.

"Alice Bushell," came the answer. An answer, Meena thought, from heaven.

"Well, Alice Bushell, I knew your mother Hilda and drove her to the hospital when she had one of her many attacks of stomach pain, which, as I remember, she attributed to food poisoning caused by her *children*. I hope you're doing a better job at the hospital."

"I'll get someone," Alice Bushell said.

"Immediately. I don't have all day. I'm not here waiting for a furniture van to deliver a chair. If the ambulance can't find its way, tell them I'm at Willow Grove and my name is Meena Grovesnor. They'll know how to find me."

"The woman from *Elle*?" Alice Bushell said. "I'd like to come myself."

"Get someone, and get them quick," Meena said. "I'm calling a member of my family and I'll of course be mentioning your name. You'll be responsible if anything goes wrong."

"Of course, madam," Alice Bushell said.

Meena dialed Julian's number, made a mistake, and had to dial it again. It's not weakness, she told herself. It's just shock. "Julian?" she said when he answered.

"Didn't your mum tell you not to make telephone calls in lightning storms?" her cousin asked irritably.

She went rigid with fury, her body suddenly charged with energy. "Were you always such an idiot, or have I just noticed?" she asked. "I've been stabbed."

"By the man who hides in the woods?" Julian asked warily.

"No, Julian, by the tree in front of the window."

"What?"

"The storm took down a bough and it flew in through the window. I was pierced by a branch. Don't worry. It's out. I can move. But I don't think I'll be moving for long, and this incredibly dense nurse named Alice Bushell seems to have trouble understanding how dire things are here. I can't open the door to let in the ambulance people. I'm up in the turret and I'll never make it down. I'm dizzy and I can barely lift my hand. That's why I rang up, you thick-headed loaf!"

"I'll be right there," Julian said. "I'm going downstairs now."

"For God's sake, put something on over your pajamas," Meena said.

She might be dying, Julian thought, but she would fret about appearances.

—

ANOTHER LIGHTNING STORM, Sigrid thought, looking up from her favorite Turkish novelist's latest work. *Why* didn't I go to Morocco? Oh, yes, I didn't go to Morocco because of tidal waves and the rabid bats. She went back to her reading and found herself rereading the same page again and again. She reached for the paper. Perhaps she could manage that. What was this? Rabid bats in England? *Two British women were bitten on the stomach by two rabid bats this morning,* she read. Why on earth had she bought a copy of the *Daily Mail*? Oh, yes, she was keeping an eye out for more of her niece's interviews. There hadn't been any. Back to the bats, she thought. *The two women have been hospitalized in Cornwall. The two women were bitten by rabid French bats.* "Rabid *French* bats?" Sigrid said aloud, now oblivious to the thunder and lightning. Can I live in such a stupid country? she thought. I *must* live somewhere else. Although where? America is full of lunatic feminists, all wanting to lynch Peter. Well, of course, they can't do that anymore, not now, not since he's been buried, but those women haven't changed. They haven't grown in intelligence simply because of his death. And France? I should quite like to go to France, Sigrid thought. I'd have gone there if it hadn't been for Evelyn behaving as if she were the mutton described in a recipe book, a person getting in the oven like that, but what could one expect? She was an *American*. And now everyone in England was to believe that rabid French bats had nothing to do but fly the Channel and bite down into the flabby stomachs of two British housewives? How she wished she could call Peter and read him this notice.

—

THE PHONE WENT in Sigrid's bedroom. Either it was Sophie, who was the only person sure to be up at all hours, busy as she was turning day into night and vice versa, or it was Julia, who would be up watching the storm, the two of them completely crazy. As was she, with her own demented sleeping hours. She picked up the phone. "Sigrid?" said Sophie's voice.

"Yes, darling," said Sigrid. "Don't ask. You didn't wake me."

"I thought I mightn't," Sophie said.

"But you might have, and you'd have done it all the same," Sigrid said.

"It's the storm," Sophie said.

"You've seen storms before, love. You saw much better ones when we lived in Cornwall during that short time after Evelyn died. Did you read about the rabid French bats? Rabid French bats have taken to flying over to sink their teeth into English countrywomen's stomachs."

"Whatever are you talking about, Sigrid?"

"I see you don't read the *Daily Mail*," Sigrid said.

"Death, Sigrid, death. It's all I think of. What are we to make of it? When people die?"

"Do you mean the physiology of it, love?" Sigrid asked. "I'm the wrong one for that. Robert would have been perfect for answering that one."

"What happens to *us* when someone dies?" Sophie went on urgently. "Since Daddy died, it's been one illness after another."

"And you think your father's spirit is making you ill," Sigrid said.

"It is possible," Sophie said.

"And what does Julia have to say? I imagine you've asked her first. So you wouldn't have to upset *me*."

"Well, I did ask her. She said in the old days, in the nineteenth century, it wasn't uncommon for a husband or wife to die a few days after the other one died."

"Like loons, darling? And did Julia suggest that you were one loon and your father was another, and he was calling for you?"

"No, she said nothing of the sort! She only said that the ones who were left behind were *perhaps* weakened by their sadness. *Perhaps*. But these days it doesn't happen so often, probably because people really are stronger, what with antibiotics and other weapons."

"Well, it's a relief to hear that Julia hasn't gone off her rocker," Sigrid said.

"What happens to you when you're the one who's left?" Sophie asked.

Sigrid thought. "Are you there?" Sophie asked.

"I'm thinking," her aunt said. "Well, love, I think, *stunned*. I think you're stunned, that's the first thing. And then, it's as if you're the one who died, and a little later, the hangman's hood drops down over your head and you're in the dark and for a while you stay there, and you don't move. You can't see anything, so you stay still. And then you start to ask, 'Who's out there?' and when no one answers, you shout a little, and when no one answers still, you start to shout louder, and when there's still no answer, you begin to weep, and that goes on for a long time. The hood's still over you, it's hot in there and hard to breathe, and once you've cried long enough, the hood rises up and you see a little light, and you pull it down again because, really, you don't know what you'll do if the hood comes off, and finally it's gone, and you look around and try to remember what it was that you liked about the world and how you're to manage in it. That's what happens to me, anyway, when someone else dies."

"The same thing," Sophie said in a soft voice.

"Are you crying?" Sigrid asked her.

"Yes," Sophie said.

"Then you'll soon be much improved," her aunt said.

—

THE POWER'S SURE to go, Rose thought, looking out the window. Just when I've gotten to an interesting part. But really, she asked herself, what is the point of writing more? If what Julia had said were true? And it *sounded* true. If Peter had tired of poor Meena ("*Poor* Meena!" said Robert's mocking voice), he'd have been careful to line someone else up before he moved out. Who else would cook his meals? He wasn't a man who liked happenstance and accident and mess, not in the end. In the end, he was like his parents, good country-people stock who wanted to know the menu for the day long in advance, always the same menu they'd chosen beginning with their birth and following until the day they died. Rose had just been to Morvah, had gone into the little shop, inherited by another branch of Peter's family, picked a dusty magazine to read on the train going back, bought as many things as she could find to buy, and there weren't many, finally settling on a Green Frog ice pop, which she proceeded to eat in the store, watching the shop owner, who finally turned to her. "Something else you would like?" the man asked. There it was, that voice, and there, now that she looked carefully at him, was the image of Peter, staring back at her.

"You're not a member of the Grovesnor family, are you?" asked Rose. "Because I had a very good friend named Peter Grovesnor."

"My cousin," said the shopkeeper. "Dead now, though. A writer, wasn't he?"

"Yes. A very good one," Rose said, "and a famous one, too."

"Was he, though?" the shopkeeper asked. "He could fit in anywhere, Peter could. I expect people were happy to see him wherever he went."

"Do others in the family write?" Rose asked.

The shopkeeper regarded her curiously. "Don't have time for it," he said, wiping down the counter. "Don't read much, either. Do you find people who read a good deal start in writing? I'd think that's the way of it."

"Probably," said Rose.

"Well, Peter, as little as I remember him, he always had his nose in a book. If it was raining, that is."

"Your voice is very like his," Rose said.

"North Country people, all of us, started there, we did, and then somehow we found ourselves in Cornwall, all clustered around Morvah."

"A Lancashire accent, I should have thought," Rose persisted.

"Well, North Country, miss. It's all the same to someone not born there, don't you find?"

"I don't have a good ear for accents," Rose said. "It's raining. Do you have brollies for sale?"

"Not a one, but you can sit it out in that corner," he said, gesturing toward a bottle-green upholstered chair. "Used to be in Peter's parlor, it was," the man volunteered. "His mum was crazy over that chair, but my father couldn't sit on it, you see."

Rose sat down in the chair and listened to the rain on the roof. "It will go on for a while, will it?" she asked.

"Can't say," the man said. He had begun unpacking tins and stamping them with pink tags. Apparently, a store kept one busy.

Now, that man, Rose thought, that man has all the attractiveness that Peter had. I can feel it over here in this chair. He's as good-looking as Peter, and he's got that hypnotizing voice. So why isn't every woman in the world beating her way to his door? The answer, she thought, was simple enough. He did not want women beating their way to his door. He had been properly taught, in the North Country way, to stick to one wife and raise his own children, and when he was ready to die, he would have the satisfaction of knowing he had done what was expected of him. He was, through and through, a man of English stock. Then where had Peter come from? True, he had been a bit of a cuckoo in the nest, but most people were. Well, then he was *more* of a cuckoo, but was that enough to account for the path—paths—his life had taken?

She stood and picked up a box of jaffa cakes. "Like them, do you?" the man said. "A great favorite in my family, they are." Rose said she'd take two boxes. "For the grandchild?" he asked.

"No, for me, I'm sorry to say."

"Don't have grandchildren?"

"Five. But not here."

"Best when they're not here," he said, laughing.

Rose considered. "It's true," she said. Then she made a decision. "Look," she said. "We're alone in the store, and I've been puzzling over some questions. Would you have an affair while you were still married?"

"Well, that is a question to ask a man when he's alone in a store," the man answered. He was, Rose saw, a little on edge.

"I'm a new widow," Rose said. "I'm not interested in affairs *myself*. I've been thinking about affairs *in general*."

"Oh, *in general*," the man said. "Another story altogether. Your man had affairs?"

"Once," Rose said.

"I see."

"But it's you I asked about," Rose went on. "Would *you* have an affair while you were married?"

"What, and walk around growing Easter eggs out of my forehead?" he asked, laughing softly. "Get up in the morning and find my wife's cold dishes in the sink and no hope of a good hot English breakfast? Have to listen to my wife's relatives telling her, 'I told you so, why did you ever marry that drunken sot?' My mum never tired of saying, 'You can't say enough for peace and quiet in the home.' Peace and quiet and a good meal, is what I say."

"And that was enough?" Rose asked, leaning forward in her chair.

"Well, enough. What's enough? I'm not the King of England, and the queen, she showed no interest whatever in me, so I had a wife, a good wife, healthy, willing to work, pretty enough. She loved me and I loved her back, still do, no reason to stop loving her that I could ever see. We had a good roof over our heads, didn't need a castle to keep up, how many suits can you wear, and how many dresses for the woman, and the children, all red and rosy-cheeked, good appetites all of them, hard workers, one a carpenter, the other a builder, the daughter halfway toward nursing. I'd say that's enough. Doesn't do to ask for too much."

"No, it probably doesn't," Rose said.

"But you did?"

"Yes, I probably did. I thought, they all want me to make something of myself, you know, in their terms, make myself known, make a difference in the world. It was that kind of family. Go look for a man with a profession, someone who never stops wanting to better himself, regardless of what he'd already achieved."

"German, was he? German, are you?"

"Yes," Rose said. "Intellectuals."

The man leaned his elbows on the counter. "People round here in Morvah, we get ourselves born, we find things to do until it's time to die. Meanwhile, we do the best we can and if it's hard, when death stops by, we're not unhappy. We knew it was coming. My mum, she used to say, 'I'm waiting for the knock at the door when Death comes in and takes up my burden.' So how do you think about life, then?"

"We think—I think—we ask, 'Why do we have to die?'"

"Everyone dies, no use asking," he said.

"Not whether or not we'll die, but why do we have to? I mean, you get to be fifty, and you still don't know much, do you? Then you get into your sixties and you begin to see some glimmers. You get into your seventies, and you know enough to give some advice. But you know you won't get much further. So you've learned all these things and then it's all wiped out. It doesn't stand to reason. Who thought up such a plan?"

"Maybe no one did. Maybe it just happened. When God wasn't looking. Accidents happen. But that's the way it is. And the young ones, they're

happy finding out about the world. They don't want to be getting it secondhand. Advice isn't the thing for the young ones. They want to charge
into the meadow, go right through the gate, and once they're in there, they
worry about the bull. That's what I make of it. Not an intellectual, of
course. So, you've got some answers? Some birds in the hand? After all that
work?"

"None," Rose said.

"So what was your unhappiness with your husband?"

"He asked too many questions," Rose said, starting to laugh.

"Did he, now?" asked the shopkeeper. "And what was his unhappiness
with you?"

"I didn't often make breakfast or dinner, at least not well, but when I
did, you *could* choke it down. But I never cleaned up anything. Piles everywhere."

"Piles?"

"Of paper."

"Oh," he said. "A bad wife, were you? The man should have given you a
beating every so often. You'd have been a good wife then, and that's the
end of it. Saved yourself and him a lot of trouble."

"And you? You beat your wife?"

"Never had a reason," he said. "Dinner always on the table, house as
neat as a pin, the children in order, no reason to beat her."

"But if she'd been a bad wife?"

"Can't even imagine it. Don't think I would have hit her. Even if she
didn't cook my supper or scour the floor. Then everyone would have said,
'He's a bad husband, he is. Lets his wife run wild.' But I'd have stayed with
a bad wife all the same. I think that's the bus."

"Bus?" Rose said.

"The one to take you back to the train," the man said patiently.

"Well," said Rose, drawing her packages together, "I want to thank you
for the shelter and for the good advice."

"Didn't give any," the man said.

"Nevertheless, I learned more in the last two hours than I have in years."

"Glad to hear it, but puzzled all the same," he said.

"Your wife is a lucky woman," Rose said.

"She is that," the shopkeeper said, smiling broadly. "Hope all my gabbling on didn't cause you a headache. My wife complains for headaches."

"You talk to her a lot?"

"Don't say much to her," the man said. "She knows everything I'll say."

"Well, goodbye," Rose said.

She got into the bus and settled herself two rows in back of the driver. So now I know, she thought. I was a bad wife. He was a bad husband. I needed a good beating. He wanted a hot meal. And if we'd accepted the fact of death and kept it firmly in mind, we would have known how to behave.

The bus began pulling away. Rose found herself pressing her face against the streaming window pane and waving, but it was getting darker, and the rain heavier, and it was impossible to know if he was waving back.

—

"HAS THE WEATHER been wild there?" Clare asked. "I called when I heard the reports on the telly."

"Pretty severe, I think," Sophie said. "Although I think there were stronger winds in Northumberland. They got the brunt of it there. I hope Willow Grove is standing."

"So do I," Clare said. "A man's been round, to take a picture of the big chandelier. Did you send him?"

"No, I've been working on some theorems. Something's wrong in my theory. Andy's here, sculpting a beautiful orchid, though. He thinks realistic sculpture is a waste of time. He keeps quoting someone; he said that if someone sculpted a figure out of a carrot, no one would find anything he created very remarkable. He's thinking of doing a portrait of Daddy. Julia found an envelope full of pictures she took of him when he was off in America."

"Did she fancy him, Sophie?"

"Well, who didn't?" Sophie asked.

"I mean, did she *really* fancy him?"

"No, I'd have to say no. She did love him. But once we were talking, and I asked her how she'd turned out all right after starting out so badly, and she said, 'I was one of the lucky ones. I wore myself out just in time.'"

"In time for what?"

"In time to meet Matt. She says she wouldn't have survived otherwise, or wouldn't have survived as well."

"So when she met Peter . . ."

"I think she saw him and thought, Red light. Someone once told her to be suspicious of any man she fell in love with on first sight. Or second sight. Or third sight. In fact, she and Matt started with a quarrel. Looking back, she thinks that was a good sign."

"Yes, well, your father and I started with a fight. He came up to me in the pub, and it was so noisy, I shouted, 'What do you think I am? A woman who waits for a man to pick her up?' So then he was sorry and apologized, and I wasn't having it, but he came back the next night."

"Did you *live* in the pub?" Sophie asked.

"I worked there on and off, yes," Clare said. "I must have told you."

"I don't remember. It's not like me. I remember everything."

"Probably you didn't want to think of your father's woman as a barmaid," Clare said.

"Oh, that's not it!" Sophie exclaimed. "I'm getting older. What are they calling it in the papers? Senior moments? I must have had a senile moment."

Clare laughed out loud. "You have twenty or thirty years left for that," she said. "I'm not even up to them, not yet."

"I don't think I'll have them, then," Sophie said seriously. "I don't think I'll last twenty or thirty years."

"You will," Clare said. "You know, last night the tide was so high you could see the spume right at the top of the cliffs."

"You should have gotten out of there!" Sophie exclaimed.

"There was no ground higher," Clare said. "I'm old enough to think, If this is where I'm to die, I don't mind dying here. It's a way of knowing if you're happy, isn't it? When we went down to Willow Grove and I stood in the turret, I asked myself, Would I be happy to die there? And the answer was no. But here, that would be fine. I'd have no objection at all. Have you ever tried that out, Sophie?"

"I wouldn't want to die in Willow Grove, not now," she said. "Or in Jamaica, either. Or anywhere in Northumberland. But in London, where I am, I can't say I'd mind that. Or if I were where you are, with Bertold there, too, of course."

"Of course," Clare answered.

"Although I don't want to die anywhere, not for a while," Sophie admitted.

"Of course not," Clare said, laughing again.

"Well, it took me so long to know what I wanted," Sophie said. "I started everything so late. I always feel I'm making up for lost time."

"But sometimes you can't."

"No. Sometimes it can't be done. Like children, the having of them. I can't make up for that."

"Someone down here says, 'Better to raise cabbages.' They're wonderful while they're little, babies are, but they grow up. They can be a bitter chaliceful to drink down."

"Did Daddy say that?"

"No, why?" Clare asked.

"The words sounded like they could be his."

"He never said it. So I had my children, and now I can pick my own, grown ones. That's the best of it, or so I think."

"And am I one of the chosen ones?"

"You are," Clare said.

—

"I THOUGHT," SIGRID told Julia, "that the storm hadn't done the house any damage, but I remembered the havoc storms like that used to wreak in Hampstead before the new roof went on, so I thought I'd better take a look in the attic. Some moths got into the storage again, nothing I care about. But a branch was hurled through the top room, into the study. That bas-relief portrait on copper, the one of Peter: destroyed."

"Not that picture!" Julia exclaimed.

"I should have given it to you when you asked for it," Sigrid said.

"Is it fixable?"

"Not unless someone wants to melt down the copper and start over again. The branch ripped out the entire face—well, not the *entire* face. There's one eye staring out at you. It looks like an eye staring up out of a muddy pond."

"Get rid of it," Julia said. She shuddered, trying to imagine it.

"Oh, I'll put it away somewhere in the corner. Underneath one of the moth-eaten carpets."

"Get rid of it!" Julia said again.

"You're getting superstitious, Julia. I didn't think you had a superstitious bone in your body."

"Oh, you know better than that!" Julia exclaimed.

"It means something, I'm sure," Sigrid said. "If one eye is still open, he must be seeing something."

"Sigrid! Get rid of it!"

"I can't," Sigrid said.

"Nor could I," Julia said. "We could take turns keeping it out of harm's way."

"You mean, is it too powerful to be harbored by one person?"

"I don't know," Julia said. "But why find out?"

"If it has power in it, if it's an evil power, then no one else should suffer it but me," Sigrid said.

"Why?"

"Because I'm used to it."

"Do get rid of it!" Julia said.

"You know I can't. If I couldn't do it before, why could I manage it now?"

"Try."

"Oh, Julia," Sigrid said.

"How long can one person be haunted?"

"How long will I live?" Sigrid asked.

SIXTY-ONE

—

HOW MUST I BEGIN? Rose asked herself. Here is that sheet of paper. There, tacked on the wall, is a good, clear photograph of Peter as he was when both of us were at university. And there is a photograph of Evelyn, whom I should like to have met, and next to her is a picture of Elfie, whom I did meet once, but only briefly, and remember only as a whirl of scarves, exotic perfume, and teasing laughter. And I ask myself, why am I so fascinated by those three? Really, by those two, by Peter and by Evelyn. It is impossible to think about either Evelyn or Peter without thinking about the other, and try as I may, Elfie quickly recedes into the distance. As she must have done in life. As she must have quickly gone over the horizon of his life.

So what is there to say? I have a contract. I have to write something. There he was, a shopkeeper's son who had an odd talent. It set him apart in the world and the world noticed him, gave him the nod. If he had been born hunchbacked, he would have been noticed, but differently. It was luck that he was given a talent for writing and charm and seduction. Perhaps all three were aspects of the same talent. Many talented people, perhaps more talented, have fewer facets to the talent they're born with and so are never heard from again. But in the end, what can you say about him? He was a force, everyone agrees on that, but how much was that worth? Did he change the world, as I once thought he had?

He was a charming man, so charming as to be fatal, and what of that? He was an unfaithful husband and far better at adultery than most men. If he'd never written a word, he would have been one of the great, unfaithful husbands and only the women in his vicinity ever would have heard of him. There would have been rumors of illegitimate children, all of that stuff. My husband could have given Peter a run for his money, but he lost his teeth and didn't replace them and he ran to fat. Where is that paper? That letter he wrote?

What am I doing? I am eating green apples. Not raw green apples, unripened, but ones that are green, not red. You may know what they're called. Ten days of green apples and I shall again be a slender man. It doesn't do to set out on a tour looking like Tubby the Tuba, for which I thank you, and the children thank you, or was it Rusty in Orchestraville that you sent last? They were quite happy with the record of *The Little Engine That Could*, and even happier with the recording of *Oscar Wilde's Tales*. I like to play "The Happy Prince" to Sophie because it starts her crying every time, and she does look so sweet when she cries for that reason.

Green apples, Julia! But what does it matter if you have thickened as you say and put on weight? You don't have my vanity. You know I am as vain as any woman. I shudder at the thought of going on tour and having everyone feed me the best of foods, while before my eyes, I grow into the Hindenburg dirigible. I don't have the courage to let myself run to fat. Nor to starve for very long. I know you must starve to stay even as you now are. But you are happy in yourself—except when you look in the mirror, so avoid that, by all means—and then you shall be happy all the time. It pleases me greatly to think of you and to know that there is at least one woman who is capable of happiness. Does your husband know how lucky he is? Yes, I know he does. He makes that plain. He is the image of my brother, Martin. Did you know that?

I'm sure I've told you that. Right now, I am not happy. I'm starved. At three o'clock—one hour from now—it will be time for another green apple. I anticipate it and dread it all at the same time. These green apples, you know, are very sour stuff. And Meena keeps a watch on me: eight green apples and not one green apple more. Last night, I was out in the woods eating a ninth green apple, and when I got back into the house, she was waiting just inside the door, and as soon as she saw me, she said, "Nine! That was nine green apples! Tomorrow you shall only have seven!" Today I looked in the cupboard and saw only seven apples. Meena is on the same regime, so I know there are more apples in the house, and I searched the house down but I could not find so much as a single apple stem. It is a gift, hiding things so they cannot be found. I will make one more exploration, but I expect to find nothing but dust and perhaps one dead ant. Not even one crumb, Meena will have seen to that. She is thin as a stick, as you know, so then why is she eating green apples along with me? To keep me company and keep up my spirits. But another green apple would accomplish the same thing, and much more quickly. Write soon and tell me what you thought of the Indian author's novel.

He had charm, Rose mused, and he was witty, and you felt as if the sun broke through the clouds and shone on you when he looked your way, but really, is he worth a book? I suppose Julia thought he wasn't. Although Julia did love him, but not madly, not as the others did. She loves so many people. It's not at all the same thing. She's not the sort to make a pilgrimage to his door hoping to catch a glimpse of him. Or to pry into Evelyn's secrets. "I might as well have known her," that's what she said. "I've known many like her." What set Evelyn apart was her talent. I don't underestimate that talent, far from it. She's part of my life, as she's part of so many people's lives once they've read her poems. But must I think of her as a strange being, a new kind of animal? Haven't you known her, really? If not in yourself, in others?

Of course, Julia's right. She is, usually. I'm surprised she gave me that letter to copy out. She said, "But I warn you. You know this already. I own the letter, but Meena owns the copyright. Be careful."

What a surprising instance of generosity. I wonder what made her do it. I wonder if she's cooking something up. You never know with Julia. But it is nice to think of him eating green apples and worrying about running to fat.

Still, what have we got? A charming man, an unfaithful husband, a penchant for depressive wives, the bad luck of two suicidal women, one of whom became famous. A man of great talent, some don't think so, although I do, who made two, and now it appears three, women entirely miserable. And made himself miserable into the bargain. And didn't leave a proper will, so that even after his death, his children are pursued by the furies, as is the last of his wives and his sister. Not someone who did well, when all is said and done.

Then where do I begin? I have a contract. They will pay out the money when I finish, and even then, I won't be able to buy my way back to Perceval Road. Some men, some women, cast bigger shadows than others. The theme of my book must be suffering and talent and fate and sorrow and pity for those who the furies pursued and are still pursuing. And he was the one who let the furies loose—unless you prefer to think of Evelyn's death as the ultimate source of all the miseries. You could certainly argue for that, but I am not writing a book about Evelyn. Although, if I am not careful, this biography of Peter will turn into a book about her.

I should never, never, *never* have embarked on this work! What was I thinking of? If only I had spoken to the Cornish man earlier. If only I had been taught to think that Death was always on the other side of the door, and it was best, all things considered, to behave oneself and to do what was right. Each life comes with its own set of commandments, and if you obey them, life is not terribly complicated, no more tragic than anyone else's, because in the end, everyone's life is tragic—when that door opens and Death slips over the threshold. If only Peter himself had behaved as he was taught to believe!

Well, to begin. Once upon a time, there was a healthy young man, the youngest of the family, the baby of the family, who went out hunting and came back with dead birds. Then when he grew up, he went out and came back with a strange woman who had beautiful feathers of her own and he turned her into a dead bird.

Oh, I cannot write this book! Rose thought, bursting into tears. Whatever made me think I could write it? When I began, I thought I was writing a biography of a mythic figure, but to me he is not mythic any longer. Although it is true that *other* people regard him as already a myth. At least *some* people in England believe it. What do I think? *I have a contract.* Why did they ask me to write Peter's biography? And an even better question: why did I agree?

Rose put her head down on the desk and sobbed so hard that she quite drowned out the wind blowing up hard and fast. The radio was announcing, *Stay inside and stay away from windows,* but she did not hear that, either.

SIXTY-TWO

Dear Mother, Darling Charlotte,

But you must be happy for me, you must! I know you think no one will ever be good enough for me, and I have to admit I've gone for years thinking the same thing, although phrasing it perhaps a little differently—I would never find anyone I wanted who was good enough for me, but I have found him, and we are terribly, terribly happy. Was it so wrong of me to marry over here in a strange country without you to comfort me and to kiss your spinster daughter one last time? Then, darling Mother, you must come over at once and we shall be married again, but this time in a

Chapel at the University. We've found the perfect place for it, and my tutor will help me secure the time and I'll write out the invitations in my own hand and simply leave out the date and time until you tell me when you'll arrive. Won't that be even better? The marriage will be accomplished, all the fear and trembling, all the hesitations and explosions—must I have a ring, what shall I wear?—will be over, and I will have weeks and weeks to settle on the dress that you will find perfect for me.

You know how unhappy I have been in the past, and for no reason, but this time, for no reason, I am completely happy. I am silly with happiness, stupefied and drunk with happiness, staring at the violets as they open, and the orange lilies in the yard below flare up like so many immense stars, so brilliant I can see them through my window even at night. I shall finish my work here, of course I will. I promised I would not leave myself naked and alone without a diploma to wrap myself in on the world's stormy heath, and now I will not be long in finishing. I must polish my draft and then hand it over to the typist. That is to be my own gift to myself as a newly minted bride. For once, I shall not have to type up my own paper! Peter knows a woman who types very fast and does so for little money, and I shall hand in a spotless manuscript, so immaculate there will be no signs of my own fingerprints, as if it had been printed by machine. I quite like the thought of that. And we can afford it easily because I have won a good prize and it comes with a bit of cash attached to it. Pounds! I have won an award that pays me in pounds! And how I shall enjoy spending them!

But, dear Charlotte, he is perfect in every way. When he is doing nothing, I sit still and look at him and to me he is one of the wonders of the world. I understand what you say. I intend to keep him unspoiled. I agree that it does not do to spoil a man badly at the beginning, and I am quite sure you are right to say that once a man is spoiled, he cannot be unspoiled later—better to go the

other way. But, Mother dear, it is so hard to keep from spoiling him!
You know how I love to cook. If I continue, we shall meet you at
the boat and you will recognize us right away. We will be the two
hippopotamuses waving and shouting out. But don't worry over
my cooking. I have little enough time for it. My paper must be finished and there is my new life to explore. Who could envy
Columbus who found a new world? I have my own new continent
to explore, wonder upon wonder. I have become a better person.
Happiness irradiates me. Light pours out of me and reflects itself
on the dead faces of others. They begin to grow toward the light I
aim at them. I have never found it so easy to find friends and keep
them. I am not so critical now. Oh, probably you will write back and
say that the people I now see are no better than the ones I knew
on the other side of this ocean, this love I fell into and drowned in,
only to emerge as a new being, washed clean, as full of light as
the waters that let you see down to the bottom where the sand
waves in patterns so like the surface of the water, and so I am better, because I do not look into other people's faces and find so
much to reproach in them. And these people look back at me,
beaming, and I see what a great thing it is to be viewed with such
acceptance, such joy. Instead of fearing that the people in the
room will see me coming in and begin gathering up their books
and coats and hats and start making excuses—only an hour until
my tutorial, so little time to reread my notes, if I don't rush now,
the coffee shop will close down—now people are so happy when
I come by, and it seems to me they wait for me. Before I would
have wished—desperately!—for their disappearance, while now I
am so happy to see them, if only to see my happiness reflected
in their faces. If they are no more than mirrors of my new state, I
cannot help but love them for it. Darling Mother, you must understand. You must have once felt just as I do, when you were very
much younger. You would not want me to go through life without

having had this light, this lantern, to lead me. If my husband, Peter, my husband, were to die tomorrow, of course I should be devastated. When I think of it, my heart appears to stop dead, but I would know I was not one of those destined to die without ever having tasted this ecstasy, this nectar.

But you know, Mother, I cannot begin to express this new happiness to you, no matter how I wish to, because if I could, I know you would understand and be happy for me. I found this happens to be like the black miseries I once plunged into. Once you reach the extreme, the vanishing point of the horizon, what is there to say but repeat the same thing over and over? I am happy, so happy, so very happy, so very, very happy, so very very very happy. It is as if, at the extremes, you have run out of intensifiers, of descriptions, even adjectives. The thing is what it is. It is a thing that casts no shadows. It is simply itself, unchangeable, perfect. And simple. I never found life simple. But now it is. It is enough, I see now, to breathe in and out. You must not worry that I shall turn into a brainless marshmallow. I have not given up my ambitions. I have yet to find a subject big enough to paint my words on. I think of that subject as a canvas. I haven't found one big enough. Or have I? Perhaps I have found the canvas at last, but not yet found the words. I think it is harder to come by the great canvas than the smaller ones. I know I have found them in the past, but not frequently enough. But I shall now. It is only a matter of time. And Peter knows so much and has already gone so much further into the wood. What a relief it is simply to follow for a time, not going first, not slashing away weeds and brambles, not tearing my flesh to shreds while I keep going in, trying to find myself, the beauty asleep in the wood, the beauty I must wake up for myself, that other self so well hidden and so deep in. But now I have found it, or Peter has found it, and he opens the path for me as if everything in the world is meant to open for him.

But I cannot begin to convey all this, and so I shall stop until tomorrow and try to make you understand, darling Mother, darling Charlotte, how I feel. Such transports! They make me quite giddy and silly. But Mother, I have found what I want and I have the man I want to live with until the day I die. Who could say more than that, wish for more than that?

Dear Martin,

It is over. I've found the woman I want. She's beautiful (even you would think so). She exists to make me happy, and she exists to make herself happy, which is, I suppose, the most important thing. She has such ambitions. She wants to be a famous writer and has wanted to be so since she was very young. I imagine our life will not be easy, but I shall not be bored. She is not, it goes without saying, like Mum. Evelyn can bake with the best of them, but that is not enough for her. She wants to achieve everything that can be achieved. That is her singular, immeasurable appetite for life. And such an appetite! I had no idea there were such women! The whole world has gone pale in comparison. Everything is now an underdeveloped photograph, a world in black and white, with only Evelyn in full color. Brilliant in every sense of the word.

Remember what Mum used to say to me? That you don't sit over the breakfast table discussing Shakespeare? Even then, I thought, She must be wrong. She was wrong. We sit over the breakfast table and discuss Shakespeare and Marianne Moore and T. S. Eliot and T. Roethke and whoever else springs to mind, and breakfast was never so tasty. I read her work—I wish there was more of it. Sometimes she gets stuck for days at a time, over one word, trying to get that one word—whereas I go along at a pretty brisk rate like a tank going over enemy terrain. She admires me for this. None of that criticism I used to get from the last lady poet who accused me of writing too quickly, without thinking enough, not thinking things through before I began writing, when what she meant to say was I was not suffering enough and how could I expect to be a poet or any kind of writer if I didn't suffer? Evelyn has no such preconceptions. She is many libraries all at once, but when she chooses, she can make herself a tabula rasa, and is open to everything.

And of course I fancy her, if I can use such a pale expression for the passion she brings out in me. She says she has found the man she will live with until the day she dies. I am, as always, more skeptical, less willing to offer such a statement to fortune, lest fortune look down upon me with envy and take revenge on such arrogance. But she is not afraid, is simply, I think, incapable of it. Although there are times, certain slants of light, when I catch her looking very afraid indeed, but she has said, often enough, that fear must be encountered, faced down and fought, and regarded in this way, fear becomes your ally. I, naturally, would rather have a more friendly ally, but this is a woman of grand thoughts and emotions, and she knows more about the terrain in there, so I will defer to her. It is very easy to defer to her. She will set me challenge upon challenge and I will rise to meet them. You have always known me to be a lazy sod at heart, but she will be the making of me there. And I suppose slowing her down will be my role. She would burn herself up if she could, simply to see what life looked like when viewed at such a speed, just to feel the flames leaping about her, as she streaked through the sky. She has the kind of passions that fueled mythic heroes.

So you can see I am besotted. And in need of a bath. And of course there is no warm water here, but I must appear clean and shining, so I will go off to freeze myself and go to greet her with an aureole of icicles in my hair. I would not have thought love, that word I have heard so much about, would get me into the bath on a day like this.

Be happy for me, Martin, for I am very happy.

All my love,
Peter

SIXTY-THREE

———

JULIA WAS SAFE in the plane, strapped in, on her way back to the States. "Only a little hop across the pond," Sigrid said, as she had always said, more sadly these days whenever Julia was about to leave London. And what is left? Julia asked herself, now that the fire has gone out? What will be left? Once he is gone, completely gone, and even Evelyn has been erased, and Meena and Sigrid and Sophie, and Andrew, and soon everyone, gone, gone, gone. And how will Peter's story end? Not until the least and last of Peter's family has died. While they are above the earth, the furies will keep after them. If Andrew were to have children, the furies would pursue them. The world has decided. It made its decree years and years ago and it has not changed its mind. I suppose that is fate. I suppose that is destiny, decisions made, consequences that cannot be reversed. And what will become of Peter's inheritance? Julia thought about Andrew. He might yet give in to Meena. In spite of what he said, in spite of what he thought best, he loved her. How many times had she heard him say, "She is the only mother I ever had"? And does the inheritance, in the end, make any difference? Peter *had* understood. It was only money. The money was the least important thing. But freeing himself from Meena—that was important. Julia asked herself how long either Andrew or Sophie could manage to stay free of the past. But if they could not free themselves, what would happen? They would lead a different kind of life. A life was a life, after all.

I am afraid, Julia thought. I am always afraid.

A bright light streamed in through the small window next to her, and she saw, as if they were already floating in the stale air of the plane, bits of grey ash, so light and thin that someone's breath would set them flying. And each of the ashes was flying through the air like a moth and each had its own things to say, and she heard each of them distinctly, forming a little fugue of voices, and she knew that when they were finished, there would be nothing more of importance to listen for. She heard Sigrid's voice, Peter's voice, Sophie's, Andrew's, Rose's, Meena's, Clare's, and each of them had something essential to say, and at times it seemed to her that one in particular was speaking to her, but speaking in the wrong voice. Someone was saying, "It is the nature of the angel to bequeath to the person most resembling a turnip the essential revelation which might, if given to someone else, explain everything."

I am being given a revelation now, Julia knew, but do I understand it?

She knew each word the voices spoke was important, but she was not sure that she understood what they had to say. But she knew that when they finished speaking, everything they might say later, in letters, through the telephone, or in dreams, would not rival what they were saying now. And so she paid attention.

Strange things are borne in on the wind. In the end.

Green apples, green apples, green apples, I cry,
If I don't have green apples, I surely will die.

I am the keeper of the furies.
I have seen the face of the man who steps in and out of the
    woods.
He has the same face as the full moon.
So long, it's been so long, but now
He is mine and he waits for me and me only.

First love is the only love.
But there can be a second.
If you insist upon it.
If you keep the first, ruined bones in your own cupboard
And do not complain.

I came into the world like anyone else.
But I saw there was no world
And I had come into nothing.
Every morning, I begin building the world again.

Oh, Mother, Mother, make my bed,
For I shall die tomorrow.

It was gloomy all life long.
Then the sun came out and he was the sun.
The light first showed itself as a strip of silver,
A narrow strip, then broader,
At the edge of the sky, right over the cliffs.
It was golden

And blinding.

Where have you been all the day, Evelyn, my child?
What have you been doing, my pretty one?
Make my bed soon, for I'm sick to my heart,
And I fain would lie down.

I don't want the money! Can't you see I don't want it!

I can't let them win! I mustn't let them win! I will try
   everything! I will stop at nothing!

She is the wind that howls, that sends sharpened branches through windows. She is the one. Don't try to tell me she isn't. Don't try to tell me these are acts of nature, independent of her. Nothing is independent of her. Nothing in my world is unrelated to her. She is my closest relative. She has moved in close. She will not move away.

The trouble is, Rose, that you don't have the slightest regard for the truth.

The trouble is, Julia, that the truth is never as big as we want it to be.

The trouble is, Sigrid, that I married her. I myself signed the document. Of my own free will. My own pact with the devil. Are we not told to look out for the devil in his many guises?

The trouble is, Peter, that you will leave me. Because you are already ill. Although I don't mind. Not now, but I shall.

The trouble is, Martin, that you refuse to see the value of avocados.

The trouble is, Mum, that even if I study all day long and all night long, I shall not care what the books can teach me.

An angel spoke through a man in a convenience store in the country. I am sure he was an angel. And what a disclosure he made! But the woman who heard it could not understand it, could not keep hold of what she had been told for long. Yes, in the end, the angel always speaks to the wrong person. So perverse. Life is so perverse.

The trouble is, love, that the world never suited me. I devoted my life to one being, and in the end, he failed me. Julia, the world is a rotten apple. But I did try. You cannot say I did not.

—

AND HE SAID, in that unmistakable voice, or the wind said, *Let the widows and the orphans do what they can for themselves. I can do nothing, not even for myself. I am the apple and the worm has found me out. In their time, it will find everyone out. Is it so important, those things you write me about, urge me about? When, in the end, I am just another person? When that is the one lesson I have ever learned in my own life, that we are all just another person?*

POISON

Susan Fromberg Schaeffer

POISON

Susan Fromberg Schaeffer

AUTHOR'S STATEMENT

As long as I can remember, I have been fascinated by how a person's life is shaped. Is that life primarily shaped by one's own character, or can events like wars or illness alter the kind of person someone eventually becomes? Is it possible that any event can indisputably be said to alter character? There are those who seem to move easily through life, while others survive one storm only to find themselves immediately faced by an even more destructive upheaval. Are there such people who are truly "under a curse," or have some of those "cursed" people engineered their own malevolent destiny? As I grew older and watched several people's lives draw to a close—miserably in some cases, happily in others—I found myself asking these questions repeatedly. Why do people's lives end as they do?

Poison is my attempt to reach certain conclusions about how and why some unfortunate people came to believe themselves cursed. They rarely blamed themselves for their predicaments. Instead, they asked whether or not they had been cursed by fame (which became, in time, a kind of infamy), or by their own characters, or by a single poor choice that led to irreversible ramifications that pursued them, like the Furies, throughout a lifetime. What had happened to blight their lives? These were the questions that shaped *Poison*. In writing *Poison*, I came to certain answers, answers that were and are, of necessity, provisional and speculative. *Poison* is, in many ways, a record of that investigation.

—Susan Fromberg Schaeffer, 2007

DISCUSSION QUESTIONS

1. Martin, Peter's brother, thinks he has wasted his life. What do you think? What do you think the author believes a worthwhile life is?

2. Had Peter met Claire when he was younger, do you think he would have been happy with her?

3. Is Peter's relentless philandering the result of the tragedies depicted in *Poison*?

4. Some people have argued that Peter's adulteries are excusable because adultery is tolerated—if not expected—in other countries. What do you think of this defense (an appeal to moral relativism) of Peter's behavior? In real life, how would you judge or react to similar behavior?

5. Do you think (or do the characters in *Poison* believe) that moral or sexual latitude ought to be granted to individuals of great gifts, like writers or painters or movie stars?

6. In the end, are Sigrid's sacrifices for Peter's sake beneficial or destructive?

7. Rose believes that she has experienced a revelation when speaking to a relative of Peter's who owns a grocery store. She feels, afterwards, as if an angel has spoken to her. What sort of revelation is it?

8. What is Penelope's role in this novel?

9. Which characters do you find most sympathetic, and which ones least? Which characters does the author seem to like or dislike most?

10. There are many violent storms depicted in *Poison*. What role does nature play in this novel?

11. *Poison* sometimes explores the chasm between what people or events actually were and the mythic beings or events the world eventually sees them as being. Is the description of the "famous" photograph of Peter and Evelyn meant to explore this idea?

12. Peter has two "motherless" children. Can they recover from the disasters inflicted upon them by their parents, especially considering their parents' fame? Or is the fact of the parents' fame irrelevant?

13. In what way (if any) is the plot of *Poison* determined or fated? Is that fate created when Peter marries Evelyn? What could have prevented the many tragedies that occur in *Poison*? Is fate the same thing as character in this novel?

14 Meena may seem to be the classic evil stepmother, but Susan Fromberg Schaeffer has said that she finds her very sympathetic. Why does the author sympathize with Meena?

15. How would you characterize the author's style, her way of telling a story?

16. When *Poison* ends, the controversy over Peter's estate has not yet been settled. What do you think will happen to the estate? What do you think will become of the other characters, particularly Sophie and Andrew?

Diana Abu-Jaber	*Arabian Jazz*
	Crescent
Faith Adiele	*Meeting Faith*
Rabih Alameddine	*I, the Divine*
Robert Alter	*Genesis**
Rupa Bajwa	*The Sari Shop*
Christine Balint	*Ophelia's Fan**
	*The Salt Letters**
Brad Barkley	*Money, Love*
Andrea Barrett	*Servants of the Map*
	Ship Fever
	The Voyage of the Narwhal
Rachel Basch	*The Passion of Reverend Nash*
Charles Baxter	*Shadow Play*
Frederick Busch	*Harry and Catherine*
Lan Samantha Chang	*Inheritance*
Rachel DeWoskin	*Foreign Babes in Beijing*
Abigail De Witt	*Lili*
Jared Diamond	*Guns, Germs, and Steel*
Jack Driscoll	*Lucky Man, Lucky Woman*
John Dufresne	*Deep in the Shade of Paradise**
	*Love Warps the Mind a Little**
Tony Eprile	*The Persistence of Memory*
Ellen Feldman	*The Boy Who Loved Anne Frank*
	Lucy
Susan Fletcher	*Eve Green*
Paula Fox	*The Widow's Children*
Judith Freeman	*The Chinchilla Farm*
Betty Friedan	*The Feminine Mystique*
Barbara Goldsmith	*Obsessive Genius*
Stephen Greenblatt	*Will in the World*
Helon Habila	*Waiting for an Angel*
Sara Hall	*Drawn to the Rhythm*
Patricia Highsmith	*The Selected Stories*
	Strangers on a Train
	A Suspension of Mercy

Hannah Hinchman — *A Trail Through Leaves**

Linda Hogan — *Power*

Pauline Holdstock — *A Rare and Curious Gift*

Ann Hood — *The Knitting Circle**

Dara Horn — *In the Image*

The World to Come

Janette Turner Hospital — *Due Preparations for the Plague*

The Last Magician

Pam Houston — *Sight Hound*

Kathleen Hughes — *Dear Mrs. Lindbergh*

Helen Humphreys — *Leaving Earth*

The Lost Garden

Erica Jong — *Fanny*

Sappho's Leap

Binnie Kirshenbaum — *Hester Among the Ruins*

Nicole Krauss — *The History of Love**

James Lasdun — *The Horned Man*

Don Lee — *Country of Origin*

Yellow

Joan Leegant — *An Hour in Paradise*

Vyvyane Loh — *Breaking the Tongue*

Suzanne Matson — *The Tree-Sitter*

Lisa Michaels — *Grand Ambition*

Lydia Minatoya — *The Strangeness of Beauty*

Donna Morrissey — *Sylvanus Now**

Barbara Klein Moss — *Little Edens*

Patrick O'Brian — *The Yellow Admiral**

Heidi Pitlor — *The Birthdays*

Jean Rhys — *Wide Sargasso Sea*

Mary Roach — *Spook**

Josh Russell — *Yellow Jack*

Kerri Sakamoto — *The Electrical Field*

Gay Salisbury and
Laney Salisbury — *The Cruelest Miles*

May Sarton — *Journal of a Solitude**

Susan Fromberg Schaeffer — *Anya*

Susan Fromberg Schaeffer   *Buffalo Afternoon*
(continued)   *Poison*
                                The Snow Fox
Jessica Shattuck   *The Hazards of Good Breeding*
Frances Sherwood   *The Book of Splendor*
                                Night of Sorrows
                                Vindication
Joan Silber   *Household Words*
                                Ideas of Heaven
Marisa Silver   *No Direction Home*
Gustaf Sobin   *The Fly-Truffler*
                                In Pursuit of a Vanishing Star
Dorothy Allred Solomon   *Daughter of the Saints*
Ted Solotaroff   *Truth Comes in Blows**
Jean Christopher Spaugh   *Something Blue**
Mary Helen Stefaniak   *The Turk and My Mother*
Matthew Stewart   *The Courtier and the Heretic**
Mark Strand and
    Eavan Boland   *The Making of a Poem**
Manil Suri   *The Death of Vishnu**
Barry Unsworth   *Losing Nelson**
                                *Morality Play**
                                *Sacred Hunger**
                                *The Songs of the Kings**
Brad Watson   *The Heaven of Mercury**
Jenny White   *The Sultan's Seal*

*Available only on the Norton Web site:
www.wwnorton.com/guides